Heather

by

John Trevena

(Pseudonym of Ernest George Henham)

Author of

"A Pixy in Petticoats," "Arminel of the West,"

"The Dartmoor House that Jack Built," etc.

London

ALSTON RIVERS, LTD.

Brooke St., Holborn Bars, E.C.

1908

ISBN-10:1475097239
ISBN-13:978-1475097238

This work forms the second volume of a moorland trilogy, the first of which, dealing with Furze as representing the spirit of Cruelty, has been published. Heather, which flourishes only in pure air and sunshine, and blossoms again though it is torn by winds, seems to represent the spirit of Endurance. The author hopes to complete his work with "Granite" as representing the spirit of Strength.

CONTENTS

INTRODUCTORY – ABOUT THE LITTLE HOUSE ON THE ROOF   1

CHAPTER I – ABOUT PATIENTS   9

CHAPTER II – ABOUT WHEAL DREAM   21

CHAPTER III – ABOUT A MIXED FAMILY   35

CHAPTER IV – ABOUT GREGORY BREAKBACK   47

CHAPTER V - ABOUT A RECTOR AND HIS VISITORS   57

CHAPTER VI – ABOUT THE FORD WHICH LIETH ON THE EAST SIDE OF ST. MICHAEL'S CHAPEL OF HALSTOCK   67

CHAPTER VII – ABOUT JARS   83

CHAPTER VIII – ABOUT A HALF-HOLIDAY   95

CHAPTER IX – ABOUT ANOTHER HALF-HOLIDAY   111

CHAPTER X – ABOUT MATRIMONY AND THE LANE WHICH WAS CALLED MORTGABLE   125

CHAPTER XI – ABOUT ST. MICHAEL'S WHITE VIOLETS AND GREEN OAKS   141

CHAPTER XII – ABOUT THE GREAT DOWNACOMBE REBELLION   159

CHAPTER XIII – ABOUT WEIGHTS AND MEASURES   181

CHAPTER XIV – ABOUT REALITIES AND UNREALITIES   203

CHAPTER XV – ABOUT NOVEMBERITIS   223

CHAPTER XVI – ABOUT CONTRASTS   249

CHAPTER XVII – ABOUT EVICTIONS   265

CHAPTER XVIII – ABOUT THE WILD GARDEN   285

CHAPTER XIX – ABOUT THE FESTIVAL OF CUPS   303

CHAPTER XX – ABOUT SMOKE   323

CHAPTER XXI – ABOUT ST. PIRAN'S SANDS   341

CHAPTER XXII – ABOUT LAUREL LEAVES   355

CHAPTER XXIII – ABOUT UNCONVENTIONAL CONDUCT   371

CHAPTER XXIV – ABOUT A PAGAN SACRIFICE   383

CHAPTER XXV – ABOUT A SUNSET OF DREAMS   395

CHAPTER XXVI – ABOUT A TWILIGHT OF GOLD   405

ANNOTATIONS   419

HEATHER

INTRODUCTORY
ABOUT THE LITTLE HOUSE ON THE ROOF

The ancient Hoga de Cossdone, now called Cawsand Beacon, is a house beaten by the wind; down its sides water weeps copiously into the bogs of its basement. Who can tell the number of its storeys or what the dark rooms contain; what bones of cold-blooded reptiles and warmblooded men; what strange fossils of tree and fern? We do not know whether there is coal in its cellars or gold in its granite safe. We toil up its sides and walk about on the roof, perceiving that water has been laid on abundantly, that the sanitation is perfect; we get into realms where the air has never been polluted, where the wind sweeps across the roof-garden of heather; and there upon the heights, where clouds seem to feed like sheep, we stumble upon a stone chest, a grave, a kistvaen; and old moormen call that the House of Cosdon.

Fifty years ago there were bones, they say, in that tiny stone house clinging like a parasite on the roof of the big one, but they have gone now; body-snatchers have picked them all out like children dragging foxgloves from the hedges and flinging them away in wasteful mischief; a quaint kind of resurrection, but good enough, for bones have not the beauty of hedge flowers. The tenant of the little house has gone his way, and nobody is sorry, for however great he may have been once, his name has perished, he is remembered only as the owner of the little house among the heather, and he didn't make good his title to that until he was dead; being gone to the last poor bone he leaves no message, but the little house on the big roof speaks for him, better than he could have done himself. "Bide here, traveller, look down, du'ye bide a minute on your way to spoil the life of that maid or to rob that ignorant countryman of his

1

money. Consider how short-lived are the annual blossoms above the perennial roots; so is the flower of your life compared to the grave. Bide a bit, traveller! Perhaps you'll change your mind."

Not that the little house talks quite that way. It is only a rough, uneducated chest of stone, and does not understand Siste, viator! or much of the wonderful language of epitaph-makers. The ordinary traveller will not want to stay after he has knocked off a bit of the tomb as a memento, and broken his knife in trying to record his illustrious initials upon the granite; but if he is anything better than bleached bones himself he has to; for the little house insists upon prattling, not in an eloquent way by any means, being only a primitive box of Dartmoor stone; it has no learning, and is very often at a loss for a word—its tenant had nothing to give it but his bones— and sometimes it has to use quaint phrases of its own; and yet it can tell a story merely because it is a tomb and lies upon the roof; just as a little pair of boots in an almost forgotten cupboard, or a dainty garment hanging behind the door of a long unused bedroom talk most horribly, because they are not boots or garment but tongues crying like the tomb, "Stay, traveller, stay!" Those little boots, that dainty garment, are shrines, fellow travellers; temples of the deity to whom we have given our whole souls. We cannot pass them by without blinded eyes and a wild heart.

You may linger long enough upon the great roof before hearing the voice from the little house. Perhaps you will never hear it. Perhaps when it does come it is nothing but the wind through the heather. That does not matter, for the little house talks of nothing but gales and tempests and storm-clouds roaring past. Some day, when the sky is low and tumbling, and there is nothing else but space, you may hear it thus—

"Bide a bit, will ye? That's right. I've seen ye often enough on the roof tramping to and fro wi' the little dog, wondering why yew and the dog and the mountain were made and how 'tis all going to end. Well, I can't tell ye though I've abin here a time, avore ever the river ran down under, and avore there was stars on the ground. Lights yew call 'em, I reckon, lamps o' villages. They come out after dimsy like the stars up over, and they look the same, soft and quiet and twinkling, but I knaw they bain't the same. I've heard tell how some one looks down by the light o' the lamps up over, but those down under don't look up by the light o' their lamps. They don't look up to the roof o' Cawsand, and that be only a little way. Most of 'em don't look higher than six foot; some not so much; some never seem to tak' their eyes off the ground all their lives.

"Please to sit down. There bain't no hurry if 'tis getting dimsy, vor yew knaw the way out o' the house. Sit down on this long stone o' mine and I'll tell ye a thing or two avore yew goes down to the lamps. I've abin here a time, vor I'm granite, and there be nothing stronger than me; I've abin here always, I can't mind the time when I wasn't here, and I'll bide to the end if there be an end. But I bain't the only one. There be two others on the roof wi' me, and I've watched 'em vor thousands and millions o' years, and I be still watching 'em, and I'll go on to the end. One of 'em be strong, the other weak; and the strong one ha' fought agin the weak one all these millions o' years without beating it, without making it weaker, without driving a scrap of it away.

"Look about ye, traveller. I call ye traveller because yew can move abroad and I ha' got to bide. What du'ye see? What du'ye hear? They'm my two companions, as old as me, the weak one and the strong, the one silent and visible, the other noisy and invisible, the two everlasting fighters—the Heather and the Wind.

"Nothing else, traveller, 'cept the lichens; just me and the heather and the wind. They've given us the roof and us holds on. 'Tis no use me asking why the heather grows in the wind 'cause yew don't knaw. The wind beats the fern, the wind beats the vuzz; but it can't beat the heather though it has tried vor millions o' years. The little pink flowers laugh at the wind same as I du. 'Blow your hardest,' it ses— and even yew, traveller, can't guess how the wind comes on winter nights across the roof— 'yew can't beat me.' And that's what I ha' been saying all these millions o' years 'cause I'm granite, but I can't understand how 'tis them little flowers be as strong as me.

"Traveller, I want to tell ye that nothing ever changes. The wind be the same as it always has been; sometimes soft, sometimes fierce, but the same wind. I be granite just as I was millions o' years ago; sometimes a lot o' lichen on me, sometimes a little, but I'm the same granite. Times there's a plenty o' flowers on the heather, times there's none; but 'tis the same heather. There's nought else on the roof 'cept a few volk, and they'm the same volk as what lived once on the sides o' the house, different clothes on 'em, different words in their mouths, but the same volk. The man they buried here was more lusty than yew, traveller, but his face was the same as yours. Seems to me as if he'd just stepped out to rest a bit avore going down the side to find his goats.

"A year be a goodish bit o' time to yew, traveller, and twenty years be what yew call a generation. Time be nought to me and the heather and the wind. Us came wi' the light and will go wi' 'en. A thousand years, what lifts a few specks o' dust off me, rubs the world clean o' volk like yew ten times; and as vor a million yew can't fancy it. But a million years ago I was here on the top o' the roof, and the wind was tearing the heather same as it du now. What's the meaning of all those years o' wind, traveller? I don't knaw, and the heather don't knaw— there's nought else but the lichens—but mebbe the wind knaws if 'twould fell. The wind has been noisy upon the roof for ever, but I don't knaw yet what it tells.

"Bide a bit, traveller! I reckon yew knaws more than me, though yew warn't here yesterday and will be gone avore morning. My days be what yew calls ages. Perhaps yew can tell me why the wind fights wi' the heather; why the heather don't give it up and go; why it grows better on the roof than anywhere else—seems to me to live on the wind—though nothing else can live here, 'cept a bit o' starved grass and corpsy lichen. Can ye tell me if the wind be sent to tear the heather, or be the heather sent to bear the wind? Du the wind hate the heather? I've seen 'en tear the blossoms off and whirl 'em along the roof and into nowhere. Be it all part of a game what bain't going to end? And last of all, traveller, perhaps yew can tell me which o' the folks started it all, who built this house o' Cosdon, and put me into the roof, and planted the heather and sent the wind? Wun't ye tell me? Then I reckon yew'm a poor thing," said the little house, with the contempt of eternal things for a mere ephemeral. "Yew knaws no more than a lump of poor old Dartmoor granite, what can't move abroad, and ain't got your eyes and ears, your mind and brain. Sitting wi' your head between your hands as though yew was mazed! Go your ways, traveller. Go down under to the villages and the stars—lamps yew call 'em—and look up like them what live there, some of 'em six foot, some of 'em two. Vor yew'm only a vule if yew can't answer a bit o' granite on the roof. Bide a bit! Don't ye want to scratch on me wi' your knife?"

When a grave becomes insulting it is time to leave it. Besides, the evening wind on the roof comes cold and storm-haunted; and the lights, when they can be seen at all, seem a long voyage away. The stone chest, kistvaen, House of Cosdon, whichever name suits, had made its appeal and was to be left unanswered. It is not easy to reply to that uncomfortable "Stay, traveller!" of the tomb. Nobody wants to linger or to reply. We want to go on, out of the wind, away from the cold and damp, towards the lighted windows and the warmth. The little house could not understand what the wind meant by beating upon the heather, and being only rough granite it could hardly be expected to talk wisely. It could only ask hard questions like a child. For it is an empty-bodied thing, and in the place once occupied by bones the wind has whirled its refuse, scraps of peat and heather, sodden grass and sheep-dung; and its sides are well-polished by the rain. It is good to be there, not to think of graves and breed a company of melancholy devils, but to imagine oneself back, if not at the beginning of things, at least as far into the first days as imagination can contrive. For one has only to breathe that air which has never been polluted; to feel the sun shining from that wonderful row of houses above, the doors of which cannot be unlocked although astronomers are always peeping over the fence and science is blotting out the word impossible; to look down upon the granite and heather; and at last to know there has been no change since the mastodon dragged his carcase there, since hairy man danced for the joy of life there, since fire was born and the first beacon blazed there. You may stand and scoff at history, and rank it with the initials scratched upon the granite. A million years in the life of the heather are but as yesterday in spite of the wind which never rests.

Still the triumph is with the ephemerals who come, struggle, and die in less than a single day of geological time. Man is the master of eternal things, not in his flesh and bones, nor in his interminable antics, but in his mind. At both ends of creation you find the man, at the lower end among snakes, spiders and swine, in filth to the eyes; at the higher end alone, unapproachable, his head almost in the sun. It is the mind which speaks of the past and insists on a future. There is something on the roof besides the eternal granite and heather; there is the wind which beats upon them without ceasing, the strong invisible thing which comes from somewhere and passes on, just as the strong invisible thing called mind beats through the bodies of men from somewhere and passes on. Mind is the most eternal of all things, beginning with a mighty miracle and having no end, linking man, not with the eternal things of his surroundings, but with the unfathomable greatness and eternity of the origin of life.

Can that mind go back beyond the granite and heather, can it learn, not by the bone in the rock or the fossil in the coal, but by its own power of recording facts, by its own memory? Can it go back in memory to the ages before men, existing as it were in anticipation of his coming? It is a question which has silence for an answer. Yet the Eastern story-teller speaks of the roc, the gigantic bird which could snatch up a man in its talons; and in the fiction, and even in the sacred and secular beliefs, of the dark ages the dragon is everywhere a familiar figure in both literature and art. Eastern story-teller knew as much about geology as the mediaeval monk, and that was nothing. Yet the roc existed in the form of the dinornis, whose bones greatly exceeded those of the largest horse, whose normal height was twelve feet, whose tridactyl footprint measured eighteen inches in length; and the flying dragon existed in the pterodactyl, with the jaws and teeth of a crocodile, body and tail of a mammal, and bat-like wings having a spread of nearly thirty feet. How were these monsters guessed at by the ancients if they were not suggested by the voice of tradition? The mind creates nothing; it can only discover and remember. The poor little ape shivering with fear in a world of fearful reptiles would hardly forget dinornis and pterodactyl since it spent its wretched life hiding from them; and when the triumph of the mammals came, and evolution brought at length some semblance of humanity to the ape, it would still remember—or rather would be unable to forget—the horror of its struggle to survive amid the great dragons of the air. The wonderful mind which had been denied to the age of vegetation, and to the age of reptiles, was no doubt doing its work; and the rude forms of primitive men might have retained within them the tradition of that terrible fight for existence; and so memory would be passed on unconsciously from one ape to another until civilization dawned. It would not be a triumph too great for the chief wonder of creation; as the shadow going before the body there is the mind going before the man.

We might have answered the little house as the wind beats upon it, and in the same manner; but as it cannot understand the wind it would not have understood us. We could have answered one of its questions, not well, in some doubt, but still we could have told it something. We could have told it that the wind is upon all of us without ceasing, tearing at us as it torments the heather on the roof; and like the heather we resist it with success. The wind cannot beat us. We perform the acts of our lives and defy it, and we place our children in its blast. It tears us up, and whirls us off apparently into nowhere like so much heather blossom, but still we win, because of the love of life and the love of our own. We could give it up and extinguish ourselves, through not breeding children, or through destroying all that are born by universal agreement, but we refuse to give way. On the other questions we are silent. Is the wind sent to tear us, or are we sent to bear the wind? Does the wind hate us? The mind does nothing for us there. No memory comes down from the age of colossal bird and flying dragon; no tradition has been conveyed by that germ of mind in the ape's shivering body of any Creative Being moving among the horrors of that world; and without memory and tradition we are as the granite is. . . .

The House of Cosdon and the roof are far behind and in the clouds. We are going down now, through the heather, still in the wind, towards the lights and the villages and the people who cause the lights.

HEATHER

CHAPTER I
ABOUT PATIENTS

Along a windy passage trotted a small boy, sniffing at a door numbered four, whining at number three, scratching at number two; and at number one, which made the end of the passage, he put up his head and howled the house down. By the manner of his conversation he proclaimed himself a dog, by his appearance he was a foxterrier and a gentleman, and the name of Tobias was marked upon his collar. He was a little watchman going his rounds, saying after his own manner, "Seven o'clock, and time for children to come out and play."

Number one door opened and a rather nice-looking girl peeped out. She wore a dressing-gown, her dark hair was tumbling, her hands and face were tanned a fine red clay colour; and the name upon her collar was Berenice Calladine.

"Hello, my lovely!" said she, while little dog Tobias lifted up his voice and grinned tumultuously. "Want a game, do you? Come along, only don't make a noise, or I shall be sacked. I've had such a day, my pet," she laughed, shutting the door and rolling Tobias upon her bed. "I've broken all the laws. Late getting up this morning, which meant one black mark, and went too far, was found out, and got a lecture. This afternoon I left unwalked that walk I ought to have done, and climbed that tor I was distinctly told I was not to climb, consequently there is supposed to be no health in me. When I got back I had a temperature, and was sentenced to remain in my own cell and repent in solitude and cigarette-ashes. And there's a new boy, Tobias. I want to see what he's like."

Tobias was understood to say that he had witnessed the arrival of the new boy and entertained no very high opinion of him, as he had taken his ball and placed it with great precision at the stranger's feet, in order to test his throwing powers, and the new boy had ignored it and him altogether.

"I expect he wants his mummy," said the young lady. "He's feeling blue, Tobias. Every one feels awful at first. I cried lots, swamped my bed, and it was dreadful cold and my tears froze, and I thought I was going to die every minute. I've been told to go to bed and I don't seem to be doing it. Such a beautiful evening, and I feel quite well. I think I'll stay up a little longer. Little stupid, you were nearly out of the window. Oh, I see," she murmured. "That's your ball on the grass."

The expression window was something of an euphemism, as there wasn't one. The entire house was in the same unfinished condition, and fresh heather-scented air careered freely through passages and rooms. It was pleasant enough at that time of year, but somewhat brutal in winter when the temperature was below freezing-point and snow came drifting upon the floor. The girl's bed was close beside the open space which, in a less savage abode, would have been occupied by a window with its usual accompaniments of blinds and curtains, and a piece of wire was stretched across to prevent her from rolling out into the garden while she slept. Below was a rough lawn dotted over with lounge chairs which were then unoccupied; and upon the lawn reposed a golf-ball gnawed into an elliptical shape by the dog's sharp teeth.

"I wonder if I should be caught," murmured Berenice, longing for the ball which Tobias flatly declined to go for unless she came too. "I shan't be happy till I get it, and I've been so bad all day I may as well end badly and start fresh and good-to-morrow. We'll chance it. Come along, Tobias."

She slipped out, tiptoed down the stairs, reached the grass safely and picked up the ball, an act which caused Tobias to jump and squeak. A cough reached her ears, and she looked up to see at one of the open spaces above a fat and comic head nodding furiously and making danger signals with its eyes and lips.

"It's all right, Mr. Gumm. He's been and gone," said she; but at that moment the gate clicked, and she saw to her horror the tyrant of that little state strolling up the path slapping the palm of his left hand with the rubber tubes of a stethoscope. "Heaven save me," Berenice murmured. "I'm caught again."

"I told you to remain in your room, Miss Calladine," said a cold voice.

"It's such a lovely evening. We don't get too many of them," protested the culprit, standing in a graceful posture of resignation, pushing the hair from her eyes.

"And I told you to go to bed."

"I was going, but I looked out and saw this ball lying on the grass, and it worried me so I had to come down and pick it up. I did try to resist temptation, but it wouldn't be resisted. I'll be good to-morrow," she promised, with a smile which meant she would behave in exactly the same way.

The doctor came forward, took the ball from her in a paternal way, and threw it among the rhododendrons, while Tobias plunged merrily after it.

"I shall have to take the dog away if the patients throw things for him," he said.

"Take Tobias away!" cried the girl indignantly. "Then I should go, and the others would go, and you would be left weeping for your children."

"Now run away to bed. I can't have you about with a temperature."

"It was only climbing up the mountains, and doing those things which I ought not to have done," she said.

"Which you are rather addicted to. Don't get up to-morrow until I have been, as I want to run over you."

"Not in those big boots, I hope," said the girl; and then ran off and watched the tyrant's departure from an up-stairs passage. "Now he's gone to his dinner, and can't bother me again. I'll go to bed presently, but I must pay some calls first."

She knocked at a door numbered five, entered, and discovered a small and pretty maiden propped up in bed, nibbling dejectedly at a large slice of bread and butter.

"Well, Miss Shazell, how are we this evening?" said Berenice, mimicking the doctor's voice and manner.

"Miserable," came the answer. "But you mustn't come in. There will be such a row if you're caught."

"Doctor has lectured me and gone. The matron is in the kitchen eating bread and honey, so we are quite safe. I've been in rows all day, and now I'm supposed to be slapped and put to bed. I'm going to be thumped tomorrow."

"I was done this morning."

"What did he say?"

"I'm better, ever so much—if he really means it. But he's going to walk me soon, and I've stuck on four pounds this week."

"Then what are you miserable about, if you're getting better and plastering on fat in such a piggish fashion?"

"I want my mother," cried the poor little girl.

"That's because you are a silly baby," said Berenice severely. "If your mother was allowed here she would only kill you. She would never have the heart to see her girl all wet with the dews of heaven, like the man who did open-air treatment in the Bible. If they hadn't kept you at home, and coddled you so long, you wouldn't be in bed now."

"I hate the place and the people," moaned Winnie.

"That's silly too. You haven't seen the people, and you mustn't hate a place which is saving your life. It's jolly good fun when you get a bit fit. And you must expect mixed biscuits in a sanatorium. How splendid and fat you're getting, Winnie! You're nearly ready for market. What meal are you devouring now?"

"Tea," said tearful Winnie. "I finished breakfast just before doctor came at noon, and I got through lunch by four, and now it's dinner-time and I shan't finish that till two o'clock to-morrow morning. I'm always stuffing, but the milk is the worst. It's awful to lie here and pour milk into myself all day."

"Just put your head back and let it run down," laughed Berenice.

"But it makes me so sick."

"Don't let it. When I feel that stage approaching I clench my hands and teeth and declare I won't give way, and I don't. I haven't been sick since the first two weeks. Some people don't try to fight against it. Old Budge is always going out to admire the flowers, but she is a pig, and loads herself like a coal-van."

"Don't," pleaded Winnie. "You mustn't stay, Berenice. I do like seeing you, but I am supposed not to speak to any one. Look at all this bread and butter! My meals run into each other so, and I can't heave the lot out of the window or they'd see it."

"Poor little girl," said Berenice. "They give you rather a rough time, and you deserve a rest if you have put on four pounds." She picked up the plate of bread and butter. "I'll hide the stuff in my room and throw it away to-morrow," she said.

"That's so wicked," said Winnie.

"My dear, we can't always be good, not even in a sanatorium. Besides, tea is not a compulsory meal for most of us. Bye-bye, baby. Don't cough to-night, or I'll come in and smack you."

Berenice went off, concealed the bread and butter, then banged at another door, and was received this time with enthusiasm. Number six was another maiden, on the wrong side of forty, although she couldn't remember it. Arabella Budge was not beautiful though she said she was good, but people doubted it. She was fond of telling small selfish untruths, such as that her name was Ella— the surname didn't matter, as she intended to change that when the man with a higher aim than her bank-account came along—and she couldn't remember anything that had happened twenty years back, and she denied using a razor, although Berenice had caught her once with a lathered face, which, Miss Budge declared, was for the sake of her complexion. The lady also affirmed she was mortally afflicted, which was obviously untrue, as serious cases were not admitted to the sanatorium, and she explained her condition by the usual statement that people of sanctity could hardly "expect to attain longevity. Miss Budge had excited some interest in the medical world, as she had gained twenty-one pounds during the first week under treatment. "Not bad for a girl," she expressed it. "Pigs simply nowhere," according to Berenice.

"My dear, I've had such a lovely dream," cried Miss Budge. "It's not often I go to sleep in the rest hour, but I did this evening, and I thought three men came in, and each claimed to be my long-lost husband. Wasn't that queer?"

"If you call bigamy a joke I suppose it was. Now I know the sort of life you have been leading," said Berenice.

"And then in came the real rude doctor without knocking as usual, with his, 'What's your temperature?' I shall throw my boot at his head one of these days."

"I should think your temperature was pretty high with such a lot of husbands," said Berenice. "Have you seen the new boy? I heard the carriage drive up."

"Just a glimpse as he walked up the path. Tall, thin, dark, and he turns his toes in. I coughed, but he didn't look up."

"A gentleman?"

"Must be. Doctor says he's a Balliol scholar. I suppose the first thing he will do is to fall in love with you, and I shall have to play gooseberry until you throw him down and trample on him, and then I can use the remains," said Miss Budge.

"Wait till Winnie Shazell gets about. I shall have to play gooseberry then."

"Is she really pretty? I can't see her as she's always in bed, and I don't dare go into other rooms like you do. I submit to discipline," said Miss Budge, with the air of a Christian martyr.

"She is a sweet, blue-eyed, flaxen-haired thing, with dimples and a most delicious nose. I expect I admire her because she is so unlike me," said Berenice.

13

"There go the Twins!" exclaimed Miss Budge, as a noise came from the stairs suggestive of furniture shifting. "It must be stuffing-time. Let's go down and bully the new boy."

"I can't. I'm supposed to be in bed getting a temperature down."

"And here's the tyrant," sniggered Miss Budge, who was gazing out of the window.

Berenice rushed to her room and began to tear off her clothes. Hearing the dreaded step on the stairs she flung Tobias off the bed, jumped in half-dressed, pulled the sheets over her, and wondered if the explanation that she had felt so faint she couldn't finish undressing would be of any use. However, the doctor did not come in. He merely asked, "Are you in bed, Miss Calladine?" as he passed; and Berenice answered in an exceedingly surprised and injured voice, "Oh yes, doctor."

The irrepressible girl could not remain quiet for long. She finished disrobing, then tumbled into bed, and leaned out of the window with a light wrapper about her shoulders for the sake of propriety, watching the Twins who were disporting themselves in elephantine fashion upon the lawn. They were middle-aged men, humorous in their way, which was always vulgar, generally grotesque, and usually quarrelling like a couple of children. One was James Gumm, the other Alfred Mudd; each was father of a family; Gumm was a commercial traveller, while Mudd was interested in the liquor trade. Berenice was right when she said that all sorts met in a sanatorium.

"Mr. Gumm," called the girl. "Please throw me up that ball." She saw it upon the grass where Tobias had left it after reclaiming it from the rhododendrons.

The Twins ceased their preposterous gambols when they heard the voice, and raised their big, bladder-like heads towards the window.

"'Ullo! are you in bed, my pretty?" cried Gumm, though it was obvious enough, as Berenice, bed and all, were visible from the lawn.

"Silly blight," howled Mudd. "Can't you see she's cooking pork-chops for your supper?"

"I want that ball, please," said the girl sternly.

"Have you said your prayers, my dear? Have you prayed for James Gumm and other sick persons?" asked that gentleman, with much solicitude.

"Shut your stoke-hole, and give the poor girl her toy. Give it here, fathead," cried Mudd. "You can't chuck."

They rolled together on the ball like a couple of fat babies, Gumm screaming, "If you chuck it you'll bust your tin lungs;" while the other's reply was so uncomplimentary that Berenice decided she had not heard it.

The ball reached the girl's bed at last, and she and Tobias began to play, which was against the rules, but she didn't mind that; while Mudd placed himself in what he imagined was a devotional attitude, and with uplifted eyes declaimed—

"I wish I wasn't married, Jim."

"So does your wife," replied Gumm; and then lumbered off, pursued by Mudd, until they nearly tumbled over Miss Budge, who was sitting on the other side of the rhododendrons extracting romance out of a Dartmoor sunset.

A bell rang and the patients took their places at the dinner-table. It was not a depressed party by any means; on the contrary, a more cheerful lot of beings could not easily have been found. They were as irresponsible as so many school-children, and nobody looking in upon them would have guessed they were afflicted with a disease which yields readily enough to Nature and its wind. They were there to imitate as far as possible animals in the matter of feeding and savages in the way of living. The mind had to be forgotten, the intellect was the only thing to be starved; everything was to be sacrificed to the gross requirements of the body.

The sanatorium was a small one, not accommodating more than eight patients at a time. In addition to those already mentioned, and the new-comer who brought the total up to seven, was a silent young curate named Sill, who had to suffer a good deal, partly from an inability to retain large quantities of food, partly from the irreverence of the others. At the commencement of the meal two chairs were unoccupied, and Gumm, who had long ago acquired the art of eating and conversing at the same time, was soon commenting upon this fact.

"The queen of my 'eart is put to bed," he said, while sucking a hot potato. "She's been bringing this respectable establishment into discredit again."

"How do you know? You weren't with her," said Mudd. The Twins generally had the conversation to themselves, none of the others having much chance.

"Doctor told me, Bristol bloater," replied Gumm in his courtly style. "She was seen out with a carroty-'eaded soldier, behaving shameful, his arm round her half-guinea seventeen-and-a-quarter inch lace-me-tight."

"She doesn't wear one," Miss Budge interrupted. "I don't either. It's not allowed. And I'm sure her waist is twenty-five inches."

"That shows my Innocence," went on Gumm. "Respectable married men don't understand ladies' clothes like soldiers and parsons."

"If you are referring to me, Mr. Gumm," began the young clergyman, but he was given no mercy by the booming commercial.

"Don't you make excuses, Mr. Sill. Soldiers and parsons are in the same bag when it comes to women, only soldiers go for the pretty ones and parsons for the rich ones. That's where their superior education comes in. If I had my time over again I'd start as a soldier, and then I'd turn parson. If you're going to be ill, Alfred Mudd, I hope you'll go into the garden and get it over like a gentleman. Do you fancy yourself an inebriate, Mr. Sill?"

"A celibate," corrected the shocked young curate. "Well, I am."

"Then you're not going to do your duty to the country," said Mudd.

"Just what I tell him," cried Miss Budge.

"You'll grow out of it," prophesied Gumm. "Wait till some pretty little girl helps you to decorate the font on Christmas Eve, and invites you to play a game of I touched last."

"I told him that too," said the lady. "At least something like it."

The curate smiled and said nothing. He was a very young man and the bacillus of mediaevalism had bitten him.

"Our little bit of youth and beauty was fair copped with the red-'eaded sergeant," Gumm went on, sprawling over the table to reach a tomato which Mudd grabbed for at the same time and just lost. "When she got back doctor gave her the choice between the sack and a spanking. 'Must keep the place respectable,' he told her, 'I've got little Jimmy Gumm to think of.'"

"Listen to him," cried the publican. "Travels in whisky, and drinking milk now like a baby at his mother's knee."

"Mammy's what?" asked Gumm. "We all know about mother's knee and slipper, but—"

"That will do, Mr. Gumm," nervously interrupted the matron who was carving meat at a side-table. "Please go on with your food."

"Right-o, Auntie. I was only impressing upon the company that we can't be too careful about our morals, when the gentleman opposite puts his word in. Pretty youth he is at home. Stands all day between a beerengine and a pile o' glasses, and sells arsenic and water at twopence a time. Ain't it true now about our pretty one? Speak the truth, Auntie. Didn't she choose the spanking, and didn't you hold her down while doctor used the strap off her box?"

"Do be quiet," cried the worried matron, while at the same moment Sill rose from the table with abruptness and hurried out into the garden.

"For what he's been and received he's going to be truly wasteful," observed Mudd.

"Take Miss Shazell's dinner up to her room before it gets cold," called the matron to the ever-bustling servant.

"With her little Jimmy's love," added Gumm.

"If she wants feeding with a spoon I'll be there," shouted Mudd.

"Gentlemen, you must behave if you please," begged the matron, shaking her carving-knife at them, which caused the publican to sing "Three blind mice," while Gumm's husky voice remarked, "No need for the plural, Auntie dear. There's only one gentleman here, now parson has gone to play among the buttercups."

"Well, here's another," said Miss Budge in her most amiable voice, as a new figure crept awkwardly into the room and produced the silence which is usual when a stranger enters. He was quite young, timid, and a trifle uncouth. His rather long hair seemed to have been left unbrushed, his clothes had a curious appearance of being disarranged; he looked indeed, as Mudd subsequently expressed it, as if he had been dragged through a furzebush. He stood for the moment near the table and made a singularly awkward bow to his future companions.

"This is Mr. Halfacre," said the matron by way of formal introduction. "Will you sit here, please, next to Miss Budge?"

"Delighted," exclaimed, not the new-comer, but the lady; while the Twins nodded their distended cheeks and champing jaws at him, and then made outward and visible grimaces at each other to signify that the latest arrival was not of their kind.

"I expect you are tired?" remarked Miss Budge, contracting her space at the table with much detail.

"Not unreasonably, considering I have made a long journey in a weak state of health," came the answer, which made the lady stare and the Twins choke. The new boy's voice was harsh and grating, and his manners were atrocious. He ought to have known that it was not etiquette to refer publicly to his health, because nobody there had really come for their health. They were simply serving a sort of imprisonment for having lived carelessly in the past. Then his pedantic manner was discouraging. Miss Budge found herself examining him with much interest. Being a scholar, the young man was presumably a gentleman in spite of his very earthy name. Miss Budge was an ordinary middle-class lady of a foolish kind, half-educated merely because she had forgotten all that she had been taught and had fed her mind for years upon nothing better than stories with a strong love-interest. Yet as a lady she discovered a sort of harsh inflection in the stranger's voice which suggested that his fellow-scholars might not have mixed with him for reasons apart from his pedantry. "Berenice will take the starch out of him," she thought; but at that moment young Halfacre turned and gazed along the table in a helpless way. He was only looking for salt, which Miss Budge did not pass at once, partly because she was annoyed at what seemed to her his want of courtesy, chiefly because she saw his eyes and they reminded her of that curious something which makes the rabbit nerveless when it sees the stoat.

"We're all of us in an interesting condition," remarked Gumm. "Brought on in my case by long hours of unremitted labour. In his case," pointing to Mudd with a fork whereon a large piece of bull's flesh was impaled, "by a life of ease and luxury. More meat, please, Auntie. Where's Tobias to eat the gristle?"

"He never leaves Miss Calladine unless he has to," answered Miss Budge, not sorry to turn her attention from the silent Halfacre.

"In the little matter of running after every pretty girl, that dog very much resembles my respected friend Alfred Mudd."

"And in the little matter of scratching himself" began the publican.

"That will do, Mr. Mudd," said the poor matron firmly, while Miss Budge tittered, and the new man muttered something inaudible which was possibly classical and presumably uncomplimentary; but nobody attended to him, for just then Sill entered and made delicately for his seat, to be greeted by the commercial in a concerned fashion,

"I am afraid you must be dreadfully hungry, your reverence."

"Sitting on the grass counting daisies is appetising. I've tried it," remarked Mudd.

"How you do tease the poor man!" tittered Miss Budge.

"The truth of the matter is he goes out on the lawn to look up and see the girls in bed," went on Gumm.

"The truth of the matter is that Miss Calladine is giving her dinner to Tobias," said the curate pleasantly.

"Oh, you sneak," cried Miss Budge.

"Didn't I say he'd been looking up there?" said Gumm.

"I shall tell doctor about her," threatened the matron, although every one knew she wouldn't. "Let me give you some more meat, Mr. Sill."

"Don't put it like that, Auntie. Give it him, hot and savoury meat such as his soul hateth. We'll see that he eats it, though we won't guarantee he keeps it," said Mudd.

Miss Budge was somewhat astonished to think that her neighbour was laughing at this vulgarity; but her second and more correct impression was that he was trying to refrain from doing exactly the opposite. Not that it was anything surprising, as he was probably very weak, and the first day in a sanatorium brings tears from men as well as from women. But young Halfacre had looked superior to that sort of thing.

The next morning the doctor came to visit his little colony in a whirling Dartmoor mist. He examined the new-comer and sentenced him to a day in bed. He thumped Berenice, found everything satisfactory, and told her to go to St. Michael's Ford, which pleased the girl, as it was her favourite walk. "And Tobias likes it too," she said. He went on to Miss Budge's room, pushed the door open, found the lady half-dressed, and made Berenice scream with laughter when she overhead his remark, "All right, Miss Budge, I'm not bashful," and the lady's answer, "I dare say you're not, but I am." Miss Budge was told to go to Downacombe, and not stay gossiping with Mr. Leigh the rector. The Twins were visited and sent exactly opposite directions for their perambulation, although they would probably manage to meet, and hide among the rocks to smoke cigarettes like wicked schoolboys. Last of all the doctor went to Winnie Shazell, and found her so much brighter and better that he said she might get up, go out for half-an-hour, and walk very slowly half-way along the road towards Wheal Dream. She was to sit down and rest at least twice on that short journey, and she was straitly charged not to speak a word to any one.

So Winnie got out at last and walked very tremulously upon the rough moorland track between the sanatorium and Wheal Dream; while Berenice at the same time was swinging along the side of the cleave with Tobias at her short skirts, making for the path which leads down to the ford which lies on the east side of St. Michael's chapel of Halstock.

HEATHER

CHAPTER II
ABOUT WHEAL DREAM

Wherever we go are tales; those that make history and those that make dreams. Some sort of story seems to be connected with every outstanding rock, every path and landmark, every cliff that hangs over the sea, and every cave half under it. Here some fool of a giant had his head hewn off by a small man who made giant-killing a profession; there some maid jumped into space because her young man was not constant and she hadn't the sense to get somebody else. They are nearly all ghastly stories; every peak has its own tragedy, each little copse of fir trees its murder. Pretty stories are forgotten somehow, or when they are remembered have to put up with the title of fairy-tale. The tragedies really did happen, but the comedies are pure invention. Folk are not to be thrilled with a tale, unless it be highly coloured, or has a certain amount of wild and bloody complications called a plot. They want the real thing, the impossible story, just because their own lives are colourless; they crave for a bit of romance between their own dull lines of commonplace, and they prefer it red; it stimulates them that way, and the horror never touches them because they are not called upon to face it. A very different thing it is when the horrible thing becomes real; when they stand near a lonely cottage on a winter's afternoon, the sea mist around, the sea waves below, sea birds above, and know that if they open that door they will see in the gloom the real red thing of their favourite tales. The hero of romance would kick the door open with a supercilious foot and light a cigarette with unshaken hands. People in real life scream and run away.

There was a tale connected with Wheal Dream, its ruins and its name; but not the sort of story which is remembered. Perhaps the mine had been opened very many years ago by some of the Jews who were driven into the world after the fall of their city; for a record exists to that effect, and your Israelite had always a nose to smell metal; but the name of Wheal Dream must have been bestowed in Stannary times. What remains is only a stupid love-story, and the fragments are hardly worth collecting. There was a man, and he had no name apparently, and he lived nowhere, but he had ambitions, a fantastic mind, and a maiden. His ambition was to make a wife of the maiden, which would seem a simple matter in an age when the marriage laws were not strict, and in a country which was hopping with cheap friars, and when a damsel did not demand a palatial residence and the latest Gallic fashions; but possibly his fantastic mind stood in the way. Such a mind was a dangerous possession in those days. As for the maiden, she was socially above the poor spadiard, for that is all he was, a wretched labourer who wore a sheep-skin and lived in a pit, and had nothing but coarse food, and when he wanted water had to drink it out of his spade, and only differed from his fellows in his possession of ambition, a fantastic mind, and the maiden. For the girl loved him, which would be the impossible part of the story if she hadn't been so feminine. She saw nothing presumptuous in the spadiard's love, although she dwelt in what then passed for a country residence, she could change her clothes when she got wet on the moor, and roast venison was served at her father's table at least twice a week. And in spite of all this she loved the man with the fantastic mind who lived in the pit and did not even own a change of sheep-skins. It is a pity tradition does not remember her name.

Even in those days men were not always what they appeared to be, and there were those who had only one bottle of wine in the house, which they couldn't drink because it had to be kept for visitors. This little girl's father might have been a very terrible personage outwardly, possessing a suit of armour which had the advantage of not wearing out quickly or getting shabby at the knees, and he might have stalked among the rocks with a clanking as of milk-cans; but for all that he was dreadfully short of tin, which sounds like a slang expression but is not, for tin was the gold of those days and people reckoned in it, an ingot of white metal being then what a bank-note is now. The girl of the period was an article of traffic; she had her market price, and the highest bidder bought her, which is one of those simple old customs which never seems to change. The daughter of the man in armour knew all about this custom, knew also that as she was pretty she was worth her weight in tin, and the man who brought that amount to her father could take her, parental good-will and benediction of holy Church included; therefore she suggested to the spadiard that he should give up being a labourer, show her he was a man, and strike out in business for himself and incidentally for her. The lover listened; he didn't want fame, position, or a suit of armour, he only wanted the girl; he returned to his pit, slept, and the fantastic mind did the rest. In a dream he saw the mine which the Jews had opened, and it seemed to him that he passed down the shaft and his eyes penetrated the rubbish and behind it was tin in abundance. There was sufficient to buy several girls. He awoke, took his spade, went to the wheal and began to dig. The evidence of the dream was true. Tin was there and the spadiard felt himself a man.

The course of prosperity soon ran in a crooked fashion for the tinner. He was behaving in a high-handed way with the law as established by the body of the Stannary in the High Court of Crockern Tor; and those who acted so did not live long to boast of it. The bailiff of Lydford issued his tin-warrant, and the spadiard was hurried off to the castle on the hill and the dungeon which "deserved no laughter "; for the well-known expression of "a living tomb" was inspired by the sight of that dungeon together with the dreadful lines—

"To lie therein one night, 'tis guess'd
'Twere better to be ston'd or press'd,
Or hang'd ere yoa come hither."

As it was the custom of the Stannary authorities to murder a prisoner first and then sit in judgment on his body, to discover whether he deserved his fate or whether he ought to have been acquitted, it will be obvious that the tinner did not reach the hopeless side of the walls of Lydford, though tradition fails to mention how he managed to escape. Possibly his fantastic mind was of good service again, perhaps the maiden helped him, more probably a thick Dartmoor mist was his preserver. He got away and went back to Wheal Dream, where the girl visited him and brought him food; while in the night he went on dreaming. The spirit of the place advised him to stay there and frighten passers by in the orthodox white-sheeted way which was very effectual in those days; by groans and shrieks, and waving fiery brands at night, and knocking two old tin cans together, if such things were obtainable— there are plenty about the place in its present state of civilisation— and by behaving generally in the demented fashion which obtains among lost souls. These things he did assisted by the young lady, who very possibly supplied him with some of her own discarded white raiment in which he could flap about at night; and as a consequence every one took care to keep well away from the gorge of the mine, except a few priests who flocked there in gorgeous copes and broad daylight and deluged the place with holy water. It was all very good fun for the clergy, but a game of life or death for the tinner.

At this point the story becomes so much patchwork, and we must take the historian's usual privilege and invent a little. So we infer that the damsel went to her father and told him all about the wealth of tin hidden away in Wheal Dream and how impossible it was to mine because of the evil spirit guarding it; and then she told him to go and see for himself, knowing well enough that as soon as he heard the first scream of the supposed demon his mail-clad knees would knock one against the other with a noise like an iron foundry. However he went, and the first thing he saw was this shockingly ungrammatical couplet written upon the rocks—

"He who gives his daughter to me
All my tin I'll give to hee."

The avaricious old fellow didn't worry about the grammar. He grasped the facts that the devil wanted his daughter and was prepared to give plenty of tin for her, and he naturally did not hesitate in closing with such an excellent bargain. So he sent for the parson in charge of St. Michael's Chapel, and asked about the form of ceremony ordained for such unions. The clergyman, of course, was horrified and said he could have nothing to do with such a black business unless very liberal fees were forthcoming. This brought a reply from the gentleman that he was temporarily embarrassed and a deadlock was reached, until the girl was questioned; and then it came out, with tears and great reluctance—for girls could dupe their parents even in the middle ages—how that ever since the mine had been haunted she had dreamed each night of a man clothed like a simple spadiard, who came to her and recited the same ungrammatical lines which her father had seen upon the rocks. She stated, moreover, being an artful maiden, that she hoped she would not have to marry the man, as she would much rather stay at home and polish father's armour; and that naturally provoked the answer that she desired, namely she was a pert bit of baggage and would have to do as she was told; while the parson went off into a discourse about dreams and visions and the marvellous intervention of Providence until his eloquence was dammed with a crock of mulled ale. And the next day in walked the tinner with a glib story of having come direct from the Court of King Arthur, or some place equally remote and romantic, but unfortunately he had been unable to bring letters of introduction because he had no pockets to his sheepskin. He said further he was the owner of a rich and devil-haunted mine on Dartmoor; that nobody could exorcise the foul fiend but himself; and lastly he had seen in a dream the fair vision of a maiden who was to be his wife and he was walking all over the country looking for her. The young lady entering that moment, according to arrangement, they recognised each other at once and fell into one another's arms in the orthodox way. Nothing remained but to fish the parson from under the table where he too had been dreaming since finishing the crock; and when he had attended professionally to the young couple the impecunious gentleman hurried off to the mine, which was haunted no longer and was found to contain a wealth of tin which exceeded all expectations. After that there was nothing more for them to do except to live happily ever afterwards.

This story of Wheal Dream, like most of the old traditions, crumbles before criticism. The simplicity of the country gentleman was somewhat inhuman, the carelessness of the Court of Stannary rather too great. Further, it may be asked, how did the spadiard or his lass know how to write those lines upon the rock, and how could the father read them? The tale disregards dramatic unities and embraces many periods. Certain it is that the mine of Wheal Dream never contained tin, but copper; the water there is coloured with it, and the damp sides of the old shaft are coated with its moss-like stain. But let no one ask for coherence, or even common-sense, in the pleasant old traditions of the moor.

It is a separate hamlet now within the treeless forest's gate, and as typical a bit of Dartmoor as exists. At first sight it consists of two, houses, one a low, rambling structure which was once the home of miners, the other a squat, box-shaped building, whitewashed years ago, patches of the wash still showing, the whole place very crumbling and cracking, the remains of a glass-house leaning insecurely across its front showing a few jagged bits of glass rattling in the wind but for some reason never falling. Against, or rather into, this house is dovetailed a tiny cottage of granite which has never been whitewashed and is to-day black with exposure, fronted by a quaint little court paved irregularly, here a flat slab, there a raised lump; every one stumbles when they walk across if they don't know the place; and down a cleft in the steep side of the moor a tiny stream descends bustling through ferns, making the long fronds dance after heavy rain, and entering the court over a smooth slab of granite to plunge into an artificial rock-basin soft with mosses; and then it splashes under a culvert older than Westminster Abbey and goes down to Wheal Dream.

The road across the gorge was made by the Court of Stannary and built up by spadiards in the days when labour was cheap. Those tinners knew how to work; the family of Jerry had not then entered the building trade; that road has never been restored and does not need it. Cutting between the farmhouse and the cottage dovetailed into it, separating them from the gorge where stand the gaunt ruins of the mine, it swings round sharply to pass the mine house perched at the extreme edge of the ravine, and then loses itself among the clatters of the high moor. Although corrugated iron has reached the place it is still beautiful; and the air is filled each day with the music of tumbling water.

They were a queer lot at Wheal Dream and a small lot, for the population was only five—two drunkards, two ancients, and a gentleman. The gorge and the little enclosed fields or binhays above were still nominally owned by the Duchy of Cornwall, but the family of Petherick had squatted there from very early times, for in the accounts presented during the reign of Henry the Seventh appears the entry, "New rent of Wheal Dream, of William Petherick and Richard Redegripp, for two acres of waste inclosed, 3d." The family of Redegripp had disappeared, or had become incorporated somehow like a defunct literary journal into that of the Pethericks; who still held the property and continued to pay a "new rent" to the Duchy, a far more nominal rent than the threepence required under the ancient order; but the Pethericks were not the legal owners of the property in spite of their squatter's title, which could be proved to have existed for at least four hundred years; and when George Brunacombe bought the old mine house from John Petherick for 150 pounds sterling and a dozen bottles of whisky a letter came from the Duchy warning the new owner that he could be turned out at any time, which would have been a proceeding resembling the acts of the Court of Stannary, who were above every law but their own. Evidently the Pethericks had been lawless folk, for in the records of the Survey Court occurs the entry, "Item they (the jurors) do present that William Petherick, by his owne confessyon, kild a stagge wth a pece or gun, nere a month since, about Halstock (wch is part in the fforest of Dartmoore and part in Venvill)." The record does not state whether for this offence against the Prince he was "presented," an expression which has nothing to do with what presented at Court means now, but might well stand as the finest euphemism for death by torture ever by the wit of man devised. This Petherick was no worse than his vicar, who was attached to answer the lord for disturbing the Prince's tenants by suing them in the Spiritual Court for tithes which they did not owe him.

The history of Wheal Dream, dealing with its legends, mining operations, and people, would need a volume; and it is with the present, rather than its past, condition that we are now concerned. The present inhabitants are our subject; the last dregs of the folk, still ignorant and primitive, who are being killed like the Red Indians by the civilisation which has for a long time surrounded and is now breaking over them, driving out the old, bringing in the new, ringing out the age of mettle, of muscle, sinew, and simplicity, and heralding the age of skill, brains, and trickery. Bigbones has finished his reign and must go to the wall against which he has been wont to push Littlebones. Evolution stays for nothing; first vegetation, then reptiles, then mammals, and now brains. The age of cunning has begun; and God help the giant.

John and Ursula Petherick occupied the farmhouse, and Amos Chown, her father, lived with them. He owned part of the furniture, an old-fashioned sofa as hard and uncomfortable to sit upon as a granite boulder, some chairs, a sideboard, and a table; at least he said so, but he was always claiming things, being old and liking to feel he was adding to his possessions. Sometimes he would point with one of his sticks to a picture or abominable ornament, and assert, "He be mine." If his daughter disagreed, Father, as he was always called, would take the article away to his own room and cover it carefully with a piece of sacking so that it should not be used or looked at. If she agreed he would chuckle and promise she should have it at his death. That event seemed a long way off. Father appeared to have reached a fixed point at which he threatened to become a permanent part of the landscape of Wheal Dream. He grew no older except in years. He tottered to and fro along the little road, from kitchen to linhay, from garden to cowshed, thinking he was doing a hard day's work but in reality doing nothing. He could chop an armful of sticks when the wind was westerly, but on ordinary occasions it took him half-a-day to cut a cabbage. The poor old fellow was dirty in his habits and it didn't trouble him if any one was looking. He spent much of his time on the little road, leaning heavily upon two sticks, coughing and spitting in a manner highly inartistic.

The tiny cottage was occupied by Uncle, whose other name was Gifford. There appeared to be some mystery about this old man, as he owned the cottage and a field behind, which property should have belonged to the Pethericks, and how he came by his title was not clear. His relationship was not clear either; he was Uncle to every one—even Father, who did not like him, called him Uncle. Ursula, who was manager of the estate—John being a debased type of being—was always saying that a great mistake had been made in permitting Uncle's claim to the field and cottage, but she could not explain how it had come to pass. Uncle remained in possession, though it was quite understood that the property would revert to the Pethericks upon his death, which could not be very far distant if only he did not contract the perennial habits of old Chown. Uncle was not beautiful to the eye; in a society of baboons he might have passed, but among trousered beings he took a low rank, for his face was an ugly red mask surrounded by a bristling hedge of whiskers, and a yellow fang on each side of his jaw were the sole survivors of the thirty-two which had fallen in the long struggle with Dartmoor bread and bacon. Uncle lived by himself; in the phrase of the moor "he had no woman," but the house-work was very light, for the bed only required making once a month and there were no dinners to be cooked.

The tenant of the mine house made himself heard at noon and in the dimsies. These were the times when he stretched his limbs and whistled. Many men who live alone take a pleasure in whistling, and George Brunacombe had grown skilful with long practice. He whistled the old songs he remembered shouting in his youth, sentimental rubbish, pothouse melodies, and hunting-ditties. At night, after finishing his work, he would sit by the window, looking down upon the ruins of Wheal Dream, and trying to imitate the night birds. On these occasions he was answered by his companion, for George did not live alone. One evening while skirting a tor he had introduced himself to Bubo, who had evidently been flung with violence from the home of his parents, either for misbehaving himself or as a person of no importance, and had damaged a leg in his fall. Bubo was quite a baby, and his round piteous eyes appealed to George, who picked him up, brought him home, and treated him as his own son. The injured leg dropped off, but Bubo did not appear to miss it much, nor did he hobble about with two sticks after the manner of the old men on the other side of the gorge. Two little wings were good enough for him, but they never carried him far from the mine house. The little owl loved the big one with all his owlish heart; for it could never have occurred to Bubo that his protector was a human being, one of those monstrous creatures who arm themselves with guns, traps, knives, and poison, like villains of melodrama, and wage war upon pretty beings who sin by asking for little bits of the big world to dwell in and small gulps of air to keep their hearts beating. Still Bubo ought to have known better, for

George had described himself at some length for his companion's benefit; and the little owl was given every opportunity to watch the big one at work, only he was so sleepy in the day time and at night there were mice to hunt in the mine house. George had lost no time in explaining himself—

"If you care to share the house of a superfluous and injured being, who is tormented by seven devils, you shall be welcome, little one. I can see you are injured, and I may guess you are superfluous. You appear to have been the one beak too much, and the morality of your society does not insist upon your preservation, which is so like the morality of mine that I must take pity upon you. We are both bipeds originally, which appears to be another tie between us. I regret the absence of wings, but as you can see I have the bones, which for lack of a better name I call arms. The feathers have not grown yet, but good theologians assure me they will be produced abundantly in a future state."

The fluffy little big-eyed ball made a sound of ridiculous incredulity, much more like a human baby than an owl.

"Don't get perturbed. I won't force my religion upon you," George went on, in a gentle manner which made his cynicism harmless enough. "When you grow up you may join the Seventh Day Adventists or the Plymouth Brethren if you like. I do not know your sex, therefore I shall regard you for the present as without one. Later on I shall regard you as common to either, with a tendency towards the male gender. I hope you won't betray my confidence by laying an egg."

Bubo drew a film over his eyes, as if he was trying to take photographs of his companion, and assumed an attitude of dejection. George created a perch, placed Bubo thereon with his face towards the dark, and continued—

"So long as your presence helps to drive out the devil of loneliness, which is the chief of all the devils, you shall remain. When you cease to do so, you and some beefsteak will meet together in a pie. The second devil tormenting me is the very devil of disease, the third of poverty, the fourth of art, the fifth of literature, the sixth of poetry, the seventh of ambition—I'm afraid there are others quite as bad, and they go at me with red-hot claws; and the only angel who fights on my side against these devils is glorious Dartmoor wind."

That was George's history in a few words; he was a man tormented by devils; hardly a genius, but possessing all the talents, and not succeeding in any of them; not knowing himself what he was. One time he called himself an artist, another time a writer of prose, and then a poet. He had tried sculpture, architecture, preparing designs for painted windows, many other things. He could do them all, but there were always plenty of others who could do them better. Had all his powers been concentrated in one form of art he must have been a success; as it was he represented that most unsatisfactory and luckless of beings, the man of many facets with mediocrity written upon each one. Nature could have taught him a lesson had he been a closer student of her ways. She would have shown him that the tree which has its lower branches lopped grows into one fine head. George had not the strength of will to lop off his side branches and devote all his sap to one strong growth. Art admits of no trifling; she must have the whole heart or none. The mind which is so powerful in one big current becomes weak and shallow when divided into a number of little streams. The man, who called himself one day a painter and the next a poet, had not learnt that.

George was weak in body and mind, but strong in courage. He did not know when he was beaten. In the old days he had taken a London studio, and set himself to win the title of first painter of the day, though even then he would write poetry at night; but he could not make a living out of art, and had to fall back upon posters for cigarettes and soaps. The first thing that did for him was his originality. He filled a big canvas with a Hebrew subject, Elijah running before the chariot of Ahab towards the gates of Jezreel, a fine picture full of strength; the driver leaning over his horses urging them on, the king scowling at the old man who seemed to be carried by the wind ahead, the storm breaking behind. Unconventional treatment caused the picture to be rejected by the Academy; and the dealers to whom it was offered refused to buy for the same reason. One of Hebrew extraction was prepared to offer a few pounds if George would paint a halo about Elijah's head, but the artist refused with violence, saying that no amount of argument would ever convince him that men passed through life with a sort of glorified soup-plate hovering above their heads. Back the picture went to his studio, and with a few touches George reduced it from the sublime to the ridiculous, and sold it finally to a firm as an advertising poster for their extract of beef.

The second cause of his defeat was illness; his chest had been always weak, and at the age of thirty grave symptoms asserted themselves, and the stubborn fellow worked with one hand while he pushed death away with the other. That sort of struggle could not last long in the atmosphere of Fitzroy Street. He became so weak that he could hardly drag himself across the studio, and he was in daily peril of being killed when crossing a street. Pen and brush fell from his hand at last because the fingers could no longer control them, and one day George muttered between his coughs, "I'll go home, and crawl over the rocks, and die upon the heather." He came of a Devonshire family, the Brunacombes of Plympton, last and least of the Stannary Towns, and his boyhood had been spent upon the moor. Even in time of health he had longed for the little rivers and the open spaces, and the sweet smell of peat. He loathed the never-ending maze of streets which stifled body and mind alike. With five shillings in his pocket he went off to a doctor, and said in his brusque way, "I want you to examine me. Five shillings is all I can afford, and if it isn't enough I'll go to a hospital and be examined for nothing." The doctor went over him, laughed cheerily—he was an Irishman with a keen sense of humour—and told him he would probably be dead in three months. "Thanks," said George. "When a doctor gives you up the worst is over. This time next year I'll run you a mile for that five bob." "Keep it for your funeral expenses," said the jolly Irishman. "You'll want it first," replied George; and off he went, assisting his steps homeward by the area railings.

The next thing was to raise a little capital for the exodus. A few pictures went at half-a-crown apiece to a bejewelled Israelite who was by no means without guile, but the sum thus obtained did not mean affluence. Then George remembered he had a sort of aunt, a lady who had married his uncle and lived somewhere in the West End in the seclusion of widowhood, so he went off in search of her, forgetting the exact address but remembering the locality. After searching two days, and ringing a number of bells, and making use of about two score brass knockers, and being confronted with the supercilious stare of numerous men-servants and maid-servants, he was directed to a narrow house which he at first mistook as a sort of rival to the Zoological Gardens. Mrs. Brunacombe lived there in the society of beasts and fishes, creeping things and fowls of the air. When George was introduced he found himself in the strong-smelling atmosphere of a room where cats and monkeys were disporting themselves without much respect for furniture, parrots were shrieking and canaries making bedlam. White mice were upon one chair, an unholy looking lizard upon another, and in tanks round the walls were fishes and various aquatic monsters. The childless owner of all this created life was trying to administer a worm-pill to a sick and shivering dog. "He will eat the lizards," she explained, "and they disagree with him."

"I should imagine it was equally unhealthy for the lizards," said George. "I hope there are no tigers," he went on nervously.

"Oh no, none of the larger carnivora," said the lady, who was not troubled with a sense of humour. "But a young panther is coming next week. I hope he will get on with the others. Who are you? Did you say you were a relation?"

"I am your nephew, George Brunacombe."

"Oh yes, poor Willie's nephew. You used to come and dine when he was alive. After his death I felt lonely, so I surrounded myself with this little family. The neighbours object rather, as the snakes escape sometimes, and the people about here are not lovers of animals. One lot prosecuted me, but last summer they went away and left a cat shut up in the empty house, so I prosecuted them for that, and now we are level again."

"I have come to see you because I am ill," said George, coming to business while he could. The atmosphere of that menagerie was telling upon him.

"You look it," said his aunt happily. "I'll give you a box of pills. My little round things cure anything. I take one myself every night."

"I want to go home to Dartmoor," George went on. "Only I have no money. I came to ask you if you are leaving me anything?"

"Bless the man. I want it all for the poor animals," cried his aunt. As a matter of fact she was leaving George a thousand pounds, all of which was Brunacombe money left by the deceased William.

"I am willing to be regarded as a poor animal," said George. "I have broken down. I have reached the crisis of my life, and if I can't get a little money now I must go under. If you are leaving me anything, can you let me have it now?"

"If I give you five hundred pounds will you promise not to worry me again?" said the lady.

George promised, Mrs. Brunacombe said she would write to her man of business, and the interview ended with a present of a box of pills and a firm refusal to kiss a strongly-scented monkey. Then the sick man got away as well as he could, but as he passed the window up it went like a bomb exploding, the lady's head appeared, and her voice shouted amid the shrieks of parrots, "When you get down to Dartmoor send me up some nice big sundews. I'll keep them in saucers and fatten 'em with bits of meat."

So George went back to his native air and for some months played the invalid in a farmhouse near Two Bridges. Then he grew better and was able to travel about the moor looking for a home, working towards the high district in the north which is dominated by the huge curving line of Hoga de Cosdon or Cawsand. One evening he reached the little village of Metheral, which was at that time unknown to the outer world; and as he walked in the dark along the road he stumbled upon a huge pair of boots the toes of which were making miniature tors heavenwards. A man occupied those boots, and his name was John Petherick, and his condition from his own point of view was satisfactory. George assisted him to rise and helped him home. They reached Wheal Dream in the dark and were welcomed by Ursula, who was far more astonished at the presence of the gentleman than by the state of her husband. George stayed there for the night as he thought; but he never went away from the place again. He too had his dream, like the spadiard of those days of legend; a dream of riches, fame, and a fair maiden. He woke with a thrill, the glory of that delicious dream—love idealised; what could be better?—in him and through him, and saw that the room was in glory too. The moon had come up while he slept. He wondered what it was like in the dreamland outside, for it had been too dark to see anything when he had arrived assisting foul-smelling Petherick along the Stannary road. He went to the window and looked out, down into the gorge, saw the old mine below, the old wheal house beyond, the sparkling water, the heather shaken by the wind. He could not describe what he saw. It was like the dream, which still seemed to be floating there in the moonlit haze and the unpolluted air. George put out his head and drank.

"I have come home," he said.

HEATHER

CHAPTER III
ABOUT A MIXED FAMILY

The distance between Wheal Dream and the sanatorium was not great in strides; but in other matters they were years apart. Progress in the region of the mine was slow, and it was an evil kind of progress; the wind of civilisation which blows no native any good. Ursula looked upon those ladies who came to her house once, but never again, perceived that she belonged to the same species, but that her life was not theirs, and forthwith she broke out into complaints about her lot. She wanted to be in a position to wear fine raiment and to despise work; and because she could not rise she sank, believing in her foolish mind that she was ascending in the social scale by insulting her lodgers, lying shamelessly, cheating, attending to them when in a state of intoxication, and hiccuping noisily at their objections. She thought she was making herself a lady.

John was a supreme effort of Nature's work in clownishness. To see him walk was a revelation in clumsiness. He stumbled along, his head much in advance of his boots, his body lurching first to one side, then to the other, following the feet, as though the body had been made of some sort of rubber, his elbows and arms paddling the air like a very awkward swimmer. He was so ignorant that it was difficult to make him comprehend the most ordinary remark. It had required a week for George to impress upon him with Ursula's assistance the simple statement that he wanted to buy the mine house; and other days were spent in explaining to John that he was not going to be robbed. He never quite understood what had happened, except that he had received £150 and some bottles of whisky for the old building and the scrap of ground it occupied. The liquor appealed to his understanding with more success, and he lost no time in devoting it to the use for which it was intended, only much too quickly. Perhaps that was why he had no recollection of cleaning the place out—it had been used as a barn before George came—or of helping the mason to repair the house. John was a good worker where no skill was required. He could not have nailed two bits of wood together, but he could haul granite with any one.

George had come as a sort of missionary to Wheal Dream, unsettling people who would have been much better left alone, making the Pethericks pay the usual penalty of ignorant folk who occupy a pleasant part of the earth's surface. In a sense he had cheated them, as the property was worth more than he had given, but he was too poor to offer more and the money seemed a great deal to them, though it did them far more harm than good. They spent every penny in folly of some kind. Heaven only knows how they did spend it, for nothing was added to the farm and no improvement was effected in the property. At the end they were actually worse off by having lost the mine house. Nor was this all. Dartmoor was getting discovered; city folk were finding out that little bits of terrestrial Paradise had been dropped about on this roof of Devon and had become accessible with the building of railways and the extinction of hostile savages. They also ascertained that land for building was scarce and that the Duchy had become jealous of its rights. There was nothing for it but to use a little honest cunning with the ignorant folk. A cunning lawyer came to Wheal Dream and dazzled the Pethericks with sovereigns. He said they could have them, as he was sorry to see them so poor and hardworking, only they would have to pay him interest which meant just a few pounds each year. He also promised to protect their interests against every one, and to give them the benefit of his advice at any time free of charge. Then he produced a paper which they couldn't read, and invited John to test his powers of penmanship. The poor clown could not write, but he made his mark in the presence of witnesses, and the lawyer went away with most of that pretty bit of Dartmoor known as Wheal Dream mortgaged to him. The Court of Stannary itself could not have done a neater stroke of business; but the distinction was obvious; for the officials of that Court were an unscrupulous lot, and this lawyer was a respectable man and a gentleman.

One other thing civilisation had done for the Pethericks; it had made them atheists. Greater presumption could hardly be imagined, seeing that their freewill—a gift which neither of them deserved—was not allied with the smallest particle of knowledge. John and

Ursula treated the stupendous problems of life and origin like so much cow-dung, as rotten stuff to be trampled into the land. They had not the sense to learn anything from their cows or pigs, who looked to them for food and attention, just as the lowest of human beings look up at the sun and behind that to the origin of creation which must exist somewhere. They thought it a fine thing to believe in nothing. It was originality, although they would not have known the meaning of that word; it made them different from, and therefore better than, their associates. They sneered when the chapel-folk passed weighted with respectable Bibles. They were superior to that sort of thing. And yet when Ursula had anything new in the way of outward apparel she went to church, not to be "put upon by the reverent," but to display her advancement in the social scale. As for Father, he was too old and tired to worry much. He considered that the religious attendances of his younger days would serve to "bring him home," if he thought about the matter at all. Perhaps he would have gone to church if they had let him spit and relieve himself as he desired.

The Pethericks did not attempt to understand Uncle, and therefore they despised him. Old Gifford had much to put up with. For all his ugliness he was a gentle old thing; he was also fairly well educated, that is to say he could read and scratch a few characters upon paper; and there was a warm sort of heart in his baboon-like body. The old fellow would have appreciated a little sympathy, but he didn't get it from the Pethericks. They only wanted to know when he was going to die and let them have his field and cottage.

"How be ye, Uncle?" asked Ursula, as she passed the little court across the culvert where the water was splashing into the bowels of Wheal Dream. She was going to the mine house to make the place dirtier under the pretence of cleaning up, as it had been agreed under the contract of sale that she should act as George's housekeeper.

"Mazed," said the old man in his resigned way. He was peeping over the gate where he often stood, unlike Father who shuffled to and fro. Fortunately Uncle was not objectionable in his habits; another like old Chown would have made the Stannary road insanitary.

"Bad job if yew'm mazed," said Ursula pleasantly. "What be chapel going to du? Reckon 'em wun't open on Sundays when yew'm gone home."

Uncle did not continue the subject, knowing he would be jeered at. He only meant to imply that he was in a state of bewilderment. It was evident he wanted to talk to some one. He held a highly

37

coloured card printed in Bavaria which was a long way from Wheal Dream; and on one side was inscribed "Mr. Gifford, Wheal Dream, Metheral, England," with a short message written in a somewhat baffling style; and on the other was the full-length portrait of a simpering young lady who seemed to have mislaid most of her clothes. Uncle thought it very beautiful but rather shocking, and he had almost decided that the card must not be placed in his Bible where such art treasures usually reposed. He was silly enough to show the picture side to Ursula, who broke out at once—

"That be a proper old thing, bain't it? The sort o' thing yew chapel-folk send to one another. Some woman sent 'en, I reckon, some dirty woman wi'out the shame to cover her nakedness. Us bain't going to have no woman here, Uncle, and I tells ye, whether 'em be respectable, or whether 'em be actresses. That's what comes o' your chapel meeting when yew gropes in the dark. I reckon yew ha' seen she wi' less on than her has there."

"It come this morning," said Uncle in his defenceless way, as if that was a complete answer to her charges.

"Well, break 'en up, and try to live decent," said Ursula, with a full sense of her own virtue.

Uncle wanted to say a good deal more, but he was wise enough to refrain. Ursula would not treat him fairly. He put his baboon-like head over the gate and looked along the little road, wondering if there was any one to listen to him. There was only Father scratching his back against a projecting stone like an old horse, ignorant that a bath would probably have been a better cure; but another figure was proceeding slowly towards the moor gate, and Uncle watched it until he recognised old Willum Brokenbrow who was coming from the village to inquire after Father's health. He was no friend, so Uncle shuffled over the court to where the water pushed through the ferns, and went up some rough steps which led to his garden suspended on the steep side of the moor; and there he seated himself and exhibited his improper postcard to the bees.

Ursula had gone on to the mine house and was telling George what a dirty old creature Uncle was getting, and how various women were inciting him to marry them by sending him portraits of their anatomical charms. "Uncle ha' saved a bit. That's what they'm after," she said. "Them chapel women would du worse than go naked vor a bit o' money."

On the road Father was coughing and spitting worse than ever, while old Brokenbrow aided and abetted his efforts until George had to get up and shut his window. The old men were deadly rivals and they desired to convince each other how ill they were. They had been friendly once, and all the bitterness between them had been caused by the sexton, who one day took it into his head to uproot a large escallonia which grew beside the wall of the church and close to the porch. There was at first no connection between the sexton's high-handed deed—which was perhaps natural, as no commoner can tolerate the sight of a growing tree or bush—and the controversy between Chown and Brokenbrow. The sexton, who could do as he liked in the churchyard—the vicar being old and indifferent—had removed the escallonia to lessen his own labours. The bush grew so rapidly and was always requiring to be trimmed, and to clear it away meant having no more bother with it. The unforeseen result was that another burying-space came into existence, which was also the choicest in the whole churchyard, being snugly situated in the angle made by wall with porch, and in full view of every one who entered the building. Naturally the last commandment was shattered; for there are few things a commoner hankers after much more than a desirable resting-place, and competition for the new space became so severe that the sexton had to promise in the vicar's name that the grave should be awarded to the first parishioner who should be in a fitting condition to occupy it. No better plan for robbing death of its unpleasantness could possibly have been devised; and when the wheelwright of the adjoining village of Downacombe-beside-the-moor, who was also an undertaker and a good many other things beside, promised to award a handsome coffin to the successful competitor, enthusiasm ran high, and a peaceful ending became the favourite topic of conversation among the aged and infirm.

Unfortunately for the aspirants it is not such an easy matter to perish upon the heights of Dartmoor. The wind, like the ancestral bellows in every cottage, blows the flame up whenever it dies down, and a funeral is such a rare event that it naturally attracts far more attention and provokes much greater real joyousness than any commoner function such as a wedding or revel. Try as they would the old folk couldn't get rid of their mortality. The very effort seemed to make them more lusty and strong. The excitement of trying to succumb stimulated them to take a new lease of life. Some of them tried unfair means, such as protracted visits to the inn, until the sexton intervened with the statement that he and the vicar had drawn up certain rules. Any one who might be suspected of any attempt at shortening his days by means of beer would be disqualified. The publican opposed this measure with violence, but without success. He described it as a deliberate attempt to take the bread out of his mouth.

Father had been for some time considered the most likely candidate for the position, but Brokenbrow had been gaining upon him lately, and in the opinion of many good judges was thought likely to win. After reaching a certain point Father ceased to make any downward progress, while Brokenbrow failed with a regularity which was reassuring to himself and his friends. Old Chown had therefore every reason to regard his rival with hatred. He had not the least desire to hobble in the rear of the procession which would follow Brokenbrow to that snug corner beside the porch. He wanted to look down from on high and regard the disappointed Brokenbrow following him.

"How be ye, Wullum?" he asked, as they hobbled together upon the Stannary road. "Purty fine, I reckon," he added hopefully.

"I be cruel bad. I knaw I be bad," said the champion of Metheral. "I be going home soon."

Home was to old Willum, not heaven, but the beautiful corner near the porch where his tombstone would be witnessed by worshippers from one generation to another.

"Yew'm looking lusty, Amos," he said happily.

"I bain't," said Father sharply. "I be expecting more and more. Doctor gave I a little bottle for my expectations, and he looked at 'en through a telescope and said 'em warn't the expectations of a man what could live long."

Father's rendering of unusual words was generally inaccurate. He gave further details which were not pleasant hearing; and then he hoped Brokenbrow would hobble home and take great care of himself, as he feared the old man was overtaxing his strength by walking across to Wheal Dream. Brokenbrow assured him that he could look after himself, until such time as the whole neighbourhood should turn out in black garments to do him honour. He went on to mention how his grandson had driven him down in the farm cart to Downacombe and had stopped at the wheelwright's yard. They had gone in to gloat over the prize of the competition which was open in more senses than one to the parishioners of Metheral.

"Brass handles, Amos," he whispered tauntingly. " Aw, 'twas a bravish sight. Brass handle as 'twas here, and another as 'twas there. Good enough vor the Duke, God save 'en. And a plate on the top o' mun all brass, and 'tis proper, Amos. The plate vor the name, Willum Brokenbrow, went to heaven as 'tmight be Monday."

Father made disgusting noises and pawed with his two sticks like a new quadruped. He was in the unfortunate position of being unable to assault Brokenbrow, as that might only hasten on his rival's decease. His vocabulary was so limited that he could not express his feelings beyond saying, "I be dalled if Metheral be going to beat Wheal Dream."

"They'm putting on varnish tu, best brown varnish. They'm sparing no expense 'cause 'tis an advertisement vor 'em," continued Brokenbrow, with great relish. "'Tis made of oak, and wull last hundreds o' years. There bain't many a squire what can afford to be put away as I'll be, please God."

Father made more noises and shuffled away, his queer old head shaking like the top of a pine-tree. "Yew wun't ha' 'en. Us wun't let ye. Us wur commoners avore yew," he growled.

"Yew can't du nought if I goes first, as I be going to. I gets weaker every day," came the exasperating answer.

"Us'll dig ye out on't," declared poor old Father. He had set his simple heart upon that grave, and he saw nothing humorous in his ambitions. After his grovelling life it would be such a great thing to be buried like a gentleman, and to lie beside the entry of the church for ever. His rival's hoarse cackle of laughter fell upon his dull ears as they parted in a state of enmity which would never have existed had the lazy sexton not demolished that bush of escallonia.

The damp and shadowy mists dragged themselves across the moor, and the curving line of Cawsand became like a sky-serpent. Uncle came down from his garden, lighted the smoky lamp in his little stone-floored room—it was very cold and bare, but he did not notice any defect, as he was accustomed to nothing else—opened the big Bible upon the table, and stood leaning over it peering at the big black print. He read aloud from the big book every night and morning, and when he became excited over a battle or murder all Wheal Dream could hear him; and the Pethericks would bang at the partition wall, telling him to "shut his noise," and sometimes would poke their heads in at the door to assure him what they thought of chapel-folk. Uncle did not heed them, but went on reading by the gleam of the smoky lamp. He stood when he read his Bible, his boots upon the cold stones, his hands upon his sticks, his head low down. He missed none of the long words, but read them all, although pedants might have been surprised and grieved at some of his renderings.

That evening Uncle could not read because he was excited and unsettled. It was all on account of the postcard, the almost illegible message upon it, not the almost immoral picture. He held it firmly in his left hand; he had not let it go since morning, and he was making it very dirty, as Uncle did not spend money on soap. Then the chapter it was his duty to read proved very dry; there wasn't a single murder in it and not even a battle. Uncle went out; his sticks tapped upon the rough stones; he went towards the mine house feeling that he must speak to some one; his baboon-like head was aching just because he couldn't find any one to appreciate the postcard. There was a light in Father's room and there were insanitary noises. The old gentleman was going to bed, thinking of the beautiful grave and trying to qualify himself for it.

George was in his studio, writing poetry, as it was too dark for painting, while Bubo made merry upon his perch, trying to describe the joys of evening to his master, telling him about the dusky pine-trees and the fir-cones falling in the wind unseen by any one, and how beautifully scented the night was, though mortals missed it all; and then at the dawn, which was the dimsy of all respectable owls, the pine-trees would shake themselves and wake, and birches would rustle and whisper like ladies clad in silk, and little pink blossoms of the whortle would sprinkle the silvery and slippery moor with jewels of the morning. And then Bubo scuttled off in a practical mood to hunt mice, while George wondered who was knocking at the door.

It was only Uncle showing his two yellow fangs as if he was proud of them and trying to be very amiable. It was not so dark that the artist could not see a gaudy picture which had nothing whatever to do with Puritanism, for Uncle was holding it out and beaming over it, and declaring in his quaint, cracked voice how it had come to him that morning. George was at a loss for words. From an artistic point of view the card was an abomination; as a toy it was good enough for Uncle, but it did not appeal to him.

"Coming to-morrow, sir," whispered old Gifford eagerly. That was what he had wanted to say all day. His head felt better already.

"Is she?" said George dryly. "I'm afraid the folk will say unpleasant things about you."

"No, sir. 'Twas a lawful marriage. Us wur wed in Metheral church, and Jimmy be our grandson, sir," said Uncle, trying hard to explain and finding it difficult, but delighted to have a listener.

George perceived that the old man had come to relieve his mind, to tell him something, not to exhibit a portrait of his wife. In a more sympathetic voice he suggested,

"You had this card from her this morning?"

"Her's dead, sir," replied Uncle. "'Tis from Jimmy. He sent it and ses he'm coming. I wun't live lonely any more, sir. Thankye kindly vor hearkening," he added, with great respect.

The old man was himself again, and was happy now he had imparted the great secret with which he had been in travail all day. Jimmy was coming home to look after him, cheer him with conversation, walk to chapel with him, protect him from the Pethericks. Jimmy would go out to work while Uncle stopped at home to clean the cottage and cook the food. When the troublesome gift of imagination had been given out Uncle had been hovering near the outskirts of the crowd and had picked up a tiny fragment which somebody with a big load of it had dropped. Uncle was using that fragment, and by its virtue he saw himself looking over the moor gate every evening waiting for Jimmy to come home with the reed basket on his arm and crowbar over his shoulder, for Jimmy was a strong boy and would become a granite-cracker. It would be a happy life for the old man now that Jimmy was coming home.

"He'm my grandson, sir, son o' my son," he went on. "His vaither took to beer, sir, and went to foreign parts, and I ain't never heard on 'en since. Read 'en, sir," he said, holding out the dirty postcard.

George took it and went back into the house, while Uncle followed and stood at the inner door, his ugly face shining with happiness in the lamplight. He was very glad he had summoned up courage to come and tell the gentleman. He would find his Bible very interesting reading when he got back.

"He's coming to-day," said George suddenly.

"To-morrow, sir," said Uncle, with firmness. The gentleman was speaking to him as if he hadn't got every bit of the card by heart.

"That means to-day. You see he wrote it yesterday," George explained; but it was some time before he could make Uncle alter his opinion. When he succeeded lamentations followed.

"I mun get back and blow up the turves, and I mun go up the garden and pull carrots and turnips and mak' a stew vor Jimmy. He'll be proper hungry sure 'nuff. What did him want to say he wur coming to-morrow when he'm coming to-day?"

Uncle went off on his two sticks, faster than he had walked for years, while George pulled off his working coat and wiped the snuff from his bushy beard. He had not been out of the house all day, and he thought he would get on the moor and tramp a mile or two through the heather to watch the white mist rolling down the dark cleave of the Okement. There was fascination for George the artist in that cleave, the fascination of romance and dreams. He took his stick and went out, passing the kitchen where Ursula, with a grimy shawl over her head, appeared to be flinging crockery and saucepans about as a preliminary to preparing his supper. He knew what it was—cold mutton which the butcher called lamb. It was always cold mutton at the wheal house. That knuckly bone clad with a little sorrowful meat was another of George's devils. He cursed the thought of it as he went up the steep slope out of the gorge, up on the heights, skirting the big bog, and still up until there was nothing to break the wind and he felt it tugging at his beard.

In the cleave beyond it was silent enough; one side of it was the moor bristling with clatters, a breakneck sort of place leading down to a bubbling bog; the other side, steep almost as a wall, was the hanging garden of the wood of Halstock. Down the bottom the river slid over its smooth bed of stone, always visible because it is white like a snowslide. It penetrates the darkest night with its cold whiteness, and a belated pedestrian will start sometimes and exclaim, "What's that?" George knew his way; there was no secret of that cleave which had not been revealed to him. Down the steep side he went, reeling from a boulder, plunging into furze, careless of prickles or bruises, drawing near the spot which was the source of his inspiration, the place which was hallowed with the romance of two thousand years. There it was under the black shadow of the hanging wood, a swirl of white water, a line of flat stones—the ford which lies on the east side of St. Michael's chapel of Halstock.

"Out of a world of cold mutton at last," gasped George.

The chapel has gone, its memory has almost fled, but the Ford remains; the Ford is necessary, the chapel was not. Men must cross the river, but they needn't go to church.

"But not out of the world of those things that spoil Wheal Dream," George muttered.

A boy was sitting on a flat stone hugging a big bundle in his arms, a hungry-looking boy with a low forehead, flat nose, and big mouth. Only his mother could have called him beautiful.

"You are Jimmy Gifford," said George, going up to him.

The boy looked frightened and sullen, but he answered civilly enough, "Ees, sir. I be going to Wheal Dream. Where's it to, sir?"

" Up over," said George, pointing over the moor, which was getting black and threatening. "Why did you come this way?"

"They told I 'twas shortest way from the station."

"So it is, for a bird. But it's no joke walking up by the waterslide after dark."

"I comed quick, sir, to get up avore the light went. I be proper tired," said the boy.

"No wonder. Why don't you sling that bundle on your back?"

George started as he spoke. It seemed to him that the bundle of clothing wriggled as if some small animal was inside. The boy opened it; there was a mass of rags and tatters, and in the middle some wizened features, a sort of old man's face, a little white bald head.

"What have you got there—a monkey?"

"A little babby, sir. Her's mine," was the answer.

"You're the father. How old are you?"

"Sixteen, sir."

"Who's the mother?"

"A little maid, sir."

"I mean how old is she?"

"Fifteen come January, sir."

George turned his head and looked at the stones in the swirling water, and beyond to the wet wood and St. Michael's heights. He was wondering whether any more astounding couple than the boy and the baby had ever crossed that historic ford.

"You had better get on. Your grandfather is waiting for you. I will show you the way round to Wheal Dream."

Jimmy got up, hugging his burden, and followed the gentleman up the steep track, lurching from side to side and panting, while George muttered to himself, "And I'm nearly forty. The miserable rabbits! According to their view of life, if they have one, I ought to be a great-grandfather." Then he turned with the question, "Where is she—the girl?"

"Her wur turned out, same as I. Her went off with a soldier," gasped the boy.

"First you, then the soldier, and then the deluge. Fifteen come January. How did it happen?"

"Us wur to a farm. They had nought but two bedrooms, and me and the maid wur put into one. They reckoned us wur tu young, but us warn't," he said in a cunning fashion.

"Follow this path," said George abruptly. "Turn to the left—this is the left, not that—at the wall of the new-take, and you'll come down to Metheral. Any one will show you the road to Wheal Dream."

HEATHER

CHAPTER IV
ABOUT GREGORY BREAKBACK

Everyone knew Gregory Breakback, but he lived apart from them all, a lonely, sexless life. His home was upon a big shoulder of the moor where it made its last heave before falling into the cultivated land. The place has no recognised name; some call it Moor Down, but Gregory always alluded to it as Moor Gate; and he was generally right where any moorland tradition was concerned. There were a few small oaks and a fir-tree or two on the side of the down, which was part of Dartmoor but just outside the forest; and among these trees was a ruin, a long, low building of loose stones, dragged down by neglect and weather, roofless, every bit of planching rotted away. At the western end the hand of the restorer had been at work. Gregory was the restorer. He had made himself one large room, rain- and wind-proof, had contrived a sloping roof and covered it with slates which he had quarried in the glen of Halstock, had plastered the interstices between the stones with mud mixed with chopped broom to bind it together, and thus had supplied himself with a comfortable, if rather unsightly, habitation. It was primitive architecture, but that sort is as lasting as any. The savage built for eternity with his mud and straw, and his walls stand now, defying rain and shaming dishonest civilisation. One stone placed upon another will remain so for ever without any need of mortar, unless some malicious creature pushes it over. Primitive folk understand the simple facts of architecture, apply them to their own necessity, and obtain a home for nothing. Every man could have a house of his own if the law and his own instincts permitted him to revert to the healthier conditions of barbarism.

Gregory referred to the ruin as his castle. He called no man landlord, but paid an annual quit-rent to the Duchy, a nominal fee for the right to squat. He had no master, yet he worked for plenty, and left them curtly when they answered him back. He could not stand being answered back. He had no companion except Ben, a shaggy beast who had been trained as a sheep-dog, and remembered his schooling well enough to try and round up every sheep he saw about Moor Gate. It was by odd jobs that Gregory lived; he did not mind what the work was so long as his employer kept out of the way or was decently servile if he appeared. People had learnt to understand Gregory. When the frost loosened a hedge so that the stones came tumbling out it was necessary to draw his attention to the fact in a delicate manner; not to tell him to do the repairing. He would have tossed the crowbar over his shoulder and said, "Break your own back, master." He was always using that expression, threatening to break the backs of the people, playing upon his own name, but meaning nothing, for he had never placed his great hands roughly on any man, though he had been near it when some fool in liquor had answered him back.

He was a big man in size and strength, not in the world's goods; and great in character without knowing it, bearing his hard lot patiently, well aware that it was hard, but smiling at it—he was always smiling and swinging over the moor with great, loose strides like a mass of granite rolling downhill—grateful for health, replying warmly to every polite word. That was Gregory Breakback, who had made himself a habitation, who lived alone without benefit of women, who did all the work that came to his hands, who had never owned one single golden sovereign in his life. He owed no man a penny; when money had to come it came. Gregory smiled at life and dared it to break his back.

How did he come by his name? Nobody wondered, for break and broken cropped up perpetually in the surnames of Metheral and Downacombe. There was old Willum Brokenbrow, for instance, who was a favourite for the grave by the porch; and there was Loveday Brokenbone, who was coming into prominence by reason of a bronchial attack which at her time of life might very well end by securing for her the coveted burying-place, leaving Willum a bad second and Father nowhere. Dame Brokenbone was possibly the last woman alive owning to the dainty English name of Loveday, which like many others, such as Sibella, Petronell, Emblyn, Annys, Penticost, Rabish, Flower, Gilian, Pascha, Creature, and Flowery, all of them frequent names for girls in registers up to the seventeenth century, have been ousted from country families by an endless succession of Bessies and Annies. But as for the destructive surnames, Gregory himself had explained the matter to George, whom he loved, for the artist lent him books, and Gregory, who could read like a clerk, had a tenderness for literature.

"Well, sir, I'll tull ye how 'twas. Years ago, avore history wur wrote, I reckon, the king in London used to send chaps what he had no use vor to work in the tin mines, just as the King of Russia sends 'em to Siberia, according to what I've read. 'Twas to get 'em out o' the way and kill 'em off quiet, vor they hadn't much chance of escaping from the mines, and if 'em tried they wur took to Lydford and pressed. Du'ye know what the Lydford press wur like? Wull, I'll tull ye. 'Twas just an old oak door, and they put mun on top of the poor chap, and a gurt lump o' granite atop o' that, and let 'em bide. When he wur pressed they buried 'en and then sat in judgment on 'en. If they found 'en guilty 'twas well enough, and if they found 'en innocent they said 'twas a pity sure 'nuff, but mistakes wur bound to happen. That wur the law, sir, and I reckon there allus has been a lot o' mad dog about the law. I seed a picture in a book yew lent me of a woman wi' a gurt knife in her hand and a cloth over her eyes, and underneath was wrote Justice. Wull, sir, if yew were to turn a woman loose, wi' her eyes covered and a knife in her hand, she'd stick that knife into the first that came along.

"'Twas proper hard in the tin-mines, no shelter, and little food, and most of 'em died, they ses. Them who served their time got together and reckoned they'd squat on the moor and till it. But they wur a wild lot o' chaps, couldn't agree among themselves, and they got a-fighting and killing one another. Them what was left squatted hereabouts to live as best they could, only as they didn't want volks to knaw who they wur they took new names. 'Twas just after the fight, and one of 'em wur saying how he'd broke another fellow's back, and wur proud on't, so t'others called 'en Breakback. And another said he'd got a rib broke, so they called 'en Brokenbone. It went on like that until all the fellows had got new names, and they ha' never been changed from that day to this. Most of 'em died rough. They lived by sheep-stealing mostly and wur hanged on the oaks of Halstock; but they managed to breed a bit avore they went, or I wouldn't ha' been telling to yew now."

George wanted evidence, but Gregory could only produce a roll of parchment, which contained a sort of record of the Breakback family, or rather had contained, for much of the roll had decayed away entirely, and a large portion of the remainder was fragile network with the ink dropping off in flakes. This roll, valuable only for its antiquity, had remained in the family nearly four hundred years and by a series of miracles had escaped destruction. At the beginning the name of Humphrey Odyorne appeared in a thick yellow scrawl, and to this Gregory pointed with the remark, "That wur our name avore us took t'other. So my granfer told I, and his granfer told he. Us ha' allus said 'twas Odyorne avore it wur Breakback, and I ha' got as much right to one as t'other. That's right, sir. A true story be powerful hard to kill. Bain't like an old lie what kills itself. Us be long livers. If a Breakback dies under ninety he'm nipped in the bud sure 'nuff. Death don't break our backs easy, I tull ye."

George could only agree to all that was said, knowing his man. Gregory would stand more from the artist than from any one, but even he dared not argue with the strong man of the ruin.

"Wull, sir, there be some queer things wrote on this old sheepskin," Gregory went on. "I reckon yew couldn't read 'em now, nor me neither; but granfer pointed 'em out to I, and he warn't born this century nor yet last, and I mind where his old finger went and what he said. Aw, sir, half-a-dozen Breakbacks tak' ye back to Judas Caesar, and the like number of Odyornes avore 'em land ye right into the Garden of Eden among the first volk whose surname wur Odyorne vor all yew can tell. Here 'tis wrote, 'Ursula Breakback gave herself away to Anthony Ruddock, a family never worth a louse, but stinking and beggarly.' They could tell a compliment in them days as gude as now. Here there be, 'Anstis Breakback lived fourscore years and yet died a maid to the great amazement of the world.' Wull, sir, they wouldn't think so much of she now. I've knawed two or dree old women what died maidens, but mebbe they warn't plentiful in them days."

Gregory did not often produce his parchment. He kept it in a chest rolled up inside a piece of cloth, and only unrolled it once a year to satisfy himself as to its condition. It would not be of much interest to the next generation, if there was one, for the writing upon it was really indecipherable. Said he, "Wull, sir, us wur gentlefolk wance; then us turned traitors and got shoved down under. 'Tis wrote on the parchment, though yew couldn't read it now nor me neither, how us lived wance to Sheviock which is by St. Germans. I knaws, 'cause I walked there and back; and I squeezed out a gurt waterblister in Sheviock churchway. There be a little church and a gurt big barn close to 'en. A man built the church and a woman built the barn; and the barn cost a penny halfpenny more to build than the church, though it be twice as large. That be a true story, and if any man ses it bain't I'll break the back of 'en. Wull, sir, the Odyornes came from Sheviock and there be Odyornes in Cornwall yet. Du'ye mind the lawyer gentleman what got the writing from they Pethericks? Gurt vules they Pethericks. Avore yew come up along I reckon. When yew writes your name on a bit of lawyers' paper 'tis the end of independence yew may depend. Wull, sir, this gentleman wanted to go fishing and catch trouts as well as volks, and I went along to show mun the pools; and he started flip-flapping the watter wi' a fly, which is a vulish way o' catching trouts and ten times as slow as groping vor 'em. So I got telling to 'en first one thing then t'other; and presently he ses, 'I smell Cornish.' 'Du' ye?' I ses. 'Yew should breed setters, vor they'd ha' proper gude noses.' 'What be your name?' he ses. 'Gregory Breakback,' I told 'en. 'Du'ye smell Cornish now?' 'Naw, can't say as I du,' he ses, puzzled like. 'But I'll ha' another try. What be the first number?' he ses as quick as that. 'Ouyn,' I ses, and, Lord love ye, he had me. 'I smells Cornish worse than ever,' he says. ''Tis a wonder to me your name be Breakback.' 'Wull,' I ses, solemn like, 'it be Gregory Odyorne tu.' That made mun jump like a trout. 'The devil!' he ses. 'Not him, nor his brother, nor yet his granfer,' I ses, getting a bit maggity, vor yew see me and the devil ha' never done much business together. 'That be my name,' he shouts, purty near flipflapping that mucky little fly of his into my ear-hole. 'Bain't my fault,' I ses, 'but so long as yew bide out o' prison, and don't get maids into trouble, I wun't be ashamed of ye.' Wull, sir, us shook hands after that, though I'd as soon grope the tail of an eel as a lawyer's hand, vor they'm both cold, jumpy things; but he wur Cornish sure 'nuff, if he wur a lawyer, and when all's said God Almighty made the Cornishman last of everything, when He'd got the experience as 'twere. That be a true story, and it ought to be wrote down on the parchment."

Pride was Gregory's failing, and it was pride that kept him straight. He did not profess to be better than his neighbours, but the feeling was there unrecognised, making him abstain from popular vices. He swung his great body over the moor to Metheral church every Sunday evening, muttering inaudibly to himself during the prayers which did not interest him, and shouting the hymns defiantly, not bothering about the words but greatly enjoying a good tune. He went to the inn and sat on a bench shouting, being unable to moderate his voice like many men of the high moor, who live with their faces to the wind, and are accustomed to shout that they may make themselves heard, and forget when they descend or go under shelter that the effort is unnecessary. He drank his beer, but never too much. If he was offered more when he didn't want it his pride rose and he would refuse in a surly way. He wasn't going to make a fool of himself, and so he told them. It was a matter of self-respect with him, not a matter of morals. The question of right and wrong did not enter his mind. He only knew he wasn't going to exhibit himself in a ridiculous aspect. It was the same in everything he did. The self-respect was always on the surface, making it impossible for him to do himself a moral injury or to take an unfair advantage over any man. The same pride had kept him solitary and hindered him from walking with women. He knew he ought to have done better for himself. A farm, a stout building, stock, and money in the bank; these ought to have been his instead of a naked ruin in the wind, bare and cold. He could not let a woman into the secret, open the door and show her earthen floor, chest and table, mattress stuffed with heather, the broken hearthstone. He would rather have broken his own back. He had nothing to offer a woman except his vile body, a splendid fabric but unendowed. He could not pass his nakedness off with a jest and say there were hundreds like himself. His pride was too massive. That was Gregory Breakback, whose principal friend, and whose only enemy, was Gregory Breakback.

There was a cage hanging in his window, a small battered thing which some one had thrown away and Gregory had picked up—but not in daylight—and bent into a semblance of its original form with his big, agile fingers. It had been there for years empty and useless, and George often wondered but did not ask questions which might have made the strong man shout. "'Tis vor the canary," said Gregory one day when he saw the artist's eyes were upon the battered object; and many months later George ventured to remark, "You haven't got the canary yet."

"Wull, sir, I'll catch 'en one day," came the answer.

After that Gregory often mentioned the canary, always with a mournful kind of mirth; and at last the truth came out. The canary that he wanted to catch was not a singing bird, but a yellow sovereign, a coin which had never fluttered into his hand during a life given to odd jobs. Half-a-canary he had possessed, although it didn't stay with him long. After a day or two it flapped its bright wings and flew away, or, as Gregory plaintively explained, "to red itself into coppers." The cage was kept in the window to remind him of the bird which suggested the coin which for some reason or other refused to arrive at the ruin of Moor Gate.

And yet Gregory was not a poor man as poverty goes in quiet corners. He did not sneak into the turnip-field for a meal or steal from the pig-trough. He had no money certainly, but to a commoner money is not the absolute necessity that it is to a townsman. He had his home and hill-top on which nothing would grow except heather, potatoes, and human beings. He was a Venvill man, which is being interpreted a man of liberty, with the right to live upon Mother Earth and suck sustenance from her bosom; and with the right to take from the earth all things that might do him good except green oak and venison, paying nothing for the same beyond the peppercorn rent called a grasewait and those nominal services to the Prince's court as might be required. The hares and rabbits of the moor were his; he could descend to the nearest turbary and dig what turves he desired. Under such circumstances it is not difficult for a strong man to survive if he wants to. Give men the freedom of the earth, abolish wire-fences and oppressive notice-boards, tear up churlish bye-laws, get rid of the robbery called tithe, give the weak adequate protection against tyrants; and then those who are men, or who can be made men, will live somehow like Gregory, thinking wistfully of the canary perhaps, but able to get along without it. You will never find a commoner inside a poorhouse unless his own vices have brought him there; and very much vice is required to drive a free man off free ground.

Gregory did not possess the comparative affluence which is spelt by the monosyllable pig. This would have been a sign of poverty if he hadn't explained that he couldn't be bothered with the creature and had no place for it; but he was usually remembered on the festival when all that is spiritual of the pig was gathered to its fathers—if indeed any part escapes the pot, for the pig is flesh within and without from snout to tail. There would be high feeding in every cottage when the poor swine were murdered. The joints went to market and were turned into clothing. The fry, black-puddings, and various other anatomical details supplied the family table with savoury meat; while the rest of the animal was salted down or presented as gifts to neighbours. Even the bladders made playthings for the children. Absolute annihilation must be the lot of the pig if he does not possess a soul.

Gregory had nothing but his dog, for which he was able to obtain an exemption order although he had no stock; but it was generally recognised that every commoner had a right to one dog free of the tax. He owned no other animal and little else, except liberty and the great bar of iron which was a wonderful tool in his hands. With it he cracked granite and built hedges. It would do anything; stir the fire or the pot, drive a nail or split a log of wood. He was often to be seen striding over the moor, the bar of iron, shining like silver at each end, balanced upon his shoulder, his other arm swinging like a bell-clapper. There was neither clock in the ruin nor watch in his pocket; he had never owned such toys and did not need them, for he always knew the time of day. Even when the sun was clouded over he knew it. The mechanism of his stomach marked the hours.

"Wull, sir, what du I want wi' clocks what tear the day into hours and minutes?" he said to George. "When it be light I'm out, and when it be dark I goes in under."

Gregory did not say how he passed those long nights in the one little room at the end of the ruin. He often sat there, elbows on knees and head between his hands, thinking and wondering, while the wind beat upon the stones and the heather went on struggling. Sometimes he would open the door and look around; there was a tall fir-tree like a flag-staff, and nothing else except space and stars and that wonderful clean wind. It was the star-lit space that troubled Gregory. He couldn't understand the meaning of it, but he thought wise men must know and if he went on thinking long enough he might arrive at the solution too. That was what Gregory had to endure, the space, the wind, and the eyes of those stars, common things of the hill-top, which, added together, made loneliness. He was only a rough growth, and he wanted a lot of information about the garden and gardener; and he had mind enough to dissect the loneliness though he couldn't find out what it was composed of; whether there was flesh and blood in the making of it, or wind and space, or whether it was a mixture of them all. It was strange, he thought, that the commoners should not live in common, should have nothing in common except the moor and their rights. It was strange that in a small village every one should lead a lonely life. At nightfall every lighted cottage was like one of those stars, cut off from every other star by space. When the inhabitants met together they drank or talked, and when they parted it was as though they had never met. The life of one was not the life of any other. They were like a circle of granite stones, made of the same stuff, covered with the same moss; but each one complete in itself, apart from the rest; all lonely though so near, cut off from each other by the wind. There was something almost terrible in the thought that a man might spend a long life in a small village, and die at last without ever mingling in the common life beyond saying, "How be ye?" or "'Tis butiful weather"; that a veteran could toddle forth after a period of retirement, and astonish some one into saying, "Why, I thought that old man was dead"; that even the members of one family should be together in one house like oil and water, mixed but separate.

These thoughts could not have occurred to Gregory in a town, because the noise would have frightened them away; but upon Moor Gate they increased and multiplied. He didn't know how his own pride, and his secret contempt for most of his neighbours, had created the greater part of that atmosphere of loneliness which made mist about him. Through that mist he saw sometimes—usually when tired after a day's hard work—a ghost bending over the hearthstone in the manner of one making preparations for supper, the figure of a woman, nobody in particular, a thought, a fancy, a mere vision, but pleasant to the eyes and heart. That was the only solution of the great problem of the lonely void of space which the gods allow to men, had Gregory known it. But he knew only one thing—the figure wasn't there.

HEATHER

CHAPTER V
ABOUT A RECTOR AND HIS VISITORS

In any large town two families may dwell side by side from one life's end to the other and never get beyond obvious remarks about the temperature. It is not quite the same in lonely parts of the country, where a strange face, or even a new suit of clothes, are something of an event; but in the matter of complete fusion there is little difference. People meet more, talk with each other much more, usually until they quarrel, but they seldom reach melting-point; their solid selves refuse to become fluid and flow together. It is a common mistake among those who describe a set of people in some lonely district to throw them into the melting-pot, bring them to a state of fluidity, and mix thoroughly, causing them to share each other's joys and sorrows and bear each other's burdens. It is not so really. It is such a great event in life when two elements find themselves blending that it can never be forgotten; for it means friendship, that rare thing. Every one has a host of acquaintances, who nod and talk about temperatures; but nobody has more than two friends.

It is pathetic to see one soul trying to get across and reach another which cannot respond; and still worse when each tries and fails, because there are so many obstacles in the way, and they cannot find the proper materials for making a bridge.

The sanatorium and Wheal Dream would have been entirely apart without that road across the common. George looked in at the window as he passed, and for a moment felt himself a hundred miles away from his home because everything was so different. A few steps more he was round a bend in the road and saw the mossy walls and rotten timbers of the old wheal and his cold house above it. He went back to the age of tinners, and their ghosts came to supper with him. The patients looked out at him and made remarks, not always complimentary, for George was an uncouth-looking creature with his loose and shabby garments, his flying hair and bushy beard. The Twins alluded to him as Father Abraham, because that patriarch is generally represented in art as a slovenly kind of gentleman with an untrimmed beard.

George had no friend, and during all those years of his life at Wheal Dream he had found only one acquaintance, Frank Leigh, the Rector of Downacombe-beside-the-moor. George had tried to get at the heart of this man, with a view to making him a friend, but so far had failed. The parson never left his rose-garden to climb up upon the moor. He called himself in jest a prisoner, like the Pope, never stirring from his Vatican—he could enter the churchyard from his garden—and refusing to do so until his right of temporal power should be conceded. Of course he did leave it sometimes, but he rarely went about the village. It was commonly reported that stones had been flung at him once, which, as every respectable person said, only showed what a lawless lot of brutes the villagers were, as a better and kinder man than Leigh did not exist. That was true, perhaps; still, this gentle and most lovable man was completely out of touch with the life about him, that strange, half-savage life which had felt the light of education and had begun to wriggle under it and feel its strength. No fusion between pastor and people was possible there because the people would not melt. They had their grievance, and unfortunately it was a real one, for the greater part of Downacombe village street or "town" was under the domination of Frank Leigh, not as glebe but as his own private property. His position was a peculiar one; he was the squarson, yet without owning the right of presentation to the living, which was practically worthless, and to which he had been appointed by the bishop at his own request. He had no means beyond the income derived from the Downacombe property, which amounted to about six hundred pounds a year, and thus he was unable to afford those repairs which might have been legally demanded of him had the property been attached to the glebe. Almost every cottage along the straggling combe belonged to the gentle rose-grower. It meant for the rector a life of ease in his beautiful garden; for the villagers an existence in tumbledown cottages. The good things of life were not equally distributed in Downacombe, but it was difficult to place the blame upon any one; it would certainly have been unjust to censure Leigh for accepting what was lawfully his. The conditions were harder for Downacombe to bear because of its close proximity to the Forest, where people were free. There was all the difference in the world between being nominal tenants of the Prince and actual tenants of Francis Leigh.

That was why Downacombe hated its pastor though he was such a good and kindly man. Six hundred pounds were squeezed every year out of the poverty-stricken place, and none of the money came back in the shape of improvements to the crumbling cottages; and only a little went into the pockets of local tradesmen. Most of it went to pay the hotel-bills and gambling-debts of a gay and pretty lady fluttering about the world.

Still again it would have been unfair to blame the rector, who had vowed at the altar to endow his wife with all his worldly goods, while he hadn't made any vow to his tenants to prevent their roofs from tumbling on their heads. If his wife refused to live with him it was not his fault. Certainly the social atmosphere of Downacombe was not exhilarating, but he had thought she would amuse herself by renewing the altar flowers and playing with her babies. Unfortunately the attraction of the altar ceased for Mrs. Leigh after the marriage ceremony; and when her first baby appeared, irregularly formed but luckily dead, she declined to have any more. Then she went away for a month's visit to Paris, and the month had never come to an end.

George had walked in the rose-garden fifty times before Leigh mentioned his wife. That is the way with these quiet men. They hide such secrets in their hearts and let the wretched things gnaw until the pain drives them mad rather than allow their acquaintances to guess the truth. It happened one day that he pointed to a new rose which he had succeeded in "fixing," with the remark, "Maggie Leigh—after my wife."

"Very pretty," said George. "Is she on the market yet?"

The rector did not answer, but a rather unhappy look came over his genial face. He had asked himself that same question more than once. As they went on he found himself talking about the missing lady. "She's a great traveller. She bobs up and down all over the map of Europe," he said lightly. "She sends me a postcard wherever she goes, but when I write to the address she has gone and my letter chases her into another country. We are always playing this game of hide-and-seek. I get a postcard with a picture of Notre Dame, and when I write to Paris she bobs up in Palermo. I send to Palermo, and a picture-card of Milan Cathedral crosses my letter. She generally sends me cathedrals. Let me give you a rose for your button-hole."

"It's for her health, I suppose?" said George, dragging him back to the subject.

"Ah, yes," Leigh answered absently. "Downacombe never did agree with her."

"He's a liar," thought George. "Some day I'll tell him so."

But the rector was like a snail, and when his horns were touched he shrank back into his shell. The people who declared they would not have him to rule over them, and yet had to put up with him, did not know what he suffered. Leigh was also one of those things growing on the roof, and the wind was beating on him. That rose-garden was the result of the intolerable restlessness of a lonely man who had nothing to occupy his time. He might have buried himself in his study to read theology or write a commentary, but what would have been the use? Better forget such things and become a gardener, and try to bring his mind down to the level of the latest rose-manure. The village folk ran after their own shepherd; the big farmers were for the most part agnostics, and the little ones imitated them to the best of their ability. Downacombe was a large parish, containing nearly a thousand souls who were supposed to be committed to his charge. There were two large chapels, one at each end of the long street, and there was a small burying-ground about one of them, containing tombstones bearing such inscriptions as "Converted during the ministry of Mr. Scamp," or "Brought to God by the preaching of Mr. Clogg." There were no such inscriptions in his churchyard, and there was no fiery eloquence heard in his church; no sermon to the people by one of themselves by earnest Mr. Scamp the blacksmith's son, or fanatical Mr. Clogg, grandson of old Betty, who could neither read nor write and found some difficulty in paying her weekly rent. These men had no qualifications beyond a ready tongue and an earnest manner; they stumbled over long words and made havoc of their aspirates, and sometimes even translated the Bible into their own dialect; and yet they succeeded somehow. Leigh often saw the Wesleyan pastor hurrying by the rectory garden, always hot and eager, always working, not a minute to spare because there was some one waiting for him. Leigh felt grimly that this man was performing the whole duty which he had been placed there to do. The rector watched this interloper rushing by, hardly pausing as he greeted a child, or shouted in her own tongue to some old crone blinking at her door, "Aw ees, Nanny, I'll come and read a bit o' the gude Buke to ye avore I goes." Then he would hurry on, while Leigh went back to his roses.

He always looked out for the patients from the sanatorium and welcomed them gladly, even Gumm and Mudd, who never went away until they had stuck flowers all over their coats. "May I go and see Mr. Leigh?" was a question the doctor was well accustomed to.

Every bedroom contained roses from the garden of Downacombe rectory. They would not grow at Metheral because of the winds. When the rector heard a noise as of a circus entering the place he was prepared to receive visitors; and looking up was sure to see two pantomimic heads bobbing up and down at the hedge, and to hear the voice of Gumm—

"'Ullo, parson, here we are again. Didn't you tell me you wanted a man to dig the garden? Well, I picked up this little round bloke coming along, and as he said it was just his trade I brought him down. Wants fivepence an hour and his beer—works out at two bob an hour."

"Straw," said the publican, who was never bashful when alluded to, winking at Leigh and poking Gumm with his stick. "A few old rags stuffed to look like a guy. They forgot to burn it last fifth of November. Stick it among the strawberries, and there won't be a bird in the garden in five minutes."

"Come in, you rascals," said the rector, glad even to welcome publicans and sinners. "I hope you are not disobeying orders."

"Not more than extra," said Gumm. "I generally run up against this blight wherever I go. I'm doing my duty, which is what the country expects. He's supposed to be going round Sampford lanes, only the farmers object 'cause he mildews the corn."

Then the bloated creatures tumbled into the garden and frisked about like gigantic lambs. They didn't know flowers from weeds, and Leigh sometimes took advantage of this fact to play a joke upon them. Everything was a flower that grew in the garden and a weed that grew outside it according to the Twins. They didn't know there was nothing in the garden more beautiful than the yellow asphodels and the stag-moss which they trampled upon in their walks.

"Can we give you a hand, parson?" asked Gumm. "Shall I send the little boy out on the road to scrape up sparrow-food?"

Leigh was ashamed to feel that he laughed at such coarse remarks, but he was a lonely man, his life was tedious, and the vulgarity of the Twins was more endurable than his own thoughts and the silence of the garden. He picked up a spade and handed it to the speaker with the remark—

"You may dig me up some tomatoes if you like."

The commercial looked puzzled, the publican suspicious; but as no responsibility rested upon Mudd he began to deride his companion.

"He don't know what a tomato is. Thinks they grow on a tree and you pick 'em like plums. Go on, Jim, there they are, all healthy and blooming at your feet. I always did say the board schools never taught children anything useful."

"Go and saw coke, fathead," said Gumm. "Tomatoes are vegetables, same as onions what you were brought upon. They grow in the kitchen garden among the cabbages."

"Well, let's go there," said Leigh in his genial way.

A long herbaceous border ran down one side of the grass pathway, and beyond it were vegetables. Gumm gazed in sore dismay at the blossoming perennials, and said he'd be blowed if he could see any of the "round red vegetables like sheep's kidneys"; while Mudd retorted, "They're under the ground, same as you ought to be, and you've got to mine for 'em."

"I've never done anything in the gardening line, parson," said Gumm apologetically. Then he stuck the spade into the border and turned up a quantity of narcissus bulbs.

"He's digging up your onions, parson," shouted the publican.

Leigh took an arm of each, and led them away, laughing gently. He took them to a glass-house and showed them a row of tomato-plants which Gumm recognised at once and said he knew the parson was getting at him, while Mudd began his studies in natural history by observing that they were just potatoes "growing bottom upwards."

Then Berenice would enter the garden, short-skirted, brown-booted, and impertinent. The rector looked out eagerly for her visits, which were frequent, for the girl always wanted flowers. He wondered what she was made of. She could not be what she looked, for she seemed so strong and she was not; she appeared so friendly, and yet if he entrusted her with a message she ignored it and said afterwards she had forgotten; there was too much froth on the surface, too little depth beneath; the rector felt sometimes that if she had been his daughter she would have chosen the wandering life of his wife and left him to the loneliness of Downacombe. Still she brought an odour into the garden, not the fragrance of the rose, but a peculiar odour more like that of the chrysanthemum.

"Here's a basket this time, because I want some flowers for Billy as well. Billy must have pink and white roses, so that she can see her own face every time she looks at them. May I go and ravage?"

That was the way Berenice came to Downacombe, as if she owned it. She was one of those handsome young women who catch up a man's heart in their petticoats and shake it off with the dust when they go to bed. Berenice was a girl who lavished her affections upon small animals. A pretty little dog represented a far higher type of being in her estimation than the most beautiful baby. Some day she might require a man to look after her dogs and to manage affairs for her, and she hardly knew herself the exact position that man would occupy; a little higher than the dogs perhaps, but not much; and he certainly would not receive the same amount of petting. She had not a long memory; if any one was unpleasant to her she soon forgot it; and when some person was extremely nice she forgot that too.

"I hope you have brought a pair of scissors this time," said Leigh.

"Not me," she said. "I'm not a nurse to clank about with a chatelaine. When the beastly things won't be picked I screw them round and round and then bite them off."

"Which is very bad for my roses. Last time I gave you the freedom of my garden the destruction was terrible; stalkless buds lying about the paths, plants dragged up by the roots, bleeding stems everywhere."

"They don't feel anything," she laughed.

"But I do; and they feel in their way. They succumb to ill-treatment like we do. A gardener understands the sufferings of his plants when he goes into the garden after a storm or a hard frost."

"I have come for flowers, not to hear sermons," said she. "These destructive hands shall be buried in the basket while you perform the surgical operations."

"They don't look destructive," he said, watching the quick movements of her small brown fingers. "How you girls manage to preserve your hands I cannot imagine. Look at mine."

They were big, rough, and hard with much digging and handling of stones, and yet they were gentler than hers. They healed the injuries which her fingers had wrought.

"We burn the midnight oil at the toilet-table, not over books," she laughed. "Give me a lot of that white gauzy stuff."

"I will, if you say please."

"I won't. If I pick it myself—"

"I shall have none left," he interrupted. "You must cut gypsophila. If you try and snatch a bit the whole plant comes away at the root."

"If I touched it the root would come up too," said she.

"No," he answered. "It is a long, brown, nerves-haped root, striking' tightly into the soil like—" He hesitated, glancing at the girl who recalled to him certain memories of pleasant walks in that garden before he had devoted his soul to rose-culture.

"Don't mind me," she said.

"I was going to say like a man's soul into a woman's heart."

"I don't know anything about that. It sounds silly," said Berenice. "Love is a tonic to take in small doses when you feel run down, just a sip now and then. I don't believe in poisoning your whole system with it. Still I should feel very bad if anything happened to Tobias. Here are the roses I want," she cried delightedly. "The very ones for Billy. You must give me a lot of these."

"This is my new rose. I can only spare you one or two," said Leigh.

"Do you want them for the church?"

"I am going to send a box of them to my wife. It is a hybrid which I have just fixed, and I have named it after her."

Berenice could not say anything to that. She only made a face and thought him foolish for sending his treasures to a woman who wouldn't live with him. Then she said—

"I promised Billy to bring her back some roses, as they won't grow on the top of our mountain, and she loves them so. She spends most of her time in bed, poor little thing."

"Who is Billy?"

"Winnie, our pet patient. Her name is Winnie Shazell, but I call her Billy Dimples, which makes her cross. She has two dimples, one on her chin, and the other on her right cheek, and when you talk to her they twinkle in and out. Sometimes I tell her not to be so affected, and then she laughs, and they twinkle worse than ever. She's a sweet thing."

"How is it she hasn't honoured me? I thought Downacombe Rectory was the paradise of all good patients," said Leigh, while his shears snipped at the rose-blooms.

"She'll come fast enough when she can. You see she's been dreadful bad, and only goes little toddles in the morning, then back to bed again. She would get on much faster if she didn't worry. You'll send her your blessing, won't you? I'll put it at the bottom of the basket so that it won't crush the roses."

"You may give her my best wishes for her complete recovery, and say I shall be very glad when she is able to come and see my garden."

"You will let her ravage," said Berenice scornfully. "Winnie could pull up every plant in the garden and you wouldn't say a word when you saw her dimples. You would ask her to go on ravaging. These are beastly thorny things! Why can't you invent a rose without prickles?"

"Because I am not a creator. We have our thorns too," he reminded her.

"I shall have to cut them off. If that child scratches her fingers she will cry for hours. You can't think what a baby she is."

"You have a new man, I think," Leigh went on as he packed the basket.

"For our sins. A real ogre of a thing, but fascinating in a rude, badly-dressed sort of way. I don't suppose he'll condescend to come and visit you, and if he does he'll first impress upon you that you are a worm, and then will tell you the Latin name of everything, and if you venture to express an opinion of your own he'll put his foot upon you and tread you into the dirt. That's how he treats us. We hate him, and yet he's fascinating rather from a woman's point of view."

"What we could call a prig?" Leigh suggested.

"Yes, a clever prig who has stuffed his head full of rubbish until he sees everything from his own narrow point of view. Gumm and Mudd tied him into his room last night during the rest hour, and when the matron let him out he went straight over to the doctor with the piece of rope, and wanted to know whether the sanatorium admitted savages and lunatics as well as invalids, because if that was so he thought he had better go. Of course doctor had to give the Twins a lecture, but any one could see he was disgusted with the sneak."

"He is not in orders?"

"Oh no. One curate is quite enough—you know what I mean, because you have met our little Sill, the squeaker as Gumm calls him. Two would drive us mazed, as they say. Why can't young curates be men instead of jellyfish? You weren't like that when you were a curate, I'm sure. You didn't hand a girl her tea-cup with a miserable sinner manner, or go about in dearly beloved attitudes, and talk like a sick cuckoo."

"Order, order," said Leigh, patting her arm and laughing gently. "The curate is a half-fledged creature, you must remember. He grows sense with his wing-feathers. Now you must run, for it is eleven. Come again soon."

He led her to the gate, watched her out of sight, and went back to the rose-walk thinking of his wife and of a letter he had just received from her. She wanted more money, and he wanted more of her affection, but he could not make himself ridiculous by running about after her. He loved her in a downright fashion, and now that she had gone he thought only of her pleasant ways, her bright face, and the style of dress which suited her best. He forgot the unpleasant details. It was simply, "I must get away from here for a bit, old man. The rust is getting into me;" and his reply, "Very well, my pretty." She was a long time getting that rust off—Leigh always forgot those other reasons—and in the meantime it was eating into him. As for the money, it would have to come out of Downacombe somehow, although he knew it was useless to raise the rents. Still, there were some cottages occupied by folk who wouldn't pay regularly. He could turn them out—they were mostly old widows— and procure better tenants. Somehow it did not occur to him to wonder what would happen to the evicted, which was strange, as he was a tender-hearted man. It was a pity, he thought, that the people would not be more submissive, more Christian-like, and bear their burdens patiently. He did not guess that the burden might be too great, for they had never taken him into their confidence, and he didn't understand them. Eighteenpence a week seemed little enough for a cottage, even if it was ruinous; but as Bill Chown, who was one of the inflamed spirits of the place, often declared, "A little be a lot when us ha' got nought."

"I really think I deserve a medal for Maggie Leigh," said the rector, as he reached the end of the alley and stood in admiration before the work of his own hands, forgetting all about rents and widows and tumbledown cottages. "She is the queen of the garden, a well-bred, haughty queen. Like my little girl—conceit in both eyes, pride at her lips; and on her cheek the dimple of disdain. That's my Maggie Leigh, rose and wife. I like pride in well-bred people," he murmured, with a pleasant smile upon his gentle face.

CHAPTER VI
ABOUT THE FORD WHICH LIETH ON THE EAST SIDE OF ST. MICHAEL'S CHAPEL OF HALSTOCK

It was a great day in the local calendar; Winnie's perambulations were to begin. The doctor told her to walk as far as St. Michael's Ford, and Berenice was to show her the way and see that she didn't fall down and hurt herself. There was not a word to be found in Winnie's mouth the whole time she was out, and her guide was to see that she rested an hour beside the river before they started back.

Winnie ought to have been happy at the idea of her first long walk, the inference being that her progress was satisfactory. Unfortunately the postman came stamping up and with great brutality hurled two small thunderbolts at her head; and as a result Winnie's breakfast was a moist affair entirely. She had her meals in bed, and as she sat up among the pillows her throat swelled and her shoulders heaved; which seemed unreasonable of her, because one of the thunderbolts proceeded from her mother and the other from her lover. The last terrified her so much that she hardly dared to glance at it, and yet it was a very amorous letter, containing rather common expressions perhaps, and alluding to her as if she had been so much confectionery, but still it was full of ardent love; the sort of letter that a common girl would have gloated over and then snuggled under her pillow; but Winnie cried over it and then tore it into fragments. The letter from her mother was affectionate also, although it struck a querulous note now and then. It mentioned that Mr. Hawker came to see her very often after his work, although she wished he wouldn't wear his hat on the back of his head and pick his teeth in her presence; and he was always talking about Winnie, and how good it would be when she was discharged strong and well enough to be married. Winnie destroyed that letter too, then struggled with fat bacon and potatoes although her throat refused to help her in the least, and tears were making a regular sop of her pretty eyes. She didn't want to go down to the Ford. She wanted to die because she was miserable, but she wanted hag mother to die too. She was only trying to get well for the old lady's sake.

Winnie was one of those helpless clinging girls who do so much good in a rough world by growing round some man, bearing blossom and fruit upon him, while keeping him together and holding him up. Such girls cannot stand alone; they must cling to something, like the wild convolvulus which twines itself about the first thing that comes handy merely to save itself from sprawling in the mud. The clinging thing cannot choose for itself; it has to accept the support that is offered, prickly holly, stinging nettle, or foul-smelling garlic. It is the same with the clinging girl, and that is why so many sweet creatures are married to brutes. They cannot help themselves, they twine about the first man who comes within reach, while their poor hearts fly about wildly in the air like butterflies beaten up and down by the wind, longing for some sheltered flower to rest on.

Little feet pattered along the passage, Winnie heard an excited whine, saw two shining eyes, and the next moment Tobias bounded upon her bed and dropped his ball very rudely upon her plate. Tail and eyes said plainly enough, "You're a pretty girl. I love you." Tobias was a dog of character, although his moral qualities would not bear looking into. Like so much of the male side of creation, he was exceedingly fickle.

"You oughtn't to come in here," sobbed Winnie. "The matron will be angry, and Berenice will be so jealous."

"What do I care?" said the excited tail and eyes. "I'm going to take you down to Chapel Ford presently, and we'll chase bunnies among the furze-bushes." Tobias conceived that the entire system of creation revolved about himself. Rabbits had been made that he might chase them, and the pleasant world had been filled with pretty girls to play ball with him. He thought it was all very good.

"Eat my breakfast, please," begged Winnie, and Tobias obeyed with joyful gulps, nosing his ball about the plate until it was left high and dry. Then he picked it up tenderly, opened the girl's little hand with a cold and rather greasy nose, and deposited it upon her palm.

"I can't throw it, little man," said Winnie in her tired way. She put her arm round Tobias, and he snuggled down like the sensible male being that he was, and kissed her ear with much devotion.

"I'm such a prisoner," she said. "I'm a prisoner at home and a prisoner here. The chain of my captivity is in that box over there. I took it off directly I got here, because I couldn't bear the weight, but whether it's on or off I feel it just the same. I wore it here, Tobias, round this finger which is supposed to communicate with the heart, and so it does, for it hurts my heart all the time. I do so long to be free, doggie, like you. I want to go up there, to the top of Cawsand, and lie upon the heather and feel the wind beating upon me, and—and have some one to help me bear it."

Tobias did not comprehend suffering. His life was placed in pleasant ways, and his trials were nothing more serious than an uncomfortable stomach after a heavy meal, and that could be dispelled by judicious rolling upon the grass. He thought the little girl was silly, but then she was sweet and pretty and was tickling his ears. If she was oppressed it was her own fault. She ought to snarl and snap and growl at her oppressors, and then they would lower their tails and slink away. Such was the little dog's experience, and he claimed to have a fairly good knowledge of life. And if her collar hurt her she had only to slip it off with her front paws. Tobias grunted and observed in his own manner, "If you will roll over and over a few times and kick as hard as you can, and bark a little, you'll soon be all right again."

"Dear roses and dear dog," murmured Winnie, smelling the one and squeezing the black nose of the other. "You would be the best of companions if you could answer me back. Somehow the roses he gave me never seemed to smell, but then they were town roses and the smoke had spoilt them. I have got to marry him, Tobias, and I shall have to live in one of a row of houses, look out upon street-lamps, and spend my life between a kitchen and a bedroom. He has bought me, and goes on buying me every week, and he must have me, although I shudder whenever he touches me. His hands are not clean and he smells of stale tobacco. Oh, Tobias, take me away upon the moor and find me a clean man who will love me and not kill me. I want the wind and the heather, and I am to be smothered with smoke and dirt."

"Time to get up, Miss Dimples. Oh, Tobias, you miserable little hound!"

Berenice appeared carrying a jug of hot water and frowning severely at her inconstant companion.

"I've been looking for him everywhere, calling and whistling. And there he lies wagging at me, as if I was a mere acquaintance, and making eyes at you. I shall hate you soon, Billy. I told old Budge you would capture everything and everybody directly you got about, and leave me nothing to play with, but I didn't think you would steal Tobias."

"He took possession of me," said Winnie. "He came and jumped on my bed."

"Well, you must have dimpled at him. That's why he wanted me to let him out. He whined and scraped, and directly I opened the door he must have come straight to you. Poor little dog, what chance has he got against a wicked girl with flaxen hair and cornflower eyes and dimples as big as saucers?"

Tobias took not the least notice of Berenice. He gave a big sigh and snuggled down again because he was warm and comfortable and his position against Winnie's side was quite to his taste.

"We have been talking about you all breakfast time," Berenice went on. "It's a great event your first long walk, and if the others could do as they liked they would follow in procession. The Twins want to send you off with a band, Budge sends you her smelling-bottle lest you faint by the way, Halfacre is talking Greek for the occasion, and the Sill hopes that I shall bear you up lest you dash your pretty feet against the stones. He's going to watch our progress with his field-glasses from the top of Cleave Tor, and of course if we do anything wicked he will find it his duty to sneak to the doctor. You mustn't talk, Billy, not a word. I shall smack you if you open your mouth. You will love the Ford. It is one of the most delicious places that ever dropped out of Kingdom Come."

Winnie was soon ready. Her clothing was scanty and light, and one good shake began and ended the toilet of Tobias. She was going down to the Ford which in the old day led towards the chapel of St. Michael, and is now, as then, a line of smooth stones set in the bed of the Okement river. The water is a wonderful colour there, under the shadow of the small and ancient oaks, green in parts and sometimes purple, and there is always a lace-like pattern of foam upon it which lengthens as it is drawn down towards the cataracts and little islands beyond where the river tries to become fierce and makes wonderful noises between walls of black stone. It is a magic spot, one of the soft places on the moor, and it suggests the tender side, happy life without passion, warm blood without lust in it, pleasant wind and not storm. It is well sheltered beside the river which separates the moor from St. Michael's Wood; on the one side the granite and furze; on the other a big precipice dripping with water, hanging with fern-fronds—six feet long are the fronds of St. Michael's ferns, and his bracken grows to a height of ten feet— overgrown with a waving mass of oaks and flowering trees, the soft, maidenly birch clad in silver and the rowans like brides smothered in bouquets. Somewhere above that wet garden the ruins of the chapel are lost, and the steep path to it covered with water-washed pebbles is almost lost too. Down that path and across the Ford has passed the whole pageantry of Dartmoor history. It was passing there before the little town of wattled huts near the mouth of the Thames was built, and long before Irish monks came to light the lamp of a new religion. It was passing there when Caesar fell at the foot of Pompey's statue. Roman agents must have crossed there, wondering what was the latest prank of mad Nero or guzzling Vitellius. Keen, bearded Jews must have crossed cursing the name of Titus. Danish freebooters crossed on their destructive mission; they had Lydford town to burn, a greater place than London. After them came English history, tinners and tyrants, Kings and Earls of Cornwall across St. Michael's Ford; and their feet as much as the waters in flood have worn those stones smooth. The dweller on Dartmoor forgets all that, and remembers only the feet of those who came bringing good tidings, his charter of liberty, his title to his home; the men who made the boundaries, who settled what was within and what was outside, who beat the bounds and appointed the line of the Forest. It was at the Ford of St. Michael's that the Perambulators finished their long and dangerous journey. It is to them that the mind turns, to the men of peace bearing the charter, written partly in Latin, partly in Norman-French, granted them by the King. The report of that perambulation is the Prince's title-deed to the Forest of Dartmoor and the Magna Charta of his tenants still.

There is nothing in the whole parish of Lydford much finer than the cleave of St. Michael of Halstock. From the summit of its tor, which, to be strictly accurate, is outside the Forest, the oaks below look like toy trees, the river is a thin white thread, the huge slabs of rock are mere pebbles. When the moon comes up over the rocks which are piled like the ruins of a city eastward, the place becomes Cleave Dream. The atmosphere is thick with the heavy light which the wind seems to blow to and fro, and from the summit of the tor, which thrusts a spur into space, there can be heard the movements of the haunters; first the beetles booming through the mist, then the river sliding down its bed of rock and the foliage whispering. The nightjars make the most noise, and though they are not musical they suit the moonlight; with harsh metallic cry they suggest the tinners working down there; and as one listens the sounds become a rattling as of mail, a clanking of swords, an iron hand striking a stone; and then, where the white river moves so fast as to appear motionless, shining figures walk from among the oaks and follow each other across the Ford. That knight in front, who crosses first and rings his fist upon the flat stone beside the water, claiming great Dartmoor as his own, is "the beloved brother, our Richard, Earl of Cornwall," and his followers are Henry de Mereton, Hamelin de Eudon, Robert de Halyun, and William le Pruz, bloody men of battle in their day, but in our own quiet ghosts, having received benediction in the chapel on the crag, and going upon their harmless way towards the moonlit rocks across some of the oldest stepping-stones in history.

Winnie and her guide were early at the Ford, but some one was there who had already worked three hours. George had come when the moor was wet and silvery, bearing a huge canvas which the breeze caught like a sail. There he was painting in his usual energetic way, unconscious of anything except what was before him, only pausing to take a big pinch of snuff, or cram a bit of cake into his hungry mouth, or running down to the river to dip his shaggy head in. Then he would shake himself like a dog, blow the drops from his beard, and dash at the picture as if he meant to knock a hole in it. He was thoroughly happy at his game, for it was nothing more. It was not business. But Halstock Cleave and Wheal Dream were a thousand times better than all the Art Schools of London, and painting dream-pictures for nothing was far more satisfying than working at some simpering portrait, and exaggerating charms which were probably not there at all, for a handful of sovereigns. He had a good heart and a good brain had George Brunacombe, only he couldn't find himself. He sang in a deep voice, and whistled like piping Pan, and talked in old English, with many a certes and forsooth and gramercy, to the figures on his canvas. He didn't hear the ladies, as they were not talking, and it was not until Tobias charged at him with overwhelming friendliness that he perceived his solitude was spoilt.

"Gadzooks, little flesh-and-blood dog," he muttered. "Thou hast broken my dream, I warrant ye."

"Good-morning, Mr. Brunacombe," cried Berenice.

George turned and bent his awkward body, having no hat to raise, but for a few moments he said nothing. So here she was, the fragile spirit who came to Wheal Dream and sat and sighed among its ruins, looking so sad and longing. He had been afraid she might slip, fall upon a rock, and break all to pieces underneath his window. The first day he made up his mind she was a ghost, and wondered why he wasn't frightened. She was the girl who loved the spadiard and had come back just to visit the old place which had given her the happiness which her soul desired. She didn't want tin; she had never wanted that. It was love she sighed for. He was the modern spadiard working at Wheal Deam, drawing out of it metal, not with a spade, but with brush and pen. Then she was gone, and he heard Ursula gamboling among his crockery; but the next day she came to haunt the place again in the same sad and longing way. He expected her to melt into the heather. And here she was in the flesh, though not much of it, the same fragile dream-girl with the soft, heather-blown face, the sad eyes, pathetic mouth, and the fair mist of hair which kept on playing hide-and-seek with her ears.

"This is Winnie Shazell. She may nod if she likes, but she mustn't say a word," said Berenice.

What a preposterous idea it was to give her such a name or indeed any name. George knew better than that. She came out of the heather of Wheal Dream, and she would go back there presently.

Winnie took advantage of the permission and nodded; and, what was far more serious, she smiled.

"There she goes with both dimples," said Berenice to herself. "Come here, Billy. Sit down on that stone and stir not at your peril. We can't help intruding, Mr. Brunacombe. Our orders are to sit here for an hour."

George had his back towards them and was pretending to paint, only his hands were not steady. He was an awkward and a nervous man. He thought she must be criticising his shabby garments, laughing at his shaggy head and bushy beard, poking fun at his boots which were laced up with string, and the reed basket containing his humble luncheon stuffed there with all manner of other things. But Winnie was doing nothing of the kind. She was looking at the big canvas, and her pretty lips were parted in a child-like admiration.

"How did you get down here with all those things?" Berenice asked.

"The easel goes in a hole among the rocks of the moon—over there," said George, pointing with his mahl-stick. "I call 'em that because the moon seems to shoot out of them as if she lived there. You ought to be down here then. It's fine, I can tell you. I carry the canvas and paint-box when there's no wind to speak of."

"Tell us what the picture is about."

"Why, it is—" began Winnie, when she was seized and scolded.

"How dare you talk, Billy! If you say another word I'll put you into the river and drown you."

George smiled, and his hands grew steady again. He knew what Winnie was going to say. She recognised the subject and understood a part of it; and he felt that she might be understanding the painter too. The spirit of the moor was in her, and she saw his visions and could dream his dreams. She had not been looking at his old clothes and untidy beard, after all. Her eyes were upon his finely-shaped hands and the work which was growing under them. He shifted the easel round and stood half-facing the girls as if he had been a school-master about to give them a lesson with a blackboard. His profile was clearly defined against the dark background of the rocks of the moon. Winnie was looking at his head and wondering where she had seen anything like it before, until she remembered a book of old wood-cuts in her mother's possession which contained the portrait of Albert Durer, by himself.

"It's a picture of the Ford. But who are the Lord Mayor's Show figures crossing the stones?" said Berenice.

"They are the Perambulators," said George, addressing Winnie.

"I thought they were meant for men. What is the difference between a perambulator and a mail-cart?" said Berenice flippantly.

"They are the knights summoned by Henry the Third to determine the boundary of the Forest," George went on.

"No history, please. I hate it, and Winnie hates it too, only she mustn't say so. We want romance."

"Well, this is, true romance for us west-country folk."

"Do tell us," said Winnie impulsively, her soul forgetful of discipline; but Berenice soon gave her cause to remember.

"Give me that rag, Mr. Brunacombe," she cried, "the filthy one covered with paint. I want it to tie round this girl's mouth."

Winnie put a hand into her companion's lap with a pleading gesture, and whispered, "I won't do it again."

"Very well, you shall be forgiven. But if you do offend the third time no mercy shall be shown you. Now you can go on with your story, Mr. Brunacombe. Sit down on one of the stones. You're so restless while you're standing. Tell us first why you have painted the Ford just as it is now. I don't know any history, but I have an idea that Henry the Third lived several years ago."

"What has happened to change it?" said the artist-poet as he seated himself opposite them, although even then he was restless, and kept twisting and turning. "Eight hundred years ago it was the same as it is now. Centuries don't alter water and granite. I have painted what I see before me, down to the asphodels on that little island and the lichen on that rock; and then I jump back to the Middle Ages for my figures. That's the way to work. Nothing changes on the moor; men are the same; it's only a matter of clothes," he said, shaking his shabby coat and comparing it with the graceful drapery of his thirteenth-century knights. "These are not characters of fiction," he went on, jumping up and running at his picture. "They are men of history who have given their names to places upon the moor. This knight who has just reached that very stone on which you are now sitting, resting his foot upon it and pointing up the cleave, is William de la Brewer; and the two behind who are racing for the last stepping-stone are Guido de Brettvill and William de Wydworthy. The tall knight just about to cross is Hugo de Bollay, and near him is Richard Giffard, picking and eating blackberries and joking with the priest who has just said mass to them in St. Michael's chapel above. 'We men of war have to eat what we find,' he says, 'while you jolly priests live on fat venison.' Critics would condemn that," said George fiercely. "They would say blackberries didn't grow in those days, and if they did knights wouldn't condescend to eat them. The king himself would have picked the blackberries of Halstock. They are as big as strawberries, and they were just as fine eight hundred years ago. Look at the Perambulator behind whose name tradition hasn't handed down to us. He means to have a go at the berries when big Giffard has done sprawling over the brambles. He's tired and hungry, and won't be sorry to get to Westminster and tell them at court about the savages of wild Dartmoor. At his shoulder is Odo de Treverbyn looking at the antlers of a stag which he has found in the grass; and here, coming down the steep path leading from the chapel—that path is there if you know where to look for it—is William Trenchard, assisting Philip Parrer, who has hurt his leg; while close to them is Nicholas de Heampton, or Highampton, cutting an ash stick with his sword. Behind them you can just see William Morleigh and the last of the Perambulators, whose name is in some doubt. They are sliding down the path laughing like school-boys. These are the twelve who appointed the boundaries of the Forest that they should never be moved at any time."

"You tell a story nicely, if you wouldn't jump about so," said Berenice, while Winnie went on staring at the picture in simple delight. "I had no idea history could be made so modern. You might paint better-looking men, though."

"Ah, you think the knights of old were always handsome, and princesses beautiful," said George rather cynically, as he returned to his stone. "Critics think so too, and that is another point where I fall foul of them. If you take any twelve men you won't find more than a couple of handsome faces among them; and these knights had been a long journey, and had a precious hard time among the savages, I can tell you. It's not likely they would be finishing the Perambulation with their best court faces."

"Where did they begin?" asked Berenice.

"At Cawsand, which you look at from your windows. I have followed their tracks and taken two weeks over it, though it is not always easy to find a place by the names given in the records, of which there are two. The first Perambulation was made under a commission given by Henry the Third to his brother, Richard Earl of Cornwall, in 1240, which is the Prince's title-deed to the Forest; and the second, which was not really a perambulation at all but a presentment of twenty-five jurors, was given at a Survey Court in 1609. This is written in English, while the Perambulation itself is in Norman Latin. The original is lost, but there are several copies extant, none of which exactly agree. Places appeared to change their names in a marvellous fashion in the old days."

"That's enough history. Let them march," said Berenice.

"Here they go, then," said George briskly. "After leaving Cawsand they made beside Raybarrow Pool to Hound Tor, which they called the Hill of Little Hound Tor. Their next point was Thurlestone, which is the tracker's first difficulty; the jurors in the sixth year of our most gracious sovereign, Lord James, got over it by supposing this to be Watern Tor; but they were wrong, for that tor lies well towards the west and the track of perambulation goes eastward. The explanation is easy enough; there are numbers of Thurlestones, Highstones and Longstones about the moor, which were always probably nothing more than boundaries, though men with long heads and narrow brains declare they are the remains of Druidical mysteries; but according to them every bit of stone on the moor has some special religious significance, and every hole in the rocks was made for what they call lustration, or for receiving the blood of some miserable victim. Some of them admit that the Longstones have been boundary posts for centuries, but before then, they declare, they must have been used for purposes of religion."

"This is guide-book talk. It's not interesting," cried Berenice, though Winnie's eyes said it was. It was the atmosphere of the moor and the wind across the heather.

"This particular Thurlestone must have tumbled down or been broken up and built into some commoner's wall centuries ago," George went on. "The trackway is plain enough along the East Wallabrook to the point where the West joins it, and on to where the united rivers fall into the North Teign at Walbrook Bridge, which is just on the other side of Scorhill with its stone remains. There what is called the North Quarter ends, and our knights took a rest and drank what they could get, which was only Teign water, but the best and purest water in the world, and no doubt they wished tobacco had been discovered. A man of Devon gave tobacco to England, a man who knew Dartmoor well, and was also the greatest man who ever lived. Devon gave England tobacco, her navy, and Walter Raleigh; and she taxed the tobacco, appropriated the navy, and cut off Raleigh's head. When the Perambulators had rested they went on to Castor Rock, and to a Highstone which was later called a Longstone, and has only been destroyed recently, that is to say within the last century; and then to a Longstone by Fern worthy, which was later called a Highstone, and was destroyed long ago. And so across the South Teign to the marshes which the record alludes to as Aberesheved, a name which appears nowhere else; the later jurors use the expression, 'the fenny place now called Turfhill.' Aberesheved or Turfhill was a turbary, a place where the peat was good, and when it became forsaken by the turf-cutters its name was dropped and lost. They made straight through the middle of the turbary to the little hill which they called Furnum Regis, and is still known as King's Oven. The trackway now is clear to any one. It runs by the Wallabrook, not the one that falls into the Teign, for that is miles behind; the Wallabrooks are endless, and were originally Wallow Brooks, probably because travellers had to wallow in them. This one rises near King's Oven and falls into the East Dart, which they called the Easter Dert, and the track runs along the east side of the brook beside Ephraim's Pinch and beneath Yar Tor. They allude to the source of the Wallabrook as Wallebrokeshede, which sounds rather like Willie broke his head. You see, they had plenty of water."

"I expect they had bottles of sack with them. Soldiers wouldn't drink water unless they were dying of thirst," remarked Berenice, wishing Winnie wouldn't stare so. "Weren't there any Rising Suns or Plumes of Feathers in those days?"

"There are not any along the track even now. You must drink water or remain thirsty. They continued the East Quarter by 'the Wallabrook until it falls into the Dart, and so by the Dart until another Dart, and so by another Dart rising up towards the foot of the Okebrook,' as the record has it in its quaint Latin. They seem to have been rather confused by the East and West Darts."

"After drinking water they saw four Darts," said Berenice. "If you could have searched the grass behind them you would have found plenty of broken bottles."

"Be that as 'twull," said George, with his big schoolboy laugh. "They continued by the East Dart, crossing what is now the road between Two Bridges and Ashburton, and passing Dartmeet they went up along West Dart and reached the foot of the Okebrook, called also the Oldbrook and Wobrook; and it was here the East Quarter ended. The next point is Drywork, as the Perambulation calls it"

"They must have found it so," came the interruption.

"Or Drylake, as the later jurors name it. Just where that particular place is I don't know, you don't know, and nobody knows, as our vicar says in his sermons, but remains of tin mines abound in that part, and the name probably refers to a settlement of tin-streamers. Then across Creffield or Driffield Ford, which is where the road between Princetown and Holne crosses the Okebrook, and from thence to Battishill, Cattishill, or Gnattishill, which is certainly Knattleborough; and then to the head of yet another Wallabrook, but a very small one this time, and down the stream until it flows into the Owne, Aven, Avena or Avon, as it is variously styled; then by Eastern Whiteborough, which is another hill, to Peter's Cross a little to the south of the Abbot's Way, to the Redlake where it flows into the Erme, and up the Erme to its source, which is called Grimsgrove; and on to the head of the Plym, where the South Quarter ends."

"With popping of corks as before," said the commentator.

"Well, they deserved a rest, for they had finished more than half their journey. The trackway is plain enough to Elysburghe, which is now the little hill of Eylesburrow, to Siward's Cross, now always called Nun's Cross; and from there to Little Hisworthy, which is Hessary Tor, but was called Ysfother by the Perambulators, then to Mis Tor and Mis Tor Pan, names which, like Hound Tor, have not changed from the thirteenth century to this day. The line crosses the Walkham to Deadlake Head, which has departed a long way from its old name of Mewyburgh, and the next boundary mark is Lints Tor, now corrupted into Lynx, and anciently known as Lullingset. Here the West Quarter ends and the trackway makes for the Tavy, at that point where it is joined by the Rattlebrook, to which the Perambulators gave in effect the name of Racketing Brook. The boundary lies beside the brook to its head at the foot of Amicombe Hill, and there we enter a more civilised part of the moor, where boundary walls have been thrown down and Longstones broken up. Our knights are getting near the end of their journey. They cross Sourton Common, the West Okement river, and so beneath Yes Tor, which in those days was known as Ernestorre. You know where they are now, coming down towards St. Michael's Chapel to complete their big circle; and here they are on my canvas, crossing the Ford which lies at the east side of the chapel."

"Thank you," said Winnie disobediently.

"However can you remember it all?" cried Berenice, ignoring the pretty culprit on this occasion. "My head would burst if I tried to cram half those names into it."

"I have tramped Dartmoor for years with its records in my pocket. It's easy to remember when you are interested," said George simply. "I don't suppose any one takes an interest in the Forest boundaries except from a selfish point of view, and so nobody tries to trace the line now. Of course, the Forest boundaries and the Dartmoor boundaries are two very different things. It would be a great pleasure to me to go round with some one who did care," he muttered.

"What are you going to do with the picture?"

"Put it in the mine house, look at it for a year or two, then cut it up some day when I'm short of canvas. My dream-pictures don't sell," he said with a defiant gesture. "Perhaps it will come in handy to stop a broken window."

"If it was mine I should send it to the Duke, with a note saying I did it all my own self, and didn't he think it rather clever? Then, if he was graciously pleased to accept the same, think how famous you would be."

"I don't do business in that way," said George.

"Don't you find it hard to fill in your time?"

He stared at the careless young woman in amazement, wondering if she meant it, then broke into his big laugh and said—

"I'm always grumbling at the sun for exceeding the speed limit. I paint while it is light and write doggerel after dark. As a recreation indoors I etch a plate, carve in wood, work in metal, mend my clothes or a table, frame a picture, or bind a book. When I'm too tired for anything else I knit stockings. Outside I do my garden, attend to my bees, follow some old ridgeway when I want exercise, add to my collection of cellular plants, pick up details for my history of tin mining. It's an eighteen hours' day at the sign of the One-legged Owl. Meals are dotted here and there in the shape of commas, not often as full stops. Just now I'm writing a novel when my real day's work is over. It's a busy firm, Bubo and Brunacombe, unlimited; and when a guinea comes of it all we put in another hour to celebrate the event."

There was a little bit of bluster in all this, for George was proud of his accomplishments, but it did not appear upon the surface. Indeed, his tone was deprecatory and his manner apologetic; and suggested, what he never could teach himself, that he was a fool not to concentrate his energies upon some particular form of art. He could not realise that none of the forms of art are necessary, that the author and artist are not admitted to audience until butcher and baker have been presented. The man with book or picture is very far down in the table of domestic precedence. The sweep jostles him from the door, and even the cats'-meat man goes in ahead of him. The sweep may do his work badly, but he is employed for all that; while the artist who has done his work well is not even asked to call another day. He deals in luxuries, and such things are not considered until the dog has been given his biscuit and the cat her horseflesh. That is why the man who deals in luxuries cannot afford to be a general merchant; he must specialise or become bankrupt. When supply exceeds demand only the best goods are likely to be looked at; and such goods are produced by the specialist. There is not much between mediocrity and talent; merely a decimal point called application.

"Well, Billy, we must go. Take my arm and be towed heavenwards;" and Berenice nodded to the artist and pulled Winnie off the stone. George was burrowing in his basket, flinging out cake and hard-boiled eggs, picking out sprigs of heather in bloom, some white, others just on the blush. He gathered them into a bunch, approached Winnie, and put out his hand with a queer lumbering movement.

"Picked it early this morning as I came across from Wheal Dream. There's plenty if you know where to look," he said brusquely, almost as if he was asking her to accept something objectionable.

Nothing could have delighted Winnie more. White Heather was more desirable than all the artificial roses of Downacombe. The roses would drop their petals and be dead in a day; but the heather is a thing that endures. She put out her hand and encircled the bunch with her fragile fingers. That heather was full of the wind and the light of the moor, the searching wind and piercing light; it had bathed in moonlight and fed upon unpolluted air; its roots had sucked life from fragrant peat. It was the manna of the wilderness. There was no sickliness in those blooms, no hot-house flavour, no suggestion of stiff white sheets and blinds drawn down in the heather, which is the symbol of health and liberty, of strong wind and pure light, of open places and the loneliness of the hills. Winnie took the dream flowers and knew they would not die. Like her they were fragile, but they bore the rough life, and more, they could hardly exist without it. Removed from the wind to the valley they would wither; touched with the smoke they would die. She put a finger to her lips; that was all; she didn't even smile, but her eyes said several things.

Berenice was cross, and her arm played the part of towline rather too vehemently. She was half in love with Winnie, just as other girls might have loved a pretty boy, and she didn't like her to receive tokens of regard from any one else, especially when such tokens so pointedly disregarded herself. She wanted good luck as much as Winnie, and George ought to have divided the white heather between them. And there was Winnie nibbling at the flowers as if they had been something nice, and nestling her nose among them as if she had forgotten they had just come out of a dirty basket among rags and paints and a poor man's luncheon. "Give me some, Billy," she said tauntingly.

Winnie was sweetness itself. She picked out a sprig, one of the whitest and best, and held it out, yet more from a sense of obedience than because she wanted to part with it; and at the same time she said in a quiet, determined sort of way— "He's a genius."

"He's nothing of the kind," said Berenice. "If he was a genius he would dress himself decently and get his hair cut. And please remember you are not to talk."

"I don't care," said Winnie. They had reached the top of the cleave, and she was able to breathe again.

"Will you be quiet? I shall tell doctor you were chattering all the time."

"Sneak," whispered Winnie. Then she subsided, and was good for several minutes, while Berenice whistled and told Tobias a few disparaging things about George, one of which was that he was a conceited prig who thought he could do everything, when his want of success in life showed plainly that he wasn't any good at all. This provoked criticism from the other side in this form, "He's the cleverest man—no, don't pinch me—and he paints divinely. Oh, Berenice, you hurt."

At the gate of the sanatorium Berenice's sprig of heather dropped out of her blouse unperceived, and fell upon the path for any one to find. A few minutes afterwards Halfacre passed in somewhat late from his walk and paused to pick it up. While he was looking at it a comic voice proceeded from the window space just above his head, asking anxiously, "What's the name of that? Do tell us, for I take such an interest in botany."

Halfacre did not possess the slightest sense of humour, and could not perceive that the Twins were always trying to draw him.

He wallowed so deeply in his knowledge and in the conceit of it that chaff was lost upon him.

"It is an exogenous plant," he said in his heavy style, while Gumm began to grin. "Erica tetralix, so called because its leaves cross one another, vulgarly called heather."

Then he drew the sprig into his coat and walked on, while Gumm rocked himself to and fro in vulgar joy. That afternoon Halfacre was sent to Wheal Dream. As he returned he met George coming from the Ford, balancing the big canvas on his head, and whistling like a ploughboy. Painting time was over and writing time had come. He stopped when he saw Halfacre and said cheerily, "Glad to see you about. I'm George Brunacombe, the cheap-Jack artist. Hope you're getting on. You'll soon be well here. I see you've found a place where the white heather grows," as he glanced, a little suspiciously, at the sprig in the other's coat.

"One of our ladies found some this morning," said Halfacre in his supercilious tones.

CHAPTER VII
ABOUT JARS

By their noises the inhabitants of a house may be judged. If it is quiet while the lamplight remains in the window one may reason that the couple within are at least civil to one another. If the sounds suggest a game of professional football it may be inferred that matrimony is taking its not unusual course when people live in a lonely place and see too much of each other. Men and women must quarrel according to their nature. Educated people argue, which is a polite way of quarrelling. The half-educated form themselves into cliques to abuse any and every other clique. Folk at the bottom of the scale, who have no education at all and are accustomed to act in a simple and straightforward manner, throw each other about. In such a quarrel there is no misunderstanding.

When George first came to Wheal Dream he was always running to the window under the impression that the only commandment of importance was being broken; but he soon discovered that yells and threats did not mean murder. The Pethericks had to fill in their time somehow, and their small talk consisted in reviling one another. They called each other dogs of various kinds, but they were ready in a moment to unite against a common foe, such as Uncle, and to specify him as a dog of the very worst type. What could they do with themselves when the cows had been milked and the cream scalded if they didn't talk? They could not read; there was no comfort in their dirty kitchen, and the parlour was a place they might not enter; they were tired, and evening is the time for recreation. So the whisky was uncorked—they were big folk these Pethericks, and had got beyond beer—and after a glass or two they felt in the mood to destroy the peace of Wheal Dream by slandering all creation.

A narrow passage led up to the kitchen, and in the middle of the passage stood Uncle, the lamplight just reaching his ugly face, leaning upon his sticks and listening in a patient kind of way. He wanted to get back and read his Bible, only John stood between him and the outer door. Ursula was in the kitchen, and near her was Father seated upon a heap of potatoes, appreciating what was going on. The place was full of peat smoke, which was wafted from the big open fireplace by the gusts of wind. The back wall, built against the side of the gorge, was green with copper which had soaked through the stones, and the stone floor, which had not been scrubbed for years, was thick with dirt. Unpleasant beetles were crawling about, and a pile of rags, thrown in a corner many months before and not touched during the hot weather, had become a breeding-place for lice. It was strange to think that human beings could live there and deliberately make the place filthier. The wettest and most mossy part of the wheal, even deep down among the old rafters in a horror of darkness, where the water ticked off the seconds and hart's tongue ferns held out their clammy fronds like a drowned man's fingers, was at least as comfortable, and probably far more healthy, than the kitchen of the Pethericks.

"I thanks God," shouted Ursula, although she never did anything of the kind—"I thanks God I ain't got any children. I sees 'em go wrong every day, and I ses to myself, on my bended knees I ses, thank God."

This was virtue from the whisky-bottle and religion from the same source. Ursula never went on her knees, not even to scrub the floor. Father appeared to approve of her sentiments, and regarded his daughter with pride, as he liked to see a proper spirit of reverence in his descendants. Ursula was spirited enough before her own people, although when in George's presence she usually wriggled like a worm. She was a small woman, swarthy in face, although soap would have removed much of it, with black eyes and curiously red lips which she kept on biting as if they irritated her.

"A bastard," she shouted. "That's what us ha' got now. A bastard on me and my husband's property. A dirty old man's dirty bastard."

Uncle shuffled nearer the step of the kitchen. He wanted to say something, only he had so few words.

"Don't yew say nought," Ursula went on in a furious voice, as if she was shouting against the wind. "Don't say that boy, that Jimmy, got 'en, vor he didn't. Us knaws better. Her be yourn, yew old serpint. Yew had she here 'cause yew'm tu mean to pay keep, and yew told the boy to bring 'en along and say 'twas his. Ain't that right, John? Ain't that right, vaither?"

John made some hoarse noises from the door which might have meant anything, while Father grunted and coughed, and finally admitted in his own manner that his daughter had touched upon a delicate subject with singular tact and candour. He was ashamed to think that little bastards should be crawling about Wheal Dream. He didn't object to dirt and insects because he was used to them, and dirt warmed his old bones, while insects were homely little things, but children who had no right to be alive were highly obnoxious. "Us ha' lived respectable and comfortable like," he explained. "Us ain't had nought to be ashamed of avore."

"It be a blessing to think us ain't got nought on our conscience," went on Ursula in the same noisy voice. "But there be never a family wi'out a bad 'un. Yew wur allus a dayceitful old toad, Uncle. Yew took the cottage and field from John and me wi' artfulness, and yew ha' been taking the bread out of our mouths ever since us wur married, and now yew'm filling the place wi' your bastards till us can't sleep in our beds. Look at 'en," she shouted. "Stands there and smiles as if he wur a gentleman."

Ursula was getting confused at the sight of so much baseness in human form and by the effort of expressing herself with suitable indignation. It was intolerable to think that Uncle should be behaving like a gentleman and introducing every sort of vice into their virtuous atmosphere. She didn't know that the old man's smile was a nervous one. He was mumbling and trying to speak plainly, but a stroke of paralysis some years back had left his speech affected, and he could not make headway against that noise. What with Ursula's tongue on one side and John's dull laughter on the other, Uncle was getting foolish.

"Let 'en talk," said Father briskly. "Let 'en say he'm sorry."

Old Gifford had no intention of expressing contrition for sins he had not committed. He had already explained the matter as well as he could, only they would not listen and would not believe. In the silence that followed he was heard to say, "It warn't Jimmy's fault. He'm a boy and wur tempted I reckon. 'Twas the fault o' they what put him and the maid together. 'Twas an accident like, and Jimmy ses he wun't du no such a thing again."

"I'll knock the head off 'en if I catches 'en trying," muttered John, who had his full share of morality.

"Us don't want to hear 'bout Jimmy. Us wants to knaw what yew pays 'en for keeping his mouth shut," cried Ursula; while Father nodded his head at her shrewdness and was glad to think that it came from his side of the family.

"He'm a good boy," said Uncle wearily, quite unable to answer a direct question. "I does my best wi' 'en."

"Aw, the old vule," said Ursula bitterly. "He don't deny it 'cause he can't. Makes a brothel of Wheal Dream, gets pictures o' naked women, and gives us no peace o' nights wi' reading his Bible and singing his hymns. I'll tull ye how 'twill end, Uncle. The devil will come vor ye, yew may depend, and 'tis no gude telling lies to he, 'cause he knaws yew."

"He comes to all, I reckon," said poor old Uncle, with his simple faith. "I keeps 'en out as well as I can wi' the gude buke, and yew asks 'en in wi' thikky bottles."

This was an outrageous thing to say, and it properly horrified the Pethericks. Uncle was not only standing apart in the attitude of a righteous man, but was actually expressing gratitude, like the chapel person that he was, because he was not like them. Ursula had to finish the contents of her glass before she could shriek again, while John, from sheer force of habit, was compelled to abandon his position at the door and imitate her. Father was indignant too, but he consoled himself by reflecting that nobody would support Uncle's claim to the beautiful new grave if it so happened that the devil should come for old Gifford before an escort of angels arrived for him. Uncle's conduct was rendering him ineligible, to say nothing of the fact that he belonged to chapel, while Father was a churchman and had proved it in his younger days by attending service every month and passing a full hour in comfortable if rather clamorous slumber.

"Let 'en go," said Father; but Uncle had already seized the opportunity to shuffle away as hard as he could. "It bain't vitty vor we to be wi' he. Us be respectable volk," he said sternly.

"Why should us put up wi' 'en then?" shouted his daughter. "He bain't vitty to bide near we, spending our money on his bastards. Ses that Jimmy got 'en, the proper old liar. I knaws they chapel-folk— dirty volk be what I calls 'em. I knaws how 'em prays and sings in the dark, and gropes vor one another. Sings and prays and preaches to cover their shame. If I had a young maid I'd throw her down the wheal avore she mixed wi' they. Tak' a drop o' whisky, vaither dear. 'Twill mak' ye sleep more comfortable."

Uncle crossed his little court and discovered Jimmy nursing the baby. It was getting dark, but the boy had not lighted the lamp. The fire was almost out, but he had not replenished it. Jimmy was rather a lazy boy, but then he had to feed and mind the baby, and that took up nearly all his time. There was something strange about the boy's nature, thought Uncle. It was unusual to find any one of his age and sex devoted to an infant, even if it was his own, hardly ever leaving it, playing with it as a young mother might have done. Certainly the child was an excuse for not working, and manual labour was evidently distasteful to Jimmy. Uncle had to do everything, much more than formerly, for his grandson made a good deal of work and required regular meals. He had begun to order the old man about, and Uncle was so glad to have a companion that he never grumbled, though it took him a long time to climb up into the garden and pull a few vegetables. Jimmy might have done that, as it would only have taken him a few minutes; but, as he explained, he was afraid to leave the child.

Uncle was by no means badly off. He had forty pounds a year coming to him in the form of rents, as he owned a bit of property and several cottages in Metheral, which the Pethericks had nothing whatever to do with, and there was a nice bit put away, for of course he never spent his income. Jimmy knew that well enough, and the knowledge was no inducement to seek his own livelihood, which would mean getting up early, and going out in all weathers on the moor with a heavy crowbar on his shoulder to crack granite until evening. He wanted to go about with a pipe in his mouth, leading his little Dora by the hand, and sitting in the sun when he was tired. Uncle was getting feeble, and the doctor said another stroke would be the end of him. Jimmy saw no reason why he should not retire from work at sixteen and enjoy life.

Uncle lighted the lamp, put it in the middle of the table, then shuffled outside for turves. The fire was so low that he had to get the big bellows and pump away with his stiff hands. He was tired, and Jimmy had appropriated his chair, which was fairly comfortable and had a hard cushion of its own. Uncle often longed for that chair, but he did not like to ask the boy to give it up. Then the supper had to be prepared. It had become quite a formidable meal lately, and Uncle seemed to be always spending shillings and changing half-crowns. The poor old man hated opening his money-box, which was kept underneath his mattress, where it made a big bump against his side as a sign of its presence. It was a terrible operation to take out a coin, and Uncle had to shuffle up and down stairs several times, and read a chapter of his Bible, and say a few prayers before he could manage to do so. He was genuine enough, but he possessed the great dread, common to many old people, of some day finding the box bare and empty.

Supper was finished, the crockery was washed and put back on the dresser, and Uncle opened the big book. That custom went on just the same in spite of Jimmy's arrival, although the boy took no interest in lamentations of prophets or battles of Israelites. Uncle's manner was against him, so was his voice; he would not have impressed any one, though he was very much in earnest. He read patiently, with the baby yelling on one side, and the Pethericks shouting on the other, until it became impossible to hear his own voice. He closed the book, postponed the prayers and hymns for a time, and shuffled near the fire-place.

"Dost ever hear from the maid, Jimmy?" he asked.

"Naw," said the boy. "What would her write to I vor?"

"If yew could find she 'twould be right and proper vor yew to be married. Her could look after we and the baby, and us would get along more comfortable like wi' neighbours," explained Uncle.

"I don't want she. Her wur a spotty-faced maid and proper ugly," said Jimmy. It was not at all likely that he should agree with such a proposal. He scented work in it and suspected the old man of artfulness. With the girl about the place he could hardly refuse to go out and earn his own living. Besides, he had done with her, as was only natural after what had happened. He wanted to spend a little time in comfort, then try some one else, some girl bigger and stronger, who had something better than a spotty face and an ugly one to boot. With the question of morality he was not concerned at his age; but that matter was of the deepest interest to Uncle.

"Yew mun think o' the baby. Yew mun think of I tu," he said. "Neighbours be getting cruel tedious. They'm saying terrible contrairy things about I, Jimmy."

"What be 'em saying?" asked the boy sullenly.

"Ses the baby be mine. 'Tis no gude telling 'em I be tu old, vor they wun't hearken."

"I told varmer I wur tu young, but they wouldn't believe me naythur. Us be in the same box, granfer," said Jimmy, grinning.

"That warn't the truth," reproved Uncle. "Don't ye get into the way o' lying, Jimmy, vor gude wun't come of it, and it leads to the place where there be weeping and gnashing o' teeth."

"Yew'm safe, I reckon, granfer. Yew ain't got none to gnash."

"Mebbe us will be given them, if us ha' got to gnash," said Uncle simply. "Du'ye find the maid and marry she. I'll give ye a proper wedding, carriage to chapel and back home, and a gurt big golden sovereign vor a present."

"I tull ye I don't want she," said Jimmy, in the same sullen way. "I wouldn't marry she not vor two golden sovereigns. Her don't want

I naythur, vor her ha' got a chap in the artillery what keeps her. Her be none the worse vor I, 'cause her ain't got the kid to mind. Her wanted to put 'en out o' the way, but I ses to she, 'I'll tak' mun,' I ses. 'I likes the little beggar.' So I du, but I don't like she, and I wun't ha' she, and what's more, granfer, I don't know where her be now."

"It bain't right, Jimmy," pleaded Uncle. "Us bain't here down under like to live as beastes, what yets grass, and breeds, and does nought else, vor 'em don't know no better. Us ha' got to du as the buke tells. Us ha' got to stand up straight avore the gurt white throne and say, 'When I wur down under I tried to be better than the beastes, Master.' Ees, Jimmy boy, it be wrote in the buke just what I ses. Us can't be beastes first and volk afterwards, vor the buke ses that bain't the way. Us ha' got to be volk first and beastes afterwards. Yew come wi' I to chapel Sunday and preacher wull tull ye the like."

"I don't want your old chapel," said the boy scornfully. "That old buke wur wrote a sight o' years ago by chaps what made a living out on't. Varmer said to I, 'Don't ye read 'en. 'Twull only maze ye and mak' ye want to argify wi' volk.' He gave I a buke 'bout pirates, what took a lot o' ships all vull o' gold and flung the volks into the sea. 'Twas proper reading, I reckon, so 'twas. Varmer and me got on well enough. 'Twas missis I couldn't abide."

Uncle shuffled back to the table and placed his hand reverently upon the dirty book, every page of which bore the impression of his fingers. He didn't understand what the boy had said. He knew nothing about the new spirit of education and the glorious enlightenment which it was bringing to minds still struggling from the earth, and too ignorant to know that what they mistook for broad daylight was really the damp and foggy hours before the dawn. He himself was either in complete darkness or the full light of the sun; he could not know which, and nobody could tell him; but he never doubted that he was in the light. Had any one tried to convince him he was mistaken their words would have conveyed no meaning, because he could see nothing beyond his own horizon; just as a man dazzled by the sun can see nothing else. But Jimmy represented the new spirit. He was the human being revised and brought up to date, educated and shown that he was as good as those who were supposed by the last generation to be his betters, convinced that there was a good deal in life beyond work, which seemed indeed to lead to nothing, assured that the books and beliefs of the past belonged to the past; for such was the result of education upon a mind which could not assimilate it. Uncle had never drunk from that stream of knowledge and his mind was at peace. He said his prayers, and sang his hymns about the other side of Jordan as well as he could for the noise next door, and then shuffled about setting the cottage in order, while Jimmy put the baby to sleep as skilfully as if he had been a woman.

There were visitors next door, Bill and Bessie Chown from Downacombe, for Ursula to quarrel with. Bill was her brother and Father's only son, but the tie of relationship did not endear him to the Pethericks, and though the Chowns were frequent visitors to Wheal Dream they were never welcome ones. Bill and Bessie were sober folk who worked very hard for their living, and as a consequence they earned it and were holding their own, while the Pethericks were going back fast. Bill worked at the copper mine while his wife undertook the sanatorium washing which, for obvious reasons, could not go to an ordinary laundry. Both of them did a little drinking, as was natural, but they drank wisely, not like the Pethericks who placed their property in bottles and were pouring it away in drams nightly. John and Ursula had always looked down upon Bill and Bessie, regarding them as poor folk whose end would be the workhouse. They themselves were commoners, tenants of the Prince, and their life was an easy one, or it would have been had they not insisted upon making it difficult. The Chowns were tied and bound, tenants of their rector, who demanded the uttermost farthing, and their life was very hard, though they worked as well as they could. Every morning Bill was up early, in summer soon after sunrise, in winter long before dawn, and tramped through driving rain, mud, snow or ice to the mine more than a mile away, a long tramp over difficult places, across a little Hoga where the whist hounds and the wind were always hunting—often Bill had to cover his face, or the particles of ice swept across at forty miles an hour would have flayed it—and over watercourses which were often in flood. Men more delicately nurtured would have been tired out by the time they reached the mine. Then the long day of work until the whistle sounded at dusk, and after that the tramp home, or a journey first to Metheral for the washing, which meant a big and heavy basket to carry home. "He be proper tired, be Bill, when he brings the flasket down home alone," Bessie would say. All that work, and no play, for a few shillings a week which was just enough to keep them out of the wind; while Frank Leigh received his sixteen pounds a week, and lived delicately, and had withal no work to make him sweat.

There was plenty of noise at Wheal Dream when the Chowns came along, simply because there were more tongues to make it. Ursula and Bessie regarded each other with dislike, partly because they were women and related, chiefly because they were jealous of each other. Bill and his father got on fairly well, though the old man considered his son was inclined to be bumptious. John hated them both, but he was polite to Bill in an offensive kind of way, or the miner might have flung him down the wheal. The Chowns had no children, which was strange, as Bessie looked just the sort of woman to bring forth plenteously, being strong and plump; but apparently Father had not been permitted to pass along the procreative gift, as both his children, Ursula and Bill, were sterile. The Pethericks were jealous of the Chowns because they seemed to be doing too well and taking too many shillings a week. The Chowns had a better reason for their jealousy, because they were not commoners, they were outside and could not possibly get inside, and they had no share in the privileges which the Pethericks enjoyed but had not the sense to make use of to their profit.

Bessie brought the bad feeling out at once. She had been to the sanatorium to get paid, and she opened her purse and jingled its contents with the unnecessary comment, "Silver, my old dear," before Ursula's eyes.

Father at once stirred himself, reaching out a shaking hand like a mud-rake, and said, "Give that I, Bessie. He'm mine."

"What be yew saying, vaither?" said Bessie pleasantly.

"He'm mine," the old man declared. "Dropped raun on the road, and couldn't stoop to pick mun up. Vull o' silver he wur, sure 'nuff." Father had his own peculiar ideas about property, and in such cases his personal pronouns were very selfish ones.

"Yew stop thee old mouth," said Bessie. This was quite an ordinary remark, not meant to be offensive, but it gave Ursula the opening which she was looking for.

"Who be yew telling to shut his mouth?" she shouted. "He'm my vaither, and I wun't have 'en insulted in his own house, an old man what can't look after hisself tu. If yew can't talk as a decent woman should, Bessie Chown, I reckon 'twould pay yew better to bide down to Downacombe. Yew bain't wanted up here along, I tulls ye, no, nor Bill neither, though he'm my brother, wi' his face vull o' malice when he hears his old vaither put upon. Get down under to your mucky old home to Downacombe and bide there, I ses." And Ursula got the cork into the bottle at the third attempt, to indicate that the hospitality of Wheal Dream was not offered to inferior persons.

"He bain't going to have my money what Bill and me works vor," said Bessie defiantly.

"Aw, yew works, I reckon, Washerwoman—that's what yew be—Washerwoman," shouted Ursula, hoping the taunt was a bitter one. "Us be free volk, us don't have no master to interfere wi' we. Me and my husband be free. Think I'd soil my hands wi' washing dirty clothes? Look at 'em, Bessie Chown. Think I'd soil 'em, I ses," 'she cried, without ever realising that they could hardly be filthier than they were. "Think my husband would dig in an old mine, and be proud of a few shillings? Us be varmers and commoners, us be volk wi' land and property, us can look any squire or parson in the face and say they'm no better than we. Who be yew? Dirt, that's what I calls yew. Proper old stinking dirt."

"Aw, dirt, that's what 'em be," muttered John, lurching along the kitchen wall and laughing like a hyaena.

"Shut thee noise, John," said Bill quietly. He was a short, thickset man, as hard as old oak and wonderfully quiet in his manner. "I'll tull ye two or dree things," he went on. "Vaither, mind where yew'm spitting. I'll tull ye this as a start off like. Us be making our way, slow, I reckon, but us be making it, and us will live to see yew in the workhouse."

He brought his great fist down upon the table, making the pernicious bottle and the cream-pans jump and tingle. Bill had been touched upon his raw spot. It was his ambition to escape from Downacombe and make himself a commoner; but that could not be done without money, and he could not save, for he had to repair his cottage and keep it from tumbling on his head. His landlord would not do anything.

"Yew'm getting tu artful wi' that tongue o' yourn," croaked Father very crossly.

"Let 'en bide," said Ursula, in withering tones. "They knaws no better, vaither. They'm poor volk and cruel jealous o' we. Her takes washing and he digs in a mine. They can't bite, so 'em barks. Du'ye knaw what us got vor the wheal house?" she shouted suddenly at her brother. "I'll tull ye. Mr. Brunacombe paid we one hundred and fifty pounds, and that's more money than yew ever seed in your life, or ever will if yew lives as long as Arethusalum."

"Where be that money now?" said Bill quietly.

"Where yew can't get it," muttered John, with his unpleasant laugh.

"Where yew can't neither," came the quick reply. "It be gone and yew'm the poorer. Landlord ha' got most of 'en, I reckon, vor they bottles wi' stars on 'em can't be got vor nought, and there's a heap of 'em in the muck-hole yonder. Yew bain't better off than we vor getting money what yew ha' flung away."

"That's it, my man. Yew give 'em the truth," said Bessie.

"Shut thee noise, woman," said her husband in the same quiet voice. "I'll tell 'em enough avore I goes."

"Aw, yew'm a proper talker down to Downacombe, they ses. Yew stands up on the lifting-stock and tells the volk they'm put upon," cried Ursula, who was not half so comfortable as she appeared to be. "Proper old bag o' wind yew be. All talk and nought to show vor 'en, they ses. Bill the liar they calls yew, and I reckon 'em bain't far out."

"Be that as 'twull. One story be as gude as t'other when yew'm nought to tell. Where be the money yew got vor putting your crosses to they papers avore witnesses? More than hundred and fifty pounds that wur, though yew bain't so ready to tell about 'en, and that be money yew ha' got to pay back," cried Bill, striking the table again.

"Us wun't come to yew vor 'en," said his sister sullenly.

"Where be all them pounds and pounds? Yew ain't done nought to the varm. It be worse than it wur in old Petherick's time, and he wur a poor man what had no borrowed money, but he worked and kept agoing same as we'm doing. He wur a free man, and yew bain't. There be your bullocks wi'out feed, and your old horse wi' all his bones sticking out. Yew don't get milk from bullocks and work from horses if yew don't keep 'em pluffy."

"Aw, yew'm a purty fine varmer, I reckon," said John in his riotous way, amused to think that he should be taught his business by a copper-miner.

"I knaws plenty," said Bill, his little black eyes getting fierce. "I knaw what happened when doctor came up along wi' these consumptuous volk. Yew, and vaither tu, though he'm old enough to knaw better, yew wur all agin 'em, and yew ses, us wun't have they foreigners here. I knaws how doctor came along and said he'd tak' cream and milk and such off yew, and yew ses, us wun't ha' nought to. du wi' ye. Proper artful yew thought yourselves, I reckon. Du'ye know what old Bidlake be taking? Wull, I'll tull'ye. Dree pounds a week winter and summer."

This was more than Ursula could stand. The memory of that refusal was a bitter pill which she never could swallow. She and her husband had opposed the sanatorium in their short-sighted way, supposing that all the other commoners would go with them. So they might have done had they not smelt money. They had threatened at one time to throw turves at the doctor, but when he replied with a shower of money they bowed their heads and worshipped. The sanatorium became a golden calf set up in their midst, and we all know what happens when that idol is erected. The Pethericks had been offered their chance to go on the flood and had chosen to remain stranded. The last thrust of Bill Chown was worse than his first.

"Yew'd best be getting home, yew and the woman," said Ursula, pointing towards the passage. "Downacombe be your place, not Dartmoor, and yew can bide there till yew'm neighbourly. Wheal Dream be ours, and us bain't going to be insulted by Downacombe volk on our own property."

"She'm right, Bill," said Bessie, as she made for the door. "Wheal Dream be theirs till it be took from 'em."

"Aw, the dirty actress," muttered Ursula, but luckily the Chowns did not hear this crowning insult.

"Good-night, old vaither," said the miner heartily.

"Bill," croaked the old man, who was half asleep and half undressed and altogether unashamed. "Yew'm an owdacious toad."

"Be that as 'twull," said Bill, with a laugh. "I knaws the mucky end of a stick when I puts my hand on 'en."

"Go back to your muck-hole and eat dirt," shouted Ursula, determined to have the last word on her own property.

"Us ha' got our fill of it here," called Bessie, beating her. Then the hard-working Chowns tramped off towards Downacombe below the moor, Father climbed laboriously to his resting-place; and the Pethericks, having nobody else to fight, quarrelled with each other until they were tired out.

Wheal Dream was quiet at last, and the spirit of the place was able to assert itself. Even Bubo was not wailing, for the little owl had scuttled beneath his master's coat and was asleep in that warm shelter; while in his tiny cottage, alone and peaceful, old Uncle sat beside the table, near the smoky lamp and grimy book, reading aloud, transported for an hour into the world of dreams and visions.

CHAPTER VIII
ABOUT A HALF-HOLIDAY

After mid-day dinner on Sunday the patients who were "strong" could do as they liked for the rest of the day. They ceased to be children in the nursery and became free-willed again, although they were liable to be punished on Monday for any sins committed on Sunday. So they were not quite free. Even supper was not compulsory, but every one attended and stuffed their hardest, because Monday was a black and anxious time for all backsliders. The scales were uncovered, the books were opened, each one was weighed in the balance, and it was bad for those who were found wanting. They were all as keen after pounds of flesh as so many Shylocks.

Winnie had been admitted into the company of those who enjoyed the privilege of the half-holiday, and she was so pleased that she said she should go for a walk just because she hadn't got to. Berenice remained in the garden talking with Miss Budge, and trying to feel cross with Winnie for enticing Tobias away from her; for the little wretch had attached himself entirely to the prettiest girl in the place, as was his usual custom. He was always with Winnie, sleeping on her bed—the centre of it for choice;—helping her in her meals, and declaring that he would remain her faithful squire until he fell in love with some one else. It was to Winnie that he brought his ball when the desire for recreation came upon him, and if Berenice approached with pleading words he merely wagged twice, contorted his body once, and explained that old flames couldn't expect any more friendly recognition. Tobias was not under treatment, but he was putting on weight fast and attaining aldermanic proportions. Of the other patients, Sill tramped off across the moor to a distant village where he could get a service flavoured with a spice of Romanism, which the inhabitants couldn't understand and therefore refrained from, but it was congenial to the curate, who delighted more in a genuflexion than in the rights or wrongs of rustics. Gumm and Mudd, as a sharp contrast, borrowed a ferret and some nets that they might go forth rabbiting. Halfacre went off with a little tin box, after explaining to the delighted Gumm that he was going in search of Dicranum taxifolium, which he translated, out of pity for his listener's ignorance, into yew-leaved fork-moss. Gumm politely assured him there was plenty of it about the old streamworks beneath Steeperton, and he had himself collected some specimens to send his wife, who was deeply interested in such things. Halfacre, who did not comprehend chaff, went off in that direction upon a hopeless quest, while Gumm shouted for the publican to inform him that school-master had gone out in search of a taxed cranium. "Go and ask granny what it means," he added. "She knows most things, except her age."

Miss Budge was lying in a hammock-chair, and near her was Berenice upon the grass, celebrating the halfholiday by smoking a cigarette, which Miss Budge did not approve of. "Girls shouldn't do it," she said. "It ruins the complexion."

"She must have been a hard smoker," whispered the publican.

"Well, what are you two big boys going to do?" asked Miss Budge pleasantly. She was always affable to men, whatever their station.

"Just off to Sunday school," said Gumm. "I've been hearing the kid his catechism. Says 'twas his father who gave him his name, and I say it was the Workhouse Guardians."

"Better than being christened by the prison chaplain the night before your mother was hanged," Mudd retorted.

"He's jealous because he don't know what happened to his after she went wrong," Gumm explained.

These men couldn't insult each other, although they appeared to be always trying. They were perfectly friendly, and would have stood up for each other through thick and thin. Chaff in an advanced stage of decomposition was the only conversation that appealed to them. The ladies were often compelled to play the part of deaf adders.

"Now, Miss Arabella, you know the litany," began Gumm.

"Botany, you mouldy pigeon," shouted Mudd.

"I will not be addressed by my Christian name. Please remember that," said Miss Budge crossly.

"She reminds me of a pretty little story in a Sunday-school prize o' mine," Gumm went on. "Flossie calls mother a silly old fool. 'Flossie,' says mother, 'I won't stand it.' 'Mother,' says Flossie, 'how are you going to prevent it?'"

"The brute," said Miss Budge.

"What is a taxed cranium, please, Auntie?" asked Gumm respectfully.

"Do you mean a poll-tax?" said the puzzled spinster.

"He don't know what he means," said Mudd.

"Right for once, beer-tank. 'Tis something schoolmaster's gone out to find. I told him where he's sure to come upon it, and I want to know what it is, so that I can tell him all about it when he brings it back."

"I don't know," Miss Budge replied. "I don't go in for fancy names, and I never learnt Latin."

"Another sufferer from those twopenny board-schools," said Gumm pityingly. "As for me, I forgot the obscene languages directly I left Eton."

"Obsolete," laughed Miss Budge.

"Are ye?" said Mudd sorrowfully. "Never mind, Auntie. You'll be born again some day."

"I won't talk to you any more, rude creatures," said the spinster snappishly. "Berenice, give me up my book."

"What a shocking thing it is to see angry passions upon the face of one we love," observed Mudd sadly.

Miss Budge could stand a good deal, besides being rather a foolish creature, and she had to laugh at these leather-skinned men, who meant nothing, after all. She soon dropped the book and said, "The idiot has gone moss-hunting, I suppose. He's got moss on the brain."

"Well, he did mention moss, and he said something about a yew-tree and a fork."

"Fork-moss," said Berenice. "There's none about here."

"'Ullo, here's the little girl woke up," cried Gumm. "Better throw that fag away, my dear, or you'll be sick all over your Sunday pinny."

"It's a miracle to me that a man should go out and dig for moss," said Mudd.

"Only time I picked it was when I went fishing to keep the worms moist," said Gumm.

"Why didn't you swallow 'em at the end of a bit of string, and pull 'em up as you wanted 'em?" growled the publican.

"Listen to him! Two sizes too large for his shirt, ain't he?" retorted the commercial.

"Go away," said Miss Budge. "We have had quite enough of you both."

"We're going. I'll tell you a pretty story when I come back, Auntie, a nice little Sunday afternoon story, called Tommy and Dolly, or what happened round the mulberry-bush."

"We won't trouble you," said the spinster firmly.

"No trouble, Auntie dear. And the pleasure is less."

"I never saw such creatures," murmured Berenice.

"Don't answer. You are sure to get the worst of it."

The Twins moved off arm-in-arm, as inseparable as a pair of trousers, and Gumm, who could not keep his mouth shut for long, called from the gate, "Ain't you going out this beautiful afternoon?"

"No, I am not," said Miss Budge decisively. "It's the only time we can do what we like. I'm going to stop here"

"And not budge," added the publican.

"Hold your tongue, Mr. Mudd."

"He can't, Auntie. His hand is only just big enough to get round a beer-barrel."

"I hate walking on a full stomach," explained the spinster.

"I should too," said Gumm thoughtfully. "Might get it scratched."

"I warned you," said Berenice, as the Twins departed with a tempestuous noise. "You will answer them, and that's what you get."

"They are coarse creatures, but they do add to our gaiety. Really I would rather listen to them than the bleating Sill or the tinkling Half acre," said Miss Budge. "Now I have three questions I want to ask you about Halfacre. Is he a gentleman? What's he doing with Winnie? And where did he get that white heather he's always wearing?"

"I dropped it, he must have picked it up, and I wasn't going to ask for it."

"I thought perhaps she had given it him," said Miss Budge in a relieved voice.

"Winnie give it him! Oh well, she would if he asked for it. The poor little thing would give her soul away to any one who wanted it."

"You are awfully fond of her, Berenice."

"I love her," said the girl. "I'd like to have her with me always, pet and play with her, and sleep in her arms. She is so sweet and helpless. I have never really loved anything but dogs, and when Tobias left me and went with her I was perfectly wretched. I couldn't slap him, and I couldn't be angry with her. If it had been any other girl I should have seen all sorts of wicked colours, but when Winnie smiled and dimpled, and said in her dear way, 'It wasn't my fault,' I could only hug her. I wish she would trust me more. She won't tell me anything about herself, and when I press her she cries."

"Is she bad?" asked Miss Budge with hesitation, knowing that she was touching upon a forbidden subject.

"Yes," said Berenice in the same low voice. "I made doctor tell me. She will never be anything but an invalid. She will always have to live the open-air life."

"But she will fight. I can see that in her. It won't happen—"

"Be quiet," said Berenice sharply.

"I'm sorry," pleaded the spinster. "Well, answer my other questions."

"I don't know what Halfacre means. I simply can't understand the man, and I don't like those eyes of his, which make me feel quite stupid. He asked me to hand him a book last night, and I said, 'Get it yourself'; and he just said quietly, 'Pass it, please,' and looked at me, and I'll be hanged if I didn't give it him. You wouldn't call me weak-minded?"

"Not exactly," laughed Miss Budge.

"If he spoke like that to Winnie she would fall at his feet. I'm keeping my eye upon her, and she shan't do anything silly if I can prevent it," said Berenice.

"She'll never be able to marry anyhow," said Miss Budge, somewhat gratified to feel she was not the only one.

"Keep off that subject. If I had her with me always I'd make her well. I'd simply love her back to health," said the girl passionately.

"A man might do that."

"No, a man would kill her. It's the calm wind she wants, not a strong one."

"Where has she gone this afternoon?"

"Out on the moor with a book, but she won't read. She will sit among the heather, and bathe in the wind, and dimple at the sun, and mop her blue eyes sometimes. She's got some trouble, though she won't tell me. Whenever I'm extra pretty to her she always cries and says she's miserable. But she won't say anything more."

"We are supposed to be talking about Halfacre, but it's all Winnie," Miss Budge went on. "Come back to the subject and tell me what the man is."

"It's no good asking questions that I can't answer," said Berenice. "There are so many different kinds of gentlemen. Sill and Brunacombe are both gentlemen, but they are as unlike each other as a frog is unlike a farmyard rooster."

"You mustn't say anything unpleasant about Brunacombe," cried Miss Budge at once.

"I'm not. Still he does flap his wings and crow a bit. I suppose Halfacre is fairly well born," the girl went on. "He's a scholar, and doesn't let you forget it, and you can't imagine an Oxford scholar being of the stuff that the Twins are made of. Oh yes, he's a sort of gentleman right enough, though he is ill-bred."

"Disgustingly so," cried Miss Budge. "He kicked me under the table, and instead of apologising told me to put my feet somewhere else."

"I've had enough of this sort of talk. It will give me a temperature," said Berenice. "I'll go and do some photographs. I've taken Winnie in at least a dozen positions, all of them pretty ones, and the light is just right for printing."

Winnie who was being talked about crossed the common to Wheal Dream, which was absolutely peaceful. The windows of the wheal house were wide open, but not a sound came forth, and there was nothing to be seen except a curtain flapping in the wind. That curtain was torn, and Winnie reflected that the inhabitant of the house had no one to ply the needle for him. She worried about that rather as she passed the house. Some girls might have knocked at the door and said, "If you will take down that torn curtain and give it me I will mend it for you." Such an idea would never have entered Winnie's head. Had the man who lived inside told her that he expected her to mend that curtain she would have hurried past the place at a dangerous speed. As it was, she went by rather as if she feared she was likely to contract the plague. "Of course no one saw me," she said, alluding no doubt to the Pethericks or to Uncle, and so far she was right. Still some one, who was not at all likely to enter into her thoughts, saw her coming and watched her out of sight, which meant going from one side of the old house to the other and running up a good many stairs; some one who was an artist and probably wanted to fix that head well in his mind, as he happened to be engaged in no less a task than an attempt at painting it; and for that purpose he had placed a bunch of pink and white heather beside his easel in order that he might get certain fairly well remembered flesh tints accurately mixed upon his palette. This person perceived that Winnie was wearing white heather at her waist; but the subject was not a pleasant one, as he had seen Halfacre go by still wearing that sprig in his coat, and he knew well enough how it had been obtained. Perhaps he had asked for it and the girl had not liked to refuse. He hoped that the white heather would bring better luck to the maid than to the man.

Winnie climbed up the moor, but not so fast when she perceived that no one was running after her, and followed the waving track towards the peat-bogs. That track had been made by the carts of many generations bringing the fuel home, and it was amazingly crooked because men have to walk in curves, perhaps because one of the human legs is shorter than the other, or one side of the brain is heavier than the other, or because the crooked part of the character is generally uppermost. Winnie did not meander along the snaky track. She made crossways of her own until she came out on the level tableland of the marshes where no paths exist, and saw brown pyramids of peat drying in the sun. Down its natural chute of Steeperton cleave came the river, hurrying to the lowlands between billowy heather and blocks of granite; where peat-cutters have brought to light huge timbers which wise men declared are sufficient evidence that a forest of oaks once covered that marsh, though they are nothing more than wooden beams brought there by the tinners to shore up their workings; where the river executes such extraordinary wrigglings that the same wise men have felt perfectly safe in asserting that serpent worship was once practised there, although the innocent river has done nothing more blasphemous than carve its way as it could where the ground was softest; where the banks are dotted with big knolls which point, according to men of intellect, to some convulsion of nature, although the ordinary moorman calls them the "deads" of old tinworks. Winnie passed among these things of the wilderness, enjoying them just because they made her forget other things, and for a time she was happy enough. She could feel that she was walking in her own pleasure-grounds as there was nobody else, no keeper, no gardener. It was all her own, wind, sun, and light included. She put up her face and smiled because her surroundings were so sweet and pure; and the sun kissed her, not in a calm, parental way, but like a passionate lover trying to draw her soul out. He was an ardent sun that afternoon. There was no pettifogging cloud to distract his attention. It was Sunday and his day out.

Winnie swam down to the river. There was no occasion for walking in that breeze, upon that pink and brown tableland fourteen hundred feet above any of those diseased growths called towns. There was nothing out of harmony, no tumultuous bells going like hammers, no streetcorners infested with girl-baiting loafers, no preacher advertising the latest thing in religion, no tavern-doors swinging to and fro. It was all natural, nothing was being patented; the sun was in the chair, the wind kept the door, and all the horrors of a town Sunday had to stay outside.

The delights of that river of green water were endless. It was green there, but red higher up because the water contained so much iron. A good drink of it was better than thin wine made out of trodden refuse of the vineyard. Winnie and the river were soon having a game together. The river was free always, but she had only Sunday afternoons, and this was the first one. She played at hide-and-seek with the stickles. The river was very young there, in the crowing and bubbling stage of babyhood, and it seemed to be running madly round and round after its own current—a very different river from the sedate old stream which saunters in a round-stomached fashion across the sand flats of Barnstaple— and it was ready enough to play with any one. So narrow was it in places that bushy heather concealed the water, and it was just there that a stickle gushed and tinkled. Winnie heard the sound, and tried to track the singing creature to its hiding-place. She knew when she was getting near by the increasing sound, but the stickle was not easy to find because it played all kinds of ventriloquial tricks and the wind was gushing too. At last she reached the exact spot, and lifted a great tangle of heather, standing ankle deep in moss, to see the white foam and to hear the music swelling up like the sound of an organ when the church door is opened. Then she would hear another stickle singing and run away to look for that.

Tired at last, she sat upon the heather, sweet-scented and springy, filled with pleasant insects working out their destiny, all busy in the struggle for existence—there is no mercy extended to insect-loafers—and she watched the peak of big Steeperton poking playfully at the cloudlets, which it was attracting with the idea of forming a thick warm mantle by evening. The sight made Winnie think, and her mind began to play with certain thoughts just as Steeperton was playing with cloudlets; only they were dark, unhappy thoughts. She had been free while roaming the marshes, but now the thoughts began to worry again. She wondered what that man was doing. She always thought of her lover as that man, which was not a good sign. Probably he was sitting in a small room filled with stiff furniture and scorching oleographs, the windows shut, the room a thick, nauseous cloud of strong tobacco-smoke; he would be reading the sporting column of a Sunday newspaper; he would be half-dressed and unshaven. He was very dark, and even when clean-shaven his chin looked dirty. He had often scraped her poor cheek in his rough, loving way, and it always made her feel quite ill. Those tender dimples against that grit and wire. Winnie shivered and her colour only remained because the wind insisted upon it. She remembered an evening, it had been one of the worst, when he had scraped and maltreated her, and finally had entreated, "Call me Ern, love. It sounds more homely."

Winnie heard the stickles singing but she could not hear footsteps beside the river, for the soft peat swallowed up all sound. She was in white and therefore a conspicuous object; dark clothing is lost upon the moor, but any white patch catches the eye immediately. Halfacre, returning empty-handed from his moss chase in the cleave above, saw the white and guessed who caused it, and his way back went naturally by the side of the river. Once he had to cough, but Winnie did not hear it; nor did she see Halfacre until he came round the bend and stopped a little below her, looking fresh-coloured and almost handsome, his empty tin box beneath his arm.

Winnie lifted herself quickly, pulling her feet up and her skirt down, for she had been kicking about comfortably on her bed of heather. Here was another creature claiming his rights as tenant in common of the marsh; standing before her on his own little bit of freehold, for a man may certainly claim as his own whatever piece of land he actually stands upon, since it is obvious that nobody else can occupy it at the same time. Well, he had driven the thoughts away, and for that she was grateful; but it would mean walking back with him, and Winnie liked to be alone when she was on the moor, or with some very congenial spirit, some one who would talk about the Perambulators and could weave a wonderful film of tales around Wheal Dream and Chapel Ford. Then she realised she hadn't heard a word of what Halfacre was saying. That was because he would keep on looking at her. Then he came up, sat beside her on her own freehold of heather, picked up her hand, looked at it, then dropped it as if he had made up his mind that he was not hungry after all. It was an outrageous thing to do, and Winnie ought to have told him so, only she couldn't. It was impossible for her to be rude to any one.

"You always hold your head drooping slightly towards your shoulder, which I believe is a sign of weakness," he said, as if inviting her to join him in the study of some new and interesting species. "You brush your ankles with the heels of your shoes, which denotes lack of confidence. There is the mark upon your stocking."

Winnie covered it promptly and said she couldn't help it. That was her usual defence. Whatever happened it was not her fault, and she was usually right.

"You cannot look me in the eyes, which is a sign of modesty. Yes, that's right," he said to himself. "Lavater says so. I have been trying to think of the animal type that you represent. You know, I suppose, that some low type of irrational animal provides the basis of every human countenance?"

"I didn't," said Winnie timidly, not understanding but trying to be interested. Why couldn't he talk about the river and the moor, or, if he couldn't do that, sit still and let the stickles sing? She heard nothing of the water while he was lecturing.

"It is so," he went on, as if it was a matter of the greatest importance. "One man represents the goat type, another the sheep; one woman represents the cow type, another the cat. We cannot remove ourselves altogether from our earliest associations. I could not get your type fixed in my mind. It has kept me awake for two nights. You seem to go back behind the animals, and the origin of your face must I think be looked for in the age of vegetation. I am sorry for that, because it means entire helplessness, though it also means beauty of a pure and soft type without any taint of animal passion."

This was a very roundabout way of comparing her face to a flower. Still there was a compliment at the end of it.

"I heard Miss Budge allude to you as a destructive little thing; by which she meant to imply, I fancy, in the shockingly loose phraseology of the ordinary middle-class female, that you resemble Helen in your sway over the hearts of men."

Winnie said nothing but merely sat and wondered who Helen might be. She wished she could summon up the courage to ask the question, because knowledge of her ignorance might possibly frighten him away.

"Helplessness is attractive to the strong," he continued in his intolerable manner, supposing, if he was capable of any self-detachment, that he was impressing her profoundly. "It is also, as I have mentioned, an attribute of plant life. Plants are indeed so helpless that Nature has to protect them in various ways. Otherwise they would become extinct. Many are given the power of propagating rapidly. Others are provided with thorns, poison, a nauseous taste or smell. Plants, unlike animals, always act on the defensive, even when they appear to be most offensive. Others are given the power of withstanding intense cold and strong gales. There is this heather, for instance. You will notice, if you examine it closely, that its leaves and flowers are specially constructed so that the plant may not be destroyed by the winds. This brings me to the type which I imagine you represent; the plant delicate in appearance, yet actually hardy enough to endure the strongest storm. I thought out all that as I was walking on the moor," he concluded naively.

"It sounds very clever," faltered poor Winnie.

"I am a very clever man," came the astounding answer. "I took the highest honours at school and college. There was nobody to touch me when I was up at Oxford. Once I refuted the Master of Balliol," he said in a reverential voice.

Winnie was quite dazed. She didn't know what to think of the man who was blaring his unpleasant trumpet at her ear; whether he was too ill to control himself, or half-mad with learning, or utterly diseased with self-pride. There was one explanation for it, a perfectly good one, but it did not occur to Winnie, as it had not occurred to any of the other patients. It was not madness, nor was it conceit; but something that the poor wretch could not help, and could not fight against with any hope of success.

"Now I will come more particularly to yourself," said Halfacre, as pleasantly as he could. It was certain he was doing his utmost to make himself agreeable; he was not trying to be rude, but on the contrary he was striving to make her happy and comfortable in his own queer way. "First I will ask your age."

Winnie gasped at that. The idea of a man, almost a stranger, demanding her to tell him her age. She set her teeth together and tried to be resolute. Her beautiful marshland was becoming rapidly a hard and pitiless sort of place.

"I asked your age," said Halfacre quite sharply.

"Twenty-four," murmured Winnie. Again she couldn't help it. He would keep on looking at her.

"I am twenty-six," he said with sudden simplicity. "Where do you live?"

So it was all to come out, the sordid secrets she had tried so hard to keep; and now everybody would know, and proud Berenice would not hug her any more or call her sweet, and the "other one," whoever that might be, would not show her any more pictures or tell those glorious fresh-air stories. It was all up with her, and she would have to be common little Winnie to the end of the story.

Halfacre nudged her with his elbow and made her start. It was a beastly thing to do but she couldn't get away from him, and he was smiling and thinking he was quite polite.

"In Keyham," she gasped.

"Then you are probably a poor girl?"

"Oh, don't tell them. Please don't tell," cried Winnie piteously. "I can't help telling you because you make me somehow. But I have managed to keep it to myself, and they don't know anything about me, and I could not stay on if they knew."

Halfacre showed no surprise at this outburst. He too had his secrets, which he was able to keep, as there was no strong-minded person to force them out. He plucked a scrap of moss, opened his tin box, threw it in and snapped the lid upon it. All his life he had been accustomed to take notes, and the piece of moss was a note which would remind him when he came to turn out the contents of the box of what Winnie had said. It was one of the commonest mosses, only the undulated hair-moss which grows all over the moor, and therefore it would recall to him at once Winnie's position in the world.

"l shall not say anything. I am poor too," he said, as if he was willing to exchange confidences. "Are your parents living?"

"My mother is. My father has been dead several years."

"Has your mother any income?" he went on, as if he was asking after her health.

"A very little, not enough for us to live on," she answered in her helpless way, having given up the struggle to resist because she knew it was useless.

"Then you work for your living. What is it? Shop, dressmaking?" he suggested, making his question sound very sordid.

"Post-office," she faltered, her eyes beginning to feel hot. "It's a grocer's shop, and the post-office is in connection with it. It's a small box railed off, and I stand in it all day. There isn't any time to sit down. The shop is at the corner of a busy street. There is a public-house opposite."

"Where were you born?"

"At Princetown in the middle of the moor, up in the clouds," she said wistfully. "My father was a doctor. We were there until I was fourteen. I used to go to the top of Crockern Tor where the supreme court was held and sit there for hours. Whenever they missed me they would send to Crockern Tor. I was so well and strong in those days. I was planted on the top of the moor, and growing there, until I was pulled up and thrown away in the smoke. I became ill then. I couldn't live out of the wind."

Halfacre made another note by picking a piece of heather and throwing it into the tin box. Winnie would have gone on talking happily of her early home, but her companion had other questions. He soon banished the thoughts which made her happy by recalling those which made her miserable; and he did so in the most direct and insolent way possible.

"Who pays your expenses at the sanatorium?"

"I don't think I can tell you. It's a very great secret." Then she began to shake and search for her handkerchief which wouldn't be found.

"Oh I see—charity," he said sorrowfully.

"It's not," said Winnie, as indignant as she could be.

"Not your mother?" he went on, with that appalling directness which she could not resist.

She shook her head quickly, then let it rest upon her shoulder.

"It is a man. There is no other deduction. It is not the grocer whose shop you work in?"

"No, no," said Winnie, weary and persecuted, longing to have it over. "It's that man."

After that a good cry would have been natural enough, and possibly it would have occurred had it not been for Halfacre's extraordinary conduct. He passed at once into the wildest passion, tearing up the heather, forcing his fingers into the moss, the veins starting from his forehead, while his eyes became like those of a lunatic.

"How much longer are we going to stand them?" he shouted. "The rich and idle who buy and break the poor. I know what you are saying. There is the tyranny of the Church and the tyranny of the rich, and between them the wretched poor sneak down to their graves by the easiest way they can find. The time is coming. We are breeding six times as fast as they are. The sun of our liberty is rising. The time is not far distant when the people shall be in power, and those who have oppressed them for centuries shall have their fill of poor man's law, and poor man's workhouses."

Winnie was only conscious that he was not looking at her. The sun was going down behind the range of tors at the back of the marsh, and over the peak of Steeperton the moon was just visible, almost full, and looking like a circle of tissue paper. Halfacre was looking at the moon and raving at her, possibly because there was some connection between his own ideas and that unsubstantial looking circlet. His fire burnt down and his rather wild eyes returned to the girl's frightened face, and his seemingly irresponsible tongue went on to ask—

"Why do you work in that post-office and submit to tyranny?"

"To make my living," said Winnie, with some spirit.

"What does he say to it, this brute who has bought you, keeps you, buys your clothes, has your body and soul in pawn?" he cried, beginning to rave again.

Fortunately Winnie did not grasp the whole of his meaning. He spoke so fast and confused her, and she was under the spell of his eyes again and could not think much.

"It's the man to whom I'm engaged," she faltered.

Halfacre became himself again when he heard that. He threw away a handful of moss, which he had been clutching as if it had been a tyrant's throat, and said coldly—

"You misled me. Who is he? What is his occupation? Tell me all about him."

Evidently this man had taken possession of her and Winnie could not escape. After all it would be a relief, she thought, to tell the whole story and let another judge and pass sentence upon her. Halfacre was expressing friendship in a very extraordinary way, but still it was a kind of friendship. He was insulting, but that was only his manner. There was a kindness for her beneath the surface. He was thrusting his support upon her, and she had to accept it.

"He is a clerk," she said, shrinking as she spoke and drawing her fingers quickly across her eyes. "His name is Ernest Hawker."

"Go on," he said when she hesitated. "The name is all right. It belongs to the land, like mine."

"He used to come to the office to buy stamps, and after a time would stay and talk to me," said Winnie. "Then he found out the time I went home, and met me at the door. I was rather grateful, for the streets are rough. After a time he came to see mother, and he took us to the theatre, and I—I became engaged to him, though I didn't want to, but I couldn't help it."

"You don't care for him. You must get out of it. I will get you out of it. The first principle of life is that of liberty," Half acre cried violently. "Only those men and women should come together who are compelled to do so by nature. Everything—engagements, ties, matrimony itself—must remain subordinate to that principle."

Winnie shivered at his passionate doctrine. She did not know much, but was able to guess that any state founded upon such shifting foundations would have to fall.

"Then it happened," she went on, when he became silent. "I was always getting ill. I never knew what it was to be really well after we left Princetown. At last all the horrors began and the doctor told mother what it was, and my only chance would be to get back on the moor away from the smoke."

"The towns that the oppressors have built, the fine houses for themselves, the dirty slums for the people," said Halfacre without violence, but in a slow and vengeful manner. "They took the land from the people and gave them instead a few square yards of filth. Not content with that they created a disease and gave them that too. The disease of civilisation, the poor man's disease, they call it. The debt is a big one but we are beginning to pay a little interest on it.

Whenever I hear of a rich man dying of the poor man's disease I laugh. So you came here. And this man is paying for you?"

"We had no money," said poor Winnie. "I couldn't work any more. It was a matter of life or death, so Mr. Hawker said he would send me here and pay for me and help mother in the meantime. I must marry him, or else pay back all the money he is spending. It is for mother's sake I am trying to get well, not for my own. Without me mother would have to seek charity; and when I get well enough, and—and am married she will live with us. There is no way out of it."

"We will put an end to it," said Halfacre, speaking as if he was her brother or uncle, instead of a stranger who had known her only a few days. "You must have liberty. Everything is a crime which stands between us and liberty. Nothing is a crime which removes one or more of the barriers. What is he like?"

Winnie was beginning to admire this man who seemed so strong and lawless; her clinging self went out to him, and she forgot his insolence, or called it depth of feeling. He was not exactly conquering her difficulties or proposing any solution of them. He was simply brushing them away like so many black cobwebs. He seemed to her to be talking sound common-sense when he said that every one had a right to be free. Why not? Are men and women beasts in cages, kept and confined for the sport of gods, fed with the bread and water of affliction, their jaws muzzled and their claws cut, their minds fretting, and their bodies' growing mangy with disease? Not a bit of it. They are not beasts, because of that soul which slips out of the cage and enters the wind, and flits towards the sun, and defies the gods, and declares it created itself.

So much for the philosophy of Halfacre, who thought himself a professor when he was only a freshman. Men and women are beasts and they cannot get out of the cage, and their minds must fret and their bodies grow mangy with disease. They are not even perfect beasts, for their very inventions represent creation run mad; genius is certainly madness, and inspiration a form of ill-health. They cannot make or copy anything real. They play with iron and steel and make monstrous toys out of them. But they cannot copy a buttercup or make a finger-joint.

"I know him," said Halfacre, when Winnie had done describing "that man," adding nothing to his attractions. "He is a common object of towns, the mindless man who represents neither good nor evil, but is like a fly buzzing about a wall searching for congenial smells. He wears his hat on the back of his head and laughs whenever he says anything. He talks about football one half of the year and about horse-racing the other half, making the same remarks every year and not knowing that he has ever made them before. His vocabulary consists of two hundred words and a few strange oaths. That's the man who is buying you by instalments."

Halfacre made a note of the fact by picking a sprig of whortleberry and throwing it into the tin box.

"He is not well off. It is very hard upon him," said Winnie miserably. "He is spending his savings to keep me alive."

She shivered, for mist was coming across the marshes and all the bogs were steaming. The river had become cold, the heather was getting colourless, and the invisible stickles were singing rather sadly. It was the mournful time of Sunday when people get dejected and go to church to grin at one another and forget themselves and the cursed loneliness of life.

Halfacre got up and wiped his muddy boots in the moss. "They won't suspect anything at the sanatorium," he said. "I shall be the same as ever, but we shall meet outside and I'll show you the way to escape. We must have liberty—all of us." He shut his little tin box with a snap, well-satisfied, as if he had just caught Winnie and had got her safely inside.

CHAPTER IX
ABOUT ANOTHER HALF-HOLIDAY

Most poor people dream about what they will do when they become rich; the time wasted in that sort of castlebuilding might make them so if it was used properly. They will surround themselves with every possible luxury, and give as much as sixpence a week to charity; they will entertain less fortunate relations, but not often; they will buy a lot of women and live uxoriously. Dreams are nothing if not selfish. A man sees himself set in the world, shouting at others to get out of his way, and beating down opposition with a money-bag. Sometimes he sees himself a professional philanthropist, which is still more selfish, and necessitates the hiring of a brass band to make a noise while he signs his cheques. A man may keep himself on the roll of fame for centuries, merely by bequeathing a thousand pounds to provide honest old women with red-flannel petticoats at Christmas. The women must be honest and the petticoats must be made of red flannel. The women only grumble at the petticoats, declare they are made of rotten stuff, and they wouldn't be seen wearing such things because of that very respectability which has won them the gift; and then they pawn the things and buy themselves gin. But the philanthropist lives on. He has bought his title to fame in very much the same way as the poor old woman buys her glass of gin.

There are other dreams, supremely selfish, for when a dream ceases to be so it is called a nightmare, but not sordid. Wealth is not necessarily a part of these, and in the best of them all it does not even enter. There is the dream of laurel-leaves, the poet's dream, which is somewhat out of fashion now, because anything, even a pewter-pot or half-a-crown, is preferable to the ancient prize of victory. And there is the dream of a face, the lover's dream, and the only one worth having because it is unspoilt by metal and corruption. These will creep in later on, but the dream itself is free of them. The unreality of that dream is the glory of it. That face is not really what it appears to be, just as the dreamer is nothing like what he thinks he is. It is not the face which appeals, but the celestial atmosphere surrounding it. The dreamer imagines that it is the face which causes the atmosphere, when the converse is the case, as he soon discovers when the dream becomes realised and he and that face are linked together, and they nearly swear at each other over the first butcher's bill.

George the artist was a day-dreamer. Fair women did not trouble him at nights, as his digestion was well enough, and angelic dream-faces demand an unsettled liver. It was when he sat by the window and looked down upon Wheal Dream that he had visions. He was not a mystic; such black arts as witchcraft and spiritualism made no appeal to him; materialism interested him far more, and he made the body and its needs the theme of nearly all his work. He thought it unnecessary for the artist to inquire into the spiritual side of things, as there was sufficient in matter to satisfy the most exacting. The moor in a mist, the wheal at moonlight, were as far as he ever went in his dream-pictures. He scoffed at the canvases of the old masters with their rough and raw ideas, and their favourite skyful of tumbling angels, pot-bellied and heavy as lead. George had a direct way of doing things. With pencil and paper he reckoned that an angel would require several geological periods to fly from the nearest fixed star to the earth, and he couldn't see how the celestial being was ever going to find the time to get down and home again. That being so, a pair of bird's wings could be obviously of no use to an angel, and therefore it was a ridiculous affectation of art to depict them with wings. And George was a failure as an artist.

He was driving nails into a boxful of pictures, while Bubo reposed on his perch, watching in the cynical fashion which he had acquired since attaining to years of discretion. Every time the hammer descended Bubo gave a little jump, possibly to signify that the noise hurt his nerves.

"Twenty pictures—sunsets, moonrisings and mists such as never were," said George to his winking partner. "You on a lump of rock, representing the king of the night, you miserable humbug; Jimmy and his baby among the ferns as rustic innocence, a feature of unreal life; Father leaning on his sticks waiting for the cows to come home, a pretty study of noble old age but without any of the less pleasing parental details; Ursula carrying a load of furze home, another common feature, although it is a thing she has never done in her life. Twenty pictures at two-and-ninepence apiece, which is all I get from the lineal descendant of Barabbas who, when I suggest he isn't paying all he owes, clutches his beard and swears by the God of Abraham and the God of Isaac that he is ruining himself for me. Here we are, Bubo, an English gentleman and a British owl beneath the thumb of one of the discarded race. Fame must be a fine thing, Bubo. It gives us a chance of getting our pride back."

The little owl closed both eyes and was sorry for himself because his master was making such a noise. Whenever George was not working or dreaming he talked aloud, directing his remarks at Bubo, who had in return given him many a quaint inspiration.

"We are two gentleman's sons, at least I have always regarded you as such, though you may be a lady's daughter for all I know," George went on, as he went round and round the packing-case whacking at it with his hammer. "Your pedigree is a fine one, Bubo. You earned the distinction of being regarded as the symbol of wisdom merely by sitting still and looking sleepy, which is exactly how a good many of my species acquire the same reputation."

The box was finished, pushed into a corner, and George turned his attention to a parcel of manuscript, and bustled about the room looking for paper and string, chatting all the time.

"It's only during the last few days the idea occurred to me that I am a gentleman. I had forgotten all about it until I went working down by the Ford. You see I have painted the Brunacombe arms to adorn the premises; three fools of pelicans vulning themselves, according to the jargon of heraldry, or as the soul-inspiring Gumm observed when I attempted to explain the thing to him, 'trying to lug their guts out,' which reduces heraldry into a far simpler form. You wouldn't feed your legitimate offspring on your blood, you'd let the beggars starve; but then you're the bird of wisdom. It's no joke to be a gentleman in these days unless you can support your title. It's illegal to go out with an axe and cleave skulls, which I understand was the usual practice of my ancestors. Grandmotherly legislation has put a stop to that. The working-man has the best time with his two or three hours a day, a week off when he wants it, and a pension if he strains himself. It's the gentleman that does the work. 'Why du'ye get up so early and go to bed so late?' Ursula asks in the words of the Psalmist. 'Don't ye get tired o' they pictures and writings?' There you are, Bubo. Our work is a game to her. When she sees me cleaning a window—because when she does it herself she makes it dirtier—she says, 'Ah, now he'm working.' When I scribble until two o'clock in the morning I'm amusing myself. If you have extracted the necessary amount of nutriment out of that piece of string I'll find a use for it."

Bubo had picked up the piece of string and was nibbling it thoughtfully. He gave it up without a whimper, and his master began to tie up the parcel.

"Yes, my friend, you're quite right in your supposition. With that cold, critical eye upon me it would be useless to dissemble. This is not a treatise upon art, nor any learned monograph upon geology, botany or ornithology, but it is, Bubo—and at this point we must blush—it is a novel. We all come to it at last. It is as inevitable as death and the poor-rate. We paint our pictures and we compose our sonnets with the virtue which is its own reward, until one day the devil enters into us and we write a novel. This one is by S. Bubo—not Samuel, my son, but Strix—which was the name awarded to your early ancestor on a certain wet afternoon in the Ark; proposed by Father Noah, a simple old sailor who lurched about the deck inventing such nautical phrases as 'shiver my timbers but it's dirty weather'; seconded by Ham and carried, though the youngest boy, who was a terror for books, demurred, saying it was ridiculous to give a bird a Latin name so many hundreds of years before the founding of the city of Rome. They were all prophets in those days, Bubo. They knew everything that was going to happen, and it must have led to a lot of confusion. I suppose Noah was always looking for his chronometer and wondering what they dratted boys had done wi' 'en, and bothering his head about Greenwich time and latitude and longitude; and then remembering he was several thousand years ahead of the times. It must have been a dreadful trial to the poor old skipper to think of the glass of grog and the strong cigar which were not for him because he was so antedated. Tobacco wouldn't have been much use to him without matches, and he hadn't got any; and, to add insult to injury, he would have known that his poor old tub would be adopted as a trade-mark by a firm of British match-makers ages after it had run aground on Ararat. No wonder prehistoric prophets were always lamenting."

Bubo made some quaint noises, flapped his wings, scuttled from one end of the perch to the other and did extraordinary things with his eyes. Then he composed himself, with his head on one side, and an expression which seemed to say, "I hope the temporary lapse from gravity was not noticed."

"I suppose you're pleased with yourself," said George, "just because I am shifting the responsibility of this book from my shoulders to your wings. As a matter of fact you ought to be ashamed. This is what people will call a disgusting book, but they will read it, Bubo, and talk about it, and beg their friends not to look at it, which is the best of all advertisements. We're a shabby couple and we're poor; there's money in this sort of thing, and who will ever know we wrote it? People will declare that nobody but a lady could write such stuff. You will observe that the parcel is already covered with flies.

"One has only got to live with a philosopher to discover what a humbug he is," George went on. "Any one seeing you perched on a tor would remark what a sublime creature you were, but to live with you changes the matter entirely. There is a pound of vice to every square inch of your feathered body, and your cry which sounds so impressive at night is really nothing more than the patter of the professional loafer, the wife-and-five-children-and-ashamed-to-work sort of cry. The goose is called a fool because he looks and behaves like one out of sheer honesty. You are regarded as a wise bird because you are a successful fraud. I'm a cross between the two of you, a goose in private and an owl in public, with the advantage, such as it is, of a mind, and the disadvantage of a complete set of vices which cannot be employed owing to lack of opportunity. Most of us human creatures are respectable, Bubo, because there is no opportunity to be anything else. They say it is hard to be good; but I do assure you, on my honour and by my ancestral pelicans in the wilderness, that it is much more difficult to be wicked."

Bubo woke up suddenly and ploughed his beak under his wing in search of a troublesome tenant.

"Even a philosopher cannot attend to the frailties of his fellow-creatures when he's got the itch," said George. "Nothing brings us down to our proper level like a flea. He skips from a dunghill into the clothes of a queen, and one place is to him just as good as the other. We do not eat our stowaways, however, Bubo, although that is no doubt the ultimate end of most creeping things. I mention the fact as an aid to your own advancement. If you refrain your children may, and thus the particular family of owls to which you belong will advance a step in the process of evolution, leave the other owls behind, and approach a little nearer to the sublime species, of which I am a singularly poor specimen, who pretend to know good from evil and virtue from vice, although what one man calls good another calls bad—perhaps you had better eat your flea, Bubo, and remain as you are."

The artist caught, up his parcel and went out of the house as fast as he could. He always acted upon impulse, having learnt by experience that if he once stopped to argue with himself nothing was done. It was a fine afternoon, and he hadn't been a good walk for ages. He would post his parcel, then tear about the moor like a wild school-boy until dark. Had he stopped to think he would have sat down to finish a picture or start upon something fresh. As soon as one task was over another began. There was never such a thing as a whole holiday for the busy workman of Wheal Dream.

The Stannary road was noisy, which was not unusual, but the sounds were those of mirth. One of Ursula's lady friends had come across to visit her. She was not a recognised humourist, although any one might have mistaken her for such, because Ursula was howling with laughter, John was bumping his uncouth body against the wall with spasmodic hee-haws, and as for poor old Father, he was shaking and coughing, and tears were removing a respectable quantity of highly fertile soil from his cheeks. Uncle was standing at his gate, hideous and patient, and as grave as Bubo. He was adding to his unpopularity and living up to his unneighbourly reputation by not laughing. Poor old Uncle had nothing to laugh at, because he had just been compelled to open his money-box, and that tragedy weighed upon him so heavily that he was unable to perceive the subtle humour in the remark of Ursula's friend, "It be lovely weather we'm getting." That was what the noise was about.

Presently Ursula recovered sufficiently to remark, "Yew'm a proper old stranger," and this witticism set them off again, until Father had to shuffle away and sit down and hope he hadn't broken a blood-vessel. They were really getting on nicely and understanding each other well. It was a conversation by means of shrieks of laughter, meant to express the best intentions and good neighbourly feeling; the ordinary way in which such women greet one another. Directly they meet they begin to howl like jackasses. It is merely the friendly smile of recognition, only they overdo it somewhat and keep it up too long. After the paroxysms of welcome they are able to settle down and talk quietly.

When George appeared there was silence; Uncle touched his hat, but the others looked at him very much as sheep regard a wandering dog. When he observed that the weather was fine they did not laugh, because he was not one of them and there was no humour in what he said. When the moor gate had clanged and the big figure could be seen swaying off across the common, Ursula's friend remarked, after a preliminary titter, "He'm the gentleman." This was the finishing touch; and they had to lead Father into the kitchen and pat him on the back until he stopped choking.

When George had posted his parcel, and had resisted the pressing invitation of the post-mistress to tell her what it contained, though to be sure it didn't really matter, as she could easily slip the string off when he had gone, he made his way up the steep road leading to the high moor. He thought he would go to the slopes of Miltor, where he could find white heather, knowing exactly where to look for it, and he thought he would bring back a bunch and leave it at the sanatorium with his kind regards. He would not ask that it should be given to any one in particular, but probably some would find its way to the right source. George had been injured that day at Chapel Ford, but he did not talk about it. Even Bubo, who heard everything, had not been told about the new disease. The germ was latent, the symptoms had not asserted themselves, and the disease had been prevented from reaching the malignant stage by the sight of Halfacre wearing that sprig in his coat. George said nothing as he walked up the side of the moor; he could not think without speaking aloud, and he could not confide to the listening wind what it knew very well already, that he had reached the mouth of the pit which is really the only landscape feature of the world of vast importance, because every man that lives has to tumble into it and lie groaning until he is put out of his misery.

A few dimples play the mischief with history, pretty faces win battles, and a smile is at the bottom of nearly every tragedy. That is why there is no escaping from the eternal matter. Only men who are not men can escape; and even they must go mad sometimes to feel no manhood stirring in them when they face the hot and throbbing pages of history.

George was upon a part of the moor which the patients frequented, therefore he was not surprised when he saw Berenice walking in front of him, going slowly and poking at the moss with her stick. The girl was lonely, for Tobias would have nothing whatever to do with her, and Winnie, she feared, was getting into bad company. They were not allowed to go out together now that Winnie was so much stronger, but Berenice had seen something that morning which made her think. Deep lanes were made for lovers, and they seem also to have been especially constructed to meet every demand of those who may wish to peep at them.

"A fine girl, George," said the artist. "Just the one if you weren't a poor devil. Wonder what she would say if I asked her to put her affections into the things of earth and my business. I wonder if I can get away without her seeing me."

That was always his way. When he saw a handsome brown-faced girl strolling the moor his first idea was that it would be very pleasant to walk with her; and the next prompted him to hurry off in the opposite direction. Some men are made like that; the peculiar state of their nerves compels them to escape from that which they desire, or when confronted by the woman of their heart to impress upon her that she is one of the most contemptible things alive. George had not nearly reached that stage when one face becomes supreme and nerves are relegated to the background. The sprig of white heather intervened.

Berenice saw him and stopped. She waved her stick, which straightway became the wand of the magician enchanting George. Evidently she wanted to speak to him, and he had to go, deciding to tell her that he had an important engagement to fulfil on the black spurs of West Miltor. The girl seated herself on a lump of granite waiting for him, criticising his appearance, admiring his fine head. As he came near she smiled and said to herself, "Poor thing! he wants a nurse."

Since that wonderful morning beside Chapel Ford George had become more conscious of his deficiencies. The light was so strong and pitiless. It showed up everything—his dreadful old clothes, shocking boots, his bushy beard full of dust, his snuff-stained nostrils. He could not rid himself of the pernicious habit of snuff-taking. He began to pull out his handkerchief, saw the colour of it, and pushed it quickly out of sight. His hands were covered with paint and ink, his collar was in its second week—he was always meaning to put on a fresh one, but it was such a nuisance—he wore no tie, but his beard concealed that deficiency fairly well; he had no cap, and the wind had blown his long hair into a delirious tangle. He was, in short, the fine picture of a tramp; but no amount of shabbiness, neglect, or untrimmed hair could do away with the strong features which broke through them, the high forehead, clear eyes, and well-bred nose. Nothing is harder to conceal than gentility. Money cannot buy it, tailors cannot make it; those who are naturally common cannot imitate it; and those who have it cannot put it off. Fine feathers make only shrieking parrots, dirty linen does not turn the clever man into a fool, and a gentleman will always look better in rags than a ploughboy in fine raiment.

"Where are you going?" asked Berenice, looking at him in a way which made him put his hands into his pockets, which were useless for any other purpose, as he had worn them into a couple of holes. This fresh girl was such a horrible contrast. She was so dreadfully clean, like a newly whitewashed wall, and there did not appear to be a speck of dust on her clothing. He wondered however girls managed to live up to such a high standard of freshness and still find time to go about and exhibit themselves.

He nodded over the hills and far away to where the mountains made a fine rugged background like that of an Italian opera and said, "To West Miltor."

"Work of some sort?"

"No, pleasure. My first half-holiday for months. The factory is closed until eight o'clock this evening. Then the machinery will start again and some sort of rubbish will be manufactured. I may pick up a little raw material on the moor."

He laughed in his boyish way, pulled his hands out of his pockets and rubbed them together briskly, then noticed she was looking at them. "I know they're dirty. It's honest dirt, paint and ink," he said defiantly. "I'll wash them when I get down to the river."

"I'm going your way. I am sent as far as the military road," said Berenice. She jumped up and stepped off beside him, her little brown boots keeping time with his shapeless monstrosities.

"It won't matter if any one does see us," said George apologetically. Those boots were such a contrast. "Every one knows me. I'm the gentleman. I don't work for my living. I sit in my workshop all day and most of the night amusing myself."

"You and Mr. Leigh are the two most popular men about here. Every one likes you and him," said Berenice. "Even our awful Twins, who are not very keen on people socially better than themselves, have nothing but nice things to say about you two. 'Leigh is made of the right stuff,' says the publican. 'So is Georgy Brunacombe,' says the sinner. 'Right for once, fathead,' is the answer. Whenever you pass our place there is some such remark as, 'There goes the man who wasn't born asleep like you were.' They can be complimentary, you see, even if they have to insult each other while being so."

"Popularity is good when it isn't bought," said George. "I hope Leigh doesn't buy it with roses. I like him very much," he went on quickly, "but he is so hated in his village that sometimes it is hardly safe for him to go into the street."

"Those people don't count," said the girl contemptuously. "What does it matter to a gentleman whether a lot of clodhoppers like him or not? They are a horrible set down in Downacombe. The man at the post-office is a Socialist, and he got a lecturer to come there who poisoned the minds of the villagers and put the idea into their heads that they were all downtrodden wretches."

"I am not speaking against Leigh. I am not saying anything now which I have not said to his face," George answered slowly. He was a poor man, much cleverer than the Rector of Downacombe, and he knew how hard he worked for a very few sovereigns. "But I shall always maintain that a man has no right to retain an official position if he cannot perform its duties."

"Mr. Leigh is perfectly willing to work. It is the villagers' own fault if they won't let him," said Berenice. "He has week-day services all through the year, and if nobody attends them you can't blame him for that."

"I said he cannot perform his duties, not he will not. The clerical work of a country village is at present nothing. Most healthy men would regard it as a recreation. Compare it with the amount performed by men of some talent for a pound or two a week. I think every village parson who gets a hundred a year, in this Nonconformist west-country at least, is very much overpaid. Take the two parishes adjoining Downacombe; one is very small, but the stipend is five hundred pounds, and the living has been awarded as a plum to a man already well off, who is also a bachelor; and the other is large and straggling, but the stipend is much under two hundred pounds, and the incumbent hasn't got a penny apart from it, and he has about a dozen children. Something must be wrong there."

"But then there is always something wrong in these things," said she, rather plaintively. "None of us get what we want, and there are prizes in every profession. I can quite understand how you feel about it. Heaps of artists don't work half as hard as you and yet get much larger incomes. It's that beastly thing called luck. But it makes life more enjoyable, a bit of a gamble, and we all like gambling, don't you think? I should hate to think of Mr. Leigh losing a single penny of his income. He's such a dear."

"Well, we won't argue," said George. "I expect you are right. I am a bit sore. Successful men get too much, unsuccessful men too little. The gamble is well enough for the winners, but the losers, who stake their last and see it go, have to find themselves quiet corners. Sometimes I think a big levelling up would settle things, but it wouldn't. Luck would soon assert itself, and every successful man would absorb the shares of seven unlucky ones. We all started level at one time, but the unlucky man quickly came upon the scene. You can't level up intelligence and ability—not to mention morality. Who is that under the white sunshade below the second tor?"

"The perambulating mushroom is Budge, senior maiden of our establishment. Don't look that way or she will wave and stampede after us—you, I mean. She is always talking about men. I tell her she ought to buy one, as she has plenty of money. What should you say if she proposed to you?"

"The same as an editor when he has read my latest sonnet."

"That would be rude, I expect. When a lady asks a man to marry her it is his duty to say 'Yes, please.'"

George looked at the girl, then wagged his beard solemnly, and made up his mind to tell Bubo all about it when he got home. Berenice was as solemn as the little owl, there was not a sign of laughter on her brown face, and her eyes were upon the granite. The artist had never been addressed so lightly by a girl.before, and he couldn't understand it. Had she taken a liking for him? But that was ridiculous. He compared the boots again and almost burst out laughing, then addressed himself mentally, "Don't be a fool. She is only trying to be pleasant because she's a bit dull and she knows you have a hard time."

"Too fast," she said. "I have got what Gumm calls a tin lung. I also have to control a troublesome thing called a temperature."

George slackened speed at once and apologised. "It's hard to walk slowly on the moor. The space is so great that you feel you must go your hardest to make any progress at all."

"You're solemn," said Berenice, as if it was the most natural thing in the world to say. "Too much living with owls in old dream-houses. Why don't you clean your nails?" she said crossly.

George looked rather bewildered, then laughed and examined the offending rims, not sorry that she had noticed them, because now he needn't trouble to keep them out of sight. He admitted they were rather worse than usual, saying cheerily, "It's no use fighting against nature. I'm a working-man, and the labourer lives in contact with the soil. He can't throw down his tools and boil his fingers seven times a day. Gloves and manicured fingers are good enough for kings and priests, but they contribute nothing to the world's knowledge. We are planted in the dirt," said George. "We grow out of it, live on it, go back to it. There's no escaping from it, and most of us can't spare the time to try. All the masterpieces of the world were produced by dirty fingers."

"What horrible nonsense!" said she.

"Not a bit of it. I don't believe a genius has ever lived who could abide clean linen. Homer I fancy was something like old Father Chown to look at, Shakespeare wrote with the garden soil of Stratford on his hands, and Michael Angelo did wonders with garlic-scented fingers. I doubt if any of the founders of religion ever had a bath."

"There is no excuse for you, anyhow," said the girl severely.

"I'm not a genius certainly," laughed George. "So much is true; but I am always turning the wheel which communicates with that centre of the nervous system called the brain, and that keeps me clean inwardly. A rolling brain gathers no rust. It's like the little river down the cleave; you couldn't imagine slime on a mountain stream, though it has black bogs and stagnant moss on each side. My brain, such as it is, can run between a pair of dirty hands like the Okement between its bogs; and as for the moss—here it is." He caught at his beard and tugged it from side to side. "It's only a parasitic growth, lichen on a rock, ivy on a tree."

"Old man's beard in a hedgerow," she added.

"No," he said rather bitterly, shrinking from the thought of age. "Clematis, traveller's joy, virgin's bower—call it that."

"But there are white hairs, long and silvery. One is upon your shoulder, so old and tired," she said maliciously.

"That's no sign of age. It is mimicry," he said. "My beard is growing grey out of sympathy with my work and surroundings. I am so fond of strong whites and cool greys in my painting; and the light up here is strong and white, the rocks are white, so are the rivers and the mists, and even the pink heather up there is bleached by this everlasting whiteness. If I went and worked on the scarlet clay of mid-Devon my beard would turn red."

"If I make you a present of nail-scissors will you use them?" she asked, frowning.

"I will. I'll trim Bubo's tail this very night. The little rascal is as ragged as Diogenes."

"What a pity it is," she murmured; and then sharply, "For heaven's sake throw that horrible handkerchief away."

"It is rather brown, but only snuff and turpentine, good honest stuff," said George. "And it's not a handkerchief, as you may see by the frayed edges. I tear up my old sheets for paint rags, and they get into my pocket sometimes. You think I live in an uncleanly way," he went on, throwing the discoloured fragment into a bog, while Berenice murmured, "The best place for it," and poked it down with her stick. "Very likely I do, for my various occupations are messy ones, and Ursula Petherick brings more dirt into the house than she takes out, but there is such a thing as clean dirt. Look at this fresh brown peat, the sand and gravel washed down this cart-track, and those little black roots. You can't call them unpleasant, for they are sweeter and purer than the stuff we are made of ourselves. They have nothing in common with smoke, soot, and town-mud. They have the wind and the rain upon them. They are the cleanest of all things. When I lie upon the peat and burrow my nose into it I seem to smell the breath of life. I'd like to die up there," said George, pointing to the huge arc of Cawsand bending across the clouds, "lying on the top of a grey slab of granite where I could heave my soul out on the heather."

"Don't use such words," said Berenice, with a shiver. "I am an invalid."

"So am I in my spare moments. That's dirt in its worst form and unavoidable; the filthy little fungi that multiply inside and choke us; the foulness of the sickroom—that's why I love the brown peat and black heather-roots, the clean sand and gravel. That's the dirt in my wheal house. It's sand under my nails and bits of heather in my beard; clean dirt which kills malignant dirt. My house is full of wind and sun, sometimes rain and mist. That's not uncleanliness."

"It's a pity," she sighed again.

"What is?" said George, full of self-conceit now that the vapours of nervousness had been dissipated.

"I'll tell you," said the girl. She was admiring him. His personality was so strong when it was reached; so were his words. When he lifted his head it reminded her of stone, not because of its power, for it was not powerful, but because the clean-cut rocks are upon the mountain-top where the rain has chiselled them; and the hair which shivered about that head was like the heather trembling with its imitation of weakness about those rocks; like the wiry heather which is not strong and yet sees the granite worn away. "You're a man," she said, "and that's why I'm sorry. There are millions going about like sheep saying, 'Baa, baa.' There are very few who fling themselves on life and try to find out what it is made of and what it was given for."

"Why, those are my own words," cried George in amazement.

"I know they are," she laughed.

"The philosophy of George Brunacombe, represented in art holding a one-legged owl."

"As quoted by Winnie Shazell," said Berenice rather mockingly.

His countenance changed, and not another jest was forthcoming.

"Winnie Shazell who strolls about the lanes with that delightful young Halfacre," she went on, noticing his hands and the movements of them. "How many pieces of paper have been blown out of your window? Down they fly into Wheal Dream, and Winnie gathers them up and reads diligently, and frowns her pretty face into lines committing them to memory. You should use paperweights."

"I believe it is Bubo. He throws them out. I'll talk to him when I get home," said George, forcing himself to speak lightly. "Why are you sorry for me?" he asked swiftly.

Berenice began to hum in a bee-like and provoking manner; and all she said was, "Here is the river where it is divided into several branches like the one in Paradise. You cross and go on. I stay this side. It sounds solemn and death-like," she laughed.

"Why are you sorry for me?" he said.

"Oh, well, you have a lot to put up with. Ill-health, hard work, little profit. Some of those bits of paper were rather confidential," she said almost flippantly. "There, I am tormenting you," she went on with a mocking kind of penitence. "I said you were a man, and so you are, a good, conceited man like Mr. Leigh. Only you should think certain things, not write them down; not write a detailed description of the ideal lady—and then let the wind blow it out of the window."

George stood upon the first stepping-stone, with his back towards the girl, and said nothing.

"But you mustn't scold dear little Bubo," she called; for Berenice adored four-footed beasts and fowls of the air.

CHAPTER X
ABOUT MATRIMONY AND THE LANE WHICH WAS CALLED MORTGABLE

There was a marriage in Downacot by Metheral, and every one was invited to bear witness that Molly Bidlake, youngest daughter of Farmer Harry Bidlake, was respectably transmuted into Molly Moorshed. People came because it would have been an insult to stay away and because there would be beer. No foreigners were present; the affair was parochial; and the house door was set open to receive guests at an early hour, although it was understood that no refreshment would be forthcoming until the church had completed its share of the work and the register had been signed with various blots and crosses.

The ceremony itself was not a dignified proceeding, although it satisfied the demands of the law, which was represented by the local constable. Old parson had been past work for a long time. He was in bed when the wedding party presented itself at the locked-up church, and declared that he wasn't going to get up to bury any one. When it was explained that the ceremony that day was the less lively one of matrimony he said there was no hurry, he would be along presently, and the party could run about in the churchyard and play the old village game of Tom-come-tickle-me while he was getting his trousers on. At last he shuffled across in carpet-slippers, rough and ready hands helped him to assume suitable vestments, and bride and bridegroom quickly received the benediction of holy Church; while the congregation nudged one another solemnly, the father of the bride and the bridegroom's mother mingled their tears together, and screams came from the porch where some small boys were terrifying small girls by trying to slip grave and respectable churchyard frogs down their backs.

There was one slight incident outside which might have been considered unseemly in some places. Plenty of people stood at the gate, shouting remarks which were probably intended to be classed in the same category as "God bless the bride and bridegroom," although they were less elegant; and a certain very bold-faced young woman, who was obviously in that condition known as interesting, selected for her greeting the disconcerting statement, "Don't forget Laura Westlake be at the wedding with a baby, the gift of the bridegroom." It was said, however, that she had played the same trick on others.

The living-room at Downacot Farm was arranged according to custom with a long table down the centre, benches on each side, and chairs along the wall. The place had received a general scouring, the china cows on the high mantel had been washed, and the pair of brass candlesticks polished. The warming-pan hanging by its strap to the wall was like a rising sun; and an alien reproduction of His Royal Highness the Landlord, beautifully framed in fir-cones and acorns, had been cleansed of flymarks. Downacot was a lonely place full of ferns, bogflowers, and masses of yellow "drunkards" in spring; a horrible mud-hole all winter. The dirt of four big hills trickled into the hamlet. A tributary of the Taw River ran through, crossing the narrow road, then tumbling down into fields beneath the usual clapper which made a bridge, though it was often submerged in winter when the usually modest and maiden-like tributary sometimes became a rough, brawling-man kind of torrent. "Any one ever been lost here?" asked a nervous stranger one day, wondering how he was to get across. "Naw, sir," replied Farmer Bidlake cheerfully enough. "Old Sammy Paschoe, him as wur a stone-cracker up to Metheral, did get drownded here one year, but us found 'en next day."

Downacot was one of those surprises which Dartmoor delights in. Approaching over the moor there was apparently nothing ahead except the big, gently-curving hills, but suddenly the ground parted asunder, the hills seemed to fall back, making a bason cracked on four sides; and in the muddy sediment at the bottom was Downacot with its tumble-down cottages, big furze-bushes, little nameless stream, and its human and floral drunkards.

Downacot Farm was a poor holding; merely a cottage , and long barn in the middle of a muddy yard, with a few hilly fields behind divided from each other by hedges of stone topped with holly-trees of a great height. No repairs had been done for several generations, and hard weather was dragging the building down. The Bidlakes, like most commoners, found their hands useless when it came to a little matter of carpentering and masonry. They couldn't afford to employ professional folk, and it had never occurred to them that loose stones, rotten beams, and crumbling thatch could be repaired or renewed by their own efforts. Gregory Breakback with his wonderful crowbar would have restored Downacot in a month or two; but Gregory was unlike his neighbours. He was there, neat and strong as usual, attired in a black suit which had belonged to his father a generation back, having taken it out of the chest where it reposed from one year's end to the other upon sprigs of rosemary to keep the moths away. The clothes only appeared for weddings and funerals. There was only one suit for festivals and holidays; but as the smiling philosopher would have said, "One man can't get into two lots o' clothes." The guests filed in with an expression of hopeless melancholy. It was indeed a sad time for them all, a wedding being of all village festivals the most dismal. The occasion called for lugubrious countenances. There were the usual jokes, of course, but they were uttered tragically. There was laughter too, but it reached the proper depth of dejection except in the case of Gregory and an uncle of the bridegroom who had disregarded etiquette by becoming prematurely intoxicated. Gregory's fine mirth troubled the party. It was true that he laughed just the same at a burial, but his mirth then was right and proper. A funeral called for jovial faces and plenty of good cheer. It was an occasion for merriment, and every one came to it with the certainty of enjoying a thoroughly festive time. But this was a wedding, and things were different; it was a time of deep drinking and mournful ballad singing. A funeral is a time of hearty eating, intermingled with stock-taking and congratulations. Still there was an under current of cheerful expectancy, for it had been rumoured that Farmer Bidlake was going to do the thing in style, by emulating the example of the highest folk in the land and supplying the guests with a wedding breakfast. There were whispered suggestions of turnip-pie, and a good many noses were at work seeking for satisfactory evidence as to the truth of this rumour.

"I ain't et turnip-pie vor I couldn't tull ye how long it be," said one old farmer with a lugubrious glance around him, as if he more than half suspected that his lengthy abstinence from this particular luxury would cause the entire universe to cave in suddenly.

"Please to tak' your seats," invited Farmer Bidlake; and the black-coated party clattered readily over the stone floor towards chairs and benches, and seated themselves gingerly, while one of the younger Bidlakes, who was the musical genius of the district, placed his concertina in readiness upon the table in front of him. Several drifted about for some time before they could decide upon the seat which it was likely they would occupy for a good many hours if their heads didn't give way. Old topers profited by long experience to obtain comfortable corner nooks.

Metheral folk were there in force; old Brokenbrow babbling of graves and headstones, and not far off Father Chown inciting his rival to wrath by coughing insistently and throwing out sinister hints appertaining to his own age and diseased condition and the law of mortality. There was Ursula in a sealskin coat though it was summer, but it was the finest thing she had, for it was real fur, bought with the proceeds of.her folly; and beside her was John wearing a wonderful collar which made him keep his eyes upon the roof. His mouth was wide open, and whenever any one touched him he took it as a sign to laugh; and did so with pain and difficulty, for the raw collar rasped his neck, being much too small for him. He had washed his neck, too, and that might have made it sore and irritable. The Wheal Dream contingent had come over in the manure-cart. Uncle Gifford was not there. It was too far to walk, and he had been so unneighbourly lately that Ursula had to inform him there was no room for him in the cart. The bride was led to the seat which had been reserved for her, where she went on giggling with the steady persistency of a running stream.

"Aw, poor maid, I knaws how she feels," said Ursula to a stout lady who overlapped her chair considerably.

"Us knaws. Us ha' been through it," said the big lady. "I ha' been through it twice, and second time it come easy enough, but the first time—wull there, my dear, if any one so much as put a finger on me I got the asterisks to wance and fair screamed."

"Her nerves be fair upsot," explained Ursula.

"All a-tremble like. I knaws how it be," said the matron, making her chair creak dismally. "Yew could ha' blown I about the kitchen wi' the bellows day I wur first wed. But that wur thirty years ago, and I ha' buried plenty since. Buried 'em proper tu, as yew knaws, cold beef and bottled beer wi' the lot, and never less than two carriages. There bain't none in Metheral parish who can say they ha' spent more than me on funerals. I had six black-edged handkerchiefs vor my first husband, and I used the lot, my dear."

Ursula did not like such boasting, as she had no exploits of her own to narrate. So she changed the subject by suggesting that it would be a pretty compliment to the bride if one of them addressed her suddenly by her recently acquired title.

The proposal did not find favour with the large lady. "Don't ye du no such thing," she whispered. "'Twould be an awful shock to the maid, and weak hearts run in the Bidlakes. 'Twould mak' she choke vor certain. Let she bide. Her'll be better vor a glass or two o' beer."

"Same wi' I," said Ursula.

"Aw, my dear, us be old birds," said the matron cheerfully. "I tull ye I wouldn't mind taking number dree, vor a man of your own du be a bit homely like when all's said agin 'em. There warn't many nerves about I the second time, yew may depend. I went through it like a—wull there, like a lamb, my dear."

Farmer Bidlake's eldest daughter, who worked with her husband in the fields and only differed from him outwardly by the addition of a skirt and the lack of a beard, came striding in with the pie, which old Risdon, had he been living and present, would certainly have classed among his "remarkable things" in the Forest of Dartmoor. It was a mighty thing, square, white and solid, and the smell of it was good, reaching to the uttermost parts of Downacot. Folk brightened up and forgot to be sorrowful. Farmer Bidlake was unquestionably marrying the last of his daughters in style. A huge bowl of cream was brought and descended like an avalanche into the valley of the great pie. Every one's glass was soon brimming with beer or cider. The concertina began to squeak and titter, and the publican of Metheral, who occupied the foot of the table as chairman of the musical programme, announced that Gregory Breakback would favour the assembly with a song.

"I ain't ever seed a maid married wi' turnip-pie avore," said the stout lady in a critical whisper to Ursula, who was unfastening her sealskin jacket to prepare for work. "'Tis a North Devon habit, but these Bidlakes ha' foreign blood in 'em sure 'nuff. I wur married first time wi' brandy," she added, harping again on her past grandeur. "Stars on every bottle, my dear, but, love ye, they wur nought to the stars I seed afterwards. Second time 'twas gin and watter, and not enough to mak' the neighbours vitty like, but then I had to come down a bit being a widdy. Widdies don't get sent off like maids, my dear. They'm secondhand like. Yew'll find it so when yew takes your next, I reckon."

This was not cheerful hearing for John, but he was fairly well used to it, as Ursula had often run through a list of eligibles from whom she might make a selection when she was at liberty to do so. That strangling collar was just then far more in his mind than any possibility of his wife's widowhood. He was wondering however he would be able to get drunk.

"Us wur married wi' whisky," said Ursula, proudly. "Warn't us, John? Don't ye stare up to the roof, yew old mazehead," she whispered crossly.

It was no use appealing to John. There had been so much whisky since that he couldn't remember.

"I had a sister, and a butiful maid her wur," said the matron, rousing herself for a special effort. "Her married coals and timber, and a fine thing for she 'twas, but her bain't a widdy yet, though she'm expecting to say 'Thy will be done' avore very long. Her went off wi' vizzy wine, my dear, proper Frenchy trade, vizzy wine wi' golden corks and wire to keep the bottles from busting. I mind the wire, vor I cut my fingers wi't."

Ursula gulped down her beer with a feeling of disgust. The stout lady was beginning to tell fishy stories. It was preposterous to suppose that any sister of that common old body had ever married "coals and timber." But conversation was over for a time, as Gregory was upon his long straight legs singing one of those simple ballads which have been passed on from one generation of moorland folk to another from "tyme out of minde," as the presentment of the Perambulators has it, and remembered word for word although probably they have never been written down. Gregory's voice was like himself; not musical, but big and strong, hitting the ears like north wind and overwhelming all such puny sounds as the running water outside, the squealing concertina, and the bride's perpetual giggling. It seemed to make the old place shake, to detach scales of soot from the rafters, and to jar the cloam upon the dresser. There was a manhood about Gregory which made the room seem small.

In the meantime the vast pie was being cut and quarried, and portions were handed round. Tom Moorshed, the bridegroom's uncle, who was already in a disgraceful condition, grabbed his share greedily and then confided a little matter, which had been upon his mind for some time, to the lady who had the honour of a seat next to him. "I be agwaine vur to be purty nigh drunk," he explained with laborious chuckles. He was afraid she might not have noticed it.

"So I should say," said the lady rather crossly, because he would keep on breathing at her.

"If so be as I be drunk," said Uncle Tom, "I apologises."

"Yew'm welcome," said the lady, as there was obviously nothing else to say; and after all Uncle Tom had only offended against good manners by taking an unfair start.

A farmer, who was some sort of semi-detached relation to every one present, claimed the attention of the company while he delivered a panegyric in the heroic style upon turnip-pie. According to him it was the foundation-stone upon which the fabric of perfect health was built. Between the merits of turnip-pie and mother's milk for babies there could be no two opinions; and the verdict was not in favour of the mother. It was the best food for adults because it filled their bellies and kept them tight for hours. It was specially adapted for old folk, as chewing was reduced to a minimum and the loss of grinders was not felt. Turnip-pie was, in short, angels' food; for it gave them meat enough. The speaker might have been advertising a patent medicine.

"I mind first time I tasted 'en, and I'll tull ye," he went on, as he wiped a creamy finger and thumb upon his neck-cloth. "'Twas to Thurlestone Barton, where I worked as a lad for dree shilluns a week and me grub, and a pack o' wool to tak' home to mother Christmas. Us made our own clothes them days, and mother wur cruel artful wi' spinning-wheel, I tull ye. Wull, first winter I wur there a gurt snow starm blowed up over Dartmoor, and the winds and drifts wur tremenjus. 'Twas Sunday morning when it cleared a bit, and varmer ses to I, 'Tain,' he ses, 'no alleluias vor yew to-day, me lad.' 'Twas a bit of a hit at I, vor I wur cruel fond o' singing in chapel them days. 'Get outside and cut a path to linhay,' he ses. So I run out and shovelled till the sweat rolled down me face, and my belly got as empty as an old bell, and when missis called I to come in vor dinner I warn't long a-getting there, yew may depend. Her ses to I, 'Tam,' her ses—they allus called I Tam, though my name wur Robert same as it be now—'du'ye like turnip-pie, me lad?' 'Can't say as how I du, or as how I don't,' I ses. 'I ain't never tasted 'en far as I knaws,' I ses. Lord love ye, us never had they fancy dishes to home them days, but I could ha' yet an owl just then, I wur that pinched. Wull, missis fetched the dish in and brought a bowl o' cream and put 'en in, and I began to feel watter drap-drappiting from me mouth when I sees that pie as white as the druwen snow outside, wi' a gurt piece of fat bacon to the bottom of mun. 'Try a little and see if yew likes 'en,' ses missis. So I sot down and took my spune and had a little. I didn't knaw if I would like 'en or no, yew see. Missis ses to I, 'Du'ye like 'en, Tam?' 'Lor, missis,' I ses, 'I hadn't time to taste 'en.' So I passed me plate over. Missis asked I agin. 'Wull there,' I ses, 'I ain't got the taste of 'en yet.' So I passed me plate over. Varmer began to laugh and he ses, 'Steady, Tam, thee hain't shovelling snow, lad.' And missis laughed tu, and ses, 'Have ye got the taste, Tam?' I ses, 'Ees, missis, I likes 'en cruel.' So I passed me plate over. But there warn't none left."

More mournful ballads followed, and the concertina wailed a dirge-like accompaniment to each, one tune differing from another according to the skill of the musician, which was slight. The jugs of liquor began to pass round a little quicker, but faces were not yet shining, for the beer was thick and the cider rough stuff; both required time to make a cheerful countenance; and the stout lady muttered something disparaging about folk who were married on anything lower than bottled stuff. She had never been married on liquor from cloam and hoped she never should be, although, as she admitted, widows at second-hand did have to put up with something while there were so many maids about. Old Brokenbrow did what he could to supply the proper note of good-feeling by expressing the pious hope that the next happy meeting of the neighbours would be to celebrate his funeral. But it was reserved for Uncle Tom Moorshed to dispel the atmosphere of depression and make the proceedings properly hilarious. He was a dull-witted old fellow at the best of times, one who was always making mistakes and getting hold of a wrong impression; and Brokenbrow's entirely personal statement culminating with the word funeral caused him to misinterpret the nature of the ceremony of which he was a conspicuous and somewhat clouded witness.

"I wun't say it bain't sad, vor it be," he stated with a cheerful hiccup. "This time last year us didn't think us would be here to-day. Aw, poor liddle maid. Us wun't see the like o' she again. I'll trouble yew vor a spuneful o' cream, Varmer Bidlake."

There was silence for a few moments. The guests were not quite certain whether they ought to laugh or not; the giggling of the bride was not to be taken as a cue, as she was irresponsible. But John Petherick mis-swallowed some beer, and the explosion consequent upon his error, which had a damping effect upon those who sat opposite, was misunderstood by Uncle Tom to be a note of sympathy with his lament.

"Her was a gude maid," he declared. "Didn't give her folks no trouble not from the day her wur born to the day her wur took. Wull, they can't say us ain't put she away respectable."

"Yew'm a dafty old mazehead, Uncle," shouted the bridegroom. "Us be wed to-day."

"I knaws 'tis her last bed," said the fuddled old fellow, who thought he was being argued with. "I bain't blind, nor deaf neither, and I ses 'twas a high-class funeral such as us can be proud of. There bain't no village on Dartmoor what puts volks away better than us du. Bit more bacon if yew please, Varmer Bidlake."

"He'm like all they Moorsheds. They'm a proper lot o' drunkards," murmured the woman who was sitting next to Gregory on a bench beside the wall.

"Wull, my dear, I never did see a shed on Dartmoor what warn't mucky," he replied, but wasting his parable on dull ears. However, the concertina was squeaking again, and some one was singing to cover Uncle Tom's little mistake, a song with a chorus which warmed them up and made them feel more like a party of children snow-balling, and when the tumult ceased somebody proposed the health of the none too happy couple, which made Uncle Tom object noisily and declare it was poking fun at the dead. When he had been quieted by the simple method of refilling his mug, and the bride began to show signs of recovering from a mild attack of hysterics, young Moorshed wrestled privily with his tie, wiped his moist moustache, lurched upright, smiled with sheer nervousness like an old-fashioned villain of melodrama, and finally informed the company that he was no manner of good at speechmaking. The neighbours wouldn't let him off. They called with one voice for a speech. They became actually merry at the sorry spectacle of the bridegroom's incapacity. Most of the men had been through it themselves, and they didn't see why he should escape. So the young man had to say something, though he felt as if his mouth was stuffed with lead.

"Ladies and gentlemen," he said at last. "Us be here to-day to get married, and—and us ha' been and got married sure 'nuff. Yew ha' treated all of us, me and my wife, I should say, and those of us as ha' been and got married to-day—" There he got entangled, owing to the foolish use of that stumbling-block to the inexperienced orator, the parenthesis; but there was plenty of sympathetic applause, which Uncle Tom roundly abused as blasphemy, and he attacked the sentence again, "Yew ha' treated me and my wife as us desarves to be treated." Then he sat down, covered with confusion, and glad to think that little trouble was over for his lifetime.

Gregory sang again, bringing storm into the room and making the black rafters creak; and when he settled again upon the bench the woman beside him murmured in admiration, "Yew du sing lovely."

"Wull, my dear, I wur walking on Dartmoor one day wi' my mouth open, and a lark flew in and I swallowed 'en. Ever since then I've abin a singing man," he said in his quizzing way which passed her comprehension.

"'Tis a long time since I wur at a wedding," she went on; and then added, "It must be proper to be wed."

"Wull, my dear, I reckon an hour of matrimony can du a man more gude than a month of anything else can in a lifetime," he said slyly, and watched the effect of his nonsense. But the woman was grave enough; his words sounded very wise, and she extracted from them all the sense that she required.

"Why ain't yew got a woman?" she asked.

"I allus gets down to market five minutes tu late, when the shops be all shut," he said.

"Get along wi' such rubbish," she said, pushing at him.

Gregory began to observe his companion, and as he did so made more room for her on the bench. She was not fair and she was forty, but her skin and eyes were good and her mouth was red. She had a tangle of hair, which any one romantically inclined might have called golden, although ordinary folk would have made her look round with the cry, "Carrots." She was inclined to be stout, her feet would have filled a man's boots; yet she was a woman, with some of the manner and smile which make any four roofed walls a home. She belonged to the sex which when it likes drives away loneliness like the morning sweeping mist from a cleave; and when it likes crowds the house with devils. Gregory knew little about this Ada Mills beyond her name. She had been away from the district for a good many years and had only lately come home. He looked at her again because of her sex, not because she was Ada Mills, and remembered that her old parents were respectable. Then he wondered if she had ever looked out from the door, to marvel at the shivering stars and the wind coming across the hills.

The neighbours were livening up and beginning to feel at home, and the songs were taking upon themselves a distinctly festive character; love-interest was giving way to the more practical Roast Beef and Union Jack of old England, not forgetting the malt liquors of the same country, and the waving signboard which attracts more readily than the flag. Some of the older hands were already finding it just as comfortable on the floor, and Uncle Tom was falling as steadily as any barometer in April. Farmer Bidlake the host was talking maudlin of his departed wife, who had been a woman "such as bain't found in these days," and was declaring between deferential hiccups his intention of marrying again some day, not from any selfish motive, but merely out of respect for her memory. Old dirt-encrusted Griffey, the granite merchant, who was one of those beings who defy all the laws of hygiene, and drive men of science and preachers upon morality to despair, as he was nearly eighty, had never used a bath in his life, was not often sober, and yet enjoyed perfect health, produced a sovereign, fastened it to the table with what looked like a splinter of red sandstone but was actually a human forefinger, as if he was afraid it might leap away suddenly like one of those insects whose habits he had ample opportunities for studying, and challenged any one to try and beat him at the game of gold production. Chown and Brokenbrow had come to words, and very nearly to blows, over the grave; and Father so far forgot his company manners as to declare, if he had much more of old Willum's nonsense, he would go and strangle poor dame Loveday Brokenbone in her bed, so that his rival at least should be deprived of the resting-place which made him ignore the last and least commandment so persistently. John was happy at last, for his weight had increased by several pints, and his collar had long ago parted asunder and was flapping on each side of his neck like a pair of cherubic wings; while Ursula and the stout lady were both weeping noisily and declaring they hadn't felt so happy and comfortable for a long time. The publican, who was half asleep, managed to exclaim, "Chorus, gentlemen," from time to time, his consciousness being something like that of a cuckoo-clock; and the bride, who was recovering from her distressing nervous condition, nudged her husband sharply and said that if he drank any more she would "bide to home wi' vaither." Young Moorshed pondered this saying, and had the sense to comprehend that matrimony very quickly transforms the shy filly into a grey mare.

Presently somebody discovered that important religious rites had been neglected, or rather had not been completed. The Christian ceremony had been performed as the law demanded and with all due gaiety, but the more solemn ritual of paganism had still to be observed. A ladder had been placed beside the nuptial cottage, which was quite close, on the opposite side of Downacot bason across the water, bundles of heather had been cut and window shrouds made; but the lazy workers were so busy indulging themselves that they hadn't plugged up the chimney or blocked the windows before the wedding party arrived. The young couple could not be allowed to enter their future home if it was left open to all the spirits of mischief and every evil eye in the neighbourhood, so Gregory, who was the local father of tradition, offered to go and make the cottage secure. He was glad of the excuse to leave that tainted atmosphere and get out into the wind. He noticed that Ada Mills had hardly been drinking at all, and perceiving a possible bond of sympathy between herself and him he asked her, "Who be a going to keep the foot o' the ladder steady?"

"Wull, I be a proper old weight. I'll come wi 'ye," she said.

They crossed the yard and got into the narrow lane, with its roof-like slope to the water, the-trees of its hedges leaning over to make a bower. It was warm in Downacot because the wind passed over the rim of its bason, flying as it were from edge to edge. They stepped across the clapper bridge, reached the cottage, and set to work. It was a heavy silence after that noisy kitchen. Gregory noticed that Ada looked welf in a cottage, moved well, and worked easily, without bustle or confusion. Her smile seemed to improve, but he liked her better when she didn't talk. He thought of the broken hearthstone up on Moor Gate and the vision he had seen bending there after the manner of one making preparations for supper; but it was not Ada Mills, nothing like her, though it might have been her younger sister if she had one. It was some one with a mind, who could look out and say, "What a wonderful thing it is to see the stars, and how the wind seems to blow them along." Would Ada Mills say anything like that? He would not remember that she was stout and somewhat homely if she could. Gregory didn't know that his position in life belonged to one class and his mind to another, and that wherever he went he must be a misfit.

When the cottage had been made devil-proof, and every breath and beam of air and sun excluded, they went out. Ada did not want to rejoin the wedding party, and Gregory had never intended to go back. Before them the lane writhed upward to the high moor and Metheral, between its big hedges which made it like a tunnel. The turf covering those stone banks was a field of white stars, gleaming stitchwort, with silver sorrel and stiff grape hyacinths. No rank weeds grew in Downacot, no docks, no nettles; only the pleasant things, virgin-like white flowers, and upon the other side of the furze-bushes, in the bogs at the very bottom of the bason, were those fat opulent drunkards the kingcups, filled with gold dust, like so many rich men sitting over their wine. Ada and Gregory began to ascend the lane, walking side by side because they were of different sex, as so many walk, with no very definite idea.

At the edge of the hamlet was an eyesore, a little wobbling tin house of God erected by a former incumbent of Metheral who had a certain amount of money but no appreciation of art. Its unpainted ugliness was an insult to Downacot, which was small enough to have been spared; but Christianity and patent-medicines have no kindness for scenery. The chapel had hardly ever been used for its intended purpose, although for several years it had been of great service as a cowshed; and beside the tin edifice, half-toppling like itself, appeared a row of far more picturesque stacks, one of fern, another of browse, a third of faggot-wood, and one of vagges thatched with heather to keep the rain out. The narrow road was an ancient trackway once known as Mortgable Lane, probably because a rent was paid for the dead wood found in Downacot; but it had become changed generations ago, like almost every name upon

Dartmoor—there are very few which have not known corruption—into Market Lane, perhaps because the venville rents were rendered to the manor upon fair or market day. There are two kinds of border lanes: the open and the bowery; both are as tortuous as the mind of a theocrat; but Market was a bowery lane.

Gregory picked flowers as he went along; they looked weak little things in his great strong hands. He glanced from time to time at the young woman, for forty is still youth upon the hill-tops; searching for another bond of sympathy, wondering if so much contented flesh could ever be wasted by romance, whether any conception higher than that of children on the old wearisome lines of squalling ineptitude was possible; whether Ada Mills could ever be made pregnant by a line of poetry or become the mother of an idea which could boast of a separate existence. He might try her, lead her astray from the sediment at the bottom of Downacot bason to the heather on the top of Moor Gate. He might set her in the wind, watch it stretch the garments upon her, and see if she could respond, say something about the life and strength of it and what a wonderful clear distance it was to the sky; or whether she would merely scream and blow about, and declare she couldn't stand it.

Gregory had life still to win; for it is a chamber-mate that makes life, and loneliness is life decapitated. It was for him a tangible vision about the broken hearthstone, or the same stone with the ghost blown round about it like the dead leaf of a summer he had never seen.

"So yew ain't been to a wedding vor a long time?" he said, drawing the stalks of a few starry stitchwort into the rim of his hat, but not looking at her.

"I hate 'em, slobbering old things," said Ada, wondering how old he was.

"Wull, my dear, it du change volk. Courtship be fine weather, and matrimony be often a frisk o' wind just 'cause volk don't get suited. Two birds in a cage will peck sure 'nuff if they bain't the same breed. When yew'm married there's no turning round. Yew must go straight ahead just as we be going up this lane."

Ada made no reply, though she was willing enough; but the words were not there.

"There's no getting out o' the lane when yew'm in it," he went on. "Yew must go on to the end on't, be the weather what 'twull. At times it be wull enough, and at times it be bad, and it be mostly rough and dirty. It bain't wide, vor no more than two can get along together, and there bain't no room in it vor quarrelling. Yew can't see over the hedges what's beyond. May be gude or bad, but yew don't knaw. Yew can't see forward, vor the lane twists, first one way, then t'other, and what's round the corner yew don't knaw. May be an old donkey, or a heap o' stone, may be a lot o' vuzz in flower, may be a bog vull o' drunkards—yew can't tull what's beyond till yew gets round; and there bain't no reason in one saying 'tis a lot o' vuzz, and t'other saying 'tis a bog o' drunkards, and tearing your tongues over it. Best to bide quiet and wait."

"What vor?" asked Ada Mills, understanding the last few words but nothing more; and even then wanting an explanation.

"Till yew'm round the bend," he answered. "There be plenty o' turns, but yew gets to the last one in time, and then yew comes out on the moor. It be all sudden like; one step yew'm in the lane and yew see nought but the hedges; next step yew'm out and can see right across Demshur."

"Why of course us can see along when us gets up on Dartmoor," said the puzzled woman.

"Don't it seem mazing to see so much?" said Gregory, again trying to strike her mind with his and produce some kind of spark.

"They ses yew can see more'n twenty churches from the top o' Cawsand," she said blankly.

"Ever been up there?" he asked.

"Not me," she cried. "What would I want to ba dragging myself up there vor?"

"I'll tull ye," he said half fiercely. "Yew goes up to feel the wind tearing at ye like a mazed beast trying to break ye, and yew can feel yew'm the strongest. Yew can get above the mist and look down into it, and feel yew'm at the top o' the world. 'Tis better than drinking milk and watter. Yew can start from Downacot, where everything grows big and strong 'cause the wind don't get down under, and yew can come up the lane, which be vull o' flowers 'cause it be a lew place, and yew can come out by the sycamores and round by the blackystones same as we'm doing—yew finds the wind then, and there be nought but vuzz and ferns and brimmles, wi' a stalk or two o' dead-man's-fingers between the stones. Yew'm on Dartmoor, and the higher yew go the more wind there be. There bain't no flowers 'cept heather, and as yew goes up Cawsand there be more wind and more heather, bigger and bigger as yew gets near the top, stronger the one and stronger t'other, till yew feels the skin o' your face drawn tight, and the roots o' your hair start pinching, and when yew opens your mouth yew can taste the wind, bite 'en and swallow 'en; and that don't be sour in your mouth nor bitter in your stomach neither. Then yew can sot down on the old tomb what be up over there, and tak' a book o' poetry out, and read 'en, my dear; read 'en till they'm lighting up over, and it be whist under, and your hands and face be wet and cold wi' the cloudy trade brought wi' the wind along. And then yew can get down and feel yew'm free."

Ada Mills looked down at her boots and tittered gently. Then she went into a scream of laughter in which she managed to include some very discordant sounds; and at last cried without sense or sympathy, "Aw, Mr. Breakback, whatever be yew a talking so vunny vor?"

HEATHER

CHAPTER XI
ABOUT ST. MICHAEL'S WHITE VIOLETS AND GREEN OAKS

Now that Winnie was stronger her walks were longer; across the moor on hot days; along the lanes when it was windy; and in the worst weather through St. Michael's wood between the boggy slopes and the river, beside the little oaks which never grew any bigger, and among the bracken which made her feel so small. She loved that walk. She delighted to trace the path of perambulation, to wander up and down beside the Blackavon, to climb from one rock to another in the bed of the river, and to sit upon an ivy-covered boulder on the height above the waterfall and look down upon the mass of white foam hurrying to the north as if fearful that the sea could not wait for its frothy contribution. She knew every pool and path, every little island above and below the Ford, and every bog and garden of king fern's. She photographed them with her pretty blue eyes, and when she was half asleep her brain developed the pictures and hung them about the walls of her room; but not quite as she had seen them, for there were creatures in the wood then whom St. Michael did not know; they were in the developed pictures, and she could not blink them away, these creatures blown about her by hard weather. In these pictures Ernest Hawker would insist upon sitting above the waterfall, or trampling upon her prettiest bank of violets, and he was always smoking rank tobacco and talking slang, and calling her his "little bit o' cream," or something equally indigestible. Then Winnie would shiver and murmur to herself, "I wonder how he would look with his beard off," which seemed a ridiculous thing to say, as Hawker did not possess a beard.

Winnie always looked pretty, which by itself was a small thing, for a pretty face can be bought in any teashop; but Winnie's tongue and hands were prettier than her face. It is manner that makes for beauty: a trick of the tongue, a little gesture which nobody else makes, a certain movement in walking; these are destructive things. The clockwork doll can sit in a corner till she melts; the little woman with a few dainty tricks can conjure to her heart's content and turn any man into a lover. Winnie practised all kinds of enchantments because "it wasn't her fault." She could hardly twist her hands together without squeezing somebody's heart flat inside them. Even when she picked up her dress to walk she wasn't like other girls, although the most subtle philosopher could not have explained just where the originality occurred. There was a suggestion of pathos in all her actions and a kind of helplessness in everything she said. Possibly the charm was there.

The height of beauty is some sort of imperfection. Very likely Helen of Troy had a slight cast in one eye. The sky scarred with one small cloud is far more beautiful than an unbroken expanse of blue. Winnie had those dimples, which science would describe coldly as small natural depressions on the face, though Cupid, who never studied anatomy, would have called them in his boyish way, "jolly sharp arrows." Dimples are flaws, and yet hearts fall merrily into them, and by the laws of gravity and attraction they cannot easily get out again. But Winnie's most distracting flaw was her nose. It is the duty of every respectable human nose to be rounded at the tip, but this girl's nose defied orthodoxy. Instead of flowing round smoothly at the end, as it ought to have done, describing a gentle curve, it broke off sheer in a tiny pink line less than a quarter of an inch long, but capable of causing a load of mischief just because it was not like other noses. It looked as if some malicious little demon had sawn the tip off. Such a slight flaw compels adoration. Men are surprised by it, then delight in it, and finally decide the world is a poor place unless they can obtain possession of the owner of it. A girl can win the man she wants by a mere squeal. But it must be an original squeal.

One or two of the Fates, less stony-hearted than the rest, must have wept a little when the model labelled somewhat prematurely Winnie Shazell was turned out of that workshop where pretty girls are moulded, and the soul was all ready to be blown into her. They must have wondered what was the good of it. The chief sculptor —no bungling apprentice made Winnie—would have admitted he was striving after an original effect when he chipped that fragment off the end of her nose. It would make the men run after her, he said.

And then the Fates, who were kindly disposed, pointed to a corner where a dirty little devil was busy with all kinds of vile instruments and chemicals, amid smoke and grime and pestiferous odours, turning out bacilli by the million, and hammering them into every atom of life that passed him on its way earthwards. What was the good of the pretty girl being sent out with a lot of that fiend's damnable growths inside her? What was the use of men running after her if she was to be diseased? But the demon in the smoke chuckled at that, and said, "The men are diseased too. I see to that. One disease runs after another disease to make more disease. And the good of it is they learn what it means to suffer. That's what the Overseer says." Then he seized with his pincers the germ of a tapeworm and hammered it into shape with great joy. A strange party of workers—the sculptor doing his best to produce loveliness, and the grimy fiend toiling for ever to destroy that loveliness; and the old Fates uttering phrases meant to be consoling, such as, "Bear up, my pretty. It will soon be over;" and the Overseer going to and fro, wondering perhaps sometimes if it would not be better to close the works altogether.

"Get up, Billy. It's nearly stuffing-time," said Berenice as she entered Winnie's room fully dressed, her fine brown face glowing. She always looked in when the doctor had gone. "How can you have that horrid slimy little toad on your bed? I wouldn't." She alluded to Tobias the fickle, who regarded that room as his own, but graciously permitted Winnie to share his bed. "Now don't look plaintive, you darling, for it's a lovely day and your shadow is not growing less," she said, bending over Winnie and kissing her in defiance of the law which in that establishment rightly ordained kissing to be an unfriendly act.

"Don't," said Winnie. "You are much better than I am."

"I'll risk it. You are looking so nice," said Berenice lightly. "Everything all right? No letters or anything objectionable? There's usually a moan in the morning."

"Only the passages—I had them again last night. Horrible dark passages," shivered Winnie.

"What's the child driving at now?" said Berenice, with the condescension of a couple of years' seniority.

"Haven't I told you? I seem to be in a great building filled with windows that don't give any light and passages that lead nowhere. It's a dreadful dream, though it sounds nothing. There seem to be hundreds of passages all alike, and they all have the same choking musty kind of smell. I have to escape because I can't breathe, so I hurry down a passage and it leads into another, and I run down that and it comes out into another passage, and the walls are wet and covered with toadstools."

"How can you see if there's no light?"

"This is a dream," said Winnie reprovingly.

"All right, Dimples. Don't open your mouth so and show your tiny tongue, or I shall kiss you again."

"At last I get into a passage where I can feel the wind, but it is a horrible salt wind which makes me feel sick," Winnie went on. "At the end of that passage is the sea, and I scream in my sleep because I have such a horror of the sea. So I turn back and hurry up and down more passages, hundreds of them, and all leading into more passages, choking and coughing all the time, until I feel the wind again, a bitter wind, and I see a dreadful white glare. Then I scream again, for that passage leads out into snow, which is another thing I have a horror of, because the sight of it always makes me ill. So I go on running again, until at last I climb up the wall like a fly to break one of the windows and get some air; and just as I reach the window down I fall and smash all to pieces, and that's the end of dream, me, and everything," she concluded with a small laugh.

"I never get to the bottom in a falling dream," said Berenice. "Do you often get these horrors?"

"Only once before here, on my second night. I coughed all through the first and never went to sleep. But I often have passages in the—at home I mean."

Winnie nearly said something about slums which would have been dreadful. Only Halfacre knew the truth, as he knew everything about her by then. He had taken her entirely under his charge and issued his orders when they were alone as if he had been a master and she his servant.

"I must get up," Winnie went on quickly. "I've been thumped this morning, and doctor says the bellows are blowing away nicely. I suppose he wouldn't say anything else, though. Still, I'm going to get well," she went on. "I lie here when I can't sleep, and nibble away at bread and butter, and keep on saying, 'I will get well.' I am fighting very hard, Berenice."

"Of course you'll get well, silly Billy. That's what we are here for," said the other girl playfully. "Tobias, don't make such a beastly noise."

"Oh, dear doggie, don't scold him," said Winnie. "I thought at first he was dreaming of bunnies, but the noise is in the next room, where Gumm lives. It sounds as if he had got a tummy-ache," she said naughtily.

"Why, he's crying," said Berenice, listening beside the wall. "I never heard of such a thing—a man crying."

"Perhaps doctor has frightened him. The noise began when he was in there."

Then the next door opened, and a moment later the big unwieldy Gumm staggered past, stumbling blindly, blowing his nose, wiping his eyes, and exhibiting every symptom of an unusually severe cold.

"Poor thing, he's in trouble," said Winnie, putting her aggravating head on one side. "Go and say something nice to him, please, Berenice."

"Little Sill can attend to the few kind words. They are not much in my line," said the brown girl rather contemptuously. "Up you get, Bill. What's your morning walk?"

"The wood," said Winnie joyously. "I may sit on my own bank of white violets for an hour."

"The right place for you, sweet thing," cried Berenice. Then she gathered up protesting Tobias, saying, "You shall come and play ball with me, whether you like it or not," and ran out and down into the garden, murmuring to herself as she went into the sunshine, "How I wish I were a man, so that I could love her properly."

The others appeared, waiting the call to breakfast and trying not to notice Gumm, who however had no idea of being disregarded, and soon came blubbering towards them with a crumpled letter in one hand and a long handkerchief in the other. There was a close connection between the two, as a glance at the letter was always followed by an application of the handkerchief. Behind him walked Mudd as chief mourner, trying to express sorrow and sympathy, but only grinning nervously and talking nonsense.

"Oh, Mr. Gumm, I do hope there's nothing the matter," cried Miss Budge foolishly, while Halfacre muttered something about a shameless loss of self-control, and the publican tried to suggest sarcastically that his friend's only object was to give them a little innocent amusement.

"My baby," howled Gumm, with a fresh splash of grief. "My poor little baby."

"Is it ill?" asked Miss Budge.

The man in trouble shook his head and mopped again, while Mudd patted him on the shoulder and said, "Bear up, Jim. You'll soon be dead," in his most sympathetic manner.

"Read it, parson," sobbed Gumm, pushing the moist letter into Sill's hand. "My poor little baby. We did want him so bad."

The curate began to intone the letter in a soft and holy key. It was from Mrs. Gumm, telling a common story. Baby had got hold of a lighted candle, and the candle had fallen on baby's flannelette nightdress, and baby's entry into Paradise had followed very soon afterwards; and the little cot was empty for evermore. The curate returned the letter, and reminded the bereaved father that it was well with his child.

"It would have been better for the poor baby if he hadn't been burnt," sobbed Gumm. "We didn't have a baby for a long time. Then it came, and now it's gone."

"Flannelette ought never to be used. My missis always puts ours in proper flannel," said the publican in a superior way.

"What's the good of talking like that, you silly fathead? My poor baby is dead, and all the flannel in the world won't bring him back. Jolly little kid he was," sniffed the unhappy father. "Used to sit up and say 'Dad' as natural as life."

"You will go to him," began Sill, feeling that something appropriate was required of him.

"I don't want to go to him," howled Gumm.

The call came to breakfast and the patients went in, with the exception of Gumm, who remained in the garden with his back to the house and his face towards the rhododendrons, informing the flowers and bees that his poor baby was dead and there was very little likelihood of another coming. He was grotesque in his grief, and his idea of endurance was to kick and make a noise, as he couldn't rob himself of sensibility. Had he been at home he would have wept over the dead child and then gone out to drink himself stupid. In that place he could not drink, so he had to howl instead. Berenice passed him, after a game with the dog outside, with a swift and careless, "So sorry, Mr. Gumm. Cheer up," and went in to breakfast, saying to herself, "I hope he won't come in to make us wet." After all nothing ripe or beautiful had been taken away by that lighted candle; only a life which really had not commenced and was capable of nothing but a little ape-like mimicry; nothing perfect and necessary like Winnie.

This young lady had not spoken to George the workman since that day she had watched him painting by the Ford; and she had not been allowed to speak then. She had seen him several times, crossing the moor with the tools of his craft, but he had always hurried off as if she had been poisonous. Winnie quite understood why he avoided her. For one thing she was stupid and he was marvellously clever; she was by force of circumstances a common person, while he was famous—of course he was famous with that head. No wonder he ran away from a poor little maid who had to stand near a barrel of cheap butter, crawling with equally inexpensive flies, and sell pennyworths of stamps. No doubt he had guessed all about it. That perfectly wonderful genius of his would have enabled him to see right into her mind. George had not the slightest idea of the high place among stars and saints that Winnie was innocently assigning to him; just as she had no suspicion of those various sketches about the walls of the Wheal House, every one of them depicting a face to which she had the best right and a nose which nobody else could hope to imitate. Of course Winnie had no right to take an interest in the craftsman, as somebody else was buying her by weekly instalments; but it was quite a proper and artistic interest; a fatal thing because it lasts longer than any other kind of interest. As for Berenice's story of those confidential scraps of paper which had fluttered into Wheal Dream, Winnie had never even seen them.

Halfway through St. Michael's Wood the Blackavon tumbles down a steep place, breaking itself to pieces among rocks, and jumps into the Okement, singing a ballad of green trees as it goes. Brook and river are united in a park-like spot where moor and woodland meet in a sort of natural rock-garden. It is a place of green and white, of foliage and foam; a waterfall is hurled over a huge slab of rock, boiling and sparkling, and spitting spray over the ferns, and when the wind blows upward it plays at making rainbows; the Blackavon is foaming too, like an overdriven horse, after its breathless hurry; and the flowers in that spot are white. Opposite are two old mines, not new and gaunt, nor middle-aged and sad, but ancient and beautiful. The ruins of the miners' cot form a rectangular heap of stones covered with moss and long tentacles of bramble. The mouths of the two water-logged shafts are draped with hanging ivy, veiled with fern-fronds, and fringed with grass of Parnassus. There is a dream-like air of mystery about the place. One listens for the sound of gnomes dancing in their hall, or for pan-pipes, and when the grass rustles—but it is only a viper, the place is not dreamland, but a corner of wind-swept earth, beautiful and deceitful like most pleasures, a place where men have grubbed copper to get gold; and on that tender grass is the silvery slime of the poisonous snake. There are no pan-pipes, no merry music; the river hums on like a far-away organ, playing its everlasting and almost sacred plain-song, the notes indicated by the rocks in its bed, and time and accent by leaps and splashes; not monotonous to those who are always listening, but exceedingly haunting; and to live by it and to leave it is to long for it again.

George sat above the waterfall on his camp-stool, dabbing at a canvas. He had finished one already, and as he painted he chaffed himself pleasantly.

"Walk up and buy," he was saying. "They are within reach of the poorest. Brunacombe's little pictures, made in England, warranted not to fade, all false to nature, because the man who can pin a bit of nature to a canvas like a butterfly to a board hasn't arrived. Buy, buy! Only twopence-halfpenny each, and one thrown in for nothing if you say it's a bad bargain. Talk about shirts and button-holes and sweated industries, while Brunacombe's masterpieces go for the price of a bad egg. There's a waterfall for you, Messrs. Abraham, Isaac and Jacob. That ought to straighten the Mosaic nose and cause the strings of the Aaronic purse to loosen. Verily it is like unto a bundle of frozen cotton-wool. Paint a waterfall! I might as well try to paint a clap of thunder. And what are those objects, Mr. Brunacombe? Why, my dear Mr. Barabbas, they are lumps of rock, and are charged for in the bill at one farthing apiece, which, as you may remember, was formerly the market price of a brace of sparrows in your own dear fatherland. I thought they were intended to be bales of indiarubber, Mr. Brunacombe, and even you, debased and ignorant as you are, must admit that the resemblance is a striking one. But that only reveals the eminence of my art, Mr. Barabbas. To paint a rock, which is actually a rock, while it at the same time resembles a bale of indiarubber, is surely the highest point to which art can attain. I will if you like paint the words Dartmoor Rock in distinct white letters. across each offending surface so that there can be positively no delusion. For that service I shall have to charge an extra halfpenny for expenditure of paint, wear and tear of brushes, loss of brain tissue, and mental and moral damage. It is not necessary for me to live, dear Mr. Barabbas, but I consider it advisable, as so many of the London roads are being repaired at present, and the traffic would be seriously disorganised by a Westminster Abbey funeral. I will not buy your dirty pictures, Mr. Brunacombe. Go out or I shall kick you.

"That's enough green paint to satisfy even the lady who lets lodgings. I can't give any more for the money. Now a smudge for that fern. The quickness of the hand deceives the eye. There you are! It looks rather like a cauliflower, but no matter. This is only art, and anything is good enough to make a bit of a splash upon a wall-paper of red-hot roses. Come along, canvas number three. Come and have a nice waterfall painted on you, and then you shall go up to London and be described as a handsome work of art by the well-known painter George Brunacombe, and be given away as a prize by a penny paper to some booby who gives the correct answer in a great gambling competition as to how many bank-notes would be required to reach from Epsom Hill to the Bankruptcy Court."

There was a gentle rustling in the bracken just behind the camp-stool, and George started, stopped his grotesque monologue—he always chatted to himself while he worked to keep his spirits up—and half turned. A good many vipers were about the wood, and more than once he had nearly set his foot upon one.

"Begone, pestiferous reptile," he called cheerfully; but the rustling in the bracken continued, and the artist, who was much too busy to swing round, began to assault his third canvas, saying—

"Peradventure it is a pony from the hills, or a fat bull of Dartmoor, or a mountain sheep caught by its horns in the brambles. The art of giving expression to running water demands steady application, and the artist who hesitates loses his eightpence an hour. I would gladly pause awhile and play with this creature, weave a garland for its neck, crown myself with oak-leaves, and wander with it over hill and dale like a Botticelli picture. George Brunacombe and the bull—the very subject for a church window. According to legend St. Brunacombe was a contemporary of St. Michael, and they both lived together in a little chapel at the top of Halstock wood."

"I am so sorry," interrupted a nervous voice, "but I cannot help hearing every word you say."

For a moment George wondered if the waterfall had exploded. He seemed to be drenched with something cold. The little easel shot away like a rocket, number three canvas fell flat on its face, and the palette went clattering after. There was Winnie standing in the bracken covered with sunshine and confusion. It was not her fault if he was there. She had tried to get away directly she saw him, only the bracken and little dry twigs were so noisy.

"What a fool I am to be so nervous," George muttered.

Certainly it was a pretty picture; much better than stones and running water, much higher art, but something beyond him, for that face was as baffling as the waterfall. It was beauty amid the bracken, with her feet in the flowers, and her head in one of those wonderful slanting sunbeams which came through a cleft in the rocks, pierced the foliage, and struck the ground just beyond her. She was blinking a little, but it suited her; she was nervous, and that suited her; she moved slightly, put a hand to her hat, inclined her head—why everything that she did suited her.

"I was talking to myself," said George, in the superior way which the state of his nerves demanded. "It's a trick of mine while working, and I didn't think any one could hear me. I often hear ponies rustling about, but I don't often see."

"People," she suggested timidly, when he hesitated, and he grunted an assent though he didn't like the word. It was something like blasphemy to think of her as a person. The days of visions were not over; decidedly not over, when St. Michael permitted his youngest daughter to roam about the woods.

"I have got to sit here for an hour," said Winnie piteously, as if it was a torment she could not face.

George picked up his camp-stool at once, and asked where she would like to have it.

"Oh no, thank you very much, but I sit on the grass, on the bank over there. Of course you know it?"

"There are some rotten trunks of trees. It is damp there," he said.

"Then you don't know it—the bank of white violets," she said, smiling.

He shook his beard, and when Winnie moved away he followed, because it seemed a natural thing to do. The black and rotten trunks were there, as he had said, but beyond, in a corner of garden made by the meeting of brook and river, was a bank he had never discovered— they had to climb over some ivy-scarred rocks to reach it—and that bank was soft with moss and dotted everywhere with white violets.

"You know more about this place than I do," he exclaimed.

"I was born on the moor, on the very roof of it," she said timidly. "I used to roam about as a child wherever I liked. I can always find out its secret corners."

"I was born on the edge of the moor. I left it, but I had to come back."

"I had to come back too," she said bravely.

"Are you fond of Dartmoor?"

"I love it. It's home," she said, the question making her forget the man. "I love it in all its moods, wet or fine, summer and winter. It is the only place where I can endure snow."

"Can you bear the winds?" he asked. She looked so delicate, so frail. Those winds which would sometimes flay his face.

"They seem to make me live," she said simply. "While they nearly carry me off my feet they put life into me." Then she added, "I have never been well out of them."

George left her, having an idea he was going to lose the rest of the morning. Over the waterfall, where they were out of sight of each other, he stood and looked down. He was a fighter, but there was a force of Nature in that green and white wood, which was saying, in answer to his "Let me go, for I must work," "I will not let you go," the answer of the angel to the artist in St. Michael's Wood.

"This is a bright and a black day," he muttered; and then sharply, "Don't be a fool, George. She gives away your white heather. She reads your secrets and tells every one. Go on with your work."

He set up his easel, took his palette and began to outline the waterfall, which at once took upon itself the form of a girl lying upon a bank. It was certainly a very difficult nose to draw. Then something else came into the bracken, an invisible imp who kept on throwing things at him, sharp-pointed things that hurt horribly. It was curious he had not discovered that bank of white violets. What a poor creature she must think him for talking such nonsense when he was alone. Of course she would .know that what he had written on those scraps of paper was only sentimental rubbish. It was hardly necessary to go and tell her that. But he would like to get an opinion upon his little pictures. Perhaps they were not so bad as they seemed, but he turned out so many that the process was mechanical. Decidedly he required criticism, and it seemed a pity to lose an opportunity. It wouldn't be a waste of time to have a few of his faults pointed out. As he arrived at this decision the imp in the bracken threw something very sharp indeed; and George gathered up his morning's work, tramped across to the bank, and frowned fiercely over the rocks as he said, "I want you to look at this," poking the little wet canvas at her as if it had been a knife; while poor Winnie trembled at the clever man's hostility, and became fully assured that her presence there constituted a most intolerable nuisance.

"I must stop here. The doctor ordered me to—for an hour," said she shyly.

"What do you mean?" said George.

"I am interrupting you, but I can't help it. I was sent here," she went on, painfully anxious to explain her position. "Why, I think it is lovely," she cried, very glad to change the subject. "How beautifully you have painted the water!"

"Only a smudge," he said gruffly. "I don't want you to admire it. I want you to point out the faults."

"Are there any? I don't think there can be," she declared with a pretty puzzled look. "Oh yes, it is perfect."

"Keep it if you like," George blurted out. "There's that big picture of the Perambulators crossing Chapel Ford—the one you saw me working at that day when I,—when you came down with Miss Calladine. You seemed to be interested," he rambled on, saying anything he could think of because she was looking so delighted with the gift and delightful in herself. "It's no good. I'll finish it for you if you like. It's not worth a frame, but you could tack it up to a wall. It's big, and would cover a crack in the plaster."

"But you mustn't," she faltered, very pleased but distressed again, and looking up in that helpless and destructive way of hers. "I ought not to take this, and as for the big picture—why, it must be worth hundreds of pounds," she said, opening her mouth rather too much for the artist's tranquillity.

"Well, keep this one—if you will," he said.

"May I really? Thank you so very much. I don't think you ought to give it me, but I—I want it," she said charmingly.

"Give it back," he said brusquely. "I'll take it home and finish it properly. This was for the Jews, and I treat them as they treat me."

Winnie gave it back, somewhat unwillingly, as if she feared he might forget all about her, glancing timidly at the fine head and nervous face, and wishing she could brush his coat for him. It was so dreadfully dusty, and his hands were smeared as usual, and bits of dry fern were caught in his beard. An hour of her clinging attention would make him such a splendid man; but then she remembered their respective positions—he the great clever artist with the world at his feet, and she a poor market slave, with a price being paid for her, and an engagement-ring which she wouldn't wear until she was compelled to hidden away in her bedroom; and she was only back in the wind for a little time, to be fattened as it were for sacrifice; and then she was to return to the place of smoke and fade away.

"You are the first great man I have met," she said, with a quick glance which told her that he preferred to keep his eyes upon the Blackavon.

"Yes, I am pretty big," he agreed, shaking his beard.

"I mean famous," she went on. "It must feel strange to know that every one talks about you. At least it would be strange to me, but then you are used to it."

"Great heavens, what is she thinking about?" was George's mental comment. He must tell her the truth, get that wild idea out of her head, confess that he was a mere dabbler in all the arts and a success in none of them; that he worked for a sorry pittance and the tribe of Judah; that the little picture he had given her was worth only a shilling or two—the price of a pound of tea; that he was absolutely unknown to the world, and his income did not equal that of a blind beggar. And yet how was he to begin? It was so pleasant to receive the tribute of admiration from those lips.

"I am only an artist. There are hundreds of 'em," he blurted out.

"Only!" she said, laughing, feeling happy and at her ease. "Think what that means to me who can't do anything. But you are a poet too, and a lot of other things besides. Mr. Leigh says you are a genius, and of course he knows."

"Mr. Leigh says a good deal that he doesn't mean," was all George could say just then. He could open her eyes later on, but for that hour, if never again, he would breathe flattery.

Winnie shook her head and decided to believe Mr. Leigh, but she liked George all the more for his modesty. She wanted to brush his coat more than ever. She found it so easy to talk, lying on the bank of violets, trifling with an acorn, and looking across at him. It was a new sensation for Winnie to find herself playing a leading part. With Halfacre she was frightened and silent, agreeing with all he said, not venturing to contradict. But with George she was comfortable; a little encouragement and she would almost have scolded him for going about in such disreputable garments. But George went on leaning against the rocks, looking sullen, which was his way of trying to conceal his feelings. He had spent most of his life suppressing emotion and he was doing it then. It would be terrible, he thought, if by any mischance he should do or say something to make her suspect that he loved her. He would rather dash his head against those rocks than make such a shameful admission.

"I shall always boast of having met you. And there will be the picture as a proof that I am telling the truth," she said artlessly.

"The picture is worth nothing," he said moodily, but Winnie only shook her head. She wasn't going to believe such nonsense. It must be worth a great deal if he had painted it, for he was a genius, and when such a one scrabbles on a canvas he is almost as guilty as the rascal who engraves a flash bank-note.

"I am afraid you are wasting the morning," said Winnie, conscious that she was boring him; and George started and admitted rudely that he was wasting it, and then concluded she desired to get rid of him. Still he didn't go. It was warm and pleasant on that bank of violets, and he liked it better than the green shelf above the waterfall. He pulled out the rag that served him for handkerchief to wipe his hot hands, forgetting he had wrapped his luncheon inside it; and when a couple of hard-boiled eggs rolled upon the bank he flushed with shame for the second time that morning.

"Here they are," said a pathetic voice. Winnie was as much concerned as if she had dropped the eggs herself; she stopped them on their downward course and held them out. It was such a small hand, and so thin. The eggs looked almost too heavy for it.

"Thank you," said George coldly; and then after a horrible pause gruesome pictures kept on rising before the artist's eyes—that cursed imagination of his—broken columns, snapped chains, and artificial flowers; the stifling interior of a church filled apparently with a heap of something purple—that for her; a dark place hanging with cobwebs, full of creeping movements, a sort of haunted Wheal Dream, a kind of prison; and then a room filled with men who were not men, but one a steam-engine, another a tree in motion, and another God Almighty— that for himself. Endurance finds out the weak spots as well as the strong: the wind strikes every part alike; and at the point of least resistance it gets in.

"I'll go on with my painting," he said.

"Please do," said Winnie.

George went back feeling dazed and half-sick. He knew he should never eat those eggs. His hands were trembling, and he could not have drawn a line to save his life. She thought he was a rich and famous man; perhaps she thought he was strong physically; and he had stood before her a big lie in man's clothing. He was really weak in body as she was, and they both suffered in different degrees from the same cause—the inward growth of the lowest form of plant life; and the only thing which could destroy those weeds was the wind. He and she were children of that wind and the moor; he had gone away and she had been taken away. And the valley of smoke had poisoned them both. He had come back like a prodigal unworthy of those harsh and kindly parents, and she had come back too. He would never go away again, and she must not; though doubtless a happy home and every comfort awaited her in the valley of smoke. Why couldn't they stay there together? They were brother and sister; they called the wind father and the moor mother—but that was imagination again. He was a poor devil; she was a girl accustomed to every luxury. He had nothing but Wheal Dream and a life of dreams, while she had everything; and everything in life seemed to mean a few bagfuls of coloured dirt manufactured into thin round baubles; just as a string of coloured beads means everything to the year-old child. It seemed that men must buy happiness, health, place in the world, their very morals and prospect for eternity with a child's playthings; and the toy cupboard in the nursery of Wheal Dream was empty. That being so George could only scowl upon Winnie and hurry away from her; and make all the splendidly naked and straightforward things of the moorland wood laugh in irony at the sorrowful spectacle of lovers coldly and proudly discussing the prospect of a change in the weather. The oak-leaves mingled with the bracken. Sometimes it looked as if the bracken was bringing forth acorns and as if the oak-branches were producing fern-fronds, so intermingled were they without shame. The Blackavon poured into the Okement. Nobody could say where the body of the one joined the body of the other, so perfect was the passionate union, all song murmur and foam; and there also were the intelligent children of Nature who were so afraid of putting off the rags of self-pride and becoming naked to one another. The river and the oaks didn't know they were naked; they had pride perhaps in their pretty bodies. Men and women are ashamed of any sort of nakedness, frightened to think of it, and when they are together dare not remove a single rag. It is not until they become like rivers meeting, not sluggishly, but with song murmur and foam that they are natural at last.

"Have you ever seen the oak-tree in the bracken?" asked a voice, the same one, only more tremulous; and the speaker had changed too, had grown more charming and more necessary. Winnie was restless. Instead of being good and sitting still on her bank of white violets she was roaming about as if she had lost something, her face quite pink, her hair a mist of tendrils.

"I can show it you," she went on confidently. Winnie had been growing during the last few minutes. She had dared to come and speak to George without waiting for orders. She had never been so impertinent before, and she felt as happy as if she had broken all the Commandments one after the other.

George turned but kept his distance. There is a certain point where attraction becomes irresistible, and the needle after a preliminary wriggle leaps wildly at the magnet. What in the needle is a servile obedience to a law is in the lover a loss of self-control; a man knows how to break the law, the needle does not, and may perhaps be accounted the most natural of the two. George remained outside the circle, though a part of his being, which preferred to obey the law of nature rather than his foolishness, was inside condemned to play satellite to the sun of Winnie's system. He replied in a commonplace voice that he had no idea what she was talking about.

"I'll show you if I may." She was delighted at his ignorance. "You are not—not—I mean you really never have seen it?"

"I don't understand you," he said blankly; though it was unlikely he could understand anything while she was playing about there.

"Why, the little oak-tree in the stem of the bracken. And you are so very clever. But nobody knows of it. Shall I show it you?"

"Yes, do," he said, getting eager; then pinched himself and muttered, "George, remember the Wheal House." It was very bare and unfurnished; only a workroom and kitchen and shabby bedroom.

"The edge of split bracken cuts like a razor," he cried. She was pulling at a big stem like a palm branch. If he saw her blood it would be all over.

"I know it cuts, but I haven't got a knife," she said helplessly. "I will show it you though;" and she pulled again, the sort of pull that might have broken a jerrybuilt spider's web, then put her hand to the front of her hat because the sun crossed her eyes. It was one of the most destructive of her movements, and though it had no effect upon the bracken it uprooted George and brought him near with a palette-knife.

"Get up the root," she said. They dropped their hostile manner and became quite neighbourly over this new interest.

"Isn't it funny how the colour changes? The root is as black as ebony, and the stalk just above the ground is like mahogany; and then the brown gets fainter as it goes up the stem and at last becomes green, and the green fades away to nothing—almost white at the top, grey-headed like an old man."

"Where is the oak-tree?"

"That's inside. A very tiny tree, but quite perfect. It runs up the stem, getting fainter like the colour, until it disappears. Will you make a slanty cut? Not the root—there, just where my finger is, in the mahogany part."

"Where?" said George in a dazed fashion. He wanted to look again at that finger, and the sweet ridiculous insignificance of it. Somehow he did not see much of the stem of bracken because there was a tiny scratch upon her wrist, and it would keep on coming before his eyes, and he wanted to do something to it though he hardly knew what.

"Just here. Look, I'll make a mark with my nail. Anywhere will do, but the tree ought to be very clear here. Well, if you don't like to cut it, let me."

"I'll do it. I was—was thinking," George blurted out. Then he made a slash, and as the black part of the stem dropped Winnie gave a small cry of pleasure.

"Couldn't be better. See, it's a lovely little tree, root, stem and branches. And I made the discovery when I was only so high."

One glance at this small natural wonder was enough for George, as the scratched wrist became visible and he would rather have fallen down and worshipped that.

"How did you manage it?" he asked absently.

"It was just by chance. I cut a stem through one day and found it out."

"I mean your wrist—that mark."

"Oh, a bramble, just after I crossed the Ford. I was swinging my arm. You will remember my picture?"

"I will finish it as well as I can, and send it you."

"I have shown you two things, my bank of white violets and the oak-tree in the bracken."

She had shown him much more; and yet George perceived nothing, except that pink scratch on a snow-white wrist.

"May I paint you?" he asked suddenly.

"Would you like to? Down here, on the bank of violets? I will ask doctor."

Then she said good-bye and went, breathing rather quickly at her own forwardness, and walking too fast; while George returned to the waterfall and tried to stand up straight.

CHAPTER XII
ABOUT THE GREAT DOWNACOMBE REBELLION

"Jimmy," called Uncle Gifford, standing at the foot of the stairs. "The tea be soaked."

This was the usual morning call, as in moorland homes it is not polite to announce that a meal is ready. Uncle might have said, "Breakfast be upon the table," or he could have asked Jimmy if he was ready for it, but it would have been something like a want of manners to say in so many words that the meal was ready for him.

"Jimmy," called Uncle again, "tear up the bed avore yew comes down." It would save him one journey up those steep stairs, and his right leg was getting very stiff. Uncle kept the beds clean, though it was hard work to evict the insects which were fond of emigrating from the overcrowded population next door. Ursula's home was filthy, while Uncle Gifford's cottage was clean; and she was a strong young woman, while he was a weak old man. It was merely the difference between resistance and submission. A rebellious mind makes a plague-stricken home.

"Aw, Jimmy, du'ye come. I ha' to go up to garden and lift taties," called Uncle fretfully.

"I be agwaine to bide abed," came the answer at last. "Seems like as if 'twould rain and little Dora be peevish. I'll ha' a cup o' tay and a gurt slice o' bread and cream."

Jimmy believed in plenty of nourishing food, as he had a baby to nurse. He was growing more like a woman every day, allowing muscle to waste and getting effeminate in manner. He often worried over the baby, declaring it was not teething properly, and he hoped he should never have to bring up another, as children were a nuisance; he was allowing his hair to grow and his flesh was getting

159

flabby; he was becoming so weak that he said it made his arms and legs ache to take the baby out for an airing. When Uncle laboured up the stairs with the cup of tea, Jimmy explained that he had been kept awake half the night and it was necessary for his health to obtain more sleep; and when the old man laboured up the second time with the slice of bread and cream, for he was forced to use his right hand to drag himself along, Jimmy remarked that it would soon be necessary to get a maiden to nurse the infant, as the task was proving too much for his strength. Uncle made no reply, but lowered his body painfully into the living-room and stimulated his soul with a prayer.

The gist of Uncle's prayer was that Jimmy and his baby were not what they ought to have been, and he ventured to lodge a respectful complaint against the continued existence of so much selfishness. "I be a poor man, Lord," he explained. "I ha' saved, and I ha' given to chapel, and I owes nought. When I wur biding alone I had the best on't though I didn't knaw, and l asked yew to send I some one; and now l ha' got Jimmy I ha' the worst on't, and I don't want 'en, Lord, and so I tull ye, and I asks yew to tak' 'en away. If I ha' Jimmy and he wun't work I can't give nought to chapel. I du hope yew can understand what I be telling. I can't give nought to chapel, which be giving to yew, Lord, and it don't seem right to give Jimmy your money, and I asks yew to see kindly what can best be done wi't."

Uncle always prayed in a colloquial fashion without any straining after archaic forms of speech. He did not venture to suggest that one bad mistake had already been committed. He had asked for a companion and Jimmy had been sent; he could not help thinking that the task of selection had been grievously mismanaged. And now he asked that Jimmy might be taken away—it was a moneybox kind of prayer—and his former solitude restored to him. Poor old Uncle had yet to learn that men must manage their affairs by their own unaided efforts.

He sat to his breakfast and thought of other days. A quaint object hanging from one of the roof-beams, a white bunch of withered wheat-ears fastened round a notched stick, made him cast his mind back. No man would wish to pass through his life again, and when he looks back he is amazed to find how few are the days that have made a mark. Most of Uncle's white days had been Sundays; chapel-meetings and sly courtships in his youth, not much religion then, but a few hot kisses and one kiss in particular—these made the deepest mark, which seemed to show that passion is the stigma which brands the beast right through. Then there was the day of his conversion, when a sermon had convicted him of living in sin and a burst of somewhat illiterate eloquence had "brought him home." Uncle remembered that day well enough, but it was not so clear as that one kiss in particular, although the conversion had led up to a great deal and the kiss to nothing. There was also a day of harvest when he had brought the "neck," which was that bunch of wheat-ears hanging to the roof-beam, safely into the house. That was one of the best days of all. He had farmed the two fields above his cottage, and that year had them under wheat, which in those days could be sold at a profit. Superstition and old customs occupied the minds of every commoner, adding beauty and happiness to their existence if they also darkened it a little; and Uncle could remember how excited they all were when only a few stalks of wheat remained to be cut. Evil spirits were abroad, and these had to be propitiated, and it was necessary to secure those last ears and carry them to the house unspoilt, so that the good spirit of the harvest should not die and the life of the corn be carried on to another year. It was John Petherick's father, a far better man though weak in business, who rushed out shouting, "I ha' 'en." "What ha' ye?" called another. "A neck! a neck!" Then there came the rush for the house, while the women, playing their part of evil spirits, tried to thwart them. Uncle himself smuggled the neck inside. Old Petherick ran to the door with a false one and drew the women after him with their crocks of cider soaking him from head to foot, while Uncle slipped inside with the true spirit of the harvest underneath his coat.

"Aw, 'twas a happy day," he muttered, still feeling the excitement of it. And there was the dry old neck like a dead man's hand hanging from the roof, although times had changed and the very custom which had placed it there was dead, because men have grown too solemn and wise for harvest-games, and wheat no longer smells of guineas. It seemed to Uncle that those had been happier days. Certainly there was more pleasure, and every man had a strong laugh, and when he danced at harvest-revel there was always a jingling in his pockets.

The loose door was kicked open and John lurched in, growling and belching in his beastly way. Uncle's thoughts already had been disturbed by noises which had not suggested family prayers next door. John looked brutal, a short black whip was underneath his arm, his hard hat was dented like a wayside kettle; his face, always an indescribable colour of deep brown, tanned skin, animal heat, and earth mingled, looked then almost black. He slipped upon the smooth stone floor, his nailed boots making angry scratches. His old trousers were stiff with cow-dung. His eyes were sunken like the unhealthy hollows in his cheeks. His hands were like the roots of trees.

"Where be your Jimmy?" he growled, dodging about like a wrestler. Speech was an effort to John, and when he said a word he tried to throw his body after it. He looked a distorted image of humanity, a man turned inside out with all the vice and viscera showing. He had been at the bottle already, and when a man starts the day's work in that fashion he is past redemption. Both he and Uncle were ugly, but old Gifford's face was only apelike ugliness, John's was foul. Stamp alcoholism upon brutality and the depth is reached.

"Jimmy be abed. He'm a lazy boy," said Uncle in a friendly way, with a fearful glance at that knotted whip.

"What's he abed vor?" growled John, striking against the table, nearly overturning it, and leaving a brown mark upon Uncle's tablecloth. "Be he a woman going to ha' a baby? Get 'en out on'f, yew old vule. Pair o' proper old tom-pollies yew be, wi' yer beds and bastards and Bibles."

"I don't understand the boy, Johnnie," Uncle said. "I don't want to ha' 'en here no longer, vor he wun't du nought, but I can't turn 'en away. What be I to du wi' 'en, Johnnie? I be old and mazed got, and my bit o' money wun't last out. He minds the baby and makes the clothes, cuts 'em out he du and fits 'en, and he knits lace as if he wur a maid."

"What else?" John shouted.

"Nought, Johnnie. Plays wi' the baby's toes, and tells o' pigs and gurt market."

"Aw, yew old mazehead. He'm a proper dirty toad," hiccuped John, less violently, as he was feeling giddy. His head was wretchedly weak, for strong drink on an empty stomach is a poor sustenance. "He goes after my woman when I be out. Yew knaws he du. I be agwaine to break 'en vor it if I catches 'en."

Uncle was not going to believe that story. Jimmy had certainly performed unmoral actions, but he was not altogether vile, and this was nothing but a trick on Ursula's part to make fresh discord between the houses. "It hain't true, Johnnie," he said. "The boy be careless like, but he bain't a bigamist." Uncle did not know whether that was the right word, but he thought it would serve. "He just goes in to get milk vor the baby," he said rather triumphantly, for he had scored over Jimmy there, having pointed out that if he didn't go for the milk baby would have none.

"Why du he go when I bain't in?"

"He'm afeard o' yew, Johnnie. He'm as nervous as a maid."

"Be that as 'twull," said John thickly, feeling that it might be better for him to get out into the air. "If I finds 'en in there I'll break 'en. Tell 'en that," he shouted, pounding the table with his fist, obliterating the whiteness of the cloth. "Tell 'en that. I'll put he and the bastard on the ground and tread on 'en." These words were shouted towards the door, and John flung himself after them with beetle-like blunderings, and staggered towards the linhay, a sort of patchwork of wood, corrugated iron, sacking, and furze-bushes, which he called his stable. John was low down in the scale, but he had his virtues; most of them as small as microbes, but one was prominent enough. He was a good workman, no man in the district did a better day's work, although he had no skill, and clumsiness increased his labours. He could build a hedge against Gregory Breakback and not be beaten; but nothing came of his work except increasing poverty, because he invested all his money in strong drink, which never pays a dividend and brings a man to the straw in time. Perhaps John deserved more pity than blame, for Ursula had what mind there was between them, and she had always been a tippler. It was the old story of the woman leading the man astray, and the man getting the blame because he was supposed to be the stronger. John and the pigs had plenty in common; they could grunt in agreement over almost every act; John and humanity had little.

He was hauling turves that day to Downacombe Rectory. Two loads were as much as any man could manage, for he had to drive out to the marsh and load the cart from the stacks which a week's sun had well dried. Peat was precious in poverty-stricken Downacombe, and its inhabitants, who had no forest rights, could only obtain it from the commoners by payment, which they were unable to afford, or by favour, which was a scarce commodity. Then a horse and cart were necessary to bring it home, and that rare event a holiday was the only day to be spared. There were thousands of tons of fuel only two miles from Downacombe, and yet it was costly, often unobtainable, just because the villagers were foreigners and had the geographical misfortune to be on the wrong side of the line. What was not wanted in Metheral was dear in Downacombe; and the freemen were not going to share the least of their privileges with bondmen.

When John reached Downacombe on his first trip soon after midday the church bells were ringing. There was a knot of men about the door of the post-office talking in a low, grumbling way. John had enough sense to wonder if an election could be impending or whether a marriage was taking place. It could not be a suicide because of the bells, and a flag was flying over the tower, and John saw the postmaster point towards the flag with a blasphemous expression. This man was a Socialist and Atheist, and had other vices with the same grammatical termination; and one of the local preachers, who wholly differed from his unbelief but agreed entirely with his diluvial politics, not because he was wicked but because he was ignorant, had helped him to sow a lot of bad seed, some of which was bound to germinate and bring forth weeds. Only a spark was required to set the smother into a flame, and a certain gentleman named Richard Halfacre had supplied that spark.

John jolted along to the rectory, dropping here and there a turve which some child pounced upon almost as soon as it reached the ground; and when he got there a servant told him the news. The bells were ringing and the flag was flying because it was Mrs. Leigh's birthday. Ringers had been hired by the master, and they were all foreigners, not a drop of local blood among them; and the villagers, she declared, were about to give a practical form to their indignation. For one thing their beloved church and bells were being desecrated; that seemed to be the special grievance of the postmaster; and for another thing the bells were being rung by foreigners, simply because locals had been offered the job and had declined. Of course John did not understand much of what he was told because he was dull-witted; and for once he and a sane philosopher might have shaken hands, for it was very difficult to discover where the grievances of the villagers came in.

When John had unloaded his peat he went back to the village. Custom ordained that he should patronise the inn, which was kept by an old couple who did not interest themselves much in outside affairs. The bar-room was simply a continuation of the kitchen. At one end was the fire-place, at the other a couple of benches and a table. Here Halfacre was sitting, eating mutton, and trying to inflame the sheep-like landlord. He had no business to be there, as the doctor had sent him across the moor for an all-day walk; but the chance to spend a day in Downacombe was too good to be lost, and the risk of discovery was not great, as the laws which are in force at a school prevail also at a sanatorium, and no patient sneaks about the wrong-doing of another.

"This house belongs to the parson," he was saying as John pushed the door open. "You pay him rent, and if you didn't he would turn you out. What good does he do you?"

"Wull, he lets us bide," said the landlord, in a voice which expressed the wish that all men would do likewise.

"Look at the plaster coming down on your heads, and the thatch is sliding off the roof. There's been nothing done for the last twenty years. Look at the cottages falling down everywhere, not fit for animals, mere holes of smoke. What is the parson doing for them?"

John understood some of this, and it amused him so much that he began to bump his body against the wall and make strange noises. Halfacre glanced at him contemptuously but without recognising the owner of Wheal Dream.

"Yew and postmaster belongs to these here Soshullists, I reckon?" said the peaceable landlord.

"I am proud to say we do," Halfacre answered. " We want to help our fellow-creatures, and lift up those that are trodden underfoot, and make men and women out of them, and give them something they can call their own. That's what we call Socialism."

"I reckoned 'twas wanting what yew ain't got and being afraid to work vor 'en," said the simple landlord.

"Aw, aw, that be a gude 'un," laughed John.

"Who are you?" asked Halfacre sharply, objecting to be laughed at by an uncouth creature who appeared to be a particularly dirty specimen of the tramp class.

"I knaws yew," laughed John. "Yew'm one o' the consumptuous ones."

"He'm John Petherick to Wheal Dream," explained the landlord.

Halfacre had no friendly feeling for the commoners, whom he regarded as land-grabbers, people who enclosed open spaces of land for their own base purposes and deprived others of the lawful enjoyment of such land. He turned away from John to resume his attack upon the landlord, who was proving himself a blackleg by not joining in the outcry against the rector for having the bells rung with imported labour on the occasion of his wife's birthday. Halfacre was no orator; he could write well, but his tongue was blundering. It was the postmaster who had stirred up the people, whilst Halfacre played the part of prompter, standing by the speaker's side and suggesting such ideas as land and leisure for every one except those who were then enjoying them.

"I ain't got nothing agin parson," said the landlord, who had his licence to think of. "He'm a gentleman, and 'tis natural he should want to live like one. The whole village ought to be pulled down and built up proper. Most o' these old places ain't worth spending money on. Patch 'em up in one place and they'll bust out in another, and as vor the roofs, yew must thatch the whole or none. 'Tis no gude thatching a bit when the whole roof leaks."

"Your parson robs the place of five hundred pounds every year," cried Halfacre, as fiercely as if he had just caught Leigh extracting that amount out of his own pocket.

"Wull, sir, that be a lot o' money, and I ain't going to say whether he desarves it or whether he don't," was the cautious answer. "S'pose he repaired one cottage a year there'd be a proper old flummux, 'cause every one would want to know why he'd repaired that cottage and not theirs. I used to ask 'en to spend a bit on this old inn, but he said he couldn't, so I reckoned 'twur best to let 'en 'lone. He said 'twasn't worth it, and he'm right. The old house be as rotten as dung, and a door don't hardly slam wi'out bringing a bit o' the wall down. The only thing to du is to pull the place down and build 'en up again. I ain't going to complain. Me and missis makes a living, and when volks might be worser off than 'em be they'm vules to kill the fatted calf what lays the golden egg," he said, as he moved off to refill John's mug. "Wull, sir, I bain't agin ye neither," he went on, bending over a big barrel and patting it affectionately. "Soshullism and revivals be gude vor my trade. Volks can't talk wi'out coming together and getting thirsty, and the more 'em talks the more wetting 'em wants. I dra's the beer and ses nought."

"You don't see any injustice in these poor creatures sweating their lives away, without a day's pleasure, living in dirty mud-holes, so that your lazy parson can spend his days in comfort?" cried Halfacre in a wild fashion.

"I reckon 'tis no injustice to work vor my living and to pay my rent," said the imperturbable landlord. "Times be cruel bad in the villages; they ses 'em wur worse years ago, but I knaw 'em warn't, they ha' never been worse than now. Volks reckon any change would mak' 'em better off, but I ses it be more likely to mak' 'em worser off. Parson don't help us, but he don't hinder us. S'pose the place wur sold and the cottages wur pulled down, and new houses built— where would us be then? Us wouldn't be able to afford the rent, and us would have to clear out on't. When things be bad, I ses let 'em 'lone lest yew mak' 'em worser."

Halfacre left his bench, cursing at so much ignorance. It was no use wasting words on this poor dolt, who was too much afraid of losing his licence to join in the fight against the oppressor. He paid for his food and said carelessly, "We are going to the rectory when the men come in from the fields. I suppose it's no good asking you to join us?"

"It bain't, sir," said the old fellow. Whatever his feelings may have been he was patriotic enough to resent this intrusion of a stranger into local affairs. "And I'll tull ye," he went on, "when it comes to marching yew wun't find many to follow. Talk be one thing and doing be another. What yew ses about a man who bain't nigh be a different thing from what yew ses to his face."

Halfacre went out, while John made up his mind to go on drinking beer for a bit and then follow to see the fun. Anything in the form of rioting was a joy to his soul, although he was quite unable to comprehend what Socialism meant or what it wanted; and there again the sanest philosopher living could have shaken hands with him. As a commoner he had no need to meddle with strange doctrines of freedom; but he was able to remember that his despised brother-in-law Bill Chown had, on those occasions when they were on fairly friendly terms, talked about such an incomprehensible matter as liberty for every one.

"Proper blackguard I calls he," said the landlord, when the kitchen door had closed behind Halfacre.

"Aw, be he?" said John, in his thick-headed way. "He'm one o' the gentlemen up to the conversation home," he added, with some respect. The sanatorium was known by the euphemism of Convalescent Home, and to be there argued the possession of money, and only gentlemen have money and can afford to be ill.

"Yew don't blind an old soldier," said the landlord. "I've abin under plenty of officers in my time, and I knaws gentlemen, and if he'm one then I'm a general. I reckon he'm one o' these fellers what goes about the country trying to set labourers agin their masters. What be this Soshullism they talks about? Every man share and share alike, they ses. Wull, me and my brother Tom started together, me wi' nought, and he wi' nought; and he ha' got nought to-day, and I ha' got a beer-house. Put my brother Tom in here, and let me go out wi' nought, I'd get hold of another house and he'd lose this one. That be me, and that be my brother Tom. Start us off together as often as yew like, I'd go up and he'd go down, vor that be the way of us, and until God Almighty makes volk of different stuff that will be the way of every one. Give me and my brother Tom a five-pound note, and I'd put mine into the business and he'd put his into his stomach. 'Tis easy to start volk level, just as it be easy to start a pony race. But 'em bain't level after they ha' run a mile."

John flushed his throat again and brought forth sounds of wind, but nothing intelligible. He imagined that the landlord had been describing a pony race, where he and his brother Tom had each invested five pounds. John comprehended pony races and could talk about them; but on such matters as religion and Socialism he was silent; or at least he could only say that he warn't one, and he warn't t'other, and he didn't believe in naythur; which was a simple way of closing discussion without gaining a reputation for obtuseness. The man who never answers soon gets pointed out as a philosopher, while the one who is always trying to find out things is regarded as a fool because he advertises his ignorance. John was looked upon as rather a subtle fellow owing to his silent tongue and abnormal laugh; and yet he was unable to read the little word "Bar" on the door of an inn, although custom had bred a knowledge of its meaning; and he could not count higher than ten, the number of his fingers. Ten ponies came within the scope of his enumerative powers, but more than ten were a "proper lot," or a drift, of ponies.

Leigh was in his garden smelling the roses which were past their prime, eating the honey of a calm evening. Every month of his life he devoted more time to those half-aimless wanderings; up one side, down another, under the pergola, through the glass-houses, round the lawn; pausing to eradicate a weed, to tie up a flagging carnation, or snap off a seed-head. His garden had taken the place of his wife; he was always with it, devoting himself to the roses like a lover. When it rained he longed for fine weather so that he could go out and walk between the perennials. After breakfast he hurried from the house to watch the annuals hurrying through their short lives; and would start with amazement when he heard the bell ring for luncheon. His evenings were given to the roses, that was understood between him and them; and he gave them some of the nights too, and of the moonlit nights more than a little. His study was littered with garden papers and the paraphernalia of that craft. He read little else, and rarely opened any book of the day or of the past. He was becoming a recluse, his mind was getting warped; always playing with the earth, some of it was forming on his mind. It was a battle between the roses and the manure with which he fed their roots.

His study swarmed with postcards. They clung to the picture-frames like bees. When he looked up, every actress of fame or Notoriety tempted him and every cathedral in Europe blessed him. The latest came from Monaco, where Mrs. Leigh was combining business with pleasure in a manner peculiar to that principality; and the card hinted that a letter would follow in reference to the business side. Still she was having a good time and getting strong and well; and she was coming home soon, to stay for a long time, as her heart was really at Downacombe though her body might be enjoying itself abroad. Women write these things with a heart-breaking facility. She was going on to Germany; she had promised some very nice people to visit the Black Forest with them, and the doctor had recommended it very highly, and she would send him lots of postcards, and not gamble more than was necessary, and then she would come home, for that was the best place after all, and would stay for at least three months.

Francis Leigh, being alone among actresses and cathedrals and the latest manual upon roses, wiped his eyes and was miserable; for promises and postcards are cold chamber-mates. It was not his wife's fault; she had always declared that the close, moist atmosphere of Downacombe would be fatal to her; and the lack of social pleasures made her fret. If he could have taken her up on Dartmoor all might have been well, so far as her health was concerned, but the dulness would have been the same.

To-morrow would be her *fête*-day, and he would have the flag flying on the tower and set the bells ringing. It would be a pleasure to him and a pretty compliment to her. He did not come to this decision until late at night. It was dark, and he left the garden early. For a time he was restless, then he settled down to plan a rock-garden which he proposed to make on a piece of waste land encumbered with brambles and bracken; but suddenly all interest in the work forsook him; it became stale and unprofitable; he pushed it away, went to his arm-chair, turned the lamp down and listened. He wanted to hear footsteps. He heard moths beating against the window, and leaves rustling and singing the flowers to sleep. Then he shuddered and awoke. He was getting old.

Such an obvious fact escapes notice until it comes in a storm and strikes like lightning. That shudder is the thunderclap which precedes the awakening, the bad dream just before dawn; it shakes the mind open and light rushes in. A man will live alone year after year, a bachelor among his hobbies, a scholar in his study, or a schoolmaster bound by academic routine. He is young, that is the only thing which matters; it was just the other day some one was laughing at him because of his youth and inexperience. True he has lately given up some form of sport, because it ceased to give him pleasure, and it made him so horribly tired and unfit for work the next day. It would soon be time to get settled, another year or two of that life and it would be his duty to marry. No hurry, as it was only a year or two ago that Harry married, and he was at school with Harry. There was a letter from him, and he said something about—what was it? Why, congratulate me on the birth of my first grandson; he meant son probably; still Harry did marry at some ridiculously early age, nineteen, or it might have been twenty-nine; anyhow it was no good thinking about it. Work and hobbies assert themselves again and these thoughts are forgotten. But late some night that fit of restlessness comes, the hobbies become as dry as ashes, the work is a burden; and then there is the convulsive shudder, the mental thunder and lightning, and the awakening. The man is old, and for the first time knows it; he has let the good things of life go by and they won't come back again; he has thought and fooled the time away, and it is too late to change, settle down, and accept new conditions. He is past fifty, and a few more of those scampering years will make him that long-sounding and gruesome thing a sexagenarian. And it was only the other day—but such reasoning is useless. That girl he had been thinking about would laugh to his face, and call him a giddy old thing, if he proposed to her. She would say he was old enough to be her father—and he had never realised it until then.

Possibly without the shuddering conviction of age Leigh would not have caused the bells to ring and the flag to fly. He did it for his own amusement; as no favourable omen was offered him he made one; just as the boy who tosses a coin to decide whether he shall do a certain thing or not goes on tossing until the coin turns up the way he wants it. The bells suggested a festival, a holiday, a wedding; they made a pleasant noise in the garden where the rector walked, bending rather more than he had done yesterday. There was a sacred touch in the secular business to his mind, because he loved his wife and love is a sacred thing. It was a kind of holy day, the festival of wife and roses, the feast of St. Margaret. It made a break in the dull monotony of days, it was an incident, which is pleasant, unlike an event, which is generally hateful. The life with the fewest events is the happiest life. So Leigh walked the day away as usual, and stood the alien ringers a good dinner and as much cider as their fleshly casks could contain; so it went on towards evening, and he had merely crossed from one side of the garden to the other when the storm broke and modern opinion came to the rectory. The cook walked up the path and announced that some gentlemen wished to see the master.

"Show them into the hall. I will come presently," he said. No doubt a marriage was impending, and they had come to get the banns published. The bridegroom requires plenty of support on such an occasion. It could be nothing else. He took another turn, noticed a. few fresh buds, then entered the house by his study window.

There was plenty of light in the hall though the sun had gone down, dragging a fine red glow after him; but there were not plenty of people. The old landlord was right when he suggested that those who shouted the loudest would march the slowest. Several had advanced as far as the outer gate, and there the majority made the discovery that they were too dirty to enter the rectory and face a gentleman. Their early ancestors had been serfs, their grandfathers little better, and they themselves could not fight against the hereditary instinct which convinced them that, despite their revolutionary tongues, they were inferior to the oppressor. They were prepared to break the shrubs and a few windows, or even set fire to the stables, if they were sure the rector couldn't see them; but if he had come out among them they would have touched their hats and declared it was a fine evening.

In the hall was Halfacre; he had decided to explain his absence by telling the doctor when he returned that he had lost his way; and with him were the postmaster subdued and tongue-tied; a small farmer from the next parish, who had nothing whatever to do with Downacombe, but had put in an appearance on account of his hatred for the Established Church, oblivious of the fact that most of the others professed to be there on account of their love for it, although none of them had passed its doors since their mothers had carried them to and from the font, which was near the door so that they needn't be taken in far enough to be contaminated; a loafer or two, who lived on their wits and by other folk's lack of them; a few genuine villagers, who felt that Leigh could not harm them much; and among them was Bill Chown, patient Bill, with the clay of the mine thick upon his hands, as innocent of flamboyant Socialism as an egg is of wool, but pitifully anxious to say or do anything which might improve his condition and prevent the hailstones from soaking his bed at nights. There was not more than a dozen in the hall. John Petherick was with those at the gate, quite drunk by this time, and fully persuaded that a pony race was about to be held, and he was there with the other sportsmen waiting for admittance.

"You wish to see me," Leigh remarked in a surprised voice, addressing Halfacre, whom he did not recognise, because he seemed to be more of his own class than the others; who crowded together and wished there was a fire, except Bill Chown, who stood apart by himself with his hat between his hands.

"Your parishioners have held a meeting in the village, and have decided that your act of ringing the church bells and flying the flag to-day constitutes an insult to them, and a degradation of the sacred property which has been placed under your charge," said Halfacre in his excited manner.

Leigh started violently, and a look of bewilderment crossed his face; but it soon cleared, he remembered he was master, and he turned to the small farmer, who was making rude noises with his tongue and cheek, and said sternly, "Take off your hat."

"I ha' got a cold in me head, parson," the man began.

"Take off your hat, or I will have you put outside. I have men in the kitchen," said Leigh, making a step forward which caused some of the company to wish there was more space. There was such a big difference between standing in the rectory and making speeches outside the post-office. Some of them began to hope that Leigh would not be hard upon them.

The small farmer removed his hat growling and grumbling, but taking precautions to make his remarks inaudible. Then Leigh turned to the postmaster and said, "I'm surprised to see you here, Colley. Have you anything to say?"

The postmaster had destroyed almost every work of creation with his tongue during the day, but he had now become marvellously innocuous. He began to think of his occupation, which the rector might deprive him of if he liked to be vindictive. It was easy to declare that it was the duty of poor people, to rise and seize what Nature had intended should be theirs, that the land belonged to them, and they were a proper lot of silly fools not to take it— when he was talking to the people. It was none so easy to preach the same doctrine to the landowner.

"I am the spokesman, and I'll talk to you as much as you like," the wild Halfacre broke in, standing with his legs apart, and glancing about defiantly.

Again the rector ignored him and repeated his question to the postmaster, who struggled a little, licked his lips, and said in a husky voice, "Well, parson, it's like this. There's a lot of bad feeling in the village, and you know it, I reckon. It ain't for me to say who has caused it"—which was modest of the man—"but it's growing. Some of the men reckon they ought to be better off—"

"And have houses to sleep in instead of dunghills," interposed the violent Halfacre, disgusted at the other's mildness. "And decent food to eat instead of pig-wash, and clothes instead of rags, and land of their own, and liberty in place of your abominable tyranny."

The rest of the party shivered admiringly and wished they could do likewise. This was putting things properly, giving their own thoughts just the right amount of inflammation. The small farmer broke the silence by clapping his hard hands together like two bits of board, and then he looked about the hall with an air of proprietorship. When they came to divide up the property that house would suit him admirably. It did not occur to him that some one else might want it, and be prepared to fight him in brotherly love for the possession of it.

"Go on with what you were saying, Colley," said the rector, with perfect self-control. He was playing the correct game of freezing them into silence. Halfacre was already feeling himself beaten. He was prepared to argue for an hour, getting fiercer and hotter over every sentence; but it was impossible to make out a case when there was no opposition, neither was it easy to argue with a man who had a singularly calm face, who evidently knew nothing about out-of-door oratory, or the rule which ordains that shout must be answered with shout and gesture with gesture, and who looked straight through the speaker as if he had been a puff of wind.

"Well, Colley?" said the rector to the stirrer-up of strife in Downacombe.

"Well, parson," laboured the postmaster, feeling various pushes in the back and an encouraging elbow in his ribs, "the people don't like you ringing the bells to-day."

"Oh, why not?"

"Well, they ain't got a holiday, and it seems to some of them as if you was—was—"

"Grossly insulting them," finished Halfacre.

"You see they have got to work the same as usual though the bells were ringing," went on the postmaster, as a sort of apology for his leader's rude remark. It was a wonderfully different postmaster from the blood and thunder individual who had recently declared that, if the people would only follow him, he would put them in possession of the entire country. No lion had ever donned the sheepskin more completely.

"This deputation is hardly representative of the village," said Leigh, in his wintry manner. "One man is a complete stranger. At least three others do not live in my parish. You, Colley, have expressed your religious convictions, or the lack of them, in no uncertain language, again and again. You call yourself an Atheist, and thereby proclaim yourself to be morally insane. Agnosticism I can understand. If you would content yourself with saying that we know nothing of things behind Nature, that the First Cause is unknowable and unrevealed," he went on, warming up and glad of the opportunity to get at the men who had never acknowledged him, "then I can meet you. But if you say there is no God you are no man."

The postmaster said nothing, but certain movements that he made seemed to relegate him temporarily to a place among the worms.

"If you like to assemble a general meeting of the parishioners—" Leigh began, when Halfacre broke in upon him hotly and heedlessly.

"They are outside, waiting at the gate; and they are going to smash your windows when it gets dark."

The postmaster opened his mouth hurriedly, to disclaim all connection with the speaker, although it was a course he had himself advocated; but Leigh was not listening. He winced slightly and, making a sudden turn, went to the kitchen, where some of the alien bellringers were still assembled, and returned in a few moments; behind him in the shadow of the hall loomed the huge figure of Gregory Breakback, who had conducted a series of grand sire triplets during the day, shouting "Bob" every other minute with a voice as big as the tenor bell itself, and he could have gone on ringing all night and stood up straight at the end of it.

Gregory gave a stride, which brought him to the side of Halfacre, and said in a voice which made the house echo, "I be a big man, and yew'm a little 'un. Shall us walk, or shall I lift ye?"

Halfacre decided he could not aid a good cause by resisting, and that it would be advisable to put aside revolutionary methods and go in peace that he might strike a better blow another day. The Downacombe rebellion looked like fizzling out. These country folk were poor weak fools, who burnt in private and paled in public; there was not a glimmer of the flaring torch about them; unlike townsmen, who knew what they wanted and were able to express themselves. The glorious principle of no work and plenty of money, the Saturnian age towards which the red flag guides, was fully appreciated by the clay-vessels of Downacombe, only they were too cowardly and inarticulate to help themselves or even to follow a leader; they would learn that discontent, added to rebellion, plus acts of violence and petty larceny, must in the long run amount to liberty—or to more servitude of a penal kind as the case may be. Halfacre went out scowling.

"Wull, sir," said Gregory in his usual way, addressing nobody in particular, but always ready with some tradition or anecdote, "some volks go out after rabbuts and finds adders, and some goes out after women and catches men. It be the contrairy way o' things. There wur two men flip-flapping Taw river, and another comes along and asks what they'm after. One answers 'en, 'I wants some trouts, 'cause I ha' nought vor supper,' and t'other he ses, 'I be just passing the time away.' Wull, sir, the hungry feller caught nought, but t'other caught a bagvul. And I reckon that be the way o' things." So saying Gregory pulled an apple out of his pocket, took a mighty bite, and strode back through the hall grinding it up like a horse.

The deputation, deprived of its brain power, huddled together like a patch of snow waiting for the sun to come and melt it. The trumpet was gone, and the other instruments seemed as vacant as the inside of a drum. There came a shuffling towards the door, which the small farmer tried to cover by muttering that he warn't afeard o' parsons and he hated 'em proper he did, and had hated 'em ever since he had been converted and brought home and received the grace of Christian charity under the ministry of his own nephew, who was a preacher on circuit and could always find a text in the Bible to damn any Government with. These remarks did not reach the rector's ears, and were not intended to. The rebellion had actually touched melting-point when Bill Chown stepped out like a man, touched his grimy forehead—there was a fringe of granite-coloured hair above his forehead although Bill was barely forty—and asked respectfully if he might speak.

"Certainly," said the rector, remembering the man's face well enough, but quite unable to recall his name.

"Us don't want land, parson," said Bill abruptly. "Us wouldn't knaw what to du wi' land if 'twas given us, vor land can't be worked wi'out money, and us ain't got money. What us wants is rights. Us wants to share and share alike wi' every one, wi' rich man and wi' poor man, them things what God Almighty meant wur to be shared."

The real leader was speaking at last, and Leigh realised it. Halfacre of the flaming torch was a hypocrite, Colley of the red flag was a humbug; both men were in comfortable circumstances, but Bill Chown was genuine. He had nothing except his clay-covered hands and the sweat of his brow. Downacombe was oppressed and in misery; the landlord was bleeding it dry of every comfort; living by the fastings of its villagers and the accumulated mites of its widows; the rents were built up with children's boots and winter firing. Leigh did not know that, perhaps he did not want to know it— a gentleman must live—and he had his roses and his wife to care for.

"So you are a Socialist too," he said.

"I don't knaw what yew means by Soshullist," Bill replied. "But if 'tis to want fair play I be one. Come and see my cottage, wull ye, parson? Bide there a night when there be a frisk of wind and snow, and if yew ses in the morning 'tis fit vor human volk, then I'll knaw what be right vor the poor. Wull ye come, parson? Yew ain't never been inside the cottage since yew come here."

"I will come some time," said Leigh, still coldly. He had to show them he was master.

"I'll tull ye how 'tis," Bill went on. "There be dree rooms, one under and two up over. They'm bedrooms, but one be all gone into holes like, and us can't put nought there, not faggot-wood, parson, vor 'twould get so wet us couldn't burn it. Me and wife sleeps in t'other, but the roof be gone so bad that us gets no rest when it be starmy, and I craves rest, parson, vor I works. Us pushes the bed first one side, then t'other, but bain't no gude, the roof be like any old sieve, and the walls be green got wi' mildew. Be that right, sir, be that fair play vor Christian volk that pays rent to a Christian parson? I'll tull ye a bit more. There be a kitchen fire down under where us bides. The smoke don't go into the chimney. A bit may now and agin, but not much on't. It comes out into the room. Us has the door o' the house wide open, winter and summer, in frost and snow, wi' the wind and rain blowing in, and then us often can't hardly speak vor coughing. If us wur to shut the door vor an hour to get warm us would be choked to death."

"I am afraid that is the case with all the cottages," said Leigh regretfully. "These big open fireplaces require so much draught, and the old-fashioned chimneys seem quite incapable of carrying off the smoke."

"It's the same at the post-office," said Colley sulkily.

"Mine used to smoke tu," said the small farmer, "but he don't now, vor I spent a bit o' money on putting 'en right. Yours don't smoke naythur I reckon, parson. A bit o' money does a proper lot o' gude."

"Have you anything more to say?" asked Leigh, turning again to Bill. "You said something about rights. What do you mean?"

"I means, sir, the rights what poor volk ought to have. I means, sir, the rights such as Dartmoor volk have. If us wur all commoners us wouldn't grumble, 'cause us would be free men and ha' the rights o' free men. And I ses there ought to be a law to mak' us commoners. A bit o' land to every man bain't no use, but what us craves is a big lot o' land, common to all, a bit o' land wi' woods, and stone, and turves, and rabbuts, wi' plenty o' grass and watter. Dartmoor volk pays no rent 'cept a shillun or two vor service. They gets their fuel and faggot-wood vor nought, and rabbuts, hares, fishes, and birds vor nought, and stone, gravel, and sand vor nought, and vuzz and vern vor nought, and pasturage and pannage vor nought; and they can purty nigh live vor nought. They ha' got a gude landlord, and as long as they gives him the service he lets 'em bide. A Prince be a better landlord than a parson, and I bain't afeard to say so."

The others murmured in sympathy, and Leigh flushed a little as he said, "The Prince has many interests. His position as regards Dartmoor is merely an official one."

"When Dartmoor volk wants to build, what du it cost 'em?" said Bill. "There be all they want lying on the moor, 'cept wood. When there be nought in the house vor food they goes out wi' a gun, and when there be nought on the hearth they lifts turves. They ha' rights, and I ses us should ha' rights tu. I be useful wi' my hands, and if I wur a commoner I could mak' my old cottage as gude as new. Us ha' got nought. If I shoots a rabbut I be a poacher. If I takes a stick from the bottoms I be a thief. If I cuts a bundle o' vuzz for thatch, or a bit o' fern vor the floor, I be robbing you somehow, and I mun pay vor't. I works hard, parson, me and wife works till us be mazed, but us makes a cruel poor living. 'Tis more like dying," he added, with a smile of grim humour.

Bill had said all he could, the words which he had rehearsed as he tramped to and from the mine, the sentences he had built up slowly and committed to memory day by day while scraping for his bread, and night by night while dodging the leakage from the roof. The postmaster, who was not accustomed to appear as junior counsel to such a common person as Bill Chown, tried to assert himself by saying submissively, "The place is all rot and mildew, and there's not a weather-proof building in the village—not in the part you own."

"This gurt big house be gude and sound," said Bill defiantly. "Yew looks after yourself, parson. Why don't yew look after we?"

Bill was getting bold and careless, and talking foolishly. Leigh became ruffled at once by anything approaching an attack; and this remark hardened his heart. He had almost made up his mind to try and meet the men. Now he decided he would beat them. There was indeed hardly any other course open to him, as rents and tithe had been insufficient to keep him out of debt; and he had a strong case after all.

"This time will have been well spent," he said, "if we can find a way out of our difficulties, settle our differences, and agree to dwell in peace. I am afraid that men of a very undesirable type have found their way to Downacombe, as they have to other places, advocating open revolution against the law. These men can do you no good. I have told you before to-day how impossible it is for me to help you. Were I wealthy I would rebuild the entire village. Nothing would give me more pleasure. I will put my case before you plainly—let me see. What is your name?"

"Chown, sir. Bill Chown to Uppertown."

"Ah yes, I remember now. That is a bad part," said Leigh vaguely. "Well, Chown, I will answer you, not as a clergyman, but as a business man. To repair your cottage and make it, as you say, habitable, I should have to spend at least a hundred pounds, and even that would mean only putting a patch on an old garment. You pay me eighteenpence a week rent, and I quite believe that you cannot pay more. If I were to spend that hundred pounds I should get no more from you than I am doing now, that is to say less than four pounds a year, and I should be a hundred pounds out of pocket. If I repaired ten cottages I should be a thousand pounds out of pocket. It would be no use increasing the rent, as none of you can afford to pay more, and without an increase, and a very large increase, I can do nothing to the cottages, for the simple reason that I haven't got the money, and could not pay the interest if I borrowed it. Apart from that, it would be a waste of money to attempt repairing. The surveyor, in his last report of the property, suggests that restoration is inadvisable. He recommended that all the buildings should be pulled down and new ones erected. If the money was given me for that purpose you could not benefit unless your wages were more than double what they are now. Your state would indeed be worse than it is now, as you would have no homes at all. I am afraid, Chown, you must make the best of a bad bargain and hope for better times."

"Us be mazed wi' waiting," said Bill. "The old cottages be tumbling down one after the other, and the young volk ha' gone to London and foreign parts, 'cause 'em can't find a roof to get in under, and the old volk ha' to go on the rates when the roof falls in on 'em. There wur two thousand volk in the parish when I wur born, and now there bain't half as many. There wun't be any in another fifty years, vor every building will ha' tumbled down 'cept the church and rectory, and the varms wun't be worked 'cause there wun't be a place for a man to bide."

"Things will improve," said Leigh cheerfully. "Farming is looking up."

"Be it?" said the small farmer, who had been sitting in a corner playing with a large red handkerchief. "I be main glad to hear that. Dalled if I knew it though."

"Not a bit of it, sir," exclaimed the postmaster, with some of his customary vigour. "If a farmer pulls through his year without drawing on his capital they say farming is looking up. Not a cottage has been built in the parish during the last hundred years, but scores have tumbled down, and their cob walls have been tilled into the fields for manure, and whole villages have been wiped out. The farmers would build fast enough if they could, but they haven't got the money."

"They are exactly in my position," said Leigh. "They are unable to borrow the money for cottage building simply because they cannot afford to pay their labourers sufficiently high wages to get back an adequate rent."

"He said varming be looking up," exclaimed the man of that persuasion. "Now he ses varmers ha' got no money. I don't hardly knaw where I be."

"Well, I have shown you my position," said Leigh indifferently. "I can't even place a new water-butt to a cottage without being out of pocket."

"If this is happy England I wish I was out of it," growled the postmaster, who always took extreme views, and was a pessimist whichever way the wind blew. "I've got a job which nobody would want to fight me for, but I'll stay with it till I lose it, as is likely enough," he said, with a glance at Leigh.

"The country be gude. There bain't none better in the world," said Bill. "'Tis the laws that be rotten and mildewy. Us craves liberty and us craves common rights," he repeated doggedly. "If us had quarries where us could crack stone, and bogs where us could dig turves, and woods where us could tak' faggots, if us wur like Dartmoor folk, I ses, then us could hold up our heads and reckon ourselves men. 'Tis a proper fine country, and I wun't leave mun till I be druve out on't. Us gets nought wi'out asking, and them that shouts most gets most, I reckon; but it bain't no use shouting when there be none to hearken. I wish ye gude-night, sir. I ha' the flasket to carry over to Metheral."

"I will come and see the cottage, Chown," said Leigh, as Bill turned to go. "And if the smoke nuisance can be stopped I'll see what I can do."

"Thankye, sir. Yew'm welcome," said Bill.

"Perhaps you'll have a look at mine too, sir," said the postmaster.

"I'll go round the village in a day or so," Leigh promised. "If you won't throw things at me," he added.

"Promises be like cream," Bill muttered into his hat. "The more yew spread 'em the thinner 'em gets."

So the great Downacombe rebellion came to a spluttering sort of end. The rector's coolness had extinguished the torch; his position was very nearly impregnable, as he had not only might on his side but right, as the world regards it. His parishioners were only beating the air by opposing him. They couldn't raise themselves an inch by shouting. They were like captured fish flapping their way towards water which they would never reach. The whole matter resolved itself into a political struggle; and politics change the condition of a country slowly. In the battle between brain and muscle, in an age of cunning, brain wins; for muscle is the foolish giant of fairy-stories, believing everything that it is told, and stabbing itself with the carving-knife that it may see the pease-pudding tumbling out of its stomach; and brain is the tricky mischievous sprite, the Jack of the stories, dodging up and down with sword and lantern, stabbing and burning heedless of consequences.

The men at the gate went away towards the inn to talk of the great deeds which they had not accomplished, and of the yet greater acts they might have performed under more favourable circumstances. Bill discovered his brother-in-law lying upon the road, his head supported against the hedge, his old hat a few yards away. John was indulging in a little refreshing sleep, weary after much beer-drinking. Bill tried to rouse him, mindful that John could take the washing back to Metheral and save him the long tramp. He had only to put John and the washing in the cart, at a safe distance from each other, and the horse would do the rest; but, as the sleepy man only babbled and would not move, Bill was forced to adopt methods which were usually effective, and left bruises.

"Kick 'en hard," said another man.

"I ha' kicked 'en dree times," Bill explained.

"I'll wake 'en," the other promised; and he did; for his boot was heavier and his leg stronger. John awoke with howls, and at once demanded whether the gates were open.

"I ha' come to the pony race," he said.

"Get up, wull ye? 'Tis time to get home along," said Bill.

"I be bit by adders. I be bit here, and here—aw, and here tu," howled John.

"'Twas only us waking ye. Come up, man. It be all over."

"Over, be it? Wull, and I've abin waiting vor 'em to start. How many of 'em wur racing? Who won it, Bill?"

"I reckon 'twas the parson," said Bill sadly.

CHAPTER XIII
ABOUT WEIGHTS AND MEASURES

It was Monday morning, the time of going back to work again, the dreariest part of the week; and it was weighing-day at the Convalescent Home, or Abode of Love, as Gumm called it. That gentleman had returned from burying his baby, and drawing its insurance money, and had become quite convalescent so far as that shock was concerned. It gave him an excuse for losing weight; as a bereaved parent it was his duty to drop a pound or two, which he could afford, as his body was puffing out like a balloon. Weighing took place before breakfast, when the body was at its lightest. There were many tricks among unscrupulous patients to add a little fictitious value to their weight, such as swallowing a pint of water, or slipping stones into their pockets, tricks which did not help them, as the truth was bound to come out.

The doctor appeared early, and there was a general scuffling into weighing-garments. He went at once to Halfacre's room and examined him. The verdict was not satisfactory, although he did not tell him so; neither was the weight. Halfacre had lost nearly a pound. They went back to the room after weighing, the young man apparently unconcerned, the doctor annoyed. He did not like Halfacre; of all his queer patients he was the queerest; a scholar of Balliol; the credentials were good enough; and yet the man had the boorish manners and cool insolence of the lower order of commoners. He might have Latin and Greek at his fingers' ends, but he had no polite English. He might occupy the position to which he seemed to be entitled by his more or less brilliant career; and yet the doctor could not rid himself of the memory that his most difficult patients were those of the lowest class. Halfacre had rebelled against sleeping in the open air; he said it was not a civilised habit, and had demanded a substantial window; and when he perceived that his request would not be complied with he suspended a blanket across the open space. This was removed with a threat of expulsion; afterwards Halfacre sulked and said nothing, except that his premature decease would be upon their consciences.

"I generally make it a rule to frighten a patient, if I see he is not doing his best," said the doctor. "So I tell you that if a man doesn't do well at the start he is not likely to do well at all. I can only give you the treatment which is likely to cure you, and will do so if you exert yourself. But if you refuse to use your determination I can't make you. There is no disease in which a patient can do so much for himself as this."

"I have other matters to occupy my mind," said Halfacre curtly.

The doctor laughed somewhat ironically. This was either supreme unselfishness or supreme folly; and he made up his mind it was the latter. Seating himself upon the bed he went on, "The matron tells me she has great trouble with you at meals. Once you were detected trying to smuggle your food into a paper bag."

"I object to making a brute of myself," Halfacre said. "This stuffing system is vile and degrading. Eating till one is sick, then eating again. It is savagery. It recalls the worst vices of the Roman Empire in its decadence."

"If I remind you that your life may depend upon it?" the doctor said, slightly amused.

"My reply is I cannot believe you."

The doctor rose, indignant, more at the supercilious manner in which the words were uttered than at the rudeness of them. He made a step to the door, then returned and said quietly, "I should like to know something of your family history. Have your parents, or brothers and sisters, shown themselves to be susceptible to any particular disease?"

"Every one is more or less diseased, either physically or morally," replied Halfacre. He resented the question as a most impertinent one. "My mother need not be included, as she is dead," he added coldly.

"Phthisis?" asked the doctor quickly; and Halfacre, to save time and trouble, assented.

"Is there any insanity in your family?"

"There may be. It is a disease which lies latent and discovers itself suddenly," came the exasperating answer. "I only concern myself with the present generation, which is immune so far as I am aware. The past neither troubles nor interests me."

"Well, Halfacre," said the doctor sharply, "I have this to say. You are a most unsatisfactory patient, and if you won't alter your ways I cannot keep you here. You go walks which I do not send you—to Downacombe usually, where it appears you visit the postmaster and make speeches to the villagers. You make no effort to cure yourself. You must change, my friend, or you must go."

Out went the doctor with an angry flush on his face, while Halfacre relieved himself by muttering, "Another of them—an enemy to the community, a fattener upon the poor, a fine gentleman, with twenty suits of clothes and one idea."

The man was such a mass of contradictory opinions, which crossed and cut each other repeatedly like the threads of a spider's web, that he was compelled to compare others with himself and judge them accordingly. He was actually passing sentence upon himself, without knowing it, however, for his brain was clever and his mind stupid; he could remember every fact of Roman History, but he could not draw a line between two characters. Vitellius and Constantine were alike to him, both Emperors and therefore oppressors; he could not perceive that one had been a man, the other a swine. For him there were two classes, the poor and the rich; every poor man was good and suffering, and every rich man was a tyrant. Wiser philosophers than Halfacre have fallen into the same error of labelling a character according to its class. The lowest and highest alike have a butcher's shop side to the character; the desires are the same, though the methods may be different; the gentleman will walk delicately after his prey, while the ploughboy blunders for it with yells and large boots. They both want the same fleshly things. The scholar says bluntly that man is a brute—and then he seduces his landlord's daughter; and never grasps the fact that he is a brute himself. The proper study of man is, not other men, but beauty which includes women; and the proper study of woman is also beauty which includes man: for the male body is more beautiful than the female body, as all statuary can testify; only the woman's head comes into flower more, and grows no thorns and spines, and careful culture has given her a kind of hybrid fragrance which at its best is overwhelming in a small room, and is, indeed, the most overpowering thing we know; and at its worst, when the woman tries to force thorns and spines for her own protection, it is a public nuisance. The proper study of every one, in secret if not in public, is beauty, which is the most simple thing created, for directly it begins to call itself beautiful it becomes exactly the opposite. The great beauty of the flowers consists largely in what appears to be their simplicity, their lack of knowledge that they are beautiful. If a consciousness of their fragrance was inspired into the purple petals of a violet the plant would soon become as unsavoury as a drain.

The weighing-machine was in a recess at the end of the passage, and here Mudd was indulging in the illegal traffic of a bookmaker, making and taking penny bets. Monday morning was a time of gambling, although it was strictly forbidden on account of its exciting and temperature lifting tendencies; but prohibition there as elsewhere made no difference. A modest pool was always made, the stakes going to the one who had put on most weight.

"Two to one I've put on three pounds," howled the publican, ignorant of the doctor's nearness until he heard a grim, "I'll take you, Mudd," which made him skip behind Miss Budge, who, he noisily declared, was large enough to shadow three of his size.

"He can't help it, doctor," explained Gumm. "He makes his living that way. He's paid fines and done time, but it don't cure him. When he's at home the police follow him about as if he was a pretty housemaid."

"Wait till I get you outside. I'll give you a thick ear to go on with," threatened the publican.

"Why don't you sack him, doctor?" complained Gumm. "What's the good of Mr. Sill praying for peace and brotherhood and God bless our 'ome, when we've got this serpent in sheep's clothing roaring at us?"

"Be quiet, you two," said the doctor. "Come along, fat lady."

This was to Berenice, who with all her faults, and perhaps because of them, was the doctor's favourite. She did not move, but said, "Hurry up, Miss Budge."

"I was not spoken to," said that lady. "The doctor always addresses me respectfully," she added, somewhat coldly.

"I'll give 'em a start," said Gumm, mounting the scales with various shocks and concussions. "I don't want it said that I died bashful. Three pounds and a 'alf of your best, please, doctor, and mother says will you cut it thick?"

There followed the usual juggling of weights and bar, and then the verdict, "Three quarters of a pound."

"Throw us in a bit o' fat, can't you, doctor?" Gumm pleaded.

"Hardly three-quarters," was the answer. "Pay over that twopence," whispered the avaricious Mudd.

"You'll have to wait till I bring my father's grey hairs to the grave and I get the bad shilling he's promised to cut me off with."

"Shell out, or I'll tell the doctor you've been kissing the servant."

"I won't. I'll plead the Gaming Act. What price the mushroom?"

Miss Budge was upon the scales. She had a trick of losing weight for a week or two, then bounding up with a fungoid growth.

"Can I get you a few more weights, doctor?" asked Gumm politely.

"Them little scales were never meant for this sort of thing. What we want is a weigh-bridge," said the publican, in the manner of one drawing attention to an evil of long-standing. "What's the tonnage, doctor?"

"Just over twelve stone," came the verdict, followed by the usual applause and the lady's expressions of amazement and disgust. "It is positively sickening," she said. "And I'm sure I don't eat much."

"She don't, doctor," said Mudd. "She sits next to me, so I can bear witness that she's speaking the truth. Last night she couldn't touch anything, except half a chicken, six potatoes in their jackets, with quarter of a pound of butter in each, a rice pudding and a dish of cream, two bananas and a pint of milk. I kept pressing her to try and swallow a few morsels, but 'twas no use. She was clean off her feed."

"Miserable liar," said Miss Budge.

"Now, Miss Calladine," said the doctor; and Berenice condescended to be weighed, and was found wanting. "I walked more last week, and I was sick twice," she explained; and for once the noisy Twins said nothing.

"We must try and keep that temperature down," the doctor said, as he prepared the scales for little Sill. "I'll have a talk with you presently." He glanced at the handsome brown girl who looked so strong and well and was yet so weak, and saw her face quiver a little.

"Come along, Sill," called the doctor, and Mudd began at once to whistle, "Onward Christian soldiers," while Gumm remarked, "He's a loser. Fasts twice a week, and never has more than two goes at the jam-pudding on Fridays."

"I feel heavier, anyhow," said the curate pleasantly.

"The Episcopalian waistcoat is a bit more on the slope," Mudd agreed.

"Three pounds," said the doctor.

"Just what I was asking for," said Gumm in an aggrieved voice. "The parson has the pull over us. He gets his bit by praying for it."

"I suppose you're too bashful to ask," said the publican with irony.

"I'm not in the business like he is. He knows the ropes," said Gumm. "If I was to pray for weight the orders would be sure to get mixed up, and likely enough we'd have rain instead."

The doctor took an arm of each of the hulking men-children and pushed them along the passage saying, "Out you go. I have to weigh Miss Shazell." The Twins went unwillingly, Gumm offering sixpence for permission to remain, and Mudd begging to be appointed clerk of the scales.

Winnie had worn night-dress and dressing-gown the first time she had been weighed, and it was therefore necessary that she should present herself in the same attire for every subsequent operation. She would never forget that second weighing. It was a chilly morning, there was a heavy mist and a slight flurry of unseasonable snow. A lamp was required by the scales. When she was called it was like going to execution; the early hour, the cold and mists, the solemn tramp of feet outside, and that horrid machine gleaming at the end of the passage. If she had lost any more weight it really was an execution, and she knew it; but if she could have gained there was a chance. There were the awful movements of the machine, the dreadful suspense which seemed to stop her breath, and then those wonderful and impossible words, "Four pounds." What a change they made in the weather. The mist became sunshine all at once, and the flakes of snow were butterflies jumping about in it. Young and pretty girls want to live; even when life seems to contain nothing for them, except those things which are unpleasant, they want to live. For life when one is young may always contain the unknown happiness and the unknown romance.

Winnie appeared, excited as usual, and very pretty, her flaxen hair glorifying her shoulders, and squire Tobias pattering at her side; and for some reason or other her little sawn-off nose was more distracting than ever. Even the doctor had to be a man sometimes, and as Winnie settled on the scales lightly, like a piece of pink heather blown in at the window, he made up his mind that she must get well. He had sometimes told girl patients, who badly needed a little encouragement, that they had put on weight, when as a matter of fact they had lost it, and the pious fraud had usually been successful and given the required stimulus to a greater effort. However there was no need for perjury that morning. There were five pounds more of Winnie than there had ever been before, five more exceedingly pleasant pounds of nice girlhood. She had beaten Miss Budge and knocked Sill into third place. She had won the sweep-stakes, which were presented to her by Gumm when the doctor had gone, with a blundering speech, an improper compliment, and a bad pun about a five-pound-note. She was delighted, and faltered her pleasure prettily; but did not tell the doctor, Berenice, or any one how those precious pounds of flesh had been built up, among St. Michael's oaks, with the water running down on two sides, and young leaves learning how to lisp on the other, and at the fourth a figure with fine head and ragged beard and extremely shabby coat concentrating all his artistic powers upon two dimples and a nose.

"You are improving in a marvellous way. You are my prize-patient," said the doctor, patting her arm gently. "I have never known such an improvement, and I should not have thought it possible. The last time I examined you the change for the better quite startled me."

"I should like to get well," said Winnie.

"It is merely a matter of time. I may tell you now what the doctor who sent you here said to me in his letter. 'She is a very delicate girl, peculiarly susceptible to a smoky atmosphere, thoroughly weak and sensitive. I am afraid she will not do well.' That was my own opinion," he went on. "When I saw you and had examined you I gave you three months. If you had gone back in the first fortnight I should have been compelled to send you home."

"How many months will you give me now?" asked Winnie, wondering why he looked the other way, as she was only standing there in her usual defenceless attitude biting at a little bit of her hair.

"As many as you like if you're good," he said laughing. "If you are well taken care of you might live to be eighty."

This was rather an exaggeration, and, although Winnie guessed as much, it pleased her. It would be nice to live a long time in some pleasant place, Wheal Dream for instance, if only she was well taken care of.

The sun was so powerful that strolling and sitting about, instead of brisk walks, were the order of the morning. The heat of the sun increases weakness just as it increases strength; and as the only shade in that part of the moor was to be found at Wheal Dream thither the patients went. They were not in a particularly hilarious mood, because Monday always cast a shadow and made them think of matters which they were not at liberty to express. Even Gumm and Mudd felt the chastening effect of weighing-morning, and found it difficult to insult each other with the proper degree of grossness. Miss Budge was the first to escape from the house after an unusually silent breakfast; and when the two girls, walking together, reached the rotten old fence which had been erected generations ago to prevent wandering drunkards from toppling into the mine shaft, and was itself tumbling about in every strange attitude of insecurity, they found the poor lady with red eyes; she was not very ill, but she was miserable, as she had long ago awakened to the fact that she was not old, but too old; that is to say, she had never been attractive to the opposite sex, and now, in spite of her light talk, she was not even attractive to herself. She was quite superfluous, and when a woman is that, she can only draw attention to herself by being eccentric, by wearing childish apparel, or painting an inch thick, or by screaming about the streets for visionary rights. If she cannot do any of these things she must sit at home, cherish a cat, chirp "pretty dick" to a canary, knit a sock or two, and grow gradually into a piece of wormwood. Women, strangely enough, never cry out for the privilege of using their free-will; they have been given the gift, but men and that queer thing modesty have never allowed them to use it, thus making women in one sense the lowest of all created things; for even the flea jumps as it likes and the bindweed twines where it will. Woman alone has to wait her invitation to jump and the order to twine; and if invitation or order never come, as is common enough, she must not jump, neither may she twine. Life was not altogether an apple-orchard for Miss Budge. She had reached that time of life when an unmarried woman has no age, she was alone, and although she had sufficient money for her needs, it was not enough to buy friends. The rich young man and the handsome girl can pick up as many fine-weather friends as they like, while they remain rich and handsome; but the poor man and the quaint spinster have to worm their way along, and are often elbowed out of the way while glancing enviously at the high-priced articles labelled, "Latest style of friendship; warranted to wear well; terms strictly cash," knowing well enough that such luxuries are not for them simply because they haven't got the money. They may stand at the corners and howl, but nobody will listen except the policeman, who will tell them to move on. The poor man in his lodgings, the quaint spinster among her faded furniture, with her lined and hungry face near the window between a pair of dusty ferns, looking for the postman who never stops there—these are tragedies of silence, without orchestra, scenery or an audience; darker in their spiritual way perhaps than the full-blooded deeds of drink and passion which fill the newspapers. The bright side of life is at the far end of a passage filled with guarded doors; those who are able to say the word Love without stammering may go through, though if they stammer it is all up with them, and the punishment for a fraudulent attempt is often a heavy one; all the others must unlock each door with a golden key, after strangling the guardians one by one.

"Billy, I've got the blues," said Berenice, when they had settled themselves at the old mine.

"I haven't—for once," said Winnie. "If you lean back you'll never have the blues again, but you'll have the blacks dreadful," she went on nervously. "Come and sit by me and I'll hold your hand."

That was Winnie's infallible remedy. She had an idea that any one was better after a restful period of her hand-holding, although a pathologist might have puzzled his brains asunder in trying to discover the secret. "Sit here," she said, patting a big cushion of moss.

Berenice was easily tempted from her rather perilous position at the edge of the wheal. She swung one arm round Winnie's waist, drew her close, and there they sat, flaxen hair against brown hair, like a couple of lovers.

"It's not often I get you all to myself like this," said Berenice cosily.

"Your hand is bigger than mine. Yours is brown and mine is white," said Winnie, playing with the brown fingers. "Don't you think mine is getting rather dumply?"

"Rather what?" asked Berenice, because she wanted to see Winnie mouth that word again.

"A dumply shape, fat, puddeny," laughed Winnie.

"Well, so it ought, considering all that weight. And I've lost again."

"You will make it up next week, and get a pound or two thrown in, to go on with, as Gumm would say. You needn't be blue, as I'm sure you are doing splendidly."

"I'm not. Doctor's been jawing like anything. He says I walk too fast, and think too fast, and do everything too fast, and I've got to consider myself a crock, and it seems to me I can't laugh without sending my beastly temperature up."

"But you can take things easily and be just as happy," said Winnie, doubling her companion's little finger and squeezing it playfully. "I should not want to kill myself with sports and dances. It's not worth the fun. I can sit still and be happy—if I have any one to sit with," she added rather unhappily.

"I can't. I must be in the middle of things or nowhere. I suppose I shall be nowhere," said Berenice angrily. She could not find any justice in her illness. "The doctor says if I tear about I am sure to have a—"

"Don't," cried Winnie shudderingly. "I can't hear that word. It is my horror. If I had one, the sight alone would kill me."

"You can shut your eyes and keep them shut until it's all over, and you know whether you are alive or dead," said Berenice with indifference, and a disregard of such a little matter as consciousness.

"But we mustn't talk like this. I shall be all right by this evening when I have written home and made my lamentation. Old Budge is leaving soon. She needn't have come as there's nothing much the matter, only she likes being here and having company. Poor old thing, she lives all alone and plays cards with her servants every evening to pass the time."

"I like being here too," said Winnie.

"But you're a miserable little humbug. You used to cry and sob and howl until I was nearly coming in to smack you."

"I was very ill in those days, and the cold was dreadful. I had snow on my pillow one night, and I was so thin that the wind blew right through me."

"I heard you blubbering," said Berenice, "and when doctor came in I asked about you, and he said, 'It's a case of kill or cure with that little thing.' I said I didn't like to hear you, and mightn't you have a hot bottle; and he said, 'Certainly not, let her freeze'—unfeeling brute. He didn't know I had a hot bottle. I brought it with me and heated the water with a spirit-lamp. How much longer are you staying?" she asked.

Winnie flushed and trembled, and squeezed her companion's finger more than ever as she murmured. "I hardly know." After a pause she added more boldly, "Until mother gets tired of keeping me here, I suppose."

This was a lie, quite a small and white one, one of those unnecessary little remarks which fall easily off the tongue and cannot be recalled, and lead to troubles. Winnie was sorry she had spoken; and she was positively miserable when she heard Berenice say, "Where do you live, Billy?"

"Oh!" exclaimed Winnie, but she had to answer, "Near Plymouth." That was vague, and ought to be satisfactory. She felt sure she would be forgiven, as an untruth cannot be wicked if it harms no one.

"In the country?" asked the brown girl.

"You live at Bideford, don't you?" said Winnie with startling innocence.

"Just outside, in a big sand-hole."

"You ought not to have broken down," said Winnie, trying to steer away from the quicksands of her own existence. "You don't come from the smoke."

"Too much general strenuosity," said Berenice moodily. "Bideford, Appledore, and all that bit of level land between the Torridge and the sea, are beastly unhealthy. But you don't come from the smoke?" she said, and stopped, leaving poor Winnie at the mercy of Beelzebub.

"Well, it's foggy and damp—and there is smoke from Plymouth," she faltered, hoping she would not be compelled to utter the awful word Keyham.

"The wind brings it over, I suppose?"

"Yes," said Winnie eagerly, which was another untruth, as the smoke upon her home was so dense that it would have required a regular Euroclydon to have swept it away.

"What's your address? I shall write to you, and come and visit you. Billy, you're breaking my little finger in two places."

"What a pretty ring," said Winnie desperately, twisting the bauble round and round, and thinking of one that was hers, a hateful object, buried in cotton-wool at the bottom of her box.

"Don't be such a kitten. I'll write down your address now—on the last page of this book where they've just married and are going to scratch at each other ever afterwards. Miss Winifred Shazell— have you any other name, Billy?"

"Yes, Erica."

"Why, that means heather," exclaimed Berenice.

"Does it? I never knew. I'm not certain I was given that name at my baptism, but father always called me Erica because he said it suited me. I never knew why. I was only a small wild moorland maid in those days."

"Don't think me clever," said Berenice. "But I heard that Halfacre of ours talk about erica this and erica that, and he told me it meant heather. Now, what's the address?"

That question was a big stone wall. Winnie had to climb it with a fib, or knock her head against it by being silent. Number 6, Butcher's Row, which was her correct address, and was, as she had said, "near Plymouth," was clearly inadmissible. She sighed and thought of many pleasant places which would do quite well to live at, but they were all on the Dartmoor side of the big town which has been baptised by the river Plym; and she couldn't say she had merely come from one part of the moor to another. It would not be true, but then, whatever she said would not be true. Halfacre knew all about Butcher's Row, and the awful people who lived opposite, and the equally appalling personalities who dwelt upon each side, but she had been forced to tell him the truth because he had made her, just as she was being compelled to tell Berenice untruths because she was making her.

"It's only a little place," she said, trying to speak contemptuously, referring truthfully to her home, although Berenice was not to know that, and hoping that she need not mention the name just because it was little.

"Dear little Bill," said the brown girl. "I believe you hate your home."

"Oh no," cried Winnie. "Of course not;" although she did.

"Miss Winifred, William, Dimples, Shazell," said Berenice, writing part of this down in small characters.

"Heatherside," gasped Winnie. That was a good safe name for a house, suggestive of the country and liberty; and not so very false either, as she remembered there was a black lodging-house, right at the bottom of the most unsavoury bowel of Keyham, called for some reason unrevealed Heatherside. She passed it on her way to work, and had sometimes seen a half-dressed man smoking a clay pipe at the door. The next house to it, which was kept under close surveillance by the police, was called "The Lindens," though Winnie was rather vague as to what a linden might be, and the tenants of the house had never bothered their heads about such a matter. Perhaps there had been lime-trees when that street had been planned, but they would not have stood long after the builder had caught sight of them. The sight of a piece of grass or a bank of flowers—weeds they're called—drive a borough council or a builder to fury, and when a tree appears the latter gentlemen invariably "sees red" and nothing else until the horror has been removed, and he can gaze with sanity restored upon soothing heaps of mortar, mud and brickbats.

"It's down," said Berenice. "Any one might think you were confessing to a murder, silly blue-eyed thing."

"Well, it's not a nice part," owned Winnie, hoping Berenice would misunderstand her; which she did.

"Villages are horrid when a town grows towards them. They are neither one thing nor the other. I suppose Heatherside near Plymouth wouldn't find you, though."

"No," said Winnie plaintively. Then she closed her eyes and plunged into deep waters, murmuring, "Plymstock—it's a horrid place, but there's a fine screen in the church." She thought she was right in that final statement.

"How do you pass the time, Billy? You don't seem to care a hang about clothes. Have you any musical or artistic vices?"

The little girl shook her head. It was easier to tell the truth mutely; and her tongue had become so wicked she could hardly trust it.

"Do you whirl round any social circle? Is Plymstock a centre for tea and talk?"

"I don't," said Winnie quite truly. The late afternoon was a busy time in the sub-post-office, as people rushed in and out with grimy germ-infested coppers, anxious indirectly to improve the revenue. People in that district bought their stamps one at a time, and sometimes Winnie became so confused that she overlooked a penny which its owner never forgot, and she had to make the deficiency good out of her shallow purse.

"You don't play games," Berenice went on. "I suppose you just lie about and dream. But how about the men?"

Winnie wriggled, and thought it was time to discuss mining or some other moorland industry. There was a peat-bog upon the other side of the river. She pointed to it and asked Berenice if she wouldn't rather talk about that.

"Answer me properly, or I'll push you down the shaft and then hurl rocks upon you. It's not likely that men leave you alone, because every male thingumbob here is in love with you."

"Oh no," cried Winnie decidedly. "Not all."

"Don't contradict. I hate you really, because I was number one before you were let loose, and now I'm bracketed second with the Budge atrocity."

"Miss Budge is silly, but she's kind. Don't say anything nasty about her," pleaded Winnie. "She strokes my hand and calls me pretty names—and that's the sort of thing that makes me fat," she said more brightly.

"Tell me about the men," said Berenice; but Winnie rebelled, and declared she wouldn't. So the brown girl pinched her until she gave little rabbit-like screams, and said she wouldn't stay to be persecuted any longer, but would go and sit with Miss Budge who was diligently perusing a romantic tale lower down the gorge. However, Berenice held her tightly; and then she said, "The first evening you were here, before you were smacked and put to bed for being so ill, l saw an engagement-ring nearly falling off this wee thin finger. Where is that ring now, Billy?"

"Why, it has fallen off altogether," said Winnie, trying to speak lightly.

"You haven't lost it?"

"No," came the answer, the short word sounding very long and woeful.

"Billy, speak properly, or I'll shake you. It's a regular operation to get an answer out of you. If you are still engaged you have got to tell me, and then I shall see the man, and if he isn't good enough, which is quite impossible, I shall refuse my consent. I don't want you to marry, little Bill. I want to have you myself."

Winnie wondered at that. She knew nothing of the love which goes out to its own sex and almost disregards the other; an unnatural and barren kind of love, and yet as enduring as any. But there was no getting away from the evidence of that ring. She might tell Berenice a part of the truth; she was always wanting to tell some one; there might be a way out even then, and if there was one Berenice might possibly suggest it. So she said in a suffocated voice, "Yes, I am engaged."

"And you're wretched about it?"

"Rather. I—I don't care enough about him."

This was putting the fact so mildly that it almost amounted to another untruth.

"Now I understand your wobbling ways. A man has got hold of you, and you're much too nervous to tell him to let go. Say yes."

"Partly yes," Winnie amended.

"You must toss him overboard, and shut your ears if he screams and says he can't swim," went on the girl with the club-shaped heart. "My dear Billy, it's so easy to chuck a man over, as easy as cracking an egg-shell, and it's fun, too, when you get used to it. Look here, I'll chuck him over for you."

"Oh no," begged Winnie, who was beginning to have trouble with her throat. "I am bound to him, Berenice—really. He's given me so much."

"Presents you mean. Send 'em back. Pack 'em all off in a box with a nice scented note saying, 'Take back the gifts that thou gavest, man, for I don't love you any more, man, and as a matter of fact I never did love you, man, but I said I did just to save you from cutting your throat and making a mess on the carpet, man.'"

Winnie tried to laugh, but the effort ended in oozy sounds which brought on coughing. She bowed herself like a weeping-birch, then quite suddenly turned and kissed Berenice, saying with a sob, "There, that's one for you."

"Well, of all the dear children" began Berenice.

"Don't say anything more about that man. Let's talk about dreams and ghosts, and postmen with wooden legs, and owls with false teeth, and—and wheals full of moons and stars."

"Billy, darling, you're just as mad as a bee in a bottle," said Berenice tenderly. "Tell me the truth," she commanded, loving her, smoothing her fair hair, and running a finger playfully over the sawn-off nose. "Do your people know of the man and like him? And why have you been and made a small goose of yourself?"

"No more of him, please. He makes my head ache," said a small voice.

"Oh, but I am not going to have my Billy bullied," said Berenice. "We'll write to him in the rest hour this evening. I'll slip into your room and tell you what to say. I've had practice. I know something about men. They curl up like frightened spiders when they get marching-orders, and they don't tell any one because they are too conceited. Is it an engagement on the sly?"

There was a negative movement upon Berenice's shoulder.

"Does your mother know?"

There was an affirmative movement.

"Oh, Billy, he's not below you—not a rich bounder?"

There was no movement at all.

"Squeeze my hand if he is."

It was one way out of the maze, perhaps the easiest way, so Winnie took it.

"Don't say your mother is driving you into it. Billy, I'll look after you," Berenice whispered passionately. "I'll face them for you, and then we'll go away and live together. The brutes—they shan't have you, darling. I love you too much, sweet little Bill—I do, with all my soul. If I have been nasty once or twice it was because of my temper, and I was cross for a bit when Tobias left me for you; but I do love you, and I'm not going to let any man, mother or monster take you away from me."

She broke into a fit of coughing, put her handkerchief to her mouth, and shuddered when she saw a spot upon it; then flung the thing away down the shaft. Winnie shivered too, although she had seen nothing; but she could not understand that violence or Berenice's meaning, or what it was that had been offered her, or that mysterious affinity which exists sometimes between creatures structurally alike.

"You're not a man," she said playfully. That was the only sort of love that Winnie comprehended, the love between Strongheart and Clinging-heart. "We are both girls," sighed Winnie.

"I don't know what I am sometimes," said Berenice. She was cold again, terribly frightened by that little spot which seemed to rise into the air between her and the sun and stain all things red. She was not made for passion; neither was Winnie. They were weak growths, loosely rooted in the soil, every gust of wind straining their roots, threatening to remove and whirl them away to the place where the storm ends.

George was wasting his time again, sitting at the window, his hands arched about his eyes, watching, not two heads, but one head which appeared sometimes through a rift in the bracken. He had seen the girls go down; Winnie never passed the wheal unobserved, for those patient eyes were always watching for her, and the tongue which pretended to be so flippant was always trying to speak to her across the gorge which existed in more senses than one. His physical weakness increased his love, that unusual love which is simply a craving to reach a soul. There he sat while his paintbrush stiffened, and peeped between his hands, which made a frame to that small picture. Presently the heads disappeared and Wheal Dream became unadorned. George stirred, released his breath with something like a groan, and then, with a scuffle and a wriggle and a merry pattering of little pads, Tobias trotted in at the ever-open door and said in his own way, "Hello." He had brought a stone with him, a scrap of gleaming quartz, and he placed it carefully in the middle of the room, licked it, danced round it, and wagged the words—

"This is a stone, the geological formation of which I do not pretend to understand. You take it, George, and behold I leap. You fling it from the window and I disappear. I get it, I return in one twinkle, I deposit it at your feet; again you throw; again I vanish. It is simple. It goes on for ever. What say you?"

George understood dog-English fairly well. What man who lives much alone does not? Tobias was a pleasant purgative; no one could retain melancholy for long in the presence of that joyous bounding little body of frolicsome flesh and indiarubber bones, every square inch of which seemed to be charged with ten thousand volts of fun and mischief.

"So you have called upon me at last," said the artist in his dry way. "We have been residents for some time, but you have avoided me until to-day, although we have nodded at each other in passing, and I have noticed an abashed look in your eye as though you were saying, 'I must really go and call on that man.' I am glad to see you, young sir. It is kind of you to visit a crabbed and venerable man, and I would not suggest that in so doing you are actuated by any selfish motive. Mr. Tobias, I believe, aged two? You have the advantage over me in name. You are among the minor prophets, although theologians might declare you to be apocryphal. I am George, a husbandman, not a man who is a husband, nor even one who labours in tillage, but one who is false to the etymology which has been forced upon him, has gone the wrong way, left the unploughed field for the primrose-bank, and seeks to supply the public with precisely those things which they do not require. I trust we shall become better acquainted. Even at this early stage of our friendship you will permit me to remark that your complete lack of dignity is hardly becoming to a Biblical character, and indeed is more suggestive of a bibulous nature. Regard me as George—a poor name and not even my own; for the angel who edits the directories of the heavenly country bright has only to shout that name to have saints, martyrs, and agricultural labourers crowding in upon him by the million. Georgie or Geordie, if you care to be familiar, and I will even answer to the bucolic title of Jarge. I must, however, mention that there is no connection between me and the gentleman who has become notorious through his scandalous habits of kissing the girls and making them cry. He is more particularly referred to in the police-reports as pudding and pie, and his alias is Porgie. It has been suggested in this immediate neighbourhood that this gentleman and myself are one and the same person, and I have been compelled to write to the newspapers disclaiming all connection. Were I to kiss the girls they would doubtless weep bitterly, but up to the present time I have neglected every opportunty in that direction."

George was bustling about the work-room all the time he was rambling his rubbish, trying to restore a certain sequence to a number of sheets of manuscript which had been blown about while he was keeping vigil at the window. Tobias stood guarding the stone, his tail working like an excited weathercock, his tongue out two inches, his eyes as bright as a couple of wet stones. Then he discovered something sedate enthroned upon a perch, and moved towards it with a sniffing nose.

"Pardon me," said George. "This is the senior partner, who supplies such brains as the firm possesses. Our Mr. Bubo, past-master of the order of crepuscular and obfuscated owlets. He is not an old master, nor is his present condition one of masterly inactivity; neither is he a sleeping partner. At the present moment he is brooding in a dark and inscrutable manner over the ultimate destiny of the short-eared strigidae. I must apologise for such imposing words, but he always uses them. A philosopher cannot think except in polysyllabic words. You are requested not to tease the metaphysician. He might get angry and peck you; and then you would probably die of bubonic plague."

The little dog laughed at such sport, and bringing his stone laid it tenderly at the artist's feet. George had finished his collection, and was free to accept the invitation. He snatched at the stone, Tobias hurled his mad self upon the hand, was rejected, came again with furious barks and gentle teeth, and they rolled together upon the floor, a disgraceful and unseemly sight. Bubo lifted up his eyes to heaven, and would have wept had he only known how. The man of forty was playing the fool, and it was doing him more good than all the arts.

"This is atrocious. My reputation," gasped George. "All is now lost, including honour. Down with heartache. *A bas* respectability. *Conspuez* my grey beard. To the devil with my summers. Ah, would you, assassin! The foul fiend fly away with my Georgian whiskers. Angels restore me a dimpling childhood. Peace, youngster, we are discovered. The bird of wisdom fixes us with a hypnotic stare. The wise have no compassion upon folly. Bubo," he shouted in his boisterous, boyish way, "we are enlarging the premises, extending the business. This is the athletic department—Tobias and Brunacombe, aged two."

There came a shadow across the floor, a body at the open door, and a rather sneering voice asking if anything was wrong. George shambled up and stood confused like a school-boy caught making faces at his master. It was Halfacre with a theological looking volume under his arm.

"Only having a game with the little dog," George muttered, blowing out his cheeks and slapping his hands together, quite unconscious of his wildly ruffled head and the dust and white hairs which smothered his sack-like clothing.

"I thought the place was on fire, or that you were in a fit," said Halfacre, walking inside and gazing about with his nose elevated. Folly such as playing with a dog was beyond his comprehension. It was the duty of man, not to skip about like a young calf, but to devote his energies, and life if necessary, to the great questions of social reform. Halfacre had a poor opinion of George, regarding him as a man whose duty it was to go out with a pot and brush and beautify gate-posts, and call himself what he was, an artisan, instead of staying at home, painting canvases different colours and claiming to be a gentleman. Every man who is a humbug regards others as humbugs, just as every drunken man thinks he is the only sober person in a crowd. Halfacre had no idea how hard George worked for the very little money he got, but he had a clear notion that everything he owned ought to be taken away from him and given to those poor people of the stamp of Jimmy Gifford who did not feel inclined to work for themselves. The coat-of-arms, those three pelicans wounding themselves, aroused his anger. No man had any right thus to advertise his possession of such a piece of arrogance. Possibly it was the idea which was distasteful to him, the pelicans drawing blood to feed their young. Had they been sensible birds, imbued with proper social ideas, they would have fed the youngsters upon the blood of somebody else.

George felt at no disadvantage before this man, although Halfacre was tidy and well-brushed; many a young woman would have adored him in the up-to-date fashion by drowning herself with him, but the artist could not help thinking that such girls would belong to the lowest class. Halfacre was well-dressed, yet his clothes would not hang properly; they looked as if they had been made for some one else. There was about him an undefinable air of awkwardness, as if he wanted to behave in the right way and didn't quite know how to manage it. While he was standing there George recognised that he himself was a gentleman; and Halfacre somehow suggested the sort of individual who would wear a silk hat in the country, applaud at a theatre, and peruse the feuilleton in a halfpenny newspaper.

"You have a nice place here. Don't you find it hard to pass the time?" said Halfacre.

"I can pretty nearly pass the time by answering that question," said George rather irritably. "Everybody supposes that because I live out here I can't be doing anything."

"Reading?" asked the other, absolutely ignoring easel and canvases and all other signs of labour.

"And writing and arithmetic; and teaching my owl to hoot in F flat," said George crossly. "That's how I make my living."

"It must be interesting," said Halfacre cynically. "You have plenty of books. Any in Greek and Latin?" he asked eagerly.

"A few, but I never look at 'em."

"Can you read Latin?"

"I don't try," said George. "What's the good?"

"That is nonsense, Mr. Brunacombe. Absolute rubbish," cried Halfacre in a strained and excited voice which made George glance round quickly. "I am a classical scholar—a scholar of Balliol," he added, dropping his voice to a whisper of awe and reverence. "There is no man living who could give me information concerning the enclitic particles. I am an exceedingly clever man, Mr. Brunacombe."

George did not hasten to light a joss-stick and wave it beneath Halfacre's nose; nor did he place the man between burning candles as a preparation to falling down and doing him worship. He merely snorted and made a face at Bubo, who responded by scratching his eye as though desiring to draw the visitor's attention to the absence of green in that large and glassy orb.

"I too am an exceedingly clever man, Mr. Halfacre," said George gravely, wondering which of them, the lion comique, or the lion bombastic, would outroar the other.

"You a clever man!" cried Halfacre in a wild and startled way. "What are your honours? Are you even a master of arts?"

"I'm an old master—at least I shall be when I've been dead a few hundred years," George chuckled. "My pictures are on their way to the National Gallery and the Louvre, though they may be a long time getting there. My place in literature has not yet been assigned, but I expect to come somewhere between the unknown author of the book of Job and Jane Austen. As a sculptor Michael Angelo comes an easy second to me, although I must admit I have never completed a model, and as an artist I should have been unrivalled if there had only been no competition. Music I have not taken up seriously, and yet my oratorio scored for tin-whistle, mouth-organ, and jew's-harp has never been imitated. I have also a genius for marbles, and have only once been defeated. That was at school, where Smith Major conquered me, not by superior skill, but by punching my head at a critical moment."

Halfacre gave an undecided cackle, and said, "This is only fooling."

"All life is fooling," said George cheerfully. "Even our work consists in fooling others to get money to fool with. Like to hear one of my sonnets, Mr. Scholar? There is a native simplicity about them which appeals to every one, to crowned heads as well as bald heads, and they have a touching pathos which can only be described as entirely Brunacombian. I owe nothing to Shakespear; the debt, if any, is upon the other side. There is a cipher running through the tragedy of Hamlet which if it were discovered, and I am free to admit that it never will be, would prove to the astonished world that the masterpiece is one of those little things thrown off by myself in a few idle and prenatal moments. Here is one," said George, picking up a scribbling book, and glancing in a none too friendly fashion at his uninvited visitor, who was standing near the table white-faced and uncomfortable. Halfacre was entirely unaccustomed to this style of conversation. He could make nothing out of it though it was clearly nonsense, but he was wondering if it was meant to be insulting or whether it was really genteel to talk like that. George started a little when he saw that face, and the eyes protruding slightly, and the fingers on each hand worrying each other like ten excited infants. The man looked distraught and ill. He went on, however, without mercy, for he could not forget how this man walked and talked with Winnie, and how he had worn that white heather, and how he had sneered to see the romp with Tobias.

"It is written in dialect, and the metre is irregular. A genius is not to be bound by trifles. Only school-children and lawyers require a knowledge of spelling. Great poets and business-men rise superior to it. When a child spells opportunity with one p he gets spanked, unless he can plead a previous American training; but if I omit the p through ignorance, it is called a poetical license. Here is the sonnet. It is called 'The Soul's Awakening,'" said George, in deep and tender tones. Then he read in his most impressive manner—

"Me and Bubo, and old Vaither Chown,
Us went all together to Exeter Town,
Where us bought some glasses vor poor old Granmer;
Granmer be blind, and can't very wull see,
And one day her took the old jackass vor me."

There was a blundering movement in the room, and George looked up with a broad grin in time to see Halfacre's back retreating rapidly, and to hear a wild voice muttering something about "that moon;" which the artist heard and wondered at. He was soon laughing with a noise that must have followed the scholar into his retirement, slapping his leg and saying to Bubo, "That wur one vor his nob. Us downed 'en proper in a fair wrastling-match, though us bain't gurt poets and artists, but plain manufacturers of rubbish for the children of Israel. He won't come here again, Bubo. A little bit more of his turned-up nose and white teeth, and we should have been sprawling on the mat here, with you for referee, in the Graeco-Roman classical style. I'd have given him the half-Nelson and a whole Napoleon under your very eyes. I'd have smashed him into enclitic particles with an accent on every one of them. That'll teach him to walk into the factory during business hours to sneer at the old-established firm of Bubo and Brunacombe."

There came a strange noise from the little patch of steep garden below the Wheal House, and George hurried to the window and looked out. He kept bees; two hives were beneath the hedge, and between them and the house were broad patches of flowers. Halfacre had not gone away. He was in that patch of garden, and there was evidently something the matter with him. Possibly George had upset him badly, perhaps he was labouring under some unpleasant form of influence, or had become afflicted with sudden delusions. He was running after a large majestic bumble-bee which boomed derisively before his nose; and he was striking at it furiously, cursing it, shrieking at it—

"Go out, you blackguard. Get out of the garden. You are not Mr. Brunacombe's bee. You have no right to the honey here. Get out on the moor, you filthy blackguard."

His face was very white, and his dark eyes seemed to be on fire with fury. George put his lips into whistling shape, but made no sound and said nothing just then; while Halfacre went on screaming, "Get out, you lazy, thieving blackguard. You want to rob

Mr. Brunacombe's bees." He had his coat off by this time, and was beating at the noisy insect with it, shouting, "Go out and get heather-honey, you scoundrel. Get out on the moor, you old blackguard—get out."

CHAPTER XIV
ABOUT REALITIES AND UNREALITIES

When the doctor came on his mid-day round Winnie obtained permission to go that afternoon to Downacombe. She was rather an ignorant little girl, and there was clinging to her the remnants of the old superstition concerning the spiritual power of priests. Leigh was such a good man; she might confess her difficulties to him; and then perhaps he would show her a way out, and even absolve her from meeting the debt. Union with that offensive but well-meaning Hawker had always seemed impossible even when she was too ill to say anything in her own defence; but now that she was getting well in her native wind, and the time of the marriage was near, she shrank the more.

George had quite succeeded in making Winnie believe that she was obnoxious to him. This was partly due to his nervous temperament and partly to the keen perception of his poor position. And Winnie always tried to frown, and answer shortly, and look as bored as possible while he was painting her. It was true that when she looked down at her boots he devoured various portions of her with his eyes, and sometimes when he turned round she had the impudence to blow him a kiss with her fingers. They understood each other so well that, while Winnie supposed George to be quite one of the brightest planets which circle round the sun, and as much above her as the top of a mountain is above the bottom of a valley, George supposed Winnie to be a happy young lady living in the lap of luxury, and therefore as much above him as the mountains of the moon are above the ooze of the terrestrial seas. That was George's own way of putting it, not a very complimentary way, but he was not accustomed to putting a high price upon himself.

Before Winnie started for Downacombe there was some fun in the garden. Every bit of amusement was snatched at eagerly by the patients, and when it was rumoured that Gumm and Mudd were wandering about making fools of themselves the others went out to enjoy the spectacle. The publican and the sinner had gone into the kitchen, which was strictly speaking out of bounds, with the idea of being temporarily faithless to their wives, the cook being a buxom wench who was not averse to the insanitary practice of kissing. Mudd was first upon the scene, but before he could do more than supply the road to hell with another paving-stone Gumm arrived, and, with that lack of breeding which was so strongly marked upon his character, pushed aside the man in possession with the blunt and conceited statement that the young woman had repeatedly expressed a decided preference for his embraces. Mudd replied with a single noun at the end of several adjectives; and when it looked like strife the damsel, who was just going to prepare stuffing for a goose, promised she would grant the somewhat easily won favour of her lips to the first man who would bring her in a bunch of sage. The overgrown infants blundered off, made their way into the garden, and then found themselves helpless. Neither of them knew the herb sage from an oak-tree.

"What are you two looking for?" called Miss Budge pleasantly.

"My false teeth," growled Gumm. "I sneezed 'em out of my head just now, and I heard 'em drop about here. Alfred Mudd is looking for what he ain't ever likely to find, and that's his character."

"What is it really?" whispered Miss Budge.

"We're just out to pick a bit of sage for cookie dear," said Mudd in an unguarded moment.

"Sage," laughed the spinster. "Why, there it is."

"Shut up," cried Berenice, pulling her arm down.

"Where?" asked Mudd.

"You're treading on it, fathead," Gumm shouted. "I ain't. This is—I don't know its right name, but we used to call it a bloody nose at school."

Gumm unobtrusively picked a nasturtium leaf and sniffed at it.

"You're getting warm," said the curate to Mudd.

"He don't need to be told that," said Gumm, wading off with a predatory eye upon some dock-leaves.

"Why don't you pick it, Mr. Gumm?" asked Berenice innocently.

"I want to show him up," said Gumm, wagging his big head at the publican. "Didn't you see him nearly tread on it just now?"

"No, I didn't," cried every one.

"I did. Put his webbed feet right across it."

Mudd was looking longingly at the rhubarb, desiring to put out his hand and seize a portion, only not daring to run any risks.

"Are you quite certain you know yourself?" asked Miss Budge.

"I know it ain't a mineral, nor yet an insect," replied Gumm.

"Sure it isn't a fruit?" suggested Sill.

"You're funny, ain't you?" said Gumm, who was beginning to wish he had never gone near the kitchen. "I picked sage in our back yard before you ever wore white socks and kissed your mammy."

"Now he thinks it grows on the ground," said Berenice.

"Where else would it grow—up in the blooming sky?" Gumm shouted; then he went on reviewing geraniums, larkspurs, and petunias, and coming to the conclusion that they were all unsuitable.

"It might save time," suggested the curate pleasantly, "if you would get a spade and dig for it."

"And if you go on being so smart, you'll bust all your buttons off," growled Gumm.

"Go on, Jim. We're watching you," cried the shameless publican.

"There'll be a few watching you if I come across and knock holes in your turnip. What are you looking at, Miss Shazell?"

"The sage," said Winnie sweetly.

"Look the other way, Billy dear," cried Berenice, swinging her round, while Gumm shuffled stealthily towards the spot she had been looking at; but there were so many different things to choose from he didn't know which to take.

"Pretty nearly got it then," sneered Mudd.

"Look here," shouted the other. "Do you know sage when you see it?"

"Of course I do," blustered Mudd.

"Show it me then," roared Gumm; but the publican was not going to be caught so easily.

"I'll give you half-a-sovereign if you put your hand upon it," Gumm went on, drawing two coppers out of his pocket.

"I'm not going to rob your landlord of his rent," shouted back the publican.

"There you are, Mr. Mudd," said Miss Budge, pointing slyly to a clump of marigolds.

"We ain't all quite as soft as we look," came the angry answer. "I do know buttercups when I see 'em."

There was a bush of rosemary beside the wall, and Gumm took his stand over it with an idea that the odour was distinctly culinary. He wiped his nose upon the bush and said it smelt all right, and he rather thought the cook would like some of it anyhow; which produced more laughter, after which Mudd declared, "That's lavender."

The others applauded, and Sill remarked, "He was very nearly right that time."

Gumm gave a sigh of relief. He had very nearly decided to stake his reputation upon the rosemary. After his brilliant remark an equally bright idea occurred to Mudd. He said he hadn't finished his milk, which he had left in the sitting-room; so he went off in a great hurry to do his duty, while his rival followed his disappearance with suspicious eyes, more than half afraid he was on his way to the kitchen to secure an unfair advantage. However, Mudd went to the sitting-room, and as a proof that he was there appeared at the window to bawl insults. Then he turned to Halfacre, who was reading in a corner, and producing a hot and crumpled mass of leaves, snatched in desperation from trees, shrubs and plants, begged to be told whether the herb sage was included among them.

"Well, what's the thing like?" said Mudd, when informed that the desired leaf was not there. "Tell us, there's a good chap, and I'll have the chance of me life to make a fool of old Gumm. He don't know the thing from a cabbage, and to tell the truth I don't either. I know parsley, and I know broad-beans and potatoes when I see 'em growing, but I don't know much about t'other flowers."

"Sage," muttered Halfacre wearily, stroking the hair from his forehead with a moist and shaking hand. "It is a herb of the salvia or mint family."

"Bust the Latin," Mudd broke in. "Talk about it in English."

"It is used for flavouring meat," said Halfacre languidly. "You must know that."

"Course I do. What's it like?"

"It is a small plant, with greyish-green crinkled leaves."

Mudd instantly projected himself from the window, and approached the group with the question, "Ain't the silly blighter found it yet?" Gumm was picking everything he could find, and when his rival appeared he pushed the bunch into his face saying, "Smell it out of that;" but Mudd ignored him and gazed about intently for a small plant with crinkled leaves, without discovering the right one because Berenice was standing over it.

"Mr. Gumm knows more than you do," cried Miss Budge. "He named an onion right at the very first guess."

"I always have little onions for breakfast on my birthday," Gumm explained. "They go on wishing me many happy returns for the rest of the day;" and at that moment the matron came to the door, and told them it was time to start out for their walks or they would have the doctor after them. Gumm, quite willing on that occasion to be obedient, left the cultivated patch, and as he did so Berenice picked a leaf of real sage and held it out to him saying, "Here it is."

Gumm hesitated, saw the girl's laugh, said defiantly, "You don't fool me," and rolled off followed with derisive mirth; while Mudd muttered to himself, "Now I'm all right," for he could not believe that Berenice was offering the true herb, so he promptly went down and picked a good handful of a plant, the leaves of which he considered answered to the description given by Halfacre, advertising his sagacity with stentorian noises.

"He's done you, Mr. Gumm," cried Miss Budge ironically.

"It ain't the first time either," said the contented publican, waving his plunder airily before his rival's face. "This is sage, fathead. Perhaps you'll know it another time."

"Silly blight," growled Gumm. "I knew it right enough, but 'twasn't likely I was going to show you."

Just then Halfacre appeared about to start on his walk, a book as usual beneath his arm; and Miss Budge requested him to inform the publican as to what he was holding.

"Borage," said the scholar shortly, and walked on.

"What, ain't it sage?" shouted Mudd, confessing his ignorance.

"No more than you are," came the answer; and the publican went away sorrowfully, while even the sinner could do no more than mutter, "What did you want to tell him for?" before he too succumbed and had to beg them to be merciful. So the cook remained unkissed, and was doubtless none the worse, though she did have to come out and pick the sage for herself.

After these things Winnie set out for Downacombe, and managed to reach the lane which led down from the moor without being caught by Halfacre or Berenice. It was a pretty walk, well sheltered, and the high hedges were still crowned with wreaths of honeysuckle, and the spikes of fox-gloves, though lined with seed-pods below, were heavy with flower-buds at the top. The lane seemed to be unwilling to leave the moor. At first it went away, but gradually returned with cunning bends, until the hedges came to an end, and the rough country smiled again as furze, heather, fern, and granite can smile with the sun of summer tickling them all pleasantly; and a white river running through with the sound of cymbals and dances, and the wind passing over with the music of strings and pipe. The lane kept to the moor as long as it could, and only wandered away reluctantly into the cultivated country when the boundary was crossed and there was no more wild land to cling to; and even then it would not leave the river which came over the boundary with it; and they two went on together into the silent villages, until the lane ran into the main road, and the river went away northwards trying to find the sea.

What could be the matter with Downacombe? thought Winnie, as she began to descend the hill which was taking her off the moor. She could not see the village, but she could smell it, and was reminded unpleasantly of home. The air was filled with smoke. It was as if she had taken a hundred years on her short walk, and was coming to Downacombe to find it transformed into a big black town, filled with buzzing machinery, and mighty chimneys vomiting smoke all over the sun. Downacombe and Keyham could have met together and exchanged a smutty embrace. Where were the roses of that valley, and the hedges of fuchsia, and the banks of hydrangea? Had they all disappeared in a night by the trick of some magician, and had the red and green country become black country? There were smuts in the air, genuine greasy smuts, which London in all its glory could scarcely have surpassed, and one lighted upon Winnie's nose, with the gross impertinence of all unreasoning objects, and joyously rolled down the steep place upon her light-blue frock.

"They are having bonfires," murmured Winnie. "Perhaps Mr. Leigh is burning Nonconformists in his back garden."

She tripped round the last bend, coughing a little, for the air was horribly polluted, and saw the church, which was set upon a small eminence not worthy to be called a hill, a bump in the ground merely, as if a giant had stamped there and raised a swelling. The rectory was at the side, but invisible on account of trees. Everything seemed all right; Winnie saw no black and whirling vapours, but the pungent smell remained, and the smuts danced about like so many London slum-children brought down for a day's romp in the country. Above Downacombe the sky was as blue as Winnie's eyes; there was no sign of lightning or thunderbolts; the storm, whatever it was, had passed. Downacombe had not been enchanted into a Leeds or Sheffield, and turned its hedges of fuchsia into smelting furnaces and its banks of foxgloves into joint-stock companies.

"Some rick has been burnt down," said Winnie.

Not a soul passed her on the lane. During the walk down from the moor she had seen only a few ponies, and they had not been communicative, but had browsed peacefully oblivious to all local events. When she reached the church Winnie was confident she had guessed rightly. The road was littered with scraps of charred straw, some of them still glowing when a puff of wind passed. It did not occur to her that all this burnt straw might not represent a burnt rick, but thatch, until an old man came slowly up the road, shaking his head in a dazed fashion and muttering to himself, "'Tis a bad day vor 'em, a cruel bad day vor 'em." Then Winnie decided to walk on to the village.

One more turn of the road and she was in the main street. It was like a fair, as there seemed to be booths all the way along, selling old clothes, kitchen utensils, furniture. That was her first impression, which lasted only a moment, and then the scene suggested a time of war; the people had been driven out of their homes by the enemy, and having no place to go for shelter were camping all down one side of the street among their shabby goods and household possessions. It was a sordid scene because the articles were so very poor, and the bright sunlight made them look the sorriest sort of rubbish. The crockery which passed muster inside a dark cottage was hideous in comparison with the stones of the road. The fearfully coloured pictures were more false than ever. Monarchs and generals with crimson cheeks, dyspeptic noses, and imbecile expressions grinned complacently from their wobbly frames at a scene of devastation. Women were seated in ancient arm-chairs broken and bulging in all their quarters, some of them with aprons to their eyes, others staring foolishly like their own pictures. The whole of one side of the village street had been swept clean by fire.

Nobody took any notice of Winnie. She moved about among them like an invisible ghost. The street indeed was crowded, as farmers had driven in from the surrounding parishes with their families, treating the occasion as an excuse for a holiday, and already children were playing about near the smouldering ruins. Those who had been burnt out were in that stupid condition of partial consciousness which usually accompanies a disaster. Bill Chown had lost, not merely his wretched home, but a day's work also. His little bit of furniture was stacked beneath the hedge, and Bessie was sitting there wondering how she was going to finish the washing and what was to become of them. Bill tramped to and fro between the hot and jagged ruins of cob which represented what was left of his home and their temporary encampment saying, "It be more than us can du with. Us du seem to ha' more than our share of the bad." The old publican, who had clung to his crumbling inn knowing that it was no use to ask for repairs, gazed at what was left of it— a grey wall, a rafter or two, and a vast amount of black refuse—and was saying something to his wife about starting again in another place. "Us never wur spending volk, and us ha' saved a bit," he said cheerfully. "It might ha' been worser than it be."

"Aw, that be what some volks be allus telling," observed a labourer's wife bitterly. "When things be as bad as 'em can be, they ses might be worser, my dear. What can be worser than to ha' no roof to get in under?"

"I'll tull'ye," answered the old publican. "Might be worser in many ways. Might ha' been winter 'stead o' summer. Might ha' been rough 'stead o' fair weather. Might ha' happened in the middle o' the night 'stead o' early morning. Us might all ha' been burnt 'stead o' getting out. Us had warning tu, and us ha' got our sticks out. There be a gude side as well as a bad side, and so long as there be a gude side I looks to 'en."

"I can't see 'en," said the miserable woman. "I reckon us be ruined, and I've abin and lost a little chiney mug what my man bought vor I to Barum vair when us wur courting."

"Why, my dear, it be the best what could ha' happened to Downacombe," cried a lusty farmer from another parish, having no inducement to be mournful as he had lost nothing, and had indeed gained a day's outing. "Them rotten old cottages wur fair tumbling down on ye. They wouldn't ha' lasted much longer anyhow, and 'tis cheaper to burn 'em than 'tis to knock 'em down. Now the place will be built up new and gude, and yew'll ha' homes vitty to bide in."

"Will they?" said the postmaster as he went by. His own quarters were untouched, as the post-office was off the main street. "It's all rector's property and you don't know him. This is what he is," and he slapped his pocket vigorously.

"Lord love'ye, man, of course he'll build. They'll mak' 'en," shouted the farmer.

"Who's to make him?" asked the postmaster.

"The cottages be insured, I reckon?"

"Ah, and for many times their value, but there's no law to make the rector rebuild, and he won't. He'll say he can't afford it."

"Sure 'nuff," agreed the old publican. "Parson won't build. That's why I be agwaine to get out on't. I've had enough o' the country. I be agwaine to try the town."

"'Tis gude for those what can get out. Us can't," said the labourer's wife.

"I reckon yew'm talking vulish," said the excited farmer, who had the good fortune to live in a village which was owned by an old-fashioned squire. "What about the insurance money?"

"That will go into the rector's pocket," said the postmaster. "He can't live on six hundred a year. Perhaps he'll be able to shuffle along now."

"There be nigh upon fifty volk burnt out wi'out house or home. What be 'em to du?" the farmer shouted.

"Us be well enough. Anything be gude vor the likes o' we," said the woman more bitterly than ever. "Any old barn wi' a bit o' straw be all us wants, and if us gets tired on't there be the House. Proper well built the House be. No walls coming in on ye, and no roof a tumbling, and beer on Christmas Day if us behaves right. If they wur to tear that old place down," she went on fiercely, pointing upward at the big grey church-tower, "they might tear the House down tu. Vor the one makes t'other, sure as I be a woman."

"Not in our parish it don't," said the farmer. "Our church belongs to squire, not to any o' these old bishops, and he gives 'en to one o' his sons, and us gets on like honey-bumbles in a hive. Beef at Christmas vor every one, and repairs done when they'm wanted, and us gives three cheers vor squire, and three vor parson, and three vor ourselves," he said quaintly. "If what yew'm telling be true, woman, all I ses is, God help poor little Downacombe by the moor."

"That's what us ha' been praying vor years," said the angry woman. "But when the fire du come it burns out we and lets parson bide."

Winnie only heard part of this. She might have heard more, had she not caught sight of the Twins tumbling down the hill like a pair of baby elephants. Evidently they had been told of the fire and were hurrying to inspect the scene. Winnie retreated from the crowd, remembering what she had come for, and walked back up the road, wondering if on that day of distress Leigh would be accessible. She had been very much surprised to hear harsh things said against him. It was the old story, she supposed, of the devoted parish priest and his ungrateful parishioners who were constitutionally unable to speak good of any man.

Out of the main street there was no one. Winnie went into the churchyard, then into the porch, and tried the door; it was unlocked, so she went in and seated herself behind a cool pillar to think and rest. She didn't like the prospect of going to the rectory. It is easy to walk to the dentist's door, but it is another matter to ring the bell. Winnie decided to sit there for a bit, screw up her courage and rehearse what she intended to say when she found herself alone with the man of God; although she knew very well that directly they were together she would forget every word. Still he was such a dear man, so holy and kind, yet without the slightest suspicion of religious cant; his manner was healing, his voice a caress. He would make it easy for her and help her through.

Conscious of a sound, Winnie looked up; then gasped, for a ghostly figure was crossing the chancel, slowly, wearily, its head down. Leigh himself with his vestments on, coming to serve the grey walls. Suddenly shy, the girl slipped behind the pillar, then peeped round it. The rector was in his seat, kneeling, his hands clasped, gazing before him. Winnie admired his character all the more.

He attended to his duties if his people neglected theirs. He held daily services though nobody came to them. Not that any of the parishioners could have attended at that time of day. Their own minister gave them spiritual food later on, when they could attend, but that was about the time when a gentleman must be at his dinner-table. Leigh always entered the church by a door in the vestry, and thus he had no idea he was being watched and listened to by a pretty little congregation of one.

Some time passed before he began the service. He looked ahead at a window, through which earlier in the year had come a soft sound as of an organ playing, caused by the bees among the lime-blossoms singing their drinking-songs. Winnie saw him shake his head and smile sadly. No doubt he was thinking of the fire and those poor homeless people, and wondering what he could do for them. He was praying for them. No man could do more—except act. Still he could not do much as he was not rich; and though the rectory was large and unused he could hardly receive any of the people there, as they might soil the carpets or damage the furniture, and besides they were unpleasant in their habits, and above all they belonged to a different class. No doubt the Wesleyan minister would look after the homeless.

It was a letter that Leigh was thinking of before he began the service, one of the most disquieting letters that his wife had ever written. She had bobbed up in Rome, of all foolish places in summer time, and the fever had promptly laid her low. She was having doctors and nurses and every attention, and going on well enough, but the expense was terrible, and really she hadn't got a farthing left. She had intended to come straight home instead of going on to that infernal city, but—well, it was those friends again, and she hardly knew how to write it, and she was afraid it would worry poor old Frankie something awful, but there it was—money was owing all over the shop, and she had contracted a debt of honour, though she was sure the brutes had swindled her; and she sometimes thought she wasn't fit to be a parson's wife, though she wasn't a bad girl, only a bit thoughtless at times; and directly she could travel she was coming off home as fast as limited mails could bring her. Only it was a case of money at once or the law-courts might have her. A statement of debts and probable expenses was included, which had made Leigh wince and wonder how much his first editions would fetch.

He began to read the office, mumbling it rather, while a choir of fat bluebottles reeled to and fro in front of him, and Winnie knelt behind the pillar, afraid to open her mouth or make a sound. It was the fifteenth evening of the month, and the psalm appointed was a dreadfully endless description of the wicked ways of the Israelites. Leigh gave out the date for the benefit of the bluebottles and they buzzed approvingly. He turned and began in a defiant voice, as if the opening words had a special meaning for him, "Hear my law, O my people."

The rest of the words died away, for a certain pillar gaped as it were, and Winnie seemed to fall out of it with a face of great confusion.

She looked across and smiled, and then there came a pause. It seemed ridiculous for him to be at one end of the church and she at the other, and that they should stand thus and attempt to make a religious dialogue. Leigh hesitated a moment, then left his seat, walked down the aisle and said, "Don't you think if you came and sat up near me we should get on better?"

"All right," said Winnie, and up she went to the front seat, and somehow they got through the long psalm, though Winnie stammered dreadfully and was almost crying with nervousness before it was finished. The rest of the service was easy, and when it was over Leigh joined her at once, as he did not change his vestments until he reached the house, and they went out together by the vestry door.

"I am so glad to see you," he said. "Though it was naughty of you to play me such a practical joke."

"I didn't," said Winnie. "I went into the church to rest, and suddenly I looked up and there you were. I didn't know you had services."

"Yes, twice a day, as the Prayer-book orders. But I do not expect to see any one. In future I shall have to search the church beforehand."

"This dreadful fire. Your poor people," began Winnie, full of sympathy, but the subject seemed to be painful to the rector. He put up his hand in rather a fearful manner and only said, "Come into the garden. You shall have as many roses as you can carry. One for your sex, one for yourself—"

"That only makes two," said she.

"Let me finish. And a hundred for your virtues."

"How many for my sorrows?" asked Winnie in a low voice.

"Not one. Not the smallest bud or promise of one," he said firmly.

"But I have them," she murmured, trying to look at him but without much success.

"That is a fancy, a little black beast of a bad dream," he said lightly. "No, no, my dear girl, we cannot allow it. Your roses have no thorns."

He opened the gate and stood aside for her to pass through. There was a field to the right, a pretty park-like place backed by thick, dark firs; and the gate to that field, which communicated with the garden, stood open. Winnie was going in that direction when Leigh took her by the arm and held her back.

"Not that way. I am superstitious sometimes. There is a man in your free part of the country called Gregory Breakback, who knows all the traditions of the soil, and he would tell you that strange things have been seen on that winding path. I don't want you to put your foot upon it this evening. Over there, where you see that mound, a nunnery once stood."

"Are you afraid I shall become a nun if I go upon the path?" asked Winnie.

"That could never be unless all men went blind," he answered. "The path is an old churchway or lichway."

Seeing her quick and questioning look, he added, "A path over which a body has been carried."

"That's horrid," she said with a shiver. "I am glad you stopped me."

"There are many paths and unfrequented lanes about this county which have the prefix church attached to them, meaning thereby that they have been made rights of way by the mere fact of a funeral crossing there at one time. I believe it is still the law that wherever a funeral passes, making a short cut to the church, even if it goes through a private house or garden, the path thus made becomes a public way for all time. Many a field pathway has been secured in this way. I tried to close this once, but public opinion was too strong for me; and I was further informed that if I did close it my garden would be filled with ghosts."

"I don't want to hear any more, please. I'm not very strong, you know," Winnie faltered.

"Of course you don't," he said tenderly. "I should not have mentioned the subject had you not turned towards the path—and that man Gregory has a trick of telling impossible stories in an unpleasantly truthful voice. Come down among the roses, Miss Winifred—I love that beautiful, home-sounding German name. A friend of peace—what could be better? Name of sweetness without thorns."

"I told you I have them," said Winnie. "Lots of them. They prick me everywhere, and—I've come to tell you all about them," she finished as hard as ever she could.

"You will not persuade me to believe. I shall not listen to you," he said. "Look at that moss-rose. They call her old-fashioned, and she is all the more beautiful for that. She shall be yours to begin with. Pass your finger over the moss and you will feel her pretty throat gently swallowing the first dewdrop of the evening."

What was he thinking about, as he raised his hands and bent his head to court the delicious queens of his garden? He looked troubled, and a flash of pain, like a twinge of neuralgia, crossed his face now and again; but it was not the fire, nor the thought of the homeless people camping by the wayside; but it was the memory of that letter which his wife-errant had written to him from Rome. "See," he said, drawing a penknife from his pocket and paring the pink thorns away, "how easy it is to dispose of your troubles. They are on the ground, and you may tread upon them."

"I can't," said Winnie mournfully. "Haven't you ever tried yourself to get rid of the thorns? They won't go."

"Then we must forget them," he said lightly. "Come down the pergola and we will wake up some buds. The season will soon be over and we shall be in seed-time. There is already a sourness in the garden and a smell of rot. Another month and every bush will wear scarlet. Here are violets already in penitential purple. Will you have some?"

"I would rather have some pink roses," she said. Why was he so morbid that evening? First his superstition regarding the churchway, then his eagerness to rob the roses of their thorns, and now his reference to the sad and pall-coloured violets. Winnie knew she must soon be going or she would be late for the rest hour; and so far she had said nothing, and Leigh, instead of encouraging or trying to help, seemed inclined to turn a deaf ear to her confession. Her old-fashioned ideas remained, and she wanted to kneel down before him and tell her troubles properly and obtain his advice and blessing; and then she could go on her way in peace. Winnie wanted to do her duty, but she also wanted to follow her own inclination. Leigh was so good and clever, and a priest to boot; he could say just what her duty was, and perhaps he would add that the contract binding her to the clerk of Keyham was an immoral one, and decide that she was at liberty to break it and do as she willed; that her duty, in short, was to follow her own inclination. Winnie had a wild hope that he might say so, although she dared not think of the consequences; and she did not own that it would be quite impossible for her to break the contract unaided. In fact, some one would have to do it for her. A St. George would have to arise to slay the dragon.

Winnie stood on the grass-path and put out a hand timidly. She dared not touch the rector, but his hands were already filled with roses, and she pinched a green leaf between her finger and thumb and so held him. Had he stepped back the leaf would have been torn off.

"I do really want to speak to you," she said in a very frightened voice. "I asked permission to come and see you, because—because—"

"Your room was getting dark, and you wanted some of my flowers to brighten it," he said soothingly.

"No," she said, beginning to cough with sheer nervousness. He was not helping her. He would not face the truth. "You are a clergyman, and I—I want to make a sort of confession. You are so good," she hurried on, her eyes roaming anywhere rather than towards his.

Leigh made a movement, a kind of start, and for a few moments there was silence. He remembered there were certain duties connected with the clerical profession, although nobody seemed quite certain about them, and what one clerk in holy orders described as a Christian Sacrament another might call a pagan vice. He himself had not troubled much about such matters, which could not concern him greatly; and as for advice, well, during his incumbency he had written and talked a good deal about rose-culture and the virtues or demerits of certain kinds of fertilisers; and he had stated the law of the land on various occasions, and had even given advice upon the best and cheapest methods of fattening pigs; but the law of the Church, whatever that might be, he had never expounded, except in its relation to temporal power, nor had he ever been asked to.

"My dear Miss Winnie," he said at last, "young girls must not get unhappy ideas into their heads."

"I do really want to confess to you, Mr. Leigh," she whispered.

He laughed and stroked her hand. "It is my own fault. I was morbid, and my fit has communicated itself to you," he said cheerily. "Confess your sins! Why, dear girl, you haven't got any."

"No, not that exactly—my affairs—my home troubles," she murmured with difficulty.

"Ah, but you mustn't," he said in his kindest voice. "You must not confide in me, Miss Winnie. For one thing I could never keep a secret, and Miss Calladine, who is always talking about you, would come down here and worm it all out of me. Besides, the doctor wouldn't like it. You are rather an invalid, and girls with your particular weakness are, I know, prone to talk incautiously. Tell the doctor about your little home worries—a younger sister breaking your toys while you are away, eh, Miss Winnie?" he said playfully. "The doctor is a good sort. He will help you much more than I can."

Winnie could not ask again. She had not the courage, for his words and manner, although most kind, were decided. So there was nobody to help her. She had come for advice and was receiving roses. She had asked for assistance and was getting playthings instead. No one would take her seriously because she was fragrant and pretty; and yet life was serious enough for every one, for pretty things and strong things alike, and was not to be smiled away or taken lightly or dismissed from contemplation with a handful of roses.

"May I ask you one question? I want you to be a clergyman for one minute," she said, without the slightest bitterness, for she liked Leigh very much and was sure his reasons for not listening to her were good ones, and yet expressing herself somewhat unfortunately. "If I asked for a certain thing should I get it?"

"You mean in prayer?" he said in a changed voice.

Winnie nodded, then said, "If I prayed very hard indeed?"

"Yes," he said. "It must be so. Ask, and you shall have. That is my authority for saying so."

"Then if I asked that some one might die, he would?" she said.

"Oh no. Certainly not," he answered in rather a shocked voice.

"Then my prayer wouldn't be answered?"

"Not that sort of prayer. You couldn't expect it."

"Why not? People must die."

"Oh, it would be impossible—and most unjust."

"What sort of prayers are answered?"

"Really," he said, "I cannot tell you."

Winnie asked no more questions. She had already stopped too long, and there might be a lecture when she got back. She took her flowers and returned thanks prettily, persuaded that Leigh had done his best for her and there were reasons which she could not understand that prevented him from doing more. She turned away from sorrowful Downacombe and climbed sadly back up the writhing lane. By then the homeless people had disappeared from the street. Various cottages, already over-crowded, and rat-haunted barns had received them, and their household goods had been stored temporarily in the two chapels. When night fell and the moon came up—a great full moon—the village became a mournful sight indeed. Medievalism and modernism were side by side, grappling at each other in the quiet moonlight. Ruins on one side, crowded habitations on the other, and upon the road between were the discontented ones discussing their hard lot and the new doctrine; longing to destroy the old dispensation and adopt the new; talking with little understanding and less reason, scarcely knowing what they believed in or what they wanted; but seeing clearly enough that a change must come. Mediaevalism could only mutter sleepily, "Let things bide;" while modernism was lifting its wild shout, "Down with everything." No doubt the big full moon had watched and heard it all before.

That night the patients were sent out to walk in the moonlight. The usual bed-time was half-past-nine, but on this occasion an extension of time was granted. "To Wheal Dream and back," was the doctor's order. It was a sort of excursion to see the old place under the most romantic circumstances; the black skeleton and yawning mouth of the ancient mine, the former waterway shining with huge rounded pebbles, the deep gorge slashed in the side of the moor; and on the one side the white river sweeping round a bend where a few black firs tossed their plumes and sighed all night, and owls tried to pretend they were only mechanical aeroplanes; and on the other, above the ribbon of the Stannary road, the tumbling house of the Pethericks, and its parasite, Uncle Gifford's cottage, each showing a thick yellow light, two spots of grease in the moonlight; and in front the house of the wheal, through which so much pageantry of the Forest had passed from Athelstan to George Brunacombe. No light was showing in that house, for the apostle of realism was resting, seated at his window drinking moonshine. When the others were asleep his lamp would be lighted. He was watching the figures drifting up the road, and strangely blurred in spite of the full moon, which shed glamour and dreamstuff rather than brightness. Suddenly he started and muttered, "The wind is getting up." It is a trick of the Dartmoor wind to scream in a moment out of a body of dead calm.

But it was not the wind. It was Gregory Breakback swinging down from the moor with the bar of iron upon his shoulder. He struck the door with it and waited. It was not usual for him to pass that way. He generally went across the heights to his ruin of Moor

Gate, whistling and roaring to himself, and making people afar off say that the wind was rising.

"Wull, sir," he began, directly George opened the door. "This be the end on't vor the year. No more on't till the Maid o' St. Michael's Wood sits up over the Blackavon a-combing her hair down to the watter and singing, 'Days be getting longer, Love be growing stronger.' Yew ain't seen she, I reckon, nor heard she neither, but I have, and that's how the years ha' gone. The young fellow stands one side of the Ford as 'twere, and the old 'un be t'other, and 'tis nought but a jump across. Aw, sir, 'tis a gude night vor the end on't."

"A change is coming, you mean?" said George. He understood Gregory and his strange ways, and his trick of speaking in parables, as some men will after a life of solitude which is itself a parable.

"Ees, 'tis the last o' summer and vair weather. I've abin up over on Dartmoor and the dogs went past, slow at first, then fast. Aw, yew wouldn't ha' heard 'em. Yew can't see into the moor same as I du. There'll be rain in an hour, and then the fall, and after that the goosie's feathers wull drap and drap and the ground'll get tied up. 'Tis a long time since the maid wur a-singing up over the Blackavon."

"Since spring you mean?"

"Wull, sir, have it like that."

"Gregory, my boy," said George lightly, "you want to tell me something."

"'Tis a cruel pity yew ain't got my eyes. See that vuzz? There be a rabbut in mun, squatting close, afeard o' my old Ben. Yew can't see 'en but I can, vor when I can't see wi' my eyes I smulls wi' my nose, and when I can't smull wi' my nose I hears wi' my ears, and when I can't hear wi' my ears I pricks in my body. Don't ye bide, sir. That's what I ses. Don't ye ever bide and look back and beyond, vor that be the way the years go."

"Come along now. Speak plainly," said George.

Gregory let the end of his bar drop like a thunderbolt. "I speak as I wull, and no man shall answer me back," he shouted. Then he brought out his hand and struck George upon the shoulder. "'Tis a vule telling to a vule," he said. "I ha' tried all my life to stand straight, and I ha' come to it wull enough to knaw what be a man and what bain't. Us ha' both done it well enough. What maids have us defiled, though us ain't got women of our own? What walls ha' us touched, though us ain't got land? And I ha' been a vule to look back and beyond, and yew'm a vule tu. Wull, sir, shake hands. Us be men first and vules afterwards."

"Thanks for the compliment," said George dryly. There was no doubt about it—the moon was getting at the mind of that man of nature, Gregory Breakback.

"I'll tull ye the story," he said, flinging the great bar on his shoulder as if it had been a stick. "I come round this way to tull ye, vor the change be coming, sure 'nuff. There wur a man and he loved a maid— Aw, sir, if I wur to stop now I'd ha' told yew the whole history of the world—but he wur afeard to let she knaw, 'cause he reckoned he warn't man enough vor she. A man who would think that be gude enough vor the best o' women. No, sir, this bain't any old story o' Wheal Dream. 'Tis a story o' St. Michael's Wood. One day he walked wi' she in the wood and 'twas spring. Yew knaw the path and how narrow it be, and she walked ahead and he come after. It got dark and the mune got up, the same old mune, and her got more ahead and crossed the Ford, and then her called 'en. He looked back and beyond 'stead o' looking forward, and he saw the Maid o' St. Michael's Wood a-combing her hair down to the watter and singing, 'Days be getting longer, Love be growing stronger,' and he bided, sir, and watched the witch maiden. He thought 'twas a minute, but when he got to the Ford nobody was there. The mune wur shining down and 'twas the same old mune. It wur spring, but it wasn't the same spring. Vor the years had gone by while he watched the witch maiden, and he wur an old man when he crossed the Ford."

He turned to go with his great smile, and George swung himself from the door with a queer sensation in his throat—understanding the story and the interpretation thereof—and called, "Get the dreams out of your head, Gregory."

"If any man says I be a dreamer," came the roaring voice from the Stannary road, as the huge figure swept across it, "I'll break the back of 'en like a stick."

Gumm and Mudd did not reach the gorge. They squatted above the road out of sight behind some boulders, and smoked secretly. The publican had a cigar made of vile materials; he cut it in half and they enjoyed the forbidden luxury in secret. Suddenly Gumm whispered, "Down, you blighter. Some one's coming."

There were footsteps upon the road. Two big heads came above the granite and perceived Halfacre striding along, his arms swinging like windmills, his feet kicking away invisible obstacles, his head thrown back.

"What's he doing?" whispered Mudd. "He's off his blooming nut."

"He's trying to blow the moon out," muttered Gumm.

Apparently this was exactly what Halfacre was attempting. He was looking up at the big moon, blowing at it with all his might.

Winnie was all alone, sitting in the shadow beside the wheal, feeling drowsy and sad, her eyes fixed upon the dark windows. Why couldn't he come down and talk to her? It would be a nice little act of attention and would pass the time quite pleasantly. But she was nobody, she was common, he had seen through her. Nobody would help her except Halfacre, and he had certainly been good and kind in his own strange way. He had done more for her than any one. Leigh would not let her confide in him; George looked the other way when she spoke; Halfacre made her tell him everything. How very different men were!

Somebody was blundering down the gorge like a driven pony. Winnie rose, calling out, afraid of being kicked or trodden on; and the next moment Halfacre was with her, still panting and blowing.

"You frightened me," she said. "Is anything the matter?"

"It is all right now," he said. "Don't make a sound. They'll turn it off presently. It must have been half-a-crown dropped into the meter instead of a penny. It's an awful light and hurts my head frightfully."

"What—this moon? Why, it's cool and lovely," said wondering Winnie.

"Not so loud," he said crossly. "You'll frighten away this shadow. Ah, it's splendid here. Out there it's awful. A regular great sea of it. I was plunging about and got out of my depth several times. I wanted to see you, Winnie. I've been looking for you. Curse my head. Look here, my dear, I've been thinking it all out, and the only thing will be for us to be married."

"Oh," shivered Winnie. Then she tried to laugh, and said as crossly as she could, "You know I am engaged."

"It will be the best way out for you," went on Halfacre, in the same excited whisper. "We'll go away very soon and be married quietly. It will have to be a very quiet marriage. I have my schemes—huge colossal schemes—and you will assist me. We will devote ourselves to the cause of freedom. Where are you, Winnie? The heat of this light is frightful. Give me your hand. Where is it?"

"Oh, please do leave me alone," she begged.

"Don't be so foolish. I can't listen to such nonsense. I can't do with it. Next month I hope, if the light goes out. That will get rid of the moon for ever. Put your arms round me, Winnie, for God's sake. I was burning hot just now and I'm shivering all over now."

"I can't marry you. You know I can't—and I won't," she said.

"If you go on talking such nonsense I shall be angry. I shall want to pick up stones and throw them about." He turned upon Winnie and caught her. "No more of this moonshine. Say yes at once."

"I can't," she moaned.

"But you must, my dear. There's no way out. That black hole is dark and filthy, and I hear water dripping there. It would be terrible to fall down it. I am not my usual self to-night because the light is too strong, but I shall be well enough in the morning. You are going to be my wife. I've had that idea for some time, and now I know it's going to be true."

"No," said Winnie.

"Well, that's another idea. Whom are you going to marry then?" he said in a more reasonable voice.

"I don't know," she moaned miserably.

"That dirty clerk who has bought you?" he sneered.

"I can't," she faltered.

"One of us," he muttered hotly.

It did come to that. Was this the answer to her prayer? After all she was common because she was poor. Was this the way out of all her troubles? She did not care for Halfacre when he was sane—and just then she supposed he was crazed with love—but he was younger, much better looking, a thousand times more the gentleman than Ernest Hawker. Winnie had always been of a yielding nature; and she was yielding then.

"Is it he?" whispered Halfacre, throwing his head from side to side to avoid the poisonous moonbeams. Had George at his window, thinking over Gregory's strange words, only known what was taking place down Wheal Dream!

"No," she said.

"Then it is I."

Winnie said nothing, but put her hands over the two dimples and the distracting nose and began to cry; and at the same moment the moon drew a large thick cloud over her and apparently began to weep too. Gregory Breakback made no mistakes about the weather. It was beginning to rain, and the change had come.

CHAPTER XV
ABOUT NOVEMBERITIS

During the autumn Berenice went home for a holiday. When she returned, reaching the sanatorium soon after six, which was the beginning of the rest hour, she ran straight up to Winnie's room and knocked hard. Two voices answered, the whine of Tobias, which was familiar enough, and another which she had never heard before.

"Billy, you're fooling," cried the girl, as she opened the door. "Why haven't you answered a single one of my letters?"

She gave a cry of dismay. A strange girl was lying in an invalid chair, and Tobias the fickle was on her lap.

"I beg your pardon," Berenice stammered. "I thought Miss Shazell would be here. I suppose they have changed her room?"

"I don't know," said the brand-new girl. "I only came yesterday. Do you mean the elderly lady? But I think they call her Budge."

"Oh no. A pretty girl, with flaxen hair and dimples."

"There is no one here like that," said the new girl. "But some have gone lately. The matron told me, and the doctor said he hoped I should do as well as the girl who had this room last."

Berenice was gone, and Tobias, changing his allegiance, pursued her down the passage to Miss Budge's room, where the spinster received her with enthusiasm, and answered her passionate question with the news, "My dear, she went three days after you, and that queer Halfacre man went the same day, and our coarse Twins went last week. The whole place has changed. I shall get off soon, as the winter here must be too dreadful. I'm so glad you're back."

"Billy gone," murmured Berenice, "without telling me, without writing a line. What can she mean by it? What did she say?"

"Nothing," said Miss Budge. "Not even good-bye. I came down to luncheon and there was no Winnie, and when I asked where she was the matron said she had gone. So had Halfacre."

"By the same train. The devil take him," cried Berenice passionately. "He was always after Billy, and she, poor darling, was as weak as water-gruel."

"There's nothing in that," said Miss Budge. "Naturally they went together, as they were both going west, and there is only one train in the morning."

Berenice sat on the bed and kicked her shoe against the wall. "There is something in it," she declared. "Why should Billy make a mystery about going? She knows I am fond of her, and I wrote at least six times, and there was never a word in reply. I have got her home address, and I'll write to that. If she doesn't answer I'll get leave to go down and see her. Billy shan't be ruined," she said fiercely.

"My dear, you are making a lot out of nothing. Little Winnie can look after herself. Oh, before I forget it, George Brunacombe is very anxious to see you. I met him to-day and he asked when you would be back. He looks terribly ill, and he said he had been in bed for three days."

"Tobias, my little doggums," murmured Berenice, bending over the soft brown head to hide her watery eyes. "What has she done to us all? She told you everything. Can't you tell me? Wag it all out, doggie dear."

Tobias wagged hard, but he only meant that now Winnie had departed he intended to follow his usual custom of adopting the prettiest girl in the place, and that person would now be Berenice, as she was more fascinating than the new-comer.

"Run! Here comes the doctor," cried Miss Budge.

"Now I shall know. I'll make him tell me," murmured Berenice, as she escaped to her room.

She waited by the door, listening to the doctor as he went from one to another, and at last he came to her with a hearty welcome. The girl was a big handful of rebellion, but every one missed her when she went away. "You're looking pale and thin. Overdoing it as usual," he said; but Berenice would not talk about herself just then. Her question came out at once, "Where is Winnie?"

She thought he looked uncomfortable. He turned, closed the door, then sat down, pulled some letters out of his pocket and gave them to her. "My letters," she exclaimed. "Then you didn't send them on."

"I don't know her address. The little girl was rather an enigma," he said.

"You know she lives at Plymstock?"

"I didn't know. I could only reach her through the doctor who sent her to me. I am very much annoyed with her," he added.

Berenice glanced at him quickly, then dropped her eyes and said, "I believe there is something called professional etiquette which prevents you from saying what you know about Winnie. I am fond of her, doctor, and I think she must have been worried, for she was always funny when I asked her questions. If she is in any trouble I want to help her."

"I know nothing about the girl," said the doctor, somewhat sharply, "except one or two things told me by her doctor, and these of course I am not at liberty to mention. I had made up my mind to speak to you about her, knowing you two were friendly. Miss Shazell was the most remarkable patient I have ever attended. Did she mention her affairs to you?"

"When I tried to draw her out she always wanted to change the subject. I know she was engaged—and didn't want the man," Berenice said in a low voice.

"It is only natural she should have men after her."

"But she wasn't fit to be married?" said the girl hurriedly.

"Certainly not. She left here with active disease. That is why I am so annoyed. As I pointed out to her, she had placed herself under my charge, and she had no right to go until I discharged her as fairly fit. It was not giving me a chance. I would never have accepted her had I imagined she was going to behave in this way; and, as I told her, I would have allowed her to remain at greatly reduced fees rather than she should return home and prove a bad advertisement for me. She declared it was not a matter of money, but she must go, and that was the end of it."

"Some one made her," said Berenice. "I know Winnie. She never could do anything for herself."

"When she came here," the doctor went on, "I did not think she would live more than a month. I told her plainly I did not undertake bad cases and could not keep her, but she cried and said Dartmoor was her native place, and begged to be allowed to stay, so I promised to give her a trial. From the very first day she improved in the most marvellous manner and never went back. She responded to the treatment at once, and the rapidity with which the symptoms diminished was extraordinary. She seemed to feed on the air like a plant, and was throwing off the disease as if it had been nothing more than a bad cold. Her case supplied an argument for the efficacy of the open-air treatment which its opponents could not possibly have explained away. That is why I am angry with her, for now all the good will be undone. Another six months here would have arrested the disease; a year would have cured her."

"Entirely cured her?"

"I believe so now. Her progress was so wonderfully rapid that it was reasonable to look for a complete cure."

"What will happen now?" asked Berenice painfully.

"Oh well," he said, with a gesture of despair, "our opponents will say that the treatment is expensive and ineffective, and only patches up a patient for a few more months of life." Then he began to question the girl about herself; but as he was leaving the room he looked back and said, "If you hear anything of her let me know."

"What about that man Halfacre?" called Berenice.

"I had to send him away. He would not submit to discipline and was impertinent," came the answer.

The dreary, wind-filled house had changed. It was a place of gaiety no longer, but of real sorrow. There were some new faces, long and lean, with not much laughter on them; and outside were the mists of autumn. Winnie had been quiet; so is the sunshine in a room, but it is none the less pleasant for its silence. She had lighted up the place wonderfully. Even the Twins had left an agreeable memory behind them. They had been noisy and vulgar, still they had made mirth, and to those who bring laughter much may be forgiven; especially to those who are in trouble while they crack their jokes. Gumm and Mudd had a great deal to endure, and though they were queer men they took Nature's punishment like brave men; and went back to their homes, to take up their work again, to breathe the smoke again; and to break down again. What hope is there for the poor man when civilisation has conferred its blessings and its microbes upon him? He leaves the smoke to snatch a few mouthfuls of air, but he must return to the smoke to make a living; and thus to complete his dying. For Nature never constructed men so that they should be smuts in a chimney.

Berenice visited George the next day, and the artist came to the door not only more untidy than ever, but actually dirty. He looked as if he might not have taken off his old clothes for a week. The girl told him so, and George tried to laugh in the old way, but only succeeded in making a sad noise. "Bubo and I are moulting," he explained. "We shall be better looking when we get our winter coats."

"You have been ill?" she said.

"Taking my holidays. Twice a year I lie in bed, once in spring and again in autumn, from Sunday morning to Thursday. I make plans then for my future work, while my brain seems to be droning about the room like a huge beetle. Some people might call it being ill, but we can't afford to use that expression. I keep a Bradshaw on my bed when I'm having my holidays, and I go to all sorts of places and put up at the pictures of swell hotels, and have a fine time running after trains and only just catching them. I've just done the Lake District very thoroughly; didn't miss a place, and the whole trip never cost a penny. Ursula Petherick supplied the necessary touch of comedy when she came up with my meals. Sometimes she was a quaint travelling companion, or the boots at the particular hotel I happened to be staying at for the moment, or a nigger minstrel on the sands. When she came in drunk one evening and poured the soup down my back I imagined I was at a hydro being massaged."

"What a life," Berenice murmured; and George heard, although he pretended he didn't. Then she asked about Winnie, and George trembled. It was plain enough. He was weak physically, and he couldn't prevent the movement, which was like that of an animal heaving as it dies. He was in pain all the time and looking about for some drug to deaden it. Presently he told her in simple language, "I saw her the very day she went, but she didn't say a word about going. She came across early, before breakfast, and I think she wanted to see Wheal Dream for the last time. She was very fond of the place."

"You fool, you fool," Berenice was saying to herself.

"I was outside. I always walk up and down our little road for exercise before starting work. She thanked me for a picture I had sent her—a sketch of the waterfall down the wood. She was very fond of the place. Will you come a few steps up the road?"

He walked ahead and Berenice followed. "Don't stoop so," she said.

"Was I stooping?" said George, trying to straighten himself. "I am getting old. I must claim the privileges. Bubo and Brunacombe, established a good many years, and not yet in bankruptcy. Look down there," he said, pointing to what had been once the wall of the mine, but was then a rock-garden. At the summit was a pendulous wave of heather, living on the air apparently, unless it found nutriment in the stones. "She wanted some of that and I know now she wanted it to take away with her. I went down to get it and I showed her what a lot of bleached flowers there were, because the bushes are so thick and heather will not flourish or grow pink if the wind cannot get to it. 'Like me,' she said. Do you hear what I'm telling? She said, 'Like me.' She said it twice."

"I am listening," said Berenice faintly.

"She took the heather and touched my hand with her third finger, or it might have been the third and fourth together. Just there she touched it," said simple George, bringing up his grubby right hand. There could be no doubt about the exact spot, for a tiny blob of gold paint marked it. "She didn't mean to. It was an accident. Then she said, 'Thank you so very much.' Just like that she said it. And then she walked away. She walked very slowly and looked back twice. She was very fond of Wheal Dream."

"Well, what do you think?" said Berenice impatiently when he paused.

"About her going? I suppose she wanted to be home again."

"What do you think about yourself?" she said. "You have just as good as told me that you worship her."

"The old masters worshipped the Madonna and saints that they painted, though they gave them hideous faces and drew them all wrong," said George. "But the saints never troubled their heads about the old masters. I can't imagine how any man could see Miss Shazell without worshipping her; but it is one thing to pray and another thing to be heard. You know what I am."

"What are you?" she said a little disdainfully.

"Just what your voice implies. I'm George. That's what I am. If you walk in a big town late on Saturday night, when folks are shopping, you will hear every few steps, 'Good-night, George.' Stand in the street and call, 'George,' and every other rapscallion in the gutter will jump at you. I am not Michael or Raphael. I'm George, and my name damns me." There was the folly of bitterness and failure in these words. Berenice did not answer him, for she was sorry. He had endured everything so well, herself included—she remembered it then—and it hurt her a little to see him aggressive under suffering. She had no intention of confessing her sins. She was not going to say she had deceived him wantonly and maliciously, by causing him to believe that Winnie had given away his gift of white heather and had made mirth over his secret and sacred thoughts. Winnie should not marry any man if she could prevent it. She wanted the girl for herself, to pet and love and play with, to treat as a beautiful animal like a bird in a cage; she wanted to withdraw Winnie from her circulation among men, take her from her natural destiny, and appropriate her body and soul. It was not a very healthy passion, the desire of a maid for a maid, but it was a strong one; better perhaps than devoting heart and life to the lower animals and making a complete lover of a dog. Berenice liked men, but not any more than she liked women. A handsome dog was in her sight more beautiful than a handsome man. There was nothing vile about her. Her affections had simply wandered away into unusual channels and her vision had become distorted, partly by her physical condition, partly by encouraging unnatural sympathies. Nature must have played some trick with her temperament at the beginning, just as she does with potatoes, making one tuber forked like a man and another featured like a monkey.

She wrote off at once to Winnie at the address which had been given her; and the shock of the reply, which was nothing but her own letter returned and marked unknown, made her so ill that she was sent to bed for two days. She scribbled a few lines of information to George, adding a request for his assistance, though not bothering much about his feelings; and his answer was, "It means only one thing. She gave you a wrong address because she did not want to be followed after she left. There is nothing else to say."

There was a good deal to think about, however. About that time George began to take long rambles upon the moor, often climbing up and down the steep and almost obliterated pathway above St. Michael's Ford as if he was pursuing the shadows of the Perambulators who had passed that way once with their maps and plans; and Bubo, balancing upon his perch, scratched his ear continually and hooted his patron goddess Minerva to witness that the master of himself and all the arts was taking too many holidays and giving so little strict attention to business that he, Bubo, would have seriously to contemplate the advisability of advertising for a new sleeping partnership. It was the beginning of dark days for George, as it was the beginning of dark days outside; for even on the heights it is very sombre at the peep of winter, when the clouds are let down to the chimney-tops, and the sun is wafted away to boil another world, and the day is merely a little grey yawn between long nights.

During those days George hardly ever spoke. It was marvellous how seldom he opened his mouth. Even Uncle touched his hat to him in vain; but there was no resisting Gregory, who could tear the restraint off any man like the wind snatching off a cloak.

"Your patch be vull o' weeds," he said, looking over the hedge at the mountainous scrap of garden. "What it wants is a gude turning and terrifying to get the stroyle out. Tak' a fork and terrify 'en, sir. 'Twull du ye more gude than tramping abroad. When a man walks alone he thinks of nought and his brains run down into his butes."

George's answer was, "I've got a back-ache, and working in the garden makes me dizzy."

"Wull, sir, I'll cure him vor ye," said Gregory the always ready. "Tak' beer and milk, and boil in 'em flowers and leaves o' marigolds, and then go ye to bed and sweat. 'Tis an old cure and a gude 'un— and it be wrote down on my parchment."

Another evening George met Bill Chown with his "flasket" of washing, and stopped to ask how things were going in Downacombe. Bill seemed to be aging and getting grey and dragging his feet more than he used to, though he was not yet fifty.

"I've abin up to see my sister," said Bill. "Us thought her and John would tak' us in, but 'em wun't. No room, sir." He paused and scratched his head, then gazed around upon the huge grey masses of moor. "They ses 'tis a little world, sir, but he'm big when yew gets to work on 'en. There be room vor a plenty o' flies on a bit o' dung, but on this gurt big Dartmoor there bain't room vor we. What 'em has 'em holds. Me and wife be in a barn to Downacombe. Us works while it be light and chases rats afterwards. Us be getting mazed wi' work and craving vor a home. Plenty o' country, sir, plenty of old walls and wheals," said Bill, looking up with dark honest eyes and describing a half-circle with a hard brown hand, "but where be the roofs? They'm fallen off and nobody puts 'em up again."

"There's no money," George said, thinking of himself. "This is a poor country, running to waste, where we grow wheat for straw and have no market for grain."

"Us don't want money. Us craves common rights, and then us could put the roofs on vor ourselves," said Bill doggedly. "If I cuts a few reeds vor thatch I be a thief."

He walked away with the big basket on his shoulder, going down into the valley of dun clay, which grew roses and wheat for pleasure. Every season it took Bill a little longer to make that journey, for he was walking slower though he didn't know it, and there was neither watch in his pocket nor clock at home to let him know that the days were shortening.

George and Berenice kept apart from each other after that. It was easy, as the winds were getting rough and the girl was sent walks into deep lanes, and he was always upon the moor. Berenice was becoming afraid of the artist because she thought he suspected her of wrong-doing and of behaving like a rival. She was almost a man where Winnie was concerned, and George might have noticed that. In a sense she was his rival, for she had quite decided that when she had discovered Winnie, as she must some time, George should not know anything about it. He was not going to have the little girl with the dimples and circumcised nose; and there the masculine nature of her cropped up again. She was a handsome brown girl, not by any means sexless, but on the contrary strongly bi-sexual. She had been bisected as it were, divided into two equal parts, one feminine, the other masculine, and the stronger side naturally predominated in matters of feeling, casting her sympathies into an extraordinary state of confusion. Thus she would glance at the Chowns struggling on bravely in their poverty and call them savages; but if Tobias ran a thorn into his foot the feminine side welled up into exaggerated sympathy and she would suffer far more than the dog.

Souls such as Berenice's cannot love because they cannot discriminate. They see something that they want and hurl themselves at it, very much like a flying beetle charging into a wall, stunning itself by the impact. There is no sense, no reasoning, no self-restraint about it, because the sufferer, although sane in other matters, is mad upon the one thing. It is the one-idea that kills in the long run. Even natural one-idea'd love may be fatal when it becomes an obsession; and an impatient devotion to religion will lead to such insane practices as pentecostal dances and doll-Sundays, reducing the sublime to the ridiculous and dismissing the Creator to the nursery. A diseased body often makes a diseased mind; and even a harmless pastime such as rose-growing may become a disease in the long run. Even loneliness may turn into a disease which destroys the moral faculty; and the continual high wind may breed the destroying germ of drunkenness. The patient must be patient, long-suffering, not easily provoked; and the patient end of the whole matter shows a perfect work.

That young person Tobias was the agent of destiny to prove Berenice's undoing. She adored the jolly little fellow. All her life she had been worried by an incurable devotion for dogs, and other animals as well, although dogs were easily first. People who have an inordinate fondness for animals should have nothing to do with them, beyond trying to better their lot and reminding men and women that they are animals too, above the lower orders in some ways, below them in others; for it is possible that no man has ever equalled the intelligence of the hardly perceptible ant. People who love animals are often tender-hearted towards their own species, and there is hardly enough endurance in the human body to bear the troubles and sufferings of both sides. As for the history of Tobias, it was short and simple like his tail, though much less moving. He was too young to have any past. He had been born in lawful wedlock, for he was a well-bred little gentleman, and respectability had been forced upon his mother. His owner was supposed to be the doctor, but Tobias preferred ladies, so he lived at the sanatorium and made love to every pretty girl who came there. When a particular charmer left he didn't break his heart, nor did he whine and grow thin, but he simply took the next best girl. When he couldn't get a woman he walked out with a man, but with such an air of condescension as to be almost insufferable. He was a smooth-haired fox-terrier with a brown spot on his side and a white marking down his face; a pretty little man with very dainty paws. After kissing pretty girls he liked running after a ball; and the third joy of his life was chasing rabbits. It was not quite easy to draw the dividing line between Tobias and a young gentleman of the superior species. For most two-legged young men are just as fond of kissing pretty girls, running after a ball, and chasing rabbits as four-legged Tobias could have been.

It was the Sunday half-holiday and Berenice decided to spend it sulkily indoors, which disgusted Tobias because the weather was fine and his energy was enormous. Presently he slipped outside, to see if there were any nice smells about, and there temptation came to him in the form of a public-house spaniel of no reputation. Tobias spoke to him after the manner of a pampered dog, and the spaniel answered him smoothly because he was really the devil in disguise. "I go a-hunting," said the public-house dog, with that fine disregard for the Sabbath which characterises sportsmen. "I'll go with you," said Tobias; and off they trotted, side by side, with their noses to the ground. This was very wrong of Tobias, who had been carefully brought up, and told that he must never speak or play with vulgar dogs, nor go forth unattended, and never display anti-religious feeling by howling when the church bell was rung. He was also desecrating the Sabbath by going out hunting; and it was therefore absolutely necessary that some evil should befall him, otherwise all the elaborate fabric of punishment for wrong-doing, built up so carefully upon the foundations of Sunday-school teaching, would have toppled ignominiously to the ground. The small boy or little dog who goes rabbit-hunting on a Sunday afternoon is certain to come to a bad end; just as the poor old Hebrew gentleman, who went out to pull a few sticks from some Hivite or Hittite hedge, was foredoomed to be caught into the moon, dog, sticks and all, and exposed there for ever like a bad negative. The spaniel was perfectly well aware that he was leading Tobias astray; and he was glad because of his diabolic nature. He was himself a lewd fellow of the baser sort, and he had no tenderness for little gentlemen who were pampered and cutlet-fed, and slept upon cushions, and had brush and combs for their toilet and fine collars to deck themselves withal. "Us will go to the copse and catch conies," said the spaniel, unwittingly proclaiming his criminal tendencies; for the law is unable to recognise a rabbit by that name.

"I've been told never to go into the copse," said Tobias, with a look of shame upon his brown face.

"Bide here then," said the coarse-minded spaniel, who had already been convicted of poaching times without number. "Proper little kiss-mammy yew be."

Tobias was not going to stand that. He could hunt rabbits quite as well as the spaniel, and he intended to prove it. So he went off, with his head up to catch all the smells, merely remarking that he must get back in time for tea, as he always had a saucer of milk and assorted cakes then, and if he didn't turn up for this light refreshment a fundamental change in the orbit of the earth would probably occur. The spaniel sneered again; a biscuit like a tile and a sniff of hot rum were more in his line.

"I've been told there are traps in the copse," said Tobias, speaking prettily as his numerous mistresses had taught him, and annoying the public-house gentleman, who knew nothing but dialect.

"Bain't none now," he said gruffly; but the spaniel lied unto Tobias.

A fire had been granted in the sitting-room of the sanatorium that afternoon, and Miss Budge was making the most of it and sprawling in front of it as if she had been the planet Mercury beside the sun. Berenice sat afar off, reading or letting her eyes wander across the moor, thinking sometimes of Winnie but hardly ever speaking. At last the tea-table appeared, Miss Budge awoke and said she was shivering on one side and baked on the other, and at the same moment Berenice became conscious that she was shivering all over. It was a cold wind and blowing straight into the room. She did not like the fire, as the sight and warmth of it made her feel sick, but she came across towards a sheltered corner; and then her eyes fell upon a ball lying upon the carpet like a lost pleiad. "Where's Tobias?" she said quickly.

Miss Budge neither knew nor cared; she said as much and got sworn at. Then Berenice went about the house, calling and whistling, but there was no cheerful whimper, no pattering of small feet to answer her. The others assembled in the sitting-room and Berenice came and catechised them, but their answers were unsatisfactory. Tobias had not been seen. It was getting dark, the wind was rising, rain was beginning to splash in dreary autumnal fashion, and Berenice felt suddenly fearfully ill. She went out into the wild weather just as she was, only conscious that the light was nearly gone, that Tobias was lost, and the night would be long and very dark.

She saw something advancing along the narrow road like a monstrous crab with ungainly movements. She went towards it, hoping it might be a man, and so it was, though it seemed to consist chiefly of large sticks and shufflings. It was Uncle Gifford going home from chapel with two tottering legs and the same number of firm ash-plants; and he was talking to himself of bruised reeds and smoking flax and wondering what they meant.

"Have you seen Tobias?" Berenice cried at once, bringing the somewhat erratic machinery which controlled Uncle's movements to a standstill. He tried to shake his head, but his neck was too stiff; so he touched his hat respectfully and wished the young lady good-evening. "Us be agwaine to have a thick night," he explained, not having understood her question.

"He went out early in the afternoon and hasn't come home," the girl went on.

"Please?" said Uncle gently.

"My little dog. He's lost," she said, her voice breaking.

Uncle was a tender old soul, but to him an animal was an animal. A cow was a creature to give milk, and to be knocked on the head for beef when she couldn't give any more. As for a dog, it was right that he should die like one. Uncle did not know why the young lady was so agitated. All he could do was to explain the matter. It was simple enough. The dog had been caught in a trap. There was nothing unusual in that. Uncle had known a dog to stand in a trap for three days until his foot had been cut right off; but Berenice only screamed when he went into details.

"Are they trapping?" she gasped.

"Ees, it be trapping-time," said Uncle, pleased to give information. "If yew goes down under yew'll hear the rabbuts screaming."

A kinder man than Uncle did not live, and yet his idea of suffering was a quaint one. He regarded it as something necessary, not as anything preventible. Men had to endure a great deal, and they felt it badly, but had to bear up somehow. Animals did not count. Uncle had been a mole-catcher for many years. He did not suppose that the moles ever suffered when he trapped them, any more than a leaf suffers when a caterpillar nibbles it. Rabbits screamed when they were in traps just as bees hummed while they were flying about. It was their nature; but animals had nothing whatever to do with such matters as consciousness and pain.

From the public-house yard proceeded yelps and howls of dire distress; not much of penitence perhaps, but rather curses and threatenings. Berenice hurried there, and found the landlord flogging the spaniel, who had just returned wet and muddy, while his small son attended with a lighted lantern. The devil may know how to escape snares, but he gets his deserts sometimes, although no punishment can reform him. The spaniel would be just as wicked on Monday though he was being flogged on Sunday.

"I'll learn ye," shouted the publican. "Proper old poaching toad yew be." The course of instruction was continued with a cart-whip.

"Ees, miss, he went off wi' your little dog," said the small boy. "He'm just a-come home. Likely yours ha' gone home tu."

Berenice hurried back to the sanatorium, but Tobias was not there. She could not stay indoors, although it was quite dark by then, and the rain was blowing about in large stinging drops. Out she went again, in defiance of authority, and questioned every villager she met as to where the traps were set. Apparently they were everywhere. The hedges bristled with them. It was almost impossible for an animal to set its foot anywhere without getting an iron jaw clamped upon it. The traps were in every direction, and she was assured that nothing could be done until the morning. A night in a trap wouldn't kill any dog, she was told. Most of the men spoke as if they were persuaded it would benefit the animal's health considerably. Berenice went to the public-house and borrowed the lantern. She tried to borrow the small boy too, and offered him money if he would go with her, but the boy was incorruptible. He was due at the evening service in the chapel, to sit beside a small girl and squeeze and pinch her between devotional intervals; which was something higher and nobler than tramping muddy fields in the wind and rain. Young as he was, he had his soul to think of; and that could not possibly be supplied with spiritual food by desecrating the Sunday evening searching for rabbit-traps.

Berenice went off by herself, coughing and gasping for breath because she would hurry so. She was acting foolishly, but could not control herself. She was feeling so ill she could hardly think coherently; and at last she had a wild idea she was searching for Winnie, who was caught somehow and was screaming for some one to come and release her. Every sound made an echo of Winnie's plaintive voice; and that windy lane just off the moor was full of sounds. Berenice tried to call out, but had no voice. The darkness, the wind and rain, the decaying autumn, increased her horror. Winnie or Tobias, it was all one just then. She loved them both—she didn't know which she loved the most. Whichever was in the trap;

that was the one. She seemed to see pink-and-white Winnie with dainty white dog's paws struggling in a mass of machinery which was moving horribly, tearing her up. Berenice had to stop and lean against a hedge coughing terribly, feeling hardly conscious and in the grip of a nightmare. Around her was a greasy little hell of yellow light cast by the lantern, and in this light were great gadfly spots of sleet. Her hair was sopping and her shoes were two shapeless lumps of clay.

At last she came out upon the edge of the copse. Down below was a mess of mossy bog, and she did not know the way through. She realised then the power of the night and the tyranny of darkness. Nothing could be done until the morning; and in the meantime all suffering lay hidden under that heavy pall of black wind and silvery sleet—but not quite all. The wind dropped, paused to rest itself as it were, and that moment the night was filled with strange noises of appeal. Only a few wet and useless fields divided the boggy copse from the church; and in the silence sounds came from the church. Up from the copse came other sounds, and the two met upon the top of the hill.

From the church came faintly the wheezy leaking music of the harmonium, trying to blow out a hymn. All around were the short sharp screams of tortured rabbits. It made a strange mixture of sounds; both making an appeal for mercy; one asking for what it would not render to others, the other demanding only justice. It was a question which sound carried the furthest; which was most likely to receive attention in the court of final appeal.

The wind, which can be merciful sometimes, swept down again from the tors and put everything else to silence. The night seemed to grow rougher than ever, and Berenice dragged herself back to the lane, mad to do something, but helpless to act. Every time her feet touched ground they seemed to try and take root there. Then she thought of George. He would do something if she could get across to Wheal Dream, not for her sake perhaps, as she had never done him any good, but for the sake of Tobias, whom Winnie had petted. She reached the road, dragged herself on, and presently a long shaft of light reached out from the side of the moor like the gleam of a lighthouse striking seawards, and she walked up the light conscious of little else until she reached the door.

George was in, working as usual, though more mechanically because his mind was not there and he did not know where it was. He appeared at the door half dressed, his coat fastened round him with a strap as all the buttons were absent, a woollen scarf taking the place of collar, his toes protruding like tubers from broken canvas shoes.

"Come along in, neighbour," he said huskily. "Leave the hat and lantern behind the door. Walk in and we'll tell before the fire;" but when the light wobbled about, like the will-o'-the-wisp upon a bog, George trembled, for he saw a frocked figure with two muddy shoes beneath, and he muttered something which roused Berenice and made her almost hate him. It was obvious that he was thinking of nothing but Winnie, and the vision of any girl at his gate made him dream.

"I thought at first you were Uncle," George said, tugging the scarf round his neck as if he desired to throttle himself. "Then when the light moved and I saw your dress—" He broke off, scrubbing his beard with the back of his hand. "This is an awful place for dreams," he muttered. "My windows open upon the wheal, and as I lie at night the dreams pour out of the shaft like cinders from a volcano."

"My dog," said Berenice faintly. "He's in a trap. Tearing his pretty self to death."

"What, the little man who trots across here and plays with me? Her dog," he added, not meaning Berenice to hear; but she did, and snapped at him—

"I shared him with her, but she never loved him half as much as I do."

George was fond of animals, more so than most men; but he did not comprehend the overwhelming passion which sets a certain dog or cat much above all other mortals under heaven.

"You have been about looking for him?" he said.

"Until I'm nearly dead. I must find him or I shall go mad in the night."

"Come in and sit down a bit."

"I should never get up again. I have been in the copse. It's a place of torture, a boggy inferno. Screams everywhere, but I couldn't hear my poor pet."

"He's all right. He's not in a trap," said George. "He's paying a round of calls."

"He must be. He never stays out after dark. Think of him. Struggling all the time, with his dear little foot in one of those damnable things—you know what a dainty little white foot it is. Covered with blood now," she cried hysterically. "His pretty brown face all matted with rain, and his beautiful eyes filled with tears," she went on. "The torture is getting worse every minute, and he can't understand. He doesn't know what he has done to deserve it. He has always been petted, and that makes it harder for him. Winnie was fond of him. She often used to kiss him between the eyes, and call him her dear thing, and I've often seen him snuggling against her, with his nose under her arm, and he was always smelling of her—"

"Stop it," said George rudely and roughly. "You can't stand this sort of thing. I can't either. There's a lust for slaughter in November because it's the month of death and general damnation. I shall die in November; the next one likely enough. Well, I'm going out to look for the poor little chap, though I might as well toss a pin into Wheal Dream, then go and search for it. But you have spoilt my peace for to-night."

He huddled on a shocking old macintosh, turned down his lamp, and came out with her. Berenice was crying by this time out of weakness, and she had to accept his arm to help herself along.

"Bear it," said George, blowing out his cheeks and pretending not to care. "Suffering is good for us. Must be, or we shouldn't get such a lot of it. If you can't bear it patiently bear it aggressively. That's my way—accept the trouble because you must, curse at it, and go on trying. But I'm no good. You girls can endure things better than men. You bend and let the wind go over you. We try to stand stiff and get our backbones twisted. Here you are. Go in and lie down."

"I shall take my morphia," she whispered. Each patient was entrusted with a little morphia for use in an emergency.

"Best thing perhaps," George said. "Oblivion is the only treatment for a raw heart."

He went on into the darkness, the plaything of wind and rain, muttering in a morbid fashion, "We're going down. We shall soon be bankrupts. Bubo and Brunacombe, born and instituted on a Friday. We're all bankrupt in November. Poor little Bubo! He lost a leg in his infancy, and he'll soon lose his partnership, for our Mr. Brunacombe is getting into deep water."

That was how the long autumnal night began. Ages passed before daylight returned, and during the intervening period Berenice endured more than she ever cared to think about afterwards. It was foolish perhaps, but people are as they are made, and when the temperament says "Down, mind," it is no use resisting. She took her morphia, but it refused to act; so she walked about the room, moaning and beating her hands together. Every gust of wind, every sweep of rain across her bed, made her howl. She could not lie still for more than a few moments. Her pillow was like a bed of nettles. She stared at her watch, the hands of which never moved, and sometimes she murmured, "If it was only all over. If he was only dead I could stand it." She suffered probably far more than the dog. She seemed to feel his every movement a thousand times intensified, and the pain of it went through her like a knife. Like the dog, she tugged to get free and could not; and every effort weakened her more. The night was growing steadily wilder and the darkness more unearthly.

At last she could endure no more of it. She dressed and went silently down-stairs. There was nobody to prevent her from leaving the house, so she did so, feeling better when she was outside and in motion. She walked to Wheal Dream, but hesitated when she got to the door of the mine house. It was past midnight, and she could not knock and bring George out. There was no light in the house, but Bubo was hooting in cheerful fashion and his wild brethren of the tors answered him. Berenice felt her way to the gate, which led from the stannary road down into the wheal, where she had sat with Winnie and the poor little girl had lied to her. The darkness was not so intense that she couldn't see the black and ancient timbers. Step by step she felt her way down, trying to think of anything except the one thing which would not be ignored. She got into the wheal, sheltered herself from the rain beneath the old timbers, and listened to the spadiard's ghost digging patiently far below. It was only the water dripping with a resounding echo, but it sounded like a spade; and there she sat moaning and shivering, and wondering if she was ever going to live through the night.

The spirit of Wheal Dream was merciful, or perhaps the drug that she had swallowed woke up and put her to sleep; anyhow the girl had not been there long before she was insensible. It was a restless sleep, full of jumping hobgoblins and cruel elves practising stannary-like torments upon prisoners; but it was unconsciousness, which was the only thing she asked for. She slept upon the dripping ferns and spongy mosses, and the unhappy hours went silently away.

It was scarcely light when Father Chown passed down and roused her with distressing and grave-qualifying noises. All through the summer Father had been worried by a long bramble, which stretched across the path and hooked his shaky legs every time he went down to bring the cow up. Not that he ever did, for the cow was sensible enough to come without being invited, but Father liked to think he was still working. He would entice a small stick into the linhay and tap at it harmlessly with a chopper the whole morning; and then he would toddle into the house and say it would be a good thing for the country if young men possessed wood-hewing powers equal to his. Every day for weeks Father had sworn vengeance upon that spiny rope which steadfastly impeded his progress. He moved at about the same rate as the minute hand of a large clock, so a very little thing brought him to a standstill. He often stood near the bramble and reasoned out the whole matter; it had caught him just as it had done yesterday; he would come that way to-morrow and it would catch him again; but if he cut it off it would cease from troubling. There seemed no doubt about that, so Father propped himself up and worried his hand slowly into his pocket, which took him a long time, and then he found it was the wrong pocket and his knife was in the other. He propped himself up on the east side and tried again; but when he had the knife he couldn't open it, and nobody was near to do it for him; and if it had been opened the blade was so blunt that his weak wrist could never have forced it through the tough obstacle. Perhaps some other instrument would be more suitable. Father could only poke at the enemy with his stick, and abuse it as if it had been a Christian. But the indifferent bramble blossomed and brought forth fruit, and its leaves turned from green to scarlet, and it hooked Father every day with its long curved thorns.

Father had spent the greater part of Sunday thinking blasphemously about the bramble, because he thought it might outlive him and go on tearing the legs of the new generation after he had taken his place among the heavenly choristers, though it was not easy to imagine Father in such a position, and he would soon have made his white robes fearfully dirty. He had gone to bed at his usual early hour and the bramble caught at him in his sleep, until it was shown him in a dream what he ought to do. He must rise early, so that there should be plenty of time, take the chopper, shuffle down the path, and attack the enemy at its root. It might not be conquered in one day, nor yet in two; but Monday morning should see bruises, and Tuesday night perchance a fatal injury; and on Wednesday it would wither away. Father arose before it was day, dressed himself by putting on his boots, the other things being already in position, finished a jug of milk in which various insects had drowned themselves during the night, and shuffled out. He reached the linhay safely after an invigorating tramp of ten yards, grasped the chopper, and then sat down on the wood-pile because more reasoning was required. How was he to carry the chopper when in motion? Both hands would be occupied with those necessary forelegs, his sticks. There were certainly side pockets to his coat, but that garment was like a work of genius, not for an age but for all time, and anything placed in those pockets would a moment later strike the ground or one of his boots. He could not carry the chopper in his mouth because he had no teeth; he could not kick it along in front of him. Father had to confess that the problem was too great for him. The bramble was going to beat him after all.

Just then he noticed something on his right boot. He always looked at his right boot when any special effort of the intellect was required; there was no inspiration to be obtained from the left boot. He bent down and observed an ant hard at work crossing the great muddy plateau of leather, dragging a tiny stalk behind it. How the insect managed this Father neither knew nor cared, but it gave him the idea which he would never have hit upon for himself. He could follow the example of the ant and drag the chopper behind him. Father lowered his thumb and with vast contempt for noxious insects smeared the poor ant out of existence; then he took a piece of rope, tied one end round the chopper, the other about his leg, and shuffled forth rejoicing. Father was almost frightened at his own sagacity.

Berenice started and shivered; she was horribly cold, and the sick feeling of despair came back with consciousness. Well, it would be all over, Tobias had finished his agony and was dead. He could not have endured through that interminable night. She imagined him lying on his side, wet, cold and stiff, his eyes glazed; and she felt as if the world had departed from her. Not the death of any human being would have distressed her so much. Just then she could have spared Winnie rather than Tobias. She dragged herself out of the wheal, passed Father, alarming him dreadfully and leaving him staring in amazement long after she had disappeared, and went up on the moor thankful for the light, though it was nothing better than a mass of rolling mist whitened as a pretence of daylight.

"Thikky place be more like London getting every day," observed Father, though he had never been much nearer London than Wheal Dream, and was therefore hardly justified in supposing that ladies of the metropolis passed the night in old mines, and rose from them suddenly at the dawn to startle old gentlemen who might be abolishing prickly shrubs in important thoroughfares. Not that Father was interfering with the vital principle of the bramble. He was tapping away with the chopper at inoffensive ferns and thick mosses; presently he struck a block of granite with a fine jarring effect and chuckled manfully. A few more like that and his old enemy would never bring forth blackberries again.

As Berenice ascended she met George. He was coming out of the wreaths of mist like a man escaping from a burning house, hurrying along with his head down, muttering as usual and hardly looking where he went. He could have walked there with his eyes shut, knowing every stone and furze-bush, and the shape of each, and the exact distance from one to another. He did not see Berenice until he was up with her, and she said nothing, but only looked at him in a wounded sort of way. There was so much mist between them that each was a ghostly figure to the other. George opened his mouth to ask how she dared to be abroad at that unearthly hour, but he only croaked dismally. He coughed, slapped his chest, and his voice came back. "I've been in and out all night. Lighting my lamp, blowing it out again, tumbling on my bed, getting the horrors and turning out for another tramp. One bad night is worse than a score of bad days; especially when the wind is up and the darkness has a slimy feel."

"Have you nothing to tell me?" asked the miserable girl.

"You won't believe it, but the sun is shining back over. It will be on us presently. This mist is running off like a tide. A touch of sunshine now is as good as a legacy. I feel almost successful on a fine day."

"I don't want the sun. I want my darling little dog," said Berenice.

"The little devil," said George tenderly. "He and Bubo have been playing the deuce with me. First you came and upset me by telling me about Tobias, and then Bubo came and rubbed it in by reminding me it was a terrible thing to lose a leg; and having an imagination and bad health I sweated and got sick. These creatures are a curse to us. I put a piece of string on Bubo's perch as a hint that he might hang himself, but he won't. He'll outlive me and find himself on the parish."

"We can do something now that the light is back. We can go along every hedge—" Berenice began, but George interrupted her gently—

"Tobias is all right. Like us, he's had a bad night, but it's over now."

"Then you do know something?"

"Last night after you left me I climbed up to Moor Gate where Gregory lives. You know him, the singing giant with the crowbar. He wasn't in, so I waited about for him. It was Sunday night, when bachelors are out with women, and Gregory is courting a woman round and about Downacot. He must be courting her seriously, as he wasn't home till midnight. I told him about Tobias, and he told Ben, his big sheep-dog. Ben possesses supernatural qualities. Gregory talks to him with his hands and the dog interprets the signs with his eyes. Here's the sun! Didn't I tell you good-luck was coming by way of bogland?"

Berenice sat upon a boulder and looked wretched. "I know he's dead. I don't care about anything," she said. "First Winnie, then my doggie, and now my temperature is up to bursting-point. There's one thing," she murmured, "I'm too ill to be lectured."

That was true enough. Usually her fine brown face seemed healthy enough to defy all diseases, but there was a pallor upon it then, and for the first time George saw that apparently transparent and spiritual expression which is so attractive and so ominous. She was dirty at last, as dirty as himself, yet it was all clean enough, the clay and copper of the wheal, the mud of the copse, the brown peat of the moor. She had always been so fresh and clean that she frightened him. Now she was in some sympathy with him. Suffering like penitence brings every one down to dust and ashes. What man cares if there is mud upon his trousers when he staggers in at the cemetery gate? George didn't like her eyes; they were too dark and there was unnatural energy in them.

"I want to get well," she was saying. "I must go and find Winnie. I shall get well if Tobias is still alive."

George sat down nearly opposite her. He was exhausted too and he wanted to feel the glad sun and soak it in. Berenice did not consider him, or she must have noticed that his features which the hair did not cover were almost as white as Meldon marble, and his face had that same spiritual transparency, and his clothes hung about him more loosely than they had done in summer time. He too was a fragile growth tormented with disease; and yet the wonderful roots of both struck down into the depths of eternity, and would endure somehow and bring forth new growths in spite of the elements which can only shake off the blossoms but cannot destroy the root.

It was ridiculous perhaps that so much fuss should be made about a dog. But there was something more than the fact of a petted animal in misery. There was his sacred character to consider. He had slept on Winnie's bed and been fondled in her arms and kissed by her very often. Even the most hardened unbeliever would not wilfully kick the thigh-bone of a martyr into the gutter, if he knew it was a genuine article, and had not, like most such relics, been supplied by the nearest rag and bone shop. He would respect the memory of a brave soul; while the true believer would snatch up the bone and desire to eat it. Berenice and George were true believers in the sense that they both loved Winnie. Berenice with her abnormal devotion for animals, which amounted to a religion, would have suffered just as much over the fate of Tobias had Winnie never existed; but George would assuredly not have spent a rambling night had the little girl with the original nose been kept out of his life.

"You ought to be getting back," he said.

"To sit and stuff myself, I suppose," she answered. "I loathe the place," she went on with the utmost bitterness. "The house is haunted by Winnie. So is every walk. Whenever I go over Chapel Ford I see her sitting on the stones, listening to—to—well, to you," she said defiantly. "You seemed to interest her more than I could. How she loved the moor! She was always wanting to climb to the highest tor, throw her arms round the topmost rock and hold on. How she must have howled when she went away! Heavens! I hate the moor."

"November," said George quietly. "Put it all down to November. April settles the debt, though not always."

"If you hear of her you'll let me know? Promise me," she said.

George stiffened at once. He was chilly and wretched, and in that mood he wanted to pretend that Winnie was nothing. "How should I hear?" he said roughly. "She doesn't write to strangers, least of all to elderly, grey-bearded men, who live up on the tors with the owls, and will soon be burrowing into a hole to perdition. I shall never see her again," cried George, blinking his eyes like a great baby, "and a jolly good thing too. Well, I'm going home—to my workshop. I've had the devil of a night, and now I'm going to paint till all's blue. Don't look at me like that. I'm all right except for a sharp touch of November. Bubo and I have taken the vows of poverty and celibacy. We have our little cloister down below, and I'm going to work there for a few more days."

"What are you going to do?" asked Berenice, wondering at the strangeness of his manner.

"Work," said George, flinging out his tired hands. "It's the only house of life which gives the mind rest. Work! it's the only wayside inn that is never full. I'm going to drive these ten little pen and brush carrying acolytes as they were never driven before. I'm going to look the other way when I see a strange face. You don't go mad while you work, but if you keep the hands in your pockets you'll find a piece of insanity there one day. I'm going to paint my windows green and imagine it is April. A fig for all women. It's the eternal burning and longing which make us rotten; and the fire is false after all. Bubo has taught me something. You can't look into an owl's cold eyes for a few years without being ashamed of blundering like a moth after the first bit of fire that burns across your path. An owl is nearer godliness than we are, though he does eat his own fleas."

"A fig for Winnie too?" suggested Berenice with some heat.

"That," cried poor George, snapping his fingers, although he broke his heart for it afterwards. "She laughed at me. She mocked me—the poor devil that lived and worked in the dirty old mine house."

"When?" cried Berenice, glad but wondering.

"Why, you told me. Those pieces of paper which I had scribbled on and the wind had blown into the wheal. Didn't she find them, read what I had written to you all and set you laughing at the poor lonely booby who was asking the Life that made him to let him have company? Pray! I tell you I've done it. I would go down twice a day on the boards, and shut my eyes so that I shouldn't see Bubo winking at me, and I'd say like any little fool of a school-child, 'God, let me make my living. That's all. I don't want fame and I don't want riches. I only want a living and I'm willing to work twelve hours a day for it.' That was my prayer. What was the answer? Why, a Jew who owed me twenty pounds went bankrupt rather than pay, and is now doing business under his wife's name, and another cheated me a bit worse than usual. What did I get in return for my score of long days and a dozen headaches? I gave up the praying. I couldn't afford it."

"I ought to tell him," said Berenice to herself, hot and shivering. "These little lies grow such long roots. But he might go after her, and she loves him, and he shan't have her. Anyhow he couldn't, so what does it matter?" She was afraid also to tell him the truth. He might have lost all control over himself. Much solitude makes a man queer company.

"You don't want Winnie now?" was what she said.

"I want no one. I shan't live much longer"

"November again," she broke in, with a smile that was intended to set, not him, but herself at ease.

"Whatever the time I'll go on working—from November to nowhere. The rest of the time I shall paint; nothing else. I've been a dabbler in a dozen crafts, thorough at none. Now I'll stick to the one. I've got a few pictures in my mind—not for the Jews or money, but for myself. And when they are done we go into liquidation. Bubo and Brunacombe, manufacturers. Assets nil."

George began to move away, dragging his great boots; and the girl who would have been a man followed him with her eyes. After all why should she speak? Every one tells lies to their own advantage. She knew that the shrine of St. Winifred was not demolished. The altar was as neatly kept as ever, the tapers were burning with a pleasant odour, and the daily services were going on the same as usual. The pretty saint, like all others more unreal, was unattainable. George was not to have her.

"I will find Winnie," said she wildly. George could not hear. "I will give her a man's love and a better love than any man could give. I would send my blood into her veins to show how much I love her."

Then George came back limping, and Berenice noticed for the first time that his neck was all bloody. He had been through hedges in the night.

"Tobias is safe. He is coming in Gregory's arms," he said quietly.

The little hill upon which they had met was the least of all the tors, and only called one because it possessed a whale-shaped outcrop of black rock; and it rose between the village and Moor Gate. There was Gregory, swinging along with his earth-shaking movements, and Tobias the Sunday-breaker was tucked under his arm, alive and unmutilated but writhing with pain.

Berenice started up and ran, babbling endearments, and the heavy November day became April suddenly.

"He'm wull enuff. Nothing broke," shouted Gregory, taking the poor, damaged limb. The claws were spread out like the foot of a goose and the leg was fearfully swollen. "'Twas an old trap, lucky vor 'en, and the jaws wur blunt."

"Let me have him. My poor darling! Oh, he's in agony," cried Berenice, kissing and cuddling the little sufferer and wiping his brown head and eyes with her handkerchief, while Tobias loved her violently, made the utmost of his injuries, and said he would never go rabbit-hunting again; at least not until he was almost convalescent.

"His foot bain't come to life yet. He'm all dead like," said Gregory. "He'll be all right by evening. Old Ben found 'en sure 'nuff, and comed to tell me, and I went wi' Ben and took 'en out."

"Darling boy. Doctor shall put some chloroform on the poor foot. Where is Mr. Brunacombe?"

"He goes beyond," Gregory answered, pointing below where a dark, limping figure was visible among the rocks. "He'm going home."

"So must I," she said. "Thanks a thousand times. You have made me happy. Oh, my pet, the paw will soon be well. Give it me to hold, dear boy."

"He'm lucky," said Gregory. "Me and old Ben ha' bided together till he ha' got human, and I've learnt friendliness. Friendship be a fine thing, if 'tis nought but the friendship of a spider. He'm a lucky dog, I ses, and when yew'm lucky yew can't du wrong. If yew drinks poison it makes yew fat. Wull, lady, I'll tull ye a story, and he'm true vor 'tis wrote down on my parchment. There wur a man who lived to Clovelly wance, and he wur so lucky that he couldn't du wrong. One time he wanted to give a man some money, but didn't knaw how to du it vor the man wur a bit above 'en like and he wur proud got wi' poverty. So the lucky one ses to 'en, 'See this old diamond ring o' mine? Wull, I'll row out to sea and tak' 'en off my finger and throw 'en in, and I'll bet yew a hundred pounds he'll come back.' T'other laughed and said, 'I'll tak' ye, man,' vor he knowed of course the ring couldn't come back. So the man got into a boat and rowed out to sea and threw his ring away; and then he got home along and told volks how he'd been and lost his ring and would reward any one what brought 'en back. And the next week a little maid comes up along and ses, 'Here be your ring, master. I wur walking on the beach and saw mun shine among the pebbles.' Wull, lady, there bain't no fighting agin luck. The poor man never got the money and he owed the lucky one a hundred pounds." Throwing his hand up to his hat, Gregory was off towards his eyrie, beginning to shout and sing, his great feet making deep impressions in the peat.

True to his word George worked the day away. Evening came and he rested a few minutes before lighting up, letting the twilight play softly upon his eyelids, talking as usual to his partner. Bubo was a splendid companion for a hard-working man. George toiled during the day by his own energy, and when evening arrived Bubo awoke and became so lusty that George felt ashamed to be idle and worked half the night with energy borrowed from the owl.

"Well, Brunacombe, how are you?" said a voice from the passage. The door of the Wheal House was always open and the doctor stepped in suddenly. He was a rare visitor; George and he hardly ever met although they lived not half-a-mile apart.

"Come in," said George rising. "Here is a chair." It was in fact the only one.

"I won't stay. I was having a walk and just looked in to see that you're taking care of yourself. You are thin."

"Work and November; neither are flesh-formers," said George.

"Come round some time and I'll run over you. You mustn't let yourself down too much. I hear you spent last night looking for that wretched dog. I ought to have put chloroform into his stomach instead of upon his foot."

"How is Miss Calladine?"

"About as bad as she can be. I sent her to bed at once, and in the middle of the day I told her about Miss Shazell. You remember that pretty little thing. Didn't you paint her? It was foolish of me, but I could not have known she would have felt it so badly. She became hysterical and then had a haemorrhage," he said indifferently. "Only a slight one, but with a girl of her temperament it is impossible to tell what may follow. The only time I have any control over her is when she is in bed."

George was as cold and white as the water rushing past Wheal Dream. He was glad it was getting dark.

"Miss Shazell?" he muttered. Even Bubo seemed to be staring frightfully at the visitor.

"I had a letter from her doctor this morning. Last week she married that man Halfacre who was here with her. I don't know whether you ever saw him. I had to send him away. The law ought to prevent such marriages. It means death to her," he said crossly.

CHAPTER XVI
ABOUT CONTRASTS

News of the world reached Metheral once a week by way of a local paper left at the public-house. The information contained therein was of the smallest kind, a jumble of concerts, chapel-meetings and affiliation orders. The contributors were for the most part village magnates who because they could write their names without a single mistake imagined they could also write English. Some of the more hopeless phrases were polished in the office; but the editor himself was not qualified to deal with such matters of higher scholarship as a singular verb following a plural noun.

The villagers liked hearing the paper read and to know all that was doing in the great world of their own neighbourhood. Sometimes one of them was mentioned by name, though it would be generally mis-spelt, and on such a day he would take more liquor than was good for him. Perhaps one of his ewes had given birth to living quadruplets; and, the glory of the deed descending somewhat undeservedly upon the master, he would be mentioned together with his farm, parish and nearest market town, all incorrectly but near enough to be recognised; or perhaps he would have been summoned for not sending a child to school, and there would be published his good woman's usual excuse how that she couldn't possibly get the housework done with "a weekly baby." The glory was the same whatever the cause. It was being in print, a public mention, a reminder to the whole world that Samuel Tozer of Vuzzypit parish in some glorious clay-covered hole of Devon was not among the least of its inhabitants, for his ewe was singularly prolific or his child abnormally engaged in domestic duties; and that sort of thing filled a niche of the parochial temple of fame with a statue of S. Tozer.

The paper was being discussed and interpreted one Friday evening—it was really afternoon but a dark wind had blown up, as it will in winter, blackening the moor too early—when the reader made a discovery of general interest under the not inappropriate heading of Mortehoe. A death was announced which had only occurred the day before, and the name of the deceased was one Job Tinker, who was a parishioner of Metheral, had property there, but had been drawn away to the remote north by business interests several years back. This was indeed a matter for fair comment, as most of the commoners present had known dead Tinker intimately, and the landlord had on several occasions assisted him the whole way from the bar-room to his own cottage because Tinker's rheumatism always came on badly late at night. Now he had departed; that fact alone was of little importance; but there would be a carnival, suitable rejoicings, black streamers, abundance of refreshments, people from all parts; for Tinker would certainly have left instructions for his bones to be placed among those of his ancestors; and his good old widow would not mind spending money on such an occasion. The landlord's red face became cheerful; he made a mental calculation of the beer and spirits in stock, decided he would require double the quantity, and said, "Wull, I be cruel sorry. Poor old Tinker. Cuts me to the heart to hear he'm gone."

"How old wur he?" asked young Moorshed, who had married Miss Bidlake during the summer and had already got into the habit of looking in upon the landlord until closing-time.

"Eighty-dree."

"Took as 'twere in his prime," said Farmer Tom Moorshed.

"Paid 'en better to ha' bided here," said the landlord. "Me tu," he muttered.

"Ah, he'd ha' lived to a gude old age if he'd bided up on Dartmoor. What be wrong wi' old Willum?"

The bar-room being warm and well-lighted, Brokenbrow had come in out of the black wind, had settled in a corner to contemplate a pot of beer and to gloat upon the prospect of conveying its contents presently into his interior. Thus dreaming he had dozed off until certain ominous words reached him. He remembered Tinker well enough; he owed him five shillings once, and as a matter of fact he still owed them.

"Be he dead?" he cried, slopping his beer over, which was a matter of no importance just then; and when the answer came in the affirmative he howled despairingly, "Then I've abin and lost my last resting-place."

"Sure 'nuff," said Farmer Tom. "Old Tinker takes the corner, Willum."

"Not him," said the landlord. "Tinker wur well set up. He wouldn't rob a poor man of his grave."

"Parson said next body wur to ha' the corner, whether 'twas man or woman. That grave be mine by right, and I be agwaine to stand out vor 'en," shouted Brokenbrow in a thoroughly healthy fashion.

"Why didn't yew go first then, Willum?"

"How wur I to go avore I wur took?" said the old man in great disgust. "I've played vair vor the grave, and Amos Chown ha' played vair tu, though I did see 'en wance sotting out in the rain wi' no coat on. I wur ready to go home, vor I ha' been a gude man and ha' never missed meeting, and I owes no man a penny," he said, forgetting all about the debt to the deceased and a few others, or perhaps he meant his remark to be taken quite literally. "I ses it bain't right vor Tinker to snatch the grave out o' my mouth as 'twere."

"He wur a parishioner," said Farmer Tom. "If he asks vor the corner he mun ha' it."

"How can he ask vor't when he'm dead?" shouted Willum.

"If his widdie wants to claim it vor 'en, her can."

"I'll go to parson. I'll tell 'en it bain't right," said the old man. "I've been waiting patiently vor the grave, and the bootiful coffin wi' brass handles, aw, and he'm got a brass plate vor me name tu, and I had 'en in me hands as they ses, and now they'm slipping out as 'em might be trouts, and I've ha' lived righteous so I wouldn't be took unprepared, like some as I could tell. And I owes no man a penny," he said again, but the landlord interrupted, "Yew owes me fivepence vor beer, Willum."

"Aw, don't ye be vulish, landlord. I ses Tinker bain't agwaine to ha' the corner. Who wants to see Job Tinker wrote on a tombstone every time they goes into church to be baptised and buried? 'Twould be desiccation of the old church wall."

"Who wants to see Willum Brokenbrow?" asked young Moorshed with a hoarse cackle of laughter.

"Your widdie wull, when her goes in to wed a better man than yew," retorted Willum, who had worked himself into a state of great indignation. Then he stamped out of the place, laying aside his righteousness for a season that he might curse the claimant. Some men apparently couldn't do wrong. There was old Tinker with plenty of money stepping into parochial immortality and the glorious heritage of the grave beside the porch; while he was to remain disconsolate and so healthy that he couldn't even catch a cold. He thought bitterly of chances he had missed, of slight illnesses which with care might easily have led up to the prize, only he had been foolish enough to get frightened and have the doctor—he had never paid the doctor—so that the indisposition had been discouraged. No doubt it was easy to die at Mortehoe, but on Dartmoor it was difficult. It was too late for him to go to Mortehoe, as Tinker had been and died and conquered. "If 'em puts 'en in my grave I'll ha' 'en out on't," he muttered angrily. "I'll dig 'en out like an old tatie, wi' my eleven fingers." Brokenbrow was as uncertain in his arithmetic as he was in his anatomy.

Parson was inaccessible. He was in the last stage of dotage, and spent his winters in bed, with a skull cap down to his ears and a hot bottle at his feet. When Brokenbrow besought an audience the housekeeper told him, "The dear old gentleman be sleeping like a little baby;" and when Willum became violent and declared he had come to murder these slumbers the door was slammed upon him; and a moment later the information went reassuringly up the stairs, "'Tis all right, your reverence. I've abin and got rid of 'en."

Brokenbrow stood without and the shape of his face became altered with fury. He saw it all now; there was a conspiracy to deprive him of his resting-place. Tinker had bought the first refusal of it with perishable gold. The old man's first idea then was to betake himself to the longed-for spot and hallow it to himself for ever by departing in peace thereon; only his health was too good. So he went instead to see Mrs. Brokenbone who lived quite close.

"How be ye, Loveday?" said Willum as he entered the cottage, after much ceremonial boot-scraping upon the heap of furze placed at the threshold for a mat.

"Aw, I be fine, Mr. Brokenbrow. And how be yew?" said the dame, who was knitting by the fire and keeping an eye upon the iron pot which seethed and bubbled like a witch's cauldron.

"I bain't as bad as I might be," said Willum. "Have yew heard tell of old Job Tinker?"

"He'm a cousin o' mine. I hope he'm fine," said the old lady.

"Ah, he be. He'm dead."

"Dead, be he? The Lord ha' mercy on 'en," said Loveday, with the utmost reverence. "He wur an awful liar, Willum."

"I wishes them as ses he'm dead wur liars tu," came the answer. "They'm going to bury 'en in my grave, and I bain't agwaine to let 'em. 'Tis worse than having a stranger man to bed wi' ye."

"I wouldn't let 'en," said the dame hurriedly. "Yew talks so bold, Willum, and me a widdie."

"Yew knaws what I be telling. The grave be my bed like, and I be the oldest parishioner, and I be cruel sick sometimes," said Willum with his very defective logic. "Parson said I should ha' 'en if I wur took. But I bain't took. I bides," he said pathetically.

"Don't ye worry, Willum," said Loveday. "If 'tis the Lord's pleasure yew mun bide yew ha' got to. 'Twould be a fine thing to ha' that grave I reckon, vor 'tis the best part o' the churchyard, but 'tis fine to be abroad and warm and comfortable like. Job would be back if he could. Job be got to a place where 'em wun't believe 'en," she added severely.

"I bain't a liar, Loveday," said Willum. "I be an upright man."

"Yew uses blasphemious words, Willum," she reminded him.

"Times when I be upsot, but I be main cruel sorry vor't, and I asks forgiveness. Us mun express our feelings. When I be glad I laughs, and when I be angry I swears. 'Tis just the difference between a fine and a thick day."

"It bain't the words so much as the angry passion," she said, gazing with a hungry passion into the pot.

"Aw, but I means nought. It be all done and gone like. I be a righteous man. I'd be put to it to name a better."

"I ain't never seed ye in drink, I du allow," said the dame graciously.

"Like enough," said Willum, though he wondered how he had ever managed to escape notice. "But yew ha' seed I in chapel, Loveday, wi' the Buke on me knees, and yew ha' heard I say Amen many a time?"

The old lady admitted this was nothing but the truth; but she felt constrained to issue a warning against too much confidence. She herself was fully insured, but it was not right for Willum to suppose he was quite like her. She could say Amen the loudest, and this was a matter which made for righteousness. Men had a vast amount of original sin in them, while women were only sinful when they had contracted the disease from men. There were a great many more women than men in the world, but in the better land the inequality between the sexes would be far greater, and a man would not be easy to find; and that was the reason why there would be no giving in marriage. Brokenbrow was unable to dispute the dame's creed beyond stating that he "wur prepared and waiting to be took." It was easy to say that, as he was feeling unusually well.

"Us dreaded yew wur going home in the spring," he reminded her.

"I thought better on't," she replied. "What be the use o' going when yew'm comfortable? I don't crave to be took early. I bain't eighty, Willum. I bain't going in middle-age as 'twere. Job ha' gone early, but he wur a liar and a money-maker, and lies and money-making breaks a body cruel."

"Let 'en be put away to Mortehoe where he lived," said Brokenbrow angrily. "If they brings 'en here me and Amos Chown 'll stand to the gate and push 'en back."

"Amos be sick," said the dame. "John brought I some turves this morning, and told I he wur in bed telling o' brimmles and vuzz-bushes what kept catching hold o' he and scratching 'en cruel. John wur wanting daisies to boil wi' a bit o' bacon vor the old man to cure 'en."

"They ha' told 'en about Tinker and he'm fretting," said Willum, who had just then a kindly feeling for his old rival. "I'll get across and see 'en. Wish ye goodnight, Loveday. I'll look in and tell a bit again tomorrow."

"Yew'm welcome, Willum. Don't ye worry about the old grave. Mebbe parson 'll let 'em put ye in atop o' Job, and then yew'll come out avore 'en on Judgment Day."

"I bain't agwaine to share my grave wi' no man," said Brokenbrow from the door. "I wouldn't ever lie quiet wi' another down under me. I'd be turning and twisting year after year to get mun out, and I'd get blasphemious and call 'en a dirty toad. If they takes the grave vor Tinker I'll tell 'em to put me away in the tatie-patch behind my little house. I ses Job Tinker ha' done perjury to get that corner, and I wouldn't lie nigh 'en, not vor all the money in the world, vor when the devil comes to tak' his own he might tak' I tu by accident like."

With many expressions of virtue and not a little bad language Brokenbrow went along the dark little road on the side of the moor where the wintry wind was thick and bustling. Wheal Dream had become a place of mud and running water; walls indoors glistened with moisture, windows were fogged, and each article of furniture was slimy to the hand. The clay had become like wet putty, the peat oozed, the ferns stretched limply down the slopes, and even the grass seemed to have lost the greenness of its life. It was a dreary prospect, and at first sight it repelled with a loneliness too realistic; too great a depth of mud, too much bog, too loudly roaring a river; but there was something which was not at once apparent, something which was born into the body after a few weeks' sojourning in that rough realism. It was health made by the wind. It was strength given by health. It was life given by strength. That was sufficient surely.

No place can give more than the best; and if health be not the best, what is better? Through the smoke of a city comes the glitter of gold like furze-blossoms in a fog; but the body cannot get at it because of disease. There is no gold on the wild upland; no smoke either, except here and there a healing fume of peat-fire almost lost amid so much wind. "Forget not the best," cried the Princess Ilse when the hind of the Ilsenstein mountain dropped the little blue flower in his wild hurry to cram his pockets with gold; and the magic blossom cried out also, "Forget-me-not;" but the hind could not understand and took more gold, and the mountain clashed together and destroyed him because he was a fool. The wind still calls, "Forget not the best," and all the heather cries also, "Forget-me-not;" but men misunderstand and go on grabbing at the gold, because it is warm and comfortable down there among the chimneys, and it seems terribly cold and pitilessly dreary up on the heights —besides they must go one better than their fathers— and so disease clashes upon them and they are destroyed, because they are fools like the shepherd lad who thought the best was the heap of gold, not the little blue flower which he trampled on. Nature is not a harlot walking the streets at a price, her good-will cannot be bought with a sovereign; those who seek may find her in the solitudes, naked as Eve, lying on her back with the wind running over her, calling men to come to her and degenerating them if they don't. But she is a wild creature with all her giant strength, and it is not good for any man to be with her long alone.

The Chowns were at Wheal Dream, Bill having come to see his father and to beg the Pethericks to take them in for the winter. They had been up before, but John and Ursula would not listen to their troubles. The barn they occupied at Downacombe was a poor shelter. None of the burnt cottages had been rebuilt, and the rector was selling what was left of the cob ruins for manure. The Chowns could not afford to leave the place, as Bill had his work in the mine and Bessie the sanatorium washing. They could just make a poor living, only they couldn't find a home. A cottage was a rare luxury. Bill could have put one up himself had he been given materials, for he was useful with his hands—unlike John, whose art began and ended with milking a cow or forking manure into a cart; but he did not possess any of John's privileges.

When Brokenbrow arrived at the tumbledown place, which the weather was staining as black as a tor, the Pethericks occupied the kitchen alone. The Chowns were above bringing consolation to Father. Ursula was leaning against the table upon which stood the usual smoky lamp and a few dirty pans. John was standing beside the hearth, his dented hat over his eyes. It would not have been easy to find a rational being to put beneath John; and yet he too could endure. He was no shivering creature frightened at the prospect of an hour's work. He might start building a hedge in the morning, and if he meant to finish it that day he did, in spite of exhaustion, or heat of sun, or flurry of stinging sleet, toiling long after dark to get the job finished; and then he would stagger home and swallow raw spirit until the walls whirled round. He could endure any amount of hard work when he was sober enough. There were the makings of a man somewhere in John, still in the raw state and never likely to get any further. A decent woman would have lifted him, but Ursula dragged him down. She was far the better educated—John indeed could never remember the precise difference between left and right—but the only effect it had upon her was to make her dissatisfied with her lot. George, who had studied her closely, had owned to himself that he couldn't find in Ursula one redeeming feature.

"I be a young woman," she shouted, her sloe-black eyes running over with maudlin water. "And I ha' nought but work. What ha' I got to look vor? Work, work, that's what it be, year after year till the bones be standing out o' me body. I've had a plenty on't, I tell ye, a plenty on't, and if this be living I've ha' done wi't. I'd be better off in me grave."

"Best get off there," John growled with his hoarse laughter. "I'll ha' a better one next time, I reckon."

"What did I marry yew vor?" she shouted. "What did I marry a mucky old stinking lot o' pig's dung like yew vor?"

"I wur vule enough to court yew. That's why," John shouted.

"Aw, dirty toad. Gets an innocent woman into his home and makes a rag o' she, and a slave o' she, and uses she vor his own trade. If I'd ha' knowed what yew wur I'd ha' took father's razor and cut me throat avore going into church."

"Aw, aw," cackled John, rolling about by the huge sooty fireplace. "Why didn't ye du it, woman?"

Drunk and furious, Ursula caught a milk-pan by its handle, swung round and sent it across the room, tumbling to the floor with the effort. It clattered against the wall, displacing a blackened piece of plaster, then rattled wildly about the stone floor; while John, howling with rage, snatched a handful of glowing peat off the hearthstone, not feeling the heat because his hand was too hard, and came across the floor all legs and arms like a horrible octopus. Ursula began to scream frightfully at that. A mighty cloud of smoke billowed out from the great open fireplace, scattering smuts everywhere.

"I'll put 'en across your face. God strike me if I don't," howled John; while Ursula grabbed a turnip by its stalk and hit out wildly, calling him all the filthy names she could imagine. She was to a certain extent courageous; perhaps that was the one redeeming feature. He closed with her, and they rolled among the sacks fighting like two cats. There was a smell of singed hair; the turnip parted from its stalk and bounded across the stones like a head from the guillotine; Ursula reached her hand into a stinking corner and brought it out full of black cobwebs and spiders and skeletons of beetles; forced the lot into John's gaping mouth. The peat went about in all directions, the wind from the open door blowing the fiery fragments here and there. Then the Chowns came clattering down, not to find out what was going on, because they knew, but thinking it might be time to interfere; and at the same moment old Brokenbrow, who had been watching the game from the passage, stepped up, knocked with his stick, and remarked with a good deal of truth that it was a rough evening.

"Please to come in, Willum," said Ursula with a hiccup and much face-wiping. She always prided herself on her ladylike qualities, and she knew it was proper to receive a guest, who wasn't a relation, respectfully. The little domestic affair was nothing. Similar scenes had taken place before and would occur again. John was a filthy brute with a vile temper. No woman could possibly endure his bestial ways and savage assaults. That was the way Ursula looked at it.

John stumbled outside into Uncle's little court to wash his mouth, while Willum presented his compliments to the company, said they were all looking lusty, and explained he had come on a little friendly visit to Father, having heard he was not well.

"He'm a lot better. Sotting up in bed he wur, and singing, 'Gentle Jesus, meek and mild,'" said Bessie in reverential tones.

"Old vaither be tough as twitch-beam," said Bill. "Go up and tell to 'en, Willum. 'Twill du the old man gude," said Ursula in her company voice, not thinking much about her father, but wanting to get the visitor out of the way.

Brokenbrow was soon tumbling about the stairs, and then Ursula addressed herself to her own relations.

"Yew get home along. Sure as yew comes up here there be trouble."

"Not a bit o' supper avore us goes?" said Bessie. "Bill be cruel tired. He've worked hard all day and he wur a bit mazed got as us came up along. 'Tis hard to tak' a heavy flasket on his shoulder, and us ain't got nought but turnips and a bit o' bread to home."

"Yew gets nought here," said Ursula fiercely. "I knaws ye, Bessie Chown. Yew ha' got a dirty mouth, woman, and yew tells shameful about I. Ses me and John don't live proper and I bain't a respectable lady. Bill tells the like and yew ha' made 'en. Vaither ain't going to leave none o' his furniture to Bill. Aw, get on home, yew two hungry rats," she said, turning her back upon them.

"Yew and John bain't agwaine to ha' us under vor winter? Say one way or t'other vor gude, and lets ha' done wi't," Bill said.

"Ha' yew under!" shouted Ursula. "Us bain't agwaine to ha' thieves and robbers to Wheal Dream. I knaws what yew be, Bill. Yew'm getting on in the world," she laughed scornfully.

"That be a purty fine noise, woman, but there be two ways o' laughing just as there be two sides o' your face. Mebbe yew'll learn t'other way avore long," said Bessie, in the gentle voice of a woman who wants to express hatred.

"Let her bide," said Bill. "Us wun't come nigh again. Mebbe us bain't going up, but they'm going down. What about they letters?" he said.

"What letters be yew telling about?" said Ursula with drunken carelessness.

"They letters from the gentleman what yew owes money to. I knaws they'm coming, vor postman told me. What be yew going to du when he comes down on ye?"

"Shut the door in his face, same as I would on yew."

"That be gude enough vor we," said Bill. "I knaws that the whole o' Wheal Dream, 'cept that bit yew sold to Mr. Brunacombe, be what 'em calls mortgaged, and I knaws that when volks don't pay mortgages they'm turned out. Yew'm on the way to the House, woman, as I told ye avore."

"And I wun't go to see she neither," said Bessie viciously.

"Yew don't knaw what yew'm telling," said Ursula, more sullen than violent. "Us owes nought what us can't pay. Wheal Dream be worth a thousand pounds," she cried defiantly.

"How much be the old house worth?" asked Bill from the door. "If it warn't down under like, and out of o' the wind, the first rough day would blow 'en down. Come home along, Bessie," he said roughly. "They calls the place Wheal Dream. I reckon 'twould best be called Vules' Volly."

"They'll be in a better house avore long," cried Bessie shrilly, as she didn't want Ursula to lose any of it.

The Chowns went out and Bessie waited on the Stannary road while Bill ascended to the Wheal House. There was still a small corner left in the flasket, and that was for George's bundle of washing. His and Winnie's had often nestled together there, amid other strange company, but he had never known it. Bill went up and found the artist outside. He had impaled the ghostly sheet of a letter upon a furze-bush and was hurling great rocks upon it; a queer scene in the darkness; but when not working George was doing strange things. That letter had just reached him, and as he fancied it represented what was bad in him he was stoning it, just as a man curses himself when he has done foolishly. Not knowing what to make of the mad gentleman, Bill stood still, announced himself, and asked for the washing.

George stopped his antics, snatched the fluttering sheet from the furze-bush, and departed. He was soon back with his bundle, and faced Bill, who stood at the door touching his hat respectfully.

"You walk a lot?" said George. The lamplight from the workroom fell upon Bill's face, dark, grimy and settled, the eyes losing their sight gradually, the hair getting thin and frosted; soil of the mine was in every wrinkle, patience on every feature; it was the face of an animal who has been kicked and looks up to know what mischief it has done.

"I du, sir," he said.

"You walk badly. You roll about. I have noticed that men who are always walking have little control over their feet."

"They'm sore, sir. I be on 'em from five in the morning in gurt heavy butes. My hands get harder and my feet softer. A man works wi' his hands, but he don't du his best if his feet bain't right, vor he mun walk to his work and stand to his work, and 'tis the feet what wears 'en out."

"You work hard?"

"All the time I bain't sleeping, sir."

"Where are you living, Bill?"

"To an old barn. He'm vull o' wind and rats, and Bessie gets the fright when winds be rough. They rats run over us in bed. Makes Bessie scream, 'em du."

"It's a hard life. You stand it well—better than I can," George muttered.

Bill smiled sadly. "Us ha' got to put up wi' what us can't mend," he said.

That was Bill's philosophy. Life was worth keeping somehow; why he could not tell, unless something might happen in the future—his pick might unearth a crock filled with gold, or the sky might open and drop privileges upon him. Nothing would happen; he would go on toiling, with insufficient food and rest, until disease jabbed him in the spine and the wind would carry him off: but romance or hope lurks in the human system, and the mysterious future has always gifts; some day everything would be different—that is what keeps men going. Endure for one more year and it will all come to pass, the long holiday, happiness and enough to live on, no more mists, rough days and backaches. But when the year is gone there is no change. Well then, one more, just another year of patience, three hundred and sixty-five more backaches and the game is won. Men never know when they are beaten, they are the hardiest things alive; that is why they are splendid. If they could see right into those years, which seem to stretch beyond in a glittering row of stars, but are probably nothing more than a lot of dry and shrivelled peas, they would fling down their tools, slink into a dark corner, and not come out unless they were carried. George, Gregory, and Bill, they were all men, and they waited for the dreams to be realised. But they couldn't all succeed and get what they wanted. Success is a cruel goddess. If she holds out a laurel wreath in one hand she has a huge bloody hammer in the other. Every one thinks he will get the wreath on his head, but most get the hammer: not deserving it perhaps; but what ox by his own conduct deserves to be poleaxed?

"Us thought sister might tak' we in," said Bill, "but her wun't."

"I know all about that. I hear everything that goes on," said George. "There would be nothing but fights if you went there. How would you like to come here?"

"Please, sir?"

"I don't use half the house," George went on. "I am sick to death of Ursula. She is drunk most nights, and generally informs me that my meal is ready by rolling about my feet. She smashes all my crockery, and her idea of cleaning the place is to bring in dirt. Your wife is clean. You are honest. She can look after me. Go and tell her. Come in to-morrow if you like."

"God bless you, sir!" Bill faltered.

"Never mind about that. I'll tell Ursula I've done with her."

"It bain't right, sir, not vor the likes o' we to bide wi' yew."

"Look upon yourselves as my servants. I'll settle with your wife when you come in. Good-night."

George shut the door quickly and left Bill in a state of amazement. Both were thinking of the Pethericks. There would be a scene when Ursula knew she had been supplanted by her despised relations. The Chowns at Wheal Dream, living with a commoner and taking the bread, or rather the whisky, out of her mouth. If that didn't make war, what would? The Pethericks had practically been living upon George, using his fire for cooking their own food, robbing the good-natured fellow right and left, cutting their Sunday dinner from his joint, making shameful additions to all his bills; and now his kitchen and home would be closed to them, and the honest Chowns would reign in their stead.

Bessie and Bill crept away quickly through the night, and the heavy basket had never rested so lightly on the man's shoulder before. They were winning, they were going up, they were ascending to the heights of the moor. They would live at last upon the common lands. Bessie wanted to go in and triumph over Ursula, but Bill restrained her. "She'm in drink," he said. "She'd fling the fire at ye."

While Bill was listening to good news his father was hearing bad from the lips of Willum Brokenbrow, who at last succeeded in climbing the muddy and slippery stairs. Father ceased his childish hymns, with which he sought to ease a somewhat rough and raw conscience, and greeted his rival with warmth. He did not like to be alone, as he got the horrors, and imagined he saw a long bramble growing through the window and hooking at him with thorns as big as choppers. It was really the bramble which had made him ill. He had spent day after day attacking the side of the hedge, but somehow he couldn't cut the wretched thing off, although he managed to tumble down twice and once very nearly rolled into the wheal. "The devil tak' all brimmles," had been his cry, but the devil had very nearly taken him instead. Now he was better and in his right mind, though the bramble was still a torment. He had enjoyed his day, however. Bessie and Bill had been to see him, and he had done himself good by calling them both "proper criminals," and had assured Bill he wasn't going to leave him anything in his will, although he had nothing to leave except a few shillings and coppers stitched up in a piece of sacking beneath his mattress, and the old sofa and two chairs in the parlour which really did not belong to him at all, although he had claimed them by the mystic rite of laying on of hands and pronouncing the words, "They'm mine." It was a mystery who did own that little bit of decrepit furniture. Ursula declared the things had come into the house with her as part, and the only part, of her marriage portion, which was certainly a lie; John asserted they had been part of the Petherick property from time out of mind; while Father distinctly remembered buying them at an auction in his youth and dragging them up to the house on a hand-cart.

"Sot down on the bed, Willum," invited Father in a genial fashion. The seat was not inviting, as like the rest of the room it was insanitary and unpleasant, but there was no other spot available for repose. The place was crammed with all kinds of rubbish collected by Father in his various progresses, and stored there as personal property of some value to be bequeathed by will to such of his descendants as had succeeded in giving him pleasure. There were scraps of wool picked off furze-bushes, old horse-shoes, bones of ponies, tins, shells with heaps of shrapnel and fuses gathered from the ranges, bottles—common objects of the house these—battered kettles and crocks, and a mass of such-like refuse, which made the room resemble and smell like a very inferior rag-shop. Everything was property that came to Father's hands. A large piece of indiarubber, picked up at George's door, was given the place of honour upon a shelf. Evidently Father looked upon it as a sort of talisman. He had .indeed often rubbed it upon his rheumatic legs and had never failed to benefit by the treatment.

Brokenbrow soon made Father acquainted with Tinker's perfidious departure. The old gentleman had heard nothing of it, Wheal Dream being always a day behind Metheral, but he shed no tears. On the contrary he seemed amused, and laughed until his spectacles dropped off. "Him and me shot vor rabbuts wance and he won. Now he'm took and I bides. I've abin and beat old Job sure 'nuff, and he wur younger than me tu."

"Who be agwaine to ha' the grave?" asked Willum ominously.

"Yew bain't," said Father. "Yew be beat, Willum."

"So be yew, Amos. Seems to me Tinker ha' died out o' spite to beat the two of us. Wull yew come wi' I to parson and tell about it?"

"I can't, Willum. I gets mazed when I be out o' bed. I don't want to be took," whined Father. "I craves to get abroad, and tak' my chopper, and cut the brimmle off."

"Don't ye want the grave?" said the shocked Brokenbrow. "Don't ye crave the bootiful coffin, wi' brasshandles, and the plate on mun as big as him yew ets your dinner off? I'd drop down dead and be thankful if I wur sure o' mun."

"When I be abroad I wants 'en cruel," whimpered Father, rubbing his eyes with his perennial breeches. "But now I be sick got I wants to bide out o' mun. I craves to get abroad again, Willum. I ha' been mazed vor dree days, and I reckoned 'em wur putting I away, and the brimmles wur scratching me legs as they let I down. I be all sweaty like when I thinks on't."

"If yew wur a righteous man," said Willum severely, "yew'd crave to be took same as I du."

"Yew gets the fright when it comes," Father blubbered. "Yew don't knaw where yew be hardly. First yew'm going, then yew bain't. I reckoned I wur gone night avore last. I opened my eyes and saw the old lamp, and I ses, 'It be Heaven sure 'nuff,' and I thought 'twas amazing homely."

Father's ambitions were somewhat mean. Most people would have called that horrible little room a very passable cell in Purgatory.

"Yew bain't a righteous man," said Brokenbrow decisively.

"I be," cried the invalid. "I knaws Our Vaither and a main cruel lot o' hymns. Sings 'em to myself I du. 'Lots o' wages left vor me,' and 'Rule Britannia,' and 'Onward, Christian Soldiers,' though I bain't sure o' the words."

The other shook his head. He considered that more than this was necessary for salvation. Father had been notoriously lax in listening to sermons and therefore he was afraid. Brokenbrow was himself in a state of good health which caused him to find no evil in himself and made him anxious for the ceremony; though when his time came he would be just as nervous as Father; and he too would run through a list of good stirring hymns and miscellaneous devotions.

Weird noises sounded over the dark wheal as Brokenbrow shuffled on his way to the inn, where he still hoped to enlist public sympathy on his behalf. Bubo had contrived to flutter to the roof of the house, where he was declaiming his loudest, and bringing undomesticated members of his family down from the rocks to hear what this fellow had to say. His master was listening, and the monotonous cry said to him, "You fool! you fool!" George was walking up and down the long rambling passage of the mine house, and small bat-like ghosts of prehistoric tinners seemed to brush against his face with every movement. There was no light in the passage; none outside; just night everywhere within and without. The only white thing was that letter which waved in the artist's hand.

"That's right, Bubo, shout it out again," he cried for all the fowls of the night to hear. "Louder, and let every one know. I've dissolved the partnership. I can't work any longer with our Mr. Brunacombe. He's a fool, a fool. He's taken to religion; he's put on a sanctimonious expression; he's going to church three times on a Sunday; he wouldn't draw a naked woman to save his life—the fool! the fool!"

George put his head out of the window and hooted. The imitation was exact, and presently Bubo came tumbling down, settled on his master's wrist, and was taken in. There was a narrow window-seat, and there George sat and scratched his partner behind the ear. Bubo lowered his head and chuckled joyously.

"Let me put it to you plainly," George said. He opened his mind to the owl as he would not have done to his own kind. "You remember we wrote a novel, Bubo. It was a desperate venture, a sort of catch-money thing, and it was vilely well done, for you and I can turn out tolerable stuff when the pinch comes; but it was dirty, filthy, a lustful thing. We wanted money, Bubo, and we want it now—never did we want it more, for the cruise of oil is getting light—and in our extremity we remembered the saying of a man who had made a success of his life, though perhaps he never took the trouble to look at his hands very closely. 'My boy,' he said, 'if you want to make money at this writing game, write fornication.' We remembered that man's advice and we followed it. The book was written, we sent it off; and now there comes this letter from the publishers."

The typewritten sheet was scarred, torn, and muddy with ill-treatment. Bubo ran his eyes over it, then pecked it viciously.

"It's a good offer, senior partner. They are keen for the book. I have written the answer and signed it, and now you must sign it too—Bubo, his mark. We hadn't met her in those days," he whispered, clutching the fluffy little body feverishly. "We didn't know what love was, and how absolutely pure it can be. Not a matter of blood and lust, Bubo; not at all. Not a matter of this secret or that secret and shame between; but a soul, a personality, eyes, hair, nose, dimples, a little movement, a hand at rest on your arm, two small feet at your fireside, a certain manner that is nowhere else—see what a lot of beautiful things against the one that is base. And we never knew of them until she came and went for ever. We shall not see or hear of her again, Bubo, but we shall never forget. And if we have to go mad together, why let's do something first to her memory, to the day we saw her at Chapel Ford, to that last morning we picked her heather, to that smile, that touch of her hand—ah, that little nose. Don't be a fool, Bubo. Let's put up something to her memory. We can't do much. We'll give all we can. The letter is written, Bubo. Call it folly or sickly sentiment, but we won't change it. Better to starve in love than thrive on fornication. 'Send the manuscript back,' we have written. 'The thing is unclean, and we will burn it.'"

Then the simple creature blundered blindly down into his work-room, with the little bird tucked under his arm, murmuring in secret and with many repetitions, like a priest at his devotions, the one small name.

CHAPTER XVII
ABOUT EVICTIONS

The coming of the Chowns to the Wheal House made Ursula mad. She soon flung herself there, clawed Bessie's face, and cursed George with original words; when ejected she hurled wet cow-dung at the windows, and wiped her filthy hands on Bill's face when he sought to remove her by force. She waited for either of the Chowns as they passed to and fro, and rushed out with a big stick. Poor Bill received some large bruises, but accepted them as Heaven-sent. Bessie could hardly venture outside, and had to keep the kitchen door locked and the window protected. Ursula was not so mighty as she seemed, for all her terrific noise; she was always in liquor, and a good push sent her down into the mud. Her clothes were a shocking sight; the woman seemed to be encased within stiff clay. John was no better; his trousers were plastered, his hands and face caked; when he came near the fire and the stuff began to melt, he steamed and stank like a heap of refuse in the sun. The two were fighting continually, but Ursula was always the aggressor; John did no more than act on the defensive, until the brute in him arose and the smell of blood was in his nostrils, and then he retaliated. His method was to fling the woman down on her face and thump her on the spine with his clenched fist. Such drum-like sounds often made music those wintry nights. Sometimes they would be fighting indoors like a couple of gladiators; sometimes on the little road, hitting at each other with lighted lanterns until their faces were covered with oil. The only washing they ever got was when they fell drunkenly on the track, which was then all water forced by the rain from the side of the moor.

Uncle hardly ever appeared in his court, and the door of his tiny cottage was fastened for fear of the Pethericks. Although his home was practically a part of theirs, the contrast between them was startling. Everything in Uncle's living-room was clean and neat; the copper candlesticks were bright, the cloam showed no soot, the concrete floor shone like polished wood; and Uncle did it all himself, not with money, but with old trembling hands. Uncle had ten servants, his own fingers, all of them as old and decrepit as himself. No smear of clay remained long on his floor; when the weather made a dirty mark on his door Uncle wiped it off, after glancing from his window to be sure the Pethericks were not about. When he heard them indoors he shuffled out for water or turves, or to poke his ugly old head over the gate to swallow some air. Ursula caught him at times, as he could only move very slowly; and once she flung him down on the stones of his court. Uncle thought at first his leg was broken, and frightened her away by saying so; but it was only paralysis creeping up his side. The old fellow had every reason to be afraid of the Pethericks, because he only enjoyed a life interest in the cottage, field, and steep garden; on his death the property reverted to John. The Pethericks had always bated him for having, as they imagined, crept in through some legal quibble, and now they were nearing the end of their tether the old man's death was becoming necessary. Ursula had approached Jimmy on that subject. It was perfectly true that she had an unholy friendliness for the boy. But Jimmy naturally wanted Uncle to continue, and in any case he was far too lazy to follow Ursula's suggestion of greasing the stairs.

"Jimmy, boy, bain't yew ever going to du nought?" Uncle asked every day except Sundays. He did not ask secular questions when he had his black coat on. "Bain't yew ever going to be a man?"

"How be I to work and mind Dora tu?" came the answer, if one was vouchsafed at all.

That wretched bastard was an excuse for everything. Whatever was Jimmy coming to, Uncle wondered. He was getting whiter, flabbier, more sensual every month. Although so young, most of the male faculties appeared to have departed from him. He was so weak that to shuffle up the stairs made him puff and blow and exclaim, "Aw, my poor heart." His hair was long, his hands were white and soft, his abdomen was distended, and that horrible white fattiness, passable enough in a buxom wench, was growing more pronounced. He had become so lazy that he could hardly speak, and it was only in the evening, when vitality was less sluggish, he was able to sing to the infant. Most of the day he sprawled upon the bed, on his back, the baby sleeping on his chest. Jimmy did not believe Uncle's story about the dwindling money. He knew the old man got his rents regularly and must have saved a lot. That was true enough, for Uncle had always been a very thrifty soul, living easily on less than twenty pounds a year; but old men who have saved hate to spend.

"Get the young monster out," George had said many a time. Uncle loved the artist, who gave him such good advice, and often of an evening would stand at his window and look across at the Wheal House watching the movements of the wonderful gentleman as well as he could.

"How be I to du it, master?" he asked.

"Lock the door upon him. Keep him out. Tell him to go to the devil," was the blunt answer, but Uncle felt he couldn't say that, as he had a simple faith in the predatory powers of the evil one, who could easily retain a human soul thus committed to his charge. Something must be done, he decided, but first it would be necessary to say many prayers, sing through his hymn-book with the best courage that he had, and read the Bible from Genesis to Revelations. Uncle was no humbug, though he did sleep with his money-box and give it more devotion than was right. He was getting on with the well-thumbed Bible; all the big prophets had been waded through, and the little ones too, although Uncle really couldn't make head or tail out of any of them; and now he was in the New Testament, which was all plain sailing, and was so enjoyable that he read it aloud, standing by his table with the glow-worm of a lamp smoking in front of him; and he acted it as well, when Jimmy was snoring in the room above, and nobody was near to see him; it was no laughing matter, nothing to jest about, for Uncle's religion was something very real; and it was in a true devotional spirit that he shuffled about the shining floor, with his grotesque old gorilla-like head shaking, playing the part of Simon Peter or the Virgin Mary, and even with awe and reverence the greatest of them all; and while poor old Uncle played the part of his Redeemer, with a torn blanket round his shoulders—the pictures showed him they wore such things in those days—John and Ursula were defiling Wheal Dream and themselves on the other side of the wall.

Uncle was seeking courage but not finding much. Jimmy must go and find his own place in the world; he was to depart with all the tramplings and trumpets of the Apocalypse; and the last word of the Bible should be Amen for Jimmy too.

Father was again in unpleasantly rude health, and tottered between house and linhay in his four-legged way. He had conquered the bramble at last, worn it away with perseverance and iron implements, and his mind was at rest. He had also been picking up a lot of things which had accumulated during his illness. He had been very near acquiring a vast amount of property, for Bessie, in cleaning out George's work-room, incautiously placed a number of things outside the door. Father came shuffling along and rejoiced to perceive so much wealth. Everything was his, bought and paid for with his own money years ago. Father had plenty of time and plenty of string, as the lesson given him by the ant had not been forgotten. So he gradually enmeshed various articles with a web of twine, fastened the ends to his limbs, and was just making off with the entire lot dragging behind when Bessie appeared, nipped his laborious project, and called him a "proper old thief." Father had never loved his daughter-in-law, as he considered she had ruined Bill, just as he imagined that his daughter Ursula had been the salvation of John; and he regarded her then as a particularly loathsome object. To threaten was useless, and he couldn't use one of his sticks, as he required them to lean upon. The only way he could show his disapproval was to spit at her while she was unharnessing him; and he did so, his aim being accurate. Bessie, who was a very cleanly woman, went into a rage and smacked his face. Father wept, tottered to his daughter, and described how Bessie had robbed and insulted him.

"Put her hand in me pocket and took all me money," sobbed the old rascal. "Took me gold watch and spectacles tu," he added, although he did not possess such a thing as a watch, and the spectacles were jammed across his forehead. "I ses, let me bide. I be old and weak, and her scratched me face and spat at I like an old Tom."

Ursula picked up the pig-pail and departed. Luckily for Bessie she escaped just in time, and the pig-wash soused the door. That evening George came down and told the Pethericks that if they gave any more trouble he should invoke the aid of the police. "Us be free volk," was all the answer he got; Ursula didn't seem able to realise that they couldn't go on abusing their privileges for ever; and as for John, he supposed that the gentleman was trying to insult them.

Most women have a parting word for their husbands when they go forth to the day's work. Ursula always said to John, "I hopes yew'll never come back alive;" but he invariably did lurch home and disappoint her, although they were often almost friendly over the first glass; it made them laugh, but the second brought forth words, the third railings, and the fourth blows. Neither could stand liquor; they were already so highly strung by the stimulating wind that a little drink made them roll. They were always tumbling about, but escaping serious injuries, until one evening Father met John as he came jolting in from the moor, standing upright in his cart, a gaunt, spectral object against the darkening sky, with the statement that Ursula had fallen from the top of the house to the bottom, and was as dead as a door-nail.

John was not perturbed. Father had never been known to make a correct statement in his life. He said, "Aw, be her?" and unharnessed the horse in a leisurely fashion, then went on with his stable work, while Father tottered about, with an icicle forming on his purple nose, declaring he couldn't go into the house, for he was afraid of "carpses," they were so "natural like," and he had got the horrors again almost as bad as when he was in bed with the bramble digging its thorns into him. "I heard she fall, Johnnie. I wur washing my foot in the creampan. 'Twas like a sack o' taties coming down. I lost count o' the thumps, mebbe 'twas four, mebbe five. And her called, 'Oh, me God.' I heard she, Johnnie. Her wur allus a gude woman, and her called God wi' her last breath, as wur proper."

John lurched to the house, and Father came tapping and groping some way behind. Ursula was doubled up at the foot of the stairs, smelling strongly of alcohol. She had tumbled from the top step to the bottom, as Father had described, and was badly knocked about and stunned. John pulled her straight, rolled her over, shook her, and concluded he would have to go for the doctor. Ursula's misfortune meant a quiet night for him, if not for Father. The old man was terrified when he heard he was to be left alone.

"I bain't agwaine to bide wi' the carpse, Johnnie," he whined. "Her may get up and walk. Her wur always restless like."

"Her bain't dead. Her be breathing as rough as Dartmoor wind," said John.

Father did not regard this as a satisfactory symptom. Corpses appeared to him to be capable of doing anything. He stated his intention of going out and trying to gain entry into Uncle's cottage. He and Uncle had been on good terms once, and he thought this would be a good opportunity for a temporary reconciliation. Nothing like a death to bring people together. And when they had greeted one another, and consented to let bygones be bygones, Father could borrow various black articles of apparel for the forthcoming funeral, and thus add to his personal property, for after wearing them they would become his as by law established. Father became quite cheerful at the prospect. It would be a much brighter world, he thought, if there could be a death in the family every day.

John went off, but the news was in front of him. Father had told the driver of a passing granite-cart and he had informed the village, adding a chapter of his own. Presently Bill Chown passed through on his way from the mine and heard the revised version; half-way to Wheal Dream he met his wife, who was also on her way to the doctor, mistrusting John, and she told him the truth.

"Where's John to?" asked Bill.

"Yonder," said Bessie, pointing to the inn. John's sheep-dog was lying at the door.

"I'll pay 'en," said Bill; and then he went off to the inn.

It was unfortunate for John that he had to pass the house of good cheer. It mattered nothing that his wife was stunned and might by dying. He must have his drink; and once inside that warm, friendly place, with others talking around him, a pot of good stuff between his hands, and with a taste for the same thoroughly acquired, there was not the slightest chance of his leaving the house until closing time. He happened to drop in at an auspicious moment, for the room was almost full, and Willum Brokenbrow occupied the centre, his feet planted in the sawdust, his face shining with philanthropy, inviting every one to drink at his expense.

"That paper be a proper old liar," he was saying when John opened the door. "Wull, here be John Petherick. Pint o' beer vor John, landlord, if yew please. How be the woman, John?"

"Her be mazed," said John.

"Us heard her had broke her neck, but I said 'twarn't true," said Brokenbrow. "Women be like cats. They falls light. Du'ye pitch in the corner, John. I be giving a little party. I be standing drink as if 'twere 'lection time, vor Tinker bain't dead, after all."

"I reckon he be," said the landlord, in a disappointed voice.

"Wull he be and he bain't," said Willum pleasantly. "That old newspaper got it all turvy-twisty like. Tinker be dead and he be living, but there be more than one Tinker. There bain't enough names vor every one, so some of 'em ha' got to tak' alibis. I don't knaw whether that be the word, but I means to say that one man has to give his name to another. Wull, that bain't it neither. What I means to say is that one man is the alias—aw, that be the word—of somebody else."

"Yew means there be a lot o' volk wi' the like name," explained the landlord.

"Aw, that's it," said Willum. "There wur two Tinkers, ourn and some other place's, and one of 'em died and t'other didn't; and the newspaper got mazed over 'em and said 'twas ourn. Our Tinker be fine, and us cares nought about t'other. Seems there wur two Tinkers to Mortehoe, one what bided there, and that be our Tinker, and t'other what went there to get well and died instead, and that be the foreigner Tinker."

John was gaping in a corner, trying to understand what was being said, and doing his best to imitate the others in the matter of laughter. He had already consumed his pint, and had turned the mug upside down to draw attention to its emptiness. He had forgotten Ursula, and wasn't likely to remember her again until he awoke from a drunken stupor the next morning, unless something happened to remind him. Something did happen, for the door of the bar-room opened to admit Bill Chown, who walked straight across and placed his copper-stained hand on John's clayey shoulder.

"Pint o' beer vor Bill, if yew please, landlord," shouted the most hospitable Brokenbrow; but while the publican hesitated, in some doubt as to whether Willum would ever find the cash, Bill looked across with an austere countenance and said—

"It bain't no time vor drink. Yew'm sot here," he went on, addressing his brother-in-law, "while my sister be lying dead to home. Du'ye hear what I be telling, John? Dead," he said solemnly. "Her wur took not ten minutes back, and Bessie be at the door all out o' breath to tell ye."

There was a big silence in the place, and the form of Brokenbrow's visage changed again. He no longer desired to give Bill beer. He would rather have given him a dose of foot-rot for being the bearer of such tidings. Hardly had he escaped from one dilemma when he found himself in another. Human life was indeed uncertain; and so was his grave.

"Aw, Bill, don't ye say it, man," he whined. "Don't say her's dead. Us can't spare she."

John stared at a framed advertisement of somebody's whisky and found the sight congenial, although he couldn't read it, but was well able to recognise the picture. He gaped a little wider, and that was all. No doubt Bill was telling the truth. The whisky would last twice as long now that he would have it all to himself. That was John's first impression.

"What did her die of, Bill? Wur it serious?" asked the landlord, in the solemn voice which was entirely professional. The joys and sorrows of his fellow-villagers were measured by the amount of liquor their emotions might require.

"Her fell down-stairs when I warn't there," John blurted out in sudden terror. They might think he had murdered the woman. "Her wur all twisted up nohow."

"They'll sot on she. They'll ha' the body here, and 'twull be vor the jury to tell whether her died from falling down-stairs or whether her was drownded," said the landlord, trying not to appear satisfied. The inquest would mean a busy day.

By this time John had arrived at his second impression. He was trying to think of a suitable maid or widow who might be foolish or man-mad enough not to reject his courtship. All his impressions just then were pleasant ones. Romance was glimmering again in his dull mind.

"I be struck," wailed Brokenbrow. "I'll get home along and go to bed, but I wun't die, neighbours. 'Tis no gude dying now. Aw, Bill, what be telling, man?"

Bill stood just behind John's shoulder, grimacing at the company and winking broadly. They quickly interpreted his signs. It was a practical joke, a trick to frighten John, a little punishment for him; Ursula was right enough—she was, as a matter of fact, sitting up in bed just then, groaning and sipping the usual remedy—and Bill had come to scare John out of his poor wits by making him believe she was dead. Every one understood this was a family affair. John had been a brute to Bill's sister, and Bill was going to punish him for it. Old Willum became lively again and renewed his request for beer.

"Du'ye hear, man?" Bill shouted, striking John's shoulder. "Her be dead."

"S'pose her be dead, what then?" John shouted.

"Bain't yew going vor the doctor?"

"If her's dead her don't want doctor," was all John had to say.

Bill was shocked and disappointed. It had never occurred to him that John would refuse to be frightened.

"If I wur told my woman had died while I wur drinking in the public I'd be upsot," said Bill.

"So would I," declared the landlord; and the rest concurred.

John was making himself unpopular. It was one thing to stifle grief with a pint-pot; quite another to display callousness. Public decency had to be respected, while John was defying it. He was only wondering what the expenses would be and how he could manage to cut them down.

"Yew mun get home and du what be proper and vitty like," said virtuous Brokenbrow.

"Let 'en walk alone. I wun't be seen wi' "en," said the disgusted Bill.

John was persuaded to rise, grinning and gaping, and feeling somehow proud of himself, and at last shambled out with a cheerful, "Gude-night, all." The conventions were a nuisance, but it seemed necessary to observe them. He slouched through the darkness to Wheal Dream in a contented frame of mind, trying to whistle, only he never could, shouting at the ghostly sheep dotted about like masses of granite, and making them jump; and so he came home, stamped up the little passage, his head far in advance of his feet, found Father huddled over the smoky peat eating bread and cream and smuts, and heard an angry voice: "If that be John, vaither, tell 'en I be waiting vor 'en wi' the muck-fork."

John made a clumsy movement, which almost landed him into the fire. He was really frightened at last.

"Be that the woman?" he muttered, staring at the old man, who was blinking his weak eyes like a sleepy cat.

"Ah," chuckled Father contentedly. "Her be conversational getting, Johnnie."

That same week, before the Pethericks had entirely recovered, the one from her fall the other from his disappointment, a little gentleman climbed up to Metheral. He was fat and prosperous, with a pink and babylike face, a vast smile, and a touch of dialect. He was a country solicitor, and he had done business with farmers for so many years that he had learnt to talk like them. A merry soul was this little gentleman, and he could fleece a poor man in such a nice and friendly way that the miserable wretch would think all the time he was receiving a favour. He was well dressed too, not that his clothes were a very good fit, because he was a countryman, but they were made of the best stuff; he had a bowler hat with a mighty dome to it, too large and slipping over his bright blue eyes, and rings on his fingers and good boots on his toes; and he hummed like a great hornet as he trotted along the road. He was a member of the Law Society, clerk to a number of boards and institutions, had the law of mortgagor's estate and rights leaking out of every pore and wrinkle, and he was just the man to play a confidence trick to perfection. He was not very well up in venville rights, however, possibly because in that respect the commoners are a law unto themselves; the charter of their liberty, which directs that their rights shall be as they have been "time out of mind," being very much like the rubric at the beginning of the Prayer-book, which orders that chancels shall be as in time past; but as neither party is able to show what these phrases exactly mean, both commoners and clergy can do pretty much as they please, and put their fingers to their noses when the law is mentioned; and they generally do.

The pretty pink gentleman trotted and hummed towards Moor Gate, his keen nose in the air, smelling guineas all the way. This big enclosed field was worth so many, that little triangular binhay so few. One cottage was a complete eyesore because it could never be made profitable, another was almost pretty and deserved to carry a fifty-pound loan; while the farm-house of the Moorsheds was admirable, and its stout timbers seemed to be asking for a substantial encumbrance. This little guinea-pig grubbed up money with his pink nose wherever he went. If he put a shilling in the ground it had become a pound by the time he routed it out. The clay represented to him the building-trade, the rivers suggested fishing-rights, and the great moor a Royal Commission, with a lot of little solicitors swinging to it at the ends of pink tape by their hands, and not by their necks, as they should have done. He reckoned up the value of every man that passed and reduced him to guineas; the same with every young woman, only he brought them down to pence because of over-production and a dull market. The squat tower of the church was a charming object, and brought to his mind memories and anticipations of all manner of tangled actions. So he rambled on, smelling fees and contracts and five-per-cents. all the way.

Gregory was at home, digging his wind-swept patch, his great figure visible half-a-mile off. The visitor gambolled up to him like a young sheep, shouting—

"How be ye, cousin? Lifting tetties? Dartmoor peat grows 'em fine, I reckon. Worth a guinea a sack, yew may depend."

"Wull, wull," said Gregory heartily. "Tis Mr. Odyorne, sure 'nuff."

"That's who 'tis. Your relation two or dree centuries removed. Shake a paw, cousin, but mind ye my hand bain't a nut, and yourn bain't a cracker neither. My word, yew'm a gurt lusty chap."

This was how the little lawyer got along so well in the world. He was not exactly a philanthropist, at least he never gave away a guinea except for breeding purposes, but he had a philanthropist's manner. He was every man's equal.

"Come vor fishing, sir?" said Gregory. "The trouts be splashing fine down under Halstock."

"And yew grope vor 'em. Aw, now, tell the truth. Yew go down wi' a lantern and grope vor 'em."

"Sure 'nuff. I ha' the right," said Gregory. "Anything off the moor that may du me good, 'cept green-oak and venison. I'd break the back of any what tried to stop me.

"I'd help ye. I'd stand up vor my own family," cried the merry gentleman. "Wull, now, I'll tull ye. I bain't come vor fishing. I'm here to see our friends the Pethericks. They'm forgetful like. Bain't treating me proper, and when I writes to 'em they don't answer. Reckoned I'd run up here and see yew first." He picked up a potato and played ball with it. "What sort of a man be John Petherick? Do he drink more than be vitty like?" he asked carelessly.

Gregory saw the trap immediately. Information was being sought from him to be used against a parishioner, and this he could not give. He had no feeling either for or against the Pethericks, and did not wish to aid or harm them. Gregory did not interfere with people. He believed in leaving every man to stand in his own whirlwind. By the unwritten law of clanship he could not answer Mr. Odyorne.

"Us all catches the bird, master, and some catches a plenty of 'em," he said, laughing and wiping his face with his sleeve.

"What bird?" asked the lawyer.

"The swallow. I can't tull ye how many mak' a summer or a winter neither. Depends on the man. Two swallows o' whisky would mak' a hot summer vor me, but I can't abide the stuff. A swallow o' wind be the bird vor me."

"And how many swallows make the Pethericks' summer? What's the bird there, cousin? The liddle yaller wan wi' dree stars vor the tail o' mun?" the visitor suggested, in his broadest and most genial dialect.

"Ask 'en, master. I knaws nought about neighbours. I bides up here along and don't meddle wi' volks, and they don't meddle wi' I vor fear o' being broke. Wheal Dream be yonder. Purty nigh a mile beyond. I'll show ye the way across."

Not a word could the subtle little gentleman extract from Gregory concerning the Pethericks, although he went on trying; but all that he got was his first lesson in commoners' law. He learnt also that Gregory did not like to be questioned. Preserving that genial manner, which was the cloak that concealed his business methods, he parted from the big, lonely figure and trotted off across the moor, humming pleasantly like so much machinery in motion, and smiling lovingly at the wild ponies just to keep his hand in.

It was a day of evictions, attempted and contemplated. Uncle had finished the Revelations, prolonging the last chapter into a kind of anthem to gain time, for the act he was contemplating frightened him dreadfully. At first he thought he would go through the Bible again, but the portability of the money-box made him reject such weakness. Then he decided to study the parts which dealt with battles and murders, to enkindle the martial spirit within him; but again he weighed the money-box and obtained thereby the nerve which all the chapters of Israelitish warfare would never have given him.

The stars in their courses beamed approvingly upon Uncle. Dora, the baby, was asleep by the fire, packed up in her little wooden box; Jimmy was sprawling on his bed up-stairs; it was cold outside, with watery mist, and vicious discharges of sleet occurred every hour like a necessary tonic. That weather ought to bring Jimmy to his senses. Uncle hardened his heart, prayed for the baby's welfare, expressed a desire that it would not catch a severe cold; and then he dragged the box outside and left it beside the hedge which separated his court from the Stannary road. The first stage was easy enough, though it seemed a murderous thing to do.

He went to the foot of the stairs and called the boy. Only the wind answered, and he called again, blowing out his hairy cheeks and shouting until even torpid Jimmy had to hear and to ask what the silly old fool wanted.

"The baby be in the court, Jimmy," explained Uncle, in the voice of tragedy.

There was a thump upon the ceiling, which meant that the boy was leaving the bed of indolence, and Uncle quaked more than ever. Everything was prepared; the key was on the right side of the door, and the boards were ready for screwing across the window. There was a side of bacon in the cottage, and enough turnips, potatoes, and flour to last well into the new year, so he could stand a long siege. Jimmy had wondered why the old man was carrying such a quantity of turves into the place, but he had been much too lazy to ask the reason.

"How did her get out there?" the youth was bleating in his ugly, falsetto voice, as he shuffled weakly down the stairs.

Uncle said nothing. The truth was impossible, and he could not say the baby had hopped suddenly, box and all, out of the window, like a jumping bean. He stood by the table, trying to act the part of Simon Peter, who was his favourite character, partly because a picture in his Bible represented that apostle, somewhat unkindly, as having a certain facial resemblance to himself. "Silver and gold ha' I nought," muttered Uncle, "leastways not much." Jimmy and the baby were evil spirits, and it was his duty to cast them out; but there was not much of the apostle about Uncle, except his faith, when the boy saw what had been done and accused him. The old man shuffled away and grasped his Bible that he might receive courage.

"Yew dafty old mazehead," piped the boy. "Yew ha' took she out. My poor liddle lamb. Her will be starved wi' cold."

Out he went, and Uncle's spirit revived. He shambled across the floor, hugging the great book, shut the door, locked it, and stood there quaking, with the key in his hand, like a quaint fresco of his favourite character. Then he made for the narrow window, which would not in any case have admitted the corpulent Jimmy, placed a board across and began to screw it to the woodwork. The worst of the business was over, he hoped. The boy would at least perceive that he had been given a delicate hint to withdraw.

Jimmy guessed as much so soon as the key was turned, but he had no intention of accepting eviction. His first thought was for the pig-faced baby. Having protected the infant's face against the stinging wind, he went to the window, saw the old man's terrified countenance behind the blurred glass, threatened it, shouted and shook his fist at it; but that was no use, for Uncle could not hear, and the gestures were only what he had anticipated. He was Peter the doorkeeper, and Jimmy was a lost soul. He was sorry for the boy, but he had been given every chance; his record was entirely bad, his sins were unrepented of, and he must leave the sheep and go among the goats. It looked as if it might snow presently; and snow would make Jimmy a very miserable goat indeed.

The boy went off, lurching backwards, dragging box and baby. He had his friend Ursula in reserve, and he found her in a more decent state than usual, scrubbing Father's head. The old man had his head washed whenever it grew irritable. John was out rebuilding the side of a hedge, working hard, like the good machine he was. He would have followed Uncle's example, but far more roughly. The Pethericks were an old and respectable Dartmoor family, which had never permitted bastards to enter their home. Ursula, who had brought base Chown blood to Wheal Dream, was inclined to be less decorous, and she was quite ready to take the wanderers in.

"Aw, the old brute," she cried bitterly. "Turning his own flesh and blood out to starve. That's chapel volk. Wait till John comes home and us will tear the door down and break the old toad's face vor 'en. Proper old devil he be wi' his psalms and hymns. Gives us no peace to nights wi' his praying. That's what Bibles and chapels bring volks to—turning innocent little children on Dartmoor to starve. His own blood and bones tu."

"What be I to du wi' Dora?" asked the miserable youth.

"Tak' she to the linhay. It be warm there in the hay. If John wur to find she in here he'd tread on her. When it gets dark us will give the old brute a proper reception. Don't let John see ye," she called.

"Keep the brush out o' my eyes, wull'ye?" said Father sternly.

Jimmy took the baby into the linhay and soon returned, actually in a hurry and excited, to say that a gentleman was talking to John up in the field. "He shook hands wi' John. He'm a foreigner," he said.

Ursula left the towel hanging over Father's head like a bridal veil and ran out. Strangers in Wheal Dream were rare objects in the winter. John was stumbling down towards the house with a merry little gentleman jumping at his side.

"Aw, my God," muttered Ursula, recognising the visitor at once.

They were coming down to her, as she was business manager, John being incapable of the smallest trick which required intelligence. He had never even registered his vote, as he could not be taught how to do it.

Mr. Odyorne smelt guineas all around him. Wheal Dream was a charming spot, full of possibilities, beautiful even in the winter. The only thing was to clear these disgusting people out, pull down their horrible house and stinking outbuildings, and then build a pretty little chalet with a thatched roof and verandah, make a garden down the gorge, plant the wheal with flowering shrubs, and the lot would sell for a fancy price if he didn't keep it himself as a summer residence. He had lent the Pethericks two hundred pounds and an instalment of fifty was long overdue, to say nothing of the interest, not a penny of which had ever been paid. He had not pressed them very hard; he didn't want the money; he would indeed have been disappointed if it had been offered. He wanted Wheal Dream, and at two hundred pounds it was very cheap, a wonderful bargain in fact. Those guineas of his were breeding like rats.

"Aw, Mrs. Petherick, here us be," he cried, putting out his hand and giving Ursula a shake such as she had never known in her life, so hearty and friendly was it. "John and me ha' been telling a bit, and now us ha' come down to listen to yew. I'll tullye how 'tis. I shall have to look after Wheal Dream vor ye. Let's go into the warm and tell about it, vor I be purty nigh froze up here."

The little gentleman skipped between the Pethericks, took an arm of each and walked on almost hugging them. He could put up with a lot of unpleasantness when he was smelling guineas. Ursula, who had never been so flattered, was delighted. Evidently Mr. Odyorne did know a real lady when he saw one. Her clothes might not be quite the thing, as they were covered with grease and clay and oil; but he recognised her genteel character and pleasant, aristocratic ways.

The little man was as sharp as a furze-bush. While walking across the moor he thought about Gregory's manner, added to it the information he had already acquired, and arrived at the conclusion, which was indeed the correct one, that the commoners would never permit him to evict the Pethericks openly. Dartmoor folk have often shown that they are in some senses outside the law of the land; they rely on their own rights and strength, which outsiders must have a giant's power to break down. They will part with nothing, they have withstood the Duchy officials with complete success; and it was therefore not likely that the commoners of Metheral would have stood idly by while a foreigner turned the Pethericks out of Wheal Dream, which the family had occupied for centuries. A duller man would not have perceived this; but little Mr. Odyorne when out sniffing was very sharp indeed. He knew his way about; he could walk in the dark without a lantern; and he was well aware that soft words and diplomacy are more effectual with rough people than any amount of violence or bluster. He did not know a vast amount of law; but he understood human nature, which was far better.

"Now then, volks," he began, when they were in the kitchen and Father had been relegated to his usual seat upon the turnips. "What be this they'm telling about ye? Them Pethericks be the best neighbours in the world, they'm strong and sober and hard-working, but they don't mak' the place pay. Tull ye what 'tis. Yew want a business man to run the varm vor ye. Aw, John, yew'm a fine fellow, but what du yew knaw about business? A vulgar thing business. Yew ha' been brought up to something better. 'Tis only us vules what go in vor business, 'cause us ain't got the sense to mak' a living wi' our hands."

John also felt flattered. He knew he was a fine fellow, only nobody had ever told him so before, and his wife had always tried to make him believe he was much lower than the beasts of the field. "Aw, aw," he laughed, staggering about on his long crooked legs; but his conversational powers ended at that.

"I had to come and see ye about that bit o' money, and now us be telling one to another, friendly like, I'll let ye into a secret," went on the lawyer. "'Tis like this: I be in difficulties, and if I don't get the bit yew owes me I shall be sent to prison, mebbe. Bad job that, volks. Bread and watter, wi' neither butter nor cream"

"Us ain't got no money," broke in Ursula somewhat defiantly.

"Lord love ye, my dear, of course yew ain't. None o' us ha' got money these hard times. I'd be ashamed to turn out my trousers and let yew see what I ha' got," said Mr. Odyorne, with perfect sincerity. "I've got no money to pay my debts and yew ain't got none to pay yours, but yew owes me two hundred pounds. Never mind the interest, volks. Us be friendly and us bain't Jews. But, John me lad, if us can't settle something I'll have to assign my mortgage, and that means sell it to the Jews, and they'll be down on yew day and night and won't rest till they ha' squeezed every farthing and a bit more out o' yew."

"Us be free volk," said Ursula as usual. "They couldn't touch we."

"They could, my dear. They'd have all the king's horses and all the king's men out after ye. Aw, and all the king's ships if they could find watter to float 'em on. Yew don't knaw the Jews. They can du anything. I've seen a Jew tak' a stone and squeeze mun in his hand till it fair dripped wi' best mutton fat."

Ursula was silent. She did know something about Jews, as she had heard George raving against them; and she had sense enough to reason that if he couldn't escape they too might find it difficult.

"Wull, I've got a scheme," went on the merry pink gentleman. "I don't come to my friends unless I can give 'em a hand up, so to speak. I've got a scheme in each pocket like stones at election-time. Now, John me lad, what du'ye say to a beer-house, a nice little house in Plymouth town, and nothing to du except draw the beer and watch the money rolling in? Du that tickle ye under the chin, man?"

Obviously the scheme tickled both Pethericks all over. To live in a town was naturally the height of Ursula's ambition; and to be the landlady of a public-house was to occupy a position somewhat, if at all, lower than the angels. It was the unlimited opportunities of using his gullet for the purpose assigned to it by creative nature, rather than any desire to become a man about town, which appealed to John. Little Mr. Odyorne added them up correctly. His sharp eyes saw the bottles scattered about the place. His knowledge of country folk told him how weary they were of the long, unlighted evenings and how ardently they desired the town when they were tied to the land. He had the public-house in his mind and could get them in; and they would not know, until it was much too late, that the licence had only a few more months to run and would not be renewed. Once out of Wheal Dream they could never return, for the place would be legally his, and there would be no house to come to—directly they were out he would burn it down, as that would be the cheapest way of clearing the ground—and the commoners would be told he had bought the property, and as for the Pethericks they would never be heard of again. The Guardians of the Poor would take good care of them. Little Mr. Odyorne knew a trick or two when he was out after guineas.

He babbled on with gilt-edged phrases and drank tea with them, pouring it into the saucer in the most homely way, until Ursula was charmed. He patted Father on the shoulder, called him a dear old gentleman, and declared he was the very picture of a venerable Duke. Father accepted the compliment and coughed all over the visitor to show his appreciation. Then John wanted to know what the gentleman intended doing with his property, as he plainly hinted he wasn't going to part with a stone of it, and was told—

"We'll do it up fine, and I'll let it vor ye at a hundred pounds a year. We'll divide the money, share and share alike till I get my little bit back, and then yew'll tak' the lot."

John grumbled something about wanting the entire sum, with the beer-house thrown in, but Ursula stopped him with a "Shut thee noise, man, and don't insult the gentleman."

Mr. Odyorne became still more friendly. He declared he had never taken to people so much in his life. John and Ursula were the real good stuff, and he couldn't say anything else; and as for Father, why, the innocent way in which he unbuttoned himself before company was perfectly touching in its simplicity. At last he jumped up and said he must go, as it was already dusk and he had a train to catch. He would see about the beer-house and write to them in a few days. He shook John heartily by both hands and said—

"'Tis a gude day's work, I reckon, man. Nothing like foreclosure when yew ain't got money. Yew don't knaw what foreclosure means and I'll tull ye. 'Tis getting another man to du vor ye what yew can't du vor yourself. Yew knaw the proverb, 'tis a rough wind what blows gude to nobody. Wull, that's what foreclosure means. Aw, John, 'tis lucky yew bain't a man o' business. Good-bye, my dear," said the mocking little wretch, turning to Ursula. "My word, if yew bain't a fine woman I wouldn't knaw where to find one. If John wur to be took I'd be after ye, sure 'nuff. There, never mind John. He bain't looking."

He drew her into the passage and kissed her cheek. Mr. Odyorne would have kissed anything for guineas. Then he trotted off as hard as he could go, rubbing his mouth and muttering, "Pah! the dirty devils."

In the meantime Jimmy had gone asleep in the linhay, exhausted with his exertions, and there John discovered him when he came for hay; and for the second time the boy was ejected, but on this occasion without guile. Ursula came running up and the usual fighting began, until it occurred to them to form an offensive alliance against Uncle. John was not going to have Jimmy on his premises, for he declared the wretched youth had been after Ursula in his absence, and Father, who was highly virtuous, had indeed suggested as much. The baby required sheltering somehow, although, as John said, there was no necessity. Ursula proposed that Uncle's door should be battered in, and there was no dissentient.

It was dark in the cottage; there was not even a glow of firelight. Uncle was squatting in a corner, clasping the Bible to his noisy old heart, in an agony of terror, praying with all his might. His enemies were upon him, and he felt sure they would murder him and swear they had done it in self-defence. When a blow came upon the door he shrieked as if it had landed on his body. That was John with a great lump of granite. John was such a strong, rough man, and he desired his death that he might have the cottage and field and strip of garden behind. And that was Ursula's voice, "Open the door, yew old devil. Open it, wull'ye?" Then another blow and another; and the light of a lantern flashed through the cracked wood and made lines of fire upon the walls. There was John's brutal laughter, and Ursula's vengeful voice again, "Takes our property from us, and drives his own blood and bones out on Dartmoor to starve. Hit 'en on his blasphemious old mouth when yew gets in, Jimmy."

Uncle did not move. He could not because something more than fear was holding him down. His body was marvellously cold and numbed, and the pricking in his right leg had ceased suddenly and the limb seemed to disclaim all connection with him. He had always been nervous, and that was why he had wanted a companion in the cottage. Even the rats at night had frightened him. He invoked aid from Heaven, but knew he was not doing it properly, and jumbling the words up; and once he discovered he was actually praying to the wonderful gentleman, and calling him the Deity, and begging him to perform a little miracle to help a poor old fellow whose only fault was a rather too great unwillingness to spend money. He confessed it then; he had always been afraid of finding himself penniless in extreme old age.

"Send down along and help, Lord God Almighty," he quavered. "Mr. Brunacombe, if yew please, gentleman, come across if it bain't troubling yew, vor I be main cruel scared and helpless. If yew please, holy angels, and Simon Peter apostle, just vor an old man what ha' put up wi' a lot and ha' done the best he could if 'twarn't vor going fo bed wi' the money-box vor fear o' the thieves. Please to send the gentleman, Lord Almighty, and Bill Chown, and St. Michael o' Halstock. I bain't able to bear it any longer, and my old legs du seem amazing vunny like. My head be mazed got tu. I can't seem to mind the bit about passing through deep watter, and the gentleman wull say I ha' done right."

The blows went on and the lock was bulging, though Uncle could see nothing except those horrid yellow flashes of the lantern. He seemed to be sinking into cold, roaring waters. Perhaps it was the shower of ice, which the wind had brought over the tors and was hurling upon the tin roof of his linhay, with the tumult of a thousand drums. Uncle moistened his thumb and turned over a few pages of the Bible, trying to feel out words which might soothe him.

What a long time they were getting in, to be sure. The blows had ceased and there was no more cruel lantern-light. Uncle was too far gone to know what had happened, but he tried to be thankful for the miracle. No doubt his prayer had been answered. John, Ursula, Jimmy, and the baby had been smitten with blindness, and were all going about seeking for somebody to lead them by the hand; at least all except the baby. Perhaps the angel had smitten that with death, and a good thing too, for it was a shameful little thing. Jimmy was a wicked boy to have brought it into the world. Uncle was feeling hard and uncharitable just then, but they were torturing him so; and he had the horrors, huddled there in the darkness and feeling sure they were going to murder him to get the property and the money-box.

John had only gone for his crowbar. Soon the light flashed in again, and the dreadful, murderous sounds, clamp! clamp! came like thuds upon Uncle's head; and as the woodwork cracked and splintered, and the lock crashed upon the concrete floor, which he had always kept so clean and polished, the old man started and shrieked in agony; and this time he went down and the noisy waters closed over his head.

"Here he be! Hit 'en, the old toad. Kick 'en, Jimmy," screamed Ursula. "Aw," she shivered. "Bide a bit. Bring along the lantern, John."

There was poor old Uncle, his patient, ugly face turned up to the roof, the eyes wide open and staring at them, unable to crawl away, a hopeless paralytic.

CHAPTER XVIII
ABOUT THE WILD GARDEN

In those days George and his senses began to fight. His work was not enough; it filled his time, but not his life, and the great void remained. Bubo sat disconsolate and heard no more small talk. George was silent and grey, and worked with his head down, listening to the wind; December was hunting upon the moor; the abomination of desolation was over Wheal Dream; its visions were horrible; snow whirled above, and its jagged timbers were blue with ice, and the things around it were dumb with winter silence. The wind was the only voice, and a threatening one. The whole world seemed bankrupt.

Only two men-patients were at the sanatorium, both spinal cases, and George saw them hobbling slowly past his windows, protecting their faces as well as they could when meeting the wind. Berenice had gone, taking Tobias with her. She had sent a message scribbled in pencil to say she was going to Penzance for the winter and would be back in the spring if it was necessary. She had written to Winnie, through her home doctor, and the letter had not been returned, so it must have reached her. She could not believe that Winnie had married that brute. She concluded by saying she was much better, or at least she hoped so; and Tobias was quite well. It was either dog or Winnie; first one and then the other, with some of herself between; but never a word for George.

After all he was a poverty-stricken creature, not a charming fox-terrier with pretty ways and soft eyes; and his nervousness made him rude. He did not even know himself what he was; sometimes he thought himself the equal of John Petherick, and tried to persuade himself he would be better employed building a hedge or throwing manure into a cart. What was his art but a trick, like a dog throwing up a piece of sugar and catching it? The arts baked no bread; a wall was necessary, as a shelter against rough weather, if it was nothing more than the side of a hut-circle; but pictures upon that wall were unnecessary and the interior was as warm without them. What was the artist but a juggler, making his pitch first in one place then in another, trying to attract those who hurried past eager to get into the eating-houses and blow their stomachs out?

George rarely spoke to the Chowns during those days, and they did not intrude more than was necessary upon his sight. When Bessie approached he was irritable. He would shut her out, write his instructions upon scraps of paper, and pin them to the door. Anything to escape talking. He knew Uncle was bedridden, and that Bessie ran to and fro to serve the old man, and incidentally to make Jimmy's life a burden, but he did not care. He seemed to be struggling with his own consciousness. He shocked Bubo frequently by his antics; testing the capabilities of his body and mind by tumbling about on a mattress with a horrid kind of gravity, and declaring he had been meant for an acrobat; or reciting Shakespeare to see if he was fitted for an actor; or singing very much out of tune in a frightful deep bass, and coming to the conclusion that nature had intended him for a singer. Sometimes he thought he would make a good tradesman; a fruit and florist's business would suit him well; and he could stand at the door and shout, "Apples are cheap to-day," against the biggest liar in the town. Then he answered advertisements in the paper, one as boots in an hotel, another as attendant in an asylum, being almost beside himself, but no answers came. Then he advertised for a wife, and a shoal of replies came from amorous servant-girls, but he flung the lot in the fire and went on painting while the solitude drew its mists closer about him. George thought he was acting quite rationally, but his mind was rotting, his senses were departing, the wintry wind was pulling him about. He became bolder than ever in his work and flung convention out of the window; but he knew all the time his pictures were so much rubbish.

Only dull men have a single nature; there is a strange diversity in the clever man; and in the genius there exists a strong impulse towards reversion to primitive savagery. That is why great men sometimes break loose from all control and make brutes of themselves. Their civilisation goes hand in hand with barbarism. Every man of genius feels that yearning towards the wild garden, which is Nature unspoilt by the trim pathways of life. George took long walks, but he always went on the moor away from the tracks of men: it was not there he felt the solitude; it was in his home; the loneliness of the moor was the savagery which he delighted in. It was his garden, the unspoilt place, and it was the Creator's garden too. The Creator does not force a plant into bloom, then throw it away on the rubbish heap. He leaves that for men to do. Men love plants that are artificial and short-lived like themselves, but the Creator makes His garden for all time; and the great glory of Dartmoor had never been disturbed by destructive gardeners. It is only a wilderness, but the wild state is the most perfect type of beauty; strong and free and breathing of immortality: and the strong mind turns towards it and loves to wander there, because of its inspiration and its nearness to the Gardener. George would walk out merely to look at a certain rowan dripping in absolute beauty into the river at the foot of Halstock cliff.

Nothing but primitive wildness was there. The oak, ash, birch, rowan, and alder were the only trees known to the first savage upon Dartmoor; they are the only trees known there now. The wild wood remains as it was; so does the garden of furze, heather and bracken. If the early savage could return and look about him he would find his home in ruins, but his garden the same. Possibly George was one of those early savages. He could sit by the river and wonder if it was really true that Caesar had landed in Britain. There was nothing around him to disturb the illusion.

In the dead December no place can be more suggestive of life than Dartmoor; not human life perhaps, that is the charm of spring, but the wild mid-life—those wondrous things which seem to approach men from above and below. Life is everywhere, from the rushing wind above to the trembling of water-drops ringing somewhere below and unseen; the moorland seems to be in travail, every furze-brake is in pangs, and some mystery struggles wildly in every bush of heather. The moor gives birth to dreams, and visions form in the mist; strange things come into the world then; questions that children ask, stories that once had life in them, and there is a litter of little jack-o'-lanthorns sucking water in every cave. It is the Walpurgis month, when people run away from the wild garden because it frightens them; and those who are savages at heart have it to themselves, and can wander about as they like, and find a reward.

As Christmas came on George grew more torpid. Like Uncle, he was stricken with paralysis, only it was in his mind. His vigour decreased, little work was done for all his vows, and he spent hours before the fire talking to himself in a low voice, but not knowing what he said. He was conscious of receiving some money, less than last time, but he was informed that his pictures were selling at reduced figures. The kindly Jew who presided over his fortunes declared it was hard to find a market for them and he was practically giving them away. No doubt there was a certain amount of exaggeration in this, but George believed, when he was able to think of the matter at all, that it was wholly true. He was no genius. He was worth hardly the smallest copper coin of the realm. Bill Chown was worth far more, because he could bend his back and use a pick. Bill's two horny hands were marked with a higher price than an artist's head.

At last Gregory came with a faggot upon his shoulder. It was the week before Christmas, and the great fellow brought as a small gift, and all he could, the Yule faggot which no commoner neglects to burn on the eve of the festival.

"Wull, sir, 'tis the oldest custom in the world," he cried, as he lowered the faggot to the threshold. "The ash ha' been burnt from the beginning o' the world to now, but yew and me wull be the only ones in England to burn 'en on Christmas Eve, and don't ye answer me back neither."

George looked at the faggot. It was composed of short sticks covered with silvery bark, and the colour of the wood was a faint yellow.

"Every house on the moor will burn it," he said.

"I told ye not to answer me back," shouted Gregory. "Ees, they'll all burn ash, but none of 'em twitch-beam. Volks be forgetful like. They minds a custom, but don't mind what it means. I knaws, vor I ha' got my parchment and he tulls me to cut the faggot by the light o' the mune and wi' a chopper or knife what ain't never been used avore. Volks got to burn ash because it wur easy to come by, and so they forgot what the custom meant. Yew and me wull burn twitch-rods, same as they did at the beginning of the world."

George took the giant by the arm and drew him inside. After all it was good to have company, and this fine creature was a cure for melancholy. "I lend you books," he said, "but you could teach the writers something. Where does it all come from?"

"The parchment," said Gregory. "He'm covered wi' writing all over, and there be writing on that, and writing on that again."

"You can't make it out."

"Don't ye answer me back. What I ses I holds to," cried Gregory, and George perceived that argument would vex his heart.

"I know you," he said. "We are birds of a feather, you in your ruin, I in my Wheal House. Eh, Gregory?" he laughed bitterly. "We're both seeking and both asking."

"Wull, sir, I've brought ye the trade," said Gregory, not quite understanding him. "Burn the twitch and yew'll live, vor he'm the tree o' life what stood in the garden. Last vull mune I ses, I'll tak' Mr. Brunacombe a faggot o' twitch-rods, and he'll burn mun on Christmas Eve and live vor ever. And here 'em be cut from St. Michael's Wood."

"Ah, Gregory," George muttered.

"I cut to the west o' the ridge, and that be in the forest though 'em ses it bain't. I knaws whether I be inside the boundary or whether I bain't. I wun't be answered back. I wouldn't bring ye twitch-rods from outside. There's no gude sap to hiss at ye in foreign twitch."

"'Quick' is the word. It's the mountain-ash."

"'Tis 'twitch' in the parchment. 'Tis the tree o' life," said Gregory. "They used to beat maids wi' the sticks on their wedding-day so as 'em shouldn't be barren, and trees so as 'em should bear fruit. Us always called the berries Eve's Apples, but the name be forgot now. The first man wur born in a twitch-beam, and he came wriggling out o' mun like a white maggot. And when he got hungry he bit open a flower-bud and there wur the first liddle woman inside."

"Sit down there," said George, pointing to his table. "Write it all out."

Gregory laughed until the place shook, and put out his huge right hand with its stiff curved fingers.

"I'd squeeze one o' they pens to nought," he said. "I can tell, but I can't write. I couldn't put down what I be telling to yew. A trick o' the tongue be one thing, and a trick o' the hand another. If I wur to write, the words would scare me like a lot o' black piskies."

He turned to go, but George followed him to the door, and said suddenly in a low voice, "Gregory."

"Wull, sir," answered the giant, turning.

"You are courting."

For a moment George thought the man was going to strike him. He went white, but it was not with rage. His hand dropped from the door, and he said, "A vule be a warning to a vule."

Then as George made no answer Gregory broke forth from his calmness like sudden wind from the heights—

"Didn't I watch vor ye? Yew ha' been gude to me," he said with a tremor. "Us bain't the like, I bain't highclass like yew, but us be men, as I told ye avore, that night when us wur mazed wi' the gurt warm mune. Us both wants the like. Let's ha' the truth on't. Us both wants a woman. Du'ye pitch, sir. Yew'm sick."

Gregory's eyes pierced everything. George sat down, his head lolling on his shoulder, his face growing as grey as his beard. Thus he remained, with his eyes half shut, gulping every few moments. Sleet pattered against the window and the wind howled, while Bubo hooted, for the night was coming on and he was glad; but all these sounds were nothing to those fierce Gregorian tones which were breaking upon the artist's head.

"They ses it wants a woman to knaw a woman, but a man can see. Du'ye reckon I go abroad wi' my eyes in my trousers? I saw yew wi' the maids: I didn't look at yew, but I looked at them. There was the dark one wi' the brown face. Her would tak' a man's heart, put mun to her teeth and bite, and say, 'I'll ha' another.' There wur t'other. Never mind about she. Didn't I watch she and yew? Ees, I reckon. Times I said 'He wull,' and times I said 'He won't.' But her wants 'en. Her wants 'en," Gregory shouted, losing control over his strength, driving his fist against the wall and leaving upon it the imprint of four great knuckles. George's head was upon his chest, his hands clutching his beard. He tried to answer, but his tongue was dry. He remembered that he had not been eating much lately. No wonder he was feeling faint.

"I came along that night, I told yew a story, I put it to ye as plain as I could, and I got home saying to myself, 'Wull he?' Yew did nought. I knaw how 'twur—I ses what I likes now. I be a man tu, and proud on't. There be tu much pride in it. Us wants to be Gods Almighty, 'stead o' plain volk wi' breeches on. 'Tis the lack o' canaries what makes vules o' we, vor I be a vule tu. 'Cause us ain't got the yaller birds us ses there be nought else. I knaws yew'm poor, sir, and yew'm none the worse vor't. I never did see a rich man what didn't look as if the Ten Commandments hadn't been torn against his face. Us needn't get into the ground and play wi' worms 'cause bad luck hits at we. Hit back at 'en, sir, hit back. Aw, I be courting sure 'nuff. Yew larn't me the lesson, and I ses, 'I'll ha' a woman avore I dies.' I ha' a poor home, I reckon, but there 'tis—a home. A man's heart be there, and if that bain't homely, what be? There he be, up in the wind, and let 'en blow as 'twull he wun't blow cold if yew takes love in under. Yew mun tak' 'en or let in the devil.

"Us bain't poor man and gentleman. Us be parishioners what stand up vor one another. Get up, sir, go abroad wi' your head up and shout back at the wind. It puts life into ye, and no man ever got strong by looking on his butes. Get a razor and cut they old whiskers off, and buy clothes that be vitty like. Don't be an old man when yew'm young. Tak' off that grey beard, what be an insult to women, and dra' a flower in your coat and go courting. I knaw how 'tis.

Yew'm weak, but a woman would give ye strength, mak' a giant of ye, mak' ye want to work wi' an iron bar 'cause a pen would be tu small vor ye. The canaries wull fly along when yew can't get no further without 'em, vor that be the way us be played wi'. When us can't get any more down under, us goes up. That be the law made at the beginning o' the world under the twitch-beam. There be one God to the top o' the tree, and one God to the bottom o' mun, but it be the like God; and when yew'm got to the roots He ses, 'Go up into the branches, man, and pick they liddle apples. Can't let ye bide down here along.' He'm kind, sir, say what 'em wull. None o' us stands in more wind than us can bear. He sends the gude sun, and us brings the black clouds along wi' our shoutings."

George stirred and made a motion with his hand. Gregory came to his side with one stride and bent his great body.

"Too late. She's married," George muttered.

Gregory straightened himself, was about to answer, but glanced down and said nothing. He went to the door, picked up his bar of iron, and the next moment he was swinging down the track singing loudly. George heard the heavy tramp and the mighty voice for a long while; and then the moor gate slammed, the sounds receded, and became mixed up with the winds. Then George arose and climbed into his bed.

Gregory was a powerful tonic, and the artist was the better for that dose of him. He tried to laugh and talk nonsense; and instead of wandering in the wild garden turned himself into the lanes, looked people in the face, spoke to them, went across to see Uncle and tried to cheer up what was left of him. Uncle was in the wild garden too, for delusions had taken hold upon him, and he thought he was lying exposed upon Dartmoor in a wild spot among the furze and ferns. George promised to come and read to him, and Uncle was grateful, but expressed a hope that the weather would not be rough or it would be impossible for him to hear. It was very windy on the top of the tor where Uncle supposed he was resting. There was work for Jimmy in those days, and he had to do it, for Bessie refused to prepare his meals, so the flabby youth shuffled about the cottage cooking himself a few potatoes and warming the baby's milk. Jimmy was getting weary of his life and meditated a change. Uncle's rents were coming in, the money-box would soon be heavy, for the foolish old fellow had no trust in paper. The box was warm in bed beside the Bible. Jimmy made his plans; and in the meantime visited Ursula when John was out.

Two days George was himself, and then he broke down again. The weather was against him; each morning the sky was black and the moor a ghastly white with frost; the sun appeared to have been extinguished; the atmosphere was cold and sluggish. George went back to his wanderings among the heather, following the rivers to their bubbling heads. The garden was a place of icy water: but the strange, noisy things of winter were still being born there, filling his mind with madness.

Then a Christmas card reached him, a wonderful little picture of shepherds dressed in purple and crimson, kneeling among sheep of a most unnatural cleanliness, while fireworks were being discharged overhead, and on an intense blue sky angels were turning somersaults. Beneath was a motto about peace and good-will, and on the back was written, "With greetings from Francis Leigh."

"It is Christmas," said George. "The time when men overeat themselves or get drunk for custom's sake, and advertise their godliness by sending one another halfpenny slips of pasteboard depicting scenes in Hebrew history; when old griefs come back and say, 'This is the time we meet again.' Leigh is orthodox. But it is the thought, not the thing. I must go and see the dear man, and give him a pretty picture too."

He opened a portfolio, took out a picture and began to touch it up, wondering if any one else would remember him. His aunt generally wrote, wanting to know if he was living decently, telling him she had neuralgia in one place and rheumatism in another, and giving him a list of additions to or subtractions from her home menagerie; but last year she had missed, and that might mean she too had been subtracted.

"It is merry Christmas, Bubo, and we are the old folks at home. Shall we get drunk for once in our lives, hoot carols, and throw things about? Drunkenness must be a kind of happiness in the wilderness; for the bottle and its imp make company."

There was a knock upon the door and Bessie appeared, her face red and glowing, as she had just walked across the village.

"Here be a card vor ye, sir. I wur passing the post-office and they called me, and said the card came this morning and must ha' dropped on the floor."

She placed it on the table behind George, who was sitting at his easel. Without turning he said, "We must have a goose, Mrs. Chown, and Uncle shall have a cut from the breast. Can you get one?"

"Ees, sir. I knaws where I can put my fingers on a booty. Shall I get ye a bottle o' something homely, sir?" asked Bessie.

George shook his head. A glass of milk was the strongest liquor he ever drank; he said so, and Bessie looked disappointed. "A drop o' drink be homely-like come Christmas," she said.

"If you can't take it what then? It's a poor heart that can't make merry without toddy. You and Bill can have some beer, just enough to set you singing and no more. If we are too sober John and Ursula will make up for it and preserve the respectability of Wheal Dream."

"That 'em will," said Bessie, although she was rather shocked at her master's lack of homeliness. "Here be the card, sir," she went on, poking it dutifully into his face. "Wull'ye have the bit o' mutton hashed vor your supper?"

George did not hear her. He was staring at the card, a picture of a small fluffy maiden cuddling a large dog; and just then he hardly knew whether Bessie was inside the room or not. He had never seen that handwriting before, and yet he recognised it. Bessie went on with her domestic questions, and George heard a noise and muttered, "Yes, anything you like—to-day or to-morrow, it's all the same."

"And a rice pudding, sir?" went on the persecutor with a wondering glance. The master was getting mad again, and he had been so much better the last few days.

George said something, though he didn't know what, and got rid of her. Then he locked the door, gloated over the card, turned it over and over, and at last began to pace the room. It was from Winnie. There was no doubt about that, although there was neither name nor initial. "With the best wishes. I hope you are well. Have you finished the picture?" So much was written on the top of the card. Lower, scribbled apparently as a nervous afterthought, he read, "I am ill again, longing for the moor."

Hardly knowing what he did, George went to his bookcase, pulled out the first volume his hand rested on, sat down and let it fall open upon his knees. There he remained for several minutes without moving, fallen again into the strange state—the wild, silent life of the jack-o'Janthorn—which had been his for so long.

"I must get out," he said at last. "I want the marshes that I may think. What is heaven doing, Bubo?"

The wind was up again; the weather was always changing, snow to-day and mud to-morrow; but it was always dark.

"Look here, my dear old chap," George muttered huskily. "Don't get mazed now. There's nothing in it. Every one does this sort of thing at Christmas. I gave her that picture. It's the most natural thing in the world she should send me a card. Besides, she's married." He leant forward, struck at his easel and sent it flying across the room, while Bubo squeaked with terror and fluttered to the other end of his perch. "Don't believe a word Gregory says. His head is stuffed full of romance and he lives in an atmosphere of moonshine shaken with the wind. Fond of me! Yet she took him; but he's young, well-dressed, good-looking enough, if he is a madman once a month. Young girls see only the side they want to see. They don't bother about morals if the face suits. Bah, she looked on me as old Father Brunacombe. She frowned when I tried to look at her. I don't believe she ever laughed at me behind my back though. I won't believe that. And yet—Oh, my God, look at that ugly, dirty devil."

George could just see himself in the mantel-glass. He saw a huddled figure in torn and baggy garments, with coarse woollen socks falling in rolls over ragged slippers that flopped when he moved. He saw a face white and lined, surrounded with a huge bush of untrimmed grey hair.

"That's the wild man of the moor. Poor old George, the savage of Wheal Dream. Look here, you fool," he went on angrily, "it's time you dragged this dream of pink women out of your heart. You've fed yourself on visions all the years you've lived here, and they are bringing you down to the level of the wretch who dies for opium. It's a wonder my work hasn't been better though," he muttered. "I've had the inspiration here, and though I laugh at my stuff and say it's rubbish I have thought sometimes—there, what's the good of talking? I know what it is. I was born from the planet Saturn on a Friday and All Fools' Day. I must get out. Good-bye, Bubo, I will be back to spend Christmas with you, man. Stare at me and grin if you can. 'I am ill again, longing for the moor.' Grin, Bubo. She's dying and saying good-bye; and not forgetting old Father Brunacombe, because he gave her a picture which he couldn't have sold for twopence and was glad to get rid of."

The brown book upon his knees was a translation of Homer. George read a few lines and rose wearily, murmuring the wild music, "And the old man went out silently to the side of the roaring sea." The first poet knew his own nature. He knew that men desire solitude in the wild garden of Nature when they are in trouble; and they like to feel the force of that Nature breaking upon their bodies. The child sneaks away into a corner to cry after a punishment; the man does the same when fate strikes him from some dark cloud. They want to be alone and not feel others are looking at them. Nature at her fiercest is the best companion in trouble because of her fierceness.

"That old blind beggar was right," said George. Then he drew an old coat around him and went out silently to the side of the roaring moor.

Soon the weather beat him. Snow which was more than half ice came against his face like pellets from a gun; and he was driven down to the lane crawling into Downacombe. Once he turned back, but felt he could not face his room and Bubo's large oracular eyes and that postcard. She hoped he was well. She wondered if he had finished the picture. Which was it, the one of herself sitting above the waterfall with her lap full of white violets, or the big canvas of the Perambulators crossing Chapel Ford? Neither was finished and perhaps never would be. He was a bee-keeper, a potato-grower; anything but an artist. Wheal Dream had been his undoing, not his making; it had quickened his body, not his mind, and now he had reached the time when health could be a joy no longer.

So he came to Downacombe Rectory by the muddy lane. Leigh was in the church, he was told, reading the service to its cold walls. George went in and waited for him, but the house was full of smoke, the woodwork creaked, and the atmosphere was so charged with loneliness that he was glad to wander about the garden until the rector appeared.

He looked whiter and worried and much older. His manner had changed too, for though as affectionate and kind as ever, he was scared, and started when the trees made a noise. "You have not been near me for a long time," he said reproachfully.

"Well, I have come now—to wish you a happy Christmas," said George, with a touch of irony in his voice.

Leigh repeated the words in a dreamy manner. They went inside, and though it was still daylight the rector fastened the shutters and lighted the lamps. He was nervous, and when George protested against this shortening of what little day there was, he said, "You must humour me. I'm getting full of whims and oddities. I don't like looking into the garden these winter afternoons. The place is so old. This house was built on the foundations of a monastery, a nunnery once stood in the paddock, there are ruins everywhere. I am too much alone, and I get a bit feverish in the evenings."

"Anything wrong?" asked George. He was in a deep chair, sucking the back of his hand as if it had been an orange, looking at the exhibition of postcards, thinking of the one at home; not giving much attention to Leigh yet, but wondering if the man was going to reveal himself.

"I hardly know. The house seems in an unsettled state. I suppose ignorant people would put it down to spirits. Things fall about at nights."

"Cats," said George.

"There are none. Bells ring."

"Wind," said George. "There's nothing wrong with the house. You are unstrung. Those parishioners of yours have upset you."

"They are appealing to me now to sell the property. I should, of course, if I could get a good offer; but who wants a decayed and tumble-down village? I think I had better burn the rest down."

"Did you ever find out how that fire was caused?"

"There is no mystery about it. I started it, only it went further than I intended."

"What?" muttered George sharply. "You burnt those people out of house and home?"

"Don't say anything about it," said Leigh, with a nervous twitch. "The people are unreasonable and there is no real spiritual life in them. The buildings were heavily insured. I shall get rid of the old cottages gradually."

"In the same way?"

Leigh nodded and said simply, "They burn like straw in the hot weather."

George was feeling queer. He opened his mouth to say something about arson and penal servitude, but closed it again, for he then at last realised that Leigh was a degenerate. It seemed impossible—this man so handsome and well made, so saintly in face, so tender in manner, who adored his flowers and devoted all that was in him to the science of rose culture, who held daily services though nobody ever attended them, who was clever and could overthrow an opponent in debate, was somehow base. He had no moral faculty. His wife would not live with him. Was it on account of her health, or had he in private life unnatural ways? Was he an impossible man to live with?

"You ought to resign the living," said George, in a wild voice.

"That is just what my wife says. She wants me to exchange and go into a town, but I could not live away from my rose garden. Of course if God called me to a better living I should feel it my duty to go."

It was no use. The rector didn't know he had done wrong, and he really tried to do his duty, and in a sense he was genuine. That accounted for the sincerity of his face and the charm of his manner. Decidedly he was not a humbug, and his talk about a call to a better living, which might have been a cant phrase in the mouth of another, was not so with him. He seemed to be every inch a man and a gentleman; and yet it would have been better if he had never been born.

"Leigh, are you a Christian?" George burst out, unable to restrain himself. He too was getting feverish and feeling he must either let himself go, or howl and roll upon the floor.

"My dear Brunacombe, I think you forget yourself," came the cold and dignified answer.

"I don't," said George. "Come on, man. We're alone here, and what you say won't carry beyond these walls. My creed is, 'I believe in a Creator, who made you, me, and everything, amen.' Not a syllable more. Isn't yours the same? You're a sane man. You're a clever man," he cried bitterly. "Do you believe that those bones on the other side of the hedge yonder will creep out of their holes one day, and put the same flesh on them, and be the same slouching folk?"

"That will do," broke in Leigh, with something like anger. "I cannot discuss matters which are too great for both of us."

"Why not? You would discuss roses or fire insurances," said George harshly. "Why not things of greater importance?"

"They are a part of our accepted religion. That is all I can say. What is the matter with you, Brunacombe?"

"I'm upset, like you. I've got a heap of trouble and it's crushing me. I should like some sort of answer as to where I am going when I'm crushed. Your heaven frightens me. I'd rather not have it. No man has succeeded in describing a heaven half as beautiful as this earth. I don't want your city of gold and oriental hymns. I would rather be on Dartmoor among the sheep and ponies—"

"A wandering spirit at the beck and call of every mediumistic school-girl," Leigh interrupted gently.

"Bah! that is all rubbish. Religious orthodoxy!" George sneered. "What is it? Why, when I was a child—"

"You thought as a child. And do so still."

"I was frightened to death by accounts of hell. I dared not pass the blacksmith's shop because I thought that was hell. Where is it now? During those few years hell has disappeared. The chapels keep it glowing, but your Church has extinguished it because the people won't have it, and the Church as a business concern is wise enough to know that the wishes of the people must be respected. What right have you to alter a doctrine to suit the taste of the time, if there is any truth in that doctrine? I say where there is no constancy there cannot be truth."

"Only the fool or the genius tries to solve what cannot be solved," said Leigh.

"And the rest are indifferent; parsons who may not think and congregations who cannot."

"It is as well. A common man makes a beautiful subject common," said Leigh impatiently. "If you gave legs to a fish it wouldn't be able to use them. Stop, stop, Brunacombe, we shall soon be at each other's throats," he said in his own affectionate manner. "We shall know the truth soon enough."

"Is that why you shut out the daylight—because you are afraid of seeing the truth rustling past your windows?"

"I am frightened sometimes," Leigh confessed.

"By what?"

"Those matters which we cannot solve. This is a lonely place, there are stories and traditions, and there are ruins of the religious houses. It is wild these winter evenings."

"Leigh, you are a good sort—upon my own bad soul you are," cried the poor, miserable George, touched by his own loneliness and a look of pathos in the rector's fine eyes. "Don't tell any one else about that fire."

"I'm not going to," said Leigh, in a surprised voice.

"You are right not to answer my questions, and yet I thought you might help me. I'm a failure, and I reckon I'm getting near the end of it all. I'm not a scoffer. I'm only a wretched fool who understands nothing. Don't turn that lamp up. Is it dark outside?"

"Not yet," said Leigh, with a slight shiver. "What is it, Brunacombe? Not money, I hope?"

"The curse of eternity be upon all gold, silver, and copper. It's the one thing—the one and only thing which makes hell for us all."

"Love," said the rector softly. "Perhaps it is the greatest mystery of all. I know her name. She often mentioned you—affectionately."

"What did she say?"

"The great famous artist. The wonderful head."

"The old clothes, the shabby boots, the grey beard?"

"No. She admired you."

"She's married," George groaned.

"To a brute."

"No," George shouted. "A conceited bounder, a moon-baked Socialist, not a brute. What?" he cried. "Will he treat her badly—hasten her death?"

Leigh said nothing, but moved about the room with his hands behind him. He looked like a Father of the Church; and yet he ought to have been in prison.

"Come here. If you loved a woman, and knew she was unhappy, and guessed she was ill-treated by her husband, would you try and get her away?"

For a few moments Leigh said nothing. Probably he would have been attacked by homicidal mania in such a case, but he had no idea of that. Presently he answered, "I should require to be tempted first."

"I'll do it," George shouted.

"Come, come, don't talk like this. I always looked upon you as a man who knew how to endure patiently."

"The time comes when you seem to be uprooted and blown about, and you can't find a sheltered place to hide. Life seems to be a tragedy of wind-tossed opportunities."

"Bear up all the way. Remember Raleigh," said Leigh.

"Ah, but he was a demi-god," said George reverently. "Even he had his small successes."

"Yours are beyond—round the next bend," said Leigh tenderly.

George bent over and took the gentle hand, the earth-hardened hand which had made his parishioners homeless.

"Where are yours?"

"I have tried to do my duty here," said the rector simply, "and I have introduced two new roses."

George did not smile at the almost insane answer, hardly thought about it, but sank back into the chair and remained as silent as if he had gone to sleep. There was not a sound in the house, nor in the damp garden outside, nor yet in the wild garden further on.

"What are you thinking about, poor old man?" Leigh asked.

"About an evening some years ago," George muttered, with his head down and his mind gone out somewhere into the storm. "I was in wretched lodgings at a seaside town, trying to get well, but not succeeding. I was so weak that every sudden noise hurt me badly; and it was lonely, though I have known nothing but a lonely life. That evening I walked out away from the steaming crowd, looking for a quiet place. The road went on between trees until the houses became few, and presently I found myself standing before one quite alone in a deep garden, surrounded with flowering shrubs. It was a big house built of stone, and perhaps it looked cold and cheerless—I didn't notice that. I only knew that some one was playing a piano in there, more sweetly and tenderly than I had ever heard it played before. I didn't know what the tune was, whether it was what they call sacred music; I only knew it was sweet and tender, and it made me long to lie down there and rest. Then I looked at the porch. Round it ran, in severe black letters, the words, 'Convent of the Immaculate Conception.' I looked between the white curtains and could see a statuette of their goddess. I hate Catholicism, I do not believe in Christianity, and the Immaculate Conception is to me a foolish tale; and yet I wanted to go in. I wanted to go in and not think about things any more.

"I went back to the esplanade. A band was making brutal noises, something without music or beauty. Loud-faced youths were strolling there, smoking and spitting; young women, just as loud-faced, walked with them, shrieking like parrots; sons and daughters of that stunning band. I saw a miner, with hands like agricultural implements, rubbing his grimy mouth across a girl's face; he was half-intoxicated, and some of his spittle was trickling down her cheek. They were just lighting the lamps. There was a smell of orange-peel, sweat, and cigar-ends. I went away. I wanted to go back to that lonely house with the black letters round the porch and the sweet music inside. I wanted to lie down in there and rest."

"Yet you would abolish convents," said Leigh.

"I would abolish them," said George fiercely, "just as your Socialists would abolish wealthy men, because they are not wealthy themselves."

He was crossing the room, already in a hurry to be alone again, and the rector followed saying, "I will see you into the lane."

It was still light, with the last effort of a day which seemed to know it could never come again, and so expired unwillingly. They could see the dead-looking rose-trees, the blackening hedges, the wet paths. They could see, as they came up, the paddock across which ran the church-way, and the copse of firs growing where the nunnery had once stood. It appeared lighter, as the field was open to the sky. There was no wind down there, and the silence was intense.

"What's that?" shrieked George.

They were beside the little gate, and their weight was against it as they strained forward. Ahead of them the path wound away in the muddy grass.

"What's that?" Leigh gasped. "Oh, let it pass."

They started round and ran like men in fear of death. Down the garden they scurried, a grotesque sight had any one been there to see, and into the house, making for shelter; and didn't pause until they reached the lighted study and could see the bright wood-fire and feel the security of walls around them. They were both panting and covered with cold sweat.

"Liver," George muttered. "Don't tell me—there's no truth in these things."

"You saw them too. We both saw them at the same moment."

"Liver," said George stubbornly.

"Six," Leigh muttered.

"Seven. One walked in front."

"They swayed from side to side. Not a sound. No chanting," Leigh panted.

"All in black, and those big hoods. One of 'em limped."

"The last bearer on the right. When they came round the curve in the path I noticed it. They walked in step. They swayed from side to side."

"Bah," said George. "It was a nightmare. We want some medicine."

"I didn't see the coffin."

"There wouldn't be one—at that period."

"I saw no body."

"Nor I."

"Why didn't we? Where was it?"

"I neither know nor care," cried George. "We are mad; at least I am. If this is how my questions are to be answered I'll ask no more. The wind blows its dead leaves towards us out of the region of folklore. Let me out," he said angrily. "If I see those old nuns I'll talk to them like dogs and tell 'em to get home."

CHAPTER XIX
ABOUT THE FESTIVAL OF CUPS

The eve of Christmas was cold; moist and spring-like in the valleys and by the coast perhaps, but on Dartmoor a keen frost. During the night a change came, and at dawn, which occurred much later than the time specified in the calendar, rain descended heavily and mist spread all around.

George started off to spend his Christmas as usual on the moor, with the sandwiches in his pocket and a macintosh strapped round him. His idea was to tire himself out, then doze by the fire until bedtime. He climbed up the moor, tramped to the great peat-marsh and on to the cleave beyond, going far into the solitudes and seeing nothing because of the mist. Sometimes he heard the river plunging or bubbling between its bogs, the snort of an invisible pony, a flock of snow-buntings whispering by. On he went beside the mysterious walls and ruins, his foot now and again slipping upon the iron cylinder of a shell or getting entangled in the carcase of a pony; his hands were like wet fishes, and the fresh water dripped from his long hair. It was a savage way of spending Christmas, but far better than huddling half-sick over a fire in company with bad thoughts. Here he was wild and free, with the strong wind and rain, lost to the world in that wool-like mist, unable to think bitterly while he battled with the elements. There was no home circle waiting for him to complete it. He was only the wild man of the moor, alone, and free from mortal aches in that splendid silence. He didn't know he was bending more and looking like an old fellow of the chimney-corner; but he did remark once—and that was the only time he spoke aloud during the morning, "You're not walking so well as you did last Christmas, my boy."

In an old ruin up along the river he ate his sandwiches and rested, getting close under the battered wall for shelter. Having finished his scrappy meal he leaned back into the ruins of a corner, piled a quantity of heather upon his head—it grew all round in great bushes—and tried to persuade himself there had never been a woman in the world. It was good to think he was cut off from the blatant vulgar festival by miles of white mist and boggy hills.

"Let 'em drink and stuff," he muttered. "I'm out of it all and not missed. There's nothing like solitude when you can endure it. The man who can is the happiest of all beings. 'Christ is born to-day,'" he shouted. "Why shouldn't old George have his carol? He used to pipe 'em when he was a kid, and believe 'em too." He laughed, making a shocking noise; and as nobody could possibly hear he made as great a tumult as he could, imitating the laughter of old men, young children, and hysterical women, until he had to stop for coughing. "Silly old fool," he said. "This is the last Christmas of your sanity. Make the most of it. Ah, but I'm going to dress to-night. I'm going to disguise myself completely by cleaning up. Bubo will lie on his back and scream for brandy when I appear like the youthful David, fresh from following the ewes great with young ones. Why, George, you're more like your prehistoric self to-day. It's the wind, the mist, and the height—two thousand feet above the moaning of the bar. I shall be down again when I get back to Wheal Dream. Perhaps you're not going mad, after all. You're not so old. What is forty on Dartmoor? Hardly out of teething and coral-sucking. This is a merry Christmas, by Bethlehem it is. I'm going to put on a collar to-night, if it chokes me. And Bubo shall wear a flowing silk tie and a pair of striped bloomers. The firm is going to give a dinner to its employees, and the books shall be opened, and we will declare a dividend for the year and pay the same in coupons upon the Bank of Imagination to our own bankrupt selves."

George remained silent for some time, while rain washed him from head to foot. He was getting sleepy and unwilling to move; but presently he murmured, "That's better, old George. You must try and keep this sort of thing up. It will do you good."

Then cold and stiffness roused him, and he had to tramp on. This time he took the other side of the hills, intending to pass under the five ragged tors of Metheral, go up to Moor Gate, and greet Gregory with a gift.

It was three o'clock, and the day had committed suicide, when George reached the ruin which one man had made habitable. He was a queer object, like the wraith of a drowned fisherman, streaming with wet, and muddy almost to the knees from wading bogs; but he was in good spirits just then, having reached that stage of weariness which somehow gives contentment. What a wretched place it was, and yet how skilfully repairs had been effected. Each bit of wood went a long way, and every nail had to do a lot of hard work. Gregory expected everything to last as well as himself. The door might have been turned out of a carpenter's shop, and yet it had been made out of the sides of a few packing-cases cunningly fitted together and the whole well tarred. Gregory could build a house and furnish it with what other people threw away.

George went on knocking, and was just about to turn away when the door opened and Ben jumped out. There was Gregory in his shirt-sleeves, looking dull and heavy. He had been sleeping over the fire, living the happier life of dreams. He did not seem glad to see George, nor did he invite him to enter.

"Couldn't let the day go by without coming to see you," said George.

"I never asked ye to come," said the giant. "Du'ye see yon tree?"

There was only one, a solitary stunted fir, which was always trying to grow and being kept down by the wind.

"Go and hang yourself on 'en," said Gregory, as he slammed the door.

George lost his temper too. He banged and kicked, and loudly threatened to break the window; and at last pushed the door open. Gregory snatched up his iron bar and shouted, "I'll break your back," but George only walked in and shut the door, saying roughly—

"We understand each other, Gregory, and I know how you're feeling. Don't I go through it myself?"

He went up to the giant, took his arm, and tried to lead him back to the fire, while Gregory growled and rumbled like a thunderstorm—

"What ha' ye come vor? Bain't a man to bide quiet in his own home? I wur asleep, spending Christmas I don't knaw where, when yew comes kicking my door. Why don't ye bide to home and leave me 'lone?"

"I didn't swear at you when you brought me the faggot of quick-beam," George answered. "I burnt it last night and sat it out."

"Aw now," muttered Gregory, "any one else I'd ha' broke, sure 'nuff. I wun't ha' volks coming in under here, and yew'm the first to surprise me like. How did the twitch burn? Did he splutter and crackle, or burn clear?"

"Burnt clear," said George.

"Then yew'll live vor ever. Mine spluttered and crackled. Allus does and allus wull, I reckon."

George was staggered at the poverty of the room. That was why Gregory had feigned to be angry; he didn't like others better off than himself to see what he had to put up with. The floor was of peat, dry and dusty; the walls were of bare stone, covered with beads of moisture; there was the big oak chest, the family heirloom which contained the parchment, and a home-made table, but that was practically all the furniture. There was no chair, a piece of plank resting upon two lumps of stone did duty for that. The remains of a Christmas dinner, bacon and potatoes, were upon the table; and the cloth was represented by a piece of paper. It was pathetic, this poverty; pitiful that a mighty creature should never have carved out a place in the world with his strength and skill. Surely there was something wrong if Gregory could remain at the bottom while little weak men reached the top.

"Du'ye pitch now yew'm here. This be my home. What think ye of 'en?"

"You could have done better than this," George answered.

"How could I? Tell me that."

"You could have worked in a different way."

"Vor a master. Not me. I'd ha' broken 'en if he'd answered me back. I be a man, not a dog to whine and follow."

"You must take the world as you find it, Gregory. I work for men that I loathe, because I must."

"I bain't made o' that trade. I bides up here along, and looks out over Dartmoor vor miles and miles, and I ses, 'When I finds a man to frighten me I'll work vor 'en.' He ain't come along yet."

"That's the spirit which breaks a man," said George.

"It wun't break me, not while I can lift my bar. When I be sick got I takes my bar and wrastles wi' the sickness and I beats 'en. That's how I be young yet. How's the home vor a woman?" he asked swiftly.

George was silent, but his face twitched and answered for him. It was not a home for any woman. Love would shiver itself to death on that wild hill-top, which grew nothing but heather above the ground and potatoes below; and shrivelled all else except that hardy growth of manhood who revelled in it; and the sort of woman that Gregory could win would not know much about the divine passion. She would appreciate the independence of a home, her title to a man, but she would grumble and swear when possession had lost its novelty and she saw the life that was to be hers till she dropped down dead. That was the sad part of it; Gregory could never find any woman to understand him; and he could not go outside his class, for he was at the bottom, and when a man is there the weight above him is enormous.

"The time will come. You're a young man," said George.

"Aw, younger than yew, I reckon. There be some proper old men here about. Harry Bidlake to Downacot, Willum Brokenbrow, Amos Chown; and after them comes the lot I be among."

"You're not forty," said George.

"Wull, sir, that be true. I bain't forty, but I be sixty-two."

"Rubbish," said George.

"'Tis true enuff. I be a strong man now, but one day I'll break and then I'll drop. I wun't bide in the old chimbley. 'Tis out o' doors or death vor me."

It was difficult to believe the man. His hair was abundant, showing no sign of age; his limbs were free and supple; his face held perpetual carnival, wearing upon it a brown mask of youth. He looked a younger man than George. His manner of life had given him something after all—a sort of immortality. Up there on the heights of Moor Gate he couldn't grow old. He would go on swinging up and down, shouting like the wind, road-making and hedge-building with his great iron bar, until he simply stopped, not because he was worn out, but because he had reached the end of the allotted span of human existence. His back would be broken by a law of Nature one day while he worked, and he would die young, if old in years. He appeared to have failed in life, to have received all the evil and none of the good; and yet he had solved the whole riddle of human existence, the riddle of perfect living and perfect dying; without weakness or disease the one, without mental failing or babblings the other; coming and going like the wind, which rises in one part of the moor and shouts across the heights, seeming almost to shake the mountains, and yet doing nothing except scattering sticks and stones and unroofing a barn or two, then going away suddenly, for no apparent reason beyond that it has done what it was meant to do and its time is up. So with Gregory; he would go down with his bar upon his shoulder as it were, with his eyes and ears open; not the wreck and ruin of a structure which was once a man.

It seemed ironical to talk about a merry Christmas and a bright new year; and yet the man seemed happy. He wanted only one thing, a woman who could understand him. It was not a small thing and it was unobtainable; but where is the man who obtains just that one thing which would seem to make life perfect?

"I ha' seen the new parting from the old," said Gregory. "I ha' seen all things break in two like yon old hearthstone. Yew see he be only half a hearthstone. T'other half be in America—least I reckon so. Hundreds o' years ago, when volks emigrated to the new land, they broke the old family hearthstone and left one half vor them what bided and took t'other half across the seas. They reckoned 'twas homely like to sot round the old stone on a winter's night and hear a gude Demshur telling. The hearthstone wur the best thing in the house them days. A man would ha' sold his bed rather than the old stone, and Government taxed 'em tu, aw, two shilluns a year vor every hearthstone, and that wur a lot o' money four hundred years agone, but men paid 'en, vor they wouldn't ha' lost the stone what their old granfers telled by vor twenty times the money. Wull, sir, I ha' seen the times break like the old hearthstone. Tis a bad thing surely vor Dartmoor volk to crave to get away to London and other foreign parts; 'twould ha' tored their hearts when I wur a lad, but now they'm glad to go. Buildings be crumbling got and ha' fallen down, and nobody builds 'em up again. I'll be the last in this old place, I reckon." George went to the corner where the iron bar was leaning and lifted it with a grunt, for it was amazingly heavy and he was not strong. It was a marvel that old Gregory could toss it about and carry it all day as if it had been nothing but a walking-stick.

"I have a present for you," he said, glancing up at the battered little cage which was always in front of the window. "If you won't take it I'll break your back."

"'Twould be a stone yew couldn't crack, not if yew wur to spit on your hands and go on tiptoe," said Gregory, without a smile.

"Well, here 'tis," said George, unbuttoning to get at his inner pocket. "Just a little yellow bird. He'll sing and flap his wings. I'll put him in the cage."

He slipped something wrapped in paper between the rusty wires and went for the door, while Gregory made a long stride across the floor, shouting, "Bide a bit, wull'ye?" But George was outside, with a cry of "Goodluck to you," and hurrying down the hill into the wet mists, because he didn't want to see Gregory's face where that bit of paper was opened. He need not have gone, for the man was not angry when he saw that the gift really was a canary, a golden sovereign such as he had never owned before. His pride was not hurt, because the coin was a token of good-will, like his own faggot of quick-beam; but he tossed it in the air and made it flap its' wings and sing to him a Christmas song. Then he put it back into the cage and laughed. He had come into the way of fortune; he could hardly reckon the possibilities of twenty shillings, never having tried before; but the money was enough, added to his own hands, to make the ruin "high-class." It was a princely gift, although it set him wondering whether the artist had not deceived him, for no man who gave away a yellow bird could possibly be poor. Gregory knew nothing about money, except that it helped to convert the lesser works of nature into gentle-folk, but he wanted to become high-class; that had always been his ambition—to end his days in a high-class way.

"Bubo will scream and peck like blue blazes when I tell him about that sovereign. He hasn't been the same bird since we burnt that manuscript," George muttered, as he made for home.

A shower of sleet welcomed him to Wheal Dream, and he put down his head and ran, banged the door open, tumbled inside; and the first thing he saw was Jimmy. The boy was sitting on the stairs, apparently waiting.

"What are you doing here?" asked George angrily.

"John, master," piped the boy. "He'm mazed wi' drink, and he'm after I wi' a gurt hammer."

He was in a state of terror, and the unnatural fat quivered on his bones.

"I don't care if he is. Get out," said George.

"Let me bide. Du'ye, master. 'Tis cruel cold on Dartmoor, and I can't go home. John be looking vor I, master."

"Go out and face him. Try and be human instead of a lump of jelly. Come on. Out you get."

George took the boy by his loose arm, dragged him up, muttering in disgust, "He's like a mass of frogspawn," and turned him out, deaf to the appeal for protection. The youth stared about in a dazed way, and his courage revived when he saw nothing but sleet and mist. He wobbled his way slowly towards Uncle's cottage, knowing that his time there was at an end, for John had threatened to take his life, and he was in the state to keep his word.

George summoned Bessie and asked what had been going on, but she only stammered, being a respectable woman, and the story was not one for her to repeat or for the master to hear. She had not known Jimmy was sitting on the stairs or she would have sent Bill to eject him. Bill was in front of the kitchen fire, warm and comfortable, waking up every few minutes to warble a song of thankfulness, then dozing off again. He had never been so happy in his life. At the present rate of progress he would soon be a commoner. Then Bessie came bustling in with an air of the utmost importance, calling—

"Bill! Come along, Bill! Master wants ye."

Bill tramped along the passage, stood on the threshold of the workroom, and touched his forehead twice, once for Bubo and once for the master, having a wonderful respect for Bubo, whom he regarded as a sort of Brunacombe totem.

"So John is drunk again," said George.

"Wull, sir, 'tis Christmas," Bill submitted.

"I understand it is his duty to get drunk," said George cynically. "But what's he after the boy for?"

"Caught 'en wi' my sister, sir, in the kitchen. Caught 'en red-handed, so to say. Ursula wur drunk, or her would never ha' been so careless."

George gave a grunt, and muttered to himself before saying, "There's been a row then?"

"John's been a-tearing about mazed like, hitting at anything wi' a hammer. He'm tored down one side o' his linhay, and flung the cart over, and broke a hen's head off. He wur throwing turves abroad and stones to the windows, and kicking wi' his butes like any old pony. He'm proper dafty, sir."

"What's he doing now?"

"In under, sir, taking more drink."

"Where's your sister?"

"Bessie dragged she over to Metheral when John went out to look vor Jimmy. Her wur screaming tu, and wanting to get to John. Her would ha' tored his eyes out. Her wull be back avore night."

"And no policeman for miles," said George.

"John wull ha' drunk himself quiet," said Bill hopefully. "Ursula wull throw 'en over, and he'll bide where she pushes 'en, and to-morrow he'll ha' forgot."

"Men don't forget that sort of thing."

"John wull," Bill declared. "He bain't larned, and the drink 'll mak' 'en forget."

"Look here, Bill," said George firmly. "I won't have any drinking here. You and Bessie must keep sober, even if it is Christmas."

"Us can't tak' tu much," said Bill, smiling respectfully. "Us ha' got nought but beer, sir, and us be going to drink 'en hot, wi' nutmeg and sugar and roasted apples in mun."

"So the wassail bowl isn't quite extinct, though the name is," said George. "Tell Bessie to take me up some hot water and plenty of it."

He dismissed the Pethericks from his mind, being full of the great festival programme. He was glowing with his walk, and the enthusiasm lent by the wind on the heights was still warm. He was going to dress for Winnie—not the married one, of course, for that would not have been right, but another Winnie; and if she, too, had dimples and a marvellous little abrupt nose, why, that wasn't his fault. After dinner they would play about the Wheal House like two children, and when tired they could sit by the fire and he would tell her stories of the mine below, and describe to her how the Perambulators came down to Chapel Ford; and then she would play to him and they would sing one or two of Herrick's glorious Christmas hymns. There was no piano, but that didn't matter, as it was going to be a dreamland Christmas. She would wear a white dress and satin shoes, and there would be a chrysanthemum in her hair; no jewellery, because they couldn't afford any just yet. It had all been arranged, and she had already gone up to dress. George lighted all the lamps and candles—it was going to be an old-fashioned Christmas—and decided that the room looked very comfortable, although it was really only the untidy workshop, and there was not more than one chair, and that was bulging and half its springs were broken; but so long as the dream lasted the room was beautifully furnished. It was a ghastly night on the moor; all the better, as the interior would seem more cosy.

"The time has come, Bubo," said George. "I will get a brush and comb, and trim you up. The senior partner mustn't look draggled."

The door opened, and the voice of Bessie announced, "That Jimmy be back again, sir. He wants to ask ye if the stones o' Chapel Ford be flooded over."

"Sure to be," said George. "I haven't been down, but with all this rain they must be covered. Ah," he murmured, "the brute is going to run for his miserable life."

"I've took the watter up to your bedroom, sir."

"All right, Mrs. Chown. If a gentleman comes while I'm up-stairs show him in here."

Bessie went off perplexed by this saying. A strange gentleman coming to Wheal Dream at such a time. The thing seemed impossible, still it wasn't her duty to say anything, and she was glad enough to hear the master was expecting company, though she didn't know how they were going to enjoy themselves, as there wasn't a drop of liquor in the house.

During the next hour occurred one of those startling atmospheric changes so common on Dartmoor, where one day is sometimes composed of a dozen different specimens of weather; the mist rolled away, a few stars began to peep, and the rain ceased; but the wind increased, and soon all the passages of the Wheal House were sighing, and there were moaning voices at every window. These were seasonable, if not cheerful noises. The peat glowed and the coals roared themselves into vapours, and it was feasting-time. The goose was ready to be dished up, and Bessie ran along the passage to inquire if the master was ready.

She opened the door with less ceremony, having already tested the virtues of hot ale, and then she jumped. The studio was brightly illuminated, and a gentleman was sitting there, but not her master. He bore indeed not the slightest resemblance to George Brunacombe; and Bubo was sitting at the end of his perch exceedingly sulky, and saying "Please remove this person" with both eyes.

"Ask your pardon, sir," Bessie stammered. "I never heard ye come in."

The stranger looked up, but said nothing. He was a young man, clean-shaven and faultlessly dressed; his features were perfect, his hands long and white; he wore indoor shoes, and there was not a speck of mud upon them. Bessie had a queer feeling in her back, as if it had suddenly been converted into a thermometer and the mercury was jumping up and down. She backed out, closed the door gently, then stood at the foot of the stairs and called—

"Be ye ready vor dinner, sir?"

"Yes," shouted a voice, which appeared to issue from the room above, because she expected it from there, but the wind was very confusing.

Bessie fled to the kitchen, calling for Bill and saying, "There be a stranger gentleman in the parlour." The studio was always the parlour. "He'm a young gentleman, and I ha' never seed 'en avore."

"Didn't master say he wur expecting company?" said Bill.

"Where du he come from then? Volks don't walk up over Dartmoor this time o' night. There bain't a bit o' dirt on his butes neither."

Bill made a face at that. Wheal Dream was a lake of mud, and if any stranger had come to the house he would certainly have brought several ounces of clay in with him.

"Must be master," he said.

"Don't ye be such an old vule, Bill. He'm no more master than your old vaither be. Wull, there," laughed Bessie scornfully, "think I don't knaw master? The gentleman bain't half master's age, and he'm dressed fine, and not a hair on's face. Proper handsome he be tu. Go in and look at 'en, Bill. Tak' an armful o' turves and mak' up the fire, wull'ye?"

Bill did so, and in the meantime Bessie had to rearrange the dining-table and prepare a place for the visitor. While this was going on Bill returned with a puzzled countenance, and asked severely—

"What ha' yew put into the ale, woman?"

"Sugar and nutmeg, wi' a small bit o' ginger."

"Nought intoxicating?" said Bill, by which he meant strong spirits, beer not being regarded as an intoxicant.

"A drop o' sauce. Nought else," said Bessie.

"If us bain't mazed it be witchery," Bill muttered. "He bain't master. I never seed a man less like master. Spoke to I in a squeaky voice, and said 'twas a rough night and he'd purty nigh got lost on Dartmoor coming up over. He ha' brought no coat nor yet hat, but he'm dry; and them butes o' his would ha' been tored to bits if he'd walked over."

"There bain't no witchery Christmas time. 'Tis the only time o' the year there bain't none," said Bessie firmly.

"Where be master to?"

"He'm up in his bedroom."

"Go and tell 'en, woman. Tell 'en gentleman's waiting," said the perturbed Bill, moving further away from the bowl of hot spiced ale.

Bessie stamped through the windy house, came to George's room, but found it dark and empty. Not knowing what to think she tramped down and took counsel with her husband. Bill became melancholy and told stories of enchantments, reminding his wife how folks had always said Wheal Dream was not altogether holy ground. Bessie argued that the goose was spoiling, and stated her intention of getting an explanation from the visitor, who appeared to have stepped suddenly, not into her master's shoes, for George always wore large and torn slippers, but into his home and property.

"Ask your pardon, sir," said Bessie when she got to the studio. "Du'ye knaw where master be to?"

The gentleman was sitting by the fire as if the whole place belonged to him. He turned and gravely handed to Bessie a quantity of something soft wrapped in paper, saying—

"This is a very interesting clematis, Mrs. Chown. If you plant it outside it will soon grow and cover the house. It is called in the vulgar tongue Old Man's Beard."

"Why, 'tis master," screamed Bessie. She recognised that voice well enough. "Aw, sir, what have 'em been and done to ye?"

At first she thought Bill had hit upon the truth and her master was under the spell of some enchantment; and there was reason for her amazement because George was transformed out of all knowledge. A razor and some good clothes, in which he was feeling extremely uncomfortable, had halved his age. It was a boy's face which was turned towards Bessie, and the big, boyish laugh for the first time suited it.

"I knew I should frighten you," he laughed. "When I saw poor old Bill come tumbling into the room with his eyes bulging I began to feel ashamed of myself. Even the owl of my bosom does not recognise me. It was hard work, Mrs. Chown. Upon my soul it is as difficult to make yourself tidy as it is to get a living."

"Wull, sir," gasped Bessie. "Us thought yew wur an old gentleman. Bill, come and see master," she shouted. "'Tis him sure 'nuff. He'm rose again," she added with a dim religious memory of other rejuvenating methods.

Bill appeared and expressed much satisfaction. He was happy to think that his suspicions concerning the hot ale were unworthy ones; and he celebrated the return of confidence by lowering the contents of the bowl by at least two inches; while Bessie seconded the vote of confidence by another inch and whispered—

"Aw, Bill, ain't master got butiful? 'Tis a face as tender as a maid's."

George tried not to be downcast when he saw two places at the table, but he wouldn't permit Bessie to take the things away. The omen was good and he accepted it. The shadow was there eating Christmas dinner with him, and perhaps some time or other the substance would follow. Still a shadow makes cold company with its sad and mocking suggestion, and George was soon miserable again. The game of pretence was all right so long as fancy and high spirits could keep it going, but the sensation of being born again did not last. George found himself longing for his dreadful old clothes and the bushy grey beard. The windy night would not be denied. It crept in at every window with groans and mutterings, and filled the home with its greeting, "A wretched Christmas, George Brunacombe, and a very dark and miserable New Year." It was impossible to be lively without prospects; he was going down hill, obeying the mechanical law of nearer the bottom the greater the speed, and next Christmas perhaps would find him there. His pictures, which had never been worth much, were now almost worthless, and he was alone. For the second year his eccentric old aunt had not written; possibly she had been devoured by her pets. Nobody had greeted him except Leigh and Winnie; and at that George jumped in his seat. He would write to Winnie, a long letter.

Not to be posted, of course; he did not know her address, and the postmark on her card was a mere smudge beginning with a P., which might have been anything from Plymouth to Paradise; but the letter could be written as if it were to be posted. He could tell her everything, confess that he didn't really dislike her although report said she had laughed at his foolish ways; and he would certainly mention the fact that he had devoted nearly two hours of hard work to tilling his own body as if it had been a piece of land, digging, mowing, and harrowing, and the result was a surprising harvest of youthfulness. He had reclaimed himself from the moor, as it were; he was a newtake cleared of rubbish, but he had no doubt that the moor would take back its own, and the heather and furze would soon spring up all over the clearing, making it as wild as before.

Staring little Bubo shook himself to double his usual size, then lifted up his voice and screamed. The rascal had done himself well that evening, and his presence was so portly he could hardly see his own foot.

"Hoot preliminary," said George. "Put your wig straight, my Lord Chancellor. It's tumbling over your eyes."

Bubo hooted again, this time impertinently, wobbled and nearly tumbled off his perch, flapped his wings violently, squawked and made such an exhibition of himself that George remarked, "I believe you imagine yourself a parrot," and had to turn him out. Bubo rushed up-stairs and was soon hard at work giving his usual realistic performance overhead, which sounded as if he had murdered somebody and was dragging the corpse to and fro. At intervals he appeared to be delivering judgment upon various criminals in a thoroughly portentous fashion.

George's performance was about as sensible. He was writing, that being far the happiest way of spending the evening he could think of. The scrawl soon ceased to be a letter, for it was impossible to keep that fiction up, and he began to set down his thoughts. He had pretended to be festive that evening, but sorrow was always in his brain; and now it ran down his arm and dripped off his pen. A man may speak lightly with tears in his eyes; but he can't write lightly; neither can a poet shed tears with his verses unless his own heart be sad. The written words that really wring the heart are doubly pitiful; for the heart of him that wrote was bitter.

Bubo was fiendishly noisy that night. He seemed to be watching and applauding some ghastly spectacle in the dark room up-stairs. At last George got up, feeling nervous. What with the wind and the tragedy in many acts which Bubo was persistently enacting, all Wheal Dream seemed haunted. He went out and looked into the kitchen window. Bill was in a chair very near the fire, and Bessie sat on his knees with her arms round his neck. They were not talking; simply basking in the contentment of warmth and full stomachs. George went outside; the wind rushed by off the side of the moor, and it was very dark. He could see the light in Uncle's bedroom window, a small glimmer of smokiness. If there had been any sound he would hardly have heard it. He wondered if Ursula had come home; John was probably insensible by then. What an awful life, had they only known it; a life leading down to some dreadful depths of spiritual consciousness in a future state, if they were not too gross to outlive death. Surely Bubo was better than the Pethericks; the very fact that he didn't know how to behave vilely seemed to give the owl a sort of predominance over such as John, Ursula, and Jimmy, the ugly growths of Wheal Dream.

George went back thinking of Uncle. Somehow there seemed to be an unpleasant connection between Bubo's screams and the patient old man who had not the strength to protect himself.

"This lonely place is far noisier than the heart of London is now," he wrote. "The wind howls, and underneath my window the water dashes down and past the wheal; and with that in his ears old Uncle will die. I can see the light in his window, one small lamp, its glass coated with soot, standing on the ledge and giving less light than a candle. I know the room; very small, with low roof sloping on both sides, no carpet, the walls stained with coppery green patches; in the centre the bed with the old man and his money-box. He can see nothing except that dirty lamp and the shadows which it makes. He will never see anything else until he becomes a shadow himself. He will never leave that room alive. How sadly the poor live and how terribly they die. But much of Uncle's poverty is of his own choosing; he could afford a better home and a housekeeper, only he is so afraid of letting his little yellow birds emigrate. It is a pity money does not decay when put away in a box; Uncle has just enough to be too little; just enough to be afraid of spending it all before he dies."

Bubo continued to imagine himself Othello murdering his wife, or Achilles dragging Hector round the walls of Troy. He and his master were night-birds, full of life in the dark and dull in the morning; and in the meantime Christmas was being celebrated in the two houses on the Stannary road; only the wind prevented the sound of their revelry from reaching the Wheal House.

Jimmy indeed spent the festival without the slightest noise, being afraid of arousing Uncle's terror and bringing John upon the scene. The boy felt pretty sure John meant to murder him, and the method would certainly be brutal; he perceived that he must get away at once, to enjoy a life of ease elsewhere, and he was ready to go now that Uncle was unable to work for him. He had no friend except Ursula; Bill reviled him and Bessie pushed him about, and he was too weak to hit the woman back. Besides, Wheal Dream was cold and dreary; Jimmy wanted a town where it would be possible to pose as one out of employment, and to enjoy warm streets, a cheap music-hall, and little girls. There was a bestial cunning beneath all that flabby flesh. He believed Uncle had quite £70 in the money-box; the wind was very noisy, the Pethericks were drunk; it was not only necessary to act at once, but no better opportunity could have been given; the night mail would carry him away, if he could only struggle across the moor to the station with his illegitimate baggage in his arms, and the train would be almost empty, as it was Christmas night. Chapel Ford was flooded, the military road was too far round, and the wind would be awful up there; he would have to go down by the lanes and chance being seen.

He took up a stick, but put it down. Uncle was very weak, and the pillow would do all that was necessary. He crept up to the bedroom. There was no light in the living-room; even the fire had died out. It seemed horribly cold, and his fat hands were shaking. He could hear Bubo play-acting; Uncle heard the noise too, and thought he was in the place of owls and wind and darkness.

"How be ye, Uncle?" said the boy. His voice was shrill no longer, but husky.

The old man had his dim eyes fixed upon the equally dim lamp which he imagined was the moon rising upon the tors enveloped in cloud. He didn't know it was Christmas. He thought it was summer and the green stains upon the wall opposite were banks of grass, and the wind was the river running below his feet. He was fairly strong; not going to die yet; but his mind was partly paralysed like his body, and he turned queer at nights.

"Aw, it be proper up here on Dartmoor," he said. "I be right on the top, wi' a gurt rock on each side o' me, and the heather be main soft to lie on. Up and down I goes wi' the wind. Now I be down, and here I goes up again. 'Tis fine up here, but I gets fearful o' being trod on by one o' these ponies, and there be a gurt bullock yonder snorting. Hear 'en! A-blowing through his nose and hitting hisself wi' his tail. Get home, wull ye, yew old bullock."

Jimmy came to the side of the bed and put his hand under, feeling up and down for the money-box. This was one of the rocks between which Uncle thought he was lying, and the other rock was the Bible. Uncle felt the hand, which was the one thing he had always been afraid of having in his bed, and he turned his head, saw the boy, shivered and struggled with his memory, and at last he whispered—

"Yew'm Jimmy."

"Come on, Uncle, let's ha' these old things out o' the bed, so's yew'll lie comfortable," the boy muttered.

"I be a cruel long way from Wheal Dream. I wur a silly old vule to come out on Dartmoor. Du'ye get home, Jimmy, and let me bide," Uncle whispered.

"Get off 'en."

"What be doing? Get down, Jimmy, and us will pray. Our Vaither which art in Heaven along—"

"Yew'm as heavy as a lot of old stone. Tak' your hand off 'en, wull ye?"

"He bain't here, Jimmy. I put 'en among the rocks. Get home, Jimmy."

"Here 'tis. Let go, Uncle. Do as I tull ye now."

"He bain't here, Jimmy, and if 'tis he'm empty. Jimmy boy, what be doing? Yew ha' cost I pounds and pounds, aw, and shilluns tu, and us ha' got nought to live on now. Gentleman," piped poor old Uncle feebly. "Go and ask the gentleman to come and I'll give ye sixpence."

Jimmy rolled him over at last and grabbed the box; but a skinny old hand clung to it like a bramble.

"Let go," he sobbed. "'Tis funeral money in him and nought else. Tak' the Bible, Jimmy. He'm a butiful Bible and vull o' pictures."

Uncle was not putting off his religion though he was fighting for his money. Bibles were inexpensive, and he could buy another; but the loss of the box would leave him dependent upon charity until rents were due again.

A Bible was about the last thing Jimmy wanted. The time had come for stronger measures, as there was no unclasping that tenacious hand. He caught the pillow, forced it over the ugly old head, dropped across it, and went on tugging at the box. There was a heaving movement below his chest, a harsh murmuring sound; and then the fingers relaxed and the box came away. Jimmy lurched across the room, blew out the lamp, and groped for the door.

As he went down he heard noises, and soon there came a thud upon the floor, followed by other sounds. Uncle had pulled himself out of bed and was dragging himself across the floor, as if he was trying to imitate Bubo's noises. The boy wrapped his prize to the baby's body, caught the burden up, and made off, splashing through mud and water, and did not stop until he was well away on the common.

Resting until his breath came back, he went on again. Fortunately for him it was all down hill, but still it demanded no mean feat of endurance to reach the station with the baby and box, and the mere fact that Jimmy accomplished it showed that he could have worked had he liked. Securing one's own ends gives labour a wonderful easiness. Several times Jimmy thought he was done, and once he came very near stuffing the baby into the hedge and leaving it; but his love for the degenerate little weakling prevailed. Had the infant been a male he would certainly have done for it, but its sex made it a thing for the boy to love. The time had almost come for him to part from it, but he was going to make sure that it would be well taken care of, and he could easily replace the loss by getting another. He had grown so fond of nursing babies that he would have been miserable without one.

Almost in the last stage of exhaustion he reached the station, making the baby look as much like an ordinary bundle as possible. There was hardly need for much precaution, as nobody was about, except a sleepy porter waiting for the mail. Jimmy bought a ticket to Plymouth, sniggering to himself with joy. Pursuit was impossible, as Uncle could not tell the story until Bessie went in to him the next morning. All the great criminal possibilities of a low and bestial life were open to Jimmy, and he rejoiced at the thought. The train was practically empty, and he had no difficulty in finding an unoccupied compartment, where he could rest and complete his arrangements. Near Devonport he kissed and fondled the sleeping child, denuded it of one small wrap, which he required to put round the money-box so that no policeman should stop him and ask questions; and then he drew the blinds down, and when the train stopped slipped out, leaving the child to be discovered by some official, sent to the workhouse, and adopted by the ratepayer. Jimmy had his wits about him though he was a mass of lustful flesh. He knew how easily a cunning rascal can live and breed his own low species, and never own or earn a penny, because the country overflows with charity enough to embarrass idlers and drunkards, but has nothing to give those who lead honest and sober lives except a lodging with the scum of the earth. Jimmy was clever enough for his generation. That night he could get a room, and the first train on Boxing Day would carry him up to London; and there he could lose himself, get some young girl to live with him—that he also knew was easy—and when weary of her he could get another, and so on until Uncle's money was exhausted. By that time his cunning would have supplied him with some other methods whereby he might idle in comfort; and if the worst came, charity would always see to it that an unfortunate young British workman need neither work nor maintain the degenerate spawn which he might bring into the world. Jimmy only hoped that every Christmas Day would be equally successful.

Bubo and Brunacombe remained in ignorance of the exodus of Jimmy and his brat, for Uncle could not descend the stairs and his feeble cries from the window of the smoking lamp were ridiculed by the wind. Such a poor thing is the human voice when Nature is shouting. Uncle was in for a night of agony. Neither did the partners at the sign of the one-legged owl know about the return of Ursula. She came from the village after Jimmy had gone, full of false fire and courage, and prepared to proclaim her doctrine of freedom, of free-rights and free-love, and no law human or divine at the back of them. She was very drunk, and when in that condition her face became a deep, dirty scarlet, and her wet eyes like half-filled inkpots. She crossed the common, laughing and flinging her arms about, and dribbling down her sealskin jacket. She got down to Wheal Dream and tumbled into her home with a merry noise.

Father was in his usual corner and John was sprawling over the table, his broken hat still jammed on the back of his head, which was lying among the unwashed crockery; his hands were filthy. He was sufficiently conscious to remember what had happened, and he retained enough control over his limbs to arise and stagger and strike a blow or two. He couldn't speak; that was a difficult accomplishment when sober, and, in his then condition, he could only manage incoherent noises like a hog with its nose in a trough. Father was trying to sing pious hymns and drink whisky, and not succeeding very well in either, as he had no memory for words nor ear for a tune, and when he took a sip from the glass, not enjoying it much but doing his duty on Christmas Day, the hot liquor made him cough, and he would squirt it out of his mouth and nose and then gasp for breath. Every sip was good physical exercise for the old man; quite as hard work as walking to the linhay and back. It was long past his usual bedtime, but he was sitting up that night as a matter of custom.

"Johnnie," he croaked to the half-conscious shape lying across the table, "I be main cruel sorry Ursula ha' turned actress."

The smoke from the peat poured out into the kitchen, which was a sign that the door had been opened. Father was enveloped in the cloud and could see nothing distinctly; but he was aware that his daughter had returned, and he heard a noise of deep breathing and nailed boots sliding upon the stones. Then Ursula came upon him with such violence that his head was knocked against the wall and his glass of good-cheer was demolished.

"Du'ye behave proper, woman," he shouted as well as he could for coughing; and then John was upon him too, feeling for Ursula that he might throw her somewhere else. He wanted to get her head against something hard, the hearthstone for choice, only he could not obtain a firm hold; and the red fire and the black walls seemed to be buzzing round him, and the floor was in wild motion like the country seen from the windows of a train, sliding past, heaving up and down. Smoke was everywhere; Ursula screamed and cursed, declaring herself a free woman with a free body; John groaned and laboured for vengeance; while Father, who was very cross indeed, begged them to behave and sit round the fire homely like.

"Don't ye be so rude, Johnnie," he kept on shouting.

John was far ruder before he had done. He caught Ursula at last and thumped her on the head until she stopped screaming. His great fist fell always on the same place, with a horrid noise, until it seemed a wonder the skull was not dented like his own hat. She fell from him at length, upon the heap of turnips just behind Father, and sprawled there unconscious; while John staggered to the table and fell across it, crashing among the dishes, in much the same condition as his wife, the breath roaring from his wide-open mouth. Poor John had been born a low and simple creature; brutality had been almost thrust upon him. A good woman would have raised him, educated him, made a home for him; and Wheal Dream would then have become a happy and smiling place. He had endured Ursula too long. He was like one of those black stalks of heather, hardly worthy to be called heather, which appear at the edge of a peat-bog, deeply rooted in mud, but barren and rotting slowly year by year.

Father went on sitting by the fire, but he was in a rage. John's conduct had been outrageous, and Ursula was his daughter. He did not care what she had done; the man had no right to thump her on the head. Father muttered and spat about him furiously. Then he got up, stood leaning on his sticks for a few moments, and presently shuffled to the other side of the fire-place. A coal-hammer was lying there, and the old man picked it up after many attempts, made his way to John's side and judged him vindictively through his spectacles. John was on a chair, his arms thrown about the table, and his head lying upon it. Father pushed the plates and dishes aside; he didn't want to break any of them as he considered they belonged to him. Then he moved John's head, because it was not in a good position, as a butcher might shift a piece of meat upon his block, and struck it with the hammer. John quivered and gave a howl, but he was too far gone to move, and Father tapped again with his weak arms, finding the sensation a pleasing one and reminiscent of the bramble. Presently John's breathing became more irregular, and the old man felt satisfied that justice had been done. He shuffled back to the dying fire and sat down, feeling rather dull with so much silent company about him, and wanting to get a little warmth into his old bones before climbing up to bed. Father remembered this might be his last Christmas upon earth, and the thought made him feel doleful.

The wind was more noisy than ever over Wheal Dream, and Bubo was the only one of its inhabitants who made himself heard. Nobody could hear lonely George, reading aloud the long letter which he had written only to be destroyed; or lonely Uncle, praying and sobbing for some one to come to him; or lonely Father, rounding off his Christmas with the simple hymn—

"Us be but little children weak."

CHAPTER XX
ABOUT SMOKE

One back street of a city differs hardly at all from another. One house may be more select than its neighbours, possess a cleaner doorstep, a greater wealth of dingy curtains, a healthier group of pot-plants blocking up its window, or even an attempt at a garden in the cat and sparrow territory behind the rails; but the same polluted atmosphere is over them all.

Plymouth is merely London printed on the west in smaller type. All cities are uniform and the name of each street is monotony, however the builder may try to flatter them with his prosaic falsehoods. Down into these streets are always flocking a mysterious and restless crowd of lodgers, who come and go like rooks to a ploughed field, seeking for what they can find, and without a single encumbrance except each other and one small clothes-box. Some of these people are almost bewildered when they are asked their name. It is so unnecessary to own such a thing in a city where only the question of sex seems to be of much importance. A man swinging over the moor with his head up and the wind whistling in his ears is a force of nature and something rather fine; but bring him into a city and he vanishes, or is only visible in the ridiculous aspect of one more fly sprawling in the honey-pot, which looked and smelt seductive at a distance but contains more poison than honey, after the manner of fly-traps. It's a carnivorous monster, the city. It keeps on calling for strong men to do the work, because its own children are so thin and smoke-dried; and the countrymen hurry in eager to pick up the gold and look at the peep-shows; and the town lets them endure for three generations; and then calls for more, like the farmer's wife appealing to her ducks, "Dilly, dilly," and a sharp knife behind her back.

Tomkins Street was one out of many, known to the policeman and postman and those who had the misfortune to dwell therein. Tomkins was a builder who had done wonders in his time, and had called dirty streets and rows of sordid houses out of a chaos of daisy-sprinkled fields. There were Jemima and Kezia streets also, named after his wife and daughter; the mark of Tomkins was over the entire district; but to his latest works Biblical names were given. Tomkins was becoming stricken in years, and it occurred to him that it was time to make his peace with Heaven, which seemed a simpler matter than extorting rent from impecunious tenants. Bethlehem Street and Galilee Terrace fully attested to the conversion of Tomkins, and were regarded by him as such works of supererogation that he felt justified in taking a little back for himself by constructing them of unusually cheap and flimsy materials.

Tomkins Street was largely given over to lodgings, or apartments as they were styled; and most of them were crowded, although there was one room in each house which was only aired about once a quarter, and hardly ever entered, because that room was the temple dedicated to respectability, and was indeed so stuffed with useless furniture that there was no space left for more than a single human presence. In one of the rooms near the top of one of these houses Winnie was lying on a hard and bumpy sofa, declaring she couldn't, and her mother was standing over her saying she must. The trouble was over a glass of milk.

"I can't this morning, Mummy. It will make me sick."

"Come along. Shut your eyes and gulp it down."

"No, dear. Leave it beside me and I'll try presently. It's no good anyhow—horrid town stuff. Mummy—Oh!"

"Don't cough so, my darling."

"Won't the window open a little more? But nothing comes in except smoke. Oh, for one breath of the wind across the heather."

"You must try and go out, Winnie."

"I'm going when the days get warmer."

"Now drink the milk."

"I'll sip at it when I'm alone. Give me my picture. It helps me to breathe."

Mrs. Shazell brought the picture of the waterfall in St. Michael's Wood, and Winnie placed it on her lap. She seemed to see the bracken swaying and the drops of spray quivering on the long grasses and to smell the white violets upon the hidden bank. That was a sacred place, her dreamland, where she had watched that wonderful head, where those wonderful hands had painted her; and she would never see place or painter again, never follow that rocky pathway beside the river beneath the great green precipice, never cross the Ford or feel her feet sinking into that delicious soft peat; and never climb the tors to eat one small mouthful of wind.

"Darling, don't yawn so," pleaded her mother in an agonised voice. That horrible yawning was worse than the cough.

"I do try, but I can't stop it. Mummy," said Winnie cheerfully, "is there any pink on my face?"

"Oh yes, dear;" and so there was, on both cheeks, but it was not the wind-blown pink.

They occupied three rooms at the top of the house. Little light, but plenty of warm smoke, entered the street, and it was January, the darkest and smokiest month. The houses on the other side were higher and intercepted what light and air there was. The place was fairly quiet by day, but when the lodgers came home there was noise enough. Just below lived a couple who were intemperate in their habits and passions; and they often spent the night cursing one another. It was not the noise which was withering Winnie but the atmosphere, that dense mass of smoke-cloud which pressed always upon the street, cutting it off for ever from purity and sunlight.

"You must get her away," said the doctor to Mrs. Shazell. "Take her to the coast. She won't live long here;" but when Halfacre was appealed to, he said statistics showed plainly that by far the greater part of the population of the country dwelt in large towns, and therefore it must be the most natural way of living. It had also been shown, he added, that carbonic acid gas was beneficial rather than harmful to the human system, and if his wife could not stand it she was plainly unfitted to survive.

As a matter of fact he couldn't stand it himself, but he attributed his own bad symptoms to overwork. There was so much to be done; such a vast amount of writing, printing, talk and organisation in connection with the cause of liberty; such a quantity of wind had to be blown into the bladder before it burst; and the winter was an exceptionally busy time, as the grown-up Jimmies of the towns could no longer sprawl in some one's field or upon somebody's haystack—setting it alight when they had done with it—and they naturally desired some one else's fireside to sprawl by. Halfacre was hard at work trying to secure them these necessaries, killing himself over it because he felt he had received the divine commission to reclaim the fallen; he was sent to be a leader of men, a blatant, illogical redeemer, a dangerous and crazy Messiah. He was in the employment of various revolutionary societies, and the police kept an eye upon him because foreign anarchists who styled themselves political refugees had been seen in his company. Just then he was engaged upon a pamphlet headed, "Bomb-throwing. A Justification." The rich and idle must be frightened somehow. He wrote well, and unfortunately believed in what he said; and this inflammatory literature was to be circulated among the working classes. Nature herself pointed the way; she makes a landscape with an earthquake; a man could clear away a lot of injustice with a bomb in each pocket.

"Wife," he cried, breaking in upon Winnie, "come along and do something. I want you to make a hundred copies of this letter. You can do fifty to-day."

"I can't, Richard. I am too ill," she said.

"Nonsense. What is illness but a form of laziness? The doctor tells me I am ill, but I laugh at him. We must work for the cause, drop down dead for it. You do nothing. Come on."

"If I get up I shall be sick."

"This is moral weakness. Do as I tell you, wife," he said, approaching the sofa, taking her wrist and beginning to drag her up. Winnie knew she must obey. She had been in his power from that day he had practically claimed her under the setting sun upon the marshes, to the day he had hurried her, unwilling and protesting to the end, to the registry office and had made her the wife of a son of the people. What chance had the poor, weak growth against the destroying storm-wind? The calm, healing wind was not there, and never could be, in the valley of that smoke. It was up along St. Michael's Wood blowing the spray across the waterfall and between the oak-trees, where George Brunacombe, who represented it, was painting his little pictures and longing for her, but only finding her when he went down into the valley of dreams.

So she had to sit at a little table and copy a pestilential document between coughs and shivers, while her husband darted here and there attacking one subject after another. He regarded Winnie as an instrument, like a pen, to be used and broken, then replaced by another; he hardly remembered she was pretty and had all those excellent failings which make a woman sweet and lovable; but he knew that as a female she was not much use; and as he watched her struggling with the hateful task he expressed his feelings.

"I was a fool to marry you, wife." He never called her by her name. "Why didn't you refuse me?"

Winnie made no reply. Her head was resting upon one hand while she tried to write with the other. She had long ago discovered how illogical and unreasonable he was, that no answer satisfied him. He pulled her arm away, told her not to be silly and affected, and to reply when he spoke to her. He was not unkind, at least he thought not, but women must be obedient and resign themselves to the law as made by their husbands.

"I did refuse you, as many times as I could, but you would not listen. Don't worry me, Richard."

"You foolish woman. This is all wrong, and half the words are left out." He snatched up the sheet which she was half fainting over, tore it up and replaced it by another, muttering, "What a bargain! what a miserably bad bargain!" while Winnie dropped the pen, making a grievous blot upon the fresh sheet, and began to cry with pathetic little yawns in between.

"There you are again, wasting time, paper and money." He forgot she was wasting herself, but he did not wish to be unjust. "Wife, I can't afford you. I must get some one else," he went on wildly. "I bought you for fifty pounds," he cried, dragging out a memorandum book and shaking his head furiously at the figures. "It is too much. You are not worth it."

"You did not. If you say such a thing again I will leave you," sobbed Winnie.

"I agreed to pay Hawker the money he had spent on you, and we fixed the price at fifty pounds. I promised to pay five shillings a week; and the blackguard follows me about the streets with his dirty gang, shouting at me, reviling me; and he sends you scurrilous postcards. Then there is your mother, who apart from her cooking is absolutely useless. Not a word of sympathy has she ever expressed for the cause, and she costs me five shillings a week as well. I shall tell Hawker he can have you both for thirty shillings."

"We are married," moaned Winnie.

"That is the foolish part of it. We ought to have lived together first, and then we should have found out we were not suited to each other and could have separated without any trouble. This law of matrimony is the first we must change. You are no good to me, wife. You are always weak and ill. You give me no help in my work as you promised—"

"Richard, don't tell lies," cried she, trying to stand up for her poor, defenceless little self.

"You did," he said angrily. "All you wanted was a home for yourself and your mother, and you couldn't stand that Hawker."

"This is a home!" sobbed Winnie.

"What more could any woman want? Three rooms, comfortably furnished," said the besotted man. "There will be wealth some day when we have educated the people. The elevation of the working class, and then what people call anarchy, every man his own law-maker. Working men form the immense majority of the population," he shouted. "We have only to weld all those units into one mass and set it rolling towards our ideal and we must win. Nothing could stand against that force. It would rule, not only this country, but more than a quarter of the whole world. And we are winning," he went on wildly, forgetting he was only haranguing his utterly useless wife. "We are reducing the hours of labour by law, so that working men shall have more leisure for studying the questions of the day and preparing themselves for government. We are opening an intellectual mine which is inexhaustible, for the labourer has never been weakened by luxury. Half the great men who have played leading parts in the history of the world started life as slaves. We have only to raise our democracy of labour into an aristocracy of intellect, to convert the scattered atoms into a solid whole which shall be deaf to the dishonest tongues of political agents, and then we shall hear no more the pitiful story of walking twenty miles a day in search of the right to work."

It was extraordinary that a man clever in some things should be so great a fool in others. Halfacre's precious doctrine was not worth the breath that uttered it. With all his reading did he not know that there was a time when the artisan ruled the country in all that was noblest and best? when his was the career of special honour, and his distinctive dress brushed the robes of royalty? It was the mere labourer who built the cathedrals, carved their woodwork, stained their windows, illuminated their missals. It was the artisan who was at the head of everything except the one crude art of wielding the battle-axe; and even he designed and manufactured the axe, and then contrived the mail which could withstand it. The mighty have fallen indeed; and Halfacre supposed this giant could be revived and given a mad political kind of strength; not asking himself what affinity there could be between the plain man of intellect who devoted all that was in him to his art, who carved the stonework in some unseen cathedral gallery with the same care and finish that he bestowed upon the visible work above the altar, and the beer-swilling lout whose ambition it is to do no work at all; between quiet men who devoted their whole energies to the creation of one masterpiece, and those who devote theirs to getting shorter hours and yelling themselves mad at football matches.

A burial of manhood was more likely to happen than a crucifixion of law and a resurrection of communism. Halfacre and his associates were not sane, but obsessed with fixed ideas morally insane. They were really solitary beings in a crowd, not atoms helping to bind the mysterious whole together, but disintegrating forces at war with each other and themselves, making ropes of sand, scattering what they sought to bind. Characters subject to one fixed idea are usually destroyed by it because it over-masters the reason. They passed out of the region of common-sense and daylight, and entered one of complete fantasy and night, mistaking the feeble glimmer of hardly visible moonlight for the noon-day sun. They mistook the movement about them for advance, when it was simply movement like the aimless restlessness of the sea. They hoped the country would go mad in their favour, and they knew that the spirit of the age is a tyrant when it chooses to assert itself; but they did not know that a revolution is generally a sign, and the last desperate venture, of weakness. Revolution and decadence are invariably hand in hand. The best possible form of government is a tyranny, they said, and they were right—only the tyrant must be a God.

Halfacre himself was merely a man unlike others. He had always been so, from the time when the little, dark, wild-eyed child had made the other children of the village jeer at him by pointing to a "stinkweed" and giving it a Latin name, until that day when the police watched his movements because his name was upon their list of dangerous persons. Halfacre had nothing but his abnormal brain; nothing behind to help him, neither culture nor heredity. Charity had trained him; he had won a public-school scholarship, and there he had been alone because he was unlike his companions; again at Oxford he won scholarships, and still he was alone and for the same reason; and being then thrust into the world he became an enemy of society, a mind off its balance, a troubled spirit which could not find its resting-place. His mind was in the shadow world and his life groped frantically after; he became aggressive to the point of insanity, continually repeating his single idea of liberty for himself and others equally oppressed; believing that those above him had no ambition except to persecute and torment him; hopelessly deluded by a sense of his own powers and greatness; and sometimes sobbing pitifully because the common people did not show much enthusiasm for him as their redeemer. With all that he had the vices of the lowest class, a foul tongue sometimes, an animal kind of sensuousness, a trick of being cruel, not for the sake of being so, but because it seemed the only way in which he could assert his power. It is not good for a man to be too much unlike his fellows.

How different was Winnie! The breath of Nature was blowing over her. She flourished only in the wind across the heather and in the blessed sunlight fresh and warm from Life's own presence with no pollution of man's making in between. To her the cruel and artificial landscape of streets and chimneys meant death; she was for the open places, the rivers and rocks, the glad and perpetually sweet earth smells of the woods, the romance of unspoilt lands, and a plot of untilled soil to grow in. The natural and the false had been joined together in Tomkins Street, and something higher than Tomkins would part them asunder.

"I'm going up to London soon," said Halfacre. "We want money, and are going to organise processions to parade the principal streets with the usual catchpenny cry of no employment. It is not dignified, but it never fails. The sentimental are on our side. If you only had some energy you might come with us," he said impatiently. "You could make yourself of some use, for you can look pathetic when you try, and you might collect a good deal. Go on with those letters, do. It makes my blood boil to see you sitting all the day idle."

Halfacre's blood boiled for curious reasons; the sight of an old man living in comfort after fifty years hard work sent it up to fever heat; it was normal when he was organising a procession of men who were unemployed partly because they would not consent to be anything else and partly because they were not worth employing. Laziness was no sin in such men, but in his wife it was a grievous fault. She was lying there with her pretty head on her arm; such a thin arm.

"Mummy," she called like a sick child when he came and shook her.

"We must separate, wife. I must get a woman, one with some life in her. That for the marriage law," he said, blowing his cheeks out. "I am tired of fooling with a doll."

Winnie hardly heard him. She was too ill, and he always spoke quickly.

"Wasting my life," he went on; "no help to me at all, no pity for the oppressed; and I am paying five shillings a week for you. I could have hired some one for that. What a fool I was to think you were any good."

"Open the window. I can't breathe," gasped Winnie. "I won't die," she murmured to herself in the same old way. Life still contained happiness. It must be so, because it had not yet come to her. Let the storm-wind blow as it liked, she would hang on.

"There she goes again—more of that horrible nonsense," Halfacre shouted, going to the fire and poking the smoky coals to make the room more stuffy. "Open windows in January. That's how the doctors tried to kill me when I had a cold on my chest. Come here, wife," for Winnie was faltering towards the door. "Was there ever a leader of men who could manage his own household?" he muttered.

"Let me go. I must. I am so bad," she pleaded, when Halfacre caught her with a rough, awkward hand, to drag her back to work; but he would not listen— that folly must be conquered or she would never be of any use—and dragged the weak, thin girl towards the table until the door opened and Mrs. Shazell entered. She was a small, fragile lady, still wonderfully pretty, but very sad-looking, and she often added to Winnie's troubles by upbraiding her for having done so badly for herself; first Hawker, then Halfacre, the first and second men that came along; why couldn't the girl be more resolute? She was kind enough then, seeing that her daughter was worse than usual and stifled with gulps of smoke, first from the street, then from the grate. The only way to manage Halfacre was to shout at him. This the lady did, and he gave way and let them go, muttering something about the excessive price he was paying for an altogether worthless wife.

A certain amount of peace followed; the leader of men went off to London, and in his absence things happened. The first was a thunderbolt in the form of a letter, addressed to "Mrs. halfacre" in an extremely illiterate hand, and so badly written as to be hardly decipherable. The writer was one Emily Halfacre, who claimed to be Richard's sister, although she was not proud of the relationship, seeing that the purport of her letter was to inform Winnie that the man was a kind of devil, and if she was really married to the creature Emily was sorry for her. His family had done what they could for him in his childhood, but since grand people had taken him up he was much too proud to visit them; and though he was probably making plenty of money, he hadn't sent a single penny to his old father, who was so crippled that he could hardly get through a day's work, and would soon have to go on the parish. They had always supposed Richard was a madman, but their clergyman declared he was a genius and they ought to be proud of him. Emily, however, knew no conceit in the matter, and she was rude enough to write that if she could get near her brother she would fling a bucket of dirty water from the duck-pond over him.

Winnie kept this letter to show her husband, but her mother never saw it. It would only have made a storm, and the poor lady would have sobbed herself ill and been incapable for days. Probably it was some malicious trick on the part of a village girl Halfacre had fooled with. He couldn't be that—the son of a labourer, for he was an Oxford man and a scholar; and yet Winnie remembered how fearfully he had always disgusted her, from the very first night, when he had gone to bed with half his clothes on; he had been actually angry when she begged him to take a bath at least once a month, and not to wear the same underclothing more than a fortnight. She did not answer that letter; she could not send her dainty handwriting into a miserable cottage home, and possibly create a regular correspondence of hateful knowledge. Poverty and illness had made her common enough, but she was still the doctor of Princetown's daughter, and not, good heavens! not the sister-in-law of that dirtyfingered and illiterate "Emly halfacre." There seemed a horrible stench in the room as she stuffed that disgraceful letter away.

After that a delicious kind of dream walk was allowed Winnie. She got out as much as she could, and walked on the Hoe, where she could breathe a little. She felt a different girl when outside, and it was such a relief to get away from noisome Tomkins Street and the dwellings which people occupied only to avoid, keeping on the streets as much as possible, spending the evenings at common entertainments or in the beerhouses, because any place was preferable to home. One evening—it was always evening that time of year—she was fluttering along wearily between parallel lines of glaring shops, when she became conscious that her tired eyes had received gratification; and immediately she was thinking of St. Michael's Wood and the Ford, and the waving bracken, and all the magnificent sights and smells of real dream-land. The vision had been caused by a picture shop. How warm the colours looked from that cold street; and in the centre, upon an easel, in the place of honour, was the Ford, and she herself was about to cross, but lingering and afraid, because she did not know what awaited her on the other side. Of course it was she, though the features were altered somewhat, but not the nose. And the picture was signed in the corner with a tiny one-legged owl; and there was a title painted on the frame—"Lost."

People were drifting about as usual, and some stopped a few moments before the window, not because they were artistic, but the interior looked warm and inviting. A commercial traveller came along with his bag of samples, bending and coughing into his large hand, and he stopped to get his breath. It was Gumm going his rounds again, trying to keep the home intact, breaking up rapidly. He did not notice Winnie, as others were between them, and she did not even glance in his direction, for she was miles away. She was draggled, feeling too ill to be tidy, and possibly if they had faced each other Gumm would not have recognised the dainty girl whom he had known in the sanatorium. He had forgetful eyes; he did not even recognise the Ford, across which he had passed many a time.

"Poor young thing! Don't she look sad?" said a weary-looking woman, with a bottle of gin and a baby in her arms.

"Ah," said the man at her side, who was carrying nothing except a large pipe in his mouth. "She's in trouble, like most of us."

"What's she lost, then?" asked the woman.

"Lost her way, I reckon," the husband answered.

"Lost her bloke, more likely," said Gumm, in husky tones. His throat was affected now, and his voice was going; and for him the day of vulgar jokes was drawing to a close. "She's parted from him there, maybe, and knows she won't ever see him again. Lost," muttered Gumm, and with that word he lurched away, tugging at his pack, and disappeared, still coughing, in the crowd.

Those people passed on and others came, lingered, and went on too, but Winnie was still there. Why had he painted her, and with such pathos on her face? She had never looked like that to him. Why not Berenice, who had a much finer face? It seemed to her as if that figure had been painted by a lover, so tender was every touch. Then it became blurred, and all the pictures in the window were one big blot of colour, because her eyes were tender too.

Winnie passed on, almost happy, though she was married to a wretch; and singing as she went her usual song, "I will not die." She would not be miserable. She was the child of luck, who must win in the end, who simply cannot be beaten because she is destined to win happiness in spite of everything; the dreamland child who must pass through all the horrors of falling and yet never reach the bottom, who must struggle through every sort of terror short of death itself, not to her doom, but to the great reward, through the haunted forest of hobgoblins to the open moor and the dawn at last.

"Watchman, what of the night? That's what we all say, and here, my friends, is the answer. All's well, for God is ahead of us with a lantern." These hoarse words came into Winnie's ears from a street-corner, where a pale, earnest man was preaching to those who would stay to listen.

"If we ask to be shown the way He will say, 'Before I can help you, you must help yourself.' You must do it, my friends," shouted the preacher. "Nothing comes to those who do nothing. You must help yourself and leave the rest to God. And then He will show you the bright side of the lantern and you will see the way. To those who do nothing He shows the dark side, because they deserve nothing."

The man's words were lost in the noise of traffic, but they seemed still to be ringing into Winnie's ears as she crept homewards. She had never done anything for herself; she was so weak and yielding; she had actually been afraid of trying to help herself because it seemed a presumptuous thing; but perhaps even that ranting preacher, who dealt only in platitudes, could teach her something. Perhaps she had a friend above the smoke, on Dartmoor, who might be willing to help her—if she could only help herself and ask him. He might show her a way of leaving her husband, of getting some employment on the moor by which she could earn her living, and where she could breathe and live.

That picture helped Winnie to endure during the darker days that followed. Half acre never wrote when he was away; she could only guess where he was and what doing; probably seducing decent men from their work for brawling purposes, spoiling their morals, filling his own pockets, and declaring they were all on the road to liberty. Winnie had another trial to bear, for Hawker had not forgotten her. He had loved her in his own way, which was real enough to himself, had denied himself for her, and then she had jilted him. Poor Winnie had written him several touching letters, saying how very sorry she was, and it wasn't her fault, and begging him not to molest her; but Hawker had no knowledge of chivalry. He began to drink brandy, which was not good for him, and gave him bloody ideas. He took to walking about with a revolver in his pocket, with the idea of murdering Winnie if he could catch her in the street. Some of his friends told the police, and Hawker was deprived of his weapon, but consoled himself by increasing the brandy. He would come round to Tomkins Street on a Sunday afternoon with a few uncomely companions, and they would stand beneath Winnie's window to shout abusive and disgusting remarks about that class of young women who promenade the public ways for hire and squeeze all the money they can out of a man. Hawker had been a decent young fellow, as virtues went in his society, but he was quickly falling to the level of John Petherick. He had been badly used, perhaps, and there was no mind to sustain him when the hour for endurance came; so he got drunk and shouted abuse at every one. He would soon lose his employment, drift about the streets, finally joining the criminal class and spending the rest of his life in and out of prison; and it was all on account of Winnie. She was to be the ruin of the wretched clerk, just because she had been too weak and yielding to repel his advances. Not that it would have been easy, for Hawker would have followed her about in spite of every rebuff, with his hat jammed on the back of his megacephalous skull, an amorous leer on his face, and a stinking cigar of the baser sort in his great, crooked mouth. It was only fair that Hawker should have his time of trouble, but it was pitiful that he should show himself unfitted to survive it. He had invited the misfortune; he ought to have walked out with some wooden-faced and respectable servant on his Sunday afternoons, and not have interfered with a damsel outside his class.

"A filthy little prostitute." Winnie had heard that shouted after her; and her husband declared she was a hindrance and a curse; all because the wrong sort of men insisted upon capturing her, and she was only Winnie of the smoke, and therefore not herself at all. From her own moor, from the glowing green depths of St. Michael's Wood, from the peat-scented, fern-draped sides of Wheal Dream, and from the picture in the materialistic street came a very different voice, calling her back and saying in a song of Dartmoor, "You are sweet and lovely, little Winnie of the hill-top. We are looking for you that we may kiss you with the kisses which have never known pollution. You are the purest and loveliest flower in the wild garden, but rough hands have torn you up and thrown you upon the rubbish heap. The gardener is looking for you that he may plant you again on the top of your windy hill."

"I must help myself," Winnie murmured, as she faltered along the unyielding street.

She visited the doctor every week; it was cheaper than letting him come to the lodging-house. The words of the wandering preacher clung to her and she repeated them often.

She had to wait her turn at the doctor's. There were several women, with plenty of troubles and not many shillings to relieve them, ahead of her; and when at last she reached the surgery it was to be handed a letter. It was from Berenice. Why did she write again, as Winnie had never answered the last letter?

The examination was soon over, the usual questions were asked, and the busy doctor could only say what he had already said a dozen times; she must get away into pure air, or—though he did not tell her so—there would be no more of her. The disease was not to be played with in this manner.

"But I can't go," she said plaintively.

The doctor shrugged his shoulders, his hand on the door to admit the next sorrowful story, and remarked, "I shall tell your husband you must. It will soon be as necessary for him as for you."

That seemed to be her only hope. If Halfacre broke down they would have to leave the town. Winnie dragged herself home, found her mother in a scolding mood, for the fire did nothing but smoke, and the unhappy lady had discovered there was hardly any money for house-keeping left, and Richard did not send anything or tell them where he was; and if he didn't come back soon they would be starving. Winnie went away by herself and opened the letter.

A minute later the sheet fluttered to the floor and the girl was in an agony of terror. There was nothing but a hurried scrawl to say that Berenice was going home from Penzance, which did not suit her, and she was determined to see Winnie and take her home. Neither date nor time was mentioned; and the letter had been delivered at the doctor's the day before.

"She will get the address and come straight on here," murmured Winnie. "I must get out somehow and make him promise not to tell her."

She reached the door, but knew she was too weak and ill to go out again. Even that one journey had been an ordeal; so she crept to her mother and put her head into the lady's lap, and declared she was really going to die at last, and she hoped it would soon be over and not hurt much; and her mother began with scolding but ended with fondling her. Then Winnie told her about Berenice's letter, and asked her to go to the doctor, as she wasn't able to go herself.

"It would be awful if she came here and found me. She thinks I am like herself. I had to tell her such lies, Mummy."

"Why couldn't you do better? Why didn't you marry that artist?" said Mrs. Shazell impatiently. She was a nice little lady when she was well treated, almost as fascinating in appearance as Winnie herself, but life was breaking and spoiling her.

"Hush, Mummy. Do please go for me."

Her mother consented at last, as she, too, had some pride, and did not desire to be confronted by any young lady in those apartments; and she went to put her things on, beginning to scold and grumble again, declaring they had never been so low in the world since Winnie had made her unfortunate marriage. Then she went out, while her daughter tried to sleep on the sofa and dream herself away from Tomkins Street.

She did sleep, for her walk had tired her out, but she saw no pleasant pictures; there was just a little space of darkness before smoky light came back, and then she heard her mother returning. She had been gone some time, but the doctor's house was a long way off; and she was talking to the landlady on the stairs.

The door opened, with what seemed to be a reluctant movement, there was a patter of small feet, an excited whimper, and the next moment Winnie was back in the sanatorium and Tobias was jumping about her, kissing and loving her, and begging to be taken down the cleave that he might chase the rabbits.

"That's her, miss," said the landlady hoarsely; and then the door was closed again.

"Winnie!" exclaimed a voice of horror. No more Billy, no more Dimples; but a cold Winnie.

There was Berenice, pale and thin, the whiteness on her face predominating over the brown, her eyes darker and larger; she could not be getting better, but no doubt she had been overdoing it, as usual. But how fresh and scented she was, how beautifully dressed, how fearfully out of place in that street of labourers' lodgings.

"Winnie! what—what have you come to?"

The poor little girl tried to rise; could not, as she felt so faint, and remained there breathing noisily. Berenice looked dazed; she unfastened her fur necklet, and then glanced at the door as if she wanted to get away.

"I think you must have made a mistake. You—you don't really know me," murmured Winnie wildly.

"Tobias does."

"It's no good telling any more stories then. I have only just had your letter. I sent my mother to stop you. I am so sorry, but I had to deceive you."

"Good heavens!" muttered Berenice. "What are you?"

"Don't talk like that. You were fond of me, Berenice. I will try and tell you if you will sit down."

"The chairs are dirty," said Berenice disdainfully. "Your boots haven't been cleaned for weeks, I should think; there is mud on your petticoat. Why, your hands are dirty too."

"I am so ill, and there is a lot of housework."

"I couldn't make you out when we were at the sanatorium. I understand you now."

"Oh, Berenice—you loved me, and this is not my fault. Won't you be sorry for me and kiss me?" Winnie faltered.

"I am very sorry for you, but you deceived me frightfully. I can't kiss Mrs. Halfacre," said Berenice, with a shudder, and added in an undertone, "Dirty Mrs. Halfacre." Her feelings were again in a state of confusion. All her furious love, every bit of affection even, for the pretty girl were swept away in one moment directly she entered that room, by the sight of the squalor and poverty, the poor little sick girl so dreadfully dressed, with the street mud on her clothes and black rims to her tiny finger-nails, and by the smell of soot and smoke and the stale, unwholesome odours of the house. That common little drudge of Tomkins Street was not her Billy of the sanatorium, not even the shadow of her. That draggled woman was nothing like the unspoilt maid she had longed to love. George would not have seen any difference, but he would have regarded Winnie with a man's eyes and with a man's love; the nose and the dimples would have been just as sweet to him, and that tender body would have lost none of its freshness. But Berenice felt as cold as any stone when she regarded the little heap of sick misery upon the old lodging-house lounge. Winnie looked at her bravely, although she had never felt so common before, but the worst was over now, she began to feel defiant, and considered the handsome, well-dressed young woman as some meddlesome lady who had come to bother a poor girl of the slums and poke a lying tract into her face in the hope that it might make her conscience raw and miserable.

"I think you had better not stay, Miss Calladine," she said firmly and proudly.

"Well, yes, perhaps it would be best. Really I am sorry," said Berenice, beginning to be awkward. "If I can do anything—if I can help you at all, please let me know. It must be pretty bad to live like this," she murmured.

"Thank you, we don't want anything," lied Winnie, in a wonderfully haughty fashion. Somehow she was fated never to tell Berenice the truth.

"Good-bye, then. I hope you will soon be better," said Berenice, feeling at a horrible disadvantage and longing to get out. By far the most delightful bubble she had ever played with was lying in a state of collapse upon that sofa, and there was nothing for her now except Tobias; neither man nor maid for her in the future, but a dog for a lover who could not change and would not disappoint.

But Tobias wouldn't go. He had jumped up on Winnie and taken possession of her again, and his eyes and tail told the old story; he had discovered his pretty girl again, a much prettier one than Berenice, and he intended staying with her. Tobias did not consider smoky Tomkins Street, the horrid lodging-house, the cheerless rooms; he was willing enough to exchange his cushioned bed and luxurious meals for a hard chair and some scraps of bread; but then he was only a dog, and had nothing to give except a dog's heart, which was a poor thing in comparison with human love. He snuggled down by Winnie and adored her, and explained that she could jump up presently and play about the room with him.

"Come along, little man," said Berenice, trying to speak carelessly; but Tobias did not even look at her.

"Good-bye, dear little doggie," said Winnie, kissing him and trying to lift him down; but she was not strong enough, and the effort made her cough.

"I hate her," said Berenice to herself; "hate her now as much as I ever loved her. Tobias, come here," she said aloud, more crossly than she had ever spoken to him; and when she saw that nothing but force would serve she had to go to Winnie's side and remove the dog, muttering, "he's such a little donkey."

Winnie said not a word; she did not even reply to Berenice's farewell, but put her head back on the hard cushion and took no further notice of the queer young woman who went out of the room with a final conventional remark, and with Tobias, protesting against being divorced, in her arms; and presently she was downstairs, feeling ashamed and miserable, asking the landlady for a piece of string to prevent Tobias from running back into low company. Then she made off in a strange condition of selfish misery. No more sanatorium friendships for her; she had seen Winnie at home, common and unclean. It could not have been love; it must have been animal passion after all; and Tobias—little brute—had tried to show her something better.

CHAPTER XXI
ABOUT ST. PIRAN'S SANDS

Even in the days when saints were as plentiful as pilchards, and miracles were sold for pence, St. Piran was a remarkable gentleman. He flourished in the fourth century, if at all, was an Irishman with a keen sense of humour, and had the honour of being one of St. Patrick's curates, until he was appointed to the living of St. Ives. Not having a boat to assist him towards his benefice, he simply sat on a millstone and paddled himself across the Channel on that, which to the historian seems an unnecessary kind of miracle, as any sort of raft would have floated just as well; and if St. Piran was so abnormally clever as to float on a stone he ought to have been capable of inventing a steamship. When the saint reached Cornwall he set to work to build a cell, open a well, slaughter Druids, and make Christians; the well and the oratory are still pointed out to strangers, as satisfactory evidence that St. Piran did paddle across the Channel on a millstone. His principal achievement is never alluded to; apparently he spent the greater part of his saintly and miraculous existence collecting his famous sands. They are deep and treacherous, and suggest the dry bones of all these myths. St. Piran is the patron saint of miners, and his feast day is March the fifth. It ought to be called All Sands' Day.

Winnie had a horror of the sea; and there it was stretching out everywhere from those endless sand-dunes, cold and heaving. She was away from the smoke at last, but had only exchanged one terror for another; for the air was not pure to her, it was tainted by the sea, by the clammy salt mists, and the horizon was filled with that sickening purple mass of water. It is a pitiless sea off St. Piran's Sands.

Halfacre returned from London in a state of collapse. He had worked hard according to his lights, and his missionary journey had been a success, although it was not one which St. Piran could have regarded altogether with approval. He was too weak to resist the doctor, who told him to go to the sea, but strong enough to resist Winnie when she begged for the moor. Seeing an advertisement of a cottage, which could be had for next to nothing as it was in the middle of St. Piran's Sands, he took it and himself and encumbrances down there. After all, he wanted quiet for what he was pleased to call his literary work. Organisation was over for the present, and there were a quantity of revolutionary pamphlets to be prepared; and he could stand on the sands and howl at the waves, and there would be none but the sea-birds to answer him.

The change was a disastrous one, except for Mrs. Shazell. The place suited her, but Winnie became worse and Halfacre steadily wilder. The sea and the wind put strength into him, but it was the wrong kind of strength, improving the body at the expense of the mind. It was March, and bitter winds lashed the Cornish coast, flinging waves and sand about in a perfect kind of anarchy; Winnie found sand in her teeth and a bitter salt taste in her mouth; all the food was gritty and tainted. There were four rooms in the cottage, and in one of them Halfacre worked day and night, like George Brunacombe; and sometimes he would rush out of the house, shouting that squires and parsons and other kinds of monsters were pursuing him, and he would dash about the sand-hills looking for stones to throw at them. They were trying to torment him because he was so unlike themselves. For years they had ignored him; as a school-boy they had compelled him to sulk alone; as an undergraduate they had sneered and passed to the other side; and now they were gathering around him and would murder him if they could. He had been free from such delusions in the town; but the wildness and loneliness of St. Piran's Sands made him mad.

There were days when Winnie felt almost well, but not many; she was usually on her bed, losing weight and strength; it was marvellous what a lot of weight the little creature could lose, and yet go on living and do housework; for she couldn't see her mother do everything. On those days when she was better she tried to help herself and oppose the husband, who in his contradictory manner would cheerfully have made a slave of her.

At last she went into his room and showed him the letter she had received from Emily Halfacre. It was about four o'clock on Friday, the twelfth day of the month. She never forgot the time and date. He was chewing strong peppermints, which scented the room;

he was always eating the things, supposing they did him good. She noticed that his black hair was filled with sand; he rarely brushed it, as there were so many more important things to be done.

"Who is this woman?" asked Winnie. She had developed a good deal of courage since the day Berenice had visited her.

"Some immoral creature, some blackmailer," he muttered angrily.

"She is not your sister?"

"Go away, woman. I will not be persecuted by you or by any one," he shouted.

"You must have relations. I have heard and seen nothing of them," said Winnie. "I don't want to," she added. "But if she is your sister—" Winnie went on, trying to tilt her pretty nose scornfully.

"If she is, what then?"

"Why, you must be a man of the very lowest class," she said, as cruelly as she could.

Winnie was helping herself, but doing it badly; and she soon realised it, for Halfacre snatched the letter, tore it to pieces, shouting incoherently all the time, and then threatened to tear her to pieces too if she dared to persecute him. Winnie went to the door, rather frightened, and he came screaming after her. The next moment they were outside, where it seemed to be raining sand; there was a heavy mist, and the sea was booming in the distance. To Halfacre that sound represented the shouting of oppressors, the men who had always hated him and were now determined to have his blood.

He caught Winnie's arm and dragged her along that he might find some place where he could hide himself, shouting, "They are after me again, they won't let me alone. They have got horses and carriages, and their women wear diamonds and fine clothes, while we are starving and drudging for the right to live. There's the squire who said, 'Let the boy alone. What's the use of stuffing his head with useless knowledge? Let him go and plough the fields.' He lives in the big house and keeps hounds, and swears at his servants, who are better than he is. There's the parson who said, 'Let him struggle on. For God's sake don't try and raise the boy above his class. Take those books from him and send him into the fields to scare the rooks.' I believe they are both on the other side of that sand-hill. Give me that rock, wife. Didn't I knock the paint off squire's carriage that day he lifted his whip at me?"

"Let me go," cried Winnie. "The wind chokes me."

"Hold your noise," he shouted roughly. "We are going across the desert, and if they catch us we'll fling ourselves into the sea to spite them."

He was going across the sand as hard as he could, Winnie's arm locked in his so that she had to follow.

"See that poor little chap slinking down the road? He hasn't got a penny to buy sweets at the village shop. The other children won't have him in their games because he's not like them. The boys throw stones at him, the girls call him 'Mr. Richard,' and pretend to curtsey when he goes by, and then shriek with laughter. They don't know how mad it makes him. He can't stand it, so he goes away into the woods and finds the flowers, and calls them by their botanical names, and they seem to understand him better than the children. He's always alone, that boy, but he won't touch his cap to parson, or say 'sir' to squire, because he knows they can't give the Latin names of the flowers in the hedgerow."

"Who are you talking about?" gasped Winnie. It had not yet dawned upon her that the illiterate letter was working madly in his brain.

"There was Emily," he went on shouting. "She was the village prostitute. There was Fred, who went for a soldier and died abroad. There was Harriet, who put on a cap and apron, and spends her life washing dishes. There was Harry, who became a labourer, and can hardly read or write. And the old man is going on the parish, crippled and done for. The devil take them all! How the rotten fish stinks down there! What a miserable home it was, and how it smelt of an evening when they were all there in working-clothes after a supper of bread and potatoes, while the poor little chap pored over his Greek Grammar in the corner! 'Chuck him out He's no good. He can't even stand at a horse's head, and he cheeks the gentry. Take the book away from him, Fred, and punch his head. Put him out to sleep in the pig-sty.'"

"It is himself," panted Winnie, sick and shivering, as she was hurried along through the wind and flying sand with the sea mist all around.

"Look at him at school," Halfacre raved on. "How the gentlemen's sons knock him about, the miserable little wretch, who wins the scholarships and gets above them all and has no money. How they jeer at him for his poor patched clothes and big country boots. 'There goes the cad. Come here, cad, and turn round to be kicked on your caddish posterior. Touch your cap, cad, and call me sir. You're a dirty swot, cad.' How they licked him round the form-room, squires' sons, parsons' sons, because he knew his Greek play so much better than they did. He was always alone when they were not torturing him, because he wasn't like them. He was always working. The masters hated him because he was not a gentleman's son. His own family hated him because he was better than they were."

"Let me go," Winnie was crying between the wind and her own distressed breathing; but again he took no notice, and did not seem to know that he was dragging her along with him. They were far away on the sands in sea-bird-land and no-man's-land.

"There he is at Oxford winning all the prizes, turning out the best Latin verses ever known there," Halfacre shouted. "'Who's that dark man in cheap, ready-made clothes? Why, that's the bounder of Balliol.' They pull his room to pieces, screw him in for hours, duck him in dirty water, spoil his poor clothes. He's only the bounder, he's got no feelings, and he don't subscribe to anything. They couldn't think what the world was coming to when bounders had brains, and what the 'Varsity was coming to when that sort of lout was admitted to win scholarships. All they can do is to give him hell, these gentlemen's sons. 'Good old bounder. Chuck him in the Cherwell.' That's the battle fought by the son of the village labourer and the brother of the village prostitute, a battle against gentlefolk and their gentle ways."

"Stop, Richard. I'll go on my knees and drag you down," screamed Winnie.

"Now he's in the world, fighting against those that fought against him, against squires and parsons. He'll raise an army one day, a million strong, and he'll beat them down. It's only a matter of time and lasting out, but they run after him and persecute him and pay their police to move him on. To the devil with all gentlefolk!" he yelled louder than ever, throwing out his arms and so releasing Winnie. He rushed on, picking up stones, hurling them about, and shrieking curses upon those who had made him mad, a poor diseased creature at war with every law, a victim of intense self-consciousness; and so he disappeared, howling into the noisy mist of sea and sea-birds.

Winnie remained on the sands until her life came back. It was time at last to help herself in earnest. She and her mother must get away from their mad master and find a place for themselves. She wasn't going to die—upon that point she was certain; neither was she going to live any longer with that horrible man. If the law could not separate them, necessity must. She would write to George, throw morality into the howling mist, and tell him everything; and if he wrote back and told her what he thought she could not lose, she could hardly fall any lower; and he might be her friend—she had no other—and might say he would help the small girl who had inspired

345

him to paint that sorrowful figure "Lost" beside the stepping-stones of St. Michael's Ford.

The mist lifted, or was blown up by the wind, as Winnie ploughed her way back over those wearying sands; and ahead of her a huge triangular gap appeared, made by the mouth of a combe. That space was filled with sky, but suddenly a purple mass heaved up like the back of a whale, and Winnie screamed, for it was the sea tossing there. She looked the other way and turned more inland, but wherever she went the horrible, heaving mass ascended and descended, as if desiring to reach her body and crush out what little life remained.

She wrote at once while courage was warm within her, but all the servile intentions died away and the letter became tender and touching. She could not send such a thing; it was impossible, and after one reading she tore it up. It was not possible to help herself in that way. She took another sheet and wrote the address at the top of it. Somehow it was the address she wanted George to have; but what else could she write?

This is what went down—

"Dear Mr. Brunacombe,

"Were you thinking of me, I wonder, when you painted that picture 'Lost'? How did you know?

"Yours sincerely,
"Winifred Shazell."

What a mad and monstrous thing it was to sign with her maiden name! but the girl felt she had reached the parting of the ways and could endure no more. She could not write her Christian name unsupported; she would not use the hateful name of Halfacre. She ceased to regard herself as a married woman, for she too was in revolt against the law, and when a timid, shrinking girl does break loose she goes far. She had reached a stage when she would have banged the door upon all the Courts of Justice and the ten commandments. She wanted her happiness—whatever it was—and some excuse for her continual and impertinent cry, "I won't die till I have it." Her wild husband had taught her something, after all.

The post-box was a long way off and she was exhausted. Should she wait until the morning and give the letter to the postman? But he might not come. Everything seemed to be shouting at her; the distant sea bellowed "Go," and the salt winds howled "Go," and the seabirds screamed "Go," and the sand flung against the window piped "Go;" and only her own sick body said "Stay." She went. That's the way people save their lives.

When Halfacre came back he was quiet enough, had indeed nothing to say, and took his food in a civilised fashion. Afterwards Winnie and her mother heard him pacing his room, and there was no other sound for some time. Then he tramped towards them, stood in the doorway, with his head down as if he had been entrusted with a message and was trying to think of it; the troubled creature looked almost fascinating as he brushed his hand across his forehead and seemed to be struggling with his memory. It was also the time of full moon.

Winnie had told her mother nothing; she never mentioned the evil, and there were no good things to report; and all that Mrs. Shazell asked for in those days was to be left untroubled.

"This can't go on any longer," said Halfacre quietly, as if he had just remembered what he had come for. "It was bad enough to be driven down here, but when it comes to treachery we must take action."

"Say something. I make him worse," whispered Winnie.

"For goodness' sake, child, manage your own wretched business," said her mother crossly.

"Stop that. I won't have conspiracy under my very nose," said Halfacre sternly, but without any violence. "You have been communicating with my enemies, putting them on my track, and this place will be a refuge no longer. Some of them are outside already. They have been throwing things at my window, as they did at Oxford; old boots and dead rats. I heard them strike the glass."

"It was only the sand," said Winnie, actually in a sulky voice.

"Hold your tongue, woman. Don't think I haven't watched you. I saw you coming back from the post. You have written to them saying where I am. Every gentleman's son in England will be here soon—to rag me, as they call it. You are on their side, because you regard yourself as a gentleman's daughter. Haven't I dragged you down?"

"Be quiet," interrupted Winnie, with a glance at her mother, who still supposed Halfacre was a gentleman in reduced circumstances, who would come into property some day; but Mrs. Shazell only looked up sleepily with the wind in her ears and asked what the man was grumbling about.

"You had better not speak to me like that. I won't be ragged by a wife." Half acre kept on brushing his forehead as if he had a headache. "This is a form of persecution which must end. That is all I have to say at present, except that I shall soon have some one to be a help and a protector. If another man throws a dead rat at me I will go out and buy a pistol," he cried wildly.

Mrs. Shazell woke up completely at last and began to scream. The man had locked the door, and it was an up-stairs room.

They heard him outside presently, cursing the moon which was hardly visible and his enemies who were not there at all. Across St. Piran's sands he went hurling shells and stones, and imagining in his foolish self-pride he was hitting the sky with them. The wind and the sea roared at him, and he thought the sounds came from his own poor body. The sand came against his face like stinging bees, into his ears like the fierce words of St. Piran's sermon, and he believed his enemies were upon him—squires and parsons—and he struck out blindly, and rushed about looking for them, raving and yelling at the "blasted gentlemen" who had blasted his life. It was a devil-haunted night upon St. Piran's drifting sands.

About four o'clock in that cold, grey hell of a morning Winnie fainted. There was no bed in the room and very little furniture, not even a couch; she was lying on the floor and her mother knelt beside her, weak and hysterical, rubbing her hands, unfastening her clothes—such shabby clothes, for Halfacre spared no money for follies—exposing her lovely flesh and nice little bones protruding so dreadfully; but Winnie neither moved nor spoke.

"Darling, don't die—not like this," cried the unhappy woman, who had been a petted lady once; and at last there came a movement and a sound, and that soft defiant voice—

"I won't die, not till I have lived."

Dawn became day and Halfacre did not forget them. He brought some tea and bread and butter, opened the door, pushed the things in, and laughed at them. He was not being unkind, he was only protecting himself, not daring to let them out or they would go and lead his enemies to the sand-hills. They were prisoners, he reminded them, and he was going to use them as such, and not feed them too well and make them strong enough to be dangerous. And Winnie required good fattening food to keep her alive; the storm was upon her now; if she could weather that she deserved to grow and flower again. Mrs. Shazell succeeded in losing all control over herself and screamed at Halfacre; an evil thing to do, for it confirmed his suspicions. She was threatening him, going to bring every gentleman in the land against him, if she could escape; henceforth he was justified in keeping them close. With a stern judicial manner he refused his wife a bed or a pillow or even water to wash with. Tradesmen visited the cottage rarely; they had to fetch most of their supplies from the church-town. That day went by and they had nothing but bread and tea to live on.

"Mummy," gasped Winnie as evening came on, an evening of writhing shapes of mist and wild March violence, "something is going to happen."

"Oh, darling!" almost screamed the hysterical woman. "Not that."

But it was that, to pile horror upon horror. Men do not know of it, but women whisper of it sometimes, and put their hands to their faces like Apollo at the death of Oedipus, because there was that about the death of the king which even a god could not look at. Only women know what men must guess at; women such as the sick and terrified servant girl in her wretched garret, frightfully afraid of being found out and knowing she must go through it alone; such as the woman alone in the bush, whose husband has gone for the doctor and lost himself, lying there in an agony of pain and terror knowing she must go through it alone. These things are too common to be blinked away. Life must go on, though we don't know why, and suffering only provokes a mocking kind of laughter from the cloud of Nature's witnesses. Winnie had her pretty teeth together. This would kill her, anyhow, doctors had said. It was not the time, not nearly; but she had suffered a good deal lately; and the cottage was locked up, Halfacre had gone off. Her mother had her hands before her eyes.

It was finished. Mrs. Shazell, weak, troubled, generally useless, became a woman; her husband had married her from a hospital and she was still skilful. Winnie had a long time ceased to show any sign of life; even her breathing seemed to have ceased. She looked pretty, deathly pretty—the flower at least had not withered—as she lay on the floor with lines of agony on the poor little face and the small lips bitten; the nose rather waxen, but as beautiful as ever; and even the dimples were not stamped out. The infant was alive, but that was of little consequence then. The cottage in the sand was silent except for the wind; it was getting dark and there was neither lamp nor candle in the room.

Halfacre was not back; he had been known to stay away the whole night. The door could not be forced by a weak woman. Mrs. Shazell could do only one thing, if it was not already too late to save her daughter's life. The window was fifteen feet above ground, but if it had been thirty she would have thrown herself out, for she was a woman then and her nerves had been driven out.

Fortune, or a special Providence, makes a way sometimes for the brave; or perhaps the ghost of St. Piran still took a sentimental interest in the place and it was he who brought the wind inland to fling a great drift of sand against the side of the cottage. It was there, anyhow, and Mrs. Shazell had nothing to do but let herself from the window feet first, and slide into the cold, kindly stuff more like a child at play than a middle-aged lady who had just become a grandmother. The full moon was coming out of the sea in a wild way, and the sandy track beyond was as white as concrete; two miles on was the church-town, and the lady girded up her loins and did it in twenty minutes, the wind being behind her and everything favourable. St. Piran ought to have slept comfortably in his celestial bed that night, for his vast wilderness of sand had been of some service at last.

Mrs. Shazell reached people with sane minds and sound hearts. There was no resident doctor, but there were fishermen, the best folk in the world, and there was a parson who was a man red with Cornish blood, who knew how to man a lifeboat and rescue bodies from the sea. There was also master constable exceedingly anxious to arrest any one who was not a parishioner, and a blacksmith with a silver wrestling cup on his sideboard and a fist which could smash woodwork. Cornish folk don't wait for the grass to grow when there is a sound of trouble; they know what it is to tumble out of bed when there are guns and rockets flashing off their coast. A party set out at once in a cart, making the horse gallop. There was no sign of Halfacre, but an old gossip declared she had seen him making off in the direction of Newquay. He was wandering about under the influence of the moon, not meaning to be unkind to those at home, but having forgotten all about them. The constable wagged his head and declared he would lay hands on him presently.

There was no need to climb in at the window, for the blacksmith had both doors open in two minutes. Winnie was lying there in the same dead state, and the child was alive. What could be done for both of them was done, but Mrs. Shazell was crying all the time—

"She must be taken away. Her husband is a madman and has tried to murder us. He went mad two days ago and thought we were trying to kill him."

The moon was shining brightly by then, the wind had ceased, and the indigo sea merely lisped in a childish fashion to the rocks. Perhaps the storm was over; but Winnie did not, and could not, know.

Another man joined the party, apparently a fisherman too, for he wore long boots and a jersey, a sou'-wester flapped down his neck, and a net was coiled upon his shoulder; but his hands, although as red as those of his companions, were not so rough. This man couldn't intone a service worth hearing, but he could manage a boat with the best of them; and he had come on foot to say—

"Put her in this net and carry her up over to the parsonage." Turning to Mrs. Shazell, he added in an awkward way, which had nothing of the polished gentleman about it, "We haven't got a fine house, but you must come to it."

They put Winnie in the net and carried her all the way without one jolt, the parson walking by the side, holding the hammock to prevent it from swaying. The doctor had already been sent for, but shook his head when he arrived and saw his patient, and remained with her all night; while the parson talked in a simple fashion about the tides, and said that if the girl weathered that of the morning she would reach the shore.

Halfacre got back at midnight, walking in all the shadows he could find, feeling very weak and ill. He had almost made up his mind to throw himself on the mercy of his wife and her mother, beg them to show him some sympathy and fight on his side against his enemies. It was the old trouble; they were unlike him, they could not understand him and laughed at his ambitions. Why couldn't they leave him alone and permit him to fulfil his mission? He had tried to be kind but they wouldn't have it; they were always mocking him or taunting him with illiterate letters from his family, and reminding him he was nothing but a labourer, who ought to have been at the plough touching his forehead abjectly to squires and parsons. If they refused to show him ordinary kindness he must protect himself, keep them locked in that room, starve them into a state of weakness so that they would be less liable to attack him. Even if they died he would only have been acting in self-defence. The moon which made him mad looked down coldly upon Halfacre as if she too hated him and was wondering why such queer minds were made.

When he got to the cottage he understood everything. The conspiracy had in part succeeded, his wife had written and told every one where he could be found, and the sons of gentlemen had been to rag him and end him, to throw him into the sea—they would hardly hesitate at murder in that lonely place—but fortunately he had gone out and escaped them, just as he had gone into the woods in his childhood to call the flowers by their Latin names and get away from the tormenting village children. They had broken the cottage open, and his wife and her mother had gone away with them. What further proof could he require of their treachery? They had gone back to their own class, that of the landowner and oppressor, and left him alone; always alone, at home, at school, at college, in the world. It was a horrible solitude; the enemy, although weak in numbers, was mighty in cunning; the oppressed, although mighty in numbers, had no strength, no unity, no intellect; and Jack would go on killing the giant because Jack was cunning and the giant was a fool.

Halfacre barricaded the door as well as he could, then huddled into the darkest corner and wept; a pitiful sight upon St. Piran's sands. How hard he had worked, and in the face of what difficulties, only he knew. What a frightful struggle it had been in his childhood, and only two maiden ladies, who were sisters and wealthy, had helped him on! Even the master of the public-school had disliked the clever ploughboy. Every one had hated him; his own class because he was trying to lift himself out of it; the better classes because he sought to join them without money. He thought he had done what he could with his brilliant gifts, but there must have been something wanting, something which kept him back, something in his body which prevented him from advancing. He had been the most distinguished scholar of his year, a man apparently to whom all things were possible; and it had only come to this—a brawling about the streets with a flag and an anarchic cry of down with everything. Possibly Halfacre deserved pity rather than blame as he sat and cried in the dark corner of the lonely cottage on the sand.

The tide came in, and the fishers went out because there were pilchards beyond the bar, and Winnie was alive, conscious again, and saying she wasn't going to die, although the doctor feared she was not speaking the truth. The girl-baby was alive too, having some of her mother's stubbornness, and a wet-nurse was found to take charge of her. The constable came to the parsonage and entreated Mrs. Shazell to charge Halfacre with all manner of offences, but the lady, who was herself prostrated by this time, desired above all things peace.

March days howled on and Winnie held her own. At last she asked if any one had written to her—as if such a thing was likely. They told her there was nothing, and she merely sighed and said it was a pity; and from that day onward she made no progress, and the doctor said it was a matter of time.

Winnie guessed as much and ceased to struggle. She had known all along there was little more chance of her getting better by the sea than in the smoke. There was nothing to live for, as she was not the luck-child after all, there was no happiness ahead, only more horrors; she would pass along somewhere else and her mother must seek the shelter of charity. That was what worried her. She told the rough and kind parson prettily that she would die as soon as she could and not be a burden, and all that had happened was not her fault; and then she thought she ought to see her husband once more. So Halfacre was sent for, but he gave no answer.

One evening a young woman came to the parsonage. She was black-haired, showily dressed in outrageous colours, hard in face and bold-eyed. She asked to see "the young person who had been with Mr. Halfacre." The parson and his wife were out, Mrs. Shazell was in bed, and the country maid, supposing it was all right, as the visitor said she was expected, let her in and took her up to Winnie's bedroom.

"'Ullo," said the young woman. "Taking it easy, ain't you? 'Ow's the kid?"

"Who are you?" asked Winnie feebly.

"Me? Why, I'm Mrs. Halfacre, if you wants to know. I'm Dick's wife. You sent for 'im to come and see you," she went on in her strident voice. "Like your cheek, I do think, after the way you treated him. I only come down yesterday, 'cause he couldn't 'ave me before, and as me and Dick are off to-morrow he said I'd better step round and see what you wanted. Good God, fancy Dick getting struck on a dolly kid like you."

"What can you mean?" gasped Winnie, when she was able to speak. Hadn't she got to the end of her sufferings yet?

"Mean?" cried the young woman, with a beastly laugh. "Oh, I see 'ow 'tis. You think you are married to Dick, and I s'pose you are in the eyes of the law, as they call it. But we don't believe in the church and the law in our society. We do as we blooming well want to. Me and Dick thinks alike. We're an up-to-date couple, we are. We were married last time he was up in London. Oh yus, we gave our word to each other without the 'elp of the registry office or any of that sort of tomfoolery. As long as we loves one another we sticks together, and if so be as I gets tired of 'im I'll go off with some other fellow, and if he gets enough of me he'll take another woman. See? That's what we call liberty. Good God, I believe the kid's a-dying. I'm off," she muttered.

CHAPTER XXII
ABOUT LAUREL LEAVES

There's always a promise of summer in March upon the moor. It came to awaken George out of a kind of working sickness, which had lasted since the beginning of the year; he had painted a number of pictures, good ones, and yet no good; his oriental agent wrote telling him to send them up and he would try and dispose of them at five shillings each, but George did not respond. He wanted to have those pictures by him, to gloat over them, give them his love; for they were the children of his imagination, he had put his heart into them, and no man likes to receive a couple of half-crowns in return for his best.

A day came glorious with furze below and sun above, a field and a sky of gold; and George cleaned his brushes and put them away for ever. He had finished his work. Then he took a sheet of paper and wrote, "In re Bubo and Brunacombe in bankruptcy;" a lot of bees, all stinging ones. He tried to think of the assets; liabilities there were none, as he had been honest; he might be worth one hundred pounds, and there was the Wheal House, which ought to bring another two hundred. Mr. Odyorne might give him more, as he would naturally desire to get the whole of Wheal Dream into his possession. With that money he would have to start again; he might take a share in a farm and live up to his name, or go into some small town and open a tobacconist's shop. George was not joking; he knew he was a failure, though he couldn't understand why, for he had worked much harder than most successful men. There was no justice in his failure, since he had tried so hard, but it was useless discussing that point, as no man can deal with destiny by string-pulling. The fact remained that he was going to be wiped out to satisfy some whim of Providence. That was how George put it in his bitterness. The moor had reclaimed him again, the grey beard was round his face and the baggy old clothes were round his body, and the peat and gravel were in his nails, and he was old and stooping and calling himself poor old George the wild man, the savage of Wheal Dream.

"It's a fine day to be damned," he muttered, not daring to think of that other day not far ahead when he would have taken his last walk through St. Michael's Wood and across the marshes to see the setting sun sliding in a bath of colour down the cleave of the river. Then he would be torn up, with some of the peat clinging to his roots; and when they dried he would die, for he couldn't strike and make growth in the stones of a town. George did not think of that day yet.

"You must die, Bubo. I can't turn you out on the moor or take you with me. One of the tragedies of failure is that you drag others down with you. The Chowns will have to go back to Downacombe and live in a ditch. We will erect a little gallows one cubit high," he said, grinning miserably. "I will give you a big breakfast, then pull a black cap over your big bright eyes, tie a stone to your foot, and launch you into eternity and the Paradise of Birds."

George went out, climbed upward, and seating himself on a flat stone watched the great landscape that he loved so well and was to lose. Tiny figures moved about, pigmy men going for granite, crawling here and there like mites; and presently Gregory came along, passing George about fifty feet away, throwing out his arm and iron bar as the gentle breeze stirred up ahead a thin white cloud.

"A gude year, sir," he shouted. "March dust never begged his bread."

George was past omens and took no heed of the fair promise of that dust. It was the glorious time of year, far happier than the death and decay of harvest days. It was the time of the resurrection of the gigantic powers of life, of bursting buds, sprouting tubers, when the pregnant earth and grass smelt good; the time of tilling and the time of marriage, of fertilising, of heaven upon earth for a few days; the bridal earth steaming with a pure kind of sensuousness towards her lord the sun; the time when a woman laughs, and a man shouts, and lambs jump madly, and horses tear about in the lust of life and joy of spring. George felt as if he could have taken Nature and rolled on the ground with her; worked for her, and tossed the produce into her lap; for that is how a man was made to live, with his skin against the earth, helping the mother to breed those things which grow in the earth; not to rot himself on the silk of luxury and the stones of art.

There was no one to reason with George. Even the heather with its eternal doctrine of holding-on made no appeal to him then, for he had a mind and that mind argued it was no use holding on. There was not a bird to whisper that the law made, as Gregory would have expressed it, at the beginning of the world is inexorable and cannot change; that the man who does his best never fails in the end; though he may have to wait until middle-age puts its frost upon him, he is bound to come through. That is a truth; the law is cruel but does not kill; it is the man who kills himself. No battle can be won without wounds, and it is only the coward who faints at the sight of blood; the true man drinks a little more courage and strikes again. There may be ninety-nine failures for every success, but the failures have only themselves to blame; they have not done their best—and man as the hardiest thing alive must sweat perhaps twenty years in pain and difficulties to do his best,—they are poltroons, they are deserters, and the law condemns them, having no mercy for shirkers. And it is a peculiarity of this Act of God that, just as it is darkest and most miserable before the dawn, so the condition of the struggler is most wretched upon the eve of his success. It is only when the work drops from his exhausted hand and he knows he can do no more, knows that he has failed and must lie in the hell of slaughter like sheep, it is then that the decree goes forth and he becomes one whom the gods delight to honour. What age-long toil the stupendous marvels of creation may have entailed upon the Creator only He knows; and perhaps He expects men to go through as much as they can endure before they too may be permitted to create.

Had George forgotten Winnie? There was the simple fellow, with the big, honest mind and clean brains, tramping across the wild common late every night, regardless of sleet and snow, going to the village and the post-office with an imaginary letter in his pocket. He wrote to Winnie every day in fancy, and in fancy posted the letter. Tricks like that keep men going sometimes, and prevent them from scrabbling on the walls and imagining they are Popes and Kings. George was happy when he took those foolish walks. They entered into his life like glad realities.

That night Wheal Dream asserted itself. Perhaps a mystery which had some unattainable truth at the bottom of it, like that hallucination of the mediaeval nuns swaying along the churchway of Downacombe, was at work connecting the spadiard of the mine with St. Piran of the sands. George went down in his sleep to St. Michael's

Ford, and there was Winnie sitting on that square, flat stone. She wore a hooded cloak of soft grey, but the hood had fallen back from her flaxen head.

"I'm so frightened," she said, but all the time she laughed because she couldn't be really unhappy there, and people can shiver and laugh at the same moment in dreamland.

"What frightens you, child?" said George. He was very old and bent, for the spring had gone for ever while he looked back, as Gregory told him it would, and Winnie was his daughter. He realised that, for people are quickwitted when they walk in dreamland.

"It's the bottom of the sea, Father," said she. "The coast has rotted away and the sea has come tumbling in. Hark at the waves roaring far above our heads."

"That is the pure wind which heals you, Winnie. It is rushing through the branches of St. Michael's oaks."

"No, Father. It's the sea sweeping the sand about. Here are shells and sand as deep as the bogs once were. The bracken has become seaweed, and there are big crabs crawling down my bank of white violets. The sea terrifies me so."

"Then why do you laugh, child?"

"Because you are with me, Father. I kept calling you, but you wouldn't come. I can hold your hand now, and we will swim through the wood."

"But I am walking and breathing. How is it we can breathe if we are at the bottom of the sea?"

"Why, you are a silly father," she laughed. "We are all mermen and mermaids now. That's why we can breathe. Look at my tail."

"I don't see any tail, Winnie. There are two delicious little feet. Where have you been all this time, child? I have searched for you everywhere."

"Have you?" she said, puzzled. "And I have been calling you. Father, we have made a mistake somehow. Did you think I wanted to lose you?" she said reproachfully. "Was I upon the top of Crockern Tor? But I had short skirts then, and my hair was blowing all over the place."

"Your skirts are short now, and your hair is loose and tumbling inside your hood. Crockern Tor is miles away, and I never looked for you there. I was afraid you might be ill and couldn't find your way home. Bubo has been ill because you would not come and give him his supper; and Father has been ill too," said George tenderly.

"Then we have all been ill; but we are going to laugh and be better now. It is all owing to the storm."

"What storm, little girl?"

"Have you forgotten the great storm which came sweeping over the moor? I clung on as long as I could, but it swept me away at last. I tried to get to the Wheal House, but it seemed to me that the door was locked. So the wind carried me away. It was so rough, Father. It hurt me horribly, and I am bruised still and stiff all over."

"I shall never let you run out by yourself again. Let me put your hood straight," said George, bending over and kissing her, on both her eyes, and her nose, and on the dimples; not in a parental manner; and every kiss turned into a large pearl, which rolled into her lap, so that it was easy to keep count of those kisses. These delightful things happen in dreamland.

"Father, I believe the storm is coming up again," she said, shivering.

"I have you by the hand, Winnie."

"But not very tight, not half tight enough. Father, you never do hold me so that the wind cannot sweep me away."

"I am not very strong, child, and I am nervous. I seem to be getting old and people laugh at me. Didn't you make faces at me behind my back once, Winnie?"

"No, never, never. I would blow kisses at you, but the wind carried them off like thistledown. It was such a terrible wind and made the sea roar so, and I suffered agony when I was lying on the sands. Hush, Father," she whispered. "Here come the Perambulators."

Down the steep pathway climbed the twelve great figures in their bright mail, and they crossed the Ford one by one, gazing ahead with stern faces. They had nearly finished their journey, they had endured the storms, and were completing the task which would never be forgotten; and then each knight became a clap of thunder, rolling into the side of Cawsand with a dolorous roar, and where each man struck was a blaze of fire.

"It's the storm, Father."

"No, child, the sky is clear over the moor. This is the calm wind. Look at the heather. It is almost motionless."

Then they were inside the wood, walking above the waterfall, Winnie clinging as if she had been a growth from his body. The hood had fallen right back and her head was lovely; drops of spray fell from the leaves above, becoming diamonds directly they touched her hair, and wherever she placed her feet roses and lilies began to grow. What a pity this was only a dream!

But they were not happy, for somehow the sun would not shine and the wood was getting dark. The storm was all round them and a sense of horror brooded. The oaks became giants in torture and their roots writhed with pain; fearful corpses sprawled among the ferns, the bodies of men who had failed; there was the Blackavon streaming down from the moor, but its waters had been turned into blood, and long-haired heads of women who had suffered in secret were bobbing about in it. The flowers exhaled an odour of iodiform; and upon the bank of white violets was the body of a creature, half man, half beast, bleeding from a hundred wounds but unable to die, because it represented the principle of eternal life. These unpleasant things happen in dreamland.

"Father, you are not holding on," cried Winnie in terror.

"We cannot fight against our destiny. My pictures are no good. Bubo is pecking holes in them, and the place is for sale. The next wind will carry us off. Winnie, don't go." She seemed to be turning into mist, thick, cobwebby stuff which enmeshed his body.

"I must, if you won't hold me, Father."

"I cannot," he cried despairingly.'

"It's the last storm. If it carries me away we are lost for ever. Oh, why don't you hear me when I call? Why don't you come to me? There is the Wheal House —no, it's the cottage on the sands. Take this and hold on. It's my heart."

"It is vapour, Winnie. It is going from me, melting away."

"Then this, take this—for the sake of heaven, my heart's sake, my life's sake, take it, for it's the last, the very last, thing I can do."

"There is nothing here, Winnie."

"Yes, don't you see it—a message? I can't breathe any more. I must rise to the surface, but it is miles above. Where are you? Father, I am lost."

George started up and looked round, seeing only the cold room and the greyness of the morning. The place was bare, for he had already begun to dismantle the house, preparing for the final departure. He looked out on the wheal, which was black and grim, and saw a magpie sitting on one of the protruding timbers. Then the postman came round the bend of the road with a brown bag swinging from his shoulder.

"Two letters vor ye, sir," shouted Bessie.

George was soon dressed; it was an operation which only required five minutes, then he shuffled down-stairs, looking like a tramp on the roads, and picked up the letters. He received so few that the sight of two envelopes was a real excitement.

There was a business letter, which he opened first. It was from his agent, and merely said, "Send me up some more of those pictures. I can sell a few of them cheap."

George shook his head and went off to tell Bubo; every such letter was presented to the senior partner, who always scratched his ear over them and looked profound, which was his way of recommending extreme caution.

"Bubo, I can't understand this descendant of Judas Iscariot. This is the second time in a month he has written asking for rubbish, and yet he grumbles when I send a few pictures, and declares he can't get them off his hands. We are not business folk, but we have a little common-sense. Verily I fear me there is guile in Israel."

George took the other letter and approached the window. The mists were rolling off rapidly and the sun was breaking through. It was going to be another fine day, bringing more March dust, which would never beg its bread, more splendour to the little mountains and wealth for the land; a good day for tillage. The very day when a man might go mad with joy if he was only a success, if he could run upon the moor shouting and singing, "I have won the fight, I have come through, I have conquered the world." That is the one day of life for the struggler, the one best day of all; when he wakes and puts a hand to his aching head and finds a wreath there; when he gets a decree written in letters of gold and signed by God Himself; when he knows he has not broken heart and health for nothing. That is the day when he rushes into a solitude for the mere joy of being alone to cut his antics; and he wouldn't tread on a worm or hurt a fly for a thousand pounds; and he must fling himself upon Mother Earth and bite a good mouthful from her body.

George tore that letter open quickly when he recognised his aunt's handwriting. The eccentric lady had been dead to him for two years, and he wondered what she would have to say then. The first lines were apologetic, but she explained that months ran by so quickly, and she hated writing to any one whom she never saw, as it seemed so useless, and the animals claimed so much of her attention; and as George would see by the date of the letter, she had got as far as "My dear nephew" a week ago, but then a monkey was taken with a kind of sickness, very grievous, and had to be nursed with much diligence, but she was able to thank God for sparing the dear pet to her, and it was so much better and livelier as to be able to bite a new servant. As for herself the neuralgia was much better but the rheumatism was worse, so there wasn't much to be placed on the credit side; and then a queer feeling seized hold of George, and he became cold all over, while his body tingled, his head was dazed, his heart began to thump, and he swayed from side to side and had to put out his hand for the wall.

"Bubo!" he gasped; "I've forgotten how to read. Come here, Bubo."

What was all this his aunt was writing about? Now that he was such a rich and famous man he might just as well pay back that money she had given him, for she was certain the dear animals wanted it more than he could, and she would have to compensate that wretched servant because the dear monkey had bitten her. As George knew, she didn't go about much, but a few people called on her, chiefly those who were interested in zoology; and one lady in particular who often dropped in to say rude things about some one else's wife and her own husband, and scandal of that sort; and she was always talking about George and saying what a rage he had become all of a sudden, and what a price his pictures were fetching; and this lady had been to see the exhibition of his principal works in Bond Street, and would very much like one herself, only the price was quite prohibitive, and she was certain her husband spent half his money upon that other man's beastly wife. She herself was delighted that George was such a success. His Uncle Will had always said George had a wonderfully fine head and he ought to do something with it—

"Breakfast be upon the table, sir," called Bessie; but her master was reeling about the room, March-mad and screaming—

"A gallows, Mrs. Chown. Not a little one for Bubo, but a great big one, fifty cubits high, for the seed of Benjamin."

"What be yew wanting, sir?" asked Bessie, appearing at the door.

"Give me your hand, Mrs. Chown. I must touch something honest or I shall go mad. Why have you always returned me the odd halfpenny? Your honesty has been perfectly vile, Mrs. Chown. What a glorious day! Did you ever see anything like it? March dust blowing up along the road, and we're like it, we're not going to beg our bread, we're seeking it out in desolate places and finding it, with butter upon it, Mrs. Chown, aw, and jam and cream as well. Where is Bill? Come here, Bill. Bring me a battleaxe, Bill, and tell it out in Jewry that George is nigh. Bill," roared the wild artist, reeling for the door, "it's a whole holiday, man! Down with work and beer. Here's half-a-crown for you, Bill," shouted George, turning out his ragged pockets and finding nothing. Then he struck the dazed miner upon the shoulder, knocked him against the wall, hit him in the ribs, laughing wildly, and plunged to the gate of his tiny garden, shouting, "Look after Bubo, Mrs. Chown. He's having a fit just now. His rich uncle has died and left him a fortune. Give him two fresh mice on toast and a cup of tea." Then he went off at full speed along the side of the moor.

The Chowns looked at each other gravely. It was no laughing matter to have their master in that terrible condition.

"Gone," said Bill, touching his head and rubbing his ribs. "I knew 'twould end that way."

"Aw, poor gentleman. He wur as kind and tender a body as ever lived," said Bessie, thinking she was pronouncing George's epitaph, and not in the least aware that his insanity meant the beginning of their prosperity.

George was soon back. It was no time for fooling. He must start off for London at once and find out everything, and take his chance of being arrested for homicide. What a simple creature he had been to believe that lying Jew! to live in the solitude of Wheal Dream, never glancing at anything but a local paper, never seeing a London publication of any kind, never dreaming that he might be making a big name and somebody else an equally big profit out of it! He was quiet enough when he got back, assured Bessie he was not dangerous, told her he was off in an hour's time to distant lands, then swallowed some breakfast, tossed a few rags and his battered toilet necessities into a disreputable bag, and made wild promises to Bubo, like a man standing for Parliament.

"The sentence of being hanged by the neck has been commuted into one of mouse-stuffing for life," he shouted. He couldn't talk that morning. "You shall have a gold chain for your neck, another to swing across your stomach. You shall be sheriff of Dartmoor and Lord Mayor of Wheal Dream, and you shall be taken to church in state and a circus-car. The senior partner of a big business has to put up with such things. Good Heavens! Bubo, did you ever see such weather? It is June, and the calendar is three months slow."

George reached London that evening, and went immediately to the shop of one who sold prints near the Strand. He had known him well in the old days; and when he got there and learnt that the printseller was dead he realised what a long way off those days were. A son had the business, and he glanced rather contemptuously at the shabby figure with the bushy beard and bulging bag, and was prepared to say he could do nothing for him, when George cried heartily—

"I remember you as a youngster when you used to run messages for your father. I'm George Brunacombe."

The printseller became sociable at once, said he was glad to see Mr. Brunacombe, and began to congratulate him, when George broke in sharply, "What's my position?"

"I imagine you know better than any one can tell you," said the other in some astonishment.

"I ask you as a man in touch with the world of art to tell me."

"Well, you're the fashion just now. Every one talks about the Brunacombe realism. We have some mezzotints of your principal works and they sell like hot cakes."

"Wait till I get at him," George muttered.

"'Mysteries in sunlight.' You remember that expression used by one of the critics? You have made a big hit, Mr. Brunacombe. I understand all the pictures in Bond Street are sold?"

"The whole damned lot, and so am I," George shouted.

The printseller stepped a little further back. Men of genius have such extraordinary habits, and the artist looked as if he wanted to murder somebody.

"How long have I been the rage?—is that the expression?" cried George fiercely.

"Certainly it is. Only this last year—as of course you know. But your pictures have been fairly popular for some time."

"Thanks," said George grimly. "Your father was a good sort, and so are you. I'll come and see you again some day;" and off he went, leaving behind him for the second time that day the impression that he was not mentally sound.

It was dark when he reached the East End, and the place of business which he entered like a mighty wind was lighted at the back with a single gas-jet. The proprietor was a thrifty soul. He was an old man, bent and wizened, and he was bending over a huge ledger, which was to him as sweet as honey, making noises like a kettle which wants to boil but can't quite manage it; and when he heard those heavy steps he started round; too late to defend himself, however, for in a moment he was seized and shaken until his false teeth dropped out, and his false hair was pulled off, while his false tongue howled thieves and murder; and then the whole of his false body was thrown upon the floor and trampled on.

"The next time you chew pigs' trotters remember George Brunacombe," shouted the artist, who had not lived upon Dartmoor for nothing.

The old man dragged himself away, glad to find he could do so in one piece, and his wife came running up with a carving-knife, supposing that robbers had broken into the place; but when she heard the ruffian's name she became sorrowful like her husband. He was abject in spite of his bruises; he knelt on the floor before George and declared he was his slave; and did it so well from force of habit that the artist was soon feeling almost ashamed of his violence. He was only a poor old foreigner in a strange land, and he had worked night and day for the distinguished visitor.

"Five shillings, half-a-crown, for a picture," George broke in, longing to reduce his nose to the level of his face.

"No no, my dear Mr. Brunacombe, my very dear gentleman. That was on account only. I have money for you, Mr. Brunacombe, very much money, hundreds of pounds, my dear sir. You shall have the money now, you shall have fifty per cent. I would not deceive you, by the holy religion I would not. Did I not say, Rebecca, I had hundreds of pounds for Mr. George Brunacombe?"

The lady agreed with oaths and gibberish; and added that her husband was a man of God.

"Paying and owing are very different things. I never sold you a single picture outright," said George, swinging his bag about as though he meant to strike with it. "You were my agent, and I have your letter of agreement. Now I am going to a solicitor—"

"No no, my dear Mr. Brunacombe. These lawyer gentlemen are so expensive, and they get the last farthing. There is the money waiting, my dear sir, hundreds of pounds, and you shall have a cheque this very night. That exhibition of yours is such a great and marvellous success. I have been honest with you, Mr. George Brunacombe. I could have kept your name out of it."

"You would never have dared," said George hotly.

"Isaac told me he had much money for you, Mr. Brunacombe," cried the lady, who also knew her part. "He and I have lived together for forty years, and I know he would not harm a dove."

"Damn the doves. He has tried to rob me," said George roughly. "Get up, you old pork-butcher, and give me an account of every blessed picture of mine you have handled."

"Oh, my dear gentleman, how you have bruised my poor bones," muttered the old wretch wickedly.

"Summons me if you like," growled George.

"No, no, my dear gentleman, I will forgive you. But you will not go to the lawyers, my very dear Mr. Brunacombe? Say you will not ruin me. I am old and greyheaded, and so is Rebecca my wife."

"Stop your whining and open your books," said George. "If you can satisfy me I'll leave the law out. I don't want it published all over the place what an ass I've been."

"It is fifty per cent, Mr. Brunacomhe. I must have fifty per cent," said the Jew eagerly. "I have made you a big man, my dear gentleman, and you have beaten me and bruised my bones."

Two hours later George left the place, tired but elated, with the cheque in his pocket. The world was at the feet of this big shabby man. No more poverty, no more grubbing in the dirt; he thought of the pictures in the Wheal House, the best he had done; he stamped his foot on the stones and laughed, and scattered coppers to the street children. But soon he was sorrowful. Happiness is not worth much unless there is some one to join in it; success is a poor thing if there is no one to share it with; and the only one had gone from him for ever. The decree had been signed too late.

George spent several days in London, doing business of a satisfactory nature; buying decent apparel for himself and presents for others; weird reptiles and monsters for his aunt, handsome gifts for the Chowns and his lonely friend the Rector of Downacombe, a large book of pictures for poor old Uncle, and something especially good for Gregory Breakback. Then he went home again, holding his head up at last, young-looking, clean-shaven. Success had made a fresh boy out of shabby old George. He went back to Wheal Dream, not as an unreclaimed patch of ground, but smoothly tilled like a garden with all the weeds and rough growth removed; and after Bubo had welcomed him with many wing-flappings and owlish hosannas, Bessie hurried in with a new apron for the occasion, and placed before the master a letter which had come the very morning after he went away.

The weather had changed, as it will in March when the month has paid its entry fee of a few pecks of dust, and winter had come again with a black and biting wind.

Bessie was outside crying with sheer happiness, for George had brought her presents and she was to receive good wages in the future; while Bill was laughing and wanting to treat every one because he was happy too; no more tramps to and from the copper-mine, no more sore feet and backaches, no more blisters from overwork; for Bill was to be manservant at the Wheal House, and his duties would be light. He was going up; he too had done his best and was getting his reward. When the king comes to his throne his servants are not forgotten; and when a man succeeds he brings success to others. Bubo was chuckling too, and turning up his beak at the idea of mice apart from sportive purposes; henceforth he would require raw beef cut from the tenderest joints.

Only George was silent; and he was walking to and fro.

It was not dark yet; time to get to Downacombe. It was glorious to find himself again in Dartmoor wind, which denies a man weariness. George set off at the top of his speed, and he was bending again, and there were lines on his face which the joy of life had lately banished. Sorrow had come back, and though he had won so much he felt then he had won nothing, for the heart's desire is everything, and the brain's desire mere flattery.

"Money will buy everything, from human souls to a red-herring," George muttered, as he raced down the lane. "If that brute wasn't a madman, why then madness doesn't exist. She may be a widow."

He winced at the word. It sounded ugly somehow, just as the thought of money is ugly to young people in love, but it spelt freedom, not the right to go about the world taking one woman after another, making harlots and breeding bastards, but the right to claim one only and cling to her.

"Leigh," George shouted, as he broke into the horrible silence of the rectory, "I've done it. I'm a man, not a bug on the back of the moor. I'm rolling the world about and sucking it like an orange. I've got England in one pocket and America in the other, and at the name of George Brunacombe every cheque-book opens. Give me a shake, dear man, and say you're glad."

The rector was sitting in the twilight, and when his face came up George shivered. It was small, the hair was almost snow-white, and the man's blood seemed to be blue and thickening. He was reading; it was a book upon roses; and there were no postcards round the room.

"What's wrong?" said George.

"It is good to see a friendly face," Leigh answered.

"You are ill," cried George. "I don't generally tell a man so, because it makes him feel worse, but I tell you. I want to frighten you, to root you out of this hole. It's the silence," George muttered, "not the solitude. A man can endure solitude up on Dartmoor where there is always roaring wind, but this silence rots. I'm a success, Leigh. I'm making a fortune. Come on, old man. Laugh with me and grow young again."

Leigh did not even smile. He listened to the artist's story, although it was not the part which he had come to tell, then muttered a few incoherent words. He was glad, but could not express himself; he had lost the gift, as he had lost every faculty except that of gardening. Decay had reached his heart.

George stayed late that night; he did not leave the house until past eleven, and during that time found out many things. Maggie Leigh, the rose, came first; she was a commercial success. Then came Maggie Leigh, the wife; she was not a commercial success.

"Go on," said George. "I'm going to get it out of you. I have brought the secret of my heart to trust with you, and I mean to have yours. Go on. Tell me, man. It's killing you keeping it to yourself in this silent place. What's the good of a friend if you can't make use of him? Come along," he said, standing behind Leigh, placing a hand on his shoulder.

"I'll tell you—wait a moment. It chokes me."

George turned the lamp down. The firelight flickered about the walls, but it was cold somehow, and the only sound in the house was that incessant creaking of the woodwork.

"She has left me in every sense," Leigh whispered.

"I was afraid of it," George muttered.

"A foreigner, a man who calls himself an Italian count, a drunken gambling scoundrel. It is this creature I have been pinching and scraping for. It was to pay his gambling debts that I burnt those cottages. It was to maintain him in his vices; and those letters of my wife were lies."

"He'll get no more, anyhow," George muttered. "Leigh, I want you to promise me that you'll resign the living and clear out of Downacombe, and that you will leave the wretched village alone and not burn any more of it."

"Just two cottages," said Leigh eagerly. "They stand apart and are very rotten. I am only waiting for hot weather."

"I won't have it," said George strongly. "I'm not a strict moralist, but these poor folk must be left alone. My dear man, don't you see how vile it is?"

"Why so? They belong to me, and they are simply tumbling down. The insurance companies are wealthy and have received a lot of money from me all these years. It is only right I should get something back."

George made a gesture of despair; on some matters Leigh was hopeless.

"You'll go away? Promise me that."

"I will, Brunacombe. I have sworn it to myself every day the last month. I must go. I am terrified. I seem to hear everything moving above and below the earth. Even the sound of a falling leaf hurts me."

"Have you seen—I mean have you imagined those creatures again?"

"They went across the week after you saw them, then twice a week, and now every evening just as it gets dark, swaying from side to side. The curious part of it is that no one else has seen them. I have to look out for them. They fascinate me. I have put on my eucharistic vestments and tried to exorcise them, but it had no effect. I always wear the vestments when I celebrate the most solemn service of the Church," he went on simply. "The bishop disapproves, but I feel it is my duty to wear them. Have you ever seen my vestments, Brunacombe? They are so beautiful, and it is a real pleasure to put them on. I should like you to photograph me in them," he said.

"It is all fancy—about these dead and buried nuns," said George almost angrily. "Your brain is out of order. You will soon be seeing them every hour of the day. Get away as soon as you can."

"Yes, I will resign at Easter. I will dig up the roses, and Jessie and I will find a healthier home."

"Who is Jessie?"

"She was the cook. Now she keeps house for me. She is very good, and sings hymns beautifully."

"Was she here in your wife's time?"

"Oh yes," said Leigh tenderly. "I was always very fond of Jessie."

George said no more. The skein was untangled at last, and he had to own that the mind of Leigh passed his understanding. A nicer and more kindly man he had never known; and yet possibly Maggie Leigh, the wife, was not altogether to be blamed for having gone to the bad; there was room for pity if her husband, who also deserved pity more than blame, had been the one to set her feet upon the restless road.

The rector improved wonderfully as they sat together and talked. He was perfectly sane, and somehow he was a good and ardent churchman, although his mind had never progressed beyond the stage of babyhood and he couldn't tell right from wrong; and yet he could talk well and show extreme cleverness. He could advise others with enviable clearness, although he was unable to control himself. So the artist came to the matter which had brought him there. He produced the scrap of note-paper upon which Winnie had written her question, showed it to Leigh, and in an anxious voice asked him what it meant; knowing that in such matters his judgment was nearly always sound.

Leigh read it through many times, then asked, "Has she ever written to you before?"

"She sent me a card at Christmas."

"Did you reply?"

"I couldn't. No address was given."

"What do you make of this yourself?"

"Nothing," said George miserably. "I can't be so conceited as to suppose she wants to see me."

"That is what I make of it. Her husband is dead."

"No, such creatures never die. They haven't been married a year," George said foolishly.

"He was a poor creature for all his bluster. There was no long life about him," Leigh muttered. "He insulted me here, as I have told you. She signs herself by her maiden name. Isn't that enough for you?"

"You think that her sole object in writing to me was to sign herself by that name?"

"I do—and to tell you she is in trouble."

"What's your advice?"

"Go down there, Brunacombe. She wants you. She always talked about you when she came to see me."

"I was a mad, blind, grovelling worm," cried George.

"If she is free let my last official act be the joining of your hands. I would rather bless you two than any one," said Leigh reverently. "You have made me promise to leave Downacombe. Now you shall promise me to go to Perranzabuloe."

"To-morrow," cried George with all his heart; and his face began to shine again.

CHAPTER XXIII
ABOUT UNCONVENTIONAL CONDUCT

On a cold March day any traveller by the North Cornwall line may feel conceited as well as numbed. He shivers because the wind tries to shatter the windows from Egloskerry onwards; he is proud because he cannot think what the railway would do without him; for two or three shillings he has apparently bought the train, a rheumatic locomotive which wobbles and totters seawards, and a lot of little weather-beaten stations with two or three dummy men thrown in at each one, looking like stiff Shems, Hams and Japhets standing on wooden plates all ready for the Ark. The train stops at every one of these stations, possibly to rest the machinery, for nobody gets in and nobody gets out, and the traveller gets frightened at last, and sits well back in a corner lest he should be discovered and mistaken for a runaway lunatic. There are no towns or villages to bring comfort and consolation to these solitary stations; just a cottage or two, which the traveller rather suspects are only put there for decorative purposes, something for him to look at as the train limps by. There is no undignified whirling on the North Cornwall line, no rude and bustling movement, but aristocratic and gouty hobbling. Nobody is in a hurry on that wild coast; there are no active pedestrians on the lonely roads to make the trains look foolish; every one moves slowly and appears to take a short rest between each step; but, then, every train and traveller have to face the wind from the Atlantic, which somehow never seems to blow from behind.

It was a very cold March day, and George for the first time owned the North Cornwall line, the good-will of the same, stations and dummy-men, and a train somewhat soiled by weather. He was in a first-class compartment, which was a useless piece of extravagance, as the notice of five seats each side painted up everywhere was simply humorous. George enjoyed railway travelling; he liked to stare out of the window and see the things go by; on the North Cornwall line in March there is not much to see except mist, black clouds and tearful windows, but upon that day a little snow was thrown in, possibly out of compliment to the distinguished artist; and the wind shrieked all the time. The men who work on that line must get giddy sometimes.

"They call me a realistic painter," George muttered. "Some day I'll send up a blank canvas and call it North Cornwall. That would mean no work, while it would be true to Nature."

The train dragged into Delabole, past the wonderful slate quarries, and seemed to expire at the already dead station with a big gasp. It was dreary enough there, a blank canvas expressed it, but only a few miles away was a furious life—the indigo sea raging upon Trebarwith Strand and bombarding Tintagel with great guns. No painter could represent that. And not a mile from all that noise was the peace that sick folk sigh for; lanes spiritual with primroses and voluptuous with premature births of spring; and tiny villages, like happy shelters seen in dreams, with soft, un-English saintly names. When the sun pushed himself through those mists, as he would in April, producing dust and butterflies, the North Cornwall line would wake up and the little stations would understand what they were put there for, and the harsh, foreign language of London would be heard in that land.

Two more stops, and the train entered the Dutch-like scenery of Wadebridge and fell into a comatose condition at its station. George tumbled out, redolent of all things new; clothes, boots and bag smelling of the shop, gloves making his hands awkward, a hat of the newest style upon his close-cropped head, his chin fragrant with shaving-soap and his pockets reeking of currency. Nobody would ever have recognised the ragged artist of Wheal Dream. The coach was waiting on the road, the four horses fretting, the guard playing with his horn, which was nearly as long as himself—there is a fine eighteenth-century touch about travel in out-of-the-way parts in the west—and the driver jumped excitedly when he saw George Brunacombe. He was in a hurry to be off, as he wanted to get across St. Breock's Downs before dark.

"Box-seat," said George.

"Right, sir," said the driver, who seemed a very excitable person. Not many travellers craved for the box that time of year, and he liked having company. "Going to Newquay, sir?"

"I am," said George.

"Ever been there avore, sir?"

"I have not," said George, observing to himself, "This is a very funny fellow."

"Fine place, sir. You'll open your eyes when you see Newquay. But it will be pitch dark and you won't see nothing," said the man, with a most portentous gravity.

George climbed up and they were off, rumbling up the principal street, the driver lifting his whip to every damsel, the guard sounding his trumpet like an apocalyptic angel.

"That's Egloshayle church yonder, sir," said the driver, maintaining his severe countenance while he spoke in a mirthful manner. "The parson of the parish built the bridge over the Camel, not the present parson, sir, but one avore 'en—lived hundreds and thousands o' years ago. 'Tis the finest bridge in the country and in the world, sir. The parson built 'en 'cause he didn't like the folks getting drownded as they crossed the ford, which they used to do in them days, sir, cross the ford and get drownded at the same time, sir, and parson didn't like it, so he built the bridge. There never was such a bridge as Wadebridge, not the town, sir, but the bridge across the Camel which was built, sir, by the parson—"

"All right," said George. "Let's have something else."

"Going to Newquay, sir?"

"Yes," said George patiently.

"Ever been there avore, sir?"

"Not to my knowledge."

"Fine place, sir. You'll open your eyes—"

"What's that over there?" interrupted the artist.

"Mist, sir, and the sky, and above that the heavenly country, as they ses."

"I mean lower down," said George impatiently.

"Padstow, sir. Don't ye never go there. A dirty, stinking hole full o' rotten fish, and 'tis the only harbour in North Cornwall, sir, though it ain't any use 'cause 'tis all sanded up, and 'tis so dangerous to get into the harbour that no skipper dares to try, sir, and when he gets there he can't come inside 'cause o' the sand, sir. They tries to fix the sand by planting grass over it."

"Not at the bottom of the harbour?"

"No, sir, round Sinkineddy church yonder. They dug the church out o' the sands, and has a divine service there every other Sunday, God willing. My wife's mother used to go to 'en, sir. She lives in Padstow, which is a dirty, stinking hole. They take the sand away for manure, sir, millions of tons of it every year."

"Aren't you getting a bit mixed?" said George.

"No, sir, they don't mix it wi' nothing. Just takes it away and spreads it on the land, and when the ships tries to get into the church they can't, sir, 'cause 'tis dangerous and all sanded up, and they gets carried on the rocks off Trevose—"

"Now you're talking about the harbour."

"No, sir, the harbour be over there. The church be yonder, and the sand, sir—"

"That's enough sand."

"Going to Newquay, sir?"

"Oh, shut up," said George.

"Ever been there avore, sir?"

"Where are we? What's this howling wilderness?"

"St. Breock's Downs. No man's land, they calls it. Mixed weather up here, sir."

"Look out," cried George. "Here's a girl."

It was getting dark, and as the coach rattled round a bend in the wild upland a small girl appeared at the crossroads, standing between her mother and her clothes-box. They were both crying, for the little girl was, plainly enough, leaving her home and going into service for the first time. No doubt they had been waiting there an hour, dreadfully afraid of missing the coach, standing in the cutting wind saying good-bye, and the mother begging her daughter to be good and the girl promising she would try. They were kissing each other furiously now that the coach was really in sight. It made a pathetic picture upon St. Breock's Downs.

The guard soon slung the plain wooden box to the top of the coach, bundled the girl inside, prevented the mother from tumbling under the wheels, and the horses were off again. George saw a dark, bleak road stretching away into No Man's Land, and the poor little woman standing on it with her handkerchief to her eyes. Somewhere down that road was a lonely cottage in the wind and solitude of that wild land, and it would be still more lonely now.

As the coach climbed up, snow came down in thick masses, driving along at a fine speed into their faces. The driver was silent; his eyes were shut and he fell all over George, righted himself, then fell the other way. The reins trailed loosely from his gloved hands, and it was obvious he had no control whatever over the horses. At last it dawned upon George that the man was drunk. That accounted for his manner; and all the time he remained as severe as a Judge of Assize. George pulled him about, and shouted at him; and the man opened his eyes and asked in a sleepy voice—

"Going to Newquay, sir?"

There was no sense left in the man now that the snow and wind had numbed him. They were nearly at the top of the bleak upland among the barrows and tors, and the weather was getting wilder as the driver got denser. George punched him severely, but obtained no satisfaction except the question, "Ever been there avore, sir?" and then as the downward road commenced, and the man who was supposed to be in authority threatened to roll off the box any moment, George put an arm round him and with the other tugged at the reins to keep the horses up. The driver was immensely amused by all this, though he retained his severe countenance and remarked that Newquay was a fine place and the gentleman would open his eyes considerably when he saw it. He had an unpleasant idea that George was not quite sober, only he couldn't say as much and insult the gentleman; but his countenance plainly expressed disgust at such conduct.

So they rolled off the downs, the wind was left behind, there was no more snow, and the sky cleared for the first time on the journey. The coach went down into the combe beyond with a speed which would have made a train of the North Cornwall line sick and yellow with envy. The driver quickly recovered in the milder atmosphere, was able to hold himself upright and inquire anxiously if there was any possibility of George going to Newquay; and then on the top of the hill in front stood out St. Columb Major, like a little town upon the Rhine. The guard began to tootle, the driver put upon himself the sternness of a major prophet, and wagged his whip like a pastoral staff, the coach rolled up to the door of the inn; and George hurried away to the fire to get the stiffness out of him, while his partner upon the box was called to the bar, and went with a godly countenance, which seemed to imply that he was going there to discharge the duty of distributing a handful of tracts and saying a few kind words to those who were therein.

When the coach started on the next stage George was inside with the little servant girl, three large men, and two women, who were in tears and black clothing. He was not going to be frozen and frightened again, though the guard had whispered reassuringly—

"He's all right, sir. Never had an accident in his life, but he can't keep the horses straight unless he has a drop. He'm one of those sort what the more 'em has the soberer 'em gets. He's got a natural genius for liquor and horses. They tak' to 'en as kind as babies to their mother."

It was not cheerful inside the coach; two of the men snored, the third had a violent cold, the women were sniffing furiously, and the little girl sobbed outright. She had tucked up her bright blue frock to keep it clean, as it was the only one she had got—that mother and she had sat up late for several nights to get it done—and she wanted to create a good impression in her new home and start life well. She wore a bright red petticoat underneath, all very fine, and that too had been made at home. The poor little thing was only sixteen, and looked almost innocent. The coach was heading straight for the sea, and the wind came against it with a doleful noise. George began to feel depressed too, as he wondered what was going to happen.

"Columb Minor," the guard shouted, omitting the saintly prefix, as he was a good Methodist.

It was merry enough there, though it was dark and tempestuous. The bells had gone mad in the tower, and people flocked along the street, making the horses plunge; and when George put his head out he saw a nimble old man trotting down the path, while some young folks ran after him and all the people cheered. It was a lively sight after the misery inside the coach.

"Is it revel time?" he asked.

"'Tis the old clerk's birthday," came the answer. "He'm a hundred and something, I don't know how much, but he'm going to live for ever, I reckon. Folk never die on this coast. 'Tis bad to be an undertaker in North Cornwall."

The coach rattled along, left the cheering crowd, and plunged into dark country again, while George found himself repeating those pleasant words, "Folk never die on this coast." It must be strange, he thought, to live over the hundred and feel well and active, and go on making plans for the future. And then the little girl opposite trod on his foot and sobbed an apology. She got out here, at the cross-roads, where puddles shone by the light of the lamps and a big clump of firs groaned drearily; and there she would have to wait until a cart came for her. It would not hurry, as she was of no importance. George saw her standing in the mud beside her box, her new blue frock gathered up to her knees, displaying the glorious red petticoat so nice and neat. It seemed cruel somehow to leave the poor little sixteen-year-old thing alone at those solitary cross-roads.

Newquay at last, and George jumped out, to be greeted by the solemn and apparently teetotal driver with a salute of his whip and the most respectful question—

"Ever been here avore, sir?"

The artist gave no reply. He was beginning to feel choky and nervous now that he was only seven miles from his destination, and he asked himself what he had really come for. It was a mad journey recommended by a kindly madman. Just because Winnie had written him a note he was tearing about Cornwall in wild March weather by way of answering it. But why had she signed herself by her maiden name? There was no getting away from that; and if it wasn't an invitation for him to—well, to come and see her, what was it? He thought also of the dream which his old wheal had sent up to him, and of Winnie's terror of being left alone. She wanted him and had, in a way, commanded his presence.

George went to an hotel and had some food. It was then nearly nine o'clock, and he was feeling feverishly restless. He could not sit still in the smoking-room, but kept reading that tiny letter and wondering what Winnie was doing and whether she was miserable and what had happened to Halfacre; and then he started, for a new thought came to him, the most obvious thing of all which is always the one that occurs last. She was suffering. She was appealing to him as a friend in her extremity. Had they not played together, coldly and diffidently certainly, but still with a dangerous kind of friendliness in St. Michael's Wood? And perhaps his manner had told her something, and he remembered—good heavens, he could remember everything then!—that her pretty eyes had been moist sometimes and her fingers had made a clinging farewell as they left his. Then with another flash came the ugly memory of Halfacre, his strange manner, wild aspect, his inane pursuit of that harmless bee. And that letter had been sent ten days ago.

George went out, sought the manager and almost collared him. "I want a carriage at once," he said. "Anything will do, as long as the horse is good. I must get to Perranzabuloe in an hour."

"It's very late," came the answer.

"I'll give the man a sovereign for himself if he's round in ten minutes," said George. "Here, do you know a cottage called Sandycote?" showing him the address at the head of Winnie's note.

"No; but there are a lot of scattered cottages along the coast. They will tell you in the village."

Money told its usual tale; George realised the blessed power of it then. He was soon off, and the driver plied his whip so well than in less than an hour they were in the middle of a sandstorm, which was St. Piran's usual hint of his saintly and apostolic nearness. A cottage appeared and George jumped out; but the inhabitants had gone to bed and would not answer. On they went with eyes smarting, for the wind was doing its best, and another white cottage started out. George knocked and roared; a voice answered in curses, and presently a head appeared somewhere in the region of the roof.

"Where's Sandycote?" George bellowed.

"Two miles beyond. You've passed the road. What be you going there for? 'Tis empty."

"Where are they?" came George's tempestuous cry.

"The man's gone"

"Dead?"

"What? Bide there a minute. I be coming down," said the fisherman, who was obviously interested.

"Hurry," shouted George, but his cry was not heard. Then the door opened and he tumbled inside. It was perfectly dark and the tenant couldn't find a match.

"Never mind a light. We can hear in the dark. Where's the man? Is he dead?"

"I don't know as he is. He's gone away. Who be you?"

"Where is she—the lady?"

"Aw, poor woman. 'Tis bad about she."

"Good God!" George muttered, beginning to sweat.

"Be you her brother?"

"Go on. Go on."

"Her be dying, they ses. Where did I put them matches? Mind, sir. There be cloam on the dresser."

It was shaking and jarring. What mattered all the crockery in the world?

"Where is she?"

"To the parsonage; a matter of half-a-mile beyond."

"Thanks," said George hoarsely. "I'll try and thank you better another time. Folk never die on this coast," he muttered. He was outside already, in darkness and flying sand. "Drive on," he said. He was very cold, shivering, and muttering to himself, "Too late, as usual, success too late, the journey too late, everything too late, and the money's only good for almshouses."

There were lights in the parsonage, anyhow, above and below, lights that passed from one window to another with a hospital-like restlessness. George was nervous no longer; he knew what he had come for. The door was opened by the parson-seaman himself, still in his jersey, surrounded with the atmosphere of his wild coast.

"How is she?" cried George at once. It was no time for commonplaces. "I am her friend. You can guess the rest."

The parson understood; he had learnt a lot about human nature, suffering and bodily endurance, while battling with the sea, bringing dead and living bodies to land. He led the artist in, asking no questions, and said gently—

"The doctor says there is no hope. She is so weak, and won't try to help herself, the disease is increasing, and it is only a question of time—"

"She is alive then," George broke in joyously. "That is enough. I can do the rest. I know what she wants— the wind of Dartmoor. She dreads the sea. Where is the man—the madman?"

"Not so much noise. She will hear," begged the parson, for George was shouting. His shrinking self was dead and buried; success in life had given him confidence and made him ignore his extraordinary position there. What was he but a stranger coming to claim another man's wife? But love can't be bothered with the old lady who presides over public morality, or machines in wigs that grind out law. George was not going to look back again.

"Her husband has left the place with another woman," said the parson. "He ill-treated the poor girl, locked her up in a room with her mother, starved them; a child was born. We rescued her just in time."

"While I was beating the Jew," howled George, going to the fire-place, snatching up the poker. He was not fit for respectable people. "I ought to have been here smashing his skull." And there was a child, another little growth to continue the endless story of endurance. "Locked up in a room, starved. Why didn't you shoot him, man? Why didn't you take an oar and lay him out with it, tie him in a net and chuck him in the sea? Why didn't you send for me?"

"I will ask her mother to come and see you."

So Winnie had a mother, which did not seem at all necessary, and George began to hate her as well. He stood there with the poker in his hand, wanting to fight any one who should dare to come between another man's wife and himself; a vastly different George Brunacombe then from the timid artist who, in the days of poverty, would turn back and hide himself when he saw any one coming.

The door had been partly open all the time, and George's voice penetrated to every corner of the little house. Winnie was sitting up in bed excited. She had heard that voice before; it was like the wind of Dartmoor blowing into the room, and it was doing her good, bringing the smell of peat and heather across her bed. It was the voice of a god, not that of a man, the voice of Nature, the calm, healing wind telling her to lie down and get well, and assuring her that the storm was really over and a wall had been built between her fragile body and the destroying wind. The explanation that it was only the doctor did not satisfy Winnie at all. Then the parson came in and beckoned Mrs. Shazell to go with him.

"Who is it?" begged Winnie, fighting with her cough, leaning over the side of the bed, bright-eyed and pretty.

"A friend of yours. He did not mention his name."

"With a grey beard and a dreadfully dusty coat? Mummy, go and brush it for him. I won't die. I am not going to die."

Winnie was beginning to laugh, and first one dimple was born again and then the other. She could smell the moor. Like old Uncle, she felt herself lying out on it, swaying up and down on the heather, and the sun was shining, and spring was coming on and there would be no more snow.

"He's a young man, clean-shaven, very well dressed."

"No, don't," she whispered. "That seems wrong. He's my friend. Didn't you say he is my friend? Run, Mummy, and I won't cough once till you come back."

Winnie took the parson's hand, and went on babbling a lot of shining and excited nonsense of all the wonderful things he would see and hear and smell when he went up on Dartmoor and rolled about in its wind.

Mrs. Shazell went down. George was sitting on a chair, with the poker across his knees, and when she entered it clattered upon the floor.

"I have come for her," he said at once. "I don't care about the world, the flesh or the devil, but I have come for her to take her to Wheal Dream. Don't be frightened. I am George Brunacombe, I am the famous artist," he blustered. "My pockets are full of money, and I'm going to furnish the Wheal House beautifully for you. I can't help being queer. Tell her I have come to take her back to the moor. I am George Brunacombe, junior partner of the firm of Bubo and Brunacombe, manufacturers of realistic pictures, known all over the world. Tell her I should have come long ago only I was away in London persecuting the Jews when her letter arrived."

"I am glad to see you, Mr. Brunacombe," faltered the little lady, looking curiously like her daughter.

"Don't keep her waiting. Go and tell her. I have come to take you and her as my guests to the Wheal House, where she will get well again. Tell her it is all Bubo's idea, and he is getting the rooms ready. You know what I mean. She doesn't want me, but she wants the moor. She was always so fond of Wheal Dream, and tell her the spring flowers are coming up by St. Michael's Ford, and the rivers are full and roaring at nights, and the waterfall is throwing spray all over the oak-trees. Tell her that. And I'll send a telegram to Bubo to get your rooms furnished. We shall turn out of the place, for you won't want two business men lumbering about. Tell her we will have a special train. The firm can stand it. Go and tell her," cried George excitedly, "and mind you say how happy it will make Bubo to have her in his house."

Mrs. Shazell went away with tears in her eyes. The poor soul was so frightfully in earnest. Winnie was holding the parson's hand, looking lovely, straining her ears. She was fighting again, she had everything to fight for; and when she heard what her mother had to say she begged to be allowed to get up and run round the room, just to show them how strong she was.

"Tell him I'll come. Oh, Mummy, can't we start at once? I want to go and sit by the Ford and watch the green water tumbling down. And tell him I'm so glad he has brushed his coat."

"Who is Mr. Bubo?" asked her puzzled mother.

"The owl, the dear little owl with only one leg," laughed Winnie, who was not at all in the mood to go on with her dying. "I am feeling so well," she said. "I can smell the wind."

Down went Mrs. Shazell again. George had put a cushion on the floor and was trying to stand on his head. He was quite mad at the prospect of Winnie at the Wheal House being forced into growth again. He became impatient when the lady sought to explain matters; how that Winnie had a husband and child, that the man had ill-used her, and gone off with another woman; and she and Winnie had practically nothing; and, of course, they could not be dependent upon him. George only interrupted her every time with angry words. He couldn't listen to such nonsense. He told her plainly he should lose his temper, and smash things with the poker, if she kept on. It was impossible to argue with him, and Mrs. Shazell had to give up trying. But George could not go until he had done one more thing. He scribbled a few lines on a scrap of paper and sent it up to Winnie. He knew it was not true that she had laughed at him in the days of his poverty, that it was only Berenice's idle story, but still he wanted to set his mind at rest and see the shrine of St. Winifred absolutely spotless; and when Mrs. Shazell came back with her answer, "It's a wicked story," he went away satisfied, and drove back to Newquay through the night.

Next morning George telegraphed to Bessie, telling her to get the house furnished in the most approved style and not think about the money; and then he drove again towards St. Piran's sands, laden with flowers and fruit. They were the best folk in the world at the parsonage, but they were poor; and George intended to claim the right of protecting this young married lady and giving her everything.

That same day he saw the doctor, a bustling, general practitioner, who knew very little about Winnie's disease, and was therefore inclined to paint a needlessly black picture regarding it.

"What have you been doing to my patient?" he asked. "She is a different girl to-day."

"I am going to take her home. That is all," George answered.

The doctor said it was foolish. Winnie would never be strong enough to make the long journey, and even if she could it was no use. It would be kinder to do all that was possible for her there, and make her last days pleasant upon St. Piran's sands.

"Years ago, when I was in London, a doctor gave me a few months to live," said George. "You can poke your fingers into me and find out what I am made of now. You don't know us moorland folk. If you take savages and shut them up in houses they will contract the diseases of civilisation, which are unknown to them in their natural state. It's the same with us. The smoke and the lowlands wipe us out." George made an upward movement with his hand. "Put us back on our native heather and we grow again."

CHAPTER XXIV
ABOUT A PAGAN SACRIFICE

The Pethericks had gathered round the fire on Christmas night for the last time. Father Chown and Mr. Odyorne had done for John; and the family name was to be wiped off the map of Dartmoor which it had blotted for so long. The lawyer had kept his trap baited, but John and Ursula required such a lot of coaxing before they would enter; they were suspicious when the time came, and said they would think over it. They were always going, but never went. It was John who made difficulties by simply declining to leave the home where he had been born and where his ancestors had lived for at least four hundred years.

John was not the same man after Christmas night. He was ill for some days without knowing what had happened, or why his head was wounded, but he supposed Ursula had done it, and Father made no boasts. Weak though the old man was, he must have hammered too hard. John couldn't work. He stumbled out in the morning to try, because he was fond of work, and for an hour he was strong enough, then pains in his head would bring him to a halt; or he would stoop and immediately become dizzy and fall about. His face was covered with cuts, and there was a nasty hole in his forehead; he had always been ugly; now he looked terrible, and Ursula hated him more and pushed the poor fellow all over the place, taunting him with the loss of strength which delivered him into her hands. Father was frightened when he looked at John through his cracked spectacles, which gave the man two unpleasant heads instead of one; the sight made him dream at nights, and he would choke and entreat the powers of darkness not to flay him with brambles for his sins. Father feared he might have hindered his spiritual advancement, and forfeited his right to a comfortable chimney corner in some heavenly mansion, because he had tapped John reprovingly upon the head with a hammer.

One day John went off for a load of faggot-wood, standing up in his cart, and Ursula dismissed him from her presence with her usual word of parting, "I hopes yew'll never come back alive." She had expressed the wish often enough, but it had never been realised; and that day her patience was to be rewarded. John came back alive, but lying in the cart, with a man leading the horse, and he was senseless. He had bent while standing in the cart, become dizzy, a wheel had struck a rock; and that was to be the end of John. He had fallen upon his head.

At first the accident made no stir, because men were always tumbling about the rocks, breaking various bones, and they were soon about again; but when it was rumoured John was very ill, getting worse rapidly, and the doctor was hopeless concerning him, there was grief in Metheral and something not altogether unlike the gnashing of teeth. No death had occurred in the parish for a great number of years; the grave by the porch remained unoccupied, but the claimants were more in number than ever. The weather of early spring scattered all manner of complaints. Willum Brokenbrow declared he was undoubtedly breaking up this time, although nobody agreed with him, and his appetite was excellent. Dame Brokenbone had a very severe cold, and had not been seen in chapel for more than a month. Several others were not feeling at all well. The competition was therefore in full swing; and John had tumbled on his head and become the favourite, although he was nothing but a boy of forty. No wonder the old people were upset.

Brokenbrow spent most of his time passing along the road between Metheral and Wheal Dream making kind inquiries, but not a word could be got from Father, who sat in his corner, with red and rheumy eyes, feeling very miserable indeed. He had ceased to desire the grave and a public funeral; he would have resigned all the costly treasures in his bedroom, even the piece of indiarubber which he had picked up at George's door, to put John on his feet again. Sometimes he asked Ursula for a Bible, explaining that he was getting very old and it was time to make serious preparations for going home, but he only received the scornful answer that there was no such rubbish in the house. Father spent his evenings weeping, and hoping that the tears would be accounted unto him for righteousness.

John grew steadily worse; he had rotted away his constitution with liquor, and that too had been Ursula's doing; the woman had tempted him and he had drunk. He was conscious, and knew he was going to die; for one thing his wife would not let him forget it, and men of the moor who have to keep their bed for many days resign themselves to the belief that their time has come. Ursula's conduct was not pleasant, and sometimes it was indecent; but then she was always at the bottle, finding it necessary to sustain herself during the time of affliction. The doctor had told her she must expect the worst; which she did with enthusiasm; and putting on her seal-skin jacket went to interview the stout widow who always managed funerals with complete success. This was anticipating things somewhat, but Ursula did not mean to be bustled. She had known an affair of this kind completely spoilt from a social point of view from lack of time to make arrangements; and, as she argued, it was not fair upon the neighbours to allow her own feelings to stand in the way.

The large lady was full of sympathy and suggestions, although she could not help being merry, partly to cheer Ursula, but chiefly because she hoped shortly to pass into a third edition, having discovered an old and rather daft farmer who required something substantial for a help-meet; and the widow, who was ready enough to blush for the third time, possessed a few pounds, which had a trick of increasing under discussion.

"I'll come across wi' ye, my dear, and tak' a look round the parlour," she said. "Poor dear John, as gude a man as ever lived, a man as any woman could be proud of. The Lord gives and takes away tu, my dear. Us wull get a proper bit o' beef and plenty o' pickles. I allus ha' found pickles go well to a funeral. How many can ye seat in the parlour? But there, don't ye worry. Yew ha' got trouble enuff. I knaws how it be. Yew'm fair mazed wi' it all. I ha' been through it twice, my dear, and it du come wonderful easy second time. Yew'll be going to church again next year, I reckon."

"John would never ha' done vor Plymouth. Us would never ha' got 'en off Dartmoor, and he would ha' spoilt custom," sobbed Ursula. "I ses to myself 'tis all vor the best. I be a young woman," she added proudly.

"Aw ees, my dear, yew'll get some fine young fisher captain, or mebbe a bosun in the Navy, vor your second. So yew be sot on going to Plymouth?"

"I ha' got a fine hotel," said the deluded creature, who perhaps deserved a little punishment for the hardness of her heart.

"Wull, I'll be over this evening, and us'll arrange things proper," said the stout lady. "How about your clothes, my dear?"

"They'm ready," said Ursula.

"Have ye got plenty o' handkerchiefs?"

"Naw, I ain't. 'Tis my first time," said Ursula apologetically.

"I'll lend ye my six. They'm fine ones, wi' black borders an inch wide, and I ha' used 'em twice," declared the lady. "I can wash 'em out after yew ha' used 'em."

John was lying on his back in the dirty bedroom, staring at the loose window and crumbling stonework. It seemed cruel to die in the spring after having come through the long winter, but luckily for John he had no imagination. Neither past nor future troubled him much; but the thought of his garden did. The potatoes were not in, the heap of manure was untouched, and would be spoiling in the sun. He wanted to get into his clothes and go down to the garden. One day's work would get the potatoes in, and then he could return to bed feeling much more satisfied. It was terrible to be wasting fine weather while the garden remained untilled.

He thought of little else, except whisky, which was a good thing, and the pain in his head, which was bad, but sometimes he recalled a very extraordinary thing called religion, which was served out in the stone chapels and churches; and he had a vague recollection of his father going to Metheral every Sunday, in black garments, and coming back full of queer texts which he explained must be accepted by John if he desired to attain immortality. That was too big a word for an ignorant fellow who had spent his life among manure heaps. It brought no meaning to John, and as for old Petherick, why, he had gone away years ago and had disappeared completely from the life of the moor, although John knew where he could find him, in the churchyard under a big lump of granite. That was not living for ever. Old Petherick was just the same as one of those carcases on the moor, except that he was out of sight while the ponies' bones were white and visible. He had assured John he would lie in the churchyard for a bit, and then come out and flap about like some old owl; at least that is what John understood by his remarks; but he knew perfectly well the old man had done nothing of the kind. The churchyard was like any of the commoners; what it had it held.

There was a good deal of activity in the house, and a savoury smell such as there had not been for a long time. Baked meats were being prepared in his honour, though he was not to partake of them. John began to feel dull. They were so busy down-stairs that there was no time to attend to him. The stout widow had taken possession of the house, and her voice was so shrill that John could hear everything she said, and the remarks were not encouraging. All things were being done properly, if not exactly in good order. The parlour was being cleaned out, and all the old sticks were taken outside to be rubbed and polished. The women laughed and joked over their work, feeling perhaps that it was useless to rebel against the will of Providence. Father forgot to be penitent and became irritable. He said they were spoiling his furniture by exposing it to the elements, and he should speak to the lawyer about their conduct when that merry gentleman called again. Father would have been very grieved had he known that the old stuff was soon to be sold by auction for what it would fetch, while all the property which he had spent years in collecting would be gathered into a heap and burnt. He was in good spirits during those days because the kitchen was full of agreeable odours, and he kept lifting the lid of a pot, dipping a spoon or a flesh-hook inside, like a Jewish high priest, and smacking his lips greedily over the result.

Although there was so much to be done, Ursula found time to run up and see John during the evening, and to inform him of the preparations they were making for her own bereavement. She was the worse for liquor, but for the sake of old times, and to show there was no ill-feeling, she gave him a little from the homely old bottle to cheer him up. John had been placed on a mattress so that he could not fall out on the floor, and a sad lamp was in the window as a sort of beacon for those who called to make inquiries. Bessie and Bill were not permitted to enter the house. They were ready to forgive and do all they could in the time of trouble, as they had good hearts and were themselves going up in the world, but Ursula reviled them and would have been violent had they insisted upon seeing the patient.

"Aw John, how be going on?" she asked amiably.

"I be going home fast," muttered the man, in his thick voice. "The taties bain't tilled neither."

"Where be ye going then?" Ursula stammered. "Yew be got like old Uncle now a-telling of home."

"Five minutes after I be gone I'll be up over a-looking down on ye," said poor John prophetically, although he had always scoffed at such a doctrine until then.

"Not yew," cried Ursula, with an alcoholic laugh. "Yew'll be down under looking up."

John groaned and tried to scratch his painful head, but his fingers were as limp as lambs' tails. "What be yew agwaine to du when I be gone?" he muttered.

"Aw, don't ye worry about I," said Ursula cheerfully. She thought she was performing her duty and making John happy. "Soon as us ha' put yew away, I be going to Plymouth. Mr. Odyorne ha' wrote that the house be ready, and he'll teach me the trade. He'll come and tak' me away hisself and see me into the place comfortable. Tull ye what 'tis, John," she hiccuped, "the gentleman be fair sot on me."

"Don't ye trust 'en," said John. Even then he couldn't bear the idea of Wheal Dream going out of the family.

"Shut your noise," said Ursula pleasantly. "Aw, if that bain't the beef burning. 'Tis a proper bit o' beef tu."

Then she blundered down-stairs and dragged Father away from the fire, where he was prowling about among the pots tasting and defiling everything.

"I'll be along presently," said the big lady, as she adjusted a bonnet like a rick-cover. "Us wull mak' a drink o' something hot, and tell to John, and sing to 'en a bit to keep his heart up. They gets a bit dull like when they'm going. Four o' clock in the morning be the time 'em goes usual. 'Tis an awkward time, my dear, but there, us has to humour them. The parlour be looking fine, but yew'm cruel short o' chairs. Yew can ha' some of mine if yew likes."

"The funeral wun't cost nothing hardly," said Ursula, with exultation.

"Aw, my dear, yew'm a lucky woman. I ha' spent pounds and pounds," said the fat lady.

John, the mere boy as the old folk regarded him, was to win the prize, the beautiful coffin presented by the wheelwright, and the immortality which was likely to be conferred by the grave near the porch; not the sort of immortality which his old father had referred to, but one which it was easier to appreciate. Willum Brokenbrow had been of all parishioners the most miserable, and had indeed attempted to take to his bed prostrated with grief, but the weather was so fine and he was feeling lusty. There was nothing for it but to be resigned, like Father, who had been a very lukewarm candidate since the almost fatal illness which had been induced by his efforts to subdue the bramble. Probably Brokenbrow had much the same sort of idea for all his loud boastings. Spring was coming on, there was a tender feeling in the wind. He could not have the grave, but he might obtain the next best thing. So he trimmed his whiskers, put on his best clothes, collected some primroses and adorned his coat with them. Then he went forth to visit Dame Brokenbone. The old lady was sitting in the usual corner, watching the usual pot and engaged upon the usual knitting.

"How be ye, Loveday?" cried Willum, with juvenile and neighbourly grimaces.

"I be purty fine, Willum. And how be yew?"

"I be surprising. I du seem to get younger every year. I be as lusty as the young unicorns what the palmist tells about. Be your cold gone, Loveday?"

"Wull, purty nearly, though I bain't getting out in the wind, but I be agwaine to chapel Sunday, if the Lord wills."

"I be agwaine anyhow," said Willum. "Us wull walk after," he added, with the manner of one haunting spirit addressing another.

"Where would us walk to?" asked the dame, gazing at the primroses and the best apparel. It was the tender time of the year, and after all they were not ninety yet, and all people are entitled to as much fun as life can give them.

"Us might walk to Wheal Dream and back," said Willum.

"'Tis cold out there along. 'Twould be best to bide in the lanes," said the dame.

"Have ye heard the cuckoo, Loveday?" asked Willum, with great anxiety.

"No, Willum, I ain't heard 'en."

"Nor me neither. But I seed a yaller butterfly."

"Wull there," said the dame, with much interest. "They'll tull of it in the newspapers."

"I wur thinking," said Willum profoundly, "that there be gwaine to be Easter."

The old lady admitted that the festival was not likely to be omitted from the calendar that year.

"There be a Monday after Easter," explained Willum; and the dame answered, it was probable.

"There be a taking and a giving in marriage about then," said Willum.

"So there be," said Loveday, as if such a thought had never occurred to her before.

"'Tis a fair day tu," said Willum, warming into enthusiasm. "Us might go abroad and dance a turn. Like two yaller butterflies," he added, which was not a happy comparison, but it pleased the dame. She laughed a good deal but said very little. It was the time when women don't say much; but they make up for it afterwards.

"I wur thinking," said Willum again, "that the grave be closed to us both, Loveday."

"I wouldn't go so far as to say that exactly. Us be human, Willum."

"What I means to tell is there be no admittance on business to the grave us craved vor. John Petherick ha' took an unfair advantage of we, and parson ses he mun ha' it and us mun bide out on't. Us ha' played fair and us ha' lost, and what I ses is there be no use crying over lost chances, and as us can't ha' the grave why shouldn't us get wed instead? One be as gude as t'other, I reckon."

"Wull there," gasped the old woman, with an eye of distinct encouragement upon her grimacing suitor. "Yew du get to put things almost as plain as minister, Willum. Fair takes my breath away, yew du."

"Monday after Easter be a gude day," he suggested.

"Aw, I mind many a fair, and I mind dancing out on the common seventy year ago. I wur a maiden then, and a proper liddle May Queen tu, I reckon."

"I minds yew," said Willum. "Us didn't reckon us would get wed seventy year afterwards," he chuckled.

"Who be saying us be agwaine to get wed?" said the dame sharply.

"I du," said Willum stoutly. "I ses to myself this morning, 'I can't ha' the grave, so I'll wed Loveday.' Us wull start life again, as 'twere."

"What would the volks say?" the dame suggested.

"They'll call we a proper pair o' yaller butterflies," declared Willum, although he ought to have known better.

"I be afraid yew might get to use blasphemious words, Willum," she said.

"I've abin and given up using they," he answered cheerfully. "I gave 'em up on Christmas, and agin on New Year, and I'll give 'em up agin come Easter time."

This was not very reassuring, but it seemed to satisfy the old woman, who was quite prepared to be joined to Willum in holy matrimony, but knew it was not decent to accept at once. She confessed she had often thought about searching for her affinity, as it was lonesome sitting alone in the kitchen; and if Willum would only bridle his tongue, and not show a decided preference for the bar-room and bad company, she thought it likely enough that a little trip to church, not to the nook beside the porch, but to the more homely altar, would not harm either of them. So they embraced in the little kitchen, and celebrated the occasion with something out of a bottle, and agreed that to commence their career in this manner was better on the whole than concluding it with a function which the entire neighbourhood would attend; and then Brokenbrow trotted off at peace with the world again, and thought the kindest thing he could do would be to travel across to Wheal Dream and advise his old rival, Amos Chown, to secure some primroses in his coat, undergo a spring cleaning, and follow his most excellent example.

Early the next morning, when there was a tender pink light upon all the moor, and the gentle wind was filled with the purest odours found upon earth, the smell of firs and peat and dewy heather, and the first sunbeams seemed to be creeping down the side of the cleave to drink of the river, poor ill-used John Petherick was evicted at last from Wheal Dream and went into the immortality which he could not think about. It was a trial of endurance for him to the end; the women who watched him were not sober, and their songs became hilarious; the window was shut tightly, and the atmosphere of the little room was horribly close, and filled with smoke and smuts from the lamp, the flame of which had been turned up too high. When the end came Ursula sobbed and shrieked, making the place hideous. It was not hypocrisy then, she couldn't help it, though the noise meant nothing, for she had hated John and in her heart was glad to think she had got rid of him.

"Did ye see the face of 'en?" she howled, more terrified than anything else. "How he did grin and grind his old teeth. Aw, my dear, did ye ever see a man go so hard? He wur a bad 'un, and knawed he warn't going to no gude place. Vull o' sin he wur from the time us wur wed. I ses thank God," muttered Ursula piously, "that he'm took to his rest. He wun't thump me on the back no more."

There were disgraceful scenes in the little house between that morning and the day of the funeral. Ursula spent most of the money that was left on liquor for herself and guests; she was about to depart, and she intended to leave a memory of her hospitality and a big reputation for having put her husband away in a thoroughly riotous and drunken fashion; she and John had swilled their souls and bodies into perdition, and now the memory of both was to be drowned in wine and brandy; nothing else could satisfy Ursula; she was going one better than anybody had ever gone before. Ruined people can afford to be reckless, and will lift their glass to the cry, "The devil. God bless him." It was a dark, horrible religion that was practised on the side of the lovely little gorge where the Stannary road wound its way along like a shelf upon brackets. Perhaps savages had defiled Wheal Dream in the distant past with their offerings; and now the last of the savage race was dirtying the place for the last time before the fire came to burn the rotten buildings and purify the hole which the Pethericks had grubbed for themselves, and make it sweet for a new and cleaner generation. The last savage sacrifice of those who had ventured to break open the ark and scatter the law abroad like dung upon the land was being held. They were ugly scenes, and it is not well to stand before those windows. The tumbledown house, where all that remained of John, last of the Pethericks, was lying silent, became during those filthy days a drinking-hell and a brothel for any man who liked to enter. Even Father wondered how Ursula could be so rude.

It was a great funeral. People talk about it still. Commoners came from all parts with their wives and little ones, and the village street suggested a revel. This was not because John was well-known and popular, but simply because the competition for the grave beside the porch had been talked about from west to east. A special effort was required of Ursula, as she was chief mourner, and so many eyes were upon her; and she rose to the occasion. Smothered in black raiment, she stood sobbing wildly by the grave, prevented from falling in by the stout widow, who held a little heap of heavily-edged and well-ironed handkerchiefs and handed them over one by one as they were required. The whole thing had been rehearsed beforehand. It was Ursula's dramatic duty to use up all those handkerchiefs, and the miserable humbug did so, soaking the lot with her maudlin mess. The recession from the churchyard was something of a triumph for her, although it was the last time she would ever loom in the public eye, except as a brawling streetwalker in the cheapest and commonest labouring quarters of Plymouth; and at every other step she howled—

"They can't say I ain't put poor dear John away respectable;" and at the gate, where several, who knew nothing about her and mistook her acting for real emotion, tried to say something consoling, she lifted up her voice and sobbed contentedly, "Aw, 'tis a real blessing to think us allus lived together so comfortable."

The last scene, and the saddest, was the feast, the only gratifying feature of which was its failure. The first stage was decent, the guests ate and drank and were pleasantly neighbourly, although they were amazed at the profusion of everything; but there was to be neither speech nor song. Gregory Breakback had come for the singing, and Ada Mills was at his side; they looked well suited to each other and happy, but neither of them touched the strange fiery liquors on the table. Farmer Tom Moorshed had come with a little speech, though it was probable that when the time came for him to deliver it he would be too fuddled to know what he was expected to say, and would mumble something about long life to the bride and bridegroom; but he was not to be called upon, for when Ursula appeared at the table she was shouting, calling herself a young woman and a free woman, and in a short time she was mad drunk, throwing things about, and challenging any woman present to step out and fight her. They tried to restrain her, but opposition made her worse. She was a free woman, and she had a fine bit of flesh on her and good clothes too, and if the company didn't believe they could come and see for themselves.

"Bide quiet, woman," went up voices from all over the room. "It bain't vitty. It be owdacious. Yew ha' just put away your man, woman."

Ursula shrieked at them all. If this was not liberty she did not know what was. Gregory was near her and she tumbled upon him, slobbered over him reeking of alcohol and sweat, and kissed him savagely. It was the first kiss he had ever received from a woman, and it was a strange one. It harmed him. He went white, hurled her off, and she struck the wall with a thud. The stout widow caught her, pulled her away, tried to force her into the chair, but Ursula called her names which no woman could endure to hear, slapped her face with all her strength, causing her to bite her lip and bleed. There was a general movement among the guests, and some of them began to go. The widow reeled to the door, crying with pain and anger—

"She'm mad. The devil be in she. I ses a curse be on this house and on all who bides here."

Ursula was yelling. She clambered upon the table, fell among the meat and drink, got to her feet, pulled her clothes up, and danced, a shocking and shameless sight in the pure sunshine. Only old Father laughed, because he was used to Ursula, and he thought she was being funny; but the guests were making for the door. They had done with Ursula; none of them would attempt to help her or stand up for her again. Outside the wind was blowing sweetly, and the light was tracing all manner of coloured pictures down the side of the moor. The contrast was overwhelming.

Gregory was on his feet, drawn up to his full height, holding Ada by the arm with a numbing pressure.

"If yew looks at that dancing doxy I'll put my coat across your eyes," he said.

"'Tis nought but the drink in she," Ada muttered.

"If that bain't the devil's medicine, what be? Come out, I ses."

CHAPTER XXV
ABOUT A SUNSET OF DREAMS

Gregory and Ada walked along the Stannary road. It was going on towards evening, and the sun was falling behind the western tors, leaving the common in shadow. The long, curving mountain of Cawsand was golden still, its summit catching the later light and shining with a borrowed splendour when the lowlands were dark. Gregory had his eyes upon the tremendous sky-line, which seemed to divide the world of unpleasant stories from the land of stars, and the sight refreshed him, cooled his body; that and the turn of the road carried them well away from the sights and sounds of the home of the Pethericks, which had already passed into the hands of foreigners.

Gregory wanted the wind. It was calm down there and it was calm above; but not the same calmness, for the spring wind up on the heights would be full of life and movement, like the spring water bubbling and foaming from the side of the moor.

"'Tis a spoilt day," he said.

"Ees, I reckon. I wun't be sorry to get off Dartmoor," Ada answered. She walked slowly, lazily he thought, and she was growing fatter. That was the air and little exercise. Such women do not walk for the love of walking, but only when they have to.

"Come on," cried Gregory. "I'll tak' ye up over and show ye what I mean. Come on, Ada, us wull stand to the top and look into the sun, and yew'll crave to bide here along till the end o' the world."

"I couldn't never climb up there," said Ada.

Neither could she understand what he meant. She never could. His language and his mind were far above her, but she liked to hear him talking. He seemed so learned; he looked so strong and clean;

there was no foul language ever found in his mouth, and no smell of liquor on his clothes. He was a man of earth, with the strange, wild stories of the earth clinging to him, making him smell wild and sweet, like the roots of a tree which the wind has torn up. He seemed to represent the spirit of the upland, to be the father of those invisible things which move in the woods and across the marshes and along the mountain top; things which silent men know are there, because they can smell their bodies and hear them rustling; but Ada did not express her thoughts in that way. He was only a man to her, but wonderful, because he talked better than other men.

"I'll tak' ye along," he said. "Yew ha' nought to du but hold my arm and let your feet go, and I'll bring ye up over to the top."

So she put her hand upon his arm and trusted in him, wondering again how old he was, but not guessing the truth. They descended, crossed the river, followed the pony track which wound upward between the blocks of granite, and ascended towards the first gigantic shoulder. Ada was soon panting. She couldn't understand doing this sort of thing for pleasure. It seemed madness to be climbing over rough ground when they might have been walking along a smooth lane. What was the use of going higher only to come down again? If it was only to feel a different and a stronger wind, to be further from the world and nearer the sky, to look down upon the green and red map of the western land, and to see lights breaking out between sea and sea, it was surely nothing but a waste of time. Then it was dirty; there was the sparkle of bog-water higher up, and clumps of scarlet moss like tropical flowers, and quaking grass of a sickly green. She was only spoiling her boots, and she was poor and couldn't afford it. Gregory Breakback was a man of strange ideas.

"Dost see it?" he shouted, with a tremendous laugh.

"See what?" she asked, almost crossly.

"The wind."

"Wull, I feels it. No one can't see the old stuff."

"I sees 'en," said Gregory. "I can see 'en moving miles away and rushing to me. Us mun go round a bit to keep clear o' the stables."

He referred to the bogs which, as many a poor pony had discovered to its cost, were stables with no doors of exit. There was no track, but the ascent became easy, although dwarf furze and tangled heather caught their feet, and presently they entered a wilderness of clatters, slabs of stone, which apparently had been cast there at the beginning of the world and never subsequently removed. The village had vanished beneath the giant's shoulder, and with it every echo of the world below; panorama rose behind parorama, a lot of scarred tors and rough ranges, and the wind was lord of all. It was cold on the great bare slopes, where was neither bush nor shrub to bear off any weather at all, and if it had come on to hail Ada would have screamed for mercy to the pitiless clouds, while Gregory would have grinned and borne it.

"Ain't us nearly up?" she panted.

"Us wun't be long," he answered. He wasn't gasping; his breath came as easily as if he had been sitting by the door of Moor Gate, gazing across his wonderland. The cairn at the top looked near, but at the end of another ten minutes it appeared just the same distance away; there was an enchantment to that view: and when the summit did come it was suddenly, like most of the good things of life.

"There be an old tomb down yonder. Us wull go and sot on 'en," said Gregory.

"'Twull be cruel cold," said Ada. "'Tis a bit more lew there."

They reached the old stone chest, which was moist and mossy, but Gregory did not heed that, and when Ada objected, having her best dress on, he pulled off his coat and spread it for her to sit on. He did not mind the wind, which was chilly up there. It made him warm. His blood and bones fed upon it, and when it increased he became stronger too. He seated himself beside her, on the edge of the grave, which had ceased to be one for so long as to have lost all dreary associations. He glanced at Ada; she was red and palpitating, and her yellow hair was in great disorder; her flesh was good, plump to the eye, soft to the touch; her limbs were large and round. Had he reached in old age, as years go, the parting of the ways? It seemed to Gregory that the god of the mountain was in a kindly mood, and the rugged mass was softening towards him. Perhaps it was nothing but the new heather springing up so strongly among the black and white stones—nothing but the change and fragrance of the spring—but Gregory believed that the form of the mountain had changed too. It was no longer an overwhelming mass stifling with its bulk; its menace had become a smile, it was a gentle thing, an airy and fragile presence, a deity of coloured cloud and flowers.

Then he thought of his home. George's Christmas gift had helped him to do wonders. The canary had been singing to some purpose, and with each one of its twenty silvery songs Gregory had added some true domestic touch. His hands were two miracles, and raw material was cheap. The place was furnished now; two large rooms were comfortable and good enough; a woman might be satisfied with them, and when she bent over the fire preparing the evening meal perhaps she would smile. The cage could be taken down, having fulfilled its purpose, and a lamp could hang in its place to shine like an eye of love across the moor. The iron bar would lean against the wall, as a symbol of strength and of labour, old Ben would sprawl beside the broken hearthstone, and he himself would work—but not for a master. His pride would remain, and a tyrant's command would still make him mad to break a tyrant's back.

"What ha' ye brought I up here vor?" asked Ada.

"To look out over," he answered.

"I'd sooner be avore the fire wi' my sewing. 'Tis a proper lonely old place."

"Yew'll want to be coming up here again?" he suggested.

"Not me. I be agwaine off Dartmoor soon as I gets the chance."

"Where be going?"

"Anywhere, so long as 'tis a town. I've had enough o' the mucky country, and I bain't wanted to home. A woman can't du nought here along. 'Tis proper in a town, wi' streets to walk on, and volks passing, and plenty o' lights. There be something to see in a town."

"Bain't there nought to see here neither?"

"Sheep and ponies, and watter everywhere. A woman can't move abroad wi'out getting her clothes mucky, and 'tis cruel lonesome."

"Aw 'tis, when yew'm alone."

"So I craves to get out on't," she said.

"Yew'm handy, Ada?"

"Ees, I can cook and mind a house, and I be useful wi' my needle and makes all my own clothes."

"Would ye mak' a man's clothes tu?"

"I reckon I could, if I had an old suit to go by."

"Yew'd bide on Dartmoor if yew had a home?"

"Aw, 'twould be different then. A woman craves a home. More than a man du, I reckon. Her likes a fireside of her own."

"And a man of her own?"

"Wull, her du, and 'tis no use saying anything different."

The sun had gone away, but the top of the mountain was clinging to the light. The wind was increasing, as it does after sunset; it seemed to Gregory that the god of the mountain was dancing in his hall. He placed his hands upon his knees and sighed. Had the sun gone down upon his loneliness? Ada was not whiter than the lily, nor had the fragrance of the rose settled upon her; she had not received the baptism of beauty; she did not partake of the mystery of sunset dreams: but there she was, a fat contented piece of woman-flesh, wanting a home and a man to give it her.

"Us ha' walked together, Ada."

"Ees, us ha' walked a plenty."

"And telled together."

"Ees," she said softly.

"I be a man. I be strong," he cried. "I be Demshur tu, and they ses when a Demshur man throws a bit o' wood into the sea it turns into a fighting ship. I could break the backs o' they liddle men in towns."

"I reckon yew could." She was understanding him now he was talking sense; the idea of matrimony is always sensible to a woman; and then he was off again in parables.

"There wur a man and he loved a woman, but had nought to give she, vor all he had wur a pigeon wi' a broken wing. So he gave she that, and her was satisfied, 'cause her knew 'twas all he had."

"What du ye mean?" said Ada.

"Wull, my dear, her wur a gude woman, 'cause her didn't want more than what the man had to give; and he gave she all he had, 'though it warn't worth much. But 'tis a true story, vor he'm wrote down on my parchment."

They became silent again, Ada, who was in her finery for the funeral festival which had been brought to nought, shivered and wanted to get down, though she also desired to hear what he had to say; while Gregory, warm in his sleeved waistcoat, felt only the call of Nature telling him it was mating-time then or never at all. He knew that he and Ada had nothing in common, except, perhaps, love for the home, which on his side would last, but on hers might die quickly when she discovered what a poor one it was, amid what solitude, set up in what wind. Would happiness endure between them, or would Ada grow in time to hate husband and home alike, imitate Ursula and seek from the bottle those pleasures which he could not give? Could they be happy looking different ways; he across the moor, she towards the gaslights of town life? Gregory could not answer. All he knew was that this was his last chance; the god of the mountain was propitious and offering him all that he deserved or could hope to win. He was a lowly creature, and his partner must be lowly too. He must take all he could get and be thankful. But would love be the thing he thought it was when Ada came to Moor Gate, she who had borrowed nothing from dreamland? The very attraction of love consists in the fact that real life has nothing to do with it. Would Ada help to maintain that idea? Or would she scold and talk scandal of the neighbours? Such questions were endless. The wind was getting higher and the noise from the subterranean hall of the god of the mountain increased. He seemed to have invited a few divine friends to come and spend a merry evening with him. They were singing a song of war; not a song of love.

"Us ha' walked since last summer, Ada."

"Ees, us ha' been some proper walks," she answered.

He tried to think what she had said during those walks. He could not recall a single remark worth remembering; but she was a woman, she must have the divine spark, and he might find it and nurse it into flame.

"Have ye ever been asked, Ada?"

"Not proper," she said, beginning to be nervous.

"I ask ye now," said Gregory loudly.

Ada put down her head and wriggled, trying not to laugh, but she had to giggle, for she could not help being tickled at the proposal. Her parents had called her a proper old maid, and often taunted her with her failure to capture a man, for she was forty, and when a woman is not settled by then she gets laughed at. Ada was pleased, and the fat on her body shook with satisfaction. Gregory was a fine man, something big to show her parents, and she could clap her hands in their faces and call them lying prophets.

"How old be ye, please, Mr. Breakback?" she asked, nudging him archly.

Gregory did not answer; the matter of his age could wait. All he said was, "I ha' a warm heart and a poor home, but I owes nought. Don't tak' me, woman, if yew craves finery. I ha' nought to give save company and my old place up over on Moor Gate."

"I knaws yew bain't rich," she said. "I likes yew, Mr. Breakback. Yew ha' been gude to me."

"Yew'll ha' me then?"

"I wull, and thankye kindly."

"I can't give ye town life. I can't give streets and shops. 'Twull be homely up over and that be all."

"Us can't get all us craves vor," said Ada resignedly. "I bain't a young maiden. I ha' known what 'tis to live careful."

"Us wull ha' to live careful."

"Wull, I'll du my best," she promised.

"Yew wun't get tired on't? Yew'll bide as yew be now?"

"I'll try, but I hopes yew wun't tell queer same as yew ha' been a-doing, vor I can't onderstand when yew tells like that."

"I can't tell no other way. Tis the life I ha' led," he said gloomily.

Somehow there was not much warmth between them, and Ada was perhaps more conscious of it than he was.

"Bain't yew agwaine to give me one liddle kiss?" she asked rather impatiently.

"Bide a bit," said Gregory. "There be a question I ha' to ask ye. It be a question they alms asked at the beginning of the world, but they don't now, vor volks be careless got. Some men don't care what 'em weds, but I care. I ha' lived lonely all my life, and I ha' lived clean, and I can look out from my door and swear I be as clean in my body as the wind what brought me here along. Now, woman, avore us be promised, I'll ask ye the question."

"Yew'm telling queer again. I don't onderstand ye," she grumbled.

"Wull, woman, 'tis a fair question vor a man to ask, and no maid need feel shame to answer. And now I ask yew. I, Gregory, ask yew, Ada, as 'em asked at the beginning o' the world, if yew wull be my woman in pure virginity?"

Ada started, shuddered, then flushed, half in anger, half in shame. The question was clear enough, and she could not pretend it was past her comprehension.

"It bain't right to ask such a thing," she stammered.

"Right or wrong, I ask ye. I wants your answer," he said loudly.

"I can't give 'en. Yew'm insulting me," she cried. Then she put her face into her hands and cried.

"No, woman. I'd break my back avore I insulted ye. Answer yes or no in pure virginity, and let's ha' the end on't."

"I can't. I can't," she sobbed.

"Be that the way yew ha' gone?" he shouted.

"Give over," she sobbed. "What harm ha' I done? I bain't better nor worse than others. I ha' been a young maid and lively, and I bain't ashamed on't neither," she said defiantly.

Gregory had left the old stone-chest, and when she rose too he began to pull his coat on, looking downwards; and now there were devils dancing in the hall of the mountain.

"Come along down. 'Tis time us wur home, and 'tis getting dark;" and so it was, for him and for her as well as for the sky.

"I bain't a bad woman," she cried.

"I bain't sot over ye to be a judge. I ha' lived clean, and all I asks of my woman be the like; and yew ha' let the lady in ye out on hire."

"Yew'm a liar," she cried hotly.

"I don't want ye, woman. I'll bide alone."

"I ha' been the same as others."

"And I be a man and proud on't. I'll tak' my body out o' the world as clean as he come in."

They said no more as they descended the mountain, walking apart, Ada sobbing all the way. At the foot they parted with a cold "good-night," and the moor between them parted too, not for a night but for ever. There was no getting across that space which the woman's life, the ordinary careless life, had made between them. Gregory went on towards Moor Gate; and nobody heard him singing as he went.

The voices were there the same as usual, the voices of those things of Nature among which he had always lived, and they called him as he went along, but he did not hear all of them; the night birds called and the heather called, and the rugged tors and dashing rivers, and the wind, clouds and uttermost depths of sky and space, and all the wonderful sprinkle of stars called as he went to his lonely home. "You are a man, Gregory Breakback;" but he did not hear that. "You are a proud man, Gregory Breakback;" but he did not hear that. "You are an old man, Gregory Breakback;" and that he heard.

So he came home to Moor Gate, to the rooms he had furnished with his wonderful hands, to the broken hearthstone where no fire glowed and where no figure would ever stoop, and to the table where no food was prepared; and faithful Ben flopped down at his feet and gave him love. He took the chair, which he had made himself for a woman to sit on, placed it outside the door, seated himself and looked out. He had failed, and it was his own fault; his pride had stood in the way at every turn; he had not humbled himself and done his best: and therefore he got the hammer on his head, not the wreath and happiness. He had tried to teach George what the artist could have taught him. A man may be a saint, and yet he fails if he cannot break and bend his back.

And for the future what was there? The voices and nothing else; the message and the company of wind and space; this playing at immortality. Dreamland was at his door pushing its golden key into his strong, hard hand, and the story of the universe was before him in soft outlines with all the illusion of the past and glamour of time ahead. The heavy mists over the marshes, the painted clouds around the tors, the mysterious haze of twilight, the wonder of the moon, the sun wallowing in his bloody death every fine evening—these would be the fellows who would bear him company; and as for the voices, there would be the whispers of St. Michael's Wood, the god-like tones of the mountains, the rattling of rocks, the rush and shout of waters; and, greater than these, the pathetic cry of the spirit-forms, made by swaling-fires and peat-smoke and moon-shadows around the ruin, gathering there in the loneliness of night, and piping with the borrowed and plaintive sweetness of the solitary bird—

"Be outside your door every evening, Gregory Breakback, and look out over, waiting and watching for the reward of life which the gods will send you. Watch our shadows creeping from the mists on the river over the furze-bushes and upward to the heather which clings to the top of the hill; and when the sky is white with moonshine keep your eyes on that dark, quivering line, made by the heather as it brushes the moonlight, and then you shall see..."

But at that point the voices failed and could tell no more. It was the blurring of the line between life and dreamland. What could he see but the sombre background of reality? This knocking at the gate of illusion would have no end, but there would be always a kind of pleasure in the effort; and the story of existence derived therefrom would be the splendid old tale of outdoor life, the life of the wood with its charming secrets, the life of the moor with its scent of brown peat and the fresh, clean dew upon everything, the life of health and strength, with sufficient patience added to keep the mind free from low and horrible delusions. It was the story which had no end, for death itself, perhaps, would only supply just that one thing necessary to make the dream real. It was the story of the triumph of mind over body.

It was dark. Gregory had gone inside and the door of the little ruin was closed.

CHAPTER XXVI
ABOUT A TWILIGHT OF GOLD

Uncle Gifford was alive and blossoming as a man of business. He was letting lodgings, and getting plenty of company at last. Two gentlemen shared his cottage, distinguished folk, who didn't object to a stone floor and only one room in which to eat and work and have their being. The firm of Bubo and Brunacombe had moved across the gorge, and the quaint metal sign of the one-legged owl swung above Uncle's doorway in the little court, where water was always splashing and ferns were generally green. The old gentleman had not advertised for lodgers; they had thrust themselves upon him, explaining they were homeless, they must live and work somewhere, and they refused to depart from the precincts of Wheal Dream. Uncle was penniless after Jimmy departed with his money-box, and George easily convinced him that it would be foolish and wrong to die of starvation, and if he and Bubo came into residence Uncle could live for nothing, be well looked after, and if at any time he took it into his head to pass into life everlasting, why he could do so in peace and comfort, with George on one side of the bed, Bessie on the other, Bill at the foot, and at the head Bubo delivering an oration upon all the avuncular virtues.

This was a very good thing for old Gifford, and when George presented him with a bright new money-box having a few shillings and coppers inside, which he could rattle about and play with as he lay in bed, his old heart overflowed with happiness. Apparently he was not going to die, although hopelessly paralysed; the doctor thought he might go on for some time, though he would never leave his room again; but George brightened up the walls with a few pictures, brought flowers into the place, taught the old man the virtues of an open window and plenty of air and sunshine; and Uncle sprawled on his back, was delighted with everything, and his shadow grew no less. He read his Bible and sang his hymns every night and morning; and prayed aloud for the wonderful gentleman who had all the arts of the magicians and could create comfort in a divine-like way. George heard his virtues going up to heaven every night, and it made him chuckle; but Bubo was offended. The senior partner's morality was on the wane, he was exceedingly sulky during those pleasant summer days, and had fallen into Willum Brokenbrow's deplorable habit of using "blasphemious words." Willum was a married man again by then, and had turned his mind entirely from joyous thoughts of sepulture. Bubo was not pleased at being moved from the Wheal House to the cottage, where there was not nearly enough room for mouse-coursing; besides, it looked too much like coming down in the world; and was he not Lord Mayor of Wheal Dream, with a little gold chain of office round his neck, and senior partner of one of the most celebrated art firms in the world?

"I told you we were going to be turned out of house and home," George said, laughing and rubbing his hands together. "I was a true prophet, ancient and mayor-like Bubo. We have come down to a cottage, to one room and a cupboard, but it isn't poverty, your worship. It's wealth, success; poverty is a fine thing when you can afford to play at it. Here's the doctor. Sit up straight and look sociable, Bubo, or I'll order you two blue pills as big as cannon-balls."

George admitted the doctor and put him in a chair. He wanted to have a serious talk, for there were plenty of clouds about, depressing him often, and until they were cleared away he wouldn't be really happy. He closed the door, set himself in the darkest corner, and began to ask questions, all about Winnie; there was nothing in the world to ask questions about except Winnie; there could never be anything of the slightest importance under the firmament of heaven except that one living thing which still moved about the earth.

"So you want to marry her, Brunacombe?"

"Of course I do. I always wanted her, but I was a poor, struggling devil in those days."

"Then that man Halfacre is dead?"

"Buried, forgotten, and gone for ever," cried George cheerfully. He had heard nothing whatever and was lying, but he wasn't going to allow the poor wretch to live. Winnie's name was not to be linked with his any longer, she was not to suffer any more shame or sorrow through him, she was to be free; so George killed him with his tongue. He knew he couldn't marry Winnie; but of what account was that so long as she was his, living in his home, protected and maintained by him; when he could see her and hear her speak, and look across at the window of her room and know she was safe and comfortable? Men and women cannot have everything; and George was getting quite as much as he deserved.

"I knew he wouldn't last. Everything in him was weak. He was a mass of diseased consciousness—a queer brute," said the doctor.

"We have done with Halfacre. At least I hope so," George muttered. "I want to hear the worst about some one else."

"She's a pretty girl. She always does what she's told. If ever a girl deserved to get well she does. She has done more for herself than any one I have ever known. She is a marvel. It's a wonder she didn't die as you were bringing her up from Cornwall."

"We wouldn't let her," said George. "She kept on saying, 'I won't die. I'll promise you to get well.' Is she keeping her promise?"

"So far as I can judge she is defying medical opinion exactly as she did before. If she had behaved properly she would have been dead long ago," said the doctor laughing. "You know what happened the first time she came here. On this occasion she was far worse, and if I hadn't known her I should have said it was impossible she could live a month."

"She has done it," cried George triumphantly.

"She is repeating her past performance. Her cough has practically ceased, she has increased twelve pounds in weight, she has no temperature, and her strength is returning. She does all she can for herself and seems very happy—both great things."

"She will soon be about again," cried George, making faces at sulky Bubo. "She will be going down to St. Michael's Ford."

"Not for another month or two. Don't be too sanguine, Brunacombe."

"Why not? Why shouldn't I be?"

"There is always the danger of a relapse, and there are so many other things; the disease might go into her throat, for instance."

"It won't," cried George. "We won't let it."

"Well, if she goes on as she is doing now—"

"She will. We'll see to it."

"Then she will get about again. But you must be very careful of her."

That was a ridiculous thing to say, and George almost jeered at it. As if Winnie wasn't going to be wrapped up in cotton-wool all the days of her life, and not even permitted to go within a yard of any bramble lest she might get scratched. George had not asked the doctor in to talk such nonsense.

"If you are married it will be a case of separate rooms and all that sort of thing. You understand that?"

"I only ask one thing," said George, "and that is to see her walking about the moor and coming in hungry to eat a good dinner. Shall I have my wish?"

"I think you will. I feel almost sure you will. This girl is different from others. She seems able to extract from this air life-giving qualities which no one else is quite able to find. That is really the whole secret of her recovery. I have always compared her to a plant which will only grow in pure air and sunshine. She could never have lasted any time in a smoky place. Even the sea air was killing her. But on the top of Dartmoor she finds her own element."

George could say nothing just then; he was behind the doctor, blinking his eyes and shaking his fist furiously at Bubo, who was always disgusted by any signs of weakness. The junior partner had become a positive idiot since he had taken to shaving every day, and going in for many changes of raiment, and descending to wine and women; at least that is how Bubo summed up the whole matter, but then he was a philosopher, when he wasn't replenishing his stomach, and therefore it was impossible for him to be patient with the follies of youth.

The doctor patted George on the shoulder and made for the door; then looked back and said, "I have sad news of some of my old patients. That poor fellow Gumm is dead. I heard from his wife only this morning."

"Poor old Yorick," George muttered. "He used to make me laugh with his queer jokes. There was something to admire in him if he could play the fool and keep up the spirits of others when he was dying."

"He would have lived and become healthy if he could have stopped up here. He had a wife, and had to go back and maintain her; and a commercial traveller has a trying time." The doctor hesitated, then added in almost a whisper, "Miss Calladine is dead."

"What?" muttered George, with a shudder.

"She was a strange girl. I liked her, but couldn't understand her," the doctor went on. "I believe every one liked her, but she frightened them. I was afraid she would go off suddenly. There was not an atom of self-control in her. That night the dog was caught in a trap did for her—she has left all her money to that dog, by the way, that he may be petted and pampered for the rest of his life. A queer girl; but she was handsome."

"Like an animal," George murmured.

"Yes, there wasn't much womanliness about her. That face of hers ought to have attracted men, but it only frightened them. It's a pity to see beauty spoilt and wasted—and upon a dog or two. It's not good enough, Brunacombe."

"Does she know?" said George, nodding his head towards his own house.

"Certainly not. You mustn't tell her;" but George only muttered—

"I don't think she would care much."

After that he had to go up to the marshes, which was always his walk when he wanted to think, for its desolation suited every mood. Berenice was taken, and Winnie left; the stiff growth had been snapped off, the clinging one lived on. Winnie and himself had weathered the storm merely by being patient, and all around them was the wreckage—the clown's head of Gumm, the wild, fascinating eyes of Halfacre, the gracious white face of Leigh, the fine brown Berenice, to say nothing of such lesser storm-tossed refuse as the Pethericks. It was sad to look out after the storm, sad to think what might have been had there been nothing but calm wind, sad even to succeed where so many fall. George was not a mystic, like Gregory; there were no voices on the moor for him; he was his own voice, and he declared conceitedly as he trotted along, "You have worked hard, George, in poverty, hunger, and dirt, and I'll be hanged if you don't deserve a holiday and fine weather."

He entered his house most days, but only visited Winnie on Sundays, by special permission on one side and by invitation on the other. He did not frown and look severe any more, and Winnie always smiled at him straight in the eyes, and if there was a speck of dust on his coat she said, "Come here," flicked it off, and laughed, "That's better." They were natural enough; they called each other by their Christian names, and sometimes —usually when it was getting late on Sunday evening, which is a dangerous time—they became Dimples and Gee; but there was never anything worse—for she was another man's wife, and George had no right to be in her bedroom— no kisses or any nonsense of that kind. There was just a handshake when Mrs. Shazell came in to tell George his time was up, for his watch always was slow on those evenings; and a "Good-bye till next Sunday, George. Tell Bubo he's not to give you too much work," from her; and a "Mind you are nice and plump by next weighing-day, Winnie," from him. There was no need for anything else, as Winnie was not strong enough for demonstrations, and they had understood each other perfectly since that night when George had rescued her just in time from St. Piran's Sands.

That merry little gentleman, Mr. Odyorne, had been going to and fro, capturing pawns like a chess-queen, but at length found himself in a corner, wedged in between George and Uncle. He had overlooked Uncle in his scheme of appropriation, and his pretty words and amiable gambols didn't go down with the artist, who, now that he was famous, began to assert himself. When Mr. Odyorne came to destroy the home of the Pethericks, Uncle's cottage stood in the way, and when he proposed to buy that for a guinea or two, old Gifford defied him to touch a stick or stone, and George aided him, declaring that he himself was lord of Wheal Dream. It was no use Mr. Odyorne buttering Uncle in his best manner, calling him the most angelic old gentleman that had ever slipped out of heaven by mistake. Uncle only opened his big Bible and read lurid extracts about a lake of fire wherein usurers would flop about like exhausted goldfish. It was no use trying to oil George into an alliance with loving phrases and such expressions as "Dear old boy," and "We gentlemen must stick together." The artist replied he was going to see fair play. Mr. Odyorne was check-mated; he could do nothing until he possessed Gifford's vineyard, except dismantle the home of the Pethericks, knock the roof off, and make it thoroughly hideous and uninhabitable, partly out of spite, but chiefly from a dread lest Ursula might return and summon the commoners to her aid. There was no fear of that; Ursula was already stranded, and going rotten with gin and lust; and as for poor old Father, he was safe in the workhouse, probably far more comfortable than he had ever been in his life, being washed and scraped out of all recognition.

"Look here," said George, the next time the lawyer came along bumbling and honey-dropping in quest of the property; "you can't get the whole of Wheal Dream, because you could never buy me out, but I can get it. I'll buy the place off you."

He wanted it so that he could rebuild the home of the Pethericks as a cottage for Mrs. Shazell. She was a dear little lady, but she kept on forgetting that other parts of her body required exercise besides her tongue; and when certain things came to pass, and George was at home again, he wanted to hear only one voice, but as much of that as he could get.

Mr. Odyorne agreed, called George a "dear old sportsman," and quoted a figure which might possibly have tempted the owners of the Tower of London. George told him to go away, cool his imagination, and write when he was serious; which Mr. Odyorne did, only his craving for guineas was also serious, and he argued that an artist who was making plenty of money wouldn't be a man of business. But George had been a poor man too long not to know something about the value of money. The lawyer went on writing loving letters, always alluding in a tender manner to "dear Mrs. Brunacombe," knocking off a few guineas every time, though it was pain and grief to him, until George had to decline to continue the matter. Then Mr. Odyorne sent in a most affectionate bill for the letters, which George paid to keep the little guinea-pig quiet, and there the incident ended; and the home of the old Dartmoor family of Petherick stands in ruins to this day.

When the heather came into flower Winnie was up and going little walks; down to the wheal as she had done in former days, not sighing and sad, as then, but delightfully happy and able to feel herself mistress of all she surveyed; along the road across the common, almost to the village; and a little way up the side of the moor. Still she was not satisfied; she longed for the big walks, and two in particular—the great peat marshes, where the wind and the stickles sang together, and the wood beyond the Ford between St. Michael's oaks, to the green shelf above the waterfall.

"I'll be patient a little longer, and then we shall be there," she said to George, who was wasting those days teaching Winnie to walk, always horribly afraid she would hurt herself in some way, removing stones from the path in front and cutting off every bramble, especially Father's old enemy, which had grown again. It was a wonder he didn't order Bessie out to wash the old timbers and sandpaper the walls of the wheal. Winnie was not supposed to talk during those walks, but the dimples were not doomed to silence, neither were they; and sometimes she would make mouths and eyes and do marvellous things with her nose, trying to express what she might not say, and then she would get her fingers crushed, and—though it was not officially recognised—kissed, when she would insist upon being particularly distracting. She had to overlook these lapses from good behaviour, because she knew she deserved punishment, and perhaps she didn't really mind much. How could she help getting well with the knowledge that calm wind was going to blow to the end of the story?

Bill and Bessie did obeisance to Winnie as the "little missis," and made her laugh by alluding to her as the owner of the master and themselves; but to Uncle she was the wonderful lady, and he occupied himself by searching out texts which were appropriate to her, and quoting them to George, who saw no reason to disagree. The state of Uncle's mind had improved greatly now that he was no longer subjected to ill-treatment. He could lie on his back and rattle his new money-box, and hope that Jimmy was being a good boy and reading his Bible regularly. Uncle was always asking when the wonderful lady was coming to visit him, although he admitted that two marvellous personages in that small cottage would be rather overwhelming; not to mention Bubo, who scrambled up the steep stairs nearly every night to perform his favourite tragedy of Othello underneath Uncle's bed. The old man was relieved when Bubo departed, for he was afraid of him; he could not understand a wild bird in a state of domesticity, and he had a dim notion that the little owl was a sort of Chaldean and astrologer, of whom, he gathered, holy writ did not entirely approve.

At last Winnie came, attended as usual, and commanded to pause on each stair before she ascended another; and when Uncle saw her there was no more breath left in him. He felt that if she had asked him for a penny out of the money-box he would not have refused. As she did no such thing, he opened his Bible before her and showed her the beautiful pictures; Adam and Eve in the garden apparently looking for their clothes; the ark floating about in a large pond, with an elephant, not exactly in proportion with the vessel, sticking its head out of a port-hole; the tower of Babel crumbling down like a suburban villa; and Lot's wife just about to be chemically transformed into a useful table condiment. Uncle explained that all the pictures had been prepared by divinely inspired artists, and were therefore accurate in every detail. He did not show Winnie the picture of Simon Peter being unkind to Ananias, as he felt he hardly knew her well enough, and it might seem conceited if he pointed out how strongly the holy apostle resembled himself; but he allowed her a glance at the plan of the New Jerusalem, which was where he was going some day, although he hastened to add he was in no hurry because the wonderful gentleman was so good to him, and covered the walls of his bedroom with beautiful pictures, and fed him with delicacies which it was really not right for him to eat but only for those who lived in kings' palaces. Bessie Chown was also a righteous person, and Uncle hoped she and Bill would in time occupy a cottage in the same heavenly street as himself. And then he thought it would be nice and homely if they said a prayer; and he lifted up his voice and made George and Winnie blush because of their virtues; but unfortunately Bubo came scuttling in behaving blasphemously, and brawled to such a disgraceful extent that Uncle had to stop.

"Yew'll come and see me again?" he asked eagerly. "And when I be going home wull ye hold my hand vor company? 'Twull seem more natural like when I opens my eyes and finds myself up over."

Winnie did not like such a question, though the compliment was a pretty one, but she promised.

"I think you have been a very good and patient man," she said.

"I ha' been homely," said Uncle. "Me and neighbours never could get on, vor us wur different. I be happy now," he added. "It be all quiet abroad, and I don't get mazed. When 'em ses, 'Come along, Uncle, 'tis time vor ye to be home,' I'll be ready, aw, and I'll be glad, vor 'tis allus fine weather up over, and I be main cruel anxious to see Noah and Elijah and Simon Peter and all the other gentlemen what 'em tells about here. There wun't be weeping, nor yet gnashin' o' teeth, and I be glad on't, vor I ha' done my weeping down here along, and I ain't got no teeth to gnash."

It was August before Winnie received permission to go down to St. Michael's Ford. So far there had been nothing said concerning their future life. When George tried to talk seriously she always said, "Wait till we go down to the Ford," and he knew what she meant. It was there they had met on the earlier stage of their perambulation; it was there they were to finish the journey, among the ghosts of those who had crossed the Ford completing their journey, settling the bounds, bringing liberty, appointing the great Forest as a free and open space for all time. It was a hot day, so they did not start until after tea; and when they came within sight of the green water, which was listless at that time of the year, the sun was low and the air was a clear haze of gold.

They did not talk much as they went down treading upon unwritten pages of history. Winnie had been inclined for mischief, having discovered there was little to grumble at; but when she saw the green oaks she was serious. There was life ahead and the difficulties of life. The old wheal had given her dreams, happy ones, but there had been corners which the colours could not reach, where shapes were crouching, Hawkers and Halfacres who might still bring trouble and foul smoke across the landscape. Even if she was pretty and lowly Goldilocks whom the prince must come for in the end however rude and cruel the herd-boys might be, even if she was the luck child who must win what she was born to win, there were still the dark corners, and the storm-wind would blow again. Kings and Queens when they come into their kingdom know the tempest is never far away, and if they are to beat it, so far as mortals can beat it, they must hold on; and the only root that will cling is the root of patience, and the only growth that will not break is the one that bends. George and Winnie were coming into their kingdom, receiving hope as they entered it, and it was the kingdom of chaste love, a land far off and almost fabulous, which only the very patient and very loving can ever hope to find. They were simply hand-in-hand lovers, opening the window of dreamland to look out over the world of dust and noise; and merely as lovers they were common people; for one person in love is merely the repetition of any other; they are the same actors with different names; dark or fair men, they are alike in their prayer to Venus for one of her team of white doves; blue or black-eyed girls, they bare their bosoms to get their hearts stabbed.

"We have come at last," cried George.

"The very evening. Perfect calm," sighed Winnie.

She seated herself upon the flat stone, which had always been there and would never be removed, and George placed himself at her feet.

"May I talk, Winnie?"

"Yes, about anything you like. One moment though. You have been giving me everything and I have given you nothing. What would you say if you looked up and an acorn dropped right upon your mouth?"

"I should say the tree had made a very good shot."

"Look up," she said softly.

He did so, and she kissed him, with a pretty sound.

"Shameless," she whispered. "I promised myself I would directly we came down here. Now you know what belongs to you, though of course you knew before."

"Forgive me for having been a fool," said George. "Here's my hand; such a fat one. There is not a ring upon it."

"Where are they?"

"I threw them out of the window. Perhaps they rolled into the wheal and will be dug out some day."

"Some one will say they belonged to the time of the Druids."

"When they were the chains of a girl's captivity."

"Winnie—dearest Dimples, why didn't I know before?" cried George. "It was all my own fault."

"It wasn't mine. Nothing has ever been my fault, and I have kept my promises. I said I would fight myself well, and here I am."

Very fresh and pretty she was too in her light clothing. There were no dirty boots, there was no mud on her petticoat; she looked almost the same as that pink girl who had sat on that same stone and listened to that same man following the course of the Perambulators. There were some little lines on her face, which the cottage upon St. Piran's sands had left behind, and there was a faint shadow beneath each eye; but George called them beauty marks, and so they were. Her flaxen hair was fluffy in the breeze, and the golden twilight dropped an aureole around it.

"Promise me one more thing, darling—never to be ill again."

"Why yes, I'll promise that too. I must have little illnesses, colds and headaches, but I won't have any more big ones. Just think, Gee, of all the time I have wasted in bed when I might have been brushing your coat. Where are those old clothes?" she asked sternly, though Winnie's attempt at sternness was like a rose trying not to smell nice.

"They are in a box somewhere. I should have worn them again if I had lost you."

"I shall give them to Bill, and tell him to burn them —all except that dear old coat. I shall keep that," said Winnie brightly, "and brush it once a week."

"It will fall to pieces," laughed George.

"Then I shall sew it together again."

"Now, darling," said he, turning and looking up at her, "let us talk away the biggest of our difficulties."

Winnie left the stone, sat on the grass beside him, and put her head upon his shoulder.

"Any one looking?" she murmured.

"The oaks and bracken and the stepping-stones of the Ford. The blackberries will be ripe next month," cried George. "I told you St. Michael's blackberries are the finest in the world. We must make some jam, Winnie."

"Oh yes, we will do everything that's lonely and lovely; but we mustn't wander off now. We will have the nasty talk and then the nice talk. You are not going to blame me, Gee?" she asked wistfully. "When you think of anything I have done you must say to yourself, 'It wasn't her fault.' You will remember she had a mother to keep, and a home to get somehow, and she was very weak-minded and a dreadful little corpse when they pulled her off the moor."

"The only person to be blamed is myself," said George.

"That's far enough from the truth to be nearly a wicked story. Well, I'm going to shut my eyes and you are going to ask horrid questions. We will get it all over before the light leaves those rocks— the rocks of the moon you called them. You see I remember everything."

"Here we go then," said George. "Have you heard anything of that man?"

Winnie made her well-known movement in the negative, then said quickly, "He doesn't know where I am. Thinks I am dead, probably, and doesn't care."

"I told the doctor he was dead."

"So he is—to us."

"But you are still his—"

"I am not. He went off with that—Oh, Gee, the awful face that girl had."

"The only thing will be a divorce."

"I won't have that," said Winnie, starting up and opening her eyes. "I am not going to have your name dragged in the dirt. What a sordid business it would be, what horrible things would have to come out, and how people would gloat over what they would call the sensational details in the life of the young woman whom the famous artist, George Brunacombe, wanted to marry. It might do you a lot of harm. People would say you aren't respectable; they love to fling dirt at a well-known man. And as for me; well, I should be something especially terrible from the pit of corruption."

"But, darling"

"Let me talk," said Winnie. "You can't arrange anything, because you are always thinking of me. I can do it much better. Gee, dearest old boy, I love you, and I am going to live with you as your wife and take your name if you will give it me. It's not as if anybody would know, and that man will never try to find me again, and if he did you wouldn't let him come near me."

"Bill would throw him down the wheal," said George savagely.

"He couldn't harm me because he would be afraid of his own life being exposed. Do I seem very shameless? It's for your sake, and there is Bubo to think of too. How flustered he would be if they put him into the witness-box. Ever since the dark and awful time in Tomkins Street I have been trying to help myself. Now I have got to help the firm as well. You see I can be strong-minded when I like," said Winnie impertinently.

"Dimples darling, I am so afraid the truth might come out."

"Let it. Do you care?"

"Not a straw."

"I don't either. The truth wouldn't get beyond Dartmoor, and your fame is in the world. Now there is the child," said Winnie, with a little gasp, shutting her eyes again. "It's your turn to talk, Gee. Go on."

"You must tell me what you want, dear."

"Whatever you want."

"We had better leave her where she is. She is well cared for. And if we like her later on—and there is nothing mentally or morally wrong—"

"We can adopt her," murmured she. "Yes, that's settled. There's no time for any more talk, horrid talk, for the light is nearly off the rocks, and we must go home. Oh, it's a lovely home at Wheal Dream."

"I shall make inquiries. The police will know the man," said George. "I want you bound to me, sweet Dimples."

"So I am with all my heart-strings. What a lot he wants," said she merrily. "He thinks I'll run away from him," she said to St. Michael's Ford. Then she became serious. "Gee, let's marry now in this golden twilight, let's have a wonderful dreamland marriage."

Up she jumped, crying, "Come along, if you love me. I am so well, so strong. I am never going to die now."

"Where are you going, sweetheart?"

"To church. Come along quick, or the doors will be shut, and St. Michael will have gone home to supper. Surely St. Michael is a good enough parson for us. Come along, Gee, to the green shelf above the waterfall, and we'll be married there."

"Where's the ring, darling?"

"I'll make one. Here's a stalk of heather. It bends but it won't break. Here is the ring. You mustn't laugh, Gee, or St. Michael will be cross and say we must come again another day. Now we cross the Ford. Then for the bank of violets—it will be all dark-green in this light, and the waterfall will be thundering like an organ."

George entered into her mood. He saw what she wanted, that they should vow fidelity to one another above the waterfall. It was to be their marriage ceremony, and the only one they were likely to have; and what could be better when the heart was right? Cupid laughs at convention. He sets up the idol and riddles it into rags with his arrows. They were children of the moor, and they were to be joined together like earth and sun in the invisible bonds and splendid warmth of a passionately chaste love.

They crossed the Ford; their figures could be seen between the oaks. Then they began to sing; and so they passed away to where the waterfall was thundering, and St. Michael came hurrying down from his ruined chapel and asked why they had been so long.

George did make inquiries; but it was some time before he learnt how Halfacre had broken down in every way, and had been compelled to seek the shelter of the cottage home where he had been born; nor was it long afterwards when the two maiden ladies, who had befriended the poor scholar through his short and strange existence, received a dirty and illiterate letter; and they read—

"Dear Madams,

"I am Sorry to tell you poor Richard had to be taken away to the Silam on Wendsday Morning his Mine was gott so bad I could not stay in the house. He took out A knife to kill me Once and he would not pull his Cloths off. We could not stop in the house were He was and He wrote letters to some of the Gentry and throwed stones at there Motocar the Doctor said it was not safe to stay in the house were He was and He was A terror to the Village and He must be put away it is sad Many thanks for your kindness in the past yours truely,

"John Halfacre."

THE END

ANNOTATIONS

INTRODUCTORY – ABOUT THE LITTLE HOUSE ON THE ROOF

"...The ancient Hoga de Cossdone, now called Cawsand Beacon..." Cawsand Beacon is a prominent hill on the northern extremity of Dartmoor, England. It is a landmark which was used as a site of beacon fire to warn of impending invasion. There are an estimated 5,000 hut circles still surviving on the moor, despite the fact that many have been raided over the centuries by the builders of the traditional dry stone walls. These are the remnants of Bronze Age houses. The smallest huts are approximately six feet in diameter and the largest may be up to five times that size.

"Yet the roc existed in the form of the dinornis..." The giant moa (Dinornis) is an extinct genus of ratite birds belonging to the moa family. Like all ratites it was a member of the order Struthioniformes. The Struthioniformes were flightless birds with a sternum without a keel and that had a distinctive palate. The dinornis was endemic to New Zealand and may have been the tallest bird that ever lived.

CHAPTER I - ABOUT PATIENTS

"'...like the man who did open-air treatment in the Bible....'" Open-air treatment was a treatment believed to cure tuberculosis. In the Gospel of John, Jesus visits the pool at Bethesda to heal a man who has been bedridden for many years and could not make his own way into the pool in order to be cured of his illness. This is likely the source of the simile used by Trevena.

"... a Balliol scholar." A student from Balliol College. Balliol College, founded in 1263, is one of the constituent colleges of the University of Oxford in England. Traditionally, the undergraduates from this college are among the most politically active in the university and the college's alumni include three former Prime Ministers.

"...makes the rabbit nerveless when it sees the stoat." The stoat is also known as the ermine or short-tailed weasel.

"...and told her to go to St. Michael's Ford..." This location refers to a ford along a bridge and across the River Ver in Hertfordshire, England. The current bridge is near St. Michael's village and some form of a bridge is believed to have existed there since ancient Roman times.

"...Miss Budge was told to go to Downacombe..." Downacombe is a fictitious place name in this novel. It means, literally, down from a combe. A combe is a small, deep valley running down to a sea; also, a bowl-shaped, generally unwatered valley or hollow on the flank of a hill.

"...along the road towards Wheal Dream." Wheal Dream is most likely a fictitious location in this novel. Wheal is the Cornish word for mine. The tale of how the place received its name from a dream that a miner had is described in Chapter II.

"...of St. Michael's chapel of Halstock." Halstock is a village in Dorset, England. It lies within the West Dorset administrative district of the county and is about five miles south of the town of Yeovil in Somerset. Helstock is on the route of the ancient Harrow Way.

CHAPTER II - ABOUT WHEAL DREAM

"...but the name of Wheal Dream must have been bestowed in Stannary times." Stannary times refers to the time period when tin mining occurred in the West Country. King Edward I's 1305 Stannary Charter established Tavistock, Ashburton and Chagford as stannary towns in Devon County, with a monopoly on all tin mining in Devon, a right to representation in the Stannary Parliament and a right to the jurisdiction of the Stannary Courts. Plympton became the fourth Devon stannary town in 1328. The Devon stannary towns are all on the fringes of Dartmoor.

"..., she was socially above the poor spadiard..." A spadiard was the name for a worker in the tin mines; also called a spalliard.

"...with the law as established by the body of the Stannary in the High Court of Crockern Tor..." Crockern Tor is a granite rock outcropping in Dartmoor. It is composed of two large outcrops of rock. The lower outcrop was the open-air meeting place of the Devonshire Stannary Parliament from the early 14th century until the first half of the 18th century.

"The bailiff of Lydford issued his tin-warrant." Lydford, also spelled Lidford, is a village, once an important town, in Devon situated seven miles north of Tavistock on the western fringe of Dartmoor.

"'To lie therein one night, 'tis guess'd...'" Lines of verse about the castle at Lydford in the reign of James I. They were written by the poet, William Browne (1590-1645), who lived in Tavistock. He was the author of "Brittania's Pastorals" (1613).

"...owned by the Duchy of Cornwall." The eldest son of the reigning British monarch inherits the duchy and title of Duke of Cornwall at the time of his birth or of his parent's succession to the throne. If the monarch has no son, the estates of the duchy are held by the crown, and there is no duke.

"...during the reign of Henry the Seventh..." Henry VII (1457 – 1509) was King of England and Lord of Ireland from seizing the crown on August 22, 1485 until his death on April 21, 1509, as the first monarch of the House of Tudor.

"'...you may join the Seventh Day Adventists or the Plymouth Brethren if you like.'" The Seventh Day Adventist Church is a Protestant Christian denomination distinguished by its observance of Saturday, the original seventh day of the Judeo-Christian week, as the Sabbath, and by its emphasis on the imminent second coming, or Advent, of Jesus Christ. The denomination grew out of the Millerite movement in the United States during the middle part of the 19th century and was formally established in 1863. The Plymouth Brethren is a conservative, Evangelical Christian movement, whose history can be traced to Dublin, Ireland, in the late 1820s.

"...Elijah running before the chariot of Ahab towards the gates of Jezreel,..." This is a Biblical reference to a story about the prophet Elijah as recorded in 1 Kings 18:45.

"...in the atmosphere of Fitzroy Street." A street located in Fitzrovia, a neighborhood in central London, near London's West End lying partly in the London Borough of Camden (in the east) and partly in the City of Westminster (in the west). The neighborhood is situated between Marylebone and Bloomsbury and north of Soho. The historically bohemian area was once home to such writers as Virginia Woolf, George Bernard Shaw and Arthur Rimbaud.

"He came of a Devonshire family, the Brunacombes of Plympton,..." Plympton, in south-western Devon, England is an ancient stannary town. It was an important trading center in the past for locally mined tin, and a former seaport before the River Plym silted up and trade moved down the river to Plymouth.

"...a lady who had married his uncle and lived somewhere in the West End..." Located to the west of the historic Roman and Mediaeval City of London, the West End was long favored by the rich elite as a place of residence because it was usually upwind of the smoke drifting from the crowded city. It was also located close to the royal seat of power at Westminster, and is largely contained within the City of Westminster. Developed in the 17th, 18th and 19th centuries, it was originally built as a series of palaces, expensive town houses, fashionable shops and places of entertainment.

"...as a sort of rival to the Zoological Gardens." The London Zoological Gardens opened for scientific study in 1828 and to the public in 1847.

"...a farmhouse near Two Bridges." Two Bridges is an isolated location in the heart of Dartmoor National Park in Devon, England. It is situated around two miles north east of Princetown on the old turnpike road which was built across Dartmoor in the late 18th century.

"...he reached the little village of Metheral,..." Metheral, or Metherell, is a village in east Cornwall. It is situated three miles east of Callington and two miles west of Calstock village in Calstock civil parish.

CHAPTER III – ABOUT A MIXED FAMILY

"...a large escallonia which grew beside the wall of the church..." Escallonia is a genus of flowering plants of the Escalloniaceae family. Commonly used as a hedge plant, it grows about one foot per year, and reaches between four to eight feet in height. Escallonia flowers from June to October, when it displays masses of rosy crimson flowers with a honey fragrance.

"...the last commandment was shattered..." The last of the Ten Commandments in the Bible is that "thou shalt not covet thy neighbour's wife, nor his manservant, nor his maidservant, nor his ox, nor his ass, nor any thing that is thy neighbour's."

"...Downacombe-beside-the-moor." This is a fictitious location in Dartmoor.

"...to watch the white mist rolling down the dark cleave of the Okement." This phrase refers to the River Okement, a tributary of the River Torridge in Devon. It was formerly known as the River Ock. It rises at two places in Dartmoor, as the West Okement and the East Okement. These meet with other minor streams and join together at Okehampton. The river flows generally north, past the villages of Jacobstowe and Monkokehampton and has its confluence with the River Torridge near Meeth.

CHAPTER IV – ABOUT GREGORY BREAKBACK

"The place has no recognised name; some call it Moor Down..." This location is fictitious.

"'...to Sheviock which is by St. Germans.'" Sheviock is a coastal civil parish and a hamlet in south-east Cornwall, The parish is two miles south of St Germans and three miles south-west of Saltash.

CHAPTER V – ABOUT A RECTOR AND HIS VISITORS

"The Twins alluded to him as Father Abraham, because that patriarch is generally represented in art as a slovenly kind of gentleman with an untrimmed beard." In the Old Testament of the Bible, Abraham was regarded as the father of Israel. Since he was an old man by the time he conceived a son, he was often depicted in art as having a long beard.

"Leigh often saw the Wesleyan pastor hurrying by the rectory garden..." A Wesleyan pastor was a follower of Methodism, a movement of Protestant Christianity. The movement traces its roots to John Wesley's evangelistic revival movement within Anglicanism. His younger brother Charles was instrumental in writing much of the hymnody of the Methodist Church. George Whitefield, another significant leader in the movement, was known for his unorthodox ministry of itinerant open-air preaching.

"They forgot to burn it last fifth of November." November 5th is an annual holiday in England. It is known as Guy Fawkes Day and Gunpowder Day. It commemorates the infamous Gunpowder Conspiracy of 1605. It was led by Guy Fawkes. The holiday is celebrated with fireworks and bonfires.

"'He's supposed to be going round Sampford lanes,...'" This place name may refer to either Sampford Courtenay or Sampford Peverell, both villages in Devon.

"'I'm not a nurse to clank about with a chatelaine.'" A chatelaine is a set of short chains on a belt worn by women and men for carrying keys, thimble and sewing kit, etc.

"'You must cut gypsophila....'" Gypsophila is commonly known as baby's-breath in the United States and Canada and "soap wort" in the United Kingdom. Its botanical name means "lover of chalk", which is accurate in describing the type of soil in which the plant grows.

CHAPTER VI - ABOUT THE FORD WHICH LIETH ON THE EAST SIDE OF ST. MICHAEL'S CHAPEL OF HALSTOCK

"...like the wild convolvulus..." Convolvulus is a genus of about 200 species of flowering plants in the bindweed family

Convolvulaceae, with a cosmopolitan distribution. Common names include bindweed and morning glory.

"...Caesar fell at the foot of Pompey's statue. Roman agents must have crossed there, wondering what was the latest prank of mad Nero or guzzling Vitellius. Keen, bearded Jews must have crossed cursing the name of Titus. Danish freebooters crossed on their destructive mission." Gnaeus Pompeius Magnus, also known as Pompey or Pompey the Great (106 BC –48 BC), was a military and political leader of the late Roman Republic. He came from a wealthy Italian provincial background, and established himself in the ranks of Roman nobility by successful leadership in several military campaigns. Pompey joined his rival Marcus Licinius Crassus and his ally Julius Caesar in the unofficial military-political alliance known as the First Triumvirate. Pompey was defeated at the Battle of Pharsalus and sought refuge in Egypt, where he was assassinated. His career and defeat are significant in Rome's subsequent transformation from Republic to Principate and Empire. Nero Claudius Caesar Augustus Germanicus(37 AD –68 AD) was Roman Emperor from 54 to 68, and the last in the Julio-Claudian dynasty. During his reign, Nero focused much of his attention on diplomacy, trade, and enhancing the cultural life of the Empire. He ordered theaters built and promoted athletic games. In 64, most of Rome was destroyed in a great fire, which many Romans believed Nero himself had started in order to clear land for his planned palatial complex, the Domus Aurea. Aulus Vitellius Germanicus Augustus (15 AD – 69 AD), was Roman Emperor for eight months, from April to December 69). Vitellius was acclaimed Emperor following the quick succession of the previous emperors Galba and Otho, in a year of civil war known as the Year of the Four Emperors. Vitellius' claim to the throne was challenged by legions stationed in the eastern provinces, who proclaimed their commander Vespasian emperor instead. War ensued, leading to a crushing defeat for Vitellius at the Second Battle of Bedriacum in northern Italy. Once he realized his support was wavering, Vitellius prepared to abdicate in favor of Vespasian, but was executed in Rome by Vespasian's soldiers. Titus Flavius Caesar Vespasianus Augustus (39 AD –81 AD), was Roman Emperor from 79 to 81 AD. A member of the Flavian dynasty, Titus succeeded his father Vespasian upon his death, thus becoming the first Roman Emperor to come to the throne after his own father. Prior to becoming Emperor, Titus gained renown as a military commander, serving under his father in Judaea during the First Jewish-Roman War. The campaign came to a brief halt with the death of emperor Nero in 68 AD, launching

Vespasian's bid for the imperial power during the Year of the Four Emperors. When Vespasian was declared Emperor on July 1, 69 AD, Titus was left in charge of ending the Jewish rebellion. In 70 AD, he successfully laid siege to and destroyed the city and Temple of Jerusalem. Freebooter is another term for a pirate.

"...'is the beloved brother, our Richard, Earl of Cornwall,' and his followers are Henry de Mereton, Hamelin de Eudon, Robert de Halyun, and William le Pruz, bloody men of battle in their day..." Richard of Cornwall (1209 – 1272) was Count of Poitou (from 1225 to 1243), 1st Earl of Cornwall (from 1225) and German King (formally "King of the Romans", from 1257). One of the wealthiest men in Europe, he also joined the Sixth Crusade, where he achieved success as a negotiator for the release of prisoners, and assisted with the building of the citadel in Ascalon. He was made High Sheriff of Berkshire at the age of only eight, was styled Count of Poitou from 1225 and in the same year, at the age of sixteen, his brother King Henry III gave him Cornwall as a birthday present, making him High Sheriff of Cornwall. Richard's revenues from Cornwall provided him with great wealth, and he became one of the wealthiest men in Europe. Though he campaigned on King Henry's behalf in Poitou and Brittany, and served as Regent three times, relations were often strained between the brothers in the early years of Henry's reign. Richard rebelled against him three times, and had to be bought off with lavish gifts. As the second son of King John, he had to wait to be crowned as King.

"...the portrait of Albert Durer..." Albrecht Dürer (1471 – 1528) was a German painter, printmaker, engraver, mathematician, and theorist from Nuremberg. His prints established his reputation across Europe when he was still in his twenties, and he has been conventionally regarded as the greatest artist of the Northern Renaissance ever since. His vast body of work includes altarpieces and religious works, numerous portraits and self-portraits, and copper engravings. His woodcuts, such as the Apocalypse series (1498), retain a more Gothic flavour than the rest of his work.

"'...but I have an idea that Henry the Third lived several years ago.'" Henry III (1207 – 1272) was the son and successor of John as King of England, reigning for 56 years from 1216 until his death. His contemporaries knew him as Henry of Winchester. He was the first child king in England since the reign of Æthelred the Unready. England prospered during his reign and his greatest monument is Westminster, which he made the seat of his government and where he expanded the abbey as a shrine to Edward the Confessor.

"'...William de la Brewer; and the two behind who are racing for the last stepping-stone are Guido de Brettvill and William de Wydworthy. The tall knight just about to cross is Hugo de Bollay, and near him is Richard Giffard...'" These names are probably fictitious, although a William Brewer was High Sheriff of Berkshire during 1190, 1193 and 1201 and the name Richard Giffard appears at several times and places in ancient sources.

"'At his shoulder is Odo de Treverbyn looking at the antlers of a stag which he has found in the grass; and here, coming down the steep path leading from the chapel—that path is there if you know where to look for it—is William Trenchard, assisting Philip Parrer, who has hurt his leg; while close to them is Nicholas de Heampton, or Highampton, cutting an ash stick with his sword. Behind them you can just see William Morleigh...'" Again, these names are most likely fictitious. Apparently, an Odo de Treverbyn lived during the 1200s. He was born in Sheviock, Cornwall and died in 1253. William Trenchard may have been an actual person.

"After leaving Cawsand they made beside Raybarrow Pool to Hound Tor, which they called the Hill of Little Hound Tor. Their next point was Thurlestone, which is the tracker's first difficulty; the jurors in the sixth year of our most gracious sovereign, Lord James, got over it by supposing this to be Watern Tor...'" Raybarrow Pool is one of Dartmoor's more extensive bogs and a dangerous one to walk through. Little Hound Tor is a tor in Dartmoor that is southwest of Raybarrow Pool and Hound Tor is south of Little Hound Tor. Thurlestone is a village five miles west of Kingsbridge in the South Hams district in south Devon. It takes its name from Thurlestone Rock, the so-called "thirled stone", an arch-shaped rock formation just offshore in Thurlestone Bay. Watern Tor is located in north-east Dartmoor.

"'...East Wallabrook to the point where the West joins it, and on to where the united rivers fall into the North Teign at Walbrook Bridge, which is just on the other side of Scorhill with its stone remains. There what is called the North Quarter ends...'" East Wallabrook is situated near Brentor, Tavistock, Devon. Like many other Devon rivers, the River Teign rises on Dartmoor, near Cranmere Pool. Its course on the moor is crossed by a clapper bridge near Teigncombe, just below the prehistoric Kestor Settlement. It exits the moor at its eastern side, flowing beneath Castle Drogo in a steep-sided valley. Scorhill refers to the Scorill Stone Circle, now the commonly known name for Gidleigh Stone Circle or Steep Hill Stone Circle. It is one of Devon's biggest and most intact stone circles and is found on Gidleigh Common near the village of Gidleigh in the north east of Dartmoor.

"'Devon gave England tobacco, her navy, and Walter Raleigh...'" Sir Walter Raleigh (1554 – 1618), born in Devon, was an English aristocrat, writer, poet, soldier, courtier, spy, and explorer. He is also well known for popularizing tobacco in England and rose rapidly in the favour of Queen Elizabeth I; he was knighted in 1585. Raleigh was involved in the early English colonization of Virginia under a royal patent. In 1591 he secretly married Elizabeth Throckmorton, one of the Queen's ladies-in-waiting, without the Queen's permission, for which he and his wife were sent to the Tower of London. After his release, they retired to his estate at Sherborne, Dorset.

"'...they went on to Castor Rock...'" Trevena's geography lesson of Dartmoor continues with many other place names included.

"'I paint while it is light and write doggerel after dark....'" Doggerel is a derogatory term for poetic verse that is considered to have little literary value.

CHAPTER VII - ABOUT JARS

"...sang his hymns about the other side of Jordan..." In the Hebrew Bible, the Jordan is referred to as the source of fertility to a large plain and it is said to be like "the garden of God." It is noted as the line of demarcation between the "two tribes and the half tribe" settled to the east (Numbers 34:15) and the "nine tribes and the half tribe of Manasseh" that, led by Joshua, settled to the west (Joshua 13:7). Numerous hymns in the Christian church refer to the Jordan River which, in the New Testament of the Bible, was the river in which Jesus was baptized by John the Baptist.

"...across a little Hoga where the whist hounds and the wind were always hunting..." In the Dartmoor area there is a legend about a wild huntsman who rides with Whist or Yell Hounds. Known as the "Midnight Hunter of the Moor" he rides a huge, dark, flame-breathing horse. The fiery-eyed dogs with salivating jaws are held to be a portent of death within a year of being seen. They are said to hound unwary travellers until they plunge to their doom below Dewerstone Rock. One local legend says the whist hounds are led by Sir Francis Drake (1545-96). This tale may have inspired Sir Conan Doyle to write The Hound of the Baskervilles."

"'...if yew lives as long as Arethusalum.'" The name is a bastardization of the Biblical name "Methuselah." Methuselah, the grandfather of Noah, is the oldest person whose age is mentioned in the Hebrew Bible. According to the biblical text, he died at the age of

969, seven days before the beginning of the Great Flood. The name Methuselah, or the phrase "old as Methuselah," is commonly used to refer to any living thing that reaches a very old age.

"'Where be the money yew got vor putting your crosses to they papers avore witnesses?'" This statement refers to the manner in which an illiterate person executed legal documents. It was acceptable for the person to sign their name with a mark (normally an "X" or cross) and to have that act observed by others who were able to sign their names to the document as witnesses.

"The sanatorium became a golden calf set up in their midst, and we all know what happens when that idol is erected." The metaphor of a golden calf refers to the gold idol in the form of a calf that was constructed by Aaron to satisfy the Israelite people as they grew tired of waiting for Moses to return from Mount Sinai, where he received the Ten Commandments. Moses was so angry with his people for their idolatry that he threw down the tablets on which God's law had been written, breaking them. Moses burnt the golden calf in a fire, ground it to powder, scattered it on water, and forced the Israelites to drink it.

CHAPTER VIII - ABOUT A HALF-HOLIDAY

"They were all as keen after pounds of flesh as so many Shylocks." Shylock is a fictional character in Shakespeare's *The Merchant of Venice* and is also a term used to describe "someone who lends money at excessive rates of interest." The character's name has become a synonym for loan shark, and as a verb to shylock means to lend money at exorbitant rates. In addition, the phrase "pound of flesh" has also entered the lexicon as slang for a particularly onerous or unpleasant obligation.

"...where he could get a service flavoured with a spice of Romanism..." Romanism refers to the beliefs and practices of the Catholic Church based in Rome.

"...the old streamworks beneath Steeperton..." Steeperton is the name of a tor in Dartmoor. The conical mound of Steeperton dominates Taw marsh. The name derives from "Steep down" and, apart from the gentle southern slope, it is an unusually steep granite hill. Two streams, the Taw and Steeperton Brook, flow on either side of it and meet at the base of the hill before flowing into the flat plain that contains Taw Marsh.

"'twas his father who gave him his name, and I say it was the Workhouse Guardians.'" In England and Wales a workhouse was a place where people who were unable to support themselves were offered accommodation and employment. Each workhouse was operated by a locally elected board of guardians, comprising representatives from each of the participating parishes.

"...across the sand flats of Barnstaple..." Barnstaple is a town and civil parish in the local government district of North Devon. It lies 68 miles west southwest of Bristol, 50 miles north of Plymouth and 34 miles northwest of Exeter. It is the main town of the district and claims to be the oldest borough in the United Kingdom. It was founded at the lowest crossing point of the River Taw, about three miles from the Taw's seafall at the Bristol Channel.

"'Lavater says so. I have been trying to think of the animal type that you represent.'" Lavater Johann Kaspar Lavater (1741 – 1801) was a Swiss poet and physiognomist.

"'...that you resemble Helen in your sway over the hearts of men." This metaphor refers to Helen of Troy, the famous character of Greek mythology. Helen was considered to be the most beautiful and desirable woman in the Greek world and was the wife of Menelaus, King of Sparta. She was seduced by and escaped with Paris, a prince, to his native city of Troy. Her abduction led Menelaus to assemble a contingent of armies from all over Greece to fight for Helen's return. The events led to the mythical Trojan War. Thus Helen's beauty was claimed to have launched a thousand ships.

"'In Keyham,' she gasped." Keyham is an Edwardian area of Plymouth. It was built to provide dense cheap housing just outside the wall of HM Dockyard Devonport for the thousands of civilian workmen. In the mid-19th century, the dockyards were smaller and Keyham was regarded as a distinct location from Devonport itself.

"'At Princetown in the middle of the moor, up in the clouds,...'" Princetown is a town situated on Dartmoor. In 1785, Sir Thomas Tyrwhitt, Secretary to the Prince of Wales, leased a large area of moorland from the Duchy of Cornwall estate, hoping to convert it into good farmland. He encouraged people to live in the area and suggested that a prison be built there. He called the settlement Princetown after the Prince of Wales. Princetown is best known as the site of Dartmoor Prison. It is the highest town on the moor, and one of the highest in the United Kingdom.

CHAPTER IX - ABOUT ANOTHER HALF-HOLIDAY

"'...which is all I get from the lineal descendant of Barabbas..." A lineal descendant of Barabbas would be a Jew. Barabbas is a figure in the Christian narrative of the Passion of Jesus, in which he is the insurrectionary whom Pontius Pilate freed at the Passover feast in Jerusalem instead of Jesus. Pilate gave the crowd a choice of freeing the criminal Barabbas or Jesus, and the crowd demanded the release of Barabbas instead. This choice paved the way for the crucifixion of Jesus. The story of Barabbas has special social significance, because it has historically been used to lay the blame for the crucifixion of Jesus on the Jews and to justify anti-Semitism.

"'...after it had run aground on Ararat.'" According to the Bible, the ark constructed by Noah to survive the Great Flood rested finally on Mount Ararat when the waters receded. Ararat is a snow-capped, dormant volcanic cone in Turkey.

"'The little rascal is as ragged as Diogenes.'" Diogenes the Cynic (412 or 404 BCE – 323 BCE) was a Greek philosopher and one of the founders of Cynic philosophy. Diogenes was a controversial figure and made a virtue of poverty. He begged for a living and slept in a tub in the marketplace.

"'Here is the river where it is divided into several branches like the one in Paradise.'" The Biblical description of the Garden of Eden states that a river flowed out of it; and from there it divided and became four rivers: Pishon; Gihon; Tigris and Euphrates.

CHAPTER X - ABOUT MATRIMONY AND THE LANE WHICH WAS CALLED MORTGABLE

"...and play the old village game of Tom-come-tickle-me while he was getting his trousers on." An old parlor game in which the object was not to laugh when someone tickled your knee.

"'...but as the smiling philosopher would have said, "One man can't get into two lots o' clothes."'" Democritus (460-370 B.C.), a Greek thinker in the time of Socrates, was known as the "Smiling Philosopher" or "Laughing Philosopher." According to legend, Democritus put out his own eyes so that he might think more clearly and not be diverted in his meditations. Some ancient writers stated that he became so perfect in his teachings that he went about continually smiling from which circumstance he became known as the Laughing Philosopher; but others say that the inhabitants of Abdera, the colony in Thrace where Democritus was born, were notorious for their stupidity, and that he was called the "laughing" Philosopher because of the scorn and ridicule that he heaped upon his townsmen for their ignorance.

"...came striding in with the pie, which old Risdon, had he been living and present, would certainly have classed among his "remarkable things" in the Forest of Dartmoor." Old Risdon is a reference to Tristram Risdon (c. 1580 – 1640), an English antiquary and topographer. He was the author of *Survey of the County of Devon*. He was able to devote most of his life to writing this work. It was structured like a travel book as the author passed from one parish to another.

"...he delivered a panegyric in the heroic style upon turnip-pie." A panegyric is a formal public speech, or (in later use) written verse, delivered in high praise of a person or thing, a generally highly studied and discriminating eulogy, not expected to be critical.

CHAPTER XI - ABOUT ST. MICHAEL'S WHITE VIOLETS AND GREEN OAK

"One or two of the Fates..." In Greek mythology, the Moirai, often known in English as The Fates, were white-robed incarnations of destiny. There were three of theme: Clotho (spinner), Lachesis (alloter) and Atropos (unturnable). They controlled the metaphorical thread of life of every mortal from birth to death. They were independent, at the helm of necessity, directed fate, and watched that the fate assigned to every being by eternal laws might take its course without obstruction. Even the chief god, Zeus, had to submit to the power of the Fates.

"...fringed with grass of Parnassus." Mount Parnassus is a mountain of limestone in central Greece that towers above Delphi, north of the Gulf of Corinth, and offers scenic views of the surrounding olive groves and countryside. According to Greek mythology, this mountain was sacred to Apollo and the Corycian nymphs. It was also the home of the Muses.

"'There's a waterfall for you, Messrs. Abraham, Isaac and Jacob. That ought to straighten the Mosaic nose and cause the strings of the Aaronic purse to loosen.'" These are anti-Semitic remarks. The first mentions three major Old Testament persons who are father, son and grandson. The phrases "Mosaic nose" and "Aaronic purse" refer to Moses and his brother, Aaron.

"'...to reach from Epsom Hill to the Bankruptcy Court.'" Epsom is a town in the borough of Epsom and Ewell in Surrey, England. Some parts of Epsom are in the Borough of Reigate and Banstead. The town is located 18 miles south-south-west of Charing Cross, within the Greater London Urban Area.

"'...like a Botticelli picture.'" Alessandro di Mariano di Vanni Filipepi, better known as Sandro Botticelli, (c. 1445 – 1510) was an Italian painter of the Early Renaissance. He belonged to the Florentine school under the patronage of Lorenzo de Medici, a movement that Giorgio Vasari characterized less than one hundred years later as a "golden age." Among Botticelli's best known works are "The Birth of Venus" and "Primavera."

"...that he worked for a sorry pittance and the tribe of Judah..." This statement is anti-Semitic. According to the Hebrew Bible, the Tribe of Judah was one of the twelve Tribes of Israel. Following the completion of the conquest of Canaan by the Israelite tribes after about 1200 BCE, Joshua allocated the land among the twelve tribes. Bethlehem and Hebron were the main cities within the territory of the tribe.

CHAPTER XII - ABOUT THE GREAT DOWNACOMBE REBELLION

"...the feast of St. Margaret." This may refer to St. Margaret of Scotland. The feast of St. Margaret was formerly observed by the Roman Catholic Church on June 10th, but was later changed to the anniversary of her death, November 16th.

"...they had come to get the banns published." The banns of marriage, commonly known simply as the "banns" or "bans", are the public announcement in a Christian parish church of an impending marriage between two specified persons. It is commonly associated with the Church of England and with other denominations whose traditions are similar. The purpose of banns is to enable anyone to raise any canonical or civil legal impediment to the marriage, so as to prevent marriages that are invalid. Impediments vary between legal jurisdictions, but normally include a pre-existing marriage that has been neither dissolved nor annulled, a vow of celibacy, lack of consent, or the couple's being related within the prohibited degrees of kinship. Traditionally, banns were read from the pulpit and were usually published in the parish weekly bulletin. Prior to 1983, canon law required banns to be announced, or "asked", in the home parishes of both parties on three Sundays or Holy Days of Obligation prior to the marriage.

"'..., that the First Cause is unknowable and unrevealed...'" First cause is a philosophical argument. It refers to the Latin term "Primum movens", usually stated as the Prime mover or first cause in English. The philosophy of Aristotle used the term in the theological cosmological argument for the existence of God, and in cosmogony, the source of the cosmos or "all-being".

"...who had conducted a series of grand sire triplets..." Grandsire is one of the standard change ringing methods, which are methods of ringing church bells or handbells using a series of mathematical permutations rather than playing a melody. The Grandsire method is usually rung on an odd number of bells: Grandsire Doubles is rung on five working bells, Grandsire Triples on seven, Grandsire Caters on nine and Grandsire Cinques on eleven.

"...the Saturnian age towards which the red flag guides..." The Saturnian Age refers to the Age of Saturn. In ancient times it was believed to have been a peaceful time period, blessed with plenty, with abundance and no wars and harassing anxieties.

CHAPTER XIII - ABOUT WEIGHTS AND MEASURES

"'Phthisis?' asked the doctor quickly..." Phthisis is a Greek term for consumption. Around 460 BCE, Hippocrates identified phthisis as the most widespread disease of the times involving coughing up blood and fever, which was almost always fatal. Today, the disease is known as tuberculosis.

"...he could not draw a line between two characters. Vitellius and Constantine were alike to him, both Emperors and therefore oppressors; he could not perceive that one had been a man, the other a swine." Vitellius (15 – 69) was Roman Emperor for eight months, from April to December 69. He was described as lazy and self-indulgent, fond of eating and drinking, and an obese glutton, eating banquets four times a day and feasting on rare foods he obtained by using the Roman navy. For each banquet, he had himself invited to a different noble's house. He is even reported to have starved his own mother to death in order to fulfill a prophecy that he would rule long if his mother died first. Constantine the Great (c 272 – 337), also known as Constantine I or Saint Constantine, was Roman Emperor from 306 to 337. Well known for being the first Roman emperor to convert to Christianity, Constantine and Emperor Licinius jointly issued the Edict of Milan in 313, which proclaimed religious tolerance of all religions throughout the empire.

"'I'll plead the Gaming Act.'" In 1710, the Parliament of Great Britain enacted a law known as the Gaming Act. It was intended to curb gambling by prohibiting the use of gambling proceeds in loan transactions.

"Mudd began at once to whistle, 'Onward Christian soldiers,'..." The hymn "Onward Christian Soldiers" was written by Sabine Baring-Gould in 1865 and the music was composed by Arthur Sullivan in 1871. Sullivan named the tune "St. Gertrude." The hymn's theme is taken from references in the New Testament to the Christian being a soldier for Christ. In II Timothy 2:3, the Apostle Paul instructs the faithful as follows: "Thou therefore endure hardness, as a good soldier of Jesus Christ."

"'You live at Bideford, don't you?'" Bideford is a small port town on the estuary of the River Torridge in north Devon. It is located 27 miles north of Okehampton.

"'Bideford, Appledore, and all that bit of level land between the Torridge and the sea, are beastly unhealthy.'" Appledore is a village at the mouth of the River Torridge, about six miles west of Barnstaple and about three miles north of Bideford in Devon.

"...leaving poor Winnie at the mercy of Beelzebub." Beelzebub, literally "Lord of the Flies", is a Semitic deity that was worshiped in the Philistine city of Ekron. In later Christian and Biblical sources, he appears as a demon and the name of one of the seven princes of Hell.

"...that it would have required a regular Euroclydon to have swept it away." Euroclydon is a cyclonic tempestuous northeast wind which blows in the Mediterranean. It may specifically refer to the name of the Gregale wind from the Adriatic Gulf, which, according to Acts 27:14, wrecked the apostle Paul's ship on the coast of Malta on his way to Rome.

"...and he can gaze with sanity restored upon soothing heaps of mortar, mud and brickbats." A brickbat is a piece of a brick used as a weapon, usually thrown at someone in the hope of injuring them.

"'Plymstock—it's a horrid place, but there's a fine screen in the church.'" Plymstock is a civil parish and commuter suburb of Plymouth. It is situated on the east bank of the River Plym and is geographically and historically part of South Hams. It comprises the villages of Billacombe, Elburton, Goosewell, Hooe, Mountbatten, Oreston, Pomphlett, Staddiscombe, Turnchapel and Plymstock proper, the centrally located village after which the parish and suburb is named. The parish church is St Mary and All Saints.

"'You are among the minor prophets, although theologians might declare you to be apocryphal.'" The Minor Prophets or Twelve Prophets, occasionally Book of the Twelve, are the collection constituting the last books of the Old Testament. The terms "minor prophets" and "twelve prophets" can also refer to the twelve writers of these prophetic works: Hosea, Joel, Amos, Obadiah, Jonah, Micah, Nahum, Habakkuk, Zephaniah, Haggai, Zechariah, and Malachi. The term "apocryphal" is used with various meanings, including "hidden", "esoteric", "spurious", "of questionable authenticity", and "Christian texts that are not canonical". The general term is usually applied to the books in the Roman Catholic Bible, and the Eastern Orthodox Bible, but not the Protestant Bible because Protestants do not regard it as God's word.

"'...but one who is false to the etymology which has been forced upon him.'" Etymology is the study of the history of words, their origins, and how their form and meaning have changed over time.

"'...the short-eared strigidae.'" True owl or Typical owl (family Strigidae) are one of the two generally accepted families of Owls, the other being the barn owls (Tytonidae).

"'...bubonic plague.'" Bubonic plague is a zoonotic disease that circulates mainly among small rodents and their fleas. Without treatment, the bubonic plague kills about two out of three infected people within four days. Bubonic plague is generally believed to be the cause of the Black Death that swept through Europe in the 14th century and killed an estimated 25 million people, or 30–60% of the European population.

"'*A bas* respectability. *Conspuez* my grey beard.'" The French words "a bas" mean "down with" and the French verb "conspuez" means "you jeer".

"Every man who is a humbug regards others as humbugs..." A "humbug" is a person who tricks or deceives. It also means talk or behavior that is deceptive, dishonest, false, or insincere, often a hoax or jest.

"...peruse the feuilleton in a halfpenny newspaper." Feuilleton was originally a kind of supplement attached to the political portion of French newspapers, consisting chiefly of non-political news and gossip, literature and art criticism, a chronicle of the latest fashions, and epigrams, charades and other literary trifles. The feuilleton may be described as a "talk of the town" and a contemporary English-language example of the form is the "Talk of the Town" section of The New Yorker. In English newspapers, the term "feuilleton" referred to an installment of a serial story printed in one part of a newspaper.

"'...me information concerning the enclitic particles.'" Enclitic particles are words that are normally optional but when present give emphasis to certain elements in sentences. Just as the word particle means a small bit of matter, these words are typically fairly short. They are not the main part of the sentence and can actually be left out.

"'My pictures are on their way to the National Gallery and the Louvre.'" The National Gallery is an art museum on Trafalgar Square, London. It was founded in 1824. Unlike comparable art museums in continental Europe, the National Gallery was not formed by nationalizing an existing royal or princely art collection. It came into being when the British government bought 38 paintings from the heirs of John Julius Angerstein, an insurance broker and patron of the arts, in 1824. The Louvre is one of the world's largest museums, the most visited art museum in the world and a historic monument. A central landmark of Paris, it is located on the Right Bank of the Seine in the 1st arrondissement (district). The museum is housed in the Louvre Palace (Palais du Louvre) which began as a fortress built in the late 12th century under Philip II. The building was extended many times to form the Louvre Palace. In 1682, Louis XIV chose the Palace of Versailles for his household, leaving the Louvre primarily as a place to display the royal collection, including, from 1692, a collection of antique sculpture. During the French Revolution, the National Assembly decreed that the Louvre should be used as a museum, to display the nation's masterpieces. The museum opened in 1793 with an exhibition of 537 paintings, the majority of the works being royal and confiscated church property.

"'I'd have given him the half-Nelson and a whole Napoleon under your very eyes.'" In wrestling, a "nelson hold" (sometimes simply referred to as a nelson) is a grappling hold which is executed from the backside of the opponent. One or both arms are used to encircle the opponent's arm under the armpit, and secured at the opponent's neck. Several different nelson holds exist, including the half nelson, and they can be separated according to the positioning of the encircling arm or arms. The term "nelson" is supposedly named after the British war-hero Admiral Horatio Nelson, who used strategies based on surrounding the opponent to win the Battle of the Nile and the Battle of Trafalgar. A "whole Napoleon" is not a recognized grappling hold and probably is used by George Brunacombe in a sarcastic context.

CHAPTER XIV - ABOUT REALITIES AND UNREALITIES

"Gumm unobtrusively picked a nasturtium leaf." Tropaeolum, commonly known as Nasturtium, is a genus of roughly 80 species of annual and perennial herbaceous flowering plants. The most common use of the nasturtium plant in cultivation is as an ornamental flower. It grows easily and prolifically and is a self-seeding annual. All parts of the plant are edible.

"'Borage,' said the scholar shortly, and walked on." Borage, also known as the starflower, is an annual herb originating in Syria, but naturalized throughout the Mediterranean region, as well as Asia Minor, Europe, North Africa, and South America. It is bristly or hairy all over the stems and leaves; the leaves are alternate and simple. The flowers are complete and perfect with five narrow, triangular-pointed petals.

"'Perhaps Mr. Leigh is burning Nonconformists in his back garden.'" In England, after the Act of Uniformity 1662 a Nonconformist was an English subject who belonged to a non-Christian religion or any non-Anglican church. A person who also advocated religious liberty may also be more narrowly considered as such. English Dissenters (such as Puritans and Presbyterians) who violated the Act of Uniformity 1559 may retrospectively be considered Nonconformists, typically by practicing or advocating radical, sometimes separatist, dissent with respect to the Established Church. Presbyterians, Congregationalists, Baptists, Quakers (founded in 1648), were considered Nonconformists at the time of the 1662 Act of Uniformity. Later, as other groups formed, they were also considered Nonconformists. These included Methodists, Unitarians, and members of the Salvation Army.

"Downacombe had not been enchanted into a Leeds or Sheffield." Leeds is a city and metropolitan borough in West Yorkshire, England. Sheffield is a city and metropolitan borough of South Yorkshire. Its name derives from the River Sheaf, which runs through the city.

"'...what my man bought vor I to Barum vair when us wur courting.'" Barum is another name for Barnstaple, Devon. The origin of this name is obscure, but has been in use since pre-Saxon times and is probably of Roman origin. Mentioned by Shakespeare, the name Barum was revived and popularized in Victorian times. It was featured in several novels of the time.

"'Hear my law, O my people.'" This is a verse from Psalm 78.

"...what one clerk in holy orders described as a Christian Sacrament..." The catechism included in the *Anglican Book of Common Prayer* defines a sacrament as "an outward and visible sign of an inward and spiritual grace given unto us, ordained by Christ himself, as a means whereby we receive the same, and a pledge to assure us thereof." According to the Roman Catholic Church there are seven sacraments: Baptism (Christening); Confirmation (Chrismation); Holy Eucharist; Penance (Confession); Anointing of the Sick (part of the "Last Rites"); Holy Orders; and Matrimony (Marriage).

CHAPTER XV - ABOUT NOVEMBERITIS

"'I keep a Bradshaw on my bed when I'm having my holidays.'" The Bradshaw, named after Mr. George Bradshaw (1801-1853), more properly called Bradshaw's Monthly Railway Guide, was a booklet of railway timetables, published monthly, from 1839 to 1961.

Each booklet was characterized by a yellow cover and listed train timetables inside.

"'I've just done the Lake District very thoroughly.'" The Lake District, also commonly known as The Lakes, and, often adjectivally, as Lakeland, is a mountainous region in North West England. A popular holiday destination, it is famous not only for its lakes and its mountains (or fells) but also for its associations with the early 19th century poetry and writings of William Wordsworth and other Lake Poets.

"...hooted his patron goddess Minerva..." Minerva was the Roman goddess whom Romans from the Second Century BC onwards equated with the Greek goddess Athena. She was the virgin goddess of poetry, medicine, wisdom, commerce, weaving, crafts, magic. Minerva was often depicted with her sacred creature, an owl usually named as the "owl of Minerva", which symbolized her ties to wisdom.

"...to such insane practices as pentecostal dances and doll-Sundays..." Christians who adhere to the pentecostal faith believe they experience manifestations, or physical responses, of the Holy Spirit's presence. Two of the most well known examples are "dancing in the Spirit" and a form of prostration known as being "slain in the Spirit". Traditionally, dancing in the Spirit means that a single participant spontaneously 'dances' with eyes closed and without bumping into nearby persons or objects, obviously under the power and guidance of the Spirit. If the experience occurs, it is attributed to the belief that the worshipper has become so enraptured with God's presence that the Spirit takes control of physical motions as well as the spiritual and emotional being. Doll-Sunday was a special church service that occurred in certain parts of England during the Christmas season. Also known as "Old Clothes Service", Doll Sunday was a day when parishioners were asked to bring dolls, as well as bags of sweets to the service and to place them close to the altar as an offering.

"...just as the poor old Hebrew gentleman, who went out to pull a few sticks from some Hivite or Hittite hedge, was foredoomed to be caught into the moon..." In the Bible, the Hivites were one group of descendants of Canaan, son of Ham, according to the Table of Nations in Genesis 10 17. The Hittites were another such group. The Hebrew gentleman who picked up sticks and met with some fate was mentioned in Numbers 15:32-36. In those verses, it states that a man who picked up sticks during the Sabbath was brought before Moses and was stoned to death for not keeping the Sabbath holy.

"...a ball lying upon the carpet like a lost pleiad." Pleiad is a reference to the Pleiades of Greek mythology. They were seven sisters who were converted by Zeus into the stars of a constellation.

"'...Gregory is courting a woman round and about Downacot.'" Downacot is a fictitious place name.

"...as white as Meldon marble..." Meldon is a village in West Devon. Situated close to Okehampton, its best known feature is the Meldon Quarry, from which granite is extracted.

"'There wur a man who lived to Clovelly wance.'" Clovelly is a village in the Torridge district of Devon. It looks out over the Bristol Channel. Thick woods shelter it and render the climate so mild that even tender plants flourish there.

CHAPTER XVI - ABOUT CONTRASTS

"...Samuel Tozer of Vuzzypit parish..." The parish is fictitious.

"...under the not inappropriate heading of Mortehoe." Mortehoe is a village on the north coast of Devon near Woolacombe, It is sited on the hilly land behind Morte Point. A nearby village is Lee Bay.

"...cried the Princess Ilse when the hind of the Ilsenstein mountain dropped the little blue flower..." The Ilsenstesin mountain figures in a European folktale that gives the Forget Me Not flower its name. In the story, a shepherd was driving his flock over the Ilsenstein (mountain), when becoming weary, he leaned on his staff. The mountain instantly opened up to him, for his staff was made from the Springwort. Inside the mountain stood Princess Ilse who had invited the shepherd to fill his pockets with the hidden gold treasure. The shepherd was pleased to oblige the princess. Just as he was about to leave, his pockets stuffed, the princess called out: "Forget not the best!" She alluded to his wonder-working staff, but the shepherd misconstrued her, thinking instead she referred to the best gold. He left his staff against the wall of rock and began gathering up more gold. Just then, the mountain closed up and cut him in two.

"'...and singing, "Gentle Jesus, meek and mild"...'" This is the title of a hymn, the words of which were written by John Wesley in 1742. It is often considered to be a child's prayer or song. The first four lines of the poem are: "Gentle Jesus, meek and mild,/ Look upon a little child;/ Pity my simplicity,/ Suffer me to come to Thee." The music for the hymn was composed by Martin Shaw, who was born in 1875.

"'Yew'm on the way to the House, woman,...'" This statement refers to a work house. In England and Wales a workhouse was a place where persons who were unable to support themselves could find accommodation and employment.

"'I knaws Our Vaither and a main cruel lot o' hymns. Sings 'em to myself I du. "Lots o' wages left vor me," and "Rule Britannia," and "Onward, Christian Soldiers," though I bain't sure o' the words.'" The first of these song titles is either fictitious, an unpublished folk-song or an intentional (on the part of the author) misquotation. "Rule, Britannia!" is a British patriotic song, originating from the poem "Rule, Britannia" by James Thomson and set to music by Thomas Arne in 1740.

CHAPTER XVII - ABOUT EVICTIONS

"...playing the part of Simon Peter or the Virgin Mary..." Simon Peter or Saint Peter was an early Christian leader who was featured prominently in the New Testament Gospels and the Acts of the Apostles. The son of John or of Jonah, Simon Peter was from the village of Bethsaida in the province of Galilee. His brother Andrew was also an apostle. Peter is venerated in multiple churches and is regarded as the first Pope by the Catholic Church. The Virgin Mary was the mother of Jesus Christ.

"'...a nice little house in Plymouth town...'" Plymouth is a city and unitary authority area on the south coast of Devon about 190 miles south-west of London. It is situated between the mouths of the rivers Plym to the east and Tamar to the west, where they join Plymouth Sound. Since 1967, the City of Plymouth has included the suburbs of Plympton and Plymstock, which are on the east side of the River Plym. Throughout the Industrial Revolution, Plymouth grew as a major shipping port, handling imports and passengers from the Americas, while the neighboring town of Devonport grew as an important Royal Naval shipbuilding and dockyard town. The county boroughs of Plymouth and Devonport, and the urban district of East Stonehouse were merged in 1914 to form the single county borough of Plymouth—collectively referred to as The Three Towns.

"'Yew knaw the proverb, 'tis a rough wind what blows gude to nobody.'" The proverb "It is an ill wind turns to good" was published as early as 1580 in England. It essentially means that someone profits from every los and is used comfortingly in indicate that a misfortune may still bring benefit.

CHAPTER XVIII - ABOUT THE WILD GARDEN

"...she was going to Penzance for the winter..." Penzance is a town, civil parish, and port in Cornwall. It is the most westerly major town in Cornwall and is approximately 75 miles west of

Plymouth and 300 miles west-southwest of London. Situated in the shelter of Mount's Bay, the town faces south-east onto the English Channel, is bordered to the west by the fishing port of Newlyn, to the north by the civil parish of Madron and to the east by the civil parish of Ludgvan. The town's location gives it a temperate climate, milder than most of the rest of Britain.

"It is the Walpurgis month, when people run away from the wild garden because it frightens them..." Walpurgis Night (Walpurgisnacht) is a traditional spring festival on April 30 or May 1 in large parts of Central and Northern Europe. It is often celebrated with dancing and with bonfires to signify the arrival of Spring. It is exactly six months from All Hallows' Eve (Halloween). The current festival is, in most countries that celebrate it, named after the English missionary Saint Walburga (710 -777 or 779). As Walburga was canonized on May 1, 870, she became associated with May Day, especially in the Finnish and Swedish calendars.

"...a translation of Homer." In the Western classical tradition, Homer is the author of the ancient epics known as the *Iliad* and the *Odyssey*. Homer is revered as the greatest ancient Greek epic poet and his works lie at the beginning of the Western canon of literature. Herodotus estimates that Homer lived 400 years before Herodotus' own time, which would place him at around 850 BC. Other ancient sources claim that he lived much nearer to the supposed time of the Trojan War, in the early 12th century BC.

"'And the old man went out silently to the side of the roaring sea.'" This quote is from Book 1 of the *Iliad* where it states in the opening lines, depending on the translation, "So he spoke, and the old man in terror obeyed him and went silently away beside the murmuring sea beach." In this part of the story, that occurs prior to the commencement of the Trojan War, the leader of the Greek forces, Agamemnon, argues with a priest, Chryses. The priest had come to the Greek ships to find his daughter, Chryseis. She had been taken by Agamemnon as a slave and the Greek leader refused to release her from a ransom offered by Chryses. Instead, Agamemnon threatened Chryses, and the priest silently walked away by the shore line to pray to Apollo for revenge. In order to defend the honor of his priest, Apollo sent a plague sweeping through the Greek armies, and Agamemnon was forced to give Chryseis back in order to end the dispute.

"'...Why, when I was a child—' 'You thought as a child.'" This dialog is a paraphrase of a verse from 1 Corinthinans 13:11 that reads, in the King James Bible, as follows: "When I was a child, I spake as a child, I understood as a child, I thought as a child: but when I became a man, I put away childish things."

"'Bear up all the way. Remember Raleigh,' said Leigh." This statement refers to Sir Walter Raleigh. See annotation under Chapter VI.

CHAPTER XIX - ABOUT THE FESTIVAL OF CUPS

"'...when I appear like the youthful David, fresh from following the ewes great with young ones.'" The simile refers to the Biblical character David who, prior to becoming King of Israel, tended the sheep of his father, Jesse of Bethlehem.

"'This is a merry Christmas, by Bethlehem it is.'" Bethlehem was the city in which Jesus Christ, of the House of David, was born according to the New Testament of the Bible. It is a Palestinian city located in the central West Bank and approximately five miles south of Jerusalem.

"'...and Government taxed 'em tu, aw, two shilluns a year vor every hearthstone, and that wur a lot o' money four hundred years agone...'" In England, hearth tax, also known as hearth money, chimney tax, or chimney money, was a tax imposed by Parliament in 1662, to support the Royal Household of King Charles II. The tax was considered easier to establish the number of hearths than the number of people. One shilling was liable to be paid for every firehearth or stove, in all dwellings, houses, edifices or lodgings, and was payable at Michaelmas (September 29) and on Lady Day (March 25). The tax amounted to two shillings per hearth or stove per year. The hearth tax was intended to be fair, in that it fell more heavily upon those with multiple or larger residences.

"...they would sing one or two of Herrick's glorious Christmas hymns." Robert Herrick (1591 – 1674) was a seventeenth-century English poet and wrote over 2,500 poems, about half of which appear in his major work, Hesperides. He is well-known for his style and, in his earlier works, frequent references to lovemaking and the female body. His later poetry was more of a spiritual and philosophical nature. Herrick also wrote about English country life and its seasons, village customs, complimentary poems to various ladies and his friends. These themes were taken from classical writings and a solid bedrock of Christian faith. An over-riding message of Herrick's work is that life is short, the world is beautiful, love is splendid, and we must use the short time we have to make the most of it.

"Bubo continued to imagine himself Othello murdering his wife, or Achilles dragging Hector round the walls of Troy." The first metaphor refers to Shakespeare's "Otello" believed to have been written in approximately 1603. The work revolves around four central characters: Othello, a Moorish general in the Venetian army; his wife, Desdemona; his lieutenant, Cassio; and his trusted ensign, Iago. In the play, Othello suspects Desdemona of infidelity and murders her. The second metaphor is from Homer's "Iliad." In the epic poem, Achilles kills Hector, the respected first-born prince of Troy, in retribution for the death of Achilles' comrade, Patroclus. Achilles then attached the lifeless body of Hector to a chariot and dragged it around the wall of Troy.

"...and the first train on Boxing Day would carry him up to London." In England, Boxing Day is the day after Christmas. It started as a custom for tradesmen to collect "Christmas boxes" of money or presents on the first weekday after Christmas as thanks for good service throughout the year.

"...rounding off his Christmas with the simple hymn—'Us be but little children weak.'" This is the first line of a children's church song, the first stanza of which reads: "We are but little children weak,/ Nor born in any high estate;/ What can we do for Jesus' sake,/ Who is so high and good and great?" The words of the hymn were written by Cecil F. Alexander and published in 1850. The music was added by Christopher E. Willing in 1868.

CHAPTER XX - ABOUT SMOKE

"Tomkins Street was one out of many, known to the policeman and postman..." This street name in Plymouth, Devon is assumed to be fictitious. The other street names in that paragraph do not actually exist either.

"... a dangerous and crazy Messiah." The term "messiah" is the anglicized version of a Hebrew term generally transliterated as Mashiach, designating a king or High Priest, who were traditionally anointed with holy anointing oil. Following the death of Simon bar Kokhba, who ruled Judea from 132-135 until he was defeated by the Romans and who was considered by some to be the last messiah, the term came to refer to a Jewish king who would rule at the end of history. In later Jewish messianic tradition and eschatology, messiah refers to a leader anointed by God, and in some cases, a future King of Israel, physically descended from the Davidic line, who will rule the united tribes of Israel and herald the Messianic Age of global peace. Christianity emerged early in the first century AD as a movement among Jews and their Gentile converts who believed that Jesus is the Christ or Messiah. Christians commonly refer to Jesus as either the "Christ" or the "Messiah." In Christian theology the two words are synonymous.

"She got out as much as she could, and walked on the Hoe..." In Plymouth, the Hoe is a large south facing open public space on the coast. The Hoe is adjacent to and above the low limestone cliffs that form the seafront and it commands views of Plymouth Sound, Drake's Island, and across the Hamoaze to Mount Edgcumbe in Cornwall. The name derives from the Anglo-Saxon word Hoe, a sloping ridge shaped like an inverted foot and heel.

CHAPTER XXI - ABOUT ST. PIRAN'S SANDS

"Even in the days when saints were as plentiful as pilchards..." A pilchard is another name for the sardine, but the precise meaning of the word differs based on the region where the name is used for the fish. Pilchard fishing and processing became a thriving industry in Cornwall from around 1750 to around 1880, after which time it went into an almost terminal decline.

"It is a pitiless sea off St. Piran's Sands." St. Piran's Sands is the location on the Cornish coast where, according to legend, St. Pirans arrived from Ireland. There is a medieval church of St Piran, on Perran Sands, that was built in about 1150, following the inundation of St Piran's Oratory by the dunes.

"'Good old bounder. Chuck him in the Cherwell.'" Cherwell refers to the River Cherwell, which drains south through the Oxfordshire region to flow into the River Thames at Oxford.

"...and put their hands to their faces like Apollo at the death of Oedipus, because there was that about the death of the king which even a god could not look at." In Sophocles' ancient Greek play, "Oedipus the King", the city of Thebes suffers a plague which leaves its fields and women barren. Oedipus, the king of Thebes, has sent his brother-in-law, Creon, to the house of Apollo to ask the oracle how to end the plague. Creon returns, bearing good news: once the killer of the previous king, Laius, is found, Thebes will be cured of the plague (Laius was Jocasta's husband before she married Oedipus). Hearing this, Oedipus swears he will find the murderer and banish him. Oedipus comes to the painful realization that he unknowingly murdered his father and must banish himself from the city. Furthermore, he has committed the taboo of marrying his mother. Overcome with shame and guilt, he blinds himself. In "Oedipus at Colonus", the second of the plays in the Theban trilogy of Sophocles, Oedipus prepares for his death at a city that was foretold by the oracle at Apollo.

"...him making off in the direction of Newquay." Newquay is a town, civil parish, seaside resort and fishing port in Cornwall. It is situated on the North Atlantic coast of Cornwall approximately 20 miles west of Bodmin and 12 miles north of Truro.

CHAPTER XXII - ABOUT LAUREL LEAVES

"...they are poltroons..." A poltroon is a spiritless coward.

"The flowers exhaled an odour of iodiform..." Iodiform, or iodoform, is a yellow crystalline volatile chemical compound with a penetrating persistent odor that is used as an antiseptic dressing.

"'Bubo, I can't understand this descendant of Judas Iscariot.'" Judas Iscariot was, according to the New Testament, one of the Twelve Apostles of Jesus. He is infamously known for his kiss and betrayal of Jesus to the chief Sanhedrin priests for a ransom of 30 pieces of silver. This metaphor about a descendant of Judas is a slur.

"'Verily I fear me there is guile in Israel.'" While this may appear to be a paraphrase of a Biblical verse, the source is unclear. It may refer to Numbers 23:21, in which Balaam delivers a second prophecy to Balak and states, in part, that "He has not observed iniquity in Jacob, Nor has He seen wickedness in Israel."

"...if he could run upon the moor shouting and singing, 'I have won the fight, I have come through, I have conquered the world.'" The song may be a reference to 2 Timothy 4:7 which states: "I have fought the good fight, I have finished the race, I have kept the faith."

"'...fifty cubits high, for the seed of Benjamin.'" The cubit is a traditional unit of length, based on the length of the forearm. It was the standard of measurement mentioned in the Old Testament. The phrase "seed of Benjamin" refers to the descendants of the Tribe of Benjamin. According to the Torah, the tribe consisted of descendants of Benjamin, the youngest son of Jacob with Rachel. In the Blessing of Jacob, Benjamin was referred to as a ravenous wolf.

"'We have some mezzotints of your principal works...'" Mezzotint is a printmaking process of the intaglio family, technically a drypoint method. It was the first tonal method to be used, enabling half-tones to be produced without using line-based or dot-based techniques like hatching, cross-hatching or stipple. Mezzotint achieves tonality by roughening the plate with thousands of little dots made by a metal tool with small teeth, called a rocker. In printing, the tiny pits in the plate hold the ink when the face of the plate is wiped clean. A high level of quality and richness in the print can be achieved with the process.

"'Now you shall promise me to go to Perranzabuloe.'" Perranzabuloe is a coastal civil parish and a hamlet in Cornwall. The hamlet, containing the parish church, is situated just over a mile south of the principal settlement of the parish, Perranporth. The hamlet is seven miles south-southwest of Newquay. Perranzabuloe parish is bordered to the west by the Atlantic coast and St Agnes parish, to the north by Cubert parish, to the east by St Newlyn East and St Allen parishes and to the south by Kenwyn parish. The name of the parish derives from the medieval Latin "Perranus in Sabulo" meaning Piran in the sand. It refers to Saint Piran (the patron saint of Cornwall) who founded an oratory church in the seventh century near the coast north of Perranporth.

CHAPTER XXIII - ABOUT UNCONVENTIONAL CONDUCT

"On a cold March day any traveller by the North Cornwall line..." The North Cornwall line was the railway line, operated by the London and South Western Railway, that ran from Halwill Junction through Launceston to Padstow in Cornwall. It was constructed between 1886 and 1899.

"...shatter the windows from Egloskerry onwards..." Egloskerry is a village and civil parish in east Cornwall. It is situated approximately five miles northwest of Launceston. The Egloskerry railway station opened in October 1892 when the London & South Western Railway, or LSWR, opened a line between Launceston and Tresmeer.

"...looking like stiff Shems, Hams and Japhets standing on wooden plates all ready for the Ark." The three names included in this simile are the sons of Noah from the book of Genesis in the Bible.

"The train dragged into Delabole, past the wonderful slate quarries..." Delabole is a large village in north Cornwall. It is situated approximately two miles west of Camelford The village of Delabole came into existence in the 20th century; it is named after the Delabole Quarry. There were three hamlets: Pengelly, Medrose and Rockhead. When the railway arrived, the station was named Delabole after the quarry.

"...a few miles away was a furious life—the indigo sea raging upon Trebarwith Strand and bombarding Tintagel with great guns." Trebarwith Strand, locally sometimes shortened to The Strand, is a coastal settlement and section of coastline located on the north coast of Cornwall, and approximately two miles south of Tintagel. It has a sandy beach, contained by cliffs, in which natural caves are found. Tintagel is a civil parish and village situated on the Atlantic coast of Cornwall. The village and nearby Tintagel Castle are associated with the legends surrounding King Arthur and the knights of the Round Table.

"Two more stops, and the train entered the Dutch-like scenery of Wadebridge..." Wadebridge is a civil parish and town in north Cornwall. The town straddles the River Camel five miles upstream from Padstow.

"...as he wanted to get across St. Breock's Downs before dark." St Breock is a village and a civil parish in north Cornwall. St Breock village is one mile west of Wadebridge immediately to the south of the Royal Cornwall Showground. The village lies on the eastern slope of the wooded Nansent valley. The parish extends approx five miles south of Wadebridge. To the north, the parish is bounded by the River Camel, to the west by St Issey parish and to the east by Egloshayle parish. Together with Egloshayle it was one of the two parishes within which the town of Wadebridge developed.

"...the guard sounding his trumpet like an apocalyptic angel." An apocalypse is a disclosure of something hidden from the majority of mankind in an era dominated by falsehood and misconception. The Apocalypse of John is the Book of Revelation, the last book of the New Testament. By extension, apocalypse can refer to any End Time scenario, or to the end of the world in general. The introduction of angels as messengers of the apocalypse occurs repeatedly in the Bible. At least four types or ranks of angels are mentioned in biblical scripture: the Archangels, Angels, Cherubim and Seraphim. God may give instructions through the medium of these heavenly messengers; they act as the seer's guide. God may also personally give a revelation, as is shown in the Book of Revelation through the person of Jesus Christ. The Book of Genesis speaks of the "Angel" bringing forth the apocalypse.

"'That's Egloshayle church yonder, sir,'..." Egloshayle is a civil parish and village in north Cornwall. The village is situated beside the River Camel immediately southeast of Wadebridge. The civil parish extends southeast from the village and includes Washaway and Sladesbridge. Egloshayle was a Bronze Age settlement and later a river port, rivalling Padstow five miles down-river. The trade consisted of tin, clay, wool, and vegetable crops. The parish church, named after St Petroc, is built almost entirely in the Perpendicular style. It has a Norman font and a stone pulpit dating from the 15th century.

"'Padstow, sir. Don't ye never go there. A dirty, stinking hole full o' rotten fish, and 'tis the only harbour in North Cornwall, sir...'" Padstow is a town, civil parish and fishing port on the north coast of Cornwall. The town is situated on the west bank of the River Camel estuary approximately five miles northwest of Wadebridge, ten miles northwest of Bodmin and ten miles northeast of Newquay. From 1899 until 1967 Padstow railway station was the westernmost point of the former Southern Railway. The station was the terminus of an extension from Wadebridge of the former Bodmin and Wadebridge Railway and North Cornwall Railway. These lines were part of the London and South Western Railway (LSWR).

"'...and they gets carried on the rocks off Trevose—'" Trevose Head is a headland on the Atlantic coast of north Cornwall. It is situated approximately five miles west of Padstow.

"...for the little girl was, plainly enough, leaving her home and going into service for the first time." The phrase "going into service" means becoming a servant, generally a domestic servant.

"...all the time he remained as severe as a Judge of Assize." The Courts of Assize, or assizes, were periodic criminal courts held around England and Wales until 1972, when together with the Quarter Sessions they were abolished by the Courts Act 1971 and replaced by a single permanent Crown Court. The assizes heard the most serious cases, which were committed to it by the Quarter Sessions (local county courts held four times a year), while the more minor offences were dealt with summarily by Justices of the Peace in petty sessions (also known as Magistrates' Courts). The word assize refers to the sittings or sessions (Old French "assises") of the judges, known as "justices of assize."

"...in front stood out St. Columb Major, like a little town upon the Rhine." St. Columb Major is a civil parish and town in Cornwall. Often referred to locally as St Columb, it is situated approximately seven miles southwest of Wadebridge and six miles east of Newquay. The designation Major distinguishes it from the smaller settlement and parish of St Columb Minor on the coast.

"...which seemed to imply that he was going there to discharge the duty of distributing a handful of tracts..." A tract is a literary work, usually religious in nature. The notion of what constitutes a tract has changed over time. At one time, tracts were small pamphlets used for religious and political purposes, though far more often the former. They are often either left for someone to find or handed out.

"'Columb Minor,' the guard shouted, omitting the saintly prefix, as he was a good Methodist." St Columb Minor is a village on the north coast of Cornwall. At one time St Columb Minor was the main settlement in the area, but it later became encroached upon by its larger neighbor, Newquay. While still an ecclesiastical parish, St Columb Minor is no longer a civil parish.

"'Tis the old clerk's birthday,' came the answer. 'He'm a hundred and something, I don't know how much, but he'm going to live for ever, I reckon....'" Although not mentioned by name, this was an unusual reference by the author to an actual, local person of some notoriety. In 1906, James Carne (1806 – 1909) retired from his service as parish clerk in St. Columb Minor, a position that he had held for 64 years. At that time he was 100 years old. Carne died the year after *Heather* was first published.

CHAPTER XXIV - ABOUT A PAGAN SACRIFICE

"...there was grief in Metheral and something not altogether unlike the gnashing of teeth." The phrase "gnashing of teeth" is repeatedly used in the New Testament when referring, mainly in the parables of Jesus, to persons condemned to Hell. See Matthew 8:12, 13:42, 13:50, 22:13, 24:51, and 25:30; also Luke 13:28.

"'The Lord gives and takes away tu, my dear....'" This is a paraphrase of the following verse from Job 1:21: "And he said: 'Naked I came from my mother's womb, And naked shall I return there. The Lord gave, and the Lord has taken away; Blessed be the name of the Lord.'"

"'If yew looks at that dancing doxy...'" A doxy is an archaic English term for prostitute, mistress or love slave.

CHAPTER XXV - ABOUT A SUNSET OF DREAMS

No notes for this chapter.

CHAPTER XXVI - ABOUT A TWILIGHT OF GOLD

"...had turned his mind entirely from joyous thoughts of sepulture." Sepulture means burial or entombment.

"...he had a dim notion that the little owl was a sort of Chaldean and astrologer..." Chaldea or Chaldaea was a marshy land located in modern-day southern Iraq which came to rule Babylon briefly. Tribes of settlers who arrived in the region from the 8th Century BC became known as the Chaldeans or the Chaldees. The Hebrew Bible uses a term which is translated as Chaldaeans in the Septuagint.

"...the picture of Simon Peter being unkind to Ananias..." Ananias son of Nedebaios called "Ananias ben Nebedeus" in the Book of Acts, was a high priest who presided during the trial of Paul at Jerusalem and Caesarea. He officiated as high priest from about AD 47 to 59. Quadratus, governor of Syria, accused him of being responsible for acts of violence. He was sent to Rome for trial but was acquitted by the emperor Claudius. Being a friend of the

Romans, he was murdered by the people at the beginning of the First Jewish-Roman War.

"...they are alike in their prayer to Venus for one of her team of white doves." Venus was a Roman goddess principally associated with love, beauty, sex, fertility, prosperity and military victory. She played a key role in many Roman religious festivals. From the third century BC, the increasing Hellenization of Roman upper classes identified her as the equivalent of the Greek goddess Aphrodite, which in turn is the copy and the equivalent of the Phoenician goddess Astarte. Roman mythology made her the divine mother of Aeneas, the Trojan ancestor of Rome's founder, Romulus. Various ancient sources mention that Venus' chariot was pulled by white doves.

John Trevena
(Pseudonym of Ernest George Henham)
1870-1948

Printed in Great Britain
by Amazon